Bridge to Tomorrow
Cold War

A Novel of the Berlin Airlift
Part II

T0244084

Helena P. Schrader

Cold War: A Novel of the Berlin Airlift

Cross Seas Press
91 Pleasant Street
Blue Hill, Maine 04614
www.crossseaspress.com

ISBN: 979-8-9871770-2-0 (paperback)
        979-8-9871770-3-7 (eBook)
Library of Congress Control Number: 2024 9058 41

Praise for Helena P. Schrader's Novels

Praise for *Cold Peace*

"Sharp research meets vivid storytelling in an absorbing novel of the postwar period."

Kirkus Reviews

*"**Magnificent Story, Compelling History** ... Cold Peace is a magnificently conceived story on a grand scale (who writes trilogies anymore?) with dynamic characters, detailed yet evocative prose, and compelling history."*

BookTrib

"... a spellbinding work of historical fiction that brings a unique pocket of history to life with extraordinary detail and heart."

Readers' Favorites

"... a very fast-paced, suspenseful, emotional, and riveting story that any reader will find almost impossible to put down."

Feathered Quill

Praise for *Where Eagles Never Flew*

"This is the best book on the life of us fighter pilots in the Battle of Britain that I have ever seen. Refreshingly it got it smack on the way it was for us. I couldn't put it down!"

Battle of Britain Ace, Wing Commander Bob Doe

"... a tremendously moving tale of human conflict, ... Where Eagles Never Flew is both inspirational and terrifying in its reality and should be required reading for anyone under the illusion that air warfare is in any way glorious."

Steven Robson for **Readers Favorites**

"So much has been written about the battle ... that it is hard to imagine that a new novel could be written that would make the conflict seem fresh. Yet this is exactly what [Where Eagles Never Flew] has achieved."

Aviation Expert Simon Rodwell

3

"Its high-octane descriptions of air manoeuvres and daring escapes are breathtaking.... Because of its ambitious scope and phenomenal details, down to the last "Mae West" jacket, the novel is compelling, humanizing a historical event ...."

Foreword Clarion Reviews

Praise for *Moral Fibre*

"... a tribute to those who fought for freedom."

Foreign Service Journal

"Meticulously researched and skillfully written, Schrader's Moral Fibre *steps off the pages and comes to life. Her nuanced characters and authentic dialogue also provide a glimpse of Britain's stratified class-conscious culture during the WWII era. .... A riveting read and highly recommended!"*

Chanticleer Reviews 5-Stars

"Helena P. Schrader ... is a true master at delving into complex psychological dilemmas and emerging with a tantalizing, completely comprehensible tale of human frailty and strengths that blend into a unique experience for her readers."

Tom Gauthier for Readers Favorites

"A richly textured, absorbing war tale that works equally well as a touching love story."

Kirkus Reviews

Bridge to Tomorrow
A Novel of the Berlin Airlift

Book II: Cold War

Table of Contents

Foreword

Cold War is the second book in the *Bridge to Tomorrow Series* and continues the story of the Berlin Crisis 1948-1949 through the eyes of the characters introduced in *Cold Peace* — and more. All characters, whether they have lost limbs or loved ones, been held as prisoners of war or confined in concentration camps, faced abandonment by their wives, been disfigured by wounds, or suffered sexual abuse by the victors, are survivors struggling to find a place for themselves in the post war world. By the end of *Cold Peace,* they have found a new purpose in trying to defend Berlin's freedom after the imposition of a Soviet blockade.

Cold War picks up their story as the Berlin Airlift, the Western response to the blockade, gets off the ground. From their diverse positions — in the city administration or serving with the RAF, USAF or a private air ambulance company — the characters come together to save a city. Their career ambitions, whether as airmen or policemen, air traffic controllers or journalists, businessmen or politicians, intermingle with private concerns and dreams. Against the backdrop of the political and logistical challenges associated with the largest and most complex airlift in history, *Cold War* depicts the continuing struggle of those scarred by the war to forgive their enemies and to establish new, enduring relationships.

In the interests of simplicity, I usually refer to any of the four Airlift airfields in or near Hamburg as "Hamburg" and any of the three Airlift airfields near Hanover as "Hanover." For those unfamiliar with *Cold Peace*, I include short bios and a plot synopsis. Maps are also provided before the novel. In the appendices is a list of acronyms, a rank table for readers unfamiliar with the Royal Air Force, and a historical note, which highlights some of the more extraordinary true events depicted in this volume as well as identifying the occasional deviations from the historical record taken for literary purposes.

The front cover features: (upper left) a photo of the Berlin Airlift from the public domain, and (lower right) a photo of Winifred Stokes, one of the

WAAF who flew for the ATA, from her private collection.

I wish to take this opportunity to thank my editor, David Imrie, my cover designer, Anna Dahlberg, and my layouter Matthias Wille, as well as all my test readers for their patient and constructive contributions. Without them, the final product would not have been possible.

Helena P. Schrader
Blue Hill, Maine 2024

Background Information on *Cold Peace*

Characters
(at the opening of *Cold Peace*)

- Wing Commander **Robert "Robin" Priestman**, DSO, DFC and Bar, is a former aerobatics pilot, Battle of Britain ace and wartime wing leader, who ended the war in a German POW camp. At the start of 1948, he is appointed Station Commander at RAF Gatow, the small, sleepy, grass airfield in the British Sector of Berlin.

- His wife, **Emily**, is the daughter of Communist activists with an honours degree in history from Cambridge. She and Robin met and married during the Battle of Britain. Later in the war, she flew with the Air Transport Auxiliary. Frustrated by the lack of post-war employment opportunities, she is determined to do something useful in Berlin.

- **Charlotte** Graefin (Countess) **Walmsdorf** grew up in a frugal, rural environment, helping with harvests and mucking out stalls on her father's estate in northeast Germany. Both her brothers and her parents were killed in the war and her fiancée went missing on the Eastern Front. She is struggling to survive as a freelance journalist.

- **David Goldman** is a German Jew, whose family emigrated to Canada in 1934 where his father established a successful private bank. To his father's disappointment, David chose flying rather than banking as his career. Shot down in flames early in the war, his face had to be reconstructed by the famous plastic surgeon Dr McIndoe. He spent the rest of the war as an instructor with RAF training command, where he remained after the war.

- **Jakob Liebherr** is a former member of the German Parliament (Reichstag) for the Social Democratic Party. He voted against Hitler's enabling law and spent years in a concentration camp during the Nazi period. He is now a city councillor for the district of Kreuzberg and a tenant in the same apartment house as Charlotte.

- **Kit Moran** is the son of a British colonial official and a Scottish missionary's daughter of mixed race. He grew up in Kenya and went to school in South Africa, until taking an engineering apprenticeship in the UK at age 16. He enlisted in the RAF as ground crew at the start of the war, but later volunteered for aircrew and despite a temporary posting for "lack of moral fibre" went on to fly Lancasters for 617 Squadron. He is studying engineering in Leeds.

- WAAF Flight Sergeant **Kathleen Hart** is the widow of an RAF navigator who was shot down over Berlin in 1944. She joined the WAAF and qualified as an air traffic controller. She has a six-year-old daughter called Hope.

- **Charles "Kiwi" Murray** is a wartime comrade of David. (Both he and David were "sprog" pilots in Robin Priestman's squadron during the Battle of Britain.) Kiwi was demobilised at the end of the war and is struggling to make a living as a salesman. His wife has recently left him.

- **Christian** Freiherr von **Feldburg** is the younger brother of a leading member of the German Resistance, who committed suicide on the night of 20 July 1944 in the family apartment in Berlin Kreuzberg. A fighter pilot in the Luftwaffe during the war, Christian was shot down in North Africa, where he became a prisoner of the Americans. After his release, he married his best friend's widow to rescue her from an intolerable situation in France. Together they went to the Feldburg estate in Franken, where Christian's mother has returned after being interned in a concentration camp. Here they try to start life anew.

- WAAF Corporal **Galyna Nicolaevna** Borisenko was born in the Soviet Union, the daughter of Ukrainian intellectuals and enthusiastic members of the Communist Party. When she was twelve, her father was arrested, accused of treason, and disappeared. Two years later, her mother remarried, and her new husband sent Galyna to her grandmother in Finland. Together with her grandmother, Galyna emigrated to the UK, where she obtained British citizenship and joined the WAAF during the war. At the start of *Cold Peace*, she is working as a translator at RAF Gatow.

Plot Synopsis

Cold Peace opens in late 1947. Robin Priestman has just been appointed Station Commander at RAF Gatow in Berlin, a position he does not want because of his lingering hostility to Germans. Kit Moran's wife, a gifted teacher has just been laid off from work because she has become pregnant. Kathleen Hart has volunteered to fill an "urgent" request for an air traffic controller at RAF Gatow. David Goldman's father has left him a fortune too large to ignore — along with the obligation to find out what happened to all family properties in Germany. In Berlin, Charlotte is alone in a cold, almost unfurnished apartment wondering why she should continue living at all. Jakob Liebherr, her neighbour, lives in fear of the future as he watches the Russians assert themselves with impunity.

The Priestmans arrive in Berlin under the impression that their main task is to cooperate with their fellow allies, including the Russians. However, during his courtesy call with the (historical) British Air Attaché to the Allied Control Council, Air Commodore Reginald Waite, Robin learns that his job also entails winning the hearts and minds of the Germans. Waite explains that His Majesty's government does not want Germany to become communist. As Robin encounters various forms of Soviet intransigence, lies, harassment and aggression, his view of the Soviets turns negative. Meanwhile, Emily is struggling to come to terms with the Germans around her yet determined to do something useful. Believing language skills will help, she seeks a German teacher and finds Charlotte.

David and Kiwi join forces to start an air ambulance company in the UK, but first David needs to find out what has happened to family property in Germany, including property in Berlin. He stays with his friends the Priestmans, where he encounters Charlotte and learns that the Russians frequently disrupt rail traffic at the border with negative consequences for medical evacuations. David sees a potential business opportunity and engages Emily and Charlotte to do market research on the viability of an air ambulance service based in Berlin.

Kathleen arrives in Berlin anxious for more responsibility in her job but also hoping that visiting her husband's grave in the Commonwealth War Cemetery will free her heart to love again. A chance encounter with the dashing British Army Major Lionel Dickenson results in Kathleen being introduced to the diverse — and not always legal — cultural life of Berlin.

Christian arrives in Berlin to sell wine from the family estate and finds his cousin Charlotte in the family apartment house. He recognises she needs help, and since he can't persuade her to leave Berlin, he decides to stay. He is attracted by a city that, despite everything, is more vibrant and diverting than the provincial village in Franken where his mother and wife live.

Back in the UK, Kiwi has been busy trying to find a suitable old bomber and ground crew, while himself qualifying to fly twin-engine aircraft. Although he almost fails, by 1 April "Air Ambulance International" (AAI) is ready to relocate their modified Wellington bomber to Berlin. By chance, this move coincides with Soviet interdiction of road and rail traffic into the city. The ambulance proves its worth immediately. Meanwhile, David has hired Charlotte to run the office of the company and handle the customers, while Emily handles liaison with the RAF and flies as a back-up pilot.

Through Jakob Liebherr's eyes the reader learns about Berlin's crippled economy, the dominance of the black market, and the widespread unemployment, crime and prostitution. Nearly all problems have their roots in the worthless currency, which the Russians print without serial numbers or controls. Liebherr and his colleagues watch Soviet provocations and Western inaction with mounting concern. Liebherr becomes convinced that the Russians intend to expel the Western Allies from Berlin and integrate the city into the Soviet Zone of occupation, but there appears to be nothing the Berliners can do to stop it.

During a session of the Allied Control Council, where the four victorious allies are supposed to coordinate polices for Germany, Priestman witnesses unfounded soviet attacks, insults and intransigence. During the lunch break, Galyna (who accompanied him as a translator) meets a female Hero of the Soviet Union, Mila. Based on their shared loneliness and Ukrainian nationality, the two young women become friends, and at great risk start meeting surreptitiously. At a dance performance for the Red Army in the Soviet Sector that Galyna attends at Mila's invitation, she overhears drunken Soviet officers bragging about starving the Western Allies out of Berlin. She reports the conversation to the intelligence officer at Gatow. Priestman recognises the value of her intelligence and forwards it up the chain.

On 5 April, a Soviet fighter doing aerobatics in the approach corridor to Gatow rams a British European Airlines passenger plane, killing all passengers and crew. This (historical) incident convinces Robin that the Russians are going to try to seize control of Berlin. He overcomes scepticism from his superiors to obtain permission to start building a concrete runway at Gatow. Meanwhile, he has forged a friendship with the (historical) American City Commandant Frank Howley, who like Priestman, also recognises the hostile intentions of the Russians.

Meanwhile, David Goldman has discovered that neither the patients nor the hospitals in Berlin can pay for air evacuation in hard currency. Thus, while demand for the air ambulance is robust, the company cannot generate revenue. David starts taking return cargoes to help finance the ambulance service, starting with Christian's wine. Yet his inheritance is draining away, and David becomes increasingly nervous. Distress over the finances causes him to clash with Kiwi, whom he accuses of revealing company secrets to an attractive woman reporter. Emily manages to get them to patch over their differences.

After a glamorous evening at the Berlin Opera, Kathleen thinks Lionel is going to propose to her; instead, he disappears. To her intense embarrassment, she learns from her CO (Robin) that Lionel has been arrested for illegally dealing in stolen art treasures. Furthermore, Lionel is a married man with a family in England. Kathleen's dreams for a new love are shattered.

Back in Great Britain, Kit is learning that even with an engineering degree there are no jobs in bankrupt, post-war Britain. After his wife nearly dies giving birth to a daughter, he considers taking work as an aircraft mechanic — or going overseas to find employment. He agrees to await the end of the summer before making a final decision.

On 20 June 1948, the Western Allies introduce a new currency in Germany, the Deutschmark or D-Mark. This transforms the economy of the Western Zones. The German "economic miracle" has started. But in Berlin, the Soviets react by introducing a new currency of their own and insisting this is the *only* valid currency throughout the city. This effectively signals their claim to control the entire city and their intention to integrate all of Berlin into their Zone of occupation.

On 23 June the City Council is ordered by the Soviet Military

Administration to officially adopt their currency at a session of the City Assembly. When the elected representatives try to enter the City Hall, which is located in the Soviet Sector of the city, a Soviet-instigated mob attacks them. Jakob and his colleagues fight their way through the rioters and vote against the Soviet demands.

The next morning (24 June 1948) the Soviets shut down all power, road, rail and canal connections between the Western Zones of Germany and the Western Sectors of Berlin. This effectively cuts the residents of these Sectors off from their sources of food, clothing, medicines, and all other necessities of life. In addition, except for the power produced in one antiquated power plant, the Western Sectors no longer have electricity.

The Western Allies appear to have only two options: retreat or go to war over their right to remain in Berlin. The American military governor, General Clay, wants to send a supply convoy protected by combat troops, but Washington and London veto the plan as too risky. At this juncture, Air Commodore Waite suggests it might be possible to supply the city by air.

Cold Peace ends with Jakob Liebherr astonished yet elated by the Allied willingness to try an airlift, but Charlotte is terrified the Soviets will seize complete control of the city. Kathleen and Galyna, on the other hand, although offered the chance to transfer out, both opt to remain; Kathleen because the work will be more interesting and her daughter is happy in Berlin, and Galyna because she wants to work in intelligence. Although Air Ambulance International's ground crew refuses to remain in the beleaguered city, David, Kiwi and Emily agree that they must try to keep the company operating. Back in England, Kit Moran dreams of delivering food rather than high explosives to Berlin. *Cold Peace* ends with Robin telling the staff at Gatow that this is a war that will be won by intelligence, innovation, improvisation, and ingenuity — and a sense of humour.

Maps

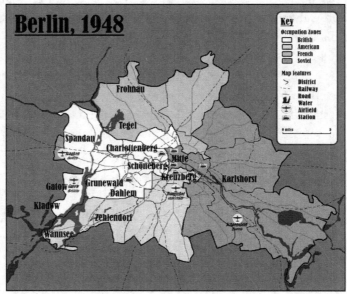

List of Characters
(names marked with an * are historical figures)

British Forces of Occupation

- General Sir Brian Robertson*, British Military Governor in Germany
- Air Commodore Reginald "Rex" Waite*, British Air Attache to the Allied Control Council
- General Otway Herbert, British Berlin Commandant*
- Group Captain W. Bagshot, British Air Lift Commander
- Lt. Colonel Graham Russel, RCE, responsible for airfield expansion

RAF Gatow Personnel

- Wing Commander Robert "Robin" Priestman, Station Commander RAF Gatow
- S/L Garth, Senior Flying Control Officer
- Captain Bateman* (RASC) commander of the Forward Airfield Supply Organisation (FASO)
- Ft/Lt Oliver Boyd, Station Intelligence Officer
- F/O "Stan" Stanley, Station Adjutant
- Assistant Section Leader Kathleen Hart, Air Traffic Controller
- Corporal Galyna Nicolaevna Borisenko, Translator

Employees of Emergency Air Services (EAS) Ltd.

- David "Banks" Goldman, Founder and principal shareholder, CEO & CFO
- Emily Priestman, Goldman's partner and wife of W/C Priestman, Head of Facilities and Personnel, Wellington (ambulance) pilot
- Charles "Kiwi" Murray, partner in the company, COO, Wellington and Dakota pilot
- Charlotte Graefin Walmsdorf, Head of Customer Relations
- Fl/Lt Christopher "Kit" Moran, Halifax pilot
- Bruce Forrester, second pilot, Halifax

- Nigel Osgood, navigator, Halifax
- Richard Scott-Ross, flight engineer, Halifax
- Jan and Rick Orloff, pilot and flight engineer on the ambulance.
- Ron and Chips, British groundcrew based in Hamburg
- Gordon "Daddy" MacDonald, former flight engineer, crew chief in Berlin
- Axel Voigt, Ludwig Winterfeld and Helmut Gries, German ground-crew based in Berlin
- Frls Klempner and Dorsh, Office Staff
- Sammy, David Goldman's dog

American Forces of Occupation

- General Lucius D. Clay*, US Military Governor in Germany
- Colonel Frank Howley*, US Berlin Commandant
- Edith*, his wife

USAF Airlift Participants

- General William Tunner*, US Airlift Commander, later Commander of the Combined Airlift Taskforce
- Lt. Colonels Bettinger* and Foreman*, two of his staff officers
- Captain J.B. Baronowsky, USAF Reserve pilot
- Lt. James "Jimmy" Hudson, USAF pilot
- Lt. Gail Halvorsen*, USAF pilot — known as "the Candy Bomber"

Members of the Berlin City Government

- Ernst Reuter*, Lord Mayor of Berlin
- Louisa Schroeder*, Deputy Mayor of Berlin
- Jeannette Wolfe*, Berlin City Councilwoman
- Jakob Liebherr, City Councillor from Kreuzberg

Residents of Berlin

- Christian Freiherr von Feldburg, cousin of Charlotte Walmsdorf, former Luftwaffe fighter pilot, now wine merchant
- Anton Sperl, former U-Boat Commander, now police inspector
- Lothar and Norbert, his former shipmates
- Trude Liebherr, wife of Jakob, a senior nurse
- Jasha, the Priestman's cook, ethnically Polish, former Soviet citizen and German slave labourer

Soviet Characters

- Mila Mikhailivna Levchenkova, Heroine of the Soviet Union, on Marshal Sokolovsky's staff
- Anastasia Sergeiovna, Galyna Borisenko's mother
- Maxim Dimitrivich Ratanov, Galyna's stepfather

Other Characters

- Virginia Cox-Gordon, British journalist
- Maisy MacDonald, Gordon's wife
- Georgina Moran, Kit's wife

Detailed Table of Contents

Bridge to Tomorrow
Book II: Cold War

July – December 1948

Prologue
Mission Impossible

RAF Wunstorf
1 July, 1948
(Day 6 of the Berlin Airlift)

Virginia Cox-Gordon scanned the unruly gaggle of reporters gathered for the official RAF briefing. All major British and American newspapers were represented alongside journalists from other European nations and many Germans. Only the Soviet press was conspicuously absent, but then they didn't need to check facts, they just published whatever their master in Moscow told them to print.

Virginia had been with *The Times* for almost a decade, working throughout the war, and she knew a good story when she saw one. The Western Allies' hopeless plan to supply the entire civilian population of Berlin by air was the hottest news item since German surrender. Every ambitious reporter wanted to cover it, but Virginia's instincts had drawn her to the story back in April when the Soviets had briefly shut down rail traffic to the Western garrisons. When the real crisis had broken seven days ago, her editor had tried to assign another — male — reporter to cover the story, but Virginia had successfully defended her territory.

A harried RAF public relations officer met the crowd of journalists and led them to a brick building dating to the Luftwaffe era and up two flights of stairs to the briefing room. Shortly afterwards, the Station Commander, Group Captain Bagshot, entered and took his place behind the podium. Bagshot sported an archetypical RAF moustache, receding hairline, and a fruit salad of ribbons under his wings. He was undoubtedly a man of military experience but appeared dismayed by the unruly reporters. He asked repeatedly and irritably for silence without success. Journalists weren't as ready to obey orders as airmen were, Virginia thought, chuckling to herself.

"Gentlemen! Gentlemen! Quiet, please! If you want to hear anything you will have to settle down." Eventually, a modicum of order settled over the crowd, and Bagshot opened by reminding the journalists of the Four Power Agreements that guaranteed Allied access to Berlin. He complained, "The Soviet actions of 24 June violated not only our international agreements but also all universal laws of humanity and human decency. This blockade seeks to cause misery to the people of Berlin. It is a cold-blooded attempt to starve them into choosing Soviet rule. The British and American governments are determined to oppose these illegal measures. The RAF and the USAF have both instituted airlifts to deliver not only food and other necessities of life but also enough coal to keep the sole available power plant running. It is important to understand that electricity is as critical as food supplies since without it the sewage and water systems will break down, as will the public transport network."

The journalists in the room knew all this. Everyone agreed that Soviet actions were despicable, but Virginia hadn't yet met anyone who thought an airlift was a viable solution — at least not in the long run. Which was why the collected journalists were keen to get some hard facts. One of them threw out a question. "Can you quantify that, sir? Just how many tons of food, coal, etc. need to be delivered each day to keep the city alive?"

"Before the Soviets intervened, the city received 13,500 tons of goods from the Western Sectors daily, but that figure does not include coal, because prior to the blockade most of the electricity was produced in the East. Nor does it include fresh produce such as milk, eggs, fruits and vegetables, which previously entered the city from the surrounding Soviet Zone. The total tonnage needed to sustain the population at the same levels as before the blockade — which was not lavish — would be closer to 15,000 tons per day."

A murmur of shock rippled across the room. Many of the journalists shook their heads. Group Captain Bagshot confirmed their assessment in his next statement, "Obviously, we cannot transport anything near that magnitude by air. However, we have worked out that to sustain an absolute minimal standard of living, between 5,000 to 5,500 tons of supplies must be flown in daily."

"Correct me if I'm wrong, Group Captain," the reporter from *The Guardian* spoke up, "but even using big freighters with a capacity of ten

26

tons, wouldn't that mean that 500 aircraft would have to land in Berlin every day?" Without giving Bagshot time to answer, he continued, "Where are all those aircraft going to come from? Who is going to fly them? And who is going to load them and off-load them — never mind see that everyone gets their fair share of everything?"

"That was more than one question. Let me answer by reminding you that the distance from here to Berlin is just over 120 miles and an aircraft can fly that distance in about an hour. Aircraft on the airlift will be making several trips to Berlin daily. So, we don't need 500 aircraft. Eight Dakota squadrons have already been deployed on the Airlift, and eight York squadrons assigned. The first of the latter arrived today, and they will begin operations tomorrow. In addition, two squadrons of Sunderland flying boats are scheduled to start operating into Berlin next Monday, the 5th of July."

"Just how many tons of goods were flown into Berlin yesterday?" another reporter called out.

"Yesterday?" The Group Captain looked over at the press officer, who showed him a document. "Two-hundred and eighty tons."

"Did I hear that right? Two-hundred and eighty tons when a minimum of 5,000 are needed?"

Across the room men again shook their heads and looked grim. Bagshot frowned and in an exasperated tone retorted, "Gentlemen, the airlift is in its seventh day. At present, only the Dakotas are operational. They have a maximum capacity of just three tons of cargo apiece. The Yorks, in contrast, can carry three times that amount, and they start operating tomorrow."

The conference was becoming more disorderly as questions were shouted simultaneously and journalists started talking among themselves to check figures and share their scepticism. Virginia decided it was time to disappear. Her colleagues were welcome to echo the official account and spout the statistics; she was looking for the human-interest story.

She slid out of the briefing room and looked around. If challenged, she'd say she was looking for the ladies' room. On the assumption that the offices here on the top floor would house senior staff, she made for the stairs. She wanted to interview men farther down the hierarchy. The lower the rank, the more flattered they'd be to talk to the press — and the less familiar they'd be with the official talking points. She scurried down a flight of stairs and peered into a large office with many desks but just a handful of people. There was not an officer in sight. Smiling she entered, and the sergeant at the nearest desk jumped to his feet. "Can I help you, ma'am?"

"I'm sure you can, Sergeant! I'm Virginia Cox from *The Times*. Our readers can't get enough news about the Airlift. I was hoping you could tell me more about how things are going?"

"This is the Met Office, Ma'am. We don't have much of an overview. You should speak to the Station Commander."

"Oh, I just left his briefing. I'm more interested in how *real* airmen see the situation." She winked and stressed the word "real."

"Well, I suppose you could go across to the sergeants' mess," the meteorologist suggested, gesturing. "You'll find lots of men there who are flying or supporting the airlift."

"Thank you!" Virginia gave him a wide smile and a wave before hurrying down the last flight of steps to exit the admin building. She crossed an open area between the buildings briskly, acutely aware that if someone spotted her she would be stopped. With relief she entered the neat brick building opposite — only to collide with chaos.

The sergeants' mess at Wunstorf in July 1948 was like no other Virginia had encountered before. She could detect nothing orderly anywhere. Luggage and flying kit lay about blocking the corridors and halls. Men were slumped on all the chairs, some still in their working overalls, and most of them were sleeping. Indeed, some men were stretched out to sleep on the floor behind the sofas. Those not sleeping were eating or drinking — right there in the lobby! This was so chaotic and irregular, that Virginia decided she should try the officers' mess instead.

Her expectations of a more civilised environment, however, were disappointed. The same over-crowding, chaos, and sense of dislocation greeted her. One man was sleeping on a billiard table! After a moment, she spotted a flying officer putting on his flight jacket and grabbing his hat, apparently preparing to leave. She went straight over to him. Putting on her best smile, she addressed him as he stepped over someone's outstretched legs. "Flying Officer! I'm Virginia Cox of the *Times*. Would you have just a couple of minutes to talk to me?"

He shook his head and kept moving towards the door. Virginia fell in beside him and walked with him. "Have you been on the Airlift long?"

"A couple of days."

"How has it been going?"

"Let's see. We're sleeping five to a room and lucky to have a room. They've changed the location of the ops centre three times. The dining room can't work round the clock, so if we miss a meal, all we get is NAAFI buns and tea — and even that is hit-and-miss in this chaos. We never know which aircraft we'll be flying in, which means we don't know the ground crew. Nor do we have a clue about what cargo we have in the crate."

They had left the mess behind and were making for the line of aircraft beside the runway. Around them, parked aircraft filled every available space. Notably, the twin-engine Dakotas had been pushed off anything concrete to make way for the heavier Yorks, and the grass was turning into a morass of mud. Meanwhile, the Yorks hogged the few hardstandings in front of the hangars and were lined up on the perimeter track. While aircraftmen crawled over the Yorks to ensure serviceability by the next day, the Dakotas doggedly lined up to take off.

Virginia's escort led her towards a bevy of Dakotas surrounded by stevedores heaving canvas sacks from lorries to men standing in the open cargo doors. The latter flung the sacks inside the aircraft. The teams worked rhythmically and steadily. All the loaders were German, although British soldiers drove the trucks and supervised the work to ensure nothing was stolen or sabotaged.

A man started waving to Virginia's companion. "That's my skipper," the Flying Officer explained. Only then did Virginia register that her interlocutor was a navigator rather than a pilot. "Better go," he announced as he picked up his pace to a jog, leaving the reporter in his wake.

Virginia didn't try to keep up. She just watched as he scrambled into the cockpit of the Dakota at the head of the queue. He was barely inside when the cargo door clanged shut and the first engine started spinning slowly. The last of the stevedores fell onto the back of the empty lorry, which pulled away as the second engine settled into a steady buzz. The Dakota started to ease out onto the taxiway, while the Dakota behind it closed its door and started its engines.

"What wonderful copy!" Virginia thought. Unlike the dreary briefing that highlighted all the problems, out here in the midst of the action she felt a thrill. At the root of all this chaos was urgency and a sense of purpose reminiscent of the war itself. She particularly loved the fact that bureaucracy appeared to be lacking. The fact that no one had yet shepherded her back to where she belonged was an indication of how disorganised everything was. True, she liked to make fun of British muddling through, but as she watched a Dakota take to the air with a dozen more waiting like ducks in a row, her heart swelled with pride. In all this improvisation there was something glorious too.

She had to get that across in her article. If she combined what she'd seen at the USAF base yesterday it would be a terrific piece of reporting. The Americans were bringing in crews and aircraft not just from the Continental United States but from South America and the Pacific too. Meanwhile, she'd been told that if a plane was loaded and no crew was standing by, staff officers dropped whatever they were doing to rush out and fly it to Berlin and back. That kind of excitement and enthusiasm would inspire readers. After all, everyone understood that feeding two and a half million people was important work. All the boring facts from the briefing underlined that this mission was impossible in the long run, but that was not what people wanted to read today. They didn't want more bad news about what Britain couldn't do. They wanted to be inspired and proud again.

But she needed a catchy title. Something that captured both that enthusiasm *and* the improvisation. Maybe "Enthusiastic Improvisation"? Or "Wartime Spirit for Humanitarian Effort"? No, too clumsy. Better to stick to something simple like "Creative Chaos."

Chapter One
"Creative Chaos"

Braindead but Still Breathing
Allied Control Council, Berlin
2 July 1948
(Day 7 of the Berlin Airlift)

"Creative chaos!" Wing Commander Robert "Robin" Priestman snapped when he caught sight of the front page of *The Times*. Priestman was just 32, a vigorous, handsome man with dark hair and eyes, his dress blues enhanced by a DSO, DFC and Bar below his wings. "I concede that we need to be creative," he remarked dryly, "but chaos can end in disaster!"

Air Commodore Reginald "Rex" Waite laughed. "There's nothing wrong with a little chaos at the beginning of anything new, Robin." Waite's mild, intelligent face was garnished with a small moustache, and his greying hair was already receding. He was the British Air Attaché to the Allied Control Council (ACC). Although the ACC had always been cumbersome and never effective, since the Soviet Military Governor Marshal Sokolovsky had walked out on 20 March 1948 it was also brain dead. No more joint directives could be issued.

Despite that, the subordinate organs of the ACC — the various committees, directorates, departments, and centres for the implementation of policy — continued to function using the guidelines and directives established before the collapse of Four Power government. In consequence, the elegant and palatial former courthouse in the heart of Berlin that housed the ACC still hummed with activity. Since the start of the Airlift, no office was busier than the Berlin Air Safety Centre or BASC. Although air traffic control for take-offs and landings lay in the hands of the respective airfields, in a windowless room on the first floor of the ACC, representatives of all four occupying powers maintained an overview of approaching and departing air traffic.

31

Priestman, as Station Commander at the only airfield in the British Sector, RAF Gatow, had come to speak with the Senior Flying Control Officer at the BASC before dropping by Waite's office.

Waite picked up the newspaper left on his desk by an aide and scanned the article. He shook his head with bemusement and remarked as he handed it to Priestman, "I question the wisdom of allowing the press access to our facilities in these circumstances."

Priestman snorted his agreement, his eyes still scanning the article.

Waite remarked, "The speech you gave to personnel yesterday evening was spot on, by the way. It was clever to compare this to war."

"I wasn't trying to be clever," Priestman countered. "I feel that this is a kind of war — a war of nerves, intelligence and ingenuity."

"And creativity," Waite noted with a wink as he tapped the newspaper article, but then he grew serious. "It doesn't help, however, that both Transport Command and British Air Forces of Occupation appointed officers with identical orders to take charge of the airlift. They sorted that out by giving BAFO control of the airfields but leaving Transport Command in command of the squadrons flying the Airlift. Overlapping responsibilities of that sort are a recipe for disaster. We can be sure the bureaucratic battle continues behind the scenes while we try to muddle through."

"Muddling through is all very well, but how I am supposed to complete a concrete runway without any concrete or construction equipment!" Priestman couldn't keep the exasperation out of his voice.

"I thought the Corps of Royal Engineers was helping out?"

"Indeed, Lt. Colonel Russel is doing his best, but he has neither crushers to pulverise the stone nor a steamroller large and strong enough to compress and level a surface fit for a fully loaded Dakota — never mind a York. Steamrollers don't fit in the belly of any aircraft the RAF has."

"Could the Americans manage it in one of their Globemasters?"

"I've already looked into that. The problem there is that Globemasters can't land on PSP runways, and until I have a steamroller, I cannot build a concrete runway — and neither can the Americans."

Waite nodded. "I understand. I'll let you know if I think of anything useful. Was there anything else?"

"Gatow doesn't just need a concrete runway, it needs taxiways, hardstandings, and lighting to enable it to work 24 hours a day, but my main concern at the moment is Air Traffic Control. We're pouring aircraft down the three air corridors as fast as we can. They all end up in Berlin air space, milling about until someone downstairs," (meaning the Berlin Air Safety Centre) "sends them to either Gatow or Tempelhof, depending on what comes free first. This means that USAF aircraft from Frankfurt sent to Gatow and RAF aircraft sent to Tempelhof are crossing paths haphazardly. It's bad enough in clear weather, but in case you hadn't noticed Berlin seems to be shrouded in cloud half the time. Sooner or later there is going to be a mid-air collision, and when that happens, we're not only going to have body parts falling out of the sky, we're also going to have dead civilians on the ground. And did I mention the weather report is for pouring rain tomorrow?"

Waite nodded seriously. "You're right, Robin. ATC is an accident waiting to happen and the Sunderlands coming in on Monday won't make it any easier. Did you have any thoughts as to what we could do to make it better?"

"It's not my area of expertise, but I would have thought more regulated traffic flow would help. I tried to raise the topic with Group Captain Bagshot, but he told me to stop interfering in *his* Airlift."

"Hm." Waite nodded and conceded, "Bagshot can be a bit wet. I'm not sure BAFO made a wise choice in appointing him to overall command." While this was said sympathetically, both officers knew that there was nothing either of them could do to change the appointment.

"The Senior Flying Control Officer suggested that I go to a fully ground-controlled approach at Gatow," Priestman continued, "— regardless of weather."

"Could you?" Waite asked.

Priestman drew a deep breath. "Pilots hate GCA."

That did not answer the question, so Waite waited while the station commander subdued the pilot within and admitted, "If I had enough controllers, yes. Visibility is too poor too often, and too many pilots are being thrown onto this airlift without familiarity with either the corridors or conditions in Berlin. The Senior FCO told me that continuous use of a GCA approach at Gatow would enable the BASC to hand Gatow-bound aircraft over sooner and focus on Tempelhof."

"Sounds good to me."

"I'm going to give it a try, but...." His voice faded, and Waite looked over alertly. Priestman met his eyes. "Off the record, Rex. Do you still think we can do this?"

"Keep a city of two million people supplied entirely by air?"

Priestman nodded, keeping his gaze fixed on Waite.

"Let me put it this way, His Majesty's Government has committed itself without reservation and the RAF has a blank cheque for whatever it needs to get the job done. In just over one week we will have deployed every transport aircraft we have, but unless the United States is willing to make an equal commitment and deploy their entire cargo fleet as well, no. We cannot win this war alone any more than we did the last one."

Untapped Resources
Ypsilanti, Michigan
Friday, 2 July 1948

The radio announcer intoned dramatically, "...*President Truman called Soviet actions in Berlin an act of undeclared war, adding that the United States and its allies did not yet need to respond with guns. 'We are going to keep the people of Berlin alive by flying in whatever they need — even if that means diverting every aircraft of the Air Force and calling up our Air Force reserves...'*"

J.B. Baronowsky started and looked over at the car radio in shock. Surely, they wouldn't do *that*? He was just six weeks away from his wedding and two months from starting his first real job after graduating from college. The last thing he needed was to be yanked out of his life and sent overseas again. But he couldn't worry about that now. His father had collapsed at work and his mother had asked him to come home at once.

Home was an aluminium-sided, single-story house that differed little from a trailer beyond sitting on cinder blocks rather than wheels. It looked like all its neighbours, except that the tiny backyard was enclosed by a high, linked-wire fence to keep the family dog in and the neighbourhood strays out. J.B. stopped his car in the driveway, stepped out and walked in through the unlocked back door.

"Mom!" he called anxiously as the screen door chinked shut behind him. He stood in the kitchen crammed with counters, cupboards, appliances, and a tiny table. It was stifling hot and smelled of apple pie.

J.B. continued to the little living room beyond. Only the familiar worn-down sofas, low coffee table and oversized radio greeted him. The crackling sound of music wafted from the speaker, but there was no sign of his mother. He called out, "Mom!" again, and then added his younger brother's name too. "Stan?" Still no response.

J.B. turned towards the narrow hallway leading to the bedrooms and was relieved to see his mother coming out of the master bedroom. She called his name at the sight of him and then fell into his arms with a heartfelt, "Thank Jesus, Mary and Joseph."

"I got here as soon as I could," J.B. answered. "Is Dad all right? Where's Stan? What happened?"

"The doctors say it was a heart attack," his mother explained. "He's lucky it happened on the shop floor. Other workers saw him collapse and shouted for the factory doctor, who called the ambulance at once. They got him to the hospital in less than an hour and by the time Stan borrowed a car to drive me there, the crisis was over. I stayed all night —"

"You mean this happened yesterday and you didn't call me until two hours ago?" J.B. interrupted her.

"I didn't want to call until I knew what to say. You couldn't have helped. He was in the hands of God and the doctors."

"Well, I could have held *your* hand, Mom!" J.B. reminded her.

She stroked his face with a finger as she gave him a tired but sincere smile. "I know, Jay, but Stan was with me, and I really wasn't thinking all that clearly. I can't remember much of what happened, just feeling confused and frightened until I was able to talk to the surgeon. He was a very nice man, and he said your dad is going to be fine. He just needs rest—"

"He's not gonna like that," J.B. predicted, but he also smiled with relief.

"Well, I'm not so sure. He had a pretty bad scare. He told me that he thought he wasn't going to make it. He started worrying about not having life insurance and talking all kinds of nonsense."

"And they still sent him home so soon?" J.B. asked in disbelief.

"It's what your dad wanted. He told me we shouldn't be paying fancy hospital bills just for him to lie around in bed, and the doctor said it was fine, so long as I keep him quiet. Stan and I got him home and put him straight to bed. That's when I called you. Stan's taking the car back to your sister Sue. She and Barb will drop by after dinner."

J.B. nodded absently, not concerned with his younger siblings. "Is Dad on any medications?"

"Yes, I've got it all written down, but he's been sleeping like a baby."

"Can I go look in on him?" J.B. asked, glancing down the narrow hall.

"Yes, of course! He heard you come in and wants to see you. Meanwhile, I'll check on the pie before it burns. You're staying for dinner, aren't you?"

"You bet!" J.B. had moved into a house in Ann Arbor with four other college students after he was discharged from the Army Air Corps and resumed his studies at the University of Michigan. It had been much more convenient for classes, libraries, labs and dating, but he missed his mother's cooking.

At the door to the master bedroom, he knocked once and called. "Dad? It's me. Jay. May I come in?"

A gruff voice answered, and J.B. poked his head into the parental bedroom. His father was in bed wearing his pyjamas. His hair lay in enough disarray to reveal the growing bald spot on his skull that he usually tried to cover up with careful combing. As J.B. entered, he tried to sit upright, but his son pushed him back down with a firm hand on his shoulder. "Just lie still, Dad." J.B. pulled the chair from his mother's vanity closer to the bed and dropped onto it. "Mom says you had a bit of a scare, but you're going to be OK."

"That about sums it up," his father admitted, adding, "thanks to the Blessed Virgin who always hears your mother's prayers." He crossed himself with a glance towards the bright-coloured print of Mary with the baby Jesus in her arms. Then with a change of tone, he added more belligerently, "But thank God for the United Autoworkers' Union too. If this had happened before the last strike settlement, I'd have been out on my ass and God knows how we'd have paid the hospital bills."

"Now don't go worrying about the bills, Dad. Just focus on getting well—"

His father wasn't in the mood to be hushed. "All very well for you to talk, but Stan's gonna be a senior this fall, and if he doesn't screw up his grades, he'll be going to college next year. He's not entitled to GI-Bill benefits like you, so I gotta pay for him myself. I promised your Mother I was going see you boys through college and a promise is a promise."

J.B. liked the firm way his father said that; it showed that no matter how shaken he'd been by the medical setback, he'd lost none of his determination. In answer, however, he soothed, "Don't you worry about Stan's college tuition, Dad. I'm going to be earning enough to help with that."

"I don't want you paying for your brother!" the older man countered frowning, "I'll do what's right by him. I just wish he'd take school a little more seriously. He's not good at it like you were."

"Oh, at his age, I wasn't all that good at school either. Don't you remember? It was the good ol' Army Air Corps that taught me how to study. I wanted those wings so bad, I was willing to knuckle down. I'm not sure I told you in my letters, but more than half the guys washed out in training. A lot of them failed on the written exams, not in the cockpit. It put the fear of God into me when my best buddy, who was a hotshot pilot, got thrown out of flight school and sent to train as a radio tech because he screwed up on the navigation test. After that I had my nose to the books, believe me!"

"You never wrote about that," his dad told him, "And I probably never told you how proud I was of those wings either. I wanted to parade you up and down the factory floor when you came home."

"Mom practically did!" J.B. reminded him, laughing at the memory of his mother showing him off to neighbours and family on every possible occasion during his short home leave before deployment.

"I thought you might want to keep flying after the war," his dad noted with an intent look that seemed to demand an explanation.

"Yeah, you're right, Dad. I *did* want to keep flying — along with about 10,000 other ex-Army Air Corps pilots. There just aren't enough civil aviation jobs to go around. I figured, if I couldn't fly the birds, maybe I could design them. Which was why I wanted that job over at the Michigan Aeronautical Research Center, MARC, so badly. It would have meant not just being around planes but also learning about cutting edge aeronautical technology and maybe even a chance to go on test flights."

"That's the job Patty wouldn't let you take, wasn't it?" J.B.'s dad asked rhetorically; he was too ill to bother disguising his disapproval.

"That's right," J.B. admitted. His fiancée Patty came from a rich Irish Catholic family and her father was a VP at General Motors. She'd grown up in big houses in nice neighbourhoods and she'd had a fit when she learned the salary MARC was offering Jay. She argued that J.B. "deserved" much more, although he suspected what upset her most was that the job came with subsidised housing in Willow Run Village. Patty flat out refused to live on the workers' housing estate, and J.B. had no choice but to turn the job down. J.B. could partially understand Patty's point of view, but his parents were offended that she thought a starting salary the same as J.B.'s dad and a house nicer than their own wasn't good enough for her. The fact that Willow Run was so close to Ypsilanti had made the job doubly appealing to his parents and doubly unattractive to his fiancée. Patty wanted more distance from her soon-to-be in-laws. J.B. had been caught in the middle.

"And you turned down that job with Douglas Aircraft, too, didn't you?" the elder Baronowsky pressed his son.

"That was in Chicago, Dad. Mom didn't want me taking it any more than Patty did. That's history now. Patty's Dad got me fixed up with a great job in the Truck Division of General Motors with a starting salary of $70 a week. That's $3,600 a year — $200 more than Douglas was willing to pay me."

"Yeah, except it's designing trucks, not airplanes like you wanted."

J.B. frowned. His father had put his finger on the sore spot, and he didn't like being reminded of it. He was glad that his mother interrupted by putting her head into the bedroom to say, "J.B., come have some pie before it gets cold, and let your dad rest before dinner."

J.B. told his dad they could talk later and followed his mom into the kitchen. He squeezed himself into the chair behind the table, and his mother shoved a piece of still-steaming pie at him. With the edge of his fork, he cut into the flaky crust sprinkled with sugar and cinnamon. His mother leaned back against the kitchen counter, waiting until he'd put a big piece of pie in his mouth before remarking, "Jay, while I've got you sitting down and listening to me, I wanted to talk to you about your wedding."

"Yeah?" he mumbled with his mouth full.

"Well, I don't see why everything has to be so fancy. A reception at the

Detroit Yacht Club, of all places! Your dad is going to have to rent a tuxedo, and your sisters and I need to make new dresses—"

"Barb and Sue aren't going to mind doing that," J.B. pointed out, thinking his sisters would be delighted to have an excuse.

"Well, that's all very well for you to say, but now your dad is on sick leave at half pay!" his mother reminded him sharply, and J.B. winced. She was right, of course. He just found it impossible to dampen Patty's enthusiasm for a big wedding. In the circles she moved in, all the girls had big weddings, and she'd been dreaming and planning for her "big day" ever since (and probably before!) they got engaged this past spring. J.B. tried to mollify his mom. "You're right, Mom. I'm sorry. Maybe Patty could lend Barb or Sue something—"

"Not on your life, Joseph Bartholomew Junior! We're not taking any charity from your fine-and-dandy bride-to-be. We'll make do. I'm just saying...Well, I'm just saying what I think, that's all." She turned away and started rinsing off the things in the sink.

J.B. stood and put his arms around her. Resting his chin on her head, he said. "Come on, Mom. Give Patty a break. She's just excited and a little full of herself at the moment. You should be glad I'm marrying a Detroit girl. Remember how you worried I might get my head turned by some 'foreigner' while I was stationed in England?"

His mother snorted eloquently. "As if I could forget those horrible years when you were overseas! I haven't listened to the news since your dad took ill, but before his heart attack, the radio talked non-stop about this crisis in Berlin. I'm scared stiff this could blow up into a new war — and then you'll be right back in it thick of it, flying against the Reds instead of the Nazis."

"Don't worry about that, Mom," J.B. reassured her. "President Truman isn't going to let it come to that."

"I hope you're right. Your dad and a lot of other folks seem to think we've got to stop the Reds, but I don't see why our boys need to risk their lives to help a bunch of Nazis. If you ask me, the Russians and Germans deserve one another."

On Life Support
Berlin-Schoeneberg
Saturday, 3 July 1948
(Day 8)

Jakob Liebherr lifted his head and looked up as yet another aircraft dropped out of the cloud and growled its way across the sky. It flew so low that Jakob felt as if he could reach up and touch it. Tempelhof Airport, the only airport in the American Sector, was just four kilometres away and all the aircraft passing directly overhead were on final approach. They sank through the clouds with their wheels and flaps already down. You could see the white stars on their wings and the oil stains on their bellies.

Liebherr was amazed they could land in these conditions. He supposed it was very dangerous and there might be a terrible accident, but he didn't want to think about that just now. For the moment, these dirty old cargo planes were like angels from heaven. It was not so much the flour, milk, and coal they were delivering, he reflected as he continued towards the unadorned building that housed the offices of the SPD. It was the message of hope that they carried on their wings: hope that the Western Allies would not abandon Berlin.

A glance at his surroundings reminded him of just how important hope was. The hulking building ahead of him had been diminished by half by aerial bombardment, and the façade had been pock-marked by Russian artillery. Most of the plaster had fallen off, exposing the underlying bricks. Many of the windows were still boarded up with cardboard and plywood. Beyond, the roofs of several buildings were missing, and the top floors had been gutted by fire. As Liebherr passed into the SPD headquarters, he remembered that more than 200 people had been trapped in the air raid shelter across the street and suffocated there. Now the same air forces that had done the killing were attempting to supply the city with all vital necessities. It was a mad world.

Although Liebherr was tired after an hour's walk to get here, he knew there would be no electric power in this part of the city until later today. That meant the elevator wouldn't be working. He had no choice but to walk up two flights of stairs to the large conference room where the SPD representatives of the Western Sectors were meeting to discuss the situation. There was no point rushing. Two years in a Nazi concentration camp had left him with weak lungs, and he became very short of breath when climbing stairs. All he could do was take it one step at a time, literally. Fortunately, he was almost half an hour early.

Halfway to his destination, he was overtaken by his colleague Jeannette Wolfe. Just ten days ago, she had been attacked by a Soviet-incited mob and beaten before they could shepherd her to safety. Yet the sixty-year-old had not been intimidated and had raised her in voice in the Assembly to protest against Soviet demands. Now she slowed her pace to walk with him. "Everything healing?" Jakob asked her, nodding at her fading bruises.

"Tsch! You know what they say: what doesn't kill us makes us stronger. You and I saw the inside of concentration camps. A few amateur thugs aren't going to frighten us. Besides, I feel better with each passing aeroplane!" With a twinkle still in her eye, she pointed towards the ceiling that was vibrating as the next aircraft flew low over the roof.

They had reached the second floor and made their way along the corridor towards the voices spilling out of an open door. The windows of the conference room were some of the few that had been reglazed. A large (if badly scratched) table sat in the centre of the room, and men and women stood chatting in informal clusters around it. All belonged to the SPD caucus of the Berlin City Council and represented the eleven boroughs located in the French, British or American Sectors. There was no one here from the Soviet Sector because the Soviets had blithely ignored the results of a party referendum. Thus, although SPD party members had voted overwhelmingly against a merger with the Communist Party, the Soviet Military Administration (SMAD) had created the so-called "Socialist Unity Party", anyway.

As they entered the room, Berlin's elected mayor, Ernst Reuter spotted them. Like Liebherr, he was in his late fifties with a face aged by two world wars. His hair was white, but his thick, bushy eyebrows were still dark. He wore a tweed jacket and his iconic black beret, both of which made him look more like a professor than a lord mayor. Yet Reuter was a savvy politician. Although the Soviets had never allowed him to take office, much less occupy the office of the Lord Mayor in the City Hall in the Soviet Section of the city, the other elected members of the city council viewed him as their leader. Coming over to Jakob he asked, "What is your son saying these days, Jakob?"

Liebherr's only son was a staunch member of the SED, always ready to explain to his father the errors in the "old man's" thinking. Liebherr summarised his son's position for his colleagues. "He believes the Soviets have shown great forbearance in the face of Capitalist provocations. He points out that it would have been easy to send in the tanks to drive the 'warmongers' out of Berlin. The Soviets chose a blockade instead to 'spare' the working people of Berlin more bloodshed. According to Karl, everything will be over in a couple of weeks."

"He thinks the Amis and Brits will give up that soon?" Wolfe sounded alarmed.

"Yes, because the people of Berlin will riot against the Western 'warmongers,' and after that we will all have peace, joy and cake ever after as we sing victory songs with our friends from the Red Army and the NKVD." (The NKVD being the Soviet Secret Police.)

"Suggest that to the hundreds of thousands of women who have been raped and the tens of thousands of families who have seen their loved ones dragged from their beds and sent to Siberia!" Wolfe snapped back, her amusement abruptly evaporated.

"What do you think, Jakob? Any chance the Berliners will riot?" Reuter asked.

"Not any time soon," Liebherr answered. "For the residents in the French Sector, rations have actually improved since the distribution of Airlift goods is on a per capita basis regardless of Sector. Meanwhile, even my wife, hardly a master of the black market, has managed to get her hands on fresh vegetables from Brandenburg. This city may be divided by the artificial boundaries the Allies drew on a map, but Berliners aren't divided. We all have friends or relatives in other parts of the city. Everyone knows someone with access to Eastern rations or farms in the Soviet Zone willing to trade milk, butter or fresh vegetables for Ami cigarettes or French brandy and the like."

"Not to mention that 200,000 Berliners work in the West and live in the East or vice-versa," Reuter added. "Goods aren't supposed to move across the Sector borders, but people still do, and they can't all be stopped and searched."

"The Soviets didn't think this blockade through properly. They've left too many loopholes," Wolfe suggested.

Reuter shook his head soberly. "I doubt it. I suspect it was simply the pace at which the West introduced the D-Mark that surprised them. They were forced to implement a blockade before they were fully ready. If the Western Allies don't cave in and we don't riot in the next few weeks, I expect they'll tighten up the controls, making it much more difficult to smuggle anything across the borders."

"Are *you* worried, Ernst?" Liebherr turned the question on him.

"Am I worried about the Berliners? Not for a moment. It's the Capitalist Warmongers and their terror-bombers that I'm worried about." He gestured with his head towards the ceiling that was again vibrating enough to rattle the light fixtures as another C-47 flew low overhead.

"What about them?"

"Much as I admire Clay's willingness to try this airlift, I doubt they can keep it up very long. At least we'll have no problem with natural gas in the meantime, though," Reuter added with a sly smile.

"I thought the Soviets had cut off the natural gas supplies as well the electricity?" Liebherr responded, puzzled.

"They did. But I was looking through my papers the other day and came across all the infrastructure plans from my days working to expand the underground." Before the Nazis came to power, Reuter had been the municipal official responsible for public transport in Berlin. "I vaguely remembered that the gas mains — massive pipes almost a metre in diameter carrying the high-pressure gas — run right under Charlottenburg and Tiergarten on their way to the gas plant in Lichtenberg which is now controlled by the Soviets. I showed the plans to an officer from the Corps of Royal Engineers the other day, and he quickly identified several suitable places for tapping into those mains. He says we'll be able to siphon off as much gas as we want from the mains and can push it through our retail network. He doubts the Soviets will even notice."

"That's amazing!" Liebherr exclaimed delighted.

Reuter put his finger to his lips. "I'm not announcing this publicly. The fewer in the know the better. The importance of it," he continued, "is that many of our factories depend on gas-fired furnaces and generators. The ability to tap into the gas mains means we have a fighting chance to keep at least some factories running. My biggest fear, assuming the Allies don't get cold feet, is that if the factories close, the ensuing unemployment will trigger riots the Soviets want. It's idle men who are most likely to turn violent."

"The Allies are giving thousands of men jobs off-loading the planes at Tempelhof and Gatow. At the latter, they also have to tranship everything three times — once off the aircraft onto a truck, then from a truck onto a barge, and finally from a barge back onto a truck. I've heard they may need as many as 10,000 men." Wolfe pointed out.

"True, but I don't like the thought of everyone in Berlin working for the occupying powers. I want to see our industry survive."

"Yes, of course," Liebherr agreed, chastised.

Reuter glanced towards the wall clock and realised it was almost time to start the meeting. Reading his glance, Liebherr and Wolfe started to turn away, looking for places to sit at the table. Reuter held Liebherr back. "Jakob, wait. The reason I came over to talk to you was because of the air ambulance."

"Ah, yes," Liebherr answered, waiting for Reuter to go on. His neighbour Charlotte Walmsdorf worked for a private British aviation company that flew patients out of Berlin to the Western Zones.

"Back in April when the Soviets closed the land routes, we asked the air ambulance to evacuate eleven sick people in just two days."

"Yes, I remember. They hadn't really started operations but improvised splendidly. It was a spectacular little coup."

"Not only that. They've been flying patients out twice a week ever since — and all without a penny in compensation because we have no means to pay them. Obviously, they can't be expected to go on like that, which was why, when Clay announced he was going to try an airlift, I met the founder, Mr Goldman, and suggested that the Western Allies might be willing to foot the bill. It's been over a week, and I've heard nothing from him since. Meanwhile, I'm told the hospitals are desperate to get the sickest patients evacuated. Do you think you could reach Mr Goldman and find out what is going on?"

"Yes, of course."

"Thank you!" Reuter gave Liebherr a smile and a short pat on his back before turning to squeeze his way towards the head of the table. Liebherr gratefully sank into the chair Jeannette Wolfe had saved for him. He was as keen as the others to find out how much food and coal the Western Allies had managed to fly into the city in the last 24 hours.

Suspended Animation
Berlin-Kreuzberg
Saturday, 3 July 1948
(Day 8)

The ticking of the kitchen clock dominated the apartment. Charlotte Graefin Walmsdorf supposed that she ought to be doing something, but what? She was an employee of the British aviation company Air Ambulance International (AAI), but the crisis had disrupted operations leaving them in limbo. While she waited for word from her employer, she had nothing to do but look after the flat she shared with her cousin Christian.

She had swept and scrubbed and cleaned, but she could not cook because there would be no electricity in this part of the city until 9 pm tonight. Without electricity, she could not iron or use the sewing machine or listen to the radio or gramophone, either. There were no books in the apartment because they hadn't been able to take books with them when she and her parents fled from Walmsdorf in two horse-drawn wagons, and the apartment she'd moved into in Berlin had been plundered during the war and left almost naked.

All she could do was sit and wait for Christian to return. She looked again at the clock. It was four twenty in the afternoon, and he had been gone since before eight in the morning. She was terrified something might have happened to him. Christian took too many chances. He didn't seem to understand that he had been defeated along with the rest of the Germans. Born a baron, he had not known humility in his youth. He'd been privileged and rich from birth and had grown into a handsome young man who got everything he wanted easily. He'd always had lots of girlfriends, Charlotte remembered, and he'd been accepted into the most glamorous of the armed forces: the Luftwaffe. In the war, he'd been a fighter pilot, but he had not fought on the Eastern Front, only in France and Africa. He'd had the good fortune to be shot down in North Africa in 1943, which meant he'd been imprisoned by the Americans rather than the Soviets. When repatriated, he was not a skeleton with lice and intestinal worms like the men released by the Russians; he came home strong, tanned and healthy. And still proud. He did not bow his head or knuckle his brow when occupation troops addressed him. Charlotte was afraid for him. The hand of the clock jerked forward another minute.

When he'd arrived six months ago, he'd planned to remain only a couple of weeks while he found customers for the family wine, but to Charlotte's boundless relief, he'd stayed on — partly because he became increasingly wrapped up in his business and partly because he sensed how desperately she needed him. He also had a vendetta against surviving Nazis who'd found ways to profit even after they had plunged Germany into utter catastrophe. Christian, she sensed, would never forgive the SS for killing his brother.

Not that the SS had killed Philip directly, of course. Philip had shot himself in the family apartment on the first floor of this house. Philip had been Chief of Staff to General Olbricht and a close colleague of Graf Stauffenberg. He and his wife, who had been a secretary to General Olbricht, had both been deeply involved in the coup attempt against Hitler that culminated in the failed assassination attempt on 20 July 1944. But to Christian, the SD officer who had seized the family apartment after Philip's suicide and carted away the families' furnishings and treasures before the Russians arrived, had come to symbolise the entire Nazi regime. He wanted revenge.

That had surprised Charlotte at first because during the war Christian's attitude towards the Nazis had seemed more contemptuous than outraged. He'd viewed the leaders as crude and corrupt and their followers as naive and simple-minded. He was less complacent now. As an American POW, he'd been forced to watch films about the concentration camps, and then he'd returned to find that the Nazis had driven his brother first to treason and then to suicide. Christian was more anti-Nazi now than he had been during the war, and that put him in conflict with the Allies who wanted to lump him — and Philip — together with the Nazis.

Christian carried a pistol in his pocket, and he knew how to use it. Charlotte was afraid that he might — against one of the occupiers. If he shot an American, Englishman or Frenchman, he'd be tried before they hanged him. If he shot a Soviet, they'd just gun him down instantly. Charlotte shuddered and looked at the clock. It was now 4:32.

She got up and opened the door beside the sink that led onto a tiny balcony facing the central courtyard. It was crammed with flowerpots sprouting tomatoes, beans, peas and parsley. Everything here, including the clothes she'd hung out after washing, was soaking wet. A fine rain fell incessantly from low clouds. From the balcony, she could hear the steady rumble of aircraft engines overhead. They seemed to be everywhere and going in all directions. She couldn't imagine how they didn't collide with one another. She went back inside and closed the door behind her, anxious not to let in the damp chill.

She wished she could make herself a cup of tea to warm up and calm her nerves, but, as she had to keep reminding herself, there was no electricity until 9 pm tonight. Tomorrow it might not be until 11 pm or 1 am. Each Sector of the city received electricity just two hours a day on a rotating basis. Charlotte sank back onto the wooden chair and glanced again at the clock. It was 4:36.

What particularly frightened her today was that Christian had set out intentionally to break the blockade, that is, to see if he could obtain some eggs, milk, butter or lard from the Soviet Zone. He'd exchanged five bottles of his good wine for two bottles of home-brewed schnapps made by the dubious young men who lived in one of the apartments on the third floor. They worked the black market, thriving in the lawless environment bred by the lack of a functioning currency. No doubt they would do well in this mad world of blockade as well. Charlotte tried to avoid them. Fortunately, they took no interest in her and why should they? She was a gaunt, over-tall, unattractive, thirty-year-old woman with mannish haircut and old, threadbare clothes.

Abruptly, as sometimes happened, the memories started to flood in on her again. She cried out "no" to fend them off, but they surrounded her, darkening the room. There were four of them. No six. Tall and strong and armed. "No!" she'd screamed, but one hit her with the butt of his rifle. She'd shrieked in both pain and terror. The second soldier joined in the 'fun.' She tried Russian, screaming in desperation, "Nyet! Nyet." But the blows just hammered down on her until she was reduced to nothing but a whimpering, writhing, pleading, begging, and grovelling piece of loathsome humanity. By the time they were done with beating, raping, kicking and urinating on her, she was only partially conscious. If only she'd been completely knocked out, then she wouldn't have felt each and every cruel, revolting and insulting thing they'd done to her — or remember it so vividly ever after.

"Charlotte!" Christian called coming through the door. "Charlotte! I've got a pound of butter and, you won't believe it, four eggs!" He was proud of himself because he'd only traded one of the bottles of schnapps and still had the other in reserve for a later date. "Charlotte?" he called again, surprised that she didn't answer. He pushed the kitchen door open to put his precious satchel with the eggs wrapped in layers of rags onto the table. He was astonished to find no sign of Charlotte here. Surely, she wouldn't have gone out in the rain?

Christian put the butter in the refrigerator, cynically noting that with only two hours of electricity, it couldn't keep things very cold. Still, it served as a kind of insulated icebox, and the electricity would come on eventually. He left his overcoat on the rack in the hall by the door and glanced into the sitting room that faced the street. The only furnishings were an old packing crate and some wooden chairs — and the huge sideboard at the far end of the room. No Charlotte. He continued into and through the large "Berliner Zimmer" at the corner of the building and turned to start down the darkened hall towards the bedrooms. He kept calling in increasing alarm, "Charlotte? Are you here? Are you all right?"

A sob answered him.

Christian froze. "Charlotte?"

The sob came again, and he followed the sound into Charlotte's bedroom. She was curled up under the comforters on her bed. Christian went down on his heels beside her. "What is it, Charlotte? Are you ill? Has something happened?" She looked a complete wreck. Her face was swollen from crying and splotched with red marks; her short-cropped, blonde hair was in complete disarray.

"Would you shoot me, Christian?" she gasped out. When he recoiled in shock, she begged more insistently. "Please! It would be so simple and fast and merciful!"

Shock made him angry. "Of course not! Have you gone mad?"

"No, or yes, maybe. I don't know. But I can't go on, Christian, I just can't. It's no good pretending. I've tried and tried these past years, but..." She shook her head. "It's no good. I can't forget. And I can't live with the memories. It would be so good to end it all. Please shoot me." Her big, blue eyes focused on him like a wounded puppy.

"No! Never!" Christian told her forcefully, hoping to shock her out of this nonsense with his uncompromising tone.

"But it would be the most merciful thing you could do." She insisted, sitting up slightly to look at him more intently. "It would put me out of my misery — just as Horst killed Pasha when he was wounded by the Soviet fighter."

"Pasha was a horse! Furthermore, he was unable to continue the journey," Christian reminded her.

"But I can't go on either, Christian," Charlotte answered, tears slipping down her face again. "Just because you can't see how crippled I am, it doesn't mean I'm not as broken as Pasha."

Christian drew a deep breath to steady his nerves. He met Charlotte's eyes and they gazed at him, frightened yet as trusting as a child's. He was all she had left. He knew he had to help her.

"Charlotte, I can't understand how broken you are — or how to help you — if you don't tell me what happened."

She looked down and away and was silent for so long that Christian began to think she would not answer. Then abruptly she shrugged and without looking at him whispered in a voice full of shame, "The Russians. They got me."

"Today? Here in this house?" Christian reared up, ready to kill someone.

"No, no," she hastened to assure him. Adding as tears streamed down her face. "It was shortly after they took the city. In May '45. Jasha and I went out to get rations because we'd had nothing to eat for two days. We thought we'd be safe together, but they cornered us. Jasha tried to protect me, but they flung her aside and two — or maybe it was three? — fell on her and held her down and then took turns raping her. The others, there were six of them." She broke down into violent sobs again, her whole body shook as her lungs struggled to drag air into her lungs.

"Charlotte," Christian spoke gently as he reached out and pulled her into his arms as if she were a child. "Charlotte, it's over, it's done with—"

"NO, IT'S NOT!" she screamed at him, pulling away. "I will NEVER get over it! Because of them Fritz would look at me like slime, even if he should come back, and David —" she broke down into miserable, hopeless crying again. Fritz was her fiancée, missing since November 1943, and David was her employer — and the man she had fallen in love with against her better judgement.

Christian pulled her again into his arms and stroked her back and shoulders. "Hush, Charlotte. Hush. No one is going to blame you for being a victim—"

"Don't be so naive!" she rasped at him through her crying. "Men do it all the time. A thousand times a day. I see it every day with my own eyes! All of you — Russians, Amis, Brits, French *and* Germans! — you look at us like whores, like trash, like *shit*!" She spat out the last word, one she had been taught from childhood never to take in her mouth. The use of it now underlined how traumatised she was.

But there was a spark of anger in that deliberate use of the forbidden word, too. It gave Christian hope. He did not answer immediately. Instead, he made himself more comfortable, cradling her in his arms until she had calmed herself down again. Then he bent and kissed the top of her head as he told her, "I don't think of you like that, and I never could. To me, you are still my favourite cousin. The one I loved to ride out with. The one, unlike my silly sister, who didn't dislike the wind in her hair and didn't mind getting wet. You could harvest hay and drive the horse plough as well as any of us boys. I always admired you for that. You were good with the horses, too, and the dogs. So at ease with nature." He hesitated but then risked saying something that he knew might hurt her, but which he hoped would build her up, he added, "I think that was what Fritz loved, too."

Charlotte started crying again, and Christian cursed himself. But then, gradually, her sobs faded away. She pulled herself together and started wiping at her face with her naked hands. Christian offered her a corner of the bedsheet, which she accepted with a nod of thanks. Finally, she said in a dull voice, "I'll go and wash my face and make you some dinner."

"No," Christian answered closing his arms around her to hold her in place. "First, we're going to talk this through."

"I don't want to, Christian. I don't want to remember. That's the whole point."

"But you *do* remember, vividly and repeatedly, and I need to know what happened so I can help you."

"I've already told you!" she snapped angrily.

"I want to know what happened next, after the rapes."

"Jasha crawled over to me and when she saw what they'd done she started shouting for help. Some people came who had stood by and done nothing the whole time," she noted bitterly. "That happened a lot. Women would be grabbed and would scream for help, but everyone would just look the other way or go in the opposite direction." She paused and added in a whisper, "I did it too. When I heard screams, I just fled, terrified they would do it to me again."

"So, some passers-by brought you back here?" Christian focused on the narrative.

"No. I was too bloody. They decided I had to go to a hospital, so they found some sort of cart or a wheelbarrow. I don't remember exactly, only that I couldn't walk. They took me and Jasha to the Hospital am Urban and Trude Liebherr—"

"Our neighbour?" Christian asked. Herr and Frau Liebherr lived just across the landing.

"Yes, yes. She's a head nurse there, and she recognised us. When, after several days, they needed my bed for more recent victims, she brought me home, but insisted I live with them."

"With the Liebherrs?"

"Yes. They were so kind, Christian. They treated me like their own daughter, and I felt safe with them. I didn't have to go out at all, not even for food. They shared whatever they had with me. They even suggested I stay on with them after my injuries had healed."

"Why didn't you?"

"I didn't want to lose the apartment. Jasha was still with me. She'd been raped too and she needed a roof over her head. But then she got the chance to cook for an American family and live in their house. She was much safer there. I had to let her go."

"Of course," Christian agreed, "but why not stay with the Liebherrs after she left?"

"Because of their son. I was afraid of him."

"Karl? The SED official?"

"Yes, he is such an ardent supporter of the Soviets and — I couldn't bear to be near him."

"Did he harm you?" Christian asked sharply.

"Not physically, but he — he made excuses for what the Russian soldiers did. He said they had a right to do whatever they liked because of what we'd done to them."

"He said that to your face, knowing what had happened?"

"He didn't know the details, I suppose, but his mother had told him enough — at least about the state I was in when I was brought to the hospital, about my two broken arms and loose teeth and ... you know."

"And he still took the side of the Russians?"

"Yes. They all feel that way, Christian. Entitled not just to rape, but to maim, insult and humiliate us. And what can we say? After what we did to them?"

"That two wrongs don't make a right, and that you cannot call yourself civilised if you behave like a barbarian."

"But weren't we barbarians, Christian?" she asked him earnestly, her eyes boring into him, searching for his secrets.

He met her eyes unflinching and answered in a hard and very precise tone. "Who do you mean by 'we'? We Germans? Then, yes, some Germans were and still are barbarians." He paused, but then he spoke slowly and deliberately to make sure she felt the full weight of what he was saying. "But on my soul, Philip never in his life did anything that besmirched his honour let alone conflicted with his Christian conscience. And, whether you believe me or not, neither did I — although I was no saint in other ways."

She seemed to be listening to him very attentively, so Christian continued, "My sister Theresa, not to mention her SS husband Walther, deserves the hell she is burning in." For a moment, he let his thoughts linger over the incomprehensible fact that his own sister had embraced Nazi ideology. Without a trace of shame or discomfort, she'd lived in a confiscated Jewish home, enriched herself from the work of slave labourers in her husband's factories, and adulated an inarticulate, hate-filled madman. He still could not fathom it, but it didn't matter. All that mattered at the moment was Charlotte.

Turning to her, he said, "Charlotte, each person's soul is their own, and we can only be responsible for ourselves. *You* cannot be blamed or held accountable for the actions of men you never knew and could not control. No matter what *they* did in the name of Germany, *you* are not to blame. Do you have anything on your conscience that would justify what the Russians did to you?"

She shook her head slowly and looked at him from her tearstained and swollen face for several seconds before mumbling, "It's not that I blame myself, Christian. It's just that I lost all sense of self-worth. All of it! If you'd seen me.... I begged and grovelled and..." she cut herself off, took a deep breath, and declared, "I'll never be whole again, Christian. And I'll never be able to — to — be a wife to a man. Not even Fritz or ...." Her voice faded away, but Christian knew she was thinking of David Goldman. He wondered if it had been the thought that she would one day have to tell David about "it" — if her dreams of a relationship came true — that had triggered her spasm of despair and pleas for him to shoot her.

Christian took a deep breath. How could he predict the way another man would react to learning the woman he loved had been brutally gang raped? Some men could overlook that kind of thing. Others couldn't. He didn't know Goldman beyond a couple of business meetings. He decided on a half-answer. "There's no need for him to know about it. At least not yet. You have to live for today — and tomorrow."

"But how can I? I don't know if the company will even stay in Berlin. They may have to pull out entirely."

"Charlotte, I don't know David as well as you do, but one thing I'm sure of: he's a born businessman. He knows as well as you do that the ambulance is needed in Berlin, now more than ever. This is the opportunity of a lifetime, and he will find a way to take advantage of it. Just give him a little more time to work things out."

"How much more time?"

"I don't know, but at least another week."

Air Ambulance International
Berlin-Kladow
Sunday, 4 July 1948
(Day 9)

David Goldman had taken over the library of his host's home and spread his accounts and correspondence around him on the large desk and the various leather chairs. He was an orderly man by nature, and he'd been meticulous in keeping a record of expenses, income, contracts, and commitments. This past week of involuntary inactivity, however, had allowed him to review where the company stood and analyse the situation based on various scenarios. It had been an edifying exercise — and a depressing one. He'd made two bad miscalculations when he'd moved his business to Berlin, and he feared they were about to catch up with him.

David got to his feet and left the library with its floor-to-ceiling bookshelves and rich Persian carpets. He wandered into the cheerful winter garden. This offered large windows and potted palms. His dog Sammy, a Collie-mix with blond hair on his head and back but a white belly, jumped down from his favourite sofa to demand attention, and David absently patted the dog's head while gazing out of the French windows.

Until a week ago, the view from here had been of a wide, well-kept lawn stretching to the banks of the Havel River. It had been as lush, green and gracious as his childhood home above the Aussen Alster in Hamburg. With the start of this blockade, however, the Priestmans' Polish cook Jasha had, with the help of the gardener, turned most of it into a massive kitchen garden.

Much as he loved the understated luxury that had characterised the house before this conversion, he found the spirit of endeavour exemplified by the cook and gardener significant. Rather than moaning to the Western Allies about dried eggs, dried milk and dried potatoes — much less rioting as the Soviets had expected — all across the city the Berliners were defiantly digging in and declaring their determination to fight for their freedom. That impressed him. It even inspired him a little. It was part of the inchoate spirit that slumbered under the ruins of this city and made him warm to it despite its hideous face.

After all, his own face had once been hideous too. When he was first delivered to Dr McIndoe's care after being shot down in September 1940, it had been so repulsive it had made one nurse vomit. As the famous plastic surgeon reconstructed his face one operation at a time, it went through phases when it resembled a Chinese rice paddy, Frankenstein and a Greek theatre mask. Only gradually had it fused and formed itself into something more human. Eventually, it had become supple and marked by wrinkles. Few people nowadays suspected that his eyebrows had been cut from the skin under his arms or that his lips and eyelids were taken from the inside of his thighs. Yet even when his face had been at its most alien, the flame of his being had burned beneath the ugly surface.

Berlin, he thought, might be like that. Disfigured not only by the occupation and the bombing but by the Nazis before that. The Nazis — loud, violent, and aggressive — had obscured and drowned out the others, but they had never represented *all* of Germany.

Living here had brought back memories of two childhood friends who stood by him after the Nazis came to power. The memory of their support had been buried under the corpses of Auschwitz, Treblinka, and all the rest. What were two teenage boys distressed by what was happening to their Jewish friend compared to the horrors of Nazi genocide? Yet they had been good to the core, and they were not alone.

People like Ernst Reuter, Berlin's Social Democratic Mayor, and the city councillor Jakob Liebherr had spent years in a concentration camp because of their opposition to the regime. Christian Freiherr von Feldburg, despite having flown Messerschmitts for the Luftwaffe, hated the Nazis with every bone of his body because they had dishonoured his country. Indeed, Feldburg was bitterly committed to bringing the worst criminals to justice, while proudly reminding the Allies — and the Germans themselves — that not all Germans had been blinded by Nazi propaganda and victories. David had discovered that he wanted to work with men like these who were determined to rebuild a better Germany.

And it wasn't just the opponents of the Nazis who had won him over. David had also come to sympathise with men like Dr Schlaer, the optometrist who had taken over his uncle's shop on the Kurfurstendam. Yes, Dr Schlaer had done nothing to stop the SA from breaking the windows.

Yes, he'd served as a medic in the Wehrmacht. Yet he remembered David's uncle with respect and affection and was ashamed of what had been done in the name of Germany. That, David had discovered, was enough. Men like Schlaer would also contribute to a new Germany and David was comfortable helping them.

He knew that the vast majority of Germans had cheered and preened and lapped up Nazi racial ideology. They had loved being "the master race," predestined to conquer, rule and prosper. He understood that their selfish egotism had enabled the slaughter of millions. He despised the Germans who had swelled with pride when they oppressed others and now wallowed in self-pity because they were themselves oppressed. For such men and women, however, the humiliation of complete defeat and occupation represented sufficient retribution. Their presence no longer deterred David from wanting to remain in Berlin.

The perpetrators of the atrocities were another matter altogether. David was determined to stop Nazis from benefitting from the property of his murdered relatives, and David believed that the man living in his uncle's home, claiming to be an "innocent" businessman, was a Nazi war criminal. Seeing him expelled was another factor keeping David in Berlin.

Yet the most compelling reason for staying here was Charlotte. David had never felt the same way about any other woman in his life. She was so vulnerable, so fragile despite her height and almost masculine features. From the moment he set eyes on her, he'd felt a protectiveness for her. He wanted to be her knight in shining armour. In the best tradition of chivalry, he wanted to be her servant, obedient to her wishes. Yet she was skittish and shy, and he didn't know how to approach her. Instead, they danced around what he sensed was a mutual attraction and hid behind their official roles as employer and employee.

Which brought him back to his accounts and the serious situation he found himself in. He turned his back on the re-purposed lawn and returned to the library to face facts. The company had already run up substantial debts before the blockade started, but no sooner had the Soviets made their move than his British ground crew had mutinied and refused to remain in the beleaguered city. His partner Kiwi had flown them back to the UK in their modified Wellington to give them a week to think things over. Aviation jobs, after all, didn't grow on trees. But David had heard nothing from them since.

Meanwhile, the Berlin City Council was pressing him to resume flights. Jakob Liebherr had called him just this morning to impress on him how urgently the city needed the services of his company — while admitting that they were still unable to pay him. They had again suggested that the company approach the Western military governors with a request for the Allies to cover the cost of evacuating patients.

David was not optimistic about that proposition. The Allies were spending astronomical sums on the Airlift already. He could not imagine them being receptive to a request to compensate a private company. Indeed, he was dubious about the prospect of even getting a hearing from any of the military governors — unless he imposed on Robin to make the request for him. Asking his friend to use precious influence on his behalf was not something he felt comfortable with. Robin had enough on his plate as it was.

"David?" It was the voice of his hostess, employee and friend Emily Priestman as she put her head around the library door. She was smiling. "David? I've got fabulous news!"

"What?" David asked sceptically.

"A telegram from Kiwi!" She waved it at him as she came deeper into the room. He took it from her.

GROUND CREW PREPARED TO WORK FROM BIZONIA STOP PROCEEDING TO RAF WUNSTORF TOMORROW AM STOP WILL AWAIT FURTHER INSTRUCTIONS THERE STOP KIWI

Thank God for Kiwi! David thought, hardly daring to believe what he was reading.

Emily was grinning at him and announced, "Robin says this calls for a drink."

The Station Commander entered the library adding, "or two."

"Yes, and no. I still don't know how I'm going to get paid!" David reminded them. It frustrated him that no one else seemed to grasp the importance of making a profit — or at least stopping the haemorrhaging of assets.

"What did Herr Liebherr say?" Emily asked, knowing only that David had received a call from the councillor earlier in the day.

"That we have to ask the Allies to foot the bill," David told her, shifting his attention to her husband to ask, "Do you think there's any chance of that?"

"Your expenses are chicken feed compared to what the Airlift is costing the British taxpayer," Robin retorted. "The problem is that Robertson sometimes gets lost in the weeds. He could decide that *your* costs are the straw that will break the camel's back. Or he could start bargaining with you about your rates or insist that you need a joint commitment from all Allies via the Control Council."

"But that's completely moribund!" David protested.

"I know. I'm telling you how Roberston thinks and reacts. If you want Allied money, the best way to go about getting it is to go straight for the jugular."

"Meaning?" Emily asked baffled.

"You have to go directly to General Clay and put your case to him," Robin told her.

Emily turned to look at David, but her husband clarified. "I don't mean David, Emily, I mean *you*."

"What?" she gasped back at him. "Why me?"

"Because he's met you, likes you and because he's a southern gentleman who will not refuse to give a lady an hearing — no matter how busy he is. I'm sure Air Commodore Waite will support you in this. You know he's always been enthusiastic about the air ambulance. If we ask him to request a meeting for you — possibly together — Clay will see you."

"Couldn't Air Commodore Waite meet Clay? There's no reason why I have to be there, is there?" Emily appeared reluctant to make this impertinent request of the powerful American general.

"Yes, there is, my dear. If Waite makes the appeal, it would appear to come from HM Government — which it does not. Either you or David must make this request, and I think you'd be more successful. But I will suggest to Waite that he accompany you. Is that fair enough?"

Emily nodded, resigned to her fate.

"Good." He looked at his watch. "If you'll pour the drinks, David, I'll put a call through to him straight away. If he's able to set something up, remember Clay prefers women *out* of uniform. And, of course, you need to bear in mind that if Clay says 'no' there will be no appeal."

David nodded grimly. "If Clay turns us down, it will be curtains for AAI."

"And many critically injured and ill Berliners," Emily reminded them both.

Chapter Two
Absurdities

Flipping a Switch — Part I
RAF Gatow
Monday, 5 July 1948
(Day 10)

The char staff was still working when Wing Commander Priestman arrived in his office. The sound of the vacuum cleaner in the anteroom droned annoyingly as he hung up his cap and settled himself behind his desk. As requested, the log of landings and take-offs from the previous day had been left in his in-box along with the inventory of spare parts and fuel, the progress report on the runway construction, and the updated summary of the tonnage of cargo delivered into Gatow for the civilian population of Berlin. On top of these routine files, a hand-written note reminded him that the first Sunderland flying boats were due to join the Airlift today, landing on the Havel mid-morning — weather permitting.

A glance out the window confirmed that the weather was splendid. The morning mist was already lifting, and the sun was starting to burn off what was left of the ground fog. Air Commodore Waite and the public relations team had made a major effort to invite the local and international media to what promised to be an impressive display of British aviation capabilities. The big flying boats were nothing if not majestic, and they made quite a splash, literally, when they settled down on a body of water. A whole flotilla of small craft, Waite promised, would be on hand to greet the great mechanical ducks, and barges would be standing by to offload the cargo before the flashing cameras of the press. Robin hoped to dash over to welcome the crews, but that would depend on the other items on his agenda.

As he reached for his appointment diary, Sergeant Andrews, the WAAF clerk who ran his office, entered with his morning tea. "Everything all right this morning, sir?" she asked cheerfully.

"So far," Priestman answered, just as the ceiling light went out. They both glanced up towards the light fixture in the centre of the room.

"Must be the bulb," Andrews suggested, "I'll call maintenance."

But Priestman noted that the sound of the vacuum had cut off at the same instant that the light went out, and he had a sinking feeling. From the hallway came excited jabbering in German. His desk faced the window towards the runways, but the windows on the other side of his office looked out over the rest of the station. Priestman stood and went to look out of these. Just as he'd dreaded, agitated people were emerging from various buildings. A moment later the generator for the control tower groaned into operation. "We've lost power all across the station," he told his secretary in a resigned tone.

"Do you think the construction crews working on the new runway might have cut the main line, sir?" Andrews suggested optimistically.

"We can hope," he answered as he returned to his desk. Without bothering to sit down, he reached for the phone, half expecting it to be dead; he was relieved to hear a dialling tone. He rang through to the tower. "How many aircraft do you have on approach?"

"Two in Berlin airspace and six in the corridor. All eight aircraft of No. 30 Squadron coming in loaded with flour and other foodstuffs."

"Get them down. I'll try to stop the next squadron from taking off."

"Do we know what happened, sir?"

"I can guess." Priestman hung up. It was one of the bizarre anomalies of the absurd situation in which they found themselves that — although Gatow received its electricity from the Soviet Sector — power had not been cut on 24 June when the lights went out across the rest of the Western Sectors. Since no one wanted to wake sleeping dogs, the issue had not been raised with the Soviets. It appeared, however, that the Soviets had just discovered their mistake and corrected it.

Priestman started to work through the consequences. The radar generator for the tower might work for another hour or two, but eventually it would run out of diesel. While they still had limited reserves of diesel, without power the petrol bowsers would not work, so they would have to refill the generator by hand, which would take a long time. Yet even if they could keep the tower operational, they still needed electricity for the equipment in the maintenance hangars and to light the flare path for landings after dark, not to mention lighting for taxiways, hangars, and to run the kitchens etc..

Tempelhof might still have some extra capacity. The USAF had more cargo aircraft on the books than the RAF, but they were dispersed across the globe. In fact, on the day the Airlift started, the USAF hadn't had a single freighter in Germany and had been forced to charter a civilian carrier to bring in their first load of cargo for the people of Berlin. In the subsequent ten days, they started collecting a fleet of freighters from around the world, but the aircraft were not all assembled. Thus, in the short term at least, the RAF might be able to divert some inbound traffic to Tempelhof.

The Station Adjutant, Flying Officer "Stan" Stanley, was in the doorway. "Are you aware that we've lost power across the airfield, sir?"

"Yes. Check with Lieutenant Colonel Russel about whether his construction crews might have damaged something. Meanwhile, I'll find out if incoming flights can be diverted to Tempelhof." As he spoke, he sat down behind his desk and took up the receiver again, requesting a connection to Group Captain Bagshot, the RAF Airlift commander.

Priestman was relieved to be put through to the senior officer promptly, although Bagshot sounded irritated — as if he didn't like having to deal with Gatow. "Sir, we have a complete power cut here at Gatow. Would it be possible for you to divert traffic to Tempelhof?"

Bagshot grunted his displeasure, but agreed, "I'll see what they can handle, but it won't be everything. What the devil caused the power outage and how fast can you get it repaired?" He made it sound as if he suspected Priestman of some sort of negligence.

"I'm checking on that now, sir. There's an outside chance that the runway construction crew damaged a power cable. However, given that our power comes from the Soviet Zone, I'm afraid we must assume that the disruption was intentional."

"Did you just say what I think you said?" Bagshot sounded incredulous and his Scottish accent became particularly thick. "Your power comes from the Soviets?"

"That's correct."

"Why didn't they cut it off before now, then?" Bagshot asked flabbergasted.

"You'll have to ask the SMAD that, sir."

"Why didn't anyone tell me about this?"

"I'm sure I mentioned it in your first briefing, sir, but since the Soviets hadn't cut the power, it appeared that they did not intend to do so."

"In other words, you *assumed* everything would be all right," Bagshot sneered. "*Wing Commander*" (he stressed the lowly rank of the offender) "Priestman *assumed* — and was wrong! Don't you understand that if Gatow has no power we can call this whole thing off? It's impossible for us to supply everything Berlin needs by air if we have only one receiving airport! But because Wing Commander Priestman *assumed* the Soviets would not cut off his power, we've started this massive operation and crowed about it to the whole world! We'll certainly look the fool now!"

This outburst, Priestman decided, did not require a response. He confined himself to asking in a clipped, professional voice. "Will you be able to stop incoming flights to Gatow until further notice, sir?"

"Oh, I'll stop them all right! But if you don't get this sorted out very soon, you can be sure you won't be commanding Gatow for very long — or any other station either! I very much doubt you'll keep your commission after making His Majesty's entire government look like perfect idiots to the rest of the world!" With that, the Group Captain hung up.

Priestman put the receiver down and stared at it for a moment as if waiting for it to catch fire. Then, unable to sit, he stood and went to the window overlooking the runways. He watched dispassionately as the first of 30 Squadron's Dakotas set down decorously on his PSP runway and rolled to the far end, braking carefully. As it turned off the runway, it was met by a Land Rover that led it to the apron in front of one of the hangars. Already the next Dakota was in sight, turning in for the final approach.

After several seconds, Priestman realised he'd been left cold by Bagshot's threats to his career. The far more important issue was the Airlift itself. As Group Captain Bagshot had so bluntly pointed out, supplying Berlin entirely by air was challenging even with two fully operational receiving airfields. It would be utterly impossible to maintain the Airlift if Gatow were knocked out of the game.

Which was exactly what appeared to have just happened. The Ivans were on the brink of shutting down the Airlift before it fully got off the ground. Embarrassingly, they had not even needed to employ force, making a mockery of Clay's promise that "nothing short of war" could force the Western Allies out. Far from starting a war, all the Ivans had needed to do was flip a switch. Now Gatow was useless, 'kaput' as the Germans said, and that meant the Airlift was over.

Yet, some part of Priestman's brain refused to accept that very simple fact. Some stubborn part of him insisted there had to be a way out of this fiasco. Maybe there was a chance they could draw power from the one small, inadequate, and overworked power plant located in the West? Obviously, meeting Gatow's electricity needs would reduce the amount of power available for the factories, transport, facilities and households of the civilian population, but the alternative was surrender. Furthermore, he had to be sure that was technically possible before raising the possibility with the city government. The man who could answer the technical question was Lt. Colonel Russel. Meanwhile, the arrival of the Sunderlands might distract attention while they looked for a solution. If he was lucky, it might be afternoon before anyone noticed that the airspace over Gatow was strangely silent.

A knock on the door interrupted his thoughts and he turned to call, "Yes? Come in!"

Lieutenant Colonel Russel, Corps of Royal Engineers, stuck only his head around the edge of the door as if he were trying to make as small a target as possible before squeaking out in mock terror. "Don't shoot! Don't shoot! It wasn't us!"

Priestman laughed, thankful for the engineer's humour at a time like this. "I never thought it was — I only *wished* it was. Come on in. I was just about to call you, anyway."

Russel was a head shorter than Priestman with chest and shoulders too broad and powerful for the lower half of his body, which appeared awkwardly stunted. Russel wasn't a handsome man either, but he was a bundle of energy. As he came deeper into the room, he was already speaking. "I've got something which I think will interest you." From under his arm, he pulled several large sheets of paper. Heading straight for Priestman's coffee table and spreading out the large blueprints, he explained, "These are plans of the city infrastructure that Mayor Reuter lent me so we could tap into the gas mains. I remembered seeing something odd on it – something possibly useful. Come and have a look!"

White Elephant
Gravesend Airfield, UK
Monday, 5 July 1948
(Day 10)

Kiwi was at the airfield just after daybreak. He was dressed in the sleek, black, double-breasted uniform of Air Ambulance International. It resembled the Royal Navy uniform with rows of brass buttons down his chest, but it boasted a red eagle holding a red cross in its claws on the left breast pocket. The four stripes on his sleeve, which indicated he was the captain of the aircraft, were red like the company logo, but the pilot's wings, shaped in cloth like RAF wings, were gold instead of silver. In place of a closed collar and tie, the uniform was designed for an open collar and a red silk ascot, giving it a jaunty, modern touch. The ensemble was striking and flattering — as long as Kiwi kept his weight down and his belly from bulging, a constant battle.

This morning, however, Kiwi was at his best. He'd shaved so closely that he was sure he'd lost a layer of skin. His hair was cut short and slicked back with Brylcreem. He'd even put on aftershave, not because he expected to encounter attractive women in the course of the day but because he hoped that, after near shipwreck of the ground crew mutinying last week, AAI was now back in business.

Kiwi parked his ancient Vauxhall beside the abandoned officers' mess at this de-commissioned, former RAF station, and dragged his kitbag out of the boot. It contained most of his worldly goods: a change of uniform, several sets of underwear, his shaving kit, logbook, and some silver-framed photos. The latter held the memories of the family farm in New Zealand which his elder brother hadn't been able to keep, his parents (both now deceased), the Tiger Moth he'd flown in his barn-storming days, and a picture of him with his squadron in France from 1945. That was about it. Which was probably a sad commentary on a man of 31, Kiwi reflected, but it did keep him flexible. He knew he was going to have to be that in the days ahead.

Shouldering his kitbag, he made his way to the hangar which still carried a large sign reading "Essex Aero" in tall blue letters. The firm had suffered a series of setbacks and only a caretaker and a manager remained at the airfield. The latter manned the tower as necessary. It was this near moribund status and skeletal staff that made it such a cheap place to rent hangar space.

The men from Essex Aero emerged out of the woodwork at the sight of Kiwi. He'd warned them the day before that he was planning to fly out today. He looked up automatically to check the weather. The morning mist still clung to the trees beyond the fence, but it was early still. He waved to the Aero men. "Can you help me get her onto the apron?"

They waved back and went to get the tractor while Kiwi continued into the hangar housing their converted bomber. In place of wartime camouflage, the Wellington was painted white with red crosses under the cockpit and on the tail and "Air Ambulance International" spelt out in large, italicised, red letters where once the squadron ID had been. Kiwi thought the warplane looked very chic in its new livery. It was known affectionately in the company as "Moby Dick."

By the time the aircraft had been pushed out of the hangar, some patches of brighter mist promised more sunshine as forecast. Kiwi looked at his watch, hoping the ground crew, Chips and Ron, would not leave him in the lurch. They were good lads. They had served together throughout the war and worked like a well-oiled machine, but he was still a little nervous about their commitment to returning to work in Germany.

As the second hand of the hangar clock jerked around the clock face, Kiwi started to worry, but almost on the stroke of eight o'clock he heard the put-put of an old engine. Following the sound, he watched as an ancient lorry stopped at the gate and stood there shivering long enough for the two young mechanics to drop down and reach for their kitbags. Ron waved at him, and Kiwi waved back with relief.

As they joined him, he shook hands and then suggested, "Let's get cracking. Start the DI while I go and file a flight plan." He left Ron and Chips to do the daily inspection, confident that Moby Dick was in good shape, and crossed to the old ops tower. The feeling of abandonment evident across the field was particularly strong here, where the equipment was still in place but collecting dust. The Essex Aero manager was waiting with the weather radio on. He waved to Kiwi, who went over to him and presented the flight plan he'd worked out the night before.

"Are you going to be taking part in this aerial relief effort, then?" the manager asked.

"Well, not directly. We'll be flying passengers out rather than food and coal in."

"But you know about the corridors and all that? I hear the Russkies shoot anyone who strays over their airspace."

"I know all about it," Kiwi assured him.

"All right then," the manager shrugged, shaking his head to suggest he wouldn't have wanted to be in Kiwi's shoes.

Chips and Ron were ready to start the engines when Kiwi rejoined them. He climbed up the ladder, pulling it inside after him and battening down the hatch. He squeezed his way to the cockpit and Chips turned over the lefthand seat to him while Ron handed him the checklist. Kiwi sensed they were as pleased as he was. They were getting off to a good start.

Approaching Wunstorf, Kiwi was surprised by how little radio chatter came over the earphones. He'd expected the base to be very busy. He took the mic to call in. "This is Air Ambulance International 001 on approach to Wunstorf. Do you read me?"

"Air Ambulance International, reading you loud and clear. What is your destination again?"

"RAF Wunstorf."

There was a pause.

"Do you have an emergency?"

"No, but a lot of people in Berlin do. This is an ambulance servicing Berlin."

"Have you been cleared to Berlin?"

"Yes," Kiwi bluffed. "The Berlin City Government has requested our services."

"Roger. Turn right on 185."

"Turning right onto 185."

They landed without further incident. The skies were empty, but the airfield was wingtip-to-wingtip aircraft. There must have been fifty Dakotas and a least a dozen Yorks just sitting around idle despite being fully loaded. "Something's wrong," Kiwi commented generally.

"Could the weather be different in Berlin?" Ron asked, looking up at the bright skies overhead.

"Maybe," Kiwi conceded, although he thought it unlikely based on the weather report he'd received before take-off.

The "follow-me" vehicle led them to what felt like the last available space on the taxiway. Here they cut their engines and dropped down out of the over-heated cockpit. The air was surprisingly clean because none of the aircraft parked around them had their engines running. Instead, aircrew sat around in small groups on the grass playing card games, reading magazines, or smoking as if they were on 'readiness,' awaiting the order to 'scramble'. Except, this wasn't a fighter station. These cargo crates ought to have been winging their way to Berlin.

"I'd better go and get the gen," Kiwi declared, meaning find out what was going on. He left Ron and Chips with Moby Dick and headed for the control tower.

Mounting the stairs, he noticed lots of people sitting and standing around. Some people were typing, telephoning or manning a teleprinter, yet most were just loitering around and chatting. Very strange.

He entered the tower, and several men turned to look at him. One of them was a big, red-haired man with a moustache and the four stripes of a Group Captain. "Are you the pilot of that white elephant out there?" he burst out in an angry, Scottish voice.

"It's an air ambulance," Kiwi tried to explain.

"I couldn't care less what it is! It's not an RAF transport aircraft and it has no business on my airfield!"

"But—"

"There are no buts! Get that bloody white elephant off my airfield! Now!"

"Where should I take it?" Kiwi tried to reason with him. "I was told to come here to await further instructions."

"I don't give a damn what you were told by someone I don't know! I'm in charge here, and I'm telling you to move that sodding thing, or I'll have a bulldozer do it for you."

"The Berlin city government has requested—"

"Well, they didn't talk to *me* about it! Get out and take your bloody white elephant with you!"

Kiwi decided the Group Captain was not a man to be reasoned with and opted for retreat. Pointedly *not* saluting the pompous RAF commander, he turned and walked out of the tower, trying to work out what he should do now. He was grateful when he felt a gentle tap on his sleeve and a Flight Sergeant gestured with his head for him to follow. Kiwi obediently fell in behind the NCO, who led him to an office and closed the door behind him. "Sorry about that, sir. Group Captain Bagshot is a bit on edge because Gatow is closed."

"What? Why? How?" Kiwi asked flabbergasted. "An accident?"

"No, apparently the electricity for the entire station is supplied by the Russkies, and they've cut off the power. Nobody knows what will happen next. Could be curtains for the whole show, you see. Anyway, it's quite a tense situation with no leeway for an unexpected visitor, I'm afraid. If you need to get to Berlin today, you might try flying to Rhein-Main. Tempelhof is open, and the Americans are still flying in."

"I was told to stage here awaiting orders. We only fly in when the patients are ready for evacuation," Kiwi improvised, realising that he'd made a huge miscalculation in assuming they could just settle in here at Wunstorf.

"I don't know what to say, sir. All RAF fields are backed up with aircraft that can't get into Gatow. You'd probably be better off flying to a civilian field to await instructions there."

Civilian fields cost a bloody fortune! Kiwi thought to himself. They charged you for everything except the air you breathed — and they'd charge for that too if they could work out a way to meter it. Still, they obviously weren't welcome here. It would be better to move to somewhere less congested. "What do you suggest?"

"Hamburg, sir."

"Can you help me file a flight plan for that?"

"Of course, sir," the Flight Sergeant replied helpfully.

With a sigh, Kiwi resolved to ring through to David from there. He might know more about what was going on at Gatow. Robin would, of course, but this was no time to bother him. Emily might have some answers, but any way you looked at it, this wasn't good news for Berlin — or AAI.

Rendezvous with Power
Berlin-Dahlem
Monday, 5 July 1948
(Day 10)

Although Emily Priestman had met General Clay at the gala reception marking the anniversary of VE Day two months ago, she was acutely aware that she was out of her depth in approaching the American Military Governor. The four Allied Powers might officially be equals, but whether the British and French liked it or not, they needed American support for almost everything. As for the Soviet military governor, he had no more power than a doorman; he simply carried out orders from Stalin. Which left Clay in a league by himself.

Clay was reputed to have clashed with his bosses in the Pentagon and with the Department of State many times. He was neither a puppet nor a lackey, and he represented the most powerful nation on earth, not to mention the only one with nuclear weapons. Emily found the idea of putting the case to fund AAI to Clay intimidating — no matter how charming he had been at the VE Day reception.

Her nerves were further strained by the situation in Gatow. When Robin had rung through with the news that the Soviets had cut the power, she'd questioned whether she should go ahead with her scheduled meeting with Clay. Robin had countered with: "For the moment, I want to act as though there is nothing wrong." Although she could not argue with him in the midst of this crisis, that answer did not ease her concerns about a meeting with Clay.

Because Air Commodore Waite had been the unofficial master of ceremonies at the reception of the first flying boats, he offered to swing by after the event to pick her up and drive her over to the US military HQ for their meeting with Clay at 7 pm. The first Sunderland had put down practically at the foot of her garden and had presented a dramatic show of British airpower. She'd enjoyed the spectacle and was quick to congratulate Air Commodore Waite on a successful event when she settled into the back seat of his official car, but she also admitted, "I'm very nervous about this meeting."

"No need for that. I expect General Clay will be quite receptive to your appeal. He is a fundamentally decent man. Do you know what he told the US Congress a few months ago when testifying about this European Recovery Plan?"

She shook her head.

"He told them that 'The American flag should not wave over any place where children are starving.' Just like that. He *shamed* them into extending the Marshal Plan to our former enemies. I was very impressed, particularly since he arrived here with little fondness or respect for the Germans."

Emily nodded, before confessing a little sheepishly, "I shared that dislike of the Germans, and I haven't entirely overcome my unease with them. I just can't forget the Concentration Camps. I know there are good Germans, people like Charlotte and her cousin, but the vast majority," she gestured towards a long queue of people standing at a bus stop they were passing, "supported Hitler — at least as long as he was winning."

"I can't say I'm terribly fond of the Germans as a nation either, but their response to this Russian blockade has convinced me that *if* we are going to make a stand, this is the place to do it."

"Possibly," Emily answered cautiously, "but that only makes the fact that Gatow has been shut down all day more explosive. We're standing on the brink of failure, aren't we? And my husband, like it or not, is associated with that failure because he's responsible for Gatow. I'm not at all sure I'm the person General Clay wants to see today."

"Mrs Priestman, I assure you, General Clay is not going to hold you responsible for what is happening at Gatow. Don't worry." He smiled encouragingly at her, but Emily's sense of foreboding continued.

Well ahead of time, they reached the complex of the former Luftwaffe regional HQ which had been converted into US military headquarters. Although it had been built in the functional style favoured by the Nazis, the Americans had painted the façade a more friendly white. Still, the barbed wire along the top of the walls and the tanks flanking the gate underlined this was the HQ of an occupying military. The guard saluted Air Commodore Waite smartly and leaned down beside the window to ask his business.

"We have a meeting scheduled with General Clay at 19:15," Waite informed him.

The sentry said "Yes, sir," and retreated into his pillbox to put a call through, verifying their story, before waving them into the compound with instructions on where to park. As they climbed out of the car, a US Army lieutenant greeted them. His trouser creases were so sharp that Emily was sure they would draw blood if she touched them.

He led them through a warren of corridors that exuded an atmosphere of intense purposefulness. Men busy as uniformed bees hurried here and there. Telephones rang. Typewriters clacked. The heels of polished shoes pounded on the gleaming granite of the well-washed floor. Emily felt utterly out of place. In the military governor's anteroom, the lieutenant indicated they should take seats alongside a dozen other supplicants awaiting an audience with the most powerful man in Germany. The lieutenant then disappeared into the inner office.

As Emily sat down, she felt the others assessing her surreptitiously. Men, particularly military men, were apt to categorise women by what they wore. Emily was grateful that the RAF clothing allowance enabled her to outfit herself in stylish, quality, tailored clothes. These suggested she was too much of a lady to be dismissed as either a floozy or a mousy housewife, without looking overly manly. The latter would have pigeon-holed her as a troublesome do-gooder.

The door to the inner office opened and General Clay appeared. Emily rose to her feet and advanced to shake his outstretched hand. She could not remember ever seeing the American military governor without dark circles under his eyes, yet he still managed to look more exhausted than usual. That didn't stop him from smiling and announcing in a soft, Southern drawl, "A pleasure to see you again, Mrs Priestman. Do come in. Air Commodore Waite." He returned the latter's salute and then held out his hand, drawing the Air Commodore inside his office as he closed the door behind them.

Clay indicated they should sit at a coffee table and took a place at the head. He did not offer them coffee or tea, an indication that he expected their visit to be short. He had given them priority over that gaggle of officers in the outer office, but he expected them to keep their part of the bargain and confine the visit to a concise minimum. Then, just as she took a deep breath to thank him for his time, Clay announced in a deceptively friendly tone combined with a sharp, penetrating look, "I've been told Gatow is closed."

"Yes, temporarily," Waite jumped in, drawing the American general's gaze and unspoken ire away from Emily.

"Is it true that the power for the entire station is supplied by the Soviets?" Clay asked in a tone of carefully controlled disbelief.

"Correct, and until this morning that appeared most fortunate. Keeping Gatow running with electricity from our sole power plant would have substantially reduced that available for civilian purposes."

"Of course. Just as our needs here at Tempelhof do. However, I'm surprised I was not informed of this anomaly weeks ago." The fact that the American Military Governor kept his voice soft did not dull the rebuke.

Emily wanted to crawl under the sofa, but to her relief, Waite was ready with an answer. "I sympathise with your annoyance, General, but I suspect your staff did not think it was sufficiently important to mention — given that power flow was uninterrupted until this morning. I imagine they believed there was no need for you to get down into the weeds of the very complex and still integrated nature of Berlin's infrastructure. I can assure you, however, that we are working on a solution. I am optimistic we will find one. We'll let you know as soon as the lights go back on again, but that's not the reason we're here. Mrs Priestman and I have come to find out what plans the United States has for evacuating civilians with medical emergencies during this siege."

Clay took a moment to digest that answer, and then his eyes flickered in Emily's direction. At last, he leaned back in his chair and smiled slightly as he replied, "I'm going to be candid with you: I don't think we've thought that far ahead." His eyes settled on Emily.

Seizing the silent invitation offered, Emily opened with her prepared remarks. "General, in the last few months I have visited nearly forty hospitals in the Western Sectors of Berlin, and what I saw shocked me deeply. You may think me naive. I certainly don't have your vast experience, and I'm sure you have seen many sobering sights beyond my imagination. Yet, nothing can change the fact that the hospitals in this city are in a dreadful state. Nearly all of them sustained damage during the war either from our bombs or Soviet artillery or both. None have been properly rebuilt since. All are run down. I was particularly struck by how dark they are. They lack sufficient glazing for widows and have only inadequate, artificial light — and that was before the Blockade started and electricity rationing came into effect. They are overcrowded and understaffed. They do not have enough clean sheets or pillows for every bed." She paused, Clay was listening to her, but he did not seem moved.

Emily continued. "The most distressing thing I learnt was that due to an acute shortage of surgeons, surgical equipment, and anaesthetics, Berlin hospitals have long been unable to conduct certain kinds of surgery. They can do no heart surgery or brain surgery, for example, nor can they operate for stomach and other forms of cancer."

Clay nodded but said nothing. Emily had no choice but to forge ahead. "The situation, as you can imagine, has been aggravated by the Blockade. The hospitals can no longer be assured of either power or diesel for their generators. Patients on life support systems could be lost due to sudden or sustained power outages. The most vulnerable patients are at risk." Emily hesitated and then with a glance at Waite asked, "General, do you want the American flag to fly over a city where the hospitals have become helpless? Where the sick are dying for want of proper medical treatment?"

Clay cleared his throat and announced, "No. The evacuation of seriously ill hospital patients makes sense. We shouldn't be flying food or fuel in for people who need medical treatment that can't be provided. I'm a touch confused, however, Mrs Priestman, because as I remember it, you work for an air ambulance company. Aren't you already actively engaged in flying the most severe cases out of Berlin?"

"General, Air Ambulance International has been forced to shut down its operations."

Clay looked startled. "Why?"

"Do you know the cost of a gallon of aviation fuel, General?"

"Not off the top of my head, but aviation fuel for this airlift is costing the American taxpayer upwards of half a million dollars every day."

"I can't afford to fill a Wellington from my kitchen kitty, General, and nor can Mr Goldman, and nor can the Berlin City government because aviation fuel can only be purchased with hard currency."

Clay did not bat an eyelid and nothing in his expression betrayed what he was thinking. Emily had no choice but to continue, "Air Ambulance International could shuttle as many as 18 seriously ill patients out of Berlin each day — but only if the aircraft is in tip-top condition, which requires meticulous maintenance and the rapid replacement of defective equipment. Furthermore, it can only fly three flights a day if it has two fully qualified pilots on board. It must also have oxygen and life-support systems for the patients. And, as I indicated before, aviation fuel. If we are to help with the evacuation of those who need medical treatment, we have to receive sufficient compensation for our services to cover our expenses and our staff."

"And General Robertson has turned you down?" Clay asked, his eyes boring into her.

"No, sir," Emily squirmed. "We decided not to ask him."

"Why was that?" Clay wanted to know.

Emily hesitated and then did something she rarely did, she flirted. With a smile, she admitted, "Well, General, my husband thought you would be more receptive to an appeal from a lady than General Robertson."

Clay smiled faintly at that and nodded ambiguously. He appeared to be thinking things over, and Emily decided it was wiser not to push him any further, although she glanced at Waite, who winked encouragement.

After several tense seconds in which no one spoke or moved, the American general nodded and got to his feet. He pushed a buzzer on his desk and the lieutenant who had escorted them immediately popped in. Clay told his aide to fetch a Major something-or-other and then returned to the coffee table and sat down again. "I've asked an officer of my staff to join us. I want you to go with him to his office to work out the details."

"Meaning the United States will cover the costs of medical evacuations in the air ambulance?"

"If they are reasonable and verifiable, yes. This isn't a blank cheque, Mrs Priestman, but fundamentally —" There was a knock on the door, and Clay called "Come in." A major with thick, dark-rimmed glasses saluted, and Clay beckoned him to join them.

"Cohen, Mrs Priestman and Air Commodore Waite have come about emergency medical evacuations for German civilians. I'd like you to work out the details with them and be sure a line item is added to our next budget request covering anticipated costs."

"Yes, sir!"

Clay turned to Emily and shook her hand with a wan smile. "A pleasure as always, Mrs Priestman. You have an uncanny knack for surprising me anew each time I encounter you. Please give my regards and compliments to your husband."

"Thank you very much, General." She would have said more, but he waved her thanks aside and offered his hand to Waite with a reminder, "Don't forget, the minute the lights go on again at Gatow put a call through to me *directly*. My secretary can give you the number."

Flipping a Switch — Part II
RAF Gatow
Monday, 5 July 1948
(Day 10)

It had all happened so fast that Emily was still a bit dazed when Waite's driver dropped her off at Gatow close to 10 pm that night. Knowing that Robin was still there, she'd asked to be taken to the airfield rather than her residence.

The sun had set at 9:30 and daylight was draining from the sky. The airfield should have been ablaze with artificial light. The runway lights should have been turned up full, and floodlights should have made the dispersals and the hardstandings bright as day. The offices of the admin block would normally have been squares of bright white and the tower should have stood out like a fishbowl illuminated from the inside.

But only darkness greeted her. And silence. Without light to work by, most of the staff had abandoned their desks and returned to their gloomy quarters. There would be cold meals in the messes tonight.

The stairwell of the main building was dark and eerily creepy — as if it were inhabited by the ghosts of dead Luftwaffe personnel. As she reached the second floor, she almost tripped over an abandoned vacuum-cleaner and cursed under her breath. Unnerved, she walked down the long hall to Robin's outer office trying to dismiss the irrational fear triggered by the sound of her high heels echoing off the walls like slow gunfire. Glad

to reach the anteroom, she burst in with a cheerful, "Hello, everyone!" —
only to find that she was talking to herself. Not a soul occupied the usually
crowded outer office. Even more odd, Robin's door stood open. Emily
approached frowning and looked inside. His office, too, was empty. Where
could he be?

She looked around for some clue. The office might have been an
abandoned ship. Papers and dirty teacups lay about. The ashtray on the
coffee table was filled with stubbed-out cigarettes — evidence of many
visitors, since Robin didn't smoke. Robin's hat was hanging behind the door
and his briefcase was standing beside his desk. He must be somewhere.

She returned through the anteroom to the hall and knocked on Fl/
Lt Boyd's door, but the Intelligence Officer did not answer. She tried the
handle and found it unlocked, but the office was empty. The same proved
true at the next three doors she tried. She had almost given up when her
fourth knock provoked a surprised, "Yes?"

Emily was startled not only by the response but by the fact that the
voice was female. Emily put her head in to say, "I'm sorry to disturb you.
I'm Emily Priestman and I'm looking for my husband, Wing Commander
Priestman."

"Oh," the sour-looking WAAF officer responded, "I think he's upstairs
in the tower. They all rushed up there in a noisy gaggle about fifteen
minutes ago."

"Thank you," Emily withdrew her head, but the WAAF called after
her in a sharp voice, "You can't go up there! Only authorised personnel are
allowed in the tower."

"I know — and guests," Emily added pointedly, thinking rude things
about the WAAF officer. Just who did she think she was?

At the entrance to the tower, however, she hesitated before the large,
official warning: "Authorised Personnel Only!" Then, annoyed for being so
easily intimidated, she knocked loudly.

The door opened at once, and she was startled to find the tower packed
with people.

"Ah, Emily!" Robin gestured her inside. "Just in time for the moment
of truth." Whatever did he mean by that? Emily walked through the crowd
to stand beside him directly behind the Air Traffic Controller's table. They
were all looking out into the darkness.

"It's 10 pm now, sir," someone announced in a tone appropriate for the death of a king or a declaration of war.

Robin nodded grimly and turned to a stocky officer in the uniform of the Corps of Royal Engineers, "Proceed, Russel," he ordered.

The army officer gave a thumbs up and spoke into the receiver of the phone. "Cut power." He ordered.

What power? Emily wondered. The whole problem was that they didn't have any! Yet these words palpably increased the tension around her. The occupants of the tower craned their necks or audibly exclaimed "ooh" or "ah." Two of the controllers held binoculars to their eyes and scanned the distance. Emily followed their gaze but saw only darkness. If anything, it looked darker than ever before.

Everyone appeared to be on tenterhooks. With bated breath, no one moved or spoke, as if waiting for something to happen. After what seemed like a long time, Robin lifted his arm to read his watch in the growing darkness.

Then, without any warning except a loud click, light abruptly blazed across the entire airfield. The overhead lamps burned down on them. Huge floodlights bathed the hangars in blinding glare. The quarters, messes and runways lit up in varying shades of yellow. From the stairway came the droning of the abandoned vacuum cleaner, although the latter was barely audible above the cheering and clapping of those in the room. Robin swept his wife into his arm and gave her a short but firm kiss on the side of her face; he was beaming.

"What just happened?" she asked, lifting her voice to be heard above the babble of excited voices around them.

"I think we just re-started the Airlift," her husband answered, sounding very pleased with himself.

"I don't understand."

"Come and meet the wonderworker, Lt Col Graham Russel." He drew her by the elbow towards the CRE officer she'd noticed earlier. Up close, she realised he was shorter than she was, but he seemed to be grinning with his whole body. "Colonel, I don't believe you've met my wife, Emily. It is a serious oversight that you two have not met before this, but we will make amends." Robin sounded as if he'd been drinking, Emily thought, but he never drank on duty. Ever. Which, she surmised, must mean he was drunk on sheer relief.

Meanwhile, she shook hands with Lt. Col. Russel, saying honestly, "I'm delighted to make your acquaintance at last, Colonel. My husband has been singing your praises ever since you got here. He's quite right that you're overdue for a dinner invitation. The problem is I can't imagine when either of you might have time for a civilised dinner."

"We'll make time," Robin announced. "We should include S/L Garth and Flight Sergeant Hart; she's about to get promoted but doesn't know it yet." He glanced over his shoulder towards the female air traffic controller chatting excitedly with the others. "Oh, and the new WAAF OC was supposed to arrive today. She should be here by tomorrow, so we can invite her as well."

"We should also include Charlotte for David," Emily advised. "That would be an even ten and would fill the table."

"Could you manage something for tomorrow?"

"Yes, I'd be delighted to," Emily agreed, surprised to discover she liked the idea of a little dinner party after the tension of the past ten days. Besides, if Clay came through and the ambulance started flying again, she would soon have little time to play hostess. "Now. Would one of you please be so kind as to tell me what just happened? How did you get the power turned back on?"

"Lt. Col. Russel discovered that the power for the Red Air Force base at Staaken is produced in our Sector."

"You're joking?" Emily gasped.

"No. I informed Waite, who — before joining the festivities surrounding the arrival of the Sunderlands — made a call on our dear friend General Kemarsky." To Russel, he explained, "He's the Soviet Air Attaché at the Allied Control Council. Waite tells me that Kemarsky appeared unperturbed. Although Waite warned him that we would retaliate if power was not restored to Gatow by 10 pm, he took the warning as a joke, making silly little quips. His demeanour implied that he believed there was absolutely nothing we could or would do. Meanwhile, Russel here found the switches to enable us to show him we meant business."

"General Robertson agreed to that?" Emily asked, astonished.

"Not exactly," Robin waffled. "One thing I've learnt over the years, Em, is that if you can't live with the answer 'no,' then don't ask the question.

So, when Waite informed Robertson of the situation, he was careful to say I was already working on a solution. He suggested we would only require the general's intervention if our local solution had not worked by midnight tonight."

"But Robin," Emily was shaken by her husband's brinksmanship. What if, instead of restoring power to Gatow, the Russians had remained defiant or even retaliated with more forceful measures? He might have stumbled into another war! The thought frightened her, but she tried to keep her anxiety out of her voice as she asked, "What if things had gone wrong?"

He shrugged. "I've taken worse risks in — and with — my life. The last thing I needed was for the Foreign Ministry, Whitehall and the Cabinet to get involved! The way I see it, this was similar to providing fighter escorts in the corridors after the BEA crash; we had to signal in no uncertain terms that we would defend our right to operate here. We bled enough, for heaven's sake, to be treated like a victorious power. I'm not going to let the Russians mock us!" There was real resentment in those words, Emily noted, and she took careful note that for her husband the Airlift was no longer a job or a duty; he had started to identify with it personally.

Robin continued, "The Russians are typical bullies. They are always sniffing about for weaknesses, but the minute we snarl back at them they back down. After Russel's men plunged Staaken into darkness, it took them exactly eight minutes and twenty seconds to switch our lights back on. Which reminds me, I'd better put calls through to Waite and Bagshot to let them know we're operational again."

"And General Clay, please. He asked specifically to be informed 'the moment the lights went back on.'"

"Then he shall be!" Robin left her standing and went over to one of the phones on the controllers' table.

Emily turned to Russel and admitted. "I feel as if my head is spinning a bit."

"It does feel rather like comic opera, doesn't it? But we shouldn't forget that physically Berlin is still a single city. Only politics divide it. There are no natural borders between the Sectors, and everything is integrated and indeed interdependent, particularly the infrastructure."

Robin was already back. "General Clay sounded very relieved just now and appreciative of the call. How did the meeting go otherwise?"

"He agreed to pay for med evacs —"

"Congratulations!" her husband broke in enthusiastically and then explained the situation to Russel, who congratulated Emily as well. "This, too, calls for champagne," Robin decided.

Raising his voice to be heard over the babble of voices, he declared. "It's going to be at least 90 minutes before the first aircraft reaches us from Celle. So, I'm standing a bottle of champagne for everyone here at the Officers' mess in ten minutes. Sergeants and other ranks are my guests!"

A cheer answered him, and in a surge, the other occupants of the room started for the door. Even the air traffic controllers left their places vacant and made for the exit.

Robin turned to Emily saying, "I want to hear all the details about this coup of yours, but this is not the best place or time."

"I understand," she assured him. "You should know, however, that General Clay stipulated we must submit our bills via the City Council, although he promised we'll be paid in dollars. David has to meet Major Cohen tomorrow to settle the details, and I must talk to Jakob Liebherr about the City Council's role. Meanwhile, we'll have Kiwi fly the ambulance in ready to take on passengers — if that's all right with you?"

His frown surprised her, but he explained, "I'm sailing very close to the wind just now — with half the gunnel under. When I told Bagshot we were back in business, he sounded almost disappointed that he didn't have an excuse to give me the sack. If I step over the line in any way — like letting Moby Dick onto the tarmac without his permission — I may find myself wearing a bowler hat faster than you can say Jack Robinson."

"But if the ambulance can't land here, we can't operate," Emily protested.

"You'll get permission eventually. Bagshot simply wants to control everything himself. You're going to have to go through channels on this one. Now, come along, let's join the party!"

Chapter Three
Scrambling

More than Its Share
RAF Gatow
Tuesday, 6 July 1948
(Day 11)

Ft/Lt Boyd, the station Intelligence Officer, entered Priestman's office at 8 am with the daily news clippings. "Not a word about Gatow being temporary shut down yesterday!" he announced triumphantly. "It's all about the Sunderlands. Lots of excellent photos. Waving children. Sailing boats. Articles about how the flying boats can carry salt in bulk. Good stuff all around."

"Well, that's something," Priestman admitted, relieved, taking the folder Boyd handed him and flipping through it. Noticing all the clippings were from the free press of the Western Sectors and Zones, he asked, "What about the Communist and Soviet media?"

"Borisenko is still working on those. You should have them in an hour, but her preliminary assessment is that Gatow has not been mentioned there either. The focus is on comparing the Sunderlands to heavy bombers with headlines similar to: "Terror-Bombers reappear over the skies of Berlin." Priestman nodded cynically. He'd come to expect that from the Russian media.

Another knock on the door was followed by the arrival of the station adjutant F/O Stanley. "Sir, you've been summoned to an urgent meeting in Wunstorf."

Priestman felt as though he'd just hit clear-air turbulence and dropped two hundred feet. Was Bagshot still gunning for him despite getting Gatow up and running again in less than 24 hours?

"The message went out to all Station Commanders," Stan clarified. "The meeting is at 10:00 this morning. You'll want to be on the ground no later than 9:45. Do you want the Anson made ready?"

Priestman checked his watch, it was 8:13. "No, I'll take the Spit," he decided. Although the station had an Avro Anson for carrying personnel and VIPs as necessary, he'd retained a Spitfire for personal use after the Spitfire squadron pulled out at the start of the Airlift. "Have it fuelled and ready for take-off by 8:45, would you?"

"Yes, sir." Stan withdrew and Priestman picked up his desk phone to instruct Sergeant Andrews to cancel all his morning meetings. He also put a call through to Emily, informing her he was flying to Wunstorf — just in case he got stuck there for some reason. One never knew...

Fifteen minutes later he left his office. Given the warm, sunny weather, he didn't bother with flying boots or flight jacket. The Allies weren't allowed to fly above 10,000 feet in the corridors anyway. Walking towards the hangar where his Spitfire was being rolled out by a couple of erks, he let his eyes scan the breadth of the field. On the far side of the PSP runway, Russel's sappers were working hard to prepare the foundation for the new concrete runway. A broad, low ditch 120 feet wide and 6,000 feet long had been carved out of the grass and levelled as best as possible with the inadequate and obsolete equipment at their disposal.

From a distance, the expanse of dirt looked impressive and almost like a real runway, but Priestman knew that Russel still had two serious problems. One was finding sufficient bitumen to surface the runway when it was finished, and the second, and more daunting problem, was crushing and pressing the gravel down into a hard surface. They desperately needed both crushers and steamrollers for that task. Russel had started talking about building them with cannibalised parts from the eclectic assortment of junk construction equipment they had collected. Priestman seriously questioned whether that could be done. Then again, after yesterday, he was starting to believe that if *anyone* could do such a thing, it was Lt. Colonel Graham Russel.

The approach of a Dakota distracted him from his thoughts because he subconsciously registered that something was wrong with it. He stopped dead in his tracks to focus his attention on the Dak. The aircraft was flying too slowly, and it wallowed slightly as if it either didn't have enough power or something was wrong with the controls. Priestman's eyes searched for signs of a dead engine, smoke, or leaking fuel or oil. Usually, when an aircraft had trouble maintaining speed and altitude it had engine trouble of some kind, but both engines were screaming lustily. As it descended towards the start of the PSP runway, it kept dropping suddenly rather than following a steady glide path.

Every muscle in Priestman's body tensed as he anticipated a bad ending to this flawed flight. How many times during the war had he watched aircraft return from a combat sortie and known long before any damage was visible that an aircraft or pilot was in trouble? Yet while this poor old Dakota looked grungy and clapped out, Priestman could see no specific defect.

The Dakota dropped, caught itself, the nose tipped up, and speed fell off. The kite wallowed on the brink of stalling and Priestman — doubtless along with half the staff at Gatow — held his breath. Then with an audible thud and squeal, the aircraft plopped down on the runway and rolled past the waiting ambulance, fire engine and station commander. The aircraft fishtailed as the brakes were applied, spewing up plumes of burnt rubber. Even so, for a horrible moment, it looked like it might career right off the end of the runway. It managed to lurch to a halt before it ran out of tarmac and then turned and waddled onto the taxiway.

Without conscious thought, Priestman changed the direction of his steps and plotted a course to intercept it at the hardstanding to which it was being efficiently flagged. The ground controller knew about the troubles and directed it to the nearest offloading point. By the time Priestman arrived, the crew had disembarked and were chattering amongst themselves in obvious relief. Priestman noted the pilot was no youngster, but rather a flight lieutenant in an old uniform. He was also drenched in sweat. He'd removed his cap, exposing longish, blond hair glued to his head, and he wiped his brow with the back of his forearm, his cap in his hand. At the sight of Priestman, he put his cap back on to salute.

Priestman returned it, but quickly asked, "What's wrong with her, Flight Lieutenant?"

"I wish I knew, sir! I've never experienced anything like this in a Dak before. They're usually docile and cooperative, but she was mushy right from take-off. She hardly got off the ground, and all the way here she wallowed like a Wimpy with too big a bomb load."

That triggered a thought, "Where did you originate?"

"Celle, sir. Why?"

"Didn't a York squadron move into Celle over the weekend?"

"Yes, but — you don't think they confused the cargoes, do you?" The Flight Lieutenant caught his drift.

"We'll soon find out." Priestman turned around and waved to the army sergeant who had arrived with an unloading crew of five. Two Germans had already gone aboard the aircraft and were handing the cargo to their colleagues on the waiting flatbed. Priestman signalled the army sergeant over. "Could you check if this is a normal Dakota load?"

"Sir?" the sergeant sounded sceptical but dutifully went to look in the cargo hold of the little freighter. The sight made him pale. "She's filled to the gills, sir!" he shouted. "There must be six tons of cargo in here!"

Priestman and the Flight Lieutenant looked at one another and burst out laughing.

"That's twice her maximum!" the Flight Lieutenant reminded the Wing Commander, staggered by what had just happened. He turned around to look affectionately at the battered two-engine freighter and announced with genuine feeling, "I love this kite! After this, I will let no one separate us!"

Priestman clapped the pilot on the shoulder and remarked, "Well done," but there was no guarantee they would be so lucky next time. Turning to the army sergeant, he ordered, "Report this to Captain Bateman at once. Stop unloading so he can see the cargo for himself. If they make many mistakes like this, we'll lose aircraft and crew through sheer carelessness."

He sounded cross but was more frightened than angry. The whole Airlift had been scraped together so hastily and people were under so much pressure that this kind of mistake was bound to happen. It was a miracle that they hadn't lost aircraft to faulty loading already. Most of the loaders knew nothing about the need to maintain an aircraft's centre of gravity. Even the army overseers were hardly experts in aerodynamics. It was ridiculously easy to make mistakes.

With a glance at his watch, Priestman realised he needed to take off immediately or risk being late for the meeting in Wunstorf — and he was already on Bagshot's blacklist. As he jogged towards the waiting Spitfire, he made a mental note to raise the issue of the overloaded Dakota at upcoming meeting. As he swung himself into the cockpit of the familiar fighter, he also sent a quick silent prayer to the Almighty that Bagshot hadn't found out exactly how he'd got the power restored yesterday.

The New Regime

In the Admin building, Flight Sergeant Kathleen Hart was facing her new commanding officer, Flight Officer P.M. Parsons. For the past six months, Kathleen had been the senior WAAF at Gatow and de facto the WAAF Officer Commanding, but she didn't hold the King's Commission and she wasn't in admin; she was an air traffic controller. The decision to supply Berlin's population by air, however, had resulted in an explosion of personnel at RAF Gatow including twenty more WAAF.

Kathleen had welcomed the appointment of a WAAF Officer Commanding because it relieved her of the extra burden. After all, being an air traffic controller was demanding and exhausting enough — even without being part of the largest airlift in history. She had opted to remain in Berlin, despite the offer of a transfer out, precisely because she wanted to be part of an operation that was testing the limits of air traffic control technology and procedures. Having responsibility for other WAAF had never been her goal or her pride. Nevertheless, having a WAAF OC meant she was henceforth subject to two superiors, the Senior Flying Control Officer Squadron Leader Garth and the WAAF Admin officer. She hoped that wouldn't be too much of a problem.

The new OC had hardly disembarked before she summoned all WAAF to a meeting in her office. Although Flight Officer Parsons was not an attractive woman, she was very well turned out. She gave the assembled WAAF a well-prepared introductory talk outlining her expectations ("nothing but the best") and reminding them of their duties ("complete dedication to the mission regardless of the time of day or the weather"). As the talk continued in this vein, however, Kathleen thought she was belabouring things they all knew a bit too much. Kathleen was happy when she finally announced, "That will be all for now. You may return to your duties." They started to file out of the office.

"Flight Sergeant Hart?" Parsons' voice stopped her in her tracks.

Kathleen looked back. "Yes, Ma'am?"

"I understand you have been in charge here in the absence of a WAAF OC?"

"Yes, Ma'am."

"Well, I'd like to have a word with you alone, please."

"Yes, Ma'am." Kathleen stood to one side to let the others file out and returned to stand before her new superior's desk.

"You may take a seat." Parsons indicated the chair in front of her desk as she sat down herself. "Flight Sergeant, I don't believe in mincing words or dancing around delicate topics, so I'm going to get straight to the point. I was sent out here with a mandate to bring some order to the chaos. The WAAF at this station have acquired a deplorable — no, a *shocking* — reputation for immorality."

Kathleen nearly fell off the chair. That hardly seemed fair! There had only been eight of them here when she arrived; the other twenty had all arrived in the last ten days since the Airlift had started. During her roughly six months as acting CO, there had been only one posting, and it had been the request of an air movements assistant who could not take the pressure after witnessing a crash. Kathleen hadn't a clue what Parsons was driving at.

"I admit it was before your time, but one of the WAAF here was posted for carrying on with a married man here on the station. I was even more shocked to learn that you also accepted invitations from a married British officer and were seen all over the place in his company."

Kathleen felt her temperature start to rise, yet she could not deny that she had gone out with Major Lionel Dickenson, formerly on General Robertson's staff. She drew a breath and faced Parsons. "Major Dickenson led me to believe that he was single."

"Did he? Or did you just assume it?" Parsons queried with raised eyebrows and a tone of voice that left no doubt as to what she thought. Nor did she give Kathleen a chance to answer, "I am not impressed by a woman who allows herself to be taken to the opera and the like by a married man. The fact that this man was later detained and indicted for the theft of works of art and antiques underlines your utter lack of judgment and propriety. Most damaging, in my opinion, you also condoned inappropriate behaviour on the part of your subordinates."

That was going too far! Kathleen protested sharply: "I don't know what you're talking about, Ma'am."

"Oh, just this little incident of a WAAF going to a party in the *Soviet* Sector out of uniform without permission. I've read the file, Hart. You were informed about Corporal Borisenko's misconduct and explicitly chose not to take any disciplinary action!" Parsons was indignant.

Kathleen snapped for air. It was true that WAAF Corporal Galyna Borisenko had gone to a party in the Russian Sector out of uniform. Yet while being out of uniform without permission was technically a breach of regulations, her civilian disguise had enabled her to collect valuable information. Kathleen's clearance was not high enough to know the details of what she'd learned, but the WingCo had stressed that he and MI6 hoped that Borisenko could gather further intelligence from the same source and did not want her activities curtailed or inhibited.

"Quite aside from the issue of being out of uniform," Parsons continued forcefully, "cavorting with Soviet soldiers is a highly dubious — not to say suspicious — activity, and it must stop. The Russians are notorious for sending their spies to seduce Western personnel and then using romantic entanglements to elicit or extort sensitive information from their victims."

Kathleen sat straighter in her chair as she replied as pointedly as possible, "Corporal Borisenko attended the party at the invitation of a Ukrainian *girl* — not a man. There is nothing romantic in their relationship. Furthermore, the Station Intelligence Officer has sanctioned their meetings and wants them to continue."

That took the wind out of the new OC's sails, but only for a moment. She recovered and announced, "I shall talk to the IO about that, but it in no way exonerates you. Your job was to maintain discipline among the WAAF and the fact that Corporal Borisenko didn't even *ask* your permission before her escapade shows just how little respect you enjoy among the WAAF. They saw you as one of them rather than as a superior and role model. Things are going to be very different under my command. I intend to run a tight ship. WAAF on my watch will not carry on with married men, nor will they fraternise with Russians — male or female — and they will not be seen in public out of uniform except with my explicit permission. We are in a warlike situation here in Berlin, and I expect wartime dedication to duty and wartime discipline. Have I made myself clear?"

"Very."

"Then you may go."

Kathleen stood and saluted so smartly it was a mockery. Then she turned around as if on a parade ground, stamped her foot once like a drill sergeant and marched rather than walked out of the office.

After this childish outburst, however, she found herself in the hallway feeling discouraged. The "affair" with Lionel had, fortunately, never got as far as the bedroom, but after losing her husband in the war, Lionel had been her first attempt at a new romance — and it had left her bruised. She was never going to risk getting involved with a man again, she vowed — only to question if that was the best thing for her or her daughter Hope. Didn't Hope deserve a father as well as a mother?

It was a moot point at the moment. She had little time for anything but work anyway. Checking her watch, she realised she had less than an hour before she went on duty in the tower. Just time for a quick cup of tea or a hot chocolate over at the NAAFI.

A door opened farther along the hall, and Kathleen pulled herself together to salute Squadron Leader Garth, the Senior Flying Control Officer, as he stepped into the hall. "Hart! Just the person I wanted to see. Could you step into my office for a moment?" That was not a question coming from a squadron leader to a flight sergeant.

"Yes, sir." Kathleen followed him into his narrow office wondering what sort of trouble she was in now. Garth dropped into his own chair and indicated she should sit as well. She sank down cautiously.

Garth got straight to the point. "Over the weekend, the WingCo convinced me that we must go to GCA for all incoming aircraft regardless of weather."

"What?" Kathleen gasped, flabbergasted. "But we don't have the radar sets — let alone the staff for that!"

"The radar sets should arrive via Celle in the next few days. Four of them. As for personnel, we'll be going on a three-watch system as soon as the concrete runway is complete. We plan three eight-hour shifts per day, each manned by two controllers, and two ground movement assistants per watch. That means we need six GCA controllers. Four volunteers have been identified in the UK and will be arriving shortly. Warrant Officer Wilkins is an experienced GCA controller, and your file indicated that you have been trained on GCA although you have not been in a GCA job. Is that correct?"

"Yes. It was one of the reasons I volunteered for this posting," Kathleen admitted. "I'd hoped to get some experience on GCA."

"Splendid!" Garth responded with enthusiasm. "Then we're all set!" Sitting up straighter he announced, "Your commission has been approved and you will take up your new duties as Assistant Section Leader. Congratulations!" Garth held out his hand and broke into a wide smile.

Kathleen was blindsided but delighted, and stammered out "Thank you, sir!" as she got to her feet.

"It's no more than you deserve," Garth assured her. "You did a first-class job during the recent tensions. I am certain you will do a superb job on the GCA."

Kathleen left Garth's office almost dizzy with pride. She couldn't help being a little bemused, however. One superior thought she was practically worthless, while the other had just entrusted her with greater responsibilities — and a commission. For once, she was lucky to have two bosses!

Criminal Police
Berlin-Kreuzberg
Tuesday, 6 July 1948
(Day 11)

The power cuts had disrupted public transport so thoroughly that Jakob Liebherr temporarily gave up going to his office. His constituents knew where he lived or could find out, and he could answer their questions just as well in his apartment as at the Kreuzberg Town Hall. He could certainly calculate Airlift requirements for his district better in the peace and quiet of his home than in his noisy office.

The Western Allies had handed over responsibility for establishing Airlift needs and priorities to the Berlin civil authorities. This meant that the Berlin City Council informed the Allies about what and how much Berlin wanted. While Liebherr appreciated and respected the Allied reluctance to decide what the Berliners should receive — and do without — the fact was that no one knew what two million people needed to survive for any length of time. It wasn't all about food and energy. People needed toilet paper, nappies and soap, too. They needed clothing, shoes, and blankets to keep warm when the heating was turned off due to the lack of power and coal. They needed sewing needles and thread, nails and plywood to keep repairing all the things that were worn out and broken and could no longer be replaced. They also needed razors, pens and paper, radios, and it went on and on. Every day, the councilmen were asked to review their earlier requests and adjust planning based on what items were depleted fastest and what new requests they had received. Liebherr found the work tedious and depressing, but he understood how vital it was.

A knock on the door startled him, but he was happy to leave the mess on his desk even before discovering the welcome sight of his neighbour Charlotte Graefin Walmsdorf and Mrs Emily Priestman.

"I hope we aren't bothering you, Herr Liebherr," Mrs Priestman opened in her passable German. "We came to tell you about my meeting with General Clay yesterday and ask for further assistance in getting the air ambulance flying again."

"You've already met General Clay?" Liebherr asked astonished. When he'd suggested to Mr Goldman two days ago that the company approach the military governors, he had presumed it would take a week or more to get an appointment.

"Yes, my husband managed to pull a few strings," Mrs Priestman admitted.

"Splendid! Come in, come in! I'd offer you tea or coffee, but we have no electricity to boil water. I could offer you sherry or schnapps, instead?"

"Thank you, no. We really don't need anything," she assured him with a smile.

Liebherr gestured towards the formal front parlour that was rarely used. It was filled with furnishings from the last century, remnants from the house in which his in-laws had lived until it had been shattered by Russian artillery. Everything that could be salvaged had been brought here before the Russians got it. The effect of so much 19th-century, over-stuffed and ornate furniture in a small room was terribly "bourgeois," but Liebherr couldn't worry about his image in times like these.

The ladies seated themselves in two of the winged armchairs and

Jakob settled himself on the sofa. "Now, please. What did General Clay say?" he prompted.

Emily looked at Charlotte and nodded for her to continue. Jakob shifted his gaze towards his neighbour. He would never forget the sight of her on the night Trude brought her home after the rapes. Her whole face had been black-and-blue and misshapen from blows. One eye had been swollen shut, while her lips had been broken and bloody. Both her arms were in casts so that she could not dress, bathe, or use a toilet without assistance. But the worst had been the way she had buckled inward like something broken. She had seemed unable to hold her head upright or straighten her shoulders. She crouched more than sat, often with her knees pulled up and her stiff, plastered arms around them. He'd kept an eye on her slow recovery, noting that her work with the ambulance had done much to restore her confidence, but disturbed to see how the blockade had made her timid again. Now, she was sitting ramrod straight in her chair, with her feet firmly on the floor and her head held high. She looked, he thought with an inward smile, more like a countess, and socialist though he was, he didn't begrudge her that.

"Herr Liebherr," Charlotte started politely and precisely, as if she hadn't let him feed her when her arms were broken. "General Clay very generously agreed to cover the cost of all AAI operational flights from Berlin."

"That's wonderful news!" Jakob declared delightedly. "What a powerful statement of commitment and charity! Mayor Reuter will be very pleased — not to mention that we have a long list of people the hospitals would like to see evacuated."

"Yes, however, General Clay insisted that the Berlin city government, rather than AAI, submit the bills to the Allied representatives. Am I explaining this correctly?" she looked at Mrs Priestman, who nodded. "He wants AAI to send itemised invoices to the City Council. The Council must then pass them on in a report listing the names and details of the patients flown out, their condition, and their destinations. Is that right?" she looked again at Mrs Priestman.

"He doesn't mean you must request permission in advance," the Englishwoman clarified, "simply list what expenses have already been incurred for whom, when and why."

"Meaning we can bill him for the flights AAI was not paid for in the last three months?" Liebherr queried hopefully.

"Unfortunately, no. But he said anything after 26 June, when the Airlift officially started, will be honoured."

"Good enough. This is still very significant. You will be able to provide us with the invoices, I presume?" Liebherr asked, his eyes shifting from one woman to the other.

"Yes, yes," Charlotte hastened to assure him. "I shall be responsible for keeping you — or whomsoever you name as my point of contact — informed of the exact costs and all the other details."

"You should also know," Mrs Priestman picked up the conversation, "that our aircraft is standing by in Hamburg right now and can fly in within two hours. We've already been in touch with the hospitals, and they have identified the six patients in most urgent need of evacuation to Hanover. All that is holding us back is for the city government to make a formal request."

"Now I'm confused," Liebherr admitted. "I thought you said we did not need to make requests in advance?"

"Not for individual flights in the future, but to start the process," Mrs Priestman explained. "Clay would like the city government to make a formal, blanket request for the evacuation of critically ill patients. Once they receive that, Generals Clay and Robertson will formally approve the request, and that will trigger the orders to the respective Airlift commanders to give clearance for the air ambulance to fly in the corridors, use Airlift bases and obtain aviation fuel. It is very urgent —"

High-pitched hysterical screaming from the street below interrupted the discussion. Charlotte recoiled and curled up, her proud bearing collapsing like a house of cards. Mrs Priestman, on the other hand, looked startled and moderately alarmed, but not frightened. She turned to look out the window in the direction of the screams. Liebherr had already leapt to his feet. With an "excuse me" he hastened out the door.

On the landing, he nearly collided with Christian von Feldburg, coming out of the apartment opposite. Together they started down the stairs in the wake of the three young men who shared the flat under the Liebherrs'. Jakob knew that all three men, who went by names such as Meyer, Schultz and Braun, were black marketeers who also sold homemade schnapps of very dubious quality. They had served together on U-boats. They were cynical but young, fit and tough.

By the time he reached the ground floor, Liebherr lagged behind the younger men. Emerging from the front door, he found a large crowd had collected around the entrance of the adjacent apartment house. In addition to the woman's frenzied shrieking, people were shouting and calling insults. The crowd blocked the way between the door and the canal. Jakob glanced towards the street and spotted an American car of some sort with police licence plates.

Ahead of him, Feldburg and *Kapitaenleutnant* "Meyer" pushed their way through the crowd, Meyer's two crewmen in his wake. Abruptly a shot rang out. Everyone froze and silence crashed down over the crowd. The only sound was the rustling of the wind in the chestnut trees.

Horrified, Jakob forced himself forward. He pushed through the stunned crowd to find three policemen holding a man crumpled up between them; a fourth policeman held a pistol pointed at the sky. One of the police officers looked straight at Jakob and barked, "Tell these fools to back off or next time I'll shoot to kill!"

"First tell me what is going on here," Jakob countered moving cautiously closer. His heart was pounding furiously in his chest, but if you learned anything in a concentration camp it was not to *show* fright or anxiety. The thugs of both fascism and communism fed on fear.

"We are making an arrest—"

"They're Markgraf's men!" someone shouted from behind Liebherr. Markgraf was the Chief of Police installed by the Soviets as soon as they had conquered the city.

"My husband is innocent!" screeched the hysterical female voice that had shattered the afternoon's peace. From the doorway she wailed, "He's done nothing — NOTHING!"

"He's a capitalist warmonger who has been gouging the proletariat —"

"He runs a barbershop!" the woman yelled back an octave higher than her normal voice. "We can hardly make ends meet!"

"Shut up or I'll arrest you as well!" the police officer with the pistol retorted, lowering the barrel of his pistol so that it pointed at the woman in the door.

She answered by flinging open her arms and howled, "Shoot me!

Shoot me! I'd rather you shot me than left me here without my Paul! *Shoot me!*" it turned into a long, drawn-out keen of grief.

The officer turned away as she sank to her knees in despair and snapped at his men. "Get him in the car!"

The other three policemen started shoving and dragging the stunned victim towards the waiting vehicle. The crowd didn't part, but it didn't stand firm either. The police officer narrowed his eyes, and his pistol swung back and forth as if looking for a target.

Jakob was no more courageous than the others. His mouth went dry, and he felt his muscles cramping up. He hated being defeated. He hated giving in, but he recognised the look in the policeman's eyes. He would have *liked* to kill someone.

The police shoved their victim into the back seat, and two of them squeezed in beside him while the third went around to the driver's seat. He climbed in behind the wheel and turned the key in the ignition. Only then did the man with the pistol start backing towards the car. He kept his pistol pointed at the crowd, his eyes daring anyone to make a move. His lips were curled in a sneer of contempt. He opened the door with his free hand and then in a swift movement, spun about and dropped inside.

No sooner had his door slammed shut than the crowd erupted. Several young men grabbed bricks from the heaps lying beside the pavement and threw them at the car. Several hit the side, boot and bumper, crashing and crunching as the metal buckled. The driver started to pull away from the curb, but the crowd chased after the car. More bricks and cobblestones rained down on the boot and the back window shattered. From the corner of his eye. Jakob registered that someone was drawing a pistol. In horror, he turned and saw Meyer start to take aim. "NO!" he shouted and knocked his arm away. "If you shoot a policeman, you'll be the next victim!"

"They aren't policemen!" someone shouted in answer. "They're Stalin's pet wolves!"

With the police car now far out of range, the crowd turned their rage on Jakob as a representative of their city government.

"They steal from us and kidnap and intimidate honest citizens!"

"When are we finally going to get *protection* from the criminals in police uniform?"

"We want police who aren't Soviet stooges!"

"So do I!" Liebherr responded, raising his voice to be heard above the snarling of the others. "Believe me! No one wants real police more than Mayor Reuter and I!"

"Then do something!"

"How many more people are you going to let them kidnap?"

"When are you going to stop the theft? We have almost nothing left as it is!"

The hostility around him was so powerful that Liebherr was relieved to feel Christian von Feldburg move up beside him. He had his hand inside his jacket, and Liebherr sensed that he, too, was fingering a pistol. Feldburg was joined a moment later by Meyer, whose pistol was still in his hand.

Encouraged by this support, Liebherr raised his voice again to project authority as best he could. "Mayor Reuter is trying to recruit men for a new police force. If any of you wish to volunteer, let me know and I will see that you speak to the right people." To his relief, this announcement harvested so much excitement that the hostility snapped. People started talking among themselves, while several of the women turned to comfort the woman sobbing in the doorway.

Liebherr joined them, sinking down on the front step to ask the name of the victim. He would, of course, protest to the Chief of Police, but he knew he would earn nothing but a sneering rebuff. Markgraf did not recognise the authority of the elected city officials; he took his orders solely from the Soviet Military Government.

As the women took the victim's wife back inside, the rest of the crowd dispersed, and Liebherr turned to go back to his apartment. Glancing up, he saw that Mrs Priestman was on the balcony and had apparently seen everything. Very good. It would do no harm for the RAF station commander to know what was going on in the city, even if there was nothing he could do about it.

Feldburg and Meyer were talking in low voices among themselves. As Liebherr entered the building, they joined him. "Is that true about a new police force?" Meyer asked intently.

"Yes. Interested?"

"I might be," Meyer tried to sound evasive, but Liebherr could tell he was tempted. After a moment, the young man admitted, "I'm tired of doing *nothing*. Just watching them trample all over us. I used to hate the

Amis and Tommies as much as the Ivans, but..." He shrugged to express his frustration, "Well, they *are* flying in food and coal, aren't they?" He automatically looked up where, nowadays, an aircraft was always visible somewhere.

"Joining the new police force will be very dangerous," Liebherr warned. "Markgraf is certain to target those who challenge his authority with special fury and determination."

"I'm not a stranger to danger," Meyer snapped back.

"No, but this is a different kind of danger," Liebherr reminded him, and then turned to Christian von Feldburg, who was silently escorting him on the other side. "What about you, Feldburg?"

"I don't think I'm cut out for police work," the baron answered with an ambiguous smile.

"Hmm," Liebherr agreed.

When he reached his own apartment, Mrs Priestman requested more details, which he tried to provide. Eventually, they returned to the topic of the air ambulance, and Liebherr assured his guests that he would inform Mayor Reuter of what was expected. "I'm sure he'll raise this at his next meeting with the representative of the military governors, and you'll be flying again very soon."

Homeless Helpers
Hamburg
Tuesday, 6 July 1948
(Day 11)

"Bloody bastard!" Kiwi exclaimed furiously as he slammed down the receiver and pushed out of the hotel phone booth. He shoved his peaked cap onto the back of his head in frustration, revealing his red face.

Ron and Chips, standing just outside the booth, pounced on him at once. "What did he say?"

"That bureaucratic arse says he 'can't' let us fly from any RAF facility until he has orders from General Roberton making an exception for AAI aircraft! It's nothing but bumpf! Sheer bureaucratic bumpf!" He resisted the urge to fling his cap down and stamp on it.

The night before, David had called through with the exciting news that General Clay had agreed that the United States would cover the costs of their operations and ordered Kiwi to bring Moby Dick to Berlin to collect the first six patients. Bright and early, they had gone out to the airport, but when Kiwi tried to file a flight plan to Berlin, the civilian controllers at Hamburg had told him they were not authorised to approve such flights. All flights in and out of Berlin from the British Zone had to be approved by the RAF.

Kiwi had duly flown to the nearest RAF station, Fuhlsbuettel, anxious to avoid another encounter with that bastard Bagshot. Here the station commander had been friendly and seemed to want to help, but he'd put a call through to Group Captain Bagshot just to confirm that it was OK. Bagshot had blistered the station commander's ear. He not only denied them permission to continue to Berlin, he also ordered them off the RAF airfield — again.

They'd had no choice but to return to Hamburg's civil aviation airfield, and as soon as they were back at their hotel, Kiwi rang through to RAF Wunstorf and demanded to speak directly to Bagshot. He was just off the phone from that conversation with the results reported to his loyal ground crew.

"Maybe we could fly from one of the US bases?" Ron suggested.

"We'd spend nearly a full tank of fuel just to get there and they're twice as far from Berlin!" Kiwi snapped back, then softened his answer by adding, "I know you're just trying to help, Ron. I don't mean to take it out on you, but this is just pure bunk! Pig-headedness! Arrogance! Bagshot's an effing bastard!"

"Did you tell him patients are waiting to be flown out?" Chips asked.

"Of course! I told him there were dozens of desperately ill patients waiting. I told him their lives depended on us getting them out, and this was a high priority of the Berlin City Council — to which he answered that he didn't take orders from the Berlin City Council and all Germans could die as far as he was concerned!" Kiwi was so angry he was not keeping his voice down and was starting to attract attention. This last comment harvested shocked and angry looks from across the lobby.

"Maybe we should go get a drink and badger ideas about," Ron suggested reasonably.

"You carry on. I've got ring Mr Goldman and let him know we're still stuck here and don't know when we can get to Berlin. We don't want the patients waiting around at Gatow, and maybe he can get a message to Robertson."

The mechanics nodded and headed for the hotel bar, while Kiwi returned to the telephone booth to ring David. He was relieved when Emily answered the phone and promised to advise David of the situation for him. David had an unpleasant way of making Kiwi feel he was to blame when things went wrong, and he didn't want to get a bollocking for this latest cock-up.

As he started for the bar, however, Kiwi was intercepted by Virginia Cox of the *Times*. "Chuck, darling!" she called out to him waving and smiling. "What a delightful surprise!"

Kiwi couldn't think of anyone he wanted to see less! He'd never forgive the way Virginia had set a trap for him once before. She'd asked for an interview about the launch of AAI and over lunch at the Hotel Adlon, she'd charmed all sorts of proprietary information out of him. After flattering him to get what she wanted, she'd brushed him off like a piece of dirt — and added insult to injury by writing a misleading article. He looked her straight in the eye and asked, "Do we know each other?"

"Chuck darling! What a card you are! You can't have forgotten that lovely lunch together at the —"

He cut her off. "What I remember is you chasing after the next story before we'd even finished and then writing an article that twisted the facts enough to put AAI in jeopardy."

She gazed at him with an expression of wounded surprise that would not have shamed a Hollywood actress. "But Chuck! That's my job — chasing after stories, I mean. And I'm stunned, no *crushed*, that you didn't like the article. I so wanted to do you justice in it. I thought it read—"

"Like we were a pair of crazy, barnstorming, bush pilots ignoring aviation regulations!"

"Chuck! That wasn't my intention at all. I truly wanted to show what a wonderful job you'd done." She looked and sounded so profoundly sincere that Kiwi wondered if it had been a misunderstanding.

"Please, Chuck. Let me buy *you* a drink and we can talk this through. What are you doing in Hamburg, by the way?" She had slipped her hand through his elbow and pulled him to her just enough so he could feel her breast against his side as she led the way towards the bar.

Damn it! He couldn't control his attraction for her despite what she'd done to him. She was a corker any way you looked at it, with bright blonde hair and legs to kill for. It didn't hurt that she was dressed now in a sleek two-piece suit, silk stockings and pearls. She'd been the debutante of the season ten years ago. Damn her! And except for that embarrassing one-night-stand with a girl whose name he couldn't remember, he'd been celibate ever since his wife left him seven months ago.

Virginia, meanwhile, had drawn him to the hotel bar, where Ron and Chips were gaping at him as the stunning woman led him in and then perched herself on a bar stool in a way that drew all men's eyes to her legs. "What are you drinking, Chuck darling?" she asked with a heart-warming smile.

No, Kiwi told himself, he was not going to get drawn into cocktails and God-knew-what-next. He'd gone off the heavy liquor ever since he'd failed his first flight test on twins and had to retake it at his own expense. David had given him a second chance and he was not going to screw it up. "A half-pint of that German beer they sell around here."

"Holsten, I think it's called," she supplied the name with a glance at the bartender for confirmation. He nodded and she ordered, "A Holsten for the captain and a Cuba Libre for me."

The bartender withdrew and Kiwi cautiously took his seat beside Virginia. Without physical contact, he found he could think a little more clearly. He concluded that the best way to stop her from luring him into a new trap was to ask some questions of his own. "What are you doing here in Hamburg? I thought you were covering the Airlift."

"So I am!" Virginia assured him enthusiastically. "That's exactly why I'm here." He looked at her blankly, and she exclaimed, "The Sunderlands! Surely you saw the news? They flew into Berlin for the first time yesterday, and I managed to get an exclusive interview with the squadron commander operating out of Finkenwerde. But there's no good hotel there, so I'm staying here. I'm here half the time anyway because the Airlift Story isn't all about Berlin, you know. It's also about the organisation behind the

COLD WAR

Airlift and the departure fields, and ships bringing in supplies and all that." She seemed to realise she was talking too much and suddenly exclaimed, "What a wonderful coincidence to run into you! I assumed you were flying yourself ragged, getting sick people out of Berlin." She paused, looking at him with big, admiring eyes.

"Well, that's what I wish I were doing and ought to be doing!" Kiwi burst out, and without thinking added, "But a certain Group Captain Bagshot, who happens to be in charge of the RAF effort, refuses to approve a flight plan for us unless he has express orders from General Robertson!"

"Good heavens! What a lot of nonsense! People might *die* if they can't get out of Berlin to get the medical attention they need! You can't be serious?"

"Of course I'm serious! We're cooling our heels here wasting money on hotel bills and airport fees while seriously sick people are trapped in Berlin all because Group Captain Bagshot is too stubborn or too cowardly to approve a flight plan!"

"He ought to be called out on this," Virginia noted.

"What do you mean?" Kiwi asked, suddenly wary.

"Well, an article describing the plight of sick children who can't get out of Berlin—"

"Oh no you don't!" Kiwi cut her off. "I was just telling you why I'm here. I don't want you screaming about it in the papers. Bagshot will have it in for us if you do that." Not to mention, he thought to himself, David will kill me for blabbing again. "Promise me you won't publish anything about this!"

"Now, Chuck darling, you know the rules," she admonished with a flirtatious smile. "When talking to journalists, unless you say *upfront* that something is 'off the record,' then anything and everything you say can be used." She said it in a nice way, but Kiwi knew she was coldblooded when it came to her job — and he knew an article against Bagshot would ruin them.

He reached out and clasped her wrist in a fierce grip. "I wasn't talking to you as a journalist!"

Virginia looked down at his hand pointedly, and he removed it. They sat tensely side-by-side. Kiwi watched her like a hawk. Her face had become hard. Then something seemed to click inside her, and she turned on a

101

charming smile. "All right, Chuck, I won't write anything about it. I just wanted to do you a favour. A little negative publicity often does wonders to clear away pointless bureaucracy, but if you don't want my help..." she finished the sentence with a shrug.

"No. I don't want you meddling in my affairs. We'll work this out in our own way. And that's that."

Their drinks arrived, and Kiwi lifted his beer in salute and Virginia replied in kind. As she put her glass down, Virginia asked with a reconciliatory smile, "What are you doing for dinner tonight, Chuck? I've discovered this wonderful old beer cellar that didn't get blitzed. It's underground, you see, with big, vaulted ceilings and gigantic, wooden beer kegs. Very romantic."

Did she mean that? Part of Kiwi was tempted, but he caught sight of Ron and Chips watching him alertly and he shook his head. "No, I'm here with my ground crew and we'll do something together. That, or," he had a better thought, "I'll hitchhike to Berlin to discuss the situation with Mr Goldman."

"Oh," she seemed surprised, almost hurt by his rejection. She didn't get turned down very often, Kiwi presumed.

"Maybe another time," he offered, half-regretting what he'd just done.

"Yes, of course," she wasn't looking at him but rather into her glass. She glanced up with a sad smile, "Is it true that Wing Commander Priestman is the station commander at Gatow?"

"That's right," Kiwi confirmed, his thoughts already drifting to how he could best get over to Fuhlsbuettel so he could catch an inbound flight to Berlin.

"We were a pair once, you know?"

"No, I didn't know."

"Ages ago, before the war. Do you see much of him?"

"I live in his house when I'm in Berlin. He was my squadron leader in the Battle of Britain."

"Oh, I didn't know that!" she exclaimed brightening up.

"It was a long time ago," Kiwi reminded her.

"Yes, a lifetime." She agreed, the sadness returning as she lifted her glass. "Well, here's to Auld Lang Syne!"

They clicked glasses. Virginia threw her Cuba Libre down like an old hand and signalled the bartender for a second. Kiwi got to his feet. "Thanks for the drink, Virginia. See you around." He walked over to his mesmerised ground crew, knocked each on the shoulder, and gestured with his head towards the door.

Chapter Four
Unexpected Allies

Devious Connections
Berlin-Kreuzberg
Wednesday, 7 July 1948
(Day 12)

David Goldman found it difficult to sleep. Robin had returned from the Station Commanders' briefing with the startling news that the RAF was going to charter civilian aviation companies to help on the Airlift. The impetus came from the fact that the RAF had no tankers in its inventory, making it necessary to purchase or charter these assets. Yet once the decision to charter civilian carriers was taken, the RAF leadership had thrown open the floodgates. Any company with certified aircraft and qualified crew was invited to contribute to the operation. The civilians would be paid by the ton of cargo delivered and would have access to RAF facilities and fuel. Instantly, David recognized that if he re-incorporated his company so it could carry freight as well as passengers, he could get Moby Dick — and any other aircraft he acquired — onto RAF airfields.

In his excitement, he'd enthused to everyone at the small dinner party hosted by the Priestmans about this unprecedented and exciting opportunity. The cargoes were guaranteed, the fuel was free, and because banks loved government contracts, he'd be able to finance additional aircraft with loans rather than drawing on his capital. He might be able to use loans to cover other start-up costs as well. The expansion of the business would, furthermore, take the pressure off the ambulance to be profitable. If things went as he envisaged, the ambulance could function practically as a charity or non-profit subsidiary of the larger, money-earning freight venture.

By the end of the evening, he had offered Emily a share in the new holding company. Furthermore, Kiwi, Emily and he had agreed to return to the UK immediately to get things started. While David handled all aspects of the legal and financial framework, Kiwi would look into aircraft and recruiting ground crew. Emily, meanwhile, would conduct interviews with prospective captains.

Yet now, in the dark of the night, things no longer looked as simple as they had in the glow of the wine-fuelled evening before. David remembered that, while there were lots of mothballed wartime aircraft that could be converted to freighters, most former air and ground crew had started new lives over the last three and half years. Those who hadn't were not likely to be the best. As a former instructor, David was acutely aware that RAF wings alone did not make a man suited to the kind of steady, safety-minded work that would be required on the Airlift.

Furthermore, David had confidently announced they would acquire two four-engine freighters and try to convert one of these into a tanker. Because the four-engine freighters could carry three times as much cargo as a Dakota, they offered dramatic economies of scale. But four-engine aircraft required a crew of five, and twice the number of ground mechanics as the smaller cargo carriers. That meant that in addition to four additional pilots, he needed two navigators, two signallers and two flight engineers plus four more ground crew for the freighters. All of them in addition to the two German aircraft mechanics he wanted to hire so they could base Moby Dick in Berlin again.

After tossing and turning a bit, he decided they should focus on hiring captains and let *them* solve the problem of pulling together a crew, including the second pilot. He would give them until the end of the month to do that. Meanwhile, Ron and Chips would be given the job of finding more fitters and riggers for the Hamburg hub, while David would approach Charlotte's cousin Christian about former Luftwaffe ground crew.

Talking to Christian had been Charlotte's idea, and the thought of her reminded David that she was sleeping just across the hall. The Priestmans had insisted that she stay the night because it was too dangerous for a woman to walk around after dark now that there were no streetlights or regular public transport.

It was odd to think of her so nearby, under the same roof. He remembered hearing her timid voice thanking Emily for her hospitality. She'd exclaimed in delight at how pretty the room was. David strained his ears, wondering if she, too, was awake, but there was no reason for her to lie awake. Tomorrow — or rather today — he would escort her home before departing for England. He was looking forward to that, but first, with an exhausted sigh, he turned over and went out like a light.

After breakfast together, Charlotte and David were picked up by Horst, Charlotte's family coachman, who now used his team and wagon to haul cargoes from Gatow to the barge port in Kladow. David had agreed to pay him double what he earned transporting Airlift cargo to take Charlotte safely back to her residence in Kreuzberg and used the excuse of wanting to talk to Christian to justify going with her.

As he settled onto the seat of the wagon beside her, the feel of her shoulder and thigh against his own was electrifying. Did she feel it too? He looked at her, trying to gauge her reaction. Her face seemed flushed, and her eyes were bright. He wanted to take her hand in his but didn't dare. Horst clicked to the team, and they set off.

It was a windy day with lots of clouds scudding overhead. The aircraft were approaching Gatow out of the east, over the Havel, but the sight had become so normal that no one paid any attention to them anymore. David's ears were more attuned to the peaceful clop-clop of the horses trotting ahead of them. It took him back to his childhood. He remembered a carriage ride in Potsdam between Sans Souci and the Neues Palast. He'd been with his Uncle Otto and Aunt Anna. The sound of a heavy aircraft flying very low and not on the approach to Gatow distracted him from his memories. Looking up, he caught a glimpse of a large Sunderland flying boat coming down from the north.

"Horst! Can you take us closer to the shore? It's fun to watch a flying boat land!"

Horst touched his cap in acknowledgement and found a weed-grown path leading towards the edge of the lake. Here the three of them tumbled down from the cart to watch the landing, but the Sunderland banked away after an initial 'look-see' and swung wide to make a new approach. Waiting for it to line up again, David glanced to the far shore. The view across the lake was good from here and without thinking he called out, "Look! You can see the Schwanenwerder. That long lawn down to the water on the left. That's my uncle's house."

"Your uncle?" Charlotte asked, surprised. "You didn't tell me you had an uncle in Berlin." She sounded so pleased that it hurt. David couldn't answer; anything he said would sound bitter and accusatory. He looked away.

Charlotte read his response correctly, and with a sharp intake of breath whispered, "I'm so sorry."

David turned back to face her, but she looked down, wringing her hands. He reached out and took one of them into his own. "There's no need for *you* to be sorry," he told her earnestly. She looked up and met his eyes, hope and pain mixing in her expression. "You are not to blame. I'm sorry I mentioned it. It's just..." David broke off. How could he explain? Nothing could bring his aunt and uncle back, but he couldn't bear for an SS officer to remain in occupation of their home.

"Yes?" Charlotte prompted, her blue eyes full of sympathy.

"It's just that a man is living in my uncle's house — a man I'm sure was in the SS or Gestapo or something. I can't prove it; I can just sense it."

"I thought all Jewish property stolen by the Nazis was supposed to be restored?" she answered hesitantly.

"In theory, yes, but this man is protected in some way. I went to the city government office to file my restitution claims, but when I gave them the address, they became flustered. Eventually, someone asked me for a pile of documents that he knew I wouldn't be able to produce — birth and death certificates for my aunt and uncle and all my cousins, copies of my uncle's will, my uncle's passport. I can't remember it all. It was a transparent attempt to put an end to my application."

"That is terrible!" Charlotte declared emphatically. "You must talk to Jakob Liebherr about this. Maybe he could help you. It is odd though..."

"What is odd?"

"Well, Christian had a terrible experience on Schwanenwerder too. He went to one of the big houses to try to sell his wine and was horrified to find one of our family paintings hanging on the wall. The man claimed the Russians had given it to him, but Christian doesn't believe him. Christian is convinced the man is living under a false name and that he was a Nazi bigwig of some sort."

David gazed at her a moment. "Do you know the name or address of the man he ran into?"

"No. You'll have to ask Christian."

Horst distracted them by drawing their attention to the Sunderland. It was making a second attempt to land, and for the moment they forgot about Schwanenwerder as they watched it settle on the water with surprising grace for its size and weight. Like a pelican on a pond, David had heard someone call it. The sight of the majestic aircraft and the cluster of little boats and barges milling around it in joyful chaos triggered unexpected gaiety in Charlotte. Her delight was childlike as she laughed and excitedly pointed various things out. David did not think he had ever seen her look so carefree before. It made her look younger. It was like getting a glimpse of her as a girl. Despite all the things he had to do today for his business, this moment alone made him glad he had taken the time to escort Charlotte home.

Charlotte lived in the five-story apartment building owned by Christian which stood directly on the Landwehr Canal. She led David up four flights of stairs to let them into her flat, calling to her cousin as they entered. "Christian! It's me and I've brought Mr Goldman. He wants to speak to you."

The door to the kitchen opened and Christian emerged smiling. "Mr Goldman! What a pleasant surprise. I was just beginning to worry about Charlotte not being back. How can I help you?"

"Well, it's about the ambulance service —"

"No need to talk in the hall," Christian interrupted, backing into the kitchen and gesturing for David to follow. As he gestured for David to take a set, he intoned, "No electricity, I'm afraid, so the only refreshments I can offer are water, terrible and dangerous schnapps, courtesy of ex-Kriegsmarine moonshiners, or first-class wine."

"It's not yet noon," David answered still standing, "and I can only stay a very short while."

Christian nodded, but again indicated the chairs at the kitchen table. David gave in and sat down. Christian sat opposite him. "So, how can I help you?"

"Charlotte has probably told you that it looks as though we will be receiving compensation from the Americans for our medical evacuations out of Berlin, and we have also made progress in getting permission to base the aircraft at RAF stations. However, my British groundcrews refuse to live and work in Berlin under the blockade. Indeed, they might not receive permission to return to Berlin from the Allied authorities, even if they were willing to do so. In short, I'm looking for experienced aircraft mechanics already resident in Berlin."

There was a moment of silence as Christian absorbed this. "Meaning you would be willing to employ former Luftwaffe aircraft mechanics?"

"Yes."

To David's intense disappointment, Christian did not respond with the enthusiasm he had expected. Instead, nothing but silence followed.

After several seconds, Charlotte shifted in her chair and burst in anxiously, "Surely you know someone, Christian? David would be able to pay in hard currency." She looked to David for reassurance as she said this, and he nodded confirmation.

"That's not the issue," Christian told them. "I don't doubt this would be a wonderful opportunity, but I flew single-engine fighters throughout the war. I don't know any mechanics who serviced bombers."

"Engines are engines," David countered. "The Merlins that powered our Hurricanes and Spitfires also carried the Lancasters."

"Merlins? Is that what your ambulance has?"

"No, Hercules VIs."

Christian shook his head. "I've never even heard of them, and no German mechanic will know anything about them either."

David had been so sure German mechanics were the solution to this particular problem, that this answer left him speechless and deflated.

"Christian, don't you want to help?" Charlotte asked her cousin reproachfully.

He looked over at her surprised. "On the contrary. I would very much like to help but let me be frank. I don't maintain close contact with Luftwaffe associations and networks because I'm viewed by most of them — or at least key elements in them — as a traitor. So, I don't have a large network I can fall back on. There is one man who might be able to help, though. He was a first-class mechanic, and he had natural curiosity and an interest in new challenges. Then again, he was a Socialist in constant trouble for insubordination. After I became a POW I lost track of him. If anyone I know could help you it would be Axel Voigt, but I must be honest with you, Mr Goldman, I don't even know if he survived the war, much less where he is now."

"I understand," David answered numbly, telling himself that operating from Berlin was not essential. If they had to, they'd manage to fly in from Bizonia. Alternatively, he could try putting an advertisement in a newspaper. He hesitated to do that, however, because the Luftwaffe had been the branch of Germany's military most widely infected by Nazi ideology, and David didn't want Nazis working for his company. Because Christian was so anti-Nazi himself, he'd presumed that Christian would not recommend anyone ideologically unsuitable. He'd failed to anticipate the problem Christian had indicated: because of his brother's prominent treason, he was himself *persona non grata* in Luftwaffe circles. To Christian, David simply said, "I would appreciate it if you would try to get in touch with this man Voigt."

"Yes, of course."

David got to his feet to take his leave and Christian rose to see him out. At the door, David stopped himself. "Oh, one more thing. Charlotte tells me there is a man living on Schwanenwerder whom you believe to be a senior SS officer." Christian went very stiff, but David forged ahead. "As it happens, my murdered uncle owned a house on Schwanenwerder and there is a man occupying it who I also firmly believe was SS. It made me wonder if they might be the same man?"

"Friedebach," Christian spat out. "He goes by the name of Friedebach. Juergen Friedebach."

"That's him!" David exclaimed, energised to think someone else shared his suspicions.

"Do you know anything about him?"

"Nothing, but I can smell SS ten feet away. And you? What do you know?"

"I believe his real name is Aggstein, von Aggstein, to be precise, but I have no way to prove that just yet. All I know is that he has personal items with the Aggstein arms on them and that a certain Max von Aggstein was a senior official in the SS Administration in occupied Poland — the economic branch of the SS, not the Waffen-SS," he clarified.

David nodded. "That makes sense."

"My sister-in-law, the widow of my brother Philip, works for the prosecution at the war crimes trials ongoing in Nuremberg and is trying to find out more for me. So far, however, she has come up only with blanks. Nevertheless, I'm convinced that Friedebach/Aggstein was a war criminal and that he is probably even now engaged in nefarious activities. All we have to do is put the pieces of the puzzle back together again and make the case against him to the right authorities — possibly through my sister-in-law. If he has done half the things I suspect he's done, he'll hang."

"I'll buy champagne for the party, and we'll celebrate it in *my* house on Schwanenwerder," David answered smiling.

"Yes, I'd like that," Christian agreed, but then his expression turned sad as he added, "But I hope you'll also return to me the painting of my brother that I found hanging there. It means a great deal to me."

"I'll return everything that belongs to you, Christian," David promised solemnly, using his first name and the informal form for the first time. "But first we have to find evidence of his complicity in crimes, and before I can focus on that I need to save my business," he reminded the German.

Christian understood and this time he sounded more confident as he explained, "Voigt was a Berliner. From Wedding, if I remember correctly. If he survived the war, and the Ivans aren't still holding on to him, he'll have washed up here. I promise to do my best to find him."

They shook hands. Then David turned to Charlotte, who was hovering behind Christian uncertainly. "Is there anything I can bring you from London, Charlotte?"

"You don't have to bring me anything," she answered blushing.

"No, but I want to. Perfume? A silk scarf? Rouge or lipstick or silk stockings?" He automatically listed the things his sister Sarah would have liked.

"Oh, no. I don't need anything like that. But — but..." she lost her courage.

"Yes?"

"Would it be possible for you to bring me a new pair of shoes?" She pointed to her feet, which were encased in scuffed shoes long since stretched out of shape and down at the heel.

"Of course I can bring you a pair of shoes," David assured her. "What size do you wear?"

"Thirty-eight. And please make them practical, comfortable shoes with only little heels. I need to walk in them a lot."

"I will do my best," David promised, already planning to buy her at least two pairs of practical shoes and one pair of dress shoes. "Now I must hurry, or we'll miss the BEA flight."

"Please ring and let me know how things go," Charlotte begged.

"Of course, Charlotte," David wanted to say much more, but he was already late. "I'll ring you on Sunday at the latest."

"Thank you, David," she offered him her hand.

David would have liked to kiss her goodbye, but he didn't dare, especially not in front of Christian. Instead, he took her hand and raised it to his lips, bowing formally but a little playfully as he murmured, "Graefin Walmsdorf." He was surprised by the flush of joy that suffused Charlotte's face in response. This old-fashioned courtesy appeared to please her beyond his expectations. Maybe he had restored a little of her self-esteem? He hoped so.

Mysterious Collaborators
RAF Gatow
Wednesday, 7 July 1948
(Day 12)

As requested, Lt. Col Russel reported to the Station Commander's office first thing in the morning. Priestman gestured for him to take a seat at the coffee table while he completed some other business with the adjutant, his secretary and the IO. When he finally approached Russel, the Lt. Col. got to his feet to say. "I want to thank you again for dinner last night, Wing Commander—"

"It was entirely our pleasure."

"No, it was mine. Mrs Priestman is a gem. You are lucky to have found her."

"My better half, I always say."

"I also enjoyed meeting Mr Goldman and Assistant Section Leader Hart, who is an outstanding example of the kind of women who built the British Empire. But I must confess, your Victory Garden caught my attention, too. I'm a frustrated farmer at heart, you see. Something about watching things grow makes me feel more at ease with the world." He hesitated, but Robin waited patiently, his expression encouraging. "This may sound rather odd, but would you object to me stopping by your house and helping out in the garden in my spare time?"

"Do you have any spare time?" Priestman quipped back, only half in jest.

Russel laughed. "I can make time for a garden."

"Well, you'll get no objection from me or Mrs Priestman, but you'll have to get Jasha's consent. It's her garden and her hens."

"Jasha?"

"Our cook. Ethnically Polish but born in the Soviet Union, she lost her family to the Soviet terror and fled to Poland just in time for the Nazi invasion. They enslaved her and sent her to work in the Reich. It seems inadequate but the best compensation I can provide is to give her complete control of my garden — at least as long as it is mine." Priestman explained.

"Indeed," Russel agreed nodding, "I will bear that in mind, but I honestly think I might be able to help a bit. Now, I've wasted enough of your time with my hobby. You asked me here to discuss something official, I believe?"

"Yes. It seems HMG wants Gatow to have two concrete runways, not just one."

"They're out of their minds! That will take months to complete and choke everything up in the meantime!" The CRE officer responded, exasperated. "A much faster way to increase capacity would be to tar the PSP runway and use it for take-offs only, while we direct all landings onto the concrete runway — as soon as it's finished, that is."

"Brilliant! We'll do that!" the WingCo agreed at once and continued, "Meanwhile, the French have agreed to the construction of an airfield in their Sector."

"Very generous of them. Are they also providing the bulldozers, crushers and steamrollers?" Russel asked back.

"Apparently some American chap believes we might be able to cut construction equipment into parts small enough to load on a C-54 and then weld them back together again on arrival. At least, that's what a USAF colonel told Bagshot. Allegedly, the Americans did this all across the Pacific as they island-hopped to Japan, building one airstrip after another."

"Do let me know if they succeed," Russel retorted with evident scepticism.

Priestman laughed shortly but continued. "Yes, well as I mentioned last night at dinner, HMG is also going to be chartering civilian airlines to transport liquid fuel into Berlin, which means also need an underground fuel storage facility."

"Abracadabra!" Russel answered with an effusive gesture of his hands.

"No, I'm serious. We need liquid fuel storage capacity at Gatow. The Americans don't want a fuel depot in Tempelhof," Priestman explained. "It's surrounded by residential buildings and the dangers of flying in and out are high enough without adding a fuel dump — not to mention the casualties to the surrounding population if the thing caught fire. The new airfield we hope to build in the French Sector will be designed to include adequate fuel storage, but the most optimistic estimates for completion are early next year. Meanwhile, diesel, petrol, heating oil and aviation fuel need to be stored somewhere in Berlin. Gatow is the logical place for it."

"Meaning, not only do you want me to build you some subterranean liquid fuel storage tanks, but you also want them finished in the next few weeks," Russel concluded.

"That shouldn't be too hard, should it?" Priestman asked in a tone that made Russel look at him twice before recognising it was a joke.

With a sigh of resignation, Russel suggested, "I'd better bring you the technical drawings so we can decide together on the best location."

"Good idea."

Russel returned a few minutes later with blueprints of the entire airfield and its infrastructure. Together they spread them out on the coffee table. "The key consideration," Russel explained as Priestman leaned over the table to look at them, his hands clasped behind his back, "is to locate the fuel dumps as far from the quarters, messes and other administrative buildings as possible. That means we can forget the entire southern perimeter." Russel made a sweeping gesture with his hand over the plans to indicate the empty areas south of the accommodation blocks. "Nor do we want the depots in line with the runways."

"I should think not," Priestman agreed dryly.

"That leaves this area north of the new runway as the best option. At least on paper. I'm going to have to survey the area to see what the soil is like and so on."

"Shall we walk over together and get a preliminary feel for it?" Priestman suggested. "I need to get out of this office from time to time." While Russel folded the plans back together, Priestman grabbed his hat. They left the office together, Priestman telling Sergeant Andrews he'd be back in a half hour or so.

Russel took the opportunity of being alone with Priestman far from other ears to ask, "Was anything else said at the meeting yesterday that I should know about?"

"Not specifically," Priestman answered before adding, "but off the record, Group Captain Bagshot is floundering in chaos. He has no sense of the bigger picture. He's lost in the weeds. Worst of all he doesn't seem to grasp that the urgency of the situation calls for us to cut the red tape — not double it. He's turned aircraft back for nonsensical infringements of regulations and he took the coffee away from incoming crews because they hadn't gone through customs! Can you imagine? Men coming in to fly almost round the clock are being harassed about a half-pound of coffee brought in their kit from England. It took all my self-control not to explode."

Russel laughed. "That speaks well for you, WingCo."

"Thank you, but I don't have a lot of self-control and I'm at serious risk of losing my wool in the wrong place and time. Bagshot thinks I've already chalked up a black about the power outage on Monday —"

"But we solved it!"

"That doesn't matter. He blames me for the fact that he didn't pay enough attention at the briefing when I first reported to him. At the time, we were all greatly relieved that, unlike Tempelhof, we didn't have to rely on power generated in our own Sector. To raise the issue with the Soviets would have risked drawing their attention to the anomaly and to switch to our limited sources would have meant even less power for the civilian population. At the time, everyone agreed to just let things be. Bagshot prefers to forget that, however," Priestman's expression reflected the fact that the Bagshot's ticking-off had been one of the most severe of his career. It had left him reeling. He and Bagshot did not see eye-to-eye on anything, and that was sure to cause more problems in the future.

They reached the PSP runway and paused to watch a Dakota settle down at the far end and thunder past them with a squeaking wheel and greasy, black underbelly. Then they strode hastily over the irregular surface before the next aircraft was lined up. Here Russel pointed to the left and they walked around the end of the incomplete new runway.

Priestman caught sight of something just beyond the perimeter fence that he hadn't noticed before. He couldn't make sense of it and pointed. "What is that under the trees over there?"

Russel's eyes followed his outstretched finger. "Oh, that! Looks like another one of the barrels of bitumen we've been receiving lately."

"What barrels of bitumen?"

"We've been finding them along the perimeter fence for the last week or so."

"Who is putting them there?"

Russel shrugged. "No idea. At first, we thought they might be booby-trapped or of poor quality, so we handled them gingerly. But they turned out to be just what they appeared to be: barrels full of tar. As far as we can tell, somebody — or maybe many people — on the Soviet side of the border want to see us complete this runway."

"Is that credible?" Priestman asked sceptically.

"My German workers tell me that people in the Russian Zone aren't stupider than people in the West. They can see what's going on — that the Soviets are trying to starve the Berliners into submission, while we're trying to keep them alive. My workers say that people talk about almost nothing else in their local pubs, or *kneipe* as they call them. They know that more runways mean more — I think someone's trying to get your attention." Russel interrupted himself to point to a Land Rover of the RAF regiment that was bouncing its way over the airfield in their direction.

Priestman turned to look and then started walking in the direction of the vehicle. Even before it reached them, the driver called out. "Wing Commander Priestman, could you come to the main gate, please? There's something very strange that you ought to see, and the Lieutenant Colonel might want to join us, sir."

Priestman and Russel exchanged a surprised glance and then hastened to clamber into the Land Rover. The driver raced around the end of the runway and crossed the taxiways at a fast pace. As they approached the main gate, they could see that a large, agitated crowd had already collected. The driver hooted. People glanced over, recognised the CO, and let the Land Rover through to the barrier. On the other side stood a steamroller.

"What the devil ...?" Priestman exclaimed as he and Russel jumped out opposite sides of the Land Rover to look more closely at the bizarre apparition.

The CRE officer walked around the machine, commenting in an admiring tone, "Not exactly the latest technology, but by Jove, it's precisely what I need for the runway."

Priestman focused on the guard and driver. "What is this all about, Corporal?"

"Well, sir, this man says he's driven this steamroller from Leipzig so we can use it for building the runway and anything else we like."

"Wait, wait, wait. Leipzig is down in Saxony somewhere —"

"That's right."

"He would have had to cross half the Soviet Zone to get here—"

"Yes, he said he came via Potsdam and Nedlitz."

"And no one stopped him?"

"No."

Priestman turned to look at the driver who was short, round-faced and grinning from ear to ear. Dressed in threadbare, dirty workman's clothes and disintegrating shoes from which his filthy toes emerged, he looked poor, humble and insignificant. His peaked cap was crumpled and faded, but reminiscent of the caps worn by Russian revolutionaries. Altogether, he appeared too simple to engage in deviousness and too poor to harbour sympathies for the capitalist warmongers. Recognising a senior officer, the man broke into a wide grin and a flood of German that triggered a series of laughs from the Germans standing around.

"Would someone like to translate that?" Priestman asked the crowd.

"He says he told anyone who stopped him that he had to go to the next village because the Ivans ordered him there. If they asked 'why,' he'd shrug and say he hadn't a clue. He never said he was going farther than a few miles."

Priestman shook his head in bemusement and told the man "Well done!," eliciting another broad smile as the man put his hand to his cap in a kind of salute. Turning to Flying Officer Boyd, who had joined the crowd,

Priestman ordered, "Be sure our benefactor gets a good meal and see if he needs a few marks to get back where he came from."

"I'll take care of it, sir, and have a nice chat with him over some schnapps in the worker's canteen," Boyd promised.

"Thank you." Priestman turned back to the engineer. "What do you say, Russel? Is it what you were looking for?"

"A damn sight better than something that's been welded back together again. With this, we should have the concrete runway finished in less than ten days."

"Excellent. Let me know about the other project as soon as you've finished your surveys."

"Yes, of course."

As Priestman turned in the direction of his office, he was feeling much better than when he'd arrived this morning. Maybe his luck would hold after all.

Extraordinary Coincidences
Foster Clough, Yorkshire
Wednesday, 7 July 1948
(Day 12)

"The car's making a strange squeaking noise in the back," the Reverend Edwin Reddings told his son-in-law as he came through the back door. He was scratching his head as if puzzled.

"The brakes?" Kit asked back.

"I don't think so. The noise seemed to start when I *stopped* braking."

"I'd better take a look at it," Kit declared, getting to his feet.

"I can take it to the garage if you prefer," Reddings offered.

"No, it might be dangerous for you to drive," Kit told him, grabbing overalls from a hook by the back door. "We've got time before dinner. I'll see if I can find out what's wrong." He stepped into the legs of the overalls and continued outside as he pulled the arms over his shirt and fastened the buttons. For the first half of the war Kit had been a fitter, and he retained his old work clothes for tasks like this — or mucking out the stalls of the two horses his in-laws kept in a stable at the back.

Kit welcomed the distraction because he could use something practical to do just now. He'd spent the afternoon filling out an elaborate and lengthy application form for a job. After being turned down for scores of engineering jobs over the last six months, his wife Georgina had talked him into responding to an advertisement from Ethiopian Airlines soliciting applications from pilots, flight engineers and ground crew. It was as much Georgina's enthusiasm as his own frustration that had induced him to respond. Georgina had been depressed ever since she'd been forced out of her beloved teaching profession because English schools would not employ mothers. Georgina had been told it was different in Africa, and that she would have no trouble finding a teaching job in Ethiopia. Kit, however, had discovered that the Ethiopians, with their 2,000-year history, maintained an arcane bureaucracy. He had never encountered anything quite like this application form before — not even in the RAF. It was 20 pages long and included lengthy questions about his family, his religion, his education and, of course, his experience.

Kit took the tool kit out of the boot of his father-in-law's car and put it down on the ground. Then he lay down on his back and squirmed his way under the tailgate with a torch, which he directed towards the brakes. As he conducted the inspection, he was asking himself how he was supposed to answer the question, "When was the last time you flew an aircraft?"

Did he admit to flying without a license with Leonard Cheshire in a Mossie that the Group Captain might — or might not — still have owned? Or did he omit that flight (which he had not dared record in his logbook) and say that the last time he'd flown he'd crash-landed, breaking the aircraft into three pieces and leaving his flight engineer crippled for life while crushing his left foot under the instrument panel so completely that they had to cut it off to extract him before the fuel tanks exploded?

Which brought him to the question of the medical exam. In addition to the application form, Ethiopian Airlines had sent a five-page "Medical Questionnaire" to be completed "by the applicant's attending physician." Aside from the fact that he didn't have a particular physician, what were the Ethiopians likely to do with, "Missing left foot and half of lower left leg." He knew he could fly with his artificial limb, but why should Ethiopian Airlines believe him? And why would any doctor pass him fit to fly —

"Kit! Kit!" It was the urgent voice of his father-in-law.

The reverend's tone was so alarmed that Kit pushed himself back out from under the car fearing some sort of calamity. Had his daughter Donna had an accident? Or Georgina? Reddings was gesturing to him from the back door, signalling him to come. "It's a telephone call for you!"

Kit pushed himself off the ground, using his flesh-and-bones foot, and wiped the dirt off his palms on the already dirty thighs of the overalls as he hastened to the house. "Who is it?" he asked his father-in-law, who stood holding the door open for him.

"A Mr Goldman calling from London about a job interview!" Reddings exclaimed flustered. He knew how hard Kit had been looking for jobs these past six months.

Puzzled, Kit frowned slightly. He couldn't remember the name Goldman, but there might well have been a Goldman among the scores of personnel chiefs to whom he'd sent his many letters of inquiry. He took up the telephone receiver and spoke into the handset, "Good afternoon. This is Christopher Moran."

"David Goldman," came the crisp answer. "I'm the Managing Director of Air Ambulance International based in Berlin, Germany. His Majesty's Government has decided to contract civilian airliners on the Berlin Airlift. My company is looking into options for adding air freight to our ongoing ambulance operations. If we go ahead, we will need to employ pilots with four-engine ratings and experience. You were recommended to us by Assistant Section Officer Hart as a possible captain." Kathleen! Kit thought, noting that she had been promoted. On the other end of the line, the unfamiliar voice continued. "I'm calling to see, first, if you would be interested in what, due to the nature of the work, must be a temporary position only, and if so, if you could come to an interview at the Savoy Hotel in London tomorrow or Friday." At last the clipped voice paused long enough to allow Kit to answer.

Kit's pulse was racing. He was being offered a chance to fly the Airlift! The day the British government had announced their intention to supply the city by air, he had told his father-in-law that he wished he could be part of it. Reddings, ever the optimist, had told him he thought he would be. Kit had not believed him. He'd been invalided out of the RAF and had seen no possible way to become part of this military operation. Now, out of the blue, things had changed. Civilians were being given a chance to fly. He could hardly breathe for fear he might say something to spoil his chances. He tried to keep his voice neutral as he replied: "The answer to both questions, sir, is yes. However, I'm currently in Yorkshire. I'm not sure about train connections, so Friday afternoon would be better."

"Excellent. The interview will be with our Director of Personnel, Mrs Emily Priestman, who will be able to provide you with additional details. She says..." Goldman covered the phone with his hand and his voice became muffled. Then his voice came clear and loud again as he announced, "Mrs Priestman would have time for you at 4 pm. In the tearoom. Is that all right?"

"Yes, sir. That's fine. How will I recognise her?"

"Mrs Priestman will be wearing our black and red uniform. You should have no difficulty finding and identifying her. Please bring your logbook and licences to the interview."

"Yes, of course."

"Do you have any other questions?"

"No, I'll save them up for the interview."

"Excellent. Good evening, then."

"Good evening."

The telephone connection went dead, replaced by the dialling tone.

Dazed, Kit replaced the receiver and turned to find his father-in-law anxiously watching from the back door and Georgina peering at him from the stairs. "Kit?" she asked.

"I've got a job interview in London on Friday at 4 pm. I'll have to—"

"Congratulations!" Georgina and her father exclaimed simultaneously, Georgina jumping off the stairs to run into his arms while her father came forward to shake his hand.

"Ethiopian Airlines?" Georgina asked eagerly.

"No. It's an outfit called 'Air Ambulance International' based in Berlin and interested in flying cargo on the Airlift." He admitted the latter with a sheepish grin in the direction of his father-in-law.

"Didn't I tell you this would happen? It is your destiny!" Reddings declared triumphantly, his whole face beaming with delight.

"Calm down, both of you," Kit admonished. "All I have is an interview — not a job."

"But how did they find out about you, Kit?" Georgina wanted to know.

"It seems they ran into Kathleen somewhere and she mentioned me—"

"What an extraordinary coincidence!" Reddings declared, the hall light glinting off his spectacles as he nodded his satisfaction. Kit and Georgina exchanged a smile, knowing that the Anglican vicar believed coincidences were the hand of God.

"If things work out, we'll owe Kathleen a nice dinner or two," Kit suggested, "but let's not count our chickens before they hatch. I've got to get myself down to London for the interview on Friday, first."

"Did I hear that correctly?" Mrs Reddings emerged out of the kitchen. "You have a job interview, Kit?"

"Yes, Friday afternoon in London at the Savoy—"

"Perfect! I think Georgina should go with you and you should stay the weekend — at the Savoy at our expense. Don't you agree, Edwin?" She did not give her husband a chance to disagree. Continuing to her daughter and son-in-law she declared, "You two have not had any time alone together since Donna was born and that's what you both need. You go down to London together on the train, stay at the Savoy—" She held up her hands to stop the protests. "You never had a honeymoon, and I've been meaning to suggest something like this for a long time; this is the right moment. You will *both* go to London, get theatre or concert tickets and enjoy yourselves *regardless* of what happens at the interview."

Kit and Georgina looked at one another, while Reverend Reddings muttered, "Sometimes you can be very bossy, Mrs Reddings." Then Georgina threw her arms around her mother. "Thank you so much, Mummy! It *is* just what we need. It will be so much better to be together whatever happens."

"Quite right. Now would one of you be so kind as to fill me in on the details of the job?"

Kit summarised all he knew again, adding, "But I'm not at all sure they know about my handicap—"

"But you can still fly, Kit!" Georgina insisted. She had *always* insisted that he was not "handicapped."

"I know, but please be realistic. All of you." Kit was talking as much to curb his own excitement as theirs. He didn't want to get his hopes up too high, or the disappointment of rejection would be all the greater. "There are lots of other men out there who can fly as well as I can and *don't* have a handicap."

"Show them to me!" Georgina challenged him.

He just shook his head. "The other thing to bear in mind is that this is only a temporary job — for as long as the Airlift lasts, which might only be a month or two."

"Which is perfect," Reddings declared. "This way you can still submit your application to Ethiopian Airlines or anywhere else, but in the meantime you can earn some income, re-activate your flying status, and—" he paused for emphasis and looked Kit straight in the eye, "take food rather than bombs to Berlin — just as you said you wanted."

Chapter Five
Uncertain Options

The Best Years of Our Lives
Ann Arbor, Michigan
Thursday, 8 July 1948
(Day 13)

The phone was ringing in the old, clapboard house that J.B. shared with friends in Ann Arbor. Thinking it might be his fiancée, Patty, he dropped the groceries on the counter and grabbed the phone. "Hello!"

"Return to base, captain!"

J.B. frowned, confused and irritated. Then he recognised the voice. "Orloff? Rick Orloff? Is that you? Where the hell are you?" Rick Orloff had been his bombardier on his last 12 missions.

"Willow Run."

"Willow Run?" J.B. couldn't believe his ears. Willow Run was the commercial airport serving the Detroit metropolitan area and close to his parents' home. "What are you doing there? How long are you in town for?" Rick came from a small town in Indiana and had returned there after the war. They didn't need bombardiers in peacetime and Rick had never finished high school, so his plans had been vague when they parted. J.B. had received only a couple of postcards from him since. Most had said little, but one had contained the intriguing information: "Just got hitched! Barb can eat her heart out." Rick had dated J.B.'s sister Barb briefly, but she had never shown much interest; Rick was too poor, too rough, and too independent for her taste.

On the other end of the telephone line, Rick's voice announced with nonchalant pride, "Just delivered a cargo of live lobsters for some auto executive's private party. Looking around for outbound cargo, but I'm here until I find something."

"Cargo? As in air freight?" J.B. asked incredulously.

"That's right. Me and my partner have been flying all over the country—"

"You're flying? How did you get a flying job? You can't fly!"

"My partner can, and FAA regulations do not – repeat: not — require a licenced copilot for flights carrying less than five tons of freight. We got ourselves a beat-up old DC-2. My partner flies her and I keep her running. Got qualified as an aircraft mechanic while fixing tractors after the war."

"What does your wife think of you flying all over the country?" J.B. asked, unable to repress a twinge of jealousy.

"She thinks it's terrific!" Rick answered so enthusiastically that J.B. could 'hear' his grin over the telephone line. Rick added by way of explanation, "She's my pilot."

"What?" J.B. couldn't believe his ears. "You've got to be kidding me!"

"Why should I? Jan was a WASP. Trained on B-17s too. That's what brought us together."

"Hot damn! She must be some woman."

"Yep, and this is your chance to meet her, Captain. If you can get your ass out here before dark, I'll take you to see our baby too — that's the DC 2. By the way, what did you say you were doing for dinner tonight?"

"Meeting up with an old buddy and his new wife!" J.B. answered. "Look, it'll take me about 90 minutes to get out to Willow Run. Where can I find you?"

"Come on over to the GAT. There's a small bar there that isn't as crowded as the ones in the main terminal. We'll be waiting for you."

The General Aviation Terminal (GAT) occupied some of the old factory offices, and the bar was in what had been the executive dining room. It had a certain dated dignity as if time had stood still for a few years. The scent of oil and aviation fuel from thousands of B-24s built at the plant had seeped into the furnishings along with cigar smoke and spilt brandy. From here, one expected to look out and see the purposeful bombers lined up for inspection rather than smartly painted airliners taxiing to and fro.

J.B. had no trouble finding Rick at the bar. He hadn't changed at all. Same distinctive, tanned face, close-cropped hair, and trim figure. J.B. sucked in his stomach, wincing at the flab he'd put on his waist since settling into student life two years ago.

Rick was wearing his leather bomber jacket over a khaki shirt and trousers. The woman beside him was dressed similarly. Patty wouldn't have liked that, J.B. noted automatically. She didn't think "nice" girls wore trousers, not even for sport, but J.B. had become used to women in trousers in England during the war. As Rick's wife turned to face him, he was taken aback by how plain she was. She was too tall, too bony, and her facial features were both elongated and too mismatched to be attractive. J.B. wouldn't have given her a second glance, although Rick looked pleased and self-assured.

"How do you do, Mrs Orloff!" J.B. extended his hand. "I'm Joseph Baronowsky Jr., but just about everybody calls me J.B."

"Nice to meet you, Captain — J.B., I mean. I've heard so much about you!" She spoke in a low-pitched but forthright voice so different from Patty's genteel half-whisper.

With a glance at Rick, he complained, "You've got me at a disadvantage there, Ma'am. My friend Rick hasn't told me anything about you."

"Sit down and have a drink while you get acquainted," Rick answered. "Then I'll take you over to meet NRJ48."

J.B. settled himself on the bar stool and ordered a beer from the attentive bartender before turning back to Rick's wife. She gave him a broad smile and announced. "I'm Janet, but you can call me Jan."

"Rick tells me you can fly — including the B-17."

"Well, not like you did. I only ferried them."

"Yeah, but the Fortress? That's pretty impressive."

"For a girl, you mean?"

"Well, I don't run into women pilots every day, that's for sure. How did you get into flying in the first place?" J.B. asked.

"My Daddy has a big ranch up in Idaho, and as he got older he thought riding fences was for the dogs. He said he'd been saddle-sore about a hundred times too often already, so he bought himself an old biplane and started flying fences. He used to take me with him, and I learned to fly almost before I could drive. When the WAFS got established — you know about the WAFS and WASP?"

"Oh, yeah! I heard a lot about them. My baby sister would have joined the WASP if she could. She must have applied ten times, but they kept turning her down."

"I was lucky. I had enough flying hours to get accepted straight into the WAFS. Later I was assigned to FERD — the ferrying division. General Tunner was tough as nails, but he always gave us girls a fair chance."

J.B. nodded, and Rick plonked his empty beer glass on the counter. "Come on, let me show you NRJ48 before it gets any darker."

The twin-engine cargo aircraft had seen better days. Her battered appearance and the smell of oil and dirt triggered J.B.'s memories and he felt a strong surge of nostalgia for flying. Yeah, war was hell, but the flying had been great.

He ducked to enter the small door in the fuselage and his leather-soled shoes slipped on the metal floor plates as he scrambled up the slope to the cockpit. The torn and sagging leather seats behind the control panel were inviting, but J.B. curbed his instinct to just plop down into his old place. Instead, he glanced over his shoulder at Jan and gestured for her to take the lefthand seat. "After you, Captain."

She smiled up at him as she sank into the pilot's seat and invited him to sit beside her on the right. Rick stood between them, an elbow on each seatback like the flight engineer. Jan pointed out the controls and chatted happily about the flying qualities and quirks of the bird, while J.B. listened without paying much attention. He was thinking what a life this must be for Rick: flying without anyone shooting at them, without the whole misery of the war, military hierarchies, and regulations. Flying all over the country, too, seeing it from end to end, and best of all, doing it with a business partner who was his wife. J.B. hadn't known that jobs like this existed, but now he couldn't imagine a better life.

Then he thought guiltily of Patty. He'd fallen in love with her because she was so beautiful, so poised, so sophisticated and classy. He'd had to fight off a lot of competition, too. Winning her hand had been a triumph to be savoured. Not to mention that she'd already opened a lot of doors for him, getting him that job at GM with a starting salary higher than what his dad earned after 30 years working on the shop floor. Choosing a honeymoon hotel in Niagara Falls, selecting china and furnishings, finding a cute little house to rent in the suburbs with front and back lawns and a second bedroom for "the kids" — all those things associated with planning a future together — had enabled him to envisage a lifestyle more luxurious than anything his parents had dreamed about. Would he give that all up for a life like this? It surprised — and unnerved — him to realise the answer might be yes.

As they dropped down by the tail wheel after the tour was over, J.B. tried to put those feelings into words. "You're lucky. Both of you. Must be a great life."

"Yeah, except when we can't pay the bills," Rick answered with a laugh. "Financially, we live from one flight to the next."

Ah, J.B. thought, so that's the catch.

Jan laughed, too, but nervously. "Yeah, we got caught out in Atlanta once. A client cancelled on us after we'd already fuelled up and we couldn't pay the fuel bill."

"What happened?"

"Oh, Rick talked them into giving us another 24 hours. What choice did they have? They'd have lost fuel syphoning it out again."

"But they impounded dear old NRJ48 to make sure we didn't take off in her with their aviation fuel!" Rick reminded her.

"And then there was the time we busted our you-know-what to get a cargo from Salt Lake City up to Seattle only to have the bastard's check bounce!"

"Yeah, that was pretty bad," Rick agreed, shaking his head.

"I guess you don't stay in fancy hotels then?" J.B. was beginning to get a better picture of their lifestyle.

"No way! We bed down right here!" Rick gestured back inside the DC-2. "Have everything we need. We roll out our sleeping bags and the toilet's just a couple of steps away. We can make a coffee in the galley and keep some orange juice in the fridge there. Better than most trailers!"

"What would you say to a night with my folks?" J.B. answered. "If nothing else, we've got a shower."

"Naw, I wouldn't want to impose," Rick shook his head.

"Look, I'll give my mom a call and tell her my best wartime buddy is coming over with his wife and I want her to make her best Polish bigos. She'll be pleased as punch."

"You're sure she won't mind?" Rick asked, tempted.

"She knows how you saved my ass over Mannheim, Orloff. She'll be happy to meet you at last. And you too, Jan." Rick included the tall woman beside him, whose lack of pretension had already won him over. He no longer noticed she wasn't pretty.

"If I'm gonna be in nice company, I better go change into a skirt," Jan concluded, climbing back into the aircraft. The men moved a few feet away to give her more privacy and lowered their voices.

"What are you up to nowadays, J.B.? Weren't you due to graduate this spring?"

"Yeah. I did. Got engaged too," he added with a grin.

Rick punched his arm as he offered his congratulations, but with a glance at the aircraft to be sure Jan wasn't coming out just yet, he grew serious again. "Look, J.B., you were always the brainy one among us, who read the papers and all that. What do you think about what's going on in Berlin? Is this ruckus with the Reds gonna blow up into another war?"

"I don't think that's very likely. We've got the bomb, the Russkies don't, and they know it."

"Yeah, well, given all that, how come the Russkies started this thing in the first place? Why try to grab Berlin from us?"

J.B. shrugged. "Up to now they've had it pretty much their way — they annexed Latvia, Estonia and Lithuania back in '40 when they were friends with Hitler. Now they've stolen half of Poland and launched successful Communist coups in Hungary, Romania, Bulgaria, and Czechoslovakia. They probably thought we'd just pull out of Berlin without a squawk."

"Do you think there's any chance this Airlift can work?" Rick asked next, looking at his former captain intently.

"Why? You want to try to get in on it?" J.B. joked.

"Hey, I hear they're paying big bucks to civilian charter companies," Rick returned evading his eyes and shrugging awkwardly. "It's got to be better than what I earn now which, when I add up all the hours I work and see how much cash I have in my pocket, amounts to about a dime a day. The problem is old NRJ48 here," he jabbed his thumb in the direction of the weary DC-2, "can't make the flight across the Atlantic."

"Look, I don't see how an airlift can work in the long run. There are more than two million people who need food and fuel. One article I read said we'd have to fly in something like ten thousand tons of stuff a day, and all we've managed so far is a couple hundred. A few days of bad weather and the whole thing's gonna crash. That's what the Reds are counting on.

You're better off flying lobsters around than getting involved in a risky operation like the Berlin Airlift."

"Yeah, you're probably right," Rick agreed without sounding convinced, but at that moment, Jan rejoined them. She was wearing a floral print dress with buttons down the front and a belt at the waist. It had seen better days and was crushed from being stuffed in a kitbag for too long.

"Sorry, I don't have anything better," Jan answered J.B.'s look. "Besides, you can't make a silk purse out of a sow's ear any way you try. Dressing me up wouldn't make a lot of difference one way or another."

"You look just fine, Jan. It just struck me you might want to bring your laundry along with you so you can use our washer and dryer while you're there."

Jan looked at him with an expression of amazement. "That is about the nicest proposal anybody — other than Rick – has ever made me. Rick said you were different; now I believe him. I'll go get the laundry bag."

As she disappeared again, J.B. turned to Rick. "She's a gem."

"Yes, she is," Rick agreed proudly.

"Do you ever hear from any of the other guys?"

"Nope. Not that I expected to. We didn't have much in common."

"No, I guess you're right. Just ten guys poured into a bomber." J.B. paused and then admitted wistfully, "Still, sometimes it seems like they were the best years of our lives, doesn't it?"

Tea at the Savoy
London
Friday, 9 July 1948
(Day 14)

By half past three in the afternoon, Emily was feeling both wilted and discouraged. Since the next interview wasn't until four, she went to the ladies' room and took the opportunity to brush out her hair and pin it up again. Emily was thrilled to have been elevated to partner in David's new holding company and she'd been keen to interview prospective captains for the freighters they were going to buy, but after completing four interviews she was feeling much less confident in her abilities. She wished Robin were here so she could talk to him, but since he wasn't she was going to have to navigate this process on her own. Time to grow up, she told herself, looking at her reflection in the mirror.

The woman who gazed back at her looked trim and attractive in the black uniform with gold buttons and wings combined with red rank and company insignia and a red silk scarf at her neck. Her light brown hair was swept into a French twist at the back of her head, the red of her lipstick matching the red trim on the uniform. Her face was well-shaped with large hazel eyes but with enough wrinkles not to look doll-like. All in all, she thought she looked the part of a professional, and yet....

One of the candidates had tried to chat her up, suggesting dinner "and more" rather than taking the interview seriously. Another had kept casting looks at her wings as if he were offended by them. He finally asked her outright where she'd got them and how many flying hours she had. She hadn't liked his tone, and he hadn't liked her answer. She'd been relieved when he cut the interview short, no longer interested in a job where a woman would be his boss.

It was by now clear to Emily that any man willing to take what could only be a temporary job was someone who had not adjusted well in the post-war world. It was hardly surprising that the third candidate had displayed every sign of an alcohol problem from a bloated, red nose and bloodshot eyes to shaky hands. She knew that Kiwi, too, had become far too dependent on alcohol after his marriage went on the rocks. She didn't want to condemn a man for a drinking problem, but an alcoholic was unlikely to be reliable, and what if he tried to fly when drunk? She didn't want to risk it.

Yet, the fourth candidate hadn't impressed her either. He'd been restless and unable to look her in the eye. His answers had been vague, leaving her with the feeling that he was hiding something — and wouldn't be reliable either. Yet there was nothing definite that she could point to, nothing she could report to David. Fortunately, these interviews were just preliminary, she reminded herself. She was not charged with making a final selection, just selecting the three best candidates to whom the company might offer a probationary contract.

She looked down at her watch. It was 15:48. Time to go back to her table in the tearoom for the last interview. David had included this final candidate out of politeness to Assistant Section Officer Hart, but Emily was sceptical about a former member of 617 Squadron. It had been known as a suicide squadron, assigned exceptionally dangerous operations, and she'd heard rumours that some 617 aircrew had been addicted to danger. She imagined that someone like that might fancy flying the Berlin Airlift, but she didn't want to be in the same cockpit as him. Besides, someone from such a famous squadron was bound to be full of himself. She remembered newsreels about Guy Gibson that made him a perfect hero, but Robin had little good to say about him, claiming he treated his ground crews poorly. She drew a deep breath. Best get this over with.

She returned to the hotel's famous tearoom. It was the kind of place her parents would have abhorred, with pseudo-Louis XVI chairs, thick carpets, starched and pressed damask tablecloths and linen napkins folded into fans. Chrystal chandeliers and white Corinthian columns framed the luxurious furnishings. Emily vacillated between feeling out of place and delighting in the fresh flowers at every table, the pianist playing Chopin sensitively in the background, and the light from the glass dome that bathed the room in sunshine.

No sooner had she taken her place, than the doorman pointed her out to a young man in a business suit waiting near the entry. He nodded and started towards her. He was tall, slender and good-looking with dark hair that fell over his brow, but there was something odd about his gait and he certainly didn't have Gibson's broad smile. "Mrs Priestman?" he enquired politely as he stopped beside her chair, his face serious.

"Yes, that's me. Flight Lieutenant Moran?" she asked, getting to her feet.

"Yes."

They shook hands, and then she indicated the seat opposite her and urged, "Please have a seat." As he settled in the chair, he seemed wound up, and she decided to put them both more at ease by suggesting tea.

"That would be lovely," he readily agreed.

Emily lifted her hand, and a waitress came to take their order. After she withdrew, Emily opened with her prepared remarks. "Flight Lieutenant, first I'd like to thank you for taking the time to come to London and talk to me. We are aware that, since no one knows how long the Berlin Airlift will last, taking a job 'for the duration' is an uncertain proposition. We might find things are over before we get started, or we might be flying the Airlift for months. So, my first question is whether that is a problem for you?"

"Since I'm currently unemployed, no, it's not."

"Excellent. Now another issue is that our operations will be based in Germany, at an RAF station near Hamburg. I see you are married with a small daughter. Are you sure you don't mind operating from Germany?"

"No, not at all," he assured her. "My wife is very supportive of my application. She plans to stay with her parents while I work abroad."

"Good. Then why don't you tell me a little more about your flying career and why you are interested in this job?" Emily sat back to listen.

"When I heard about the Berlin Airlift, I felt it was what I had to do — or at least what I wanted to do," he answered earnestly.

"Why is that?" Emily asked surprised. All the other candidates had responded to the same question by listing their accomplishments — the flying hours, the different aircraft they'd flown, the number of ops, the medals. None had got around to addressing the question of why they wanted the job.

Moran shrugged. He was sitting with his elbows resting on his knees and his eyes were fixed on his feet. Then he lifted his head and looked her in the eye. "When I crashed my Lancaster in Germany, soldiers from the Wehrmacht pulled me and my flight engineer to safety before the cockpit was consumed by flames. A Wehrmacht doctor reconstructed my eye socket, put my ribs and hip back together, and saved what was left of my leg. None of that gainsays that the Nazis were tyrants involved in genocide. Nor does the fact that Germans saved my life make me ashamed of the 48 earlier ops I'd flown, during which I contributed to pulverising German industry and collaterally destroyed many homes and lives. I don't regret what I did in the war, but when I heard about the Airlift, I thought it would be — I don't know — a way that I could help build a bridge beyond the hatred and the destruction and mutual suspicion that still exists in the heart of Europe."

Emily felt chastened and humbled. David talked in terms of business opportunities, and she, too, had thought of freight as a means to save AAI. None of the other four bomber pilots she'd interviewed over the last two days had so much as hinted at such motives. This answer reminded her that Gibson hadn't been the only CO of 617; Leonard Cheshire had commanded the squadron for longer, and he was a passionate proponent of peace. Realising that Fl/Lt Moran was anxiously awaiting her response, she admitted, "That was the best answer to why anyone could want this job that I've heard in two days of interviews. Well said. Which only leaves the question of your flying experience."

Moran again shrugged and looked down at his feet before facing her. "I joined the RAF as a fitter." That surprised Emily. While she knew that many men had come up through the ranks in the RAF, most of them retained their working-class accents and often a certain cheekiness that came from bucking class prejudices to get to the top. Moran, on the other hand, spoke with a cultured accent more common among the elite. It was starting as a fitter, not ending as a flight lieutenant, that didn't seem to match. He continued, "After volunteering for aircrew, I trained as a flight engineer and flew 30 ops with 626 Squadron during my first tour and six with 103 Squadron in my second tour before..." he hesitated and then continued, "I was recommended for flying training, and—"

"Excuse me," Emily interrupted him. "But wasn't it unusual to be recommended for training in the middle of a tour?"

Moran drew a deep breath, but he did not get flustered. "On that 36th op, four of the crew were severely wounded, the skipper mortally so. As a result, the crew was being broken up anyway. Because we made a good landing despite my skipper's condition, the RAF thought I had potential as a pilot."

"Yes, I can understand that. Please go on."

"I was sent to South Africa for the early stages of training and returned to England to finish up. The CO of the Lancaster Finishing School, the last non-operational posting, recommended me for 617 Squadron and I was accepted."

"You went to 617 straight out of training?" Emily asked, surprised. "Wasn't that unusual too?"

"Yes, but it was early 1945 and several of the veteran skippers had been forced to retire. The new CO wanted 'fresh blood' untainted by the culture of other squadrons. It probably helped that I had a DFM already. Ultimately, however, I only flew twelve complete ops as skipper, plus a gardening op from the OTU, a Second Dicky flight to the *Tirpitz* and a boomerang over Norway. I'm sure you can find many pilots with more flying hours than I have."

He might be overdoing the modesty a bit, but Emily preferred that to the line-shooting of the other candidates. Out loud she admitted candidly, "Flying hours aren't the only criterion for this job."

"What else are you looking for?" he asked with an edge to his voice that was almost resentful — as if he'd encountered hidden criteria with negative results before.

"Flying the airlift requires precise flying — something that 617 was famous for, of course," Emily hastily added, embarrassed for even mentioning it to this candidate, "but the real challenge I think is that as a company we are not in a position to recruit other crew members. We are relying upon the skippers to pull together their own crew."

Unlike the others, Moran looked relieved rather than annoyed. "I'm glad to hear that because I'd rather form a crew through mutual consent than be assigned to a crew. How much time do I have to find the others?"

"We are going to give our candidates until the end of the month to present a complete crew. You will be given a probationary contract at modest pay to cover your expenses while recruiting. At the start of next month, however, candidates with a full and fully qualified crew will be given contracts for the duration of the Airlift and those without will be terminated."

Moran nodded solemnly. "Meaning I must find a navigator, signaller, flight engineer, and second pilot in addition to myself in the next three weeks?"

"Exactly. Would any of your old crew be interested and available, do you think?" This was a standard question. The degree to which pilots maintained ties with their former crew and the willingness of their former crewmates to fly with them again was something David (and Robin) thought was telling.

"My signaller would almost certainly sign on with me. My navigator, on the other hand, has a first-rate architecture practice in the West End, a socialite wife, and a new baby. He won't be interested in flying the Airlift. I might know of an alternative, however, as one of my former gunners is now a qualified navigator. Obviously, I didn't have a second pilot in my RAF crew, so that might also be a challenge."

"And your flight engineer? Would he be interested in this job?"

"My flight engineer would do anything to find a job of any kind, but he was crippled when we were shot down. He's now in a wheelchair. It's an incredible waste because he was absolute wizard with aircraft engines."

"I'm so sorry to hear that!" Emily responded to the first half of the message, only to catch her breath as the second half sank into her consciousness. She straightened up. "Wait! He wouldn't be one of the many flight engineers who first qualified as ground crew, would he?"

"Exactly. He was one of Trenchard's brats and a first-rate crew chief before volunteering for aircrew."

"Crew chief?" Emily repeated, and then sitting very straight she asked hopefully, "Do you think he might be able to explain engines and how to maintain them to others?"

"I should think so. Why?"

"Well, one of our biggest challenges is that while our freight operations will be run from Hamburg, we'd prefer to base our ambulance in Berlin, closer to the patients who need to be flown out. The ground crew we have now, however, refuse to remain in blockaded Berlin, so we're looking for Luftwaffe mechanics to do the work. The ambulance is a converted Wellington with Hercules VI engines, and Luftwaffe mechanics can't be expected to know anything about them. It occurred to me that even from a wheelchair, your former flight engineer might be able to train and supervise them while they do the physical work." Moran was looking at her so strangely that she began to think she had said something silly. "Isn't that possible?"

"I don't know why not, provided someone can handle translating English to German and back. I'm just overwhelmed that you — your company — would consider giving a man with such a severe disability such an important job."

Emily hoped she hadn't overstepped her mandate, but David was keen on hiring Berlin-based ground crew.

Moran continued, "I'm also relieved because, you see, I may not have mentioned that I am also handicapped. I have an artificial leg." He leaned down and knocked on the wood of his artificial left leg. "Is that a problem?"

"Flight Lieutenant Moran, Mr Goldman was one of Dr McIndoe's guinea pigs. When he was first admitted to the hospital, he was told he would never fly again. He didn't accept that answer and eventually persuaded the RAF medical establishment to give him a chance. He went on to become one of the RAF's chief instructors, teaching other instructors. He believes strongly in giving men with handicaps a chance. All we ask is that you can still fly to the standards required."

"I can," he answered intently, "and I'd like to be given the chance to prove it."

"Without knowing the pay or conditions?" Emily asked back with a touch of amusement. The other candidates had been very keen to know what the pay and perks were. They wanted extras because the job was temporary.

"Without knowing anything more than what you have said already — and a chance for former flight engineer, Fight Sergeant Gordon MacDonald, to join the company as well."

"You are still in touch with him then?" Emily asked for confirmation.

"Yes. We see each other regularly."

That clinched it. The fact that the crippled man didn't blame his skipper for his condition said all that was needed about Moran's leadership. "Flight Lieutenant Moran, AAI would like to offer you a probational contract. Are you prepared to accept immediately, or would you like some time to think about it and look over the contract?" She reached down and removed from her briefcase a copy of the contract that David had drawn up with his lawyers the day of their arrival.

For the first time since she had encountered him, Moran smiled. It was a beautiful, heartfelt smile that made him very handsome. "I don't need any time to think. I want this job very much."

"Wonderful!" Emily replied enthusiastically. "I think we're going to get along splendidly. Shall we have a drink on it? Maybe something stronger than tea?"

Moran nodded agreement and then hesitated before admitting, "Ma'am, my wife is upstairs biting her fingernails about the outcome of this interview. Would you find it inappropriate for me to ask her to join us?"

"No, I wouldn't. I'd be delighted to meet her." Emily heartily approved of a man who wanted to include his wife in his victories. She was already certain that Moran would be an asset to AAI, but she reminded herself that he still needed to pull together a complete crew. Meanwhile, AAI needed to find some German mechanics — or they wouldn't need a crew chief.

East of Eden
Berlin-Kreuzberg
Saturday, 10 July 1948
(Day 15)

Christian's efforts to track down Axel Voigt via telephone books, the Red Cross, and his sister-in-law's access to Gestapo records produced a blank. Reluctantly, he turned to his last option. He'd gone down one flight of stairs and knocked on the door to the apartment below. After a moment, a wary voice asked, "Who's there?"

"Christian Freiherr von Feldburg."

The door cracked open, and the youngest of the three residents asked belligerently, "What do you want?"

"I'm looking for *Kapitaenleutnant* Sperl."

The young man opposite him recoiled and barked back, "Where did you hear that name?"

"It's all right Lothar, I told Major Freiherr von Feldburg my name." Sperl came up behind his colleague and opened the door fully. "Come in, Feldburg."

Christian squeezed past the still-unsettled younger man and followed the *Kapitaenleutnant* deeper into the apartment. In the kitchen, Sperl indicated a place at the table, and Christian sat down.

"Schnapps?" Sperl asked.

"Not if you've brewed it yourself," Christian retorted.

Sperl laughed shortly and then asked, "So, what can I do for you?"

"I'm trying to find someone, an old colleague to be precise. He was a flight mechanic, a troublemaker, and a die-hard socialist. The rank he had when last I saw him was *Stabsfeldwebel*, but he might have been busted down a rank or two after I stopped protecting him. Indeed, I thought he might get himself shot for insubordination at some point, but there is no record of that. He appears to have been released by the Americans more than a year ago, but that was all my research could turn up."

"And why do you think I might know this man?"

Christian shrugged. "You deal with many people in your line of work."

"True," Sperl admitted with a faint smile.

"Voigt was a survivor. If he couldn't find legitimate work — and where was he likely to do that? — he might have turned to the black market. Everyone else did."

"Hm," Sperl acknowledged the logic. "What did you say his name was? Voigt?"

"Yes, Axel Voigt."

Sperl nodded and appeared to think for several moments. "Give me a couple of days to see what I can find."

Christian put a bottle of wine on the table. "Enough?"

"Among officers, of course."

That had been three days ago. Now, Christian was back to see what Sperl had found out. Again, they sat in the kitchen and Christian refused refreshments. Sperl opened with, "My colleagues verified that a man we dealt with almost two years ago was called Voigt. He was an odd bird. He clearly despised the SS, yet he had dozens of SS collar, sleeve, breast and cap insignia — some from very senior officers. It wasn't newly minted either. We found dirt and blood on some of it. We concluded he'd been grave robbing."

Christian looked shocked enough to provoke an explanation.

"Many SS killed themselves in the last days of the war. The Ivans took the jewels, gold teeth and watches but weren't so keen on the uniforms. They dumped the corpses — still clothed — into common, unmarked graves. This fellow Voigt appeared to know where some of those graves were and he was anxious to sell, desperate almost, yet he drove a hard bargain too. If the Amis hadn't been so greedy for the stuff, I wouldn't have dealt with him again. At the time, however, we couldn't get enough of the junk. Back in '46, the GIs all wanted SS souvenirs to take home with them." He paused and then asked Christian, "Do you think that might be your man?"

"Maybe. Do you remember what he looked like?"

"Not really. I know he wasn't skeletal like Soviet POWs, so I expect he'd been an Ami POW. I can't remember anything else. Nothing stood out."

"Could you — would you — give me his address?"

Sperl shrugged, "I'd give it to you if I knew it, but I don't. But I'd probably recognize where we met him if I go back to the area. My memory is visual."

"Would you mind taking me there? That would be very helpful!" Christian answered with relief.

"Fine," Sperl answered and looked down at his watch. "I've got a business appointment later this afternoon, but if you want to go straight away, we should be able to get there and back in time."

"Thank you," Christian said again, getting to his feet in anticipation.

"First, we have to find you some appropriate clothes."

"What do you mean?" Christian countered, offended. He went to considerable effort to always look immaculate.

"You look rich and capitalist and we're crossing into the Soviet Sector. Come with me." Sperl took him to the back room where clothing of all kinds was piled high but not randomly. Sperl wound his way between the various stacks directly to a heap of blue workers' overalls that he started holding up and sizing with his eyes. When he found clothes he thought would fit Christian, he tossed them to the baron. "Start with those. You'll need a collarless shirt and workers' shoes, too."

Half an hour later, Sperl and Christian left the apartment on Maybachufer. In addition to their worn and weathered blue overalls over collarless shirts, they wore faded caps, scuffed, heavy-soled shoes and cheap socks. Sperl insisted that Christian get some grime under his fingernails and as a last measure, sprinkled some of his schnapps over them both.

They walked along the canal, stopping to buy the morning paper. "That's so the Ivans will have something to confiscate," Sperl explained. "Remember, be humble and submissive and say as little as possible. Every time you open your mouth you betray yourself as a Frankish nobleman."

Shortly afterwards they came to a damaged and provisionally repaired pedestrian bridge that spanned the narrow canal that separated Kreuzberg in the American Sector from Alt-Treptow in the Soviet Sector. Although people were still allowed to move freely between Sectors, to enforce the blockade a pair of Soviet soldiers controlled the bridge. They were walking listlessly back and forth with Kalashnikovs over their shoulders. Sperl led the way, nodding his head and fingering his cap humbly to the Soviets as he came off the bridge. They stopped him and Sperl held up his hands while the Soviets rifled through his pockets and checked for a watch. Finding nothing but Eastern money, which was all but worthless, they snatched the newspaper and shouted insults at him for having it, before letting him pass. Sperl bobbed his head submissively and scurried away around a corner while the soldiers subjected Christian to the same procedure.

A few blocks beyond the bridge they reached the commuter train (S-Bahn) station of Treptower Park and boarded a northbound train. At Alexanderplatz they transferred to the underground, the U-Bahn. Christian stopped to buy one of the newspapers on sale at the kiosk before they descended the crumbling steps to the urine-smelling platform. As they waited for their train, Christian perused the newspaper. The headline read: "Germans turned into Slaves!" The article described the atrocious working conditions at Gatow and Tempelhof, where, it said, German crews were forced like "Egyptian slaves" to off-load aircraft at an inhumane rate without breaks or adequate food and water. The shifts were so long that workers frequently collapsed from exhaustion, but the Western Allies forced them back to work with kicks and blows. Christian nodded. The Soviets used slave labour extensively and knew exactly what it looked like.

The next page featured an article about a "tender blonde girl of 16" raped by an American negro soldier. Priceless, Christian thought remembering Charlotte's experience, and he continued to the next article. This alleged the Western allies were flying in ice cream, fine wines, cognac, fresh lobsters, and shrimp on their "so-called airlift" for the "feasts" of the "capitalist" officers while the people of West Berlin lived on bread made "predominantly from sawdust" and had no fresh vegetables, eggs, milk or butter whatsoever. That they lacked these items because of the Soviet blockade was not mentioned. The third page ran an opinion piece about the "brutal determination" of the "capitalist warmongers" to tear Germany in two and thereby render it forever weak. Only by resisting the temptations of the "seductive but treacherous D-mark" could the Germans retain their freedom and dignity in a "democratic" Germany protected by their "friends," the Red Army. The article ended with an appeal to all "true Germans" to join in a demonstration before Brandenburg Gate to condemn the "ruinous" policies of "two currencies" and "two Germanies". The date and time for the demo were printed in bold print.

They travelled four stops on the underground and then walked for a couple of blocks with Sperl looking for familiar landmarks. Although he looked in a couple of courtyards to be sure, when he spotted the right building he exclaimed at once. "That's it!" Fragments of a once-elegant façade still clung to the face of the redbrick building he'd identified, and here he led the way under the front house, crossed the first courtyard, which was only enclosed on three sides because one wall had been shattered by bombs, and took the passageway under the second house. The next courtyard was completely enclosed, smaller, dirtier and smellier. Coal was heaped in one corner and rubbish in another. Rats scuttled for safety at their approach.

They entered the stairwell of the house at the back and the stink of stopped up toilet greeted them. Christian made a face and Sperl laughed. "Welcome to the real world, Herr Baron."

"I've been a prisoner, you know," Christian snapped.

"Of the Americans," Sperl snorted.

"It wasn't the gulag for you either."

"No, I enjoyed the dubious hospitality of the British."

One flight up, Sperl stopped before a door and gestured. "The Voigt we dealt with lived here."

Christian stared at the door in front of him with a sinking heart and an unpleasant weight in his stomach. Glued to the wood at eye level was a large SED sticker showing two hands clasping each other. Other SED posters were tacked above and below the sticker. "Fatherland! Peace! And Socialism!" one shouted. "Unity for the Working People of the World!" another promised. "Profit to the People, not the Plutocrats!" "Socialism is Peace and Progress." Christian was especially struck by a dark poster showing a night landscape with four-engine bombers flying through the sky and a large, muscular hand with curled fingers reaching upwards. The text read: "Drag the Terror-Fliers from the sky!"

That was the last straw. "There is no point in knocking!" Christian stopped Sperl as the black marketeer reached out his hand. Because Voigt had been socialist for as long as Christian had known him, he didn't doubt this *was* the man he was looking for. Yet anyone who could support the Soviets and buy their propaganda wholesale was not going to want any part in assisting the Airlift. He turned to go back down the stairs and get some fresh air.

"Don't be so hasty," Sperl advised catching his arm.

"I used to like and respect Voigt. I don't want to see him parroting this Russian shit."

"You don't know what hides behind the symbols and the slogans," Sperl warned. "Be honest, you think I'm a Nazi fanatic, don't you?"

Christian considered Sperl a moment and then replied, "Let's just say that U-boat captains had a reputation for loyalty to the Nazi regime, and I have reservations about U-boat warfare."

"Why?"

"Because it targeted unarmed merchantmen and used stealth and deception to attack unseen."

"The merchantmen may have been unarmed, but the escorts certainly weren't. Not to mention Coastal Command's bombers could carry both torpedoes and depth charges. As for tactics, didn't you prefer to attack out of the sun, unseen, on unsuspecting targets?"

"Touché," Christian conceded.

"Now, regarding my politics..." Sperl shrugged. "While it's true I was an enthusiastic Hitler Youth leader at the age of 16, I grew up. I certainly didn't shoot myself when I heard Hitler had blown his brains out. Ask the others. I would have thrown a party — if we'd had anything left to party with. The Nazis were a bunch of corrupt thugs, and I know it as well as you do. People are disgusting animals, and politicians are the worst of the species. Now, we've come all this way, let's find out if this Voigt is the man you're looking for or not." Sperl rapped hard on the door with his knuckles.

A voice from far away called, "Who's there?"

Sperl just turned to Christian and waited for him to answer.

Christian raised his voice and announced, "Feldburg. Christian Freiherr von Feldburg."

Something seemed to bang, and then rapid footsteps approached the door. It was yanked open, and an aged young man stood before them. His hair was reddish brown and thinning at the crown. His face was deeply lined, his eyes darkly circled. He was dressed much as they were, in old, workers' clothes. Frowning, he stared at Christian, shifted his head this way and that as if trying to see him better before he uttered, "Herr Major? Is it really you? Where did you come from? What are you doing here?" His eyes ran over Christian's clothes, baffled.

"I wanted to — see how you were doing. Herr Meyer here," Christian indicated Sperl, "said he had met you a couple of years ago."

Voigt frowned at Meyer as if he didn't remember him — or maybe didn't *want* to remember him. "Go down to the *Manifesto*, it's on the right when you come out onto the Schoenhauser. I'll join you there in fifteen minutes." Then he slammed the door in their faces.

"Well, that was friendly," Sperl commented sarcastically.

Christian nodded, confused. It was Axel, but the smirk, the self-assurance, and the cheekiness were all gone. In their place was something grim and embittered. The Nazis had never broken Voigt, but... His eyes scanned the SED posters again. Sperl was right. If Voigt believed all these slogans, he would have felt triumphant and excited by the impending expulsion of the Western Allies.

"Shall we go down to the *kneipe*?" Sperl asked.

"Why not? We've come this far."

The tavern was already crowded. Customers were standing around the bar and sitting squashed together on small, straight-backed wooden chairs that stood haphazardly around the black-painted tables. The smell of beer, broth, and heavy tobacco smoke dominated the air. The soup smell was not appetising, but then no food in Berlin public houses was tasty these days. The men were smoking roll-your-own cigarettes with terrible quality tobacco. Christian and Sperl found a table in a corner and sat with their backs to the wall, the *kneipe* spread out before them.

Christian tried to hear what the other customers were talking about. Prices seemed to be the main topic of conversation. In low murmurs, men exchanged black market prices and muttered about an exchange rate of 8 or 9 east-marks to one D-Mark. Someone claimed the D-mark was replacing cigarettes as the preferred method of payment. Someone else complained, "If they aren't sending anything to the Western Sectors any more, why isn't there more for us?"

The speaker was hushed up by his companions, who nervously looked over their shoulders. When one of them met Christian's eyes, he whispered something in his friend's ear, and abruptly they downed their beers, clunked the glasses on the table, and left.

At last Christian caught sight of Voigt in the door, but as he started to squeeze his way past the men at the bar, he was stopped by a young man with a hawkish face. "You'll be at the rally, won't you, comrade?"

"Of course, comrade!" Voigt answered, fingering his hat more submissively than he had ever saluted an officer.

"I'll be watching for you!" the man replied in a menacing tone. Then with an artificial smile, he clapped Voigt on the back and turned to go. Voigt continued to where Sperl and Christian were sitting and sat with his back to the rest of the room. He opened the conversation with a nervous, "Didn't you want anything to eat or drink?"

"We wouldn't mind a beer," Sperl answered, slapping a couple of east marks on the table to pay for all three of them. Voigt took the money and went over to the bar. Christian eyed Sperl questioningly. "Men talk easier over alcohol," Sperl explained.

Voigt returned with three murky-brown, watery beers with little foam. He set them on the table and sat down again. Looking earnestly at Christian he professed, "I thought you were dead, Herr Major."

"Oh. You mean no one at the squadron heard about my survival?" Christian was surprised.

Voigt shook his head. "What happened?"

"Nothing miraculous. I was badly shot up by an American P-47 and took some shrapnel to the back of my head. The next thing I knew I was aboard a hospital ship in mid-Atlantic with two broken legs. The alarm was going off as we zig-zagged frantically to avoid being sunk by a U-boat." He ended with a reproachful look at Sperl. That was the sanitised version, of course. In fact, after realizing he'd been badly shot up in the dogfight, he'd made the decision to crash-land at an American field. He'd consciously chosen imprisonment over fighting another day for Hitler and his thugs.

Sperl, meanwhile, was laughing. "So *that's* why you developed such a strong dislike for our cute little boats. I note, however, the U-boat *didn't* sink the hospital ship you were on."

"No, I told the Americans to turn the damn sirens off because no officer of the *Kriegsmarine* would sink a ship with large red-crosses on it

— only to learn that some U-Boat captain had done *exactly* that the week before. It was very embarrassing."

Voigt was looking from one to the other confused.

"Herr Meyer has a past — as do we all," Christian explained, adding, "But I came to talk to you about the future."

"Future? What's that?" Voigt snapped back with withering bitterness.

"Tomorrow and tomorrow and tomorrow — and the day after," Christian answered.

Voigt leaned so close to Christian that he could not really be heard; his words seemed only to form in Christian's head from lip reading. "Eating SED shit for breakfast, lunch and dinner so I can get the morphine my mother needs."

"What happened to your mother?" Christian asked.

"She was caught under a beam when the ceiling collapsed at the armaments factory where she had been conscripted. It broke her back and hips. She's crippled and in constant pain — unless I can get her morphine. Do you know what morphine costs?"

Christian shook his head slowly. "Not a clue."

"Well," Voigt answered in a low, even voice like molten lava, "enough morphine to keep my mother pain-free for a week, costs more than a man like me, working in a Peoples' Own Factory producing gearboxes, can earn in a month. Which means my mother can have one week of relief and then lie in agony for the next three while I beg for my dinner — or I can earn a little extra by showing up at SED rallies, helping to trash voting booths, beating up students that say the wrong thing, making sure scientists and engineers are dragged from their beds at night to be shipped to the Worker's Paradise or—" with a glance at Sperl he added "digging around in forgotten mass graves for baubles that appeal to our American friends."

Both Christian and Sperl responded with silence. The pain, the bitterness and the helplessness burned like acid. Christian drew a deep breath. "In that case, my friends would not be able to pay you enough to meet your needs, either."

"What friends? What are you talking about?" Voigt demanded angrily.

Christian drew a deep breath, "My cousin Charlotte is working for a British air ambulance company that plans to base an ambulance in Berlin — at Gatow to be precise — and they want to hire German aircraft mechanics

as ground crew. I thought you might like that work, but I understand that
—"

Voigt grabbed his arm. "Did you say an air *ambulance*? You mean an aircraft that flies patients to hospitals?"

"Yes."

"Where does it fly?"

"Wherever the best medical treatment can be provided for the patients on board — Hamburg, Frankfurt, Dusseldorf, Munich."

"To the West?"

"It's a British company."

"It must cost a fortune! Who can afford to pay for an aircraft to fly them to a hospital hundreds of miles away?" Voigt spat out furiously. "The Ivans are right about the capitalists only taking care of their own!" He had raised his voice for the first time, and Sperl stirred uneasily, watching the reaction of those around them.

Christian met Voigt's eyes and shook his head, "Wrong. The Amis are paying for it."

"What?"

"The American taxpayers will pay for the flights."

"Why would they do that?" Voigt scoffed.

Christian shrugged, "For the same reason they are flying food, coal, and clothing into Berlin for the Berliners?"

"Are they really?" Voigt scoffed.

"Come with me to Tempelhof and see for yourself."

It was Voigt's turn to look over his shoulder nervously. Then he leaned closer to Christian again. "But how do they decide who to fly out? Who gets to go to a hospital in the West? "

"As I understand it, the hospitals decide."

"Which hospitals? The hospitals in the West?"

"The hospitals in Berlin that request the air ambulance service," Christian explained.

Voigt jumped to his feet and kicked his chair against the table furiously. "The West. Always the f***ing West. And no doubt you need real money—"

"Shut up!" Sperl jumped to his feet and yanked Voigt back down with one hand while gesturing calmingly to the rest of the occupants of the room with the other.

Voigt sat clutching his fists together as he glared at the table, not speaking. Christian and Sperl exchanged a glance over his head. Sperl jerked his head towards the door and Christian nodded.

"Voigt," Christian declared in a calm voice, laying a hand on his shoulder. "I believe you have Herr Meyer's address?"

Voigt nodded without looking at him. He was staring at his clenched fists beside the untouched beers.

"I live one flight up. If you want to discuss this again, just come see me."

Voigt nodded without looking up.

Christian and Sperl stood and slipped past Voigt, who continued to sit unmoving at the table. Abruptly, Voigt lunged after Christian, grabbing him. "Wait! They want ground crew, you said. For what kind of engines?"

"Hercules VI."

"Never even heard of them!" Voigt wailed like an animal in agony.

Sperl gave Christian a warning look. They were attracting too much attention.

Christian again put a hand on Voigt's shoulder. "Come and talk to me about it another time. Maybe we can work something out." Then he followed Sperl out of the *kneipe* as fast as he could go without making a scene.

Gardening
Berlin-Kladow
Sunday, 11 July 1948
(Day 16)

The steamroller made all the difference. By working intensively for three days in a row, they compacted the surface sufficiently to pour the first layer of concrete. As the sun sank behind the forest beyond the fence, an ancient paver crawled — clanking and groaning — along the long pit dropping globs of liquid cement onto the surface behind it. A team of German workers with rakes and metal brushes spread the concrete as evenly as possible in its wake, followed by the steamroller that pressed the concrete down.

At the end of the shallow ditch, the paver crawled onto the grass verge belching diesel smoke into the evening air. Finally, the men spreading the concrete reached the grass too, and stood about resting on their tools and wiping away sweat until the steamroller reached them, standing shuddering for several seconds before its driver shut down the machine.

Lt. Col. Russel wiped the sweat from his forehead with the back of his arm, which came away black with soot. He went over to take a closer look at their work. Nodding with satisfaction, he exclaimed, "*Sehr gut!*" The Germans murmured a thank you, bobbing their heads or risking a smile although they looked dreadful: filthy, stinking and exhausted.

Runway construction was now ahead of schedule. Unless a catastrophe struck, they were on track to finish the runway more than a week ahead of what he'd originally estimated. For the moment, however, nothing more could be done. The cement needed time to settle and harden before they sent the steamroller over it again, pouring the next layer and the next until they were ready for a layer of surface tar. It was time for a break.

Russel raised his voice to be heard by the men chatting as they lit up cigarettes, and announced in his increasingly serviceable German, "*Morgen ist feiertag!*"

That caused a commotion. Half of the men didn't believe him they were getting a day off, but he repeated himself and explained as best as he could about the need to let the concrete harden. Some of the experienced workers understood, and started saying to the others that he was right. Russel was not offended that the Germans believed their own foremen more than the British officer and engineer; he was glad to have experienced construction workers on his team.

The workers started walking towards the showers and changing rooms. Their cheerful voices carried on the evening air. They were laughing and animated as they discussed what they would do with a rare day off. Russel looked up at the luminous sky and the rising evening star. As usual, one Dakota was on final approach while another taxied to the head of the runway for take-off. It was going to be a clear day tomorrow and Russel had his own plans. He hoped to do some gardening.

The following morning, Graham Russel slept late and dressed not in uniform but in his comfortable, old gardening clothes, complete with a large straw hat. He parked his assigned car, an old Wehrmacht open-top staff model, in the front drive of the Priestman residence and went up the front steps to ring the bell. No one answered the door. Hm, Graham thought, as he rang the bell a second time. When still no one answered, he walked around behind the house, where he noticed a commotion at the foot of the garden that resolved itself into the launching of a small boat. The WingCo was hoisting the sails with Mrs Priestman at the tiller and their civilian guest in the bow. An old man was shoving off, while a dog stood up to his belly in the water barking in excitement and thrashing the air with his tail. The Priestmans' cook completed the scene; she was waving as the little sailing boat caught the wind, heeled and glided away.

The launch successful, the elderly man and the cook turned back towards the house. The latter caught sight of Graham and rushed forward, while the man returned to the boathouse to put things in order.

"So, sorry!" the cook called. "Wing Commander is on water!" She gestured towards the still-visible sailboat.

"That's all right," Graham assured her. "I came to do some gardening. Wing Commander Priestman said that I should talk to you about that. I thought I might do some weeding for you." He pointed to a bed of vegetables that looked in need of such service. Then remembering his manners, he held out his hand to her. "My name's Russel. Graham Russel. Please call me Graham."

She was momentarily taken aback but then broke into a wide smile which made her look much younger than he had thought her to be. She shook his hand exclaiming, "Hello, Mr Graham. I'm Jasha. I see you before, no?"

Because of his misshapen body, people tended to remember Graham, so he was used to being recognised. "Yes, I was here for dinner earlier in the week, which was when I saw and admired your garden. You wouldn't mind me helping you with it, would you?"

"No, no," she agreed, but continued to look puzzled. Pointing to the garden, she asked hesitantly, "You want to *work* in garden?"

"Not for pay, just for the sake of doing it."

She smiled at that. She was a pretty woman when she smiled, Graham thought, but she shook her head in protest too, "You are important man. Not gardener."

"I'm only important when I'm dressed up," Graham answered. "Now, I'm just a gardener — if you'll let me." Although Jasha nodded vigorously, Graham had the feeling she still didn't fully understand him. So, he tried a different tack. "Why don't you show me what you've planted?"

"Yes, yes!" She lit up at that and started on the tour at once. They progressed slowly through the extensive garden with Jasha pointing things out and explaining when each crop would ripen or if there were problems. She often reverted to German or Polish, but it didn't matter because Graham was more interested in winning her trust than the details of what she said. He nodded, asked sparse questions, commiserated over the problem of slugs, and praised what she had done. When they got the henhouse, Jasha waxed very eloquent – in Polish. Abruptly, she realised what she was doing and broke off to laugh at herself. Graham laughed with her. When the laughter died, he pushed at one of the walls, causing it to sag and tilt. "The earth's too wet here. We should move it to drier ground and shore it up a bit more."

Jasha shook her head. "Wing Commander not want chickens near house."

Graham looked back towards the elegant house with its wide terrace and French windows and had to agree. "Well, in that case, I could find some cinder blocks or bricks to use as piers to lift it off the wet ground." She looked confused, so he explained with gestures and his patchy German until she nodded vigorously and smiled widely again.

As they walked back up the slope of the lawn, the dog came bounding up to shake himself beside them and then kept them company back to the house. At the top of the garden, the dog separated himself to dry himself on the warm flagstones of the terrace, while Graham again asked if he could do some weeding, bending down to demonstrate his intent. This time, Jasha agreed, and Graham set to work.

Gradually, the day turned hot and muggy. From the Havel came the sound of lapping water and the deep-throated chugging of barges carrying goods from Gatow into the city or returning empty. The chickens clucked contentedly in their yard and now and again a crow called from the tall trees on the fringe of the property. The Dakotas droned overhead incessantly, and one of the Sunderlands put down with a great splash as well. Graham watched all the fuss for a few minutes before resuming his weeding. Now and then, Jasha checked up on him. They found it surprisingly easy to communicate because of their shared interest in making things grow.

Graham had learned to love gardening when he was a schoolboy. Because of his stunted legs, he was not able to take part in school sports, so his housemaster had suggested that he help the school gardener when the other boys were playing games. That way he was not entirely sedentary or lonely. He also got some fresh air and sunshine. The gardener had been Indian. He'd come to England decades earlier with some former headmaster and had remained at the school after his benefactor had died. He was wise, patient, and gentle, and he had filled Graham's head with a thousand Indian tales that made him want to see the world. He might have joined the merchant navy if the war hadn't come along.

Graham had been fourteen when the Great War broke out. His father returned to active service. His older brother had volunteered at once and been killed in '15. Graham had volunteered as soon as he turned 17, but they turned him down on medical grounds. He was not infantry material. Six months later, they weren't so picky. He'd been accepted and assigned to the sappers. He'd earned his commission by early '18 and spent the rest of the war building roads and airfields. In the process, he became addicted to the comradeship he'd found.

When the war ended, he hadn't wanted to leave the army, so he took a permanent commission. In the interwar years, he'd served across the Empire: Palestine, Sudan, India, Singapore. He'd loved it all and never felt lonely because he made friends everywhere he went. His friends welcomed him into their homes, included him in their Christenings, birthday parties, weddings, and funerals. Occasionally he'd allowed himself sentimental affections for girls, who never returned his feelings, but he'd learned to dismiss such lapses in sanity as unimportant. He went on to new assignments, made new friends, laughed, partied, and tended the odd plant or two.

This last war had been harder, however. He'd served primarily in Burma with the "forgotten army." The murky political situation, the climate, the terrain, the undeniable sense of being forgotten indeed by a government obsessed with fighting Germany, and the brutality of the enemy had all taken their toll. It was in Burma that Graham had discovered gardening as therapy.

This garden, however, reminded him more of growing up than battling the Japanese. The smell of the earth was different, and the insects were less aggressive. Graham found himself thinking of retirement and a garden of his own. He'd been in the army for 31 years, and he'd built an awful lot of airfields. The thrill of going to new places and facing new challenges was fading. Many of his friends had already retired. Some to "warm climates" — Oman, Kenya and Cape Town. Or, more commonly, to homes in the suburbs near "the grandchildren." It was odd, Graham reflected; he had never missed having children as much as he missed having grandchildren. If nothing else, Berlin was turning into a tale to tell them about. Uncomfortably, he realised that for the first time in his service life he felt lonely. He was completely free, and that was rather sad.

When the Priestmans returned from sailing, Jasha disappeared to make a late lunch and Graham settled down to talk to them and their guest Mr Goldman. He told them the latest on the runway, and the WingCo brought them up to date on political developments. The Americans, he said, still hoped to solve the impasse in Berlin by diplomatic means.

"You mean we won't need the runway?" Graham asked, torn between frustration at putting so much work into something superfluous and relief that the blockade might be over.

Robin gave him a look that made the rest of them laugh. When the laughter died down, Robin explained himself. "Although I've rarely dealt directly with the Russians, Air Commodore Waite has spent the last three years trying to work with them, and the tales he tells would make you weep. He says the Soviets do not understand the meaning of the word 'compromise.' They understand 'tactical deviation from the guidelines of Marxism-Leninism for temporary gain' but not genuine give and take. It is all take, and every time we give, they chortle in delight at our naivety."

Graham nodded thoughtfully.

"From the purely business standpoint," David Goldman spoke up. "It's just as well this blockade will last a little longer. I've taken options on two four-engine aircraft and three men have been tasked with finding aircrew to fly them. It would be awkward to call everything off at this stage, although we've at least achieved our immediate objective of getting permission for our ambulance to use RAF facilities."

Emily joined in. "David will talk to Charlotte this afternoon about contacting the city council about patients. If we're lucky, we'll be able to resume operations on Tuesday or Wednesday." She sounded so pleased that Graham decided congratulations were in order. He felt a twinge of envy for Robin's luck in love but dismissed the feeling as unworthy. He reminded himself that Emily had been away for the last four days. The Priestmans needed some privacy. It was time to leave.

He got to his feet. "Thank you so much for letting me indulge my passion for gardening and for the lovely meal, too, but I wouldn't want to outstay my welcome."

"Do you have plans for the rest of the day?" Robin asked casually, getting to his feet.

"Not really," Graham admitted, "but I've been in Berlin almost a month and I've never been farther than Spandau. I haven't seen a single thing of interest — not the Reichstag or Hitler's bunker or the Royal Palace or any of the other places in the guidebooks. I thought maybe I'd give myself a tour."

"Oh!" David sat up straighter. "If you're going into Berlin, could you possibly drop me off in Kreuzberg? As Emily said, I promised to meet Charlotte this afternoon," he glanced at his watch, "and it could take hours by public transport."

"No trouble at all," Graham agreed, "as long as you can give me directions."

David jumped to his feet and began collecting his things.

"Would you mind taking Jasha with you as well?" Mrs Priestman asked hopefully. "She's Catholic and there is no Catholic church anywhere nearby, but there is one near Charlotte's house, which she used to attend. I'm sure she'd be very grateful if you could take her, and she deserves an afternoon off."

"I'd be delighted," Graham assured her, and Mrs Priestman went inside to tell Jasha she would be taken to Mass if she wanted to go.

Within fifteen minutes, Graham found himself driving up the Potsdamer Chaussee on the way to Spandau. David sat beside him, while Jasha, dressed in a black dress, black stockings, black shoes, and black scarf, was in the back. In her new attire, she looked like an old peasant, and

Graham was sad for her.

"I have an idea," David announced as they sped along the empty road. "It's such a lovely, hot day, why don't we collect Charlotte and all go down to Wannsee together? It's one of Berlin's more charming sights — no war damage at all."

Graham shrugged. He'd seen a lot of lakes and bathing beaches. He was more interested in the historical sites.

"We could all go for a swim," David continued.

Jasha shook her head. "I can't swim, Mr David."

"Well, you could wade in the water to cool off or loll about in the sunshine. Afterwards, I'll treat everyone to a Berliner Weisse or two at Moorlake. I've heard it has reopened." David's enthusiasm was hard to resist.

Graham found himself asking, "What is a Berliner Weisse?"

"Ah, Colonel, you *are* new to Berlin! And clearly in need of an education. Berliner Weisse is a light, low-alcohol beer served with a touch of raspberry or Waldmeister syrup. It is extremely refreshing on hot days like this, and it is brewed locally. The wise gentlemen of the Berlin City Council have resolved that, blockade or not, the breweries should not shut down — or not yet anyway. Moorlake is a former royal residence turned into a restaurant with a wonderful beer garden directly on the lake. It has an excellent reputation and is very popular with the occupation forces. Along the way, I could show you various points of interest including the Kommandatura, Jagdschloss Gruenwald, the—"

"All right, all right. I capitulate!" Graham told him grinning. He knew his vehicle was being hijacked, but he didn't mind. It would be more pleasant to spend the afternoon with David and two ladies than on his own. "Unless you object, Jasha?"

She answered with a flood of German directed at David, who answered in the same language. At the end, she nodded and said to Graham. "I go to Mass next week. We go to Wannsee with Mr David and Countess Charlotte."

On their arrival at Charlotte's apartment, the countess responded to the proposed outing with that uniquely feminine mixture of delight combined with the complaint "I have nothing to wear!" Adding more specifically, "I don't own a bathing suit."

"I brought you one from London," David replied with a smile, "along with three pairs of shoes, and a few other items that are in the boot. As for Jasha—"

"We could ask Herr Sperl if he has ladies' swimming suits in his stock," Charlotte instantly proposed, and the conversation broke down into German again. Graham resigned himself to waiting out in the street while the others sorted things out. Meanwhile, his engineer's eyes examined the bomb damage around them with admiration both for the soundness of German construction and the thoroughness of the Allied Air Forces.

At last they were on their way again, with David getting in the back seat with Charlotte while Jasha took the place in the front beside Graham. She had changed for the third time today and looked rather frightened and confused. Charlotte had outfitted her in a light blue dress with large, white polka dots. Gone were the Displaced Person, the cook, the gardener, the slave labourer, and the widow. Jasha had become an attractive woman in her mid-forties.

From the back of the car, David gave the directions for Graham to drive to the Zoologische Garten and from there down the Kurfuerstendamm, so David could show Charlotte the office building he owned. Here they stopped and got out while David expounded enthusiastically on his plans to relocate the main office of AAI from Gatow into space on the first floor. The new office would be closer to their clients (the hospitals), the city council and the Allied liaison offices. Charlotte was delighted by the idea because it would save her the extremely long commute to Gatow. David mentioned that he might even be able to fix up an apartment for himself in the partially ruined top storey.

They climbed back into Graham's car and sped down the Koenig's Allee. This was broad, well-paved and almost empty of traffic. Graham could not resist driving more aggressively. As he increased speed, he glanced over at Jasha and saw an uninhibited smile on her face. Feeling his gaze, she looked over at him with wide blue eyes that seemed to ask if this was real. Was she, the former slave labourer, really driving through the Reichshauptstadt in a convertible? Well, a German military staff car. He gave her a reassuring smile, and her own smile broadened. "Happy?" he asked. She nodded vigorously. That made him feel good. How often in his life had he been able to make a woman happy? He couldn't remember a single instance.

The rest of the afternoon fled by too quickly. David and Charlotte were lost in their own world and speaking German, but Graham was happy, too. The language barrier that inhibited the conversation between Jasha and himself didn't seem to matter. He sensed that for Jasha the outing was like a fairy tale. He took pleasure in watching her surprise and delight at each stage from the visit to Jagdschloss Gruenewald to wading in the warm waters at the sandy beach at the Wannseebad and finally sitting in the late afternoon sun on the lawn of a royal palace turned beer garden.

By the time they left the sun was setting, and Graham suggested, "I can bring the materials we need to raise the henhouse next week and then take you to Mass. Would that suit you?"

"Oh, yes!" she assured him. "Very much."

Graham dropped Charlotte off first and then drove Jasha and David back at the Priestmans' house and returned to Gatow. When he went to bed, he could not remember when he'd enjoyed a day off so much.

Occupational Hazards
Berlin-Kreuzberg
Monday, 12 July
(Day 17)

The pounding at the door penetrated Charlotte's sleep, turning her dream into a nightmare. Screaming, she broke free of the ghostly assailants only to realise that the knocking at the door was real. Terrified, she registered it was pitch black, still the middle of the night.

"Don't worry, Charlotte. I'll handle it!" Christian called to calm her as he padded down the hall in pyjama bottoms and bare feet. Charlotte tried to stay put, but she could not cower in her bedroom while Christian faced whoever it was. She grabbed her dressing gown and followed him. When he opened the apartment door, she caught sight of Herr Liebherr, also still in his dressing gown and beside him Herr Sperl, fully dressed but looking dishevelled and agitated. Something dark and wet smeared the front of his jacket and soiled his chin. Coming closer, a chill ran down Charlotte's spine; it was blood.

Liebherr looked purposeful and determined as he explained, "...our friend Sperl returned fire while his friends got the injured man into a car."

"Were you hit?" Christian asked Sperl.

"No. The blood is not mine. It is from my former second engineer. He took a bullet in the head, and I held him in the car on the way to the hospital," Sperl explained.

Liebherr re-entered the conversation, "Trude believes he must be flown out to a hospital that can handle brain surgery. That's why I need to talk to Charlotte—"

"I'm here," Charlotte spoke over Christian's shoulder.

"Excellent," Liebherr found a wan smile of relief before continuing earnestly, "Can it be done? I know we've barely set up the procedures and the hospitals have not yet sent us their lists, but Trude claims this is an acute emergency. She says Berlin has no facilities to perform the operation needed. She thinks he should be transferred to Munich."

"Yes, the best hospital for brain surgery is in Munich," Charlotte confirmed.

"Do you think your ambulance can transport him there today?"

"I don't know for certain, Herr Liebherr. The ambulance is parked at Fuhlsbuettel with one of our pilots standing by. I'll call Mr Goldman right away and see what he thinks." Because the only phone was in the foyer, she added, "I'll just go and put on my shoes."

As she returned to her room, the men continued talking in low voices. She caught fragments of what was being said. Sperl's agitated voice carried farthest. "They had no warrant! If he hadn't resisted, he would have just disappeared into a gulag like all the others."

"You shot at the police?" Liebherr wanted confirmation.

"They aren't police! Damn it! They're Soviet thugs!" Sperl countered hotly.

Liebherr answered in a low voice. She couldn't decipher his words, but he sounded more concerned than outraged.

Charlotte had her shoes on and slipped past the three men to hurry down the stairs to phone without hearing any more.

Robin groggily reached for the ringing telephone and grunted into it, "Yes?"

A surprised silence was followed by a timid voice. "*Herr Oberstleutant*, it's Charlotte Walmsdorf. A young man has been shot in the head and needs to be evacuated to Munich for medical treatment. I was trying to reach Mr Goldman."

Robin was now fully awake. "Hold on. I'll get him."

"What is it?" Emily asked as he flung open the covers to get out of bed.

"An emergency medevac for you. Gunshot wound to the head."

"Oh my God!" Emily sat up and looked over at the clock. It was 2:35 am. While Robin fetched David Goldman from the guest room, Emily started getting dressed. She heard David running barefoot down the stairs to pick up the phone in the front hall. Going into the bathroom, she brushed out her hair and deftly put it up on the back of her head. She was starting to put on her shoes when David knocked on the door. "Emily?"

"I'm almost ready. Did you get through to Kiwi?"

"Yes, he's rousing the ground crew. The estimated time of arrival is two and a half hours from now. He'll be able to file a flight plan and take on enough fuel for Frankfurt Main, but you'll have to refuel there. That's assuming the Americans will let us fly into Frankfurt Main," David admitted with a significant glance at Robin. They had only just received permission to use RAF facilities; no one had yet taken the next step of asking the Americans about the use of their facilities.

"I'll ring Lt. Colonel Walker and see if I can get clearance for you," Priestman promised; Walker was his counterpart at Tempelhof USAF base.

"Thank you! I'll get dressed," David disappeared, and Robin went in search of his pocket address book with Walker's number in it.

There was still no sign of dawn when Kiwi, Ron and Chips arrived at RAF Fuhlsbuettel, but it was awash with light since the Airlift continued round-the-clock. Ron and Chips hitched a ride out to the hangar housing "Moby Dick" while Kiwi went to file a flight plan. He was wary after what had happened the week before, but the Airlift was growing at such a rate that it appeared to be overwhelming the bureaucracy. Kiwi's request provoked only the surprised question, "What? You want to fly *empty* into

Berlin?"

"We're an ambulance. The Berlin City Government has requested an emergency medevac to Munich."

"Oh, right. Now I remember. What kind of aircraft is it? A Wellington?"

"That's right."

"And empty, so you'll be faster than the Daks. Be sure to identify yourself to ATC as a Wellington so they can give you a different altitude."

"Got it!" Kiwi gave a thumbs up, stopped for the latest Met, and "hoofed it" over to the hangar. The sky was beginning to grey, and the clock was creeping towards 4:30 am. The bowsers were still filling Moby Dick's tanks when he arrived, and the air smelled of 100-octane fuel. Kiwi clambered up the ladder into the cockpit and sank into the lefthand seat. He'd be flying down to Berlin on his own. David and Emily would meet him at Gatow, where Emily would join him for the flight to Munich and back. David had opted to remain behind to work with Charlotte on submitting their first request for reimbursement to make sure everything went smoothly. Kiwi felt the same sense of excitement as before a fighter sweep. It was wonderful. They were back in business.

The land ambulance arrived at Gatow with the patient just after 6 am. Emily and David met it on the tarmac behind the main admin building, where they were joined by Gatow's assistant medical officer, Flight Lieutenant Dr Hamish. The latter boarded the ambulance to check on the patient and spoke briefly with the accompanying nurse. They agreed that the patient should not be moved more than necessary, which meant leaving him where he was until Moby Dick was ready to take him on board. Hamish approached Emily to explain that the nurse could not make the flight. It had come up too unexpectedly and she had other obligations.

"You mean there will be no nurse flying with us at all?" Emily asked alarmed.

"I'm afraid not, but there's no need to worry. We'll get everything set up. The patient is heavily sedated. All you have to do is see that the oxygen, blood, and fluids do not become disconnected during the flight."

Emily's face reflected her discomfort, but Hamish patted her arm and assured her. "Really, there is nothing to worry about. I'll show you what to do."

Shortly afterwards, Moby Dick arrived. While Kiwi jumped down, the medics wheeled the stretcher under Moby Dick's open bomb bay doors. Kiwi connected the winches and went aboard to hoist the stretcher, followed by Dr Hamish and Emily. Hamish connected the patient to the oxygen, blood and fluid feeds and showed Emily what to watch for during the flight. Then he disembarked, and she strapped the patient onto the aircraft bed. Over the internal mic, she told Kiwi to close the bomb bay doors. After they were locked shut, she went forward to the cockpit and settled into the righthand seat.

They were given priority for take-off, and once in the air were rapidly handed over to the Berlin Air Safety Centre, which had the job of weaving them through the inbound traffic from the three corridors. After roughly 15 minutes they reached their cruising altitude of nine thousand feet, placing them a couple of thousand feet above most Airlift traffic, and turned southwest towards the American Zone. The sun was well over the horizon now, and they had an excellent view of the steady stream of aircraft moving in the opposite direction below them.

"All lined up like that they look like a flying train," Kiwi observed.

Emily agreed but she was more worried about some clouds gathering on the horizon ahead of them. The met report had made light of them, but they looked like thunderheads to her. The thick white clouds reached dramatically skywards, and the innards were turning dark. All they could do was hope to reach Munich before the storms struck. Emily did some dead reckoning on the navigation table and estimated they would arrive in Frankfurt at 8:35 am. That would be six hours since Charlotte had called, and almost eight hours since their patient had been shot. Furthermore, in Frankfurt Main they had to refuel before they could continue to Munich, another hour and a half away. A ground ambulance would meet them at Munich airport, but the transfer to the hospital might take half an hour or more. All in all, it might be as much as fourteen hours between the incident and the operation that could save the patient's life. She went back to check on him, but he seemed to be sleeping peacefully.

At 7:40, they picked up signals from the Fulda navigation beacon signal. That meant they were no longer flying in Soviet airspace. "Could you call in our position? Kiwi requested.

Emily reached for the microphone but waited until the tone changed indicating they had passed over the beacon and were on the other side before pressing the button. Into the mic she reported, "AAI 005 crossing Fulda beacon westbound for—"

"Whoever that broad is, get off this frequency! This is a USAF channel for Airlift flights ONLY."

Emily looked at Kiwi and he stared back at her. "Maybe they don't recognise AAI. It is our first flight into Frankfurt since the Airlift started," he suggested.

Emily tried a second time. "This is Air Ambulance—"

"LADY!" The voice sounded louder and angrier than before. "GET OFF THIS FREQUENCY! THIS IS A USAF CHANNEL ONLY!"

Kiwi grabbed the microphone from Emily and held it close to his mouth lending his deep, down-under voice extra volume and timbre. "Frankfurt, the 'lady' is Flying Officer Priestman, Royal Air Force Voluntary Reserve with more than 1,000 wartime flying hours. She is currently seconded to Air Ambulance International. We are on an emergency medevac from Berlin. Clearance was obtained from USAF HQ Berlin. We are westbound having passed Fulda. Acknowledge."

It took several seconds, but then the controller acknowledged without further comment and gave them their heading and altitude for the next leg of the flight.

"You take over the controls," Kiwi suggested, "and I'll handle the morons on the radio during landing."

They landed without further incident. The follow-me jeep led them straight to the fuel dump and they shut down the engines for refuelling. Kiwi dropped out of the cockpit to stretch his legs, while Emily went back to check on the patient. He was still unconscious but as far as she could tell all was well. She checked the levels of oxygen, blood and fluids. The latter bags appeared more than half full. She returned to the cockpit and looked out. A lot of men seemed to be loitering around, and she could guess why. They wanted to see if there really was a woman in the cockpit. She'd encountered this behaviour before when she'd had to divert to a USAF base in bad weather during the war. She hated it.

Kiwi called up to her. "Emily?"

She opened the window and put her head out.

"Do you want a coffee or anything?"

"No, thanks. I just want to get out of here as soon as we can."

"Roger!"

In less than twenty minutes the aircraft had been refuelled. Emily made another check on the patient. Everything was still connected, but he didn't seem to have moved. She supposed that might be normal, but she felt uneasy. Back in the cockpit, she admitted to Kiwi, "I don't like the way the patient looks. Maybe we should ask a doctor to check on him?"

"What? The Americans have just given us priority and every other aircraft on this field is waiting for us to depart! If we change our minds they'll be pissed off, and we'll look silly."

"Yes, of course," Emily agreed, buckling her harness.

"Go ahead," Kiwi urged. "You fly it, I'll deal with the goons." As she reached for the throttles, he pressed the button on the radio to report. "AAI 005 pushing back now."

The flight to Munich was uneventful, although the clouds continued to build. On landing the air was hot and humid and they could hear distant thunder. Compared to the Airlift airfields, Munich's civil airport was sleepy, with only a couple of airliners standing before the terminal. As soon as they turned off the runway, they were told an ambulance was standing by to receive their "passenger." It was 9:47 am.

Emily parked beside the waiting ambulance and opened the bomb-bay doors, while Kiwi crawled to the sick-bay to handle the winches for lowering the stretcher. As Emily went through the cockpit drill for parking the aircraft, she felt a wave of exhaustion. She'd only had a couple hours of sleep and had been flying mostly on adrenaline. Only gradually did the sound of agitated voices penetrate her consciousness.

She released her harness straps and scrambled out of the seat to open the cockpit hatch and lower the ladder. As her feet hit the tarmac, she knew something was wrong. The medics around the stretcher appeared to be making resuscitation attempts, and Kiwi looked dazed. He felt her gaze, looked over and shook his head. No, she protested, resisting the thought. It can't be.

Kiwi came over to her and confirmed in a low voice, "He's dead."

Oh my God, Emily thought. They shouldn't have flown without a nurse. They should have consulted a doctor in Frankfurt. Or maybe she should have stayed with the patient? In the end, it didn't matter what they'd done wrong; they'd lost their first patient. She'd always been buoyed up by the idea that AAI was "saving lives". Losing one left her feeling discouraged and vaguely unsettled about the future.

Chapter Six
The Boys from Zebra

Sparks
Oldham
Tuesday, 13 July 1948
(Day 18)

Kit's eagerness to join the Airlift had overpowered his natural caution, but realism had soon set in. His wartime crew had been good and lucky, particularly when flying their preferred Lancaster Z-for-Zebra, but a bomber crew was fundamentally different from a freighter crew. Kit's hopes for pulling together a new crew centred on Terry Tibble, his former wireless operator. Since the war, Terry had worked for the Post Office in Oldham, and Kit could not be sure he'd be willing to abandon that secure job for something as risky and temporary as the Berlin Airlift.

Since he didn't feel he should talk to Terry about something so important over the phone, he decided to travel to Oldham to meet him face-to-face. After a tedious train trip, he found himself in a boring street of terraced, red brick buildings. A grocer, a butcher, an ironmonger, and a chemist occupied the shopfronts of the two-storey houses crowned by grimy chimneys. The number he had for Terry matched a barbershop, and Kit wondered if he had the wrong address. Then he saw a small sign in the window reading "Rooms to Let."

Entering set off a tinkling bell, and an elderly man stood to ask how he might help. "I'm looking for Mr Terence Tibble. I was given this address," Kit explained.

"Yes, he rents my second room."

"Oh, good. When do you expect him back from work?"

"He should be there now. Working nights. You can go straight up those stairs." He pointed towards the back.

Terry's abode certainly qualified as "humble" — with a toilet in the backyard and no bath, Kit registered as he made his way to the door labelled "No 2." Here he knocked, but no one answered. What an idiot for not calling first to warn Terry that he was coming! He knocked again louder, and was rewarded by a grunt which resolved itself into a "What is it? Who's there?"

"Terry, it's me. Kit."

Something banged and then the door opened, and Terry stood in the door frame wearing nothing but his pyjama bottoms. His bony frame and sun-starved skin were exposed, making him look young and undernourished. He also looked odd without his thick, dark-framed glasses. He was squinting. "Is something wrong?" Terry asked in alarm.

"No, I just wanted to talk to you in person. I thought—"

"I'm working the graveyard shift from midnight to eight in the morning. What time is it?"

"Two pm. I'm sorry—"

"Don't worry. Have a seat while I get dressed. There's nothing wrong with Georgina or Donna, is there?" Terry asked as he replaced his pyjamas with underpants and sat on the bed to pull on some trousers.

"They're fine, Terry. It's just that I — well, I might have a job."

Terry stopped with just one leg in his trousers. "An engineering job, like?" His face wanted to break into a smile but waited for confirmation.

"No," Kit admitted, and Terry's face fell before Kit added, "It's a flying job — provided I can find a crew."

Terry reached for his spectacles so he could see Kit better. "Did I hear you right, Skip? You have a *flying* job?"

"Not yet. I've been given until the end of the month to find a crew of five. Which means I need a second pilot, navigator, signaller—"

"Not any more you don't!" Terry stood and zipped up his trousers. "You've got one!"

"Terry, you don't know anything about the job yet—"

"I know I'd be flying with you, Skip. That's good enough for me."

"I'm flattered, but I have to be honest with you; this isn't the perfect job."

"What's wrong with it?"

"Well, for a start, it's only temporary. It would mean giving up your safe —"

Terry interrupted to end the sentence himself, "Dead-end job that bores me to death. Look, Skip, without a school-leaving certificate I've got no chance of a promotion. It might be different in a private company, but the civil service is all about putting people into boxes and slamming the lid on you! I've wanted to leave so much that I considered going to sea as a radio operator! Except, I get seasick. How fast does my Morse have to be? I might have to practice a bit to get it back up to speed."

"Slow down, Terry," Kit tried to signal he had more bad news. "The other reason this job isn't all that wizard is that it's in Germany."

"Germany?" Terry looked confused.

"It's flying the Airlift — taking supplies into Berlin."

"Oh!" Terry took a few seconds to digest the news and then shrugged. "Where would we live?"

"I've been told we'll have access to RAF guest quarters or can live on the economy, whichever we prefer."

Pointedly looking around the little room overlooking the back yard with the outhouse, Terry replied, "I've never lived as well as in RAF quarters. It sounds too good to be true."

"It might be. You see, I'm going to need a second pilot, a flight engineer and a navigator, too. Adrian would never come along, but I was thinking Nigel's a qualified navigator now, so I thought I might see if he was interested. The problem is, I haven't been able to reach him. I've rung the number he gave me half a dozen times but there's no answer. Has he shipped out?"

Terry squirmed uncomfortably. "Nigel signed aboard a Baltic ore carrier a couple of months ago—"

Kit couldn't stifle a "damn." It was going to be hard enough to find a flight engineer and second pilot without having to look for a navigator too.

Terry broke in on his thoughts. "Uh, he got into a spot of trouble on his last trip, though. I think he said something about, um, the company blacklisting him."

Kit gaped at Terry, horrified. The last time he'd seen Nigel, fresh from passing his Mate's Exam, he'd looked so proud, confident, and mature. He had been on track to improve his lot in life. Kit hated to think he'd got himself in trouble already, but he couldn't suppress his relief. It meant that he might be available for aircrew. To Terry, he said, "Do you think you could find him and ask if he wants to join my crew?"

"I'll do my best, Skip," Terry promised.

The Fighter Still Remains
Liverpool
Wednesday, 14 July 1948
(Day 19)

Terry had grown up poor, but not rough. He'd spent his childhood in Oldham, which was industrial, gritty, monotonous, and working-class. Nigel, in contrast, had been born and raised in Liverpool, which was both more battered and more combative. During the war it had drawn the repeated attention of the Luftwaffe and, to Terry's unfamiliar eye, it looked as if nothing had been rebuilt since. On the contrary, many smaller shipping companies and shipyards had fallen on hard times and were shuttered. Ships lay rusting at abandoned berths or rotted at anchor, floating derelicts. The men who should have been working in both the ships and the yards were idle, too. Terry passed a dole queue so long that it stretched around the block. Unemployed youths loitered around the lamp posts, eyeing passersby with malevolence.

Conscious of how small and weak he looked, Terry tried to walk fast and purposefully. He double-checked the instructions he'd written down and confirmed he needed to turn right at the next corner, just after the *Jolly Tar*. The gutter in front of the pub stank of vomit, which hadn't yet washed down the drain. Just before he made the turnoff, he heard a shout and a second later a football smashed against his ankle. Terry kicked the ball away angrily without looking in the direction from which it came. He spun in the opposite direction instead and came face-to-face with the boy who had been about to pinch his wallet. "Bog off!" Terry snarled and the boy drew back.

This was a dreadful place to grow up, Terry registered, as he turned into the narrower, darker side street. He'd only gone about a hundred yards before a young woman in a short skirt stepped out of a doorway and slipped her arm through his elbow. "Want a quickie, love?"

"I beg your pardon?" Terry looked at her pale face, disfigured to grotesqueness by overdoses of lipstick and rouge.

"Oh, no," she groaned, "you're one of *those*. Wouldn't know what to do, would you?" she sneered as she withdrew into the shadows.

Terry found the sign saying "Laundry," and rang the bell. From inside a woman's voice screeched, "I'm coming, I'm coming!" The door was yanked open and a woman in a pink dressing gown, pink slippers, and hair rollers stood in the doorway. "What do you want?" she asked hostilely, having already noted that Terry didn't have a laundry bag.

"I'm looking for Nigel Osgood," Terry answered.

"That lazy sod of-a-son-of-mine? I hope you're here to take him off my hands!" Without giving Terry a chance to answer, she turned and raised her voice to yell towards the back of the house, "NIGEL! Come here!"

The answer was rude, but Nigel's mother wasn't put off. "You've got a visitor!"

A door crashed and Nigel staggered into the hall. He was wearing only his underwear, and one eye was swollen shut. The entire left side of his face had been transformed into a misshapen bruise, and his swollen lips bore scabs. When he saw Terry, his eyes widened and then he stumbled forward. "Terry? What are you doing here?" his words ran together because his lips were so badly swollen.

"Can we go somewhere else to talk?" Terry answered, looking pointedly at Nigel's mother, who was staring at them.

"Yeah, of course we can. Do you know where the Sally Ann is?"

"I'll find it," Terry answered.

"I'll be there in a few minutes."

Terry retreated to the main street, stepped into the chemist's opposite the *Jolly Tar* and got directions to the Salvation Army. When he arrived, he was told the soup kitchen was closed, but was offered tea and sat down to wait. It wasn't long before Nigel showed up. He'd put on his uniform with the lone stripe of a Third Officer on his sleeve, but the uniform was rumpled and salt stained.

Seeing Terry's look, Nigel growled, "What was the point of getting it cleaned? I'll never get another officer's berth." As he slumped into the chair opposite Terry, he pounded a fist on the table only to wince. His hand, too, was swollen and bruised.

Nodding towards his face, Terry asked, "That what the Chief Mate did to you?"

"Nah," Nigel unconsciously reached up to measure how swollen his face was with his fingers. To Terry, he explained, "Or not all of it. I tried to throw one of my mother's boyfriends out. That's why she's so pissed off at me."

"Did you manage?"

"Don't know why I bother. If I throw one out she just picks up another. And each one's worse than the one before!" The anger that lurked only just below the surface started to flare up, but then the spark died out again. Nigel shrugged in defeat. "This is going to sound sick, but sometimes I wish she'd just go on the game and charge 'em for it. At least that way they'd bring some effing money in, instead of sucking us dry! We've got bugger all in the cupboards, and I haven't had a solid meal since I came ashore."

Terry had never seen Nigel so low before. He supposed it was because, for a while, things had been looking up. This reverse of his fortunes had come too suddenly and too profoundly to fully grasp. "I can take you out to supper, Nigel," Terry offered softly.

"Yeah, thanks!" Nigel snarled back. "And what about tomorrow and the day after?" Yet, as before, no sooner had the anger erupted than it faded again. Nigel folded his arms on the table and dropped his forehead on them. To the table he slurred, "I'm a wreck, Terry. A worthless wreck. The bastards win again. Just like they always do. All the smart-arsed toffs always win, and the likes of us just get kicked further and further down into the sewer."

Nigel had always had this streak of resentment that Terry did not share. Terry saw the injustice in the world, but he didn't accept that he was helpless to change his personal circumstances. From long experience, however, he knew it was pointless to argue with Nigel. He wanted to comfort Nigel, but because he hadn't known much physical affection growing up, he also found it hard to offer it. After a moment of hesitation, he timidly laid his hand on Nigel's shoulder. "Look, Nigel, there might be a way out. You see, the skipper sent me—"

Nigel sat bolt upright. "You'd better not have told him about what happened!" Nigel warned, clenching his fists as he glared at Terry. He looked ready to punch him if he'd betrayed Nigel's state to their wartime skipper.

Terry hastily shook his head and lied in self-defence. "No, of course not, but he's trying to put a crew together again and he wanted to know if you'd be interested in joining us."

"What?"

"He's got a chance to fly the Airlift with a commercial aviation company, but he needs a full crew—"

"He needs an air gunner?" Nigel asked back flabbergasted.

"No. He thought you could join as navigator."

Nigel gaped at him. "Me? Navigator? In Adrian's berth?"

"You know Adrian's not going to leave his comfy life to fly day and night!"

"That's for sure!" Nigel scoffed, mollified by shared contempt for the most privileged member of their former crew.

Terry continued, "But you qualified as a navigator to sit for your Mate's Exam."

Nigel nodded slowly. "I did well on that part of the test. I like shooting the stars, and the new radio navigation aids are wizard stuff." He paused, still staring at Terry, and asked, "Did the skipper really ask about me, or was it your idea?"

"It was his idea," Terry assured him.

Nigel's left hand crept over his battered face and he groaned. "Christ! I can't let the skipper see me like this! I've got to get myself cleaned up. Terry, can you help me? I need to get away from here — from *her*, from Liverpool, from everything."

Terry nodded. "You can come back with me to Oldham. I've only got one room, so you'll have to sleep on the sofa, but if the Skip finds a second pilot and a flight engineer, we'll be on our way to Germany by the end of the month."

"Who would have thought I'd *like* the thought of going to Germany?" Nigel countered with a lopsided grin.

The Cripple
Edinburgh
Wednesday, 14 July 1948
(Day 19)

Gordon MacDonald deftly folded up the ironing board and shoved it back in its stowage space beside the refrigerator. He'd learned how to open it at a height that enabled him to iron from his wheelchair. Although he still made a hash of tricky items like shirts, he could manage dish towels, napkins and the like. With three of the latter on his lap, he wheeled himself to the cramped dining room and put the freshly ironed and neatly folded napkins on the three place settings he'd laid. He paused to survey the little room, looking for something he'd forgotten. He'd polished the silver tea service, and he'd dusted everything he could reach. Seeing nothing more he could do, he rolled himself back to the parlour and looked it over critically.

Gordon remembered how pleased he and Maisy had been to move into this house when they married eighteen years ago. Maisy had gone to a lot of effort to find the right furniture and had been proud to inherit the china service and a proper cabinet to store it in. His parents had given them the etchings on the back wall, and his sister had stitched the cushion covers. The photographs on the mantlepiece recorded the milestones of his life: a big-eared kid grinning at the camera in the uniform of a Halton apprentice, a proud corporal on the arm of Maisy in a white wedding dress, the Christening of both daughters, the wedding photo of the eldest, a formal picture of him with sergeant's stripes and his aircrew brevet, and finally, a crew picture in front of the Lancaster Z-Zebra. Everything in the room had a memory attached to it; most of them good. It wasn't the past that hurt, but the future, so he dwelt on the past.

Over the years, he'd invited many of his mates home with him. Few had liked it as much as Terry, who claimed it was the nicest place he'd ever stayed in his life. Terry had always jumped at an opportunity to come home with Gordon. Tonight's visitor, however, wasn't an orphan raised in poverty like Terry, and Gordon wasn't sure how he'd react. Flight

Lieutenant Moran had grown up in spacious houses full of native servants and gone to posh schools where they taught Latin and played cricket. Gordon didn't think he'd had anyone with that kind of background to dinner before, and looking things over critically, he noticed that the paint was peeling over the door to the hall, the curtains were badly faded, and the rugs were getting threadbare from the wear and tear of his wheelchair. Six years of wartime had taken their toll on the little house, and now that he was an invalid there was no money to repair things. The house had a rundown feel about it, which made Gordon sad because he'd always been so proud of it.

"Gordon?" His wife called from the kitchen. "Can you come here for a moment?"

He wheeled around and headed towards the sounds and smells of food being prepared. His wife was wearing an apron and scarf over her hair for cooking. She pointed towards a tray with cream crackers with cheddar and asked him to take it to the parlour.

Gordon manoeuvred the wheelchair until he could reach up and pull the platter onto his lap, then retreated. No sooner had he arranged everything on the coffee table than the doorbell rang. Punctual to the minute, Gordon thought with an inner smile; that was the skipper all right. If they were even 30 seconds late over the target, he was unhappy about it. Calling to Maisy that he'd get it, he rolled himself to the entryway and opened the door. Kit Moran stood on the doorstep with a large bouquet.

"For the Mrs," Kit explained with an almost apologetic smile.

"That was thoughtful of you, Skip. Come in," Gordon pushed himself backwards.

Kit entered, his eyes sweeping his surroundings, and Gordon found himself mumbling apologies about not being able to keep it up as he should. "But it's wonderfully cosy!" Kit assured him, and his tone made Gordon start to relax a little. If only he knew why his former pilot had invited himself to dinner.

Leaving Kit in the parlour, Gordon went to fetch a vase and water for the flowers. Together Gordon and Kit together found a place for them and then Kit sat down — only to spring to his feet again when Maisy arrived. She was still flushed from the heat in the kitchen but without her apron or scarf. Tall and slender for a woman her age, the strength of her Highland upbringing was reflected in her sharp features and upright bearing.

"We're so pleased to have you here, Flight Lieutenant Moran," she welcomed him as she shook his hand vigorously. "I only wish I could have made you a better meal. Who would have thought that three years after the Germans surrendered, we'd still be clipping ration coupons! And now they've even put bread and potatoes on ration as well — like they never were in the war. But meat is the worst, you know, I can't seem to get — why am I babbling on like this? I'm sorry, Flight Lieutenant. Please sit down. We've got the cheddar at least." She indicated the platter.

"Thank you, Mrs MacDonald, and I'm the one who ought to apologise for inviting myself like this, but —"

"Oh, let me get you something to drink, first. What would you like?" Mrs MacDonald broke in to ask, and Gordon could tell she was nervous because she didn't usually chatter or interrupt.

Kit took it in his stride and with a glance at Gordon asked, "What are you drinking, Gordon?"

"Guinness."

"Then I'll have one as well."

Maisy disappeared and returned with two glasses and two bottles of beer; she didn't drink herself. Gordon opened the first bottle but poured it out too quickly and the creamy head frothed out of the glass all over his knees. He was about to come out with some choice language when Kit and Maisy burst out laughing. The spill was quickly dabbed up and Maisy urged Kit to try the nibbles. Kit thanked her and took a cracker, while Gordon gulped down half his glass before he nodded to himself and faced his former skipper. "Now, don't keep us in suspense any longer, Skip. What is this all about? There's nothing wrong at home is there?"

"No. Not at all, but I wanted to tell you in person about a job I may have. I owe you my life, and I've felt so badly about being unemployed and—"

"Now, don't go talking like that! You don't have to be someone important for me to feel it was worth saving you. It's enough just to see you with Georgina and that bairn of yours."

Whatever Kit had meant to say, Gordon's remark threw him off his stride. Briefly, he was visibly distressed, then he pulled himself together. "Gordon, I may have a chance to fly on the Berlin Airlift, delivering food to the civilian population."

"Congratulations!" Gordon sat up straighter and reached out to clap Moran on the knee in sincere delight. "Well done!"

"It's not certain, however. First, I have to pull together a complete crew."

"Why don't they assign you one or let you crew up like we did?" Gordon asked confused.

"The job's not with the RAF. It's with a private company."

"Now *that's* a formula for disaster if I ever heard one! A lot of private companies trying to do things their own way will just be like so many flies in the ointment of a good RAF operation. We'd be better off on our own!" Too late, Gordon realised he was deriding Kit and his new job, and he tried to put things right, "Not that you'd make trouble, Skip, but—"

"It's all right. I know what you're saying, but this is an opportunity I can't resist, and I was hoping you might still be in touch with other flight engineers and might know of someone who could be interested in joining me."

Gordon shook his head. "I'd like to help, Skip, but everyone I know is still in the mob."

"What about that reunion, Gordon?" Maisy spoke up.

He looked at her blankly for a moment and then remembered. "Oh yes. Now I remember. I got an invitation a day or two ago from some bloke who wanted to have a reunion with those who went through flight engineer training together. He was no longer in, so maybe there are others who've been demobbed as well. But I didn't want to go, so I tossed it out."

"Maybe I can still find it!" Maisy said, jumping up and leaving them alone.

Kit was looking so earnestly at him that Gordon sensed there was more. "What is it?"

Kit drew a deep breath. "My father-in-law—"

"The reverend?"

"Yes, Reverend Reddings. He claims that coincidences are the hand of God in human affairs." Gordon grunted to suggest his scepticism but waited for Kit to continue. "The company that I may be flying with wants to hire German aircraft mechanics to do the maintenance work. They need a crew chief who could supervise and train the Germans on Hercules VI engines."

Gordon was puzzled why Moran would mention this so solemnly — and then the penny dropped. Something hot seemed to slide down his inert spine. "You — You — think — I — could do that?" he asked cautiously.

Kit nodded. "I'm sure of it. The knowledge is all there in your head. You don't need to *do* the work, just explain it, and make sure the others do it right. I recommended you."

"Why did you do a daft thing like that?" Gordon exploded, feeling overwhelmed. Already he wanted this job so badly he was starting to tremble. Yet he didn't want false hopes or charity either. "What company would want to hire a cripple and why? What's in it for them? Where's the catch?"

Kit looked back steadily, and Gordon sensed the strength and goodwill that had always drawn him to the younger man. "It's an air ambulance outfit run by one of McIndoe's Guinea Pigs and a woman pilot formerly with the ATA. They aren't your usual profit-driven businessmen."

"You *told* them I was in a wheelchair?" Gordon just couldn't believe it.

"Yes, I did."

"And they were still interested?"

"Yes."

"But why? There are lots of other men as qualified as me who aren't cripples."

"Well, it seems their British ground crew refused to remain in Berlin after the blockade started, which is why they decided to hire Germans. In other words, this job would be in blockaded Berlin, and it will only last as long as the blockade does. It's a very temporary and somewhat risky proposition, so few qualified crew chiefs are likely to want it." Kit explained, adding in a gentle voice, "And no one would be surprised or upset if you said no."

"I'm not saying no!" Daddy snapped back, frowning. "I'd take *any* legitimate job, let alone one working with aircraft. And I don't care about the pay, but I don't want charity, either. As for —" He cut himself off as Maisy reappeared in the doorway.

She looked from one to the other, then handed Kit an opened envelope. "That's the invitation to the flight engineers' reunion. It's going to be held in Warrington a week from tomorrow."

"Thank you. I was just telling Gordon that the company I hope to work for also needs a crew chief to train Luftwaffe mechanics. They asked me to find out if Gordon might be interested—"

"Oh! That would be splendid! A job with aircraft again!" She looked at her husband.

"The work would only be temporary," Kit hastened to explain.

"That doesn't matter, does it, Gordon?" Maisy answered turning to her husband with an expression of almost painful eagerness. Turning back to Kit, she declared. "He's been doing much better since I started letting him help around the house, but working with aircraft and engines — that's his life. He loves them. It would do him a world of good to get back to them, even if only for a short spell or on an irregular basis. The pay doesn't matter. Not with the girls earning their own way now, and with my job paying steady. How long would it be for?"

"We don't know. It depends on how long the Russians keep up the blockade of Berlin. The job, I'm afraid, is in Berlin."

"Oh!" She was taken aback by that but then turned to look at Gordon. Their eyes met. He didn't have to say anything. Turning back to Kit she declared. "I think Gordon should go."

Gordon was too overwhelmed for words. All he could do was reach out and clutch her hand with so much force he saw her wince.

She did not pull away, however. Instead, she declared firmly and steadily. "I want you to do this. It's what's meant to be."

Chapter Seven
Ups and Downs

Ahead of Schedule
RAF Gatow
Thursday, 15 July 1948
(Day 20)

It had been a dreary day with intermittent showers that disrupted take-offs and landings despite the ground-controlled approach Gatow had instituted. The problem was that the Americans were still using visual flight rules, and when visibility collapsed in a rain squall, aircraft became stacked up, making it more difficult to thread Gatow-bound aircraft through the flying circus over Tempelhof. All of which meant they had fallen far behind their daily goal.

The Airlift had succeeded in bringing in enough supplies to stretch the stockpiled reserves. No riots or demonstrations had erupted, and although the political situation remained tense, it was strangely stable. Yet from where Wing Commander Priestman sat in Gatow, it was also all too obvious that they were failing nevertheless — simply at a slower pace than initially anticipated. They were also no closer to a diplomatic solution.

A knock on the door interrupted his thoughts and he called "Come in!" Lt. Col. Russel put his head around the door, saw the room was empty and then stepped inside, closing the door behind him.

"Is something wrong?" Priestman asked in response to his curious behaviour.

"I hope not. I just don't want the news to escape from this room prematurely."

"Meaning?"

"I think the concrete runway is serviceable."

"*That* would be good news. Why the uncertainty? Don't you know for sure?"

"Well, to be honest," Russel scratched his head, "we can't be 100 per cent sure that the railway bed, reused bitumen and improvised machinery did the job adequately until a lot of heavily loaded Yorks or C-54s have landed on it."

"Fair enough," Priestman agreed solemnly, then grinned and asked, "Shall we try it out ourselves?"

"What do you mean?"

"Come on! I'll take you up in the Anson. I want to be at the controls of the first aircraft to land on it."

Twenty minutes later they had circled the airfield once and turned to land on the pristine new runway. The landing was smooth as silk with a short squeal of the tyres. As they rolled towards the far end, Priestman tossed a smile to Russel and offered the highest possible RAF praise: "Wizard!"

Back in his office, Priestman called the Senior Flying Control Officer, Squadron Leader Garth. "As you know, we now have a functioning concrete runway. Before I call Wunstorf and ask them to send us all their heavies, are you prepared to handle traffic on both runways simultaneously?"

"We've been planning for it for the last ten days. We'll land everything on the concrete runway and use the PSP for take-off only. In theory, everyone knows their job, although I presume there will be hiccups, we won't know what they are until we start operating. In short, we're as ready as we'll ever be."

"Good. Then I'll check with Captain Bateman to be sure his unloading crews are ready to handle more cargo, and then pass the news up the chain."

Bateman, a plump but energetic army officer responsible for the so-called Forward Airfield Supply Organisation (FASO), like Garth told Priestman that he had been closely watching the progress on the runway and had anticipated this day. "We're ready, WingCo!"

The next call was to Group Captain Bagshot in Wunstorf. As usual, the senior officer sounded short-tempered the moment he answered the phone. "What is it this time, Priestman?"

Feeling pleased with himself, given that the concrete runway had been his idea and they had completed it ahead of schedule under adverse conditions, Priestman reported cheerfully, "Sir, I'm pleased to report that the paved runway at Gatow is now operational enabling us to receive additional inbound traffic."

"It's about time!"

That grated, and Priestman fired back, "May I point out, sir, that the runway has been completed nearly two full weeks sooner than expected. In fact, after the imposition of the blockade, it was questionable whether the construction could be completed at all due to the absence of the necessary equipment."

"Don't try to take credit for this, Priestman. There should have been a paved runway at Gatow years ago. I'll implement the plans we have in place for this contingency. You can expect almost double the amount of traffic starting tomorrow."

"That's fine; we're ready for it." The antipathy was mutual, and Priestman wondered how long it would be before they had a serious clash. No point in dwelling on that now, however, so he put a call through to Air Commodore Waite.

Waite was delighted by the news. "Excellent! We must inform the city administration and the press. Indeed, we should hold a press conference at Gatow tomorrow."

"Is that necessary?" Priestman asked, alarmed.

"It is *absolutely* necessary, Robin. The people of Berlin are being asked to make substantial sacrifices and face serious hardships. The least we can do is give them something to celebrate and a little hope that things will improve."

"Could you give us the morning to chase away the gremlins?"

"Of course. How does two or three o'clock in the afternoon sound to you? Two would be better so the announcement can be included on the evening news. General Herbert will want to be there, I'm sure, and I suspect that General Robertson may turn up as well. The city government will presumably attend in strength too. You need to be prepared for a gaggle of dignitaries and maybe thirty gentlemen of the press."

"Do I have a choice?"

"None whatsoever."

Prima Donnas
Berlin
Friday, 16 July 1948
(Day 21)

The introduction of parallel landings and take-offs would have been stressful enough without the added pressure of brass, dignitaries, and press. Theoretically, Air Commodore Waite was guiding and briefing the visitors, but Flight Officer Parsons was pushing herself forward, determined to highlight "her" WAAF. Irony of ironies, the woman who had conveyed disapproval of Kathleen keeping her daughter in blockaded Berlin, now wanted Hope to present flowers to the mayor.

Parsons had come to Kathleen's quarters the night before and announced her plans in front of Hope, which Kathleen thought was either singularly obtuse or intentionally manipulative. Hope, who had turned seven in May, had become excited about the idea. She'd clapped her hands and started chattering about what she ought to wear and if her mother would put red satin ribbons in her hair.

So instead of being focused on her job, as she should have been this morning, Kathleen had to arrange to pick up Hope during her lunch break and as a result arrived in the tower just moments before her watch started, which was not her usual practice. She replaced the controller who had been on duty through the night, and he pointed out the blips on the radar representing 99 (York) Squadron already over Frohnau. Nodding, she settled into her station. For the first time since the move to radar controlling, she wished she were at the windows instead. She would have liked to watch the inauguration of the concrete runway rather than be glued to a radar screen.

Naturally, the WingCo came up to watch the first batch of heavily loaded Yorks land. Kathleen, conscious of being in control even if no one was looking in her direction, spoke clearly and precisely. The flight lieutenant commanding the first York exclaimed enthusiastically at touch-down: "That feels a whole lot better than PSP! I can hear myself think in here!" Everyone in the control room cheered.

The remaining seven aircraft landed at three-minute intervals, each adding their commentary on the runway. Kathleen risked taking a quick stretch to look out of the windows. Lorries were docking beside the Yorks for unloading, and some Dakotas were moving towards the PSP runway preparing for take-off. She returned to her radar screen.

By noon, much of the excitement had worn off because everything appeared to be running smoothly. Kathleen ate a sandwich and collected Hope from the daycare centre and helped her change into her best dress. Hope was not the least bit nervous about her press debut, Kathleen noted with amusement. She primped herself in the bathroom mirror with every indication of being pleased with the way she looked. She's going to be an actress, Kathleen concluded, and took her by the hand to turn her over to Flight Officer Parsons.

"Oh, don't you look pretty!" Parsons exclaimed, feeding her vanity further, Kathleen thought. "Now, this is the bouquet you are to give the mayor of Berlin."

"What does he look like?" Hope asked.

"I don't know," Parsons admitted, "but we'll watch and listen to what the others are saying," she told Hope with a wide smile.

Kathleen knew that the visitors had arrived by the eruption of conversation in the tower behind her. Garth called over his shoulder to her, "Hope's splendid. She just curtsied to the mayor!"

"Where on earth did she learn to do that?" Kathleen asked back, shaking her head bemusedly.

"He's bending down to chat with her for a moment," Garth retorted, but then the screen demanded her attention again.

When she had a moment to ask what was going on, they told her the visitors had been taken out to stand beside the runway while 59 Squadron landed. A little later, the WingCo called to warn them that he was bringing the VIPs up to the tower.

"Clear away those coffee cups! Get the rubbish into the bins! Button up your tunic, Corporal!" Garth ordered.

By the time the visitors crowded into the tower, everything looked smart and efficient. Garth welcomed the gaggle of intruders and led them around to the various positions, explaining the jobs done. The visitors talked amongst themselves, knocking against chairs and tables as they tried to get a better look. They were offered a brief glance into the radar room, and Kathleen studiously ignored them. She heard the crowd move on and was just about to relax when a female voice spoke almost into her ear. "What a delight to see a woman here!"

Startled, Kathleen looked over her shoulder and realised that a smartly dressed lady had stayed behind when the rest of the crowd moved on.

"Virginia Cox of the *Times*." She held out her hand. Kathleen stood to shake it as it.

"Oh, don't let me disturb you, but maybe we could talk later? I love to get the human side of a story, and reporting about a WAAF air traffic controller would make great copy. Here's my card." She pulled a business card from her blazer pocket and set it down on the table in front of Kathleen. "I have an apartment on Kronprinzenallee but we could arrange to meet anywhere you like —"

"Miss Cox-Gordon!" It was the voice of the WingCo, and it had an edge to it that made Kathleen wince. "The tour here is over. Please allow Assistant Section Officer Hart to get on with her work."

"Oh, Robin darling! I've been looking all over—"

"It's Wing Commander, Miss Cox-Gordon."

Ouch, Kathleen thought, and risked glancing up. The reporter's face had flushed, and she turned on her heel to leave. Priestman looked straight at Kathleen and shook his head firmly before departing. Kathleen was unsure what his gesture had meant. Then she saw the reporter's card on her desk and realised he didn't want her talking to the woman, so she tossed the card in the waste paper basket and focused again on her job.

Hotel California
Berlin-Kreuzberg
Saturday, 17 July 1948
(Day 22)

The three young men known to their neighbours as "Meyer," "Braun," and "Schmidt" returned to their apartment after the funeral of their former shipmate in a sombre mood. It was a hot, muggy day, so they loosened their ties, removed their jackets, and rolled up their shirtsleeves. None of them spoke until Lothar (aka Braun) tried to turn on the fan and realised there was no electricity. He cursed vividly, and his former captain Anton Sperl (aka Meyer) responded by saying in a low, calming voice. "I think we'd better sit down and have a serious talk about our future."

His comrades stared at him and then Norbert (aka Schmidt) agreed, "You're right, Anton." He dropped into the nearest chair.

"First, I take full responsibility for Thomas' death. I was wrong to suggest resistance. We should have brought him to live with us here or found somewhere else for him to hide. Trying to fight the Russian thugs was idiotic."

Lothar stared at his former captain, stunned by such an admission, but Norbert shook his head. "Look, Anton. It might have been your idea, but none of the rest of us had to go along with it. Thomas could have said no, but he was more eager to fight than you were. The problem is we're all fed up with being humiliated, kicked, and trampled on. It isn't enough to hit back surreptitiously with bad schnapps and exploitive prices for fake goods. Running away and hiding didn't feel right."

"Thomas would be alive if he had."

"Is surviving all that's left to us? I've been giving this a lot of thought, and Thomas' death has brought things into focus for me. Let's start with the fact that the blockade cuts us off from our source of potatoes, which means we can't make any more schnapps without taking silly risks. We've got at most a dozen bottles left and after they've been sold, we're dead in the water."

Anton nodded. Norbert wasn't telling him anything he didn't already know.

"As for the rest of our inventory," Norbert gestured to the stacks of lamps and other furnishings, the boxes filled with china and glasses, the stacks of bed and table linen, and the piles of clothes. "It's almost impossible to barter the stuff anymore. Nowadays, people are in the market for necessities. What we're seeing out there," he gestured with his head towards the window, "aren't ordinary people looking to trade one thing for another but organised criminal gangs. We're not in their league, and I don't want to be."

Anton drew a deep breath. "I agree. I think we should give the clothing to Herr Liebherr so he can donate it to the Red Cross or the Salvation Army, and we should attempt to sell the other items to legitimate businesses. Since the currency reform, shops have been sprouting up all over the place. A shop just opened on the corner that sells lamps and light bulbs. There are also lots of taverns that must need to replenish stocks of glasses, plates, and cutlery, but can't waste time playing the black market. We always said we were saving the stuff until we could get hard currency for it. Well, the D-Mark looks like it's stable — at least for now."

"But what do *we* do then?" Lothar protested.

"I was talking to Erich Kreisler at the funeral," Norbert announced. "He's found an old, laid-up barge, patched it up, and has got it seaworthy again. He asked me to help repair the engine so he could start transporting cargo. Everything landing at Gatow or brought in by flying boat has to be shipped up to Berlin in barges."

"Sounds like the right thing for you, Norbert," Anton told his former chief engineer, nodding approvingly.

"What about you?" Norbert shot back. "Don't you want to join us? It never hurts to have some back-up crew."

Anton shook his head. "The Allies pay by the ton. The more crew you have, the smaller everyone's share. No, I talked to Johannes Stumm. He's the Deputy Police Chief."

"What? You talked to one of Markgraf's men?" Lothar reared up, outraged.

"Stumm isn't Markgraf's man. He's a trained policeman who resigned shortly after the Nazis came to power — and he hates the Ivans as much as anybody. The Berlin City Council wants to see him take over from Markgraf, they just haven't worked out how to go about it yet. When he does take over, he's going to purge all the Red goons. He'll need new men to fill the ranks at very short notice. There'd be a place for you too, Lothar," Anton addressed the youngest among them.

"Would I be issued a uniform?" Lothar asked back, and Anton smiled to himself. Lothar was having the hardest time reinventing himself. He'd barely been 17 when he'd joined the Kriegsmarine and he'd chosen U-boats for the prestige and glamour. The uniform had meant everything to him, and losing it had been a bad blow to his self-esteem.

"Yes, if you join the regular force."

"Is there anything else?" Lothar asked, confused.

"Stumm suggested that I would be most useful as a plain clothes inspector, but I think you'd be happier in the regular force."

"Yes," Lothar agreed. "So, when is this going to happen?"

"Well, it depends —"

A bang on the door startled them. They turned to stare in the direction of the noise. The knock came again, and because Norbert was closest, he got up to answer it. Anton and Lothar drifted after him. Standing on the landing was a worker in old, baggy clothes with a peaked cap pulled low over his face. "I'm looking for Herr Meyer," he growled.

Norbert turned to look at Anton, and he stepped forward to look at the visitor more closely. It took another three to four seconds before he recognised the man. "Voigt? Axel Voigt?"

"That's right. I need to talk to you."

"Come in."

Anton gestured him inside and Voigt followed him to the front salon. Here, he looked nervously around himself before frowning hostilely at Anton's two companions.

"We were just leaving," Norbert said, jerking his head at Lothar.

Only after they had closed the door behind them did Voigt growl in a low voice, "I've got to get stuff for my mother."

"Stuff?"

"You know what I mean. I want to deal with the source directly. The Brothers — the SED — they just keep turning up the screws. They demand more and more. No matter how much I do for them, they always want more. I want to buy from the dealer — or at least talk to him. See what the prices are."

Anton shook his head, "I'm sorry, Voigt. I can't help you. I don't deal in drugs."

"But you must know someone who does!" Voigt countered, raising his voice in frustration.

Anton remained calm. "No. I don't."

"Damn it! The manufacturer sits right here in Zehlendorf! Morphine in minute quantities for show and heroin by the ton for profit. His boys must be all over the place, but if I have to, I'll go and knock on *his* door!"

"You're welcome to do that," Anton answered, unruffled, "but why don't you talk to Freiherr von Feldburg first? Maybe he can help you get legal access to morphine."

Voigt frowned and growled, "What do you mean?"

Anton shrugged. "As he told you last time we met, he's in contact with an air ambulance service that works with hospitals."

Voigt took his time thinking about that, but finally drew a deep breath and agreed.

Anton called to his companions, saying he was going upstairs and led Voigt to the Feldburg/Walmsdorf flat on the floor above. Feldburg answered the door and showed no particular surprise at the sight of Voigt and Sperl together. "Let's sit out on the balcony," he suggested, and led them across the front salon and through the open French windows onto the balcony facing the Landwehr canal. There were two chairs here already. Feldburg invited them to sit while he fetched a third from the kitchen. Before going, he asked if they wanted a glass of water. "It's all I have to offer at the moment," he added.

They accepted and Feldburg brought them each a glass before joining them. Voigt nervously sipped the water and looked at the pavement four stories below. There was no one in sight except an old lady walking a small, skinny dog. Idly, Sperl wondered what drove someone who was nearly starving to give up some of their food to keep a dog alive.

Voigt had no time to enjoy the scenery, in a dogged tone of voice pitched very low he addressed Feldburg, "Herr Major—"

"Feldburg. Just Feldburg," Christian corrected.

"I need the stuff for my mother. I need it and the Brothers make it harder and harder for me to get it. As I already told Herr Meyer, no matter what I do, they want more. They're turning me into a monster. I hate myself! I can't go on!" Feldburg nodded in understanding, but when he said nothing, Voigt added, "There has to be another way to get the stuff for my mother."

"I'm sorry. I don't deal in drugs," Feldburg unconsciously echoed Sperl.

"I know that, but Herr Meyer thought your contacts in the hospitals might be able to provide it legally. Why not? My mother is a victim, a patient. She's not some drug addict!"

"The hospitals here don't have surplus stocks of drugs. That's one of the reasons they want to fly the worst cases out."

"But the stuff is being produced in Bitterfeld!" Voigt protested. That was just a hundred miles away.

"That's in the Soviet Zone, Voigt. The blockade cuts us off from everything—"

"You can't be that naive!" Voigt snapped. "The people controlling the blockade let through anything they want to let through! They've diverted most of the drugs that used to come into the Soviet Sector to the West. They're flooding the market with the stuff — I mean the hard stuff!"

"Why would they do that?" Feldburg asked bewildered.

"Because the Ivans and SED want D-Marks! You must know that? The hospitals can get as much as they want as long as they pay in D-marks!"

Feldburg was frowning and he turned to Anton. "Have you heard this, Sperl?"

"I've heard rumours that the drug market was thriving despite the blockade, but this is the first time I've heard anything explicit about the source and reasons."

Feldburg turned back to Voigt. "Let's assume you're right, Voigt. Let's assume the stuff is available here in the Western Sectors provided one knows where to look for it and can pay the price. How do you plan to get it to your mother? People crossing the Sector border are routinely subject to unpleasant searches. On the main thoroughfares there are always scores of Red soldiers on duty, and even the smaller streets and alleys usually have a pair of Ivans watching to see that no one's breaking the blockade."

Voigt glared back at him and spat out, "I don't know. I haven't thought that far. I just know I can't go on the way things are. I've got to find a way out. I came here hoping Herr Meyer could help." He cast Sperl a reproachful look for failing him.

"My offer still stands, Voigt. If you can find one or two other mechanics willing to learn about British aircraft engines, you can have a job at Gatow. As an employee of the ambulance company you'd be paid in D-marks, and my cousin, who handles the liaison with the hospitals, could inform them about your mother's condition. I'm not going to promise any more than that, but if you're right and there's more stuff in the West than the East, then the chances of getting it seem better if you're living and working on the right side of the border and earning hard currency."

"You're suggesting I move my mother *into* the West?"

"If she's to have a chance of being flown out to the West, yes. She'll need to move into one of the Western Sectors first."

"You want me to move my crippled mother *into* the area under siege?"

"We aren't doing so badly," Feldburg retorted with a shrug. Then, without a word of explanation, he stood and went back into the apartment. A moment later he returned with a packet of cigarettes. He shook one out in Voigt's direction. Voigt stared at the cigarettes. "Those are American."

"Yes. They're good. Try one."

Voigt took one and Feldburg lit it for him. He offered one to Sperl, who turned it down. Feldburg took one for himself, and sat down again, inhaling, and blowing out the smoke several times before continuing. "Horst has moved his wagon and horses down to Gatow, where the RAF has fenced off some of the airfield as pasture for those horses helping to haul cargos to Kladow. He's bunking down there with the other drivers in the stables. That means his old apartment is vacant. You and your mother could move in there. It may still smell a bit of horse, but the odour is fading, and you'd have a private toilet."

Voigt stared at him.

"What is it?" Feldburg asked.

"I always knew you were rich, Herr Maj— Herr von Feldburg, but I didn't realise that even your coachman had a higher standard of living than my working-class family."

"Well, you've had your revolution, Voigt. If you prefer Socialism—"

"The Ivans don't have Socialism!" Voigt shouted back at him. "There's nothing fair or just about their f***king system. There are still those with wealth and those without, the powerful and powerless. All their talk of Socialism and Equality and Democracy are lies!"

Neither Feldburg nor Sperl responded to this outburst, and with an overhand throw more appropriate for a grenade, Voigt threw his cigarette stub over the balcony railing. It was a gesture of frustration. After he'd calmed down a bit, Feldburg said levelly, "It's your choice, Voigt. You decide which side of this conflict you're on."

"Choice? Who has a choice? You're going to f***king lose!" Voigt shot back. "And then what? If I've moved here, they'll take their revenge on me

— and my mother too."

"If you haven't already flown to the West — along with me, hopefully," Feldburg answered with a grin.

Voigt stood on the edge of the balcony, looking across the Landwehr canal towards the city stretching out beyond. Then he lifted his head and followed the sound of aircraft engines, finding the stream of C-47s droning their way towards Tempelhof. "They keep this up day and night, don't they? Doesn't the noise drive you crazy?"

Feldburg shook his head, "No, it is music to our ears."

Voigt looked at the sky again. "I know a couple of mechanics who might be willing to take the chance. I'll talk to them about it. I'll let you know what they say as soon as I know."

"Excellent," Feldburg answered.

Voigt turned and looked at him. "I'm trusting you, Herr Major. I'm trusting you to help my mother. You're my last hope."

"I promise to do my best, but I cannot promise that your mother will be flown out to the West."

Voigt nodded. "I understand. Now I'd better go." Feldburg and Sperl escorted him to the door, where with an eye to his new profession, Sperl couldn't resist asking, "Just one more thing, Voigt. Earlier you mentioned that the manufacturer of the stuff lives in Zehlendorf. You wouldn't happen to know his name, would you?"

"Everyone knows who it is!" Voigt countered frowning nervously.

"I don't, and knowing would make it much easier for us to make contact — either for you privately or for a hospital. You might as well let us in on the secret."

"Friedebach."

"Juergen Friedebach?" Christian gasped out, shocking the other two by the intensity of his question.

"I don't know," Voigt answered. "I don't think anyone mentioned his first name, but he's said to live somewhere in Zehlendorf."

"That's him!" Christian declared, smashing his fist into the doorframe in triumph, "The man in David Goldman's house on Schwanenwerder. The man with *my* painting hanging on his wall. I knew he was a criminal. I just thought he was a Nazi war criminal, rather than a modern drug dealer."

"He's probably both," Voigt replied with a shrug of his shoulders.

"He's sometimes also referred to as 'the SS-General.'"

"Now working for the Reds," Feldburg noted.

"Without doubt," Voigt confirmed, "which shows you how utterly amoral and ruthless he is. Until later, Herr — von Feldburg." Voigt scuttled down the stairs as if in a hurry.

As Feldburg closed the door behind him, Sperl asked him for more information. The more Feldburg explained, the more intrigued Sperl became. He sensed that this might be a perfect opportunity for him to prove his value to his future employer.

Disappeared
Berlin-Kreuzberg
Sunday, 18 July 1948
(Day 23)

Many things in Jasha's life had disappeared: first, her ethnically Polish village in White Russia had been lost to 'modernization' in the Soviet Union, then the NKVD had arrested her husband and then her teenage son for alleged treason; both were shot and buried in some mass, unmarked grave. She had fled the memories, the threats and the poverty to relatives in Poland, only to lose that refuge when the Germans invaded. She come to Germany as a slave labourer and found a home of sorts on the Walmsdorf estate, only to be force to flee again ahead of the advancing Red Army. She'd spent the last days of the war in a crouching in a celler in Berlin, and had endured the horrors of the early days of Soviet occupation.

Between her husband's arrest and the end of the war, she had lost her innocence, her youth, her honour, her trust in human kindness, and her faith in God's benevolence. Yet, without understanding why, she had not lost her love of life itself. She had learned to close a door on the past, dismiss the future as irrelevant, and focus on the present. She loved the sunrise and the sunset. She loved the sound of birds calling and the lapping of waves on a beach. She loved the sight of Sammy bounding up the stairs to say good morning and the sight of sailing boats heeling in the wind on the glittering Havel. She liked making meals for appreciative people, and she liked watching things grow in her garden. She particularly enjoyed gardening with Mr Graham because he made her laugh and made her feel special — and told her not to call him "Mr Graham" just "Graham."

Yesterday, they had spent the entire day in the garden together, but now he insisted he wanted to see more of Berlin. He wanted Jasha to join him. Yet while she did not want to open those mental doors and think about the past, she could not overcome her fears or her hatred of the Reds, either. So, she declined and asked him to leave her at Charlotte's apartment instead. From there she could go to the nearby Catholic church. Graham agreed because he was driving David to Kreuzberg to visit Charlotte anyway.

Like the week before, Graham drove David and Jasha from Kladow into the heart of Berlin, only this time Graham left them, promising to return to Charlotte's house by four o'clock. That would leave them all enough time for afternoon tea at Hotel Esplanade before Graham, David and Jasha had to return to Kladow.

As she climbed out of his car, Graham asked Jasha once more if she wouldn't join him for his sightseeing tour. She weakened momentarily. She *wanted* to spend more time with him, but he was too intent on visiting "the East." Red soldiers ruled the East, and Jasha's stomach started knotting itself. She shook her head firmly and backed away. David gave Graham some last sightseeing tips, and then he drove off.

At the door to Charlotte's apartment, her welcome wasn't just for David. "Jasha!" she exclaimed, "I'm so glad you came too! You must come and see what *Kapitaenleutnant* Sperl brought us yesterday. Well, I should say, he brought it to Herr Liebherr so he could take it to the Red Cross, but Herr Liebherr asked me if there was anything I needed and I thought of you, too. Come and see what I picked out!"

David had no interest in clothes and wandered towards the balcony where Christian jumped up, announcing. "David! I have two pieces of good news for you. First, I've identified three German aircraft mechanics willing to work at Gatow whenever you say the word. Second, I've had a tip about Friedebach. Come! I'll tell you the details." Christian gestured for David to join him in the front salon, while Jasha followed Charlotte down the back hallway.

On the spare bed in Christian's room, Charlotte had spread out three dresses and two boxes with shoes. "Look!" Charlotte exclaimed. "I thought of you when I saw this!" She held up a pretty, navy-blue dress with a white collar and cuffs. "I'm sure it would fit!" Charlotte insisted.

"It's beautiful," Jasha whispered, reaching out to touch the material and confirm that it was silk. "But where would I ever wear it?"

"To mass," Charlotte answered, "or to dinner with Lt. Col. Russel."

Jasha looked over sharply. Was she that transparent?

Charlotte met her eyes with a smile. "He's very attentive. Don't you like him?"

"I like him very much," Jasha admitted, her eyes caressing the dress.

Charlotte caught her hand and clutched it. Surprised by the intensity of the touch, Jasha turned to look at the younger woman and was horrified to see Charlotte's face dissolving into tears. "Jasha!" she gasped out.

"What is it?" Jasha asked back, confused by the change in her mood.

Charlotte pulled Jasha into her arms and clung to her as she stammered, "Jasha, I feel so terrible. I never thanked you — not once. I never even asked about how — what — I was so wrapped up in myself. I was so selfish." She was sobbing miserably.

Jasha felt tears in her own eyes, and she clung to Charlotte. All the barriers she had built against the memories collapsed as if the last three years had never been. It felt as if the rapes had happened yesterday. The women cried in each other's arms, comforting one another as they had not been able to do at the time.

Slowly, the initial storm of emotion ebbed. Jasha found herself stroking Charlotte's back and whispering, "It's all right, Charlotte. I never blamed you. You were — so broken, so shattered and confused by it all. You were a virgin and a lady, after all. You were less prepared than I was."

"How can anyone be prepared..." Charlotte stammered out, pressing her hands to her face to wipe away some of the tears.

Jasha found a handkerchief in her skirt pocket and handed it to Charlotte. "I have seen many terrible things: a famine that drove men to cannibalism, the Great Terror that made us fear every neighbour, every knock on the door and mistrust even our closest friends, the German invasion, and finally the end of the war. But the worst — My son was only seventeen when they accused him of being a Polish spy. He had never been to Poland in his life. He was utterly loyal to the Soviet Union. Yet they shot him in the back of the head and dumped him in an unmarked grave. After a mother has survived that, a rape is not so terrible."

"You never told us!" Charlotte reproached her, horrified.

Jasha shrugged and wiped her own tears away. "I don't like to remember."

Charlotte sank down beside the pile of clothes, "Do you think — do you think...."

"What?" Jasha settled on the other side of dresses.

"Will you ever want — ever be able to — I mean, with a man you love — could you? Could you love again?"

Jasha turned to look at the pretty navy blue silk dress spread over the heap of things. "I don't know," she admitted. "I wish I could be married to a good man who cares for me, who is protective and respectful and looks after me. I wish we could have a farm — or at least a garden — together. I'd like to grow things with him and have chickens and ducks, maybe even a cow. I'd like to cook things so good that he eats too much and gets a pot belly. I'd like to grow old and fat together. But I don't know about the bedroom part...."

"I'm so afraid of that — and yet afraid, too, that — I might — I don't know!" she ended with an inarticulate shake of her head.

"But you like Mr David, I think?" Jasha asked cautiously.

"He's absolutely wonderful! I never thought I would ever feel so much for another man as I'd felt for my fiancée Fritz. But it's been so long since Fritz disappeared, and David is so gentle with me and so kind. He has made me feel like a lady again — like I am someone worth loving."

"Of course, you are worth loving!" Jasha admonished. "And Mr David is a good man, I think."

"Yes, but that's exactly what makes me ashamed to deceive him. Shouldn't I warn him that I'm not — not — what I appear?"

"But you are who you appear to be, Charlotte."

"No, Jasha!" Charlotte shook her head violently and the tears were flooding down her face again. "I'm not a lady any longer! I'm not even a *maid*. I'm nothing but a piece of trash, kicked about, used by six men one after another and then pissed upon—"

Jasha sprang up and pulled Charlotte back into her arms. "Hush! Stop! What they did to you, to us, doesn't change who *we* are."

Charlotte sobbed into Jasha's bosom. "Yes, it *does*! I can't ever be who I was before."

Jasha knew that was true, so she did not deny it. She just held Charlotte in her arms until she had calmed herself again. Then she said softly, "No, we'll never be the same again, but we must try to love who we are."

"What's taking you two so long?" Christian called from the front of the house. "We'll miss Mass if we don't leave soon."

"I'm coming, Herr Baron! Just another couple of minutes!" Jasha answered. Hastily, Jasha and Charlotte pulled themselves together, dried their tears and looked each other over. Charlotte applied fresh lipstick, and Jasha combed her hair. They returned together to the front of the house, Jasha to go to Mass and have lunch with Christian, and Charlotte to go with David on an outing together. They agreed to meet at 4:30 at the Esplanade for tea.

Charlotte and her family were Protestant, but Christian was Catholic, like Jasha. She found it comforting to attend Mass with him. Too many young men were no longer devout, but Christian had gone to a Jesuit school and like Jasha, he wanted to confess. After all the misery she had witnessed, Jasha no longer trusted in the benevolence of God, yet that made her all the more afraid of Him. It seemed to her that He wanted to punish mankind for their many sins and that the innocent were swept up in His rage against the guilty. She directed all her prayers to the Virgin, certain that she understood the suffering of the innocent and that she sympathised with the victims, even if she didn't seem to be able to mitigate the anger of the Holy Spirit.

After Mass and Confession, Christian and Jasha had a light snack at a restaurant with tables on the pavement. Because of the blockade and the rationing, the only thing on the menu were "*broetchen*" (rolls) with a thin, milky-white, rubbery substance that the proprietor optimistically and insistently called "cheese." "It's American," he told them as if that made it taste better. No matter, Jasha thought, the *broetchen* were good.

When they finished, it was already after 3 pm, and Jasha didn't want Graham to find the apartment empty, so Christian took her back. They settled on the front balcony with its view of the street and canal. That way they would be able to see Graham arrived. They planned to call down to him and save him four flights of stairs.

But he didn't come. Not at four or four-thirty or five. Christian decided they had to call the Esplanade to warn Charlotte and David that they would be late. By 6 pm, Jasha was frantic. "The Reds!" she told Christian. "They've done something to him."

"What can they do to him? He's a British officer." Christian tried to calm her. "Even more than the rest of us, the occupation forces have the right to be anywhere in the city."

"But he wasn't in uniform," Jasha pointed out. Graham hadn't wished to stand out. He'd wanted to blend in as best he could.

"No, but he has his ID with him," Christian reminded her.

"It doesn't matter. The Ivans can't read Latin letters — or they don't want to. They could have kidnapped him!"

"No, they wouldn't risk that. He's probably just had trouble with the car or something."

By 8 pm, Charlotte and David were back, and they collectively made the decision to inform Wing Commander Priestman. Aside from anything else, David and Jasha had no means of transport back to Kladow. David handled the call to the Wing Commander, but as Jasha stood beside him, she could hear the RAF officer's alarm and that increased her fears. Priestman said he'd send his car and driver for them and would also inform British Army HQ of Lt. Colonel Russel's disappearance.

"Do you think the Ivans really might have kidnapped him?" David asked sceptically.

Priestman sighed heavily, "Unfortunately, yes. The Americans have reported several similar incidents, albeit with lower-ranking personnel. We've issued several warnings to personnel generally, and I personally reminded Graham he was taking a risk."

Jasha's hands started writhing with distress. "No," she gasped inarticulately. "No, no, no!"

Call for Help
RAF Gatow
Monday, 19 July 1948
(Day 24)

WAAF Corporal Galyna Borisenko was working her way through *Izvestia* when the Intelligence Officer, Flight Lieutenant Boyd, called her. Officially, her position was that of Russian translator/interpreter, but unofficially she was on probation for a transfer to MI6. A call from Boyd, therefore, filled her with excitement. She meticulously marked her place, folded the paper back together again, and lined up her pencils and rubber on the top of the desk. Standing, she tucked a notepad and pen into the left breast pocket, then straightened her tunic and hurried to the Intelligence Officer's office on the top floor.

"Ah, Borisenko," Boyd responded to her knock on his door.

"You wanted to see me, sir?" she asked brightly after saluting as smartly as she could. Short and square in stature, she never quite looked like the WAAF in the recruiting posters, but her keenness was evident in the polish of her buttons and the shine of her shoes.

"There has been an unfortunate incident over the weekend. Lt. Col Graham Russel, the senior CRE officer responsible for our new concrete runway, has disappeared."

"Disappeared?" she asked, shocked.

"Yes, he's been too busy working on the runway to 'see the sights' and he wanted to make up for that yesterday. After dropping off friends in Kreuzberg and promising to return to collect them by 4 pm, he crossed into the Soviet Sector just after 11 am. He was driving his official vehicle, a former Wehrmacht *"Kuebelwagen"* with British Forces of Occupation plates, but he was not in uniform. Witnesses saw him visiting the ruins of Hitler's Chancellery at about 11:30 am, and then stopping to look over Goering's former Air Ministry before driving down Unter den Linden and parking near the Staatsoper. He left the car open and unlocked, while he went into the opera. He has not been seen or heard of since. He did not return to his car, and two sappers retrieved it late last night. They found no evidence of anything unusual in or on the vehicle. The only surprise was a small box of chocolates in the glove compartment, which suggests Russel may have intended to meet with a lady friend. However, the chocolates would surely have been on his person if his meeting was in the East," Boyd suggested.

Borisenko nodded her agreement, and Boyd continued. "Meanwhile, General Herbert put a call through to the SMAD to see if they knew where Russel was. The Soviets responded with mocking surprise. Reportedly, the Soviet Kommandant, General Kotikov, remarked that maybe Russel 'was intelligent enough to know when he was beaten' and had decided to desert. Before Herbert could reply, he suggested that alternatively, Russel might be sleeping off a binge or an overdose of drugs. His most plausible thesis was that Russel might have been enjoying a 'passion-filled tete-a-tete with his mistress' somewhere far away from the 'obnoxious noise' of aircraft day and night. The tone was intentionally insulting, and General Herbert was deeply offended. Nevertheless, with the Russkies denying all knowledge of Russel's whereabouts, the military police have been ordered to handle the case as a 'missing person.' The Berlin city police have also been informed."

Borisenko nodded solemnly.

Boyd continued, "Since Lt. Col. Russel is Corps of Royal Engineers, his whereabouts aren't strictly RAF business, but he's a personal friend of the WingCo, who is very concerned. He suggested you might be able to exploit your contacts to find out more. What do you think?"

Borisenko bit her lower lip, realised what she was doing, and stopped. Unconsciously, she was frowning with concentration. "I have not spoken to Mila Mikhailevna since she wished me goodbye at the start of the blockade. She broke off the call precipitously. I don't know how she will react if I contact her now."

"As you know, the four-power status of the city officially guarantees the right of members of all four occupying powers to move freely throughout Berlin. The Soviets do not have the right to stop British personnel unless they are violating the law or behaving in a disorderly manner — something their troops do in our Sector all the time with impunity, by the way. General Herbert has explicitly advised that we should not prohibit personnel from crossing Sector borders as this would play into Russian hands. That said, there are disturbing indications that the Reds aren't playing by the rules —

to put it mildly. The Americans have reported the arrest of several service personnel — always when they were alone in civilian clothes in the Soviet Sector. All, so far, have eventually turned up again, but often after being kept in demeaning conditions or subjected to abuse for several days. Lt. Colonel Russel doesn't deserve that — not to mention that he knows more about construction at this airfield and our plans for expansion than we want the Russkies to know."

"I will try, sir!" Borisenko retorted and saluted smartly.

Back at her desk, Borisenko sat for several moments collecting her courage and then opened her notebook and found Mila's work number. She was very nervous as she dialled the number and counted the rings — two, three, four — "Levchenkova!" A woman identified herself on the other end.

Borisenko lowered her voice almost to a whisper. "Mila! It's me! Galyna Nicolaevna. I need to talk to you."

"I'm sorry. You must have the wrong number," Mila answered in a loud and indifferent voice before hanging up. Galyna knew Mila's reaction might be subterfuge, yet part of her was hurt by Mila's tone all the same. Mila had become a friend, the first person she'd ever confided in about her father's arrest and disappearance.

She reported Mila's response to Boyd and then went back to her regular work. Translating the Russian newspapers was a depressing task. They crowed about their cleverness in "exposing" the "heinous egotism" of the Western Powers that were prepared to let little children starve just to maintain an "illegal" presence deep inside the Soviet Zone. The Western "capitalists" were trying to use their "terror bombers" to stretch supplies, but it was a "mathematical certainty" that the provisioning of a city of more than two million people by air was impossible. The West would soon face the "logical" consequences of their "arrogance" by being thrown out of Berlin by the indignant "working masses".

Shortly after lunch, the telephone in the section rang and a colleague answered, only for the line to be dead. After that had happened twice more, Galyna reached for the telephone herself the next time it rang. A female voice barked in Russian: "Comrade, you should know that the café opposite the Reichstag is a smugglers' den! It should be raided as soon as possible. If you go tonight, I promise you will catch some very big fish."

Collecting her thoughts, Galyna started to respond, but Mila spoke over her. "Yes, comrade. That's right." Galyna held her breath as Mila paused again and then said. "Yes, comrade. I understand. I will not breathe a word to anyone else. ... Yes, comrade. Long live Comrade Stalin!"

Boyd warned Galyna that the meeting might be a trap, but since the venue was in the British Sector they had a better chance of preventing a kidnapping. He promised to be nearby and told the regular patrols of Royal Military Police positioned at the Brandenburg Gate and Lehrter Station to be on the lookout for the possible kidnapping of a young woman. Boyd also arranged for an RMP Land Rover and driver to wait behind the Lehrter Station. This would bring Galyna back to Gatow after the meeting regardless of the time.

Galyna did not wear uniform and she travelled by public transport from Spandau to Lehrter Station before walking the remaining distance to the rendezvous venue. She was as nervous as the first time she'd met Mila and they had found this sordid and rundown bar. The disreputable clientele had intimidated Galyna, but last time Mila had been armed and unabashedly discouraged unwanted approaches by showing her pistol. Galyna didn't have a sidearm and wouldn't have been able to use it even if she had. As she descended the three steps into the seedy bar, her heart was already racing. She didn't have a good plan for what to do if Mila wasn't there, which seemed probable since they had not set a time.

The air that hit her as she entered was heavy, hot and smoke-filled. Although crowded, Galyna could not spot another woman in the entire joint, while the men who looked back at her showed predatory interest. Galyna searched for an RAF uniform she could cling to, but she couldn't spot any British or American military personnel. All the customers appeared to be Germans or member of the forgotten legion of displaced persons. From a nearby table, the men jocularly signalled for her to join them. "*Komm, Fraulein! Komm! Zahlen gut!*"

Galyna's German was not good, but good enough to understand what that meant! She spun about and started up the stairs again. She couldn't do this.

Someone grabbed her from behind and she started to scream. Instead, a hand came down over her mouth and Mila hissed in her ear. "It's me and

I'm armed."

Galyna hadn't recognised Mila because she wore men's clothes and a peaked cap low over her brow that covered her hair. Face to face with her and feeling her strong embrace, Galyna felt a rush of relief. She flung her arms around her friend in gratitude.

"Come, come," Mila urged, taking her by the hand and leading her to a little table almost behind the stairs. A candle stuck in the mouth of a bottle was half burned down and a beer glass contained a finger of liquid left. Mila had been waiting for a while.

Mila signalled imperatively to the waiter, and he hastened over as if he were afraid of her. The other men had turned away, too. Mila was prominently armed again.

"What do you want to drink?" Mila asked Galyna in Ukrainian.

"Tea," Galyna answered.

"You're sure?" Galyna nodded, and Mila placed the order in German. The waiter bobbed his head and retreated.

The Ukrainians sat down opposite one another, and Mila reached out to take Galyna's hands in both of hers. She looked intently into Galyna's face as she asked, "Are you all right?"

"This place frightens me, that's all. Otherwise, I'm fine." Galyna felt ashamed that she had almost run away. What sort of secret agent would she make if she were afraid of going to a bar alone?

"Look! I've brought you everything I could!" Mila responded, pulling her bulging knapsack onto her lap and unloading it. "Sausage, smoked ham, canned sardines, cheese, condensed milk." As she spoke, she unpacked the items and spread them out on the table.

Galyna gaped at them, confused.

"And here," she ended proudly, "because man does not live by bread alone, some caviar I snitched from Marshal Sokolovsky's last banquet." As she spoke she placed a large glass of caviar on the table. It was the only jar with a label in Cyrillic lettering. All the other goods were American products sent to the Soviet Union during the war.

"Mila! What? Why?" Galyna's eyes swept back and forth.

"You must be starving, Galyna. I know that. I know you would never tell me, but we have all heard that you are getting almost nothing to eat any more."

"Mila!" Galyna gasped out, reaching across the table for her friend's hand. "You are so sweet! So kind! I don't know what to say."

"Don't say anything. Just pack it up. You have a knapsack?"

"Yes, yes, but you don't understand. We aren't starving. Look at me!" She gestured towards her solid figure. "I'm as fat as ever."

Mila paused to look at Galyna, cocking her head to one side, puzzled.

"Seriously," Galyna stressed. "The food is getting boring and almost all of it is dried now — dried potatoes, dried milk, dried eggs — but there is *enough*. At least so far. Or anyway for the occupation forces. That's not why I called you."

"No?" It was Mila's turn to look bewildered.

"No. Something else has happened. Something that has — has —." She stopped herself and took a fresh approach. "You know what happened to my father."

Mila nodded solemnly.

"Now another friend, not a close friend, an acquaintance really, but he's a British officer, Mila, and he disappeared during a sightseeing trip in the Soviet Sector. The official answer is that they don't know where he is but... I don't believe them."

Mila shook her head. "Of course you don't believe them. You shouldn't. They tell lies all the time."

"If we could find out where he is, who is holding him, then we could protest through the proper channels, but as it is..." She ended with a helpless shrug, her gaze fixed on the far side of the room. Turning back to Mila, she added in a softer, tenser voice, "That frightens me, Mila." Although Galyna had planned this appeal, she discovered that she did not have to pretend fear; she was sincerely frightened.

Mila put a reassuring hand over hers. "I understand. This is very dangerous for you." She looked around the bar, saw the waiter bringing Galyna's tea, and sat back in her chair. Galyna followed her lead and they both waited while the waiter placed a tea and a beer in front of them. Galyna hastened to bring some D-marks out of her pocket to pay. Then the waiter retreated again.

"If you don't want me to bring you food, then I think we should find another place to meet. Somewhere less unpleasant, somewhere safer."

"Where?"

"I've been looking at a map. Gatow is very close to Gross-Gleinicke Lake. Do you know it?"

"Yes, it's the closest sandy beach to the airfield. There are even little cabins for changing in. We can reach it by bicycle from Gatow. It is very popular with RAF personnel."

"The other side of the lake is in our Zone, and I'm a strong swimmer. I can swim across the lake if I'm not carrying anything and then we can talk like we used to, just two friends, two sunbathers."

"You'd do that for me?" Galyna asked, touched.

Mila smiled at her. "I've missed you, Galyna, and I'd like the adventure. I'm very bored. When I was a partisan, I was always in danger and always doing something that seemed important — important enough to risk my life. Now, I go to banquets and watch the senior officers gorge themselves and get drunk and rude. Or I go hunting with Grisha and his friends, but Grisha has orders and will be leaving soon. All the good men, the men who fought the war, are being replaced by party hacks, by NKVD stooges. Karlshorst stinks worse and worse. What is your friend's name?"

"Russel. Lt. Col. Graham Russel."

"Is he important?"

"Not really. He's just an engineer. He..." She hesitated but then followed the guidelines Boyd had laid down, "...he built our new runway." The runway, Boyd had told her, was no secret, not now that it was operational. He said he hoped that Russel would have the sense to talk a great deal about the runway to divert attention from plans which were not public knowledge. Boyd had not told her what those plans were.

Mila nodded. "They will want to know where he got the concrete and tar and the construction equipment. No one thought you could complete a runway after the blockade started. Sokolovsky was furious and threw one of his tantrums. He broke some beautiful things and also knocked some heads together, and I think someone was sent home on account of it." She shook her head smiling almost wickedly as she admitted, "I was very amused."

"I don't understand," Galyna admitted.

Mila shrugged. "They are always so smug, so sure of themselves. History is on their side. They will always win. They have all the answers. And then some British colonel builds a runway — which wasn't supposed to be possible — right under their noses. Don't you see how funny that is?"

Galyna wasn't sure. She nodded agreement and admitted, "I understand that it is a little victory, but..." she tried to explain her inability to find the situation funny. "...but I am still too afraid of them to laugh even at their discomfort. I'm afraid of what they will do next — like torture poor Lt. Col. Russel."

Mila sobered up and nodded. "You are right. Because you know him, it is different. He is not just a means to an end. I will see what I can find out, but I suspect they have him in Potsdam, at the NKVD interrogation centre. If I find out anything concrete, I will give you a call with a name and address. I will call you Comrade Nikitin. Andrei Fyodorovich Nikitin, Comrade."

Galyna nodded and smiled tentatively. "Yes, Comrade Levchenkova. I understand. To Comrade Stalin!" She raised her glass, and they clicked them together.

After they finished their drinks, Mila again offered Galyna her packages of food. Galyna took the caviar, salami and ham. She packed them into her knapsack, left the bar, and returned to the Lehrter Station. The RMP Land Rover was waiting for her along with a frazzled Flight Lieutenant Boyd. He seemed very relieved to see her safe and sound.

Chapter Eight
Escalation

Report for Duty
Ypsilanti, Michigan
Thursday, 22 July 1948
(Day 27)

Both of J.B.'s sisters had been invited to a bridal shower hosted by Patty's maid-of-honour in Ann Arbor. The event finished at 4 pm, and J.B. picked his sisters and Patty up to take them to dinner at his mom's. The plan was for him to drive Patty home afterwards.

By the way the girls were chatting and laughing, J.B. gathered that the event had been a success. Settling into the back seat, Barb asked, "Do you have many more showers, Patty?"

"Just two, one next week and one the week after. Then it will be the Big Week itself." Patty sounded jubilant.

"It feels just like the build-up to D-Day," J.B. groused under his breath as he turned the key in the ignition.

Patty leaned forward to switch on the car radio. She turned the dial until she found music she liked and then twisted around to talk to Barb over the back of the seat. They were talking fashion and J.B. tuned them out. The music on the radio had given way to the news. "...General Lucius D Clay arrived in Washington this morning for consultations with President Truman and the Joint Chiefs of Staff. Meanwhile, in Berlin, the situation remains tense, with major pro-Communist demonstrations in the eastern Sector of the city. The American Commandant, Colonel Howley, warned—"

Patty turned the dial in search of music again.

"I was listening to that," J.B. snapped, annoyed. The situation in Berlin interested him. He hoped the Allies weren't going to just back down. His father was outraged over the Soviet annexation of much of Poland and kept saying it was time to teach Stalin a lesson.

"Oh, sorry, honey," Patty replied, and deftly changed the subject by asking, "Don't you want to stop and pick up some flowers for your mom?"

J.B. liked the thought, but his wallet was getting awfully thin these days. "Naw, we don't have time," he told Patty and kept driving. He supposed everything would be OK once he started working, but the wedding and all these pre-wedding events were financially and emotionally draining. J.B. was tired of smiling at everyone, giving a thousand people the same resume of his future job while listening to inane chatter and girls giggling. He wanted to get on with his life.

Just after six, they pulled into the drive of his parents' home. J.B. knew Patty disliked the entire neighbourhood because all the houses looked like trailers and sat on identical little plots of land. She'd be in a hurry to leave tonight — and probably the rest of their lives, too. He sighed in anticipation of lifelong tension between Patty and his parents as he flung the car door open to get out.

His brother Stan burst out of the front door and jumped off the porch without using the steps. "J.B.! You've got a telegram!"

"What?"

"A telegram! It was delivered while you were in Ann Arbor!" Stan shoved it at him.

It was addressed to Captain J.B. Baronowsky, Jr. and J.B.'s heart started pounding. He ripped it open only vaguely aware of Stan, Patty and his mother watching him.

CAPT J B BARONOWSKY JR. TO REPORT ASAP BUT NOT NLT 0800 FRIDAY 23 JULY AT SELFRIDGE AFB FOR IMMEDIATE AND INDEFINITE OVERSEAS DEPLOYMENT STOP ADJ GEN USAF.

"What the f—" he cut himself off just before he offended his mom and Patty. "They can't do this to me!" he protested as he read the text again and again. Yet even as he protested, he knew they *could* and *had* done it to him.

"What is it, J.B.?" Patty asked.

"What does it say?" Stan echoed.

"Jesus Christ!" J.B. swore, and his mother reproached him sharply.

"Mom! You don't understand! These are orders to report to Selfridge Air Force Base by 8 am tomorrow morning."

"For your reserve duty? I thought you couldn't be called up until—"

"They can call me up anytime they please! And it's not reserve duty —
it's an overseas deployment."

Exclamations of disbelief erupted on all sides. Patty snatched the telegram out of his hand to read it for herself. As soon as she'd absorbed the
text, she started protesting hysterically. "This can't be! It's insane! That's
less than 24 hours away! And what do they mean by 'overseas' and 'indefinite'? There *has* to be some mistake!" Patty's tone rose in key and volume
with each sentence. "You have to call someone and get things straightened
out!" she ordered her fiancée. "If you explain to them about our wedding
—"

J.B. cut her off. "The Air Force couldn't care less about my wedding or
my job! If they want Capt. Baronowsky back in uniform and flying some
gosh-darn airplane, then nothing else matters to them."

"But you can't *possibly* go!" Patty wailed.

"You want me to be in jail on our wedding day?" J.B. shot back at her,
then turned away, clenching and unclenching his fists.

"I'm gonna call my dad," Patty declared. "I'm sure he'll know some
way to get you out of this." She ran up the steps and into the Baronowsky
house, brushing past J.B.'s mother.

But Patty's call didn't change anything. Her Dad said he'd "see what
he could do", but nothing could be done before 8 am tomorrow. With
Patty getting increasingly hysterical and venting her anger on everyone
else, Barb agreed to take her home in J.B.'s car so J.B. would have time to
pack. His dad insisted he was well enough to drive him to Selfridge AFB
although it meant getting up at 4 am and leaving the house before dawn.

J.B.'s mom spent most of the night ironing his uniform shirts and
trousers and then got up at 3 to make a batch of chocolate chip cookies that
she wrapped in aluminium foil. In the eerie artificial light of the kitchen,
J.B. hugged her goodbye while his father backed the car out of the garage.
His mother was teary-eyed. "I don't see how they can just yank you out of
the middle of your life and send you overseas when there's not even a war
on. It just doesn't seem right," she complained.

"That's the army way, Mom," J.B. told her with resignation. "Duty
comes first. Things are pretty tense in Europe, and my guess is we're de-
ploying a couple of bomber squadrons to England to remind the Reds we
can hit them if we want. I'll send a cable as soon as I know for sure, but

meanwhile, don't worry too much. This is just sabre-rattling. No one is going to be shooting at me."

His father honked the horn softly and J.B. grabbed his duffle bag and went out the kitchen door. He flung his kit into the back seat and slipped in beside his father. Once they turned onto the highway, the monotony of driving on the near-empty, straight road put J.B. to sleep. He didn't wake up again until his dad shook him. "We're almost there, son."

J. B. sat up. The gate to the base was just a few hundred yards ahead of them. "Thanks for bringing me all the way up here, Dad."

"What choice did I have?" the elder Baronowsky growled. "You'd have been AWOL otherwise, and I don't need a son in jail!" But then he stopped the car and looked over at J.B. as he added, "Glad I could help, Son."

J.B. got out, removed his duffle bag from the back and went around to the driver's side to shake hands with his dad. "No saying how long I'm gonna be gone, Dad, but don't let the newspaper talk of war scare you. We've got the bomb, and the Reds don't. We just need to underline that point by putting some more hardware on the Continent. The Reds aren't so dumb that they're gonna start shooting at us. I expect this will all blow over in a couple of weeks. Bottom line: I don't think there's anything to worry about — except Patty's rage about the wedding being postponed."

His Dad chuckled softly, and J.B. turned towards the gate. As he came abreast of the gatehouse, he received a smart salute, which he returned, and then the sentry asked his business. "Reporting for duty," J.B. answered, handing him the cable.

"Yes, sir! Report right over there!" The sentry pointed to a multi-story brick building. "First floor, second door on your right. You'll find other officers collecting there already."

"Do you have any idea where we're headed?" J.B. asked, keen to scoop up any scuttlebutt he could.

The private grinned. "Yes, sir! Y'all headed for Berlin, flying them big C-54 Skymasters." With his thumb, he indicated the four-engine transports lined up beside the runway.

"But I've never flown one in my life!" J.B. protested.

"That so? Well, I don't write them orders, sir, but between you and me, you aren't the only one. Buddy of mine says they're calling up anyone with four-engine ratings so you can fly those birds across the Atlantic and then down into Germany. Haven't you heard? The Reds have been block-ading Berlin for almost a month now, so it's up to the Air Force to keep the city alive."

J.B. thanked the sentry, his emotions reeling. He'd guessed this had to do with the Berlin Crisis, but he hadn't expected to be sent to Berlin itself, much less in a plane he'd never flown before! Were they crazy?

But as he entered the building, he was surrounded by that unique, distinctive atmosphere of a military base. He stood straighter, lifted his chin a bit and picked up his pace. With bemusement, he realised there was an unmistakable spring in his step, and he was already feeling invigorated. Besides, why not learn to fly the C-54? It was a beauty of a bird, and the civilian version, the DC-4, dominated the airline fleets. As for going to Berlin in the middle of this crisis, that sounded a lot more exciting than another bridal shower!

For a second he felt a twinge of guilt. Patty was one heck of a beautiful and classy gal. He was lucky she'd agreed to have him, but the crisis in Berlin wasn't going to last forever. They had the rest of their lives ahead of them. This airlift gig, on the other hand, was a once-in-a-lifetime adventure. It would feel good to be part of something bigger than himself again —and to do something more important than just make money.

Reunion
Warrington, UK
Friday, 23 July
(Day 28)

The flight engineers' reunion was scheduled to start with dinner at the Patten Arms Hotel in Warrington. Kit arrived early and booked a room for three nights. "Coming for the RAF reunion, then?" the desk clerk asked.

"Yes, although I may have to leave before it's finished," Kit answered, omitting the fact that he had not been invited. He carried Gordon MacDonald's invitation in his pocket, however, and this provided all the scheduling details as well as the names of the two organisers. Pulling it out, he asked whether either of the organisers had arrived yet.

"Yes, sir. Mr Royce Flynn checked in just a few minutes ago. He's in Room 31."

Kit dumped his stuff in his own room and then went to knock at Room 31.

"Just a minute! I'm coming!" a voice called from behind the door, and a moment later a smiling, balding man a head shorter than Kit stood in the door frame. "You've come for the reunion?" he asked cheerfully.

"Well, yes and no. I wanted to speak to you before it starts. I wasn't actually invited, you see. I found out about the reunion from Gordon MacDonald—"

"Oh, I've heard about him. He was two classes behind me, I believe. I heard he'd been badly injured. Broken back, wasn't it?"

"Yes, exactly—"

Thinking he understood what Kit wanted, Flynn jumped in, "But you're a flight engineer, I assume? You look familiar somehow..." He frowned as he tried to place Kit's face in his memories.

"Yes, I flew a full tour as a flight engineer before —"

"What did you say your name was? Not that it matters. We're happy to have you join us. How about going down to the bar and chatting over a drink? The others will be trickling in over the next couple of hours."

"Yes, good idea," Kit agreed. Together they went down to the hotel lounge bar just off the lobby. They ordered and settled at a small table for two. Once they were comfortable, Kit introduced himself. "The name's Moran, Christopher Moran, but people call me Kit."

"Funny! The name rings a bell. We must have met during the war. What squadron did you fly on?"

"I completed a tour with 626 and then went to Witchford as an instructor, before joining 103—."

Flynn's jaw dropped, and Kit braced himself. Flynn burst out, "You're the flight engineer who refused to fly an op to Berlin! You stood up in the briefing, told the Station and Base Commanders to do something very rude and walked out. Crikey!" The man was staring at him with wide, shocked and confused eyes.

"Before you give me a lecture about being a lily-livered coward and not having the right to mingle with aircrew who didn't lack moral courage," Kit kept his voice low and steady, yet forceful just the same, "I was not discharged, I was not court-martialled, I was not sent to clean latrines or work in the mortuary. On the contrary, I was sent for flight training, qualified on Lancasters, and flew with 617 Squadron. And I have my logbook with me to prove it, if you don't believe me."

Flynn's eyes had grown larger by the second, and as Kit finished he opened his mouth, closed it, and then opened it again to say, "I'm sorry that you expected an insulting tirade from me, Moran. That is not — none of it — what I intended to say. Frankly, I was awed by your courage. I was very new to the squadron. I think I'd flown just three ops and one had been to Berlin and I was scared stiff of going back. I remember wishing I'd had the courage to do what you'd done. All we sprogs looked up to Selkirk's crew, and when you failed to return it made us all the more apprehensive. We didn't know you'd survived until you walked into the briefing, and there wasn't one of us who didn't sympathise with you. I thought they were bloody bastards to order you to fly with a new crew less than 24 hours after your skipper got the chop."

Kit felt the tension ease away. "Thank you. I'm sorry I jumped to conclusions."

"No, you must have faced a lot of, well, unpleasantness. I just don't understand how you could avoid all the punishments, the court martial and all that."

"It's quite simple. Although, after what I'd done and said, the CO wanted me off his squadron at once, I could not be officially designated 'lacking moral fibre' until an RAF psychiatrist made a diagnosis to that effect. I was sent to a diagnostic centre where the attending psychiatrist concluded I was not suffering from mental illness and should return to active duty. I was given the option of returning to operations or ground duties. I chose operations, and the senior RAF medical officer made the recommendation for flight training."

"That's astonishing," Flynn still seemed quite perplexed. "I've never heard of anyone who was posted for LMF being given a chance to learn to fly."

Kit smiled faintly, "No, because we *never* heard what happened to those who were thrown off the squadron — just like you never knew what happened to me. We simply speculated and spread rumours."

"I suppose you're right," Flynn conceded.

Kit tried to explain. "It was the opinion of the RAF orderlies at the station where we made our emergency landing that Selkirk had been dead for hours. They assumed that I had been at the controls of the damaged Lancaster, which suggested to the powers-that-be that I was pilot material."

"How extraordinary," Flynn murmured, still sounding dazed. Kit concluded that Flynn needed to digest what he had learnt and sipped his beer in silence. At last, Flynn asked, puzzled, "But if you've commanded a Lancaster, let alone one on 617, why are you interested in attending a lowly flight engineers' reunion?"

"First, having flown more ops as a flight engineer than a pilot, I don't think of engineers as 'lowly'. Secondly, I didn't come strictly to attend the reunion, but rather to recruit a flight engineer. You see, I'm putting together a crew for a civilian company that wants to fly freighters on the Berlin Airlift."

"Oh! How exciting! I didn't know there were civilian carriers on the Airlift."

"As far as I know there aren't any yet, but the RAF has invited interested companies to apply for contracts. They must have suitable aircraft and qualified aircrew."

"Oh, now I understand," Flynn smiled. Despite his earlier sympathy, he appeared relieved to discover that Kit didn't have his heart set on crashing the party.

"How would you like to handle my request? Should I join one of your events and explain what I'm looking for?" Kit asked, adding before Flynn had a chance to answer, "Alternatively, you could make an announcement and inform the attendees that I'm here and would like to hear from anyone who is interested."

"I think the latter would work better," Flynn agreed. "There are quite a few engineers from 103 Squadron coming, and there's no way of knowing how they'll react to your unexpected appearance in our midst."

"Fair enough," Kit agreed.

After placing a quick call to Georgina to keep her informed of progress, Kit went for a stroll. He stopped for fish and chips before returning to the hotel at around 9 pm. As he passed the dining room, he looked in discreetly. It was easy to identify the reunion participants at a long table, and although Kit couldn't see them all, most appeared to be in RAF, BEA, or BOAC uniforms. Not very promising. Men with steady jobs weren't going to give them up for something as uncertain as this.

Kit retreated to the lounge bar, which was now awash with Americans. They were here in force because the RAF had turned nearby Burtonwood airfield over to the USAF as a maintenance base for US aircraft flying the Airlift. There wasn't a table free, so he sat at the bar and ordered a gin and tonic. His perch enabled him to look out of the door at the lobby. Not long afterwards, he saw a stream of men calling their good nights to one another as they spilled out of the hotel restaurant. Now would be the time for someone interested in a job to stop by and talk to him.

No one did.

Playing with his gin and tonic more than drinking it, Kit started to picture what had happened. Flynn had probably told the others the whole story, meaning well, but putting others off. Or maybe Flynn *hadn't* tried to explain things but had simply given Kit's name and one of the others from 103 Squadron had put two and two together, leading to a whisper campaign. The upshot was that no one wanted anything to do with someone who had been labelled LMF, no matter how briefly.

Kit glanced at his watch. It was nearing 11 pm. The lobby was quiet and dark, and even the lounge was gradually emptying as some of the Americans started to leave. Kit was thinking about turning in for the night when a young West Indian gentleman entered. He was smartly dressed in a starched, white shirt, well-fitted suit, and highly polished shoes. He carried the kind of fat briefcase that travelling salesmen used for carrying samples of their wares. Kit wondered what he sold and where he hailed from. Suddenly, one of the Americans shouted over to the bartender. "What's that n***** doing in here? I thought this was a decent place." The elderly man behind the bar stiffened and looked over in alarm. "You serve that n***** in here and we leave!" the American threatened. There were about six men in his party.

Without a word of protest, the West Indian turned on his heel and walked back out of the lounge. Kit sprang to his feet and followed him, catching sight of him as he exited onto the street. Kit hurried after him, afraid he'd disappear in the dark outside. He was relieved to find him standing on the curb looking across the street as though he was unsure where to go. Kit stopped beside him and asked, "Smoke?"

West Indian looked over, startled, then smiled mildly and replied, "Thank you."

Kit took out a packet of cigarettes while the salesman put his bag down on the curb. They each took a cigarette and Kit struck a match for them both. They inhaled in silence. Only after they had exhaled did Kit ask, "Why did you leave? You had as much right to be in there as those Yanks."

"I know, but there were a lot of them, and they were itching for a fight. Why wreck a nice hotel and harm a decent man's business?" He paused, looked at Kit with his gentle smile and intelligent-but-sharp eyes and added, "The more interesting question is, why did *you* leave?"

"Because I would have choked if I had to breathe the same air as those racist bastards." After that outburst, Kit felt he was obliged to explain. "My grandmother was Zulu. In South Africa I'm categorised — and treated — as coloured."

"You wouldn't be the pilot they called 'Zulu Moran,' would you?"

"Where on earth did you hear that?" Kit asked back aghast. It was bad enough running into someone who knew about him being kicked off 103 Squadron for lacking moral fibre, but the name Zulu Moran had been known only among members of 617 Squadron.

"I was on No 9 Squadron the last six months of the war, and as you may remember, we flew several joint operations with 617. The orders of battle listed all the aircraft of both squadrons by call sign and pilot. I was intrigued when someone referred to you as 'Zulu Moran.'" He paused and looked harder at Kit. "And you must be the same Mr Moran who Royce Flynn says is looking for a flight engineer to fly the Airlift?"

"Yes, that's right. Are you a flight engineer?" Kit asked back, astonished.

Now the other man held out his hand. "My name's Richard Scott-Ross. I came into the lounge looking for you, and I'd very much like to know more about that job." As they shook hands, he explained, "I went up to my room to get my logbook and got side-tracked by some of my former colleagues who were carrying on upstairs, or I would have dropped in earlier."

"Let's go back into the lobby and sit down," Kit suggested. Scott-Ross readily agreed, and they returned inside.

"Are you West Indian?" Kit asked.

"Yes, Trinidad. Do you know it?"

Kit shook his head. "No, you just didn't sound African."

They found two comfortable seats beside a coffee table as the noisy crowd of Americans departed without noticing them. Scott-Ross was intent on capturing Kit's interest in his qualifications and opened with, "I flew a total of 43 ops as a flight engineer with two squadrons. I can show you my logs—"

"The whole time on Lancasters?"

"No, I was first on 640 Squadron, which had the Halifax."

"Excellent! The company we would be working for is considering Tudors, Lancasters or Halifaxes. Since I've only crewed on Lancasters, it would be an asset to have a flight engineer with Halifax experience. What have you been doing since the war?"

"I'm a salesman. I represent a firm selling aviation sparkplugs."

"Now I know why you want to fly the Airlift," Kit quipped, perplexing Scott-Ross. Ashamed of himself, Kit apologised at once, "I'm sorry. Bad joke. It's just that I could never be a salesman." Resuming a professional tone, he added, "You understand that a job on the Airlift can only be temporary and could end at any time."

"Yes. I understand," Scott-Ross assured him seriously.

"And you still want it?"

"Very much."

"When could you start?"

"Don't you want to see my resume and references?" Scott-Ross asked back, baffled, pointing to his briefcase.

"In the war," Kit reminded him, "we never looked at resumes, references, or logbooks. We just chatted for a few minutes and either clicked or didn't. The men I crewed with were the finest men I've ever known. If you'll have me as your pilot, I'd be delighted to have you as my flight engineer."

Scott-Ross smiled broadly for the first time. "It would be my pleasure, Mr Moran! — Or should that be Zulu?"

"My friends call me Kit," he answered and nodded towards the bar. "Let's drink to a long and productive partnership!"

The Inevitable
RAF Gatow
Sunday, 25 July 1948
(Day 30)

When the alarm went off in what seemed like the middle of the night, Kathleen knew it was going to be a bad day. The cloud was so thick and low that the sun penetrated only weakly, and rain showers rattled the windows. On a day like this, Hope would not be able to "help out" at the stables. She'd be confined indoors at the daycare centre and would be bad-tempered. Meanwhile, the poor weather put an extra strain on the controllers.

Kathleen dropped a sullen Hope at daycare and cycled through puddles to the tower. As she entered, she heard a chorus of voices over the radio counting "...two...three...four" and was momentarily confused. Then she realised that a Dakota was bouncing its way down the runway after landing too hard — and was receiving "friendly" commentary from the pilots awaiting take-off. Welcome to the Airlift!

Someone quipped over the radio, "I say, Danny Boy, have you thought of taking up basketball?" Laughter filled the entire tower.

Kathleen shook out her raingear and hung it beside the other wet coats near the exit to the stairs. As she took over her station, her predecessor identified the incoming traffic she would be handling. They had long ago abandoned squadron call signs and IDs in favour of aircraft numbers. The Air Movement Assistants could quickly check the type of aircraft and squadron of any aircraft by its number. The only distinction was made between RAF flights (Rafair) and British European Airlines (Bealiner).

"That's Rafair 314. He's next."

Kathleen clicked on the radio, "Rafair 314, this is Gatow control. Confirm you are crossing Frohnau?"

"Affirmative. Looks very murky from up here."

"It looks worse from down here. What is your cargo?"

"Ten thousand bottles of gin."

"You're joking!" The comment did not come from Kathleen but from another pilot listening in on the frequency.

"Look, 314, that gin is not yours to break, you understand? It is our collective property."

"In the best communist tradition, comrade."

Although the commentary didn't stop, Kathleen mentally filtered it out and concentrated on bringing the aircraft in safely: "314 ease more to port and flatten your descent... Glide path still too steep... That's better. You are sideslipping to starboard now, correct to port... Good. Hold course, speed and rate of descent."

Half an hour later, the ceiling dropped to just 100 feet, which meant the pilots were flying blind until seconds before touchdown. This made them utterly dependent on the controllers, and pilots didn't like that. The pressure on the controllers increased commensurately.

Kathleen checked with the Air Movements Assistant whether the air ambulance was scheduled to fly in this morning. Much as she admired what AAI was doing, the ambulance inherently required extra attention. First of all, it was a Wellington, which meant it was given a different cruising altitude and speed. Second, it had to park near the sick quarters, not at one of the unloading hardstandings. Finally, on departure, it was given precedence, which disrupted the normal flow of traffic, both on the taxiways and on the runway. On a day like today, it would be a particular burden. Fortunately, it had already departed with its first load of patients and would not be back for several hours. By then, fingers crossed, the weather might have lifted a little.

Kathleen had only been at her radar station about twenty minutes when a pilot called in, identifying himself as Rafair 198, and adding, "Gatow control, just so you know, this is my first approach."

"Well," Kathleen quipped back, "you certainly picked a fine day for it!"

"Wouldn't you know? It's my birthday too."

"Many Happy Returns," she wished him cheerfully.

"A return to Berlin was the *one* thing I fervently wished I would *never* have *last* time I was here."

"I can imagine, but it's changed a bit — thanks to you and your friends."

Several aircraft later, a pilot broke into the monotony with a loud "Crikey! There is water below me! I thought Berlin was landlocked."

"You're over the Havel."

"Are you sure? It looks like the North Sea to me."

"It's a lot smaller and warmer."

"Is it water all the way to Gatow from here? There aren't any tall obstacles — Crikey!"

Another voice commented dryly, "Just got a glimpse of Kaiser Bill's bones," meaning the Kaiser Wilhelm Tower that reared up more than 150 feet directly beside the Havel.

Squadron Leader Garth came to stand behind Kathleen for a few moments and remarked in a calm voice, "We'll swap controllers on the hour." The watch system they had instituted after the completion of the concrete runway entailed two radar controllers on at all times, one for each runway. However, because talking the aircraft down for landings was more stressful than controlling take-off, the controllers usually switched runways after two hours. Garth's comment meant the swap would come after just one hour. Just as well, Kathleen thought as the rain thundered on the roof overhead, all but drowning out the radio transmissions.

Beside her "Willie" Wilkins on the master radar started visibly and exclaimed, "What the devil...?"

Kathleen glanced over at him. He was frowning and leaning in towards the screen while trying to fiddle with some of the settings. His radar provided a complete picture of Berlin airspace, not just the approach paths to Gatow. The rain squall appeared to have disrupted the transmissions.

She was glad her own set was working without any trouble as she concentrated on another block of eight Yorks.

Willie called out to the Assistant Flying Control Officer, "Flight Lieutenant Mitchell? Could you come here for a moment?"

Kathleen tried to ignore what was going on beside her. She had a pilot with a thick Welsh accent that she found difficult to understand and, assuming the problem was reciprocal, she made an effort to enunciate precisely. "A little more to starboard... Good... Maintain course and speed but increase your rate of descent by another fifty feet per minute... That's good. Glide path now excellent."

"I had an aircraft right here," Willie explained as Mitchell looked over his shoulder. "And it's gone. Just gone. More than two miles out from Tempelhof."

Kathleen forced herself not to listen to the continued exchange. She concentrated on her job. She spoke over the R/T, "Rafair 268, you should be breaking clear of cloud any moment."

His answer was drowned out by a voice calling from the tower. "Sir! Tempelhof is reporting an aircraft down!"

Kathleen rigidly maintained concentration until Rafair 268 was safely down. Then she looked up and to her left. Garth had joined Mitchell and Willie. Together they blocked her view of the screen, but from behind her someone reported, "Tempelhof is saying an inbound USAF C-47 with a load of flour went down in Friedenau, sir. Handjerystrasse 2."

"Good God! That's a residential quarter, isn't it?" Garth exclaimed, looking up and over his shoulder.

"Nothing but five-storey blocks of flats," Mitchell muttered in response.

"Better inform the CO. God knows how the Berliners will react to this," Garth ordered.

While Mitchell moved towards a telephone, Kathleen, with no in-bound traffic for another five minutes, stood and went into the main room of the tower. It offered a gloomy vista in shades of grey from the low cloud to the wet pavement and the waiting aircraft. Everything continued with surreal normality. There were no sirens, no flashing lights, no one was running about. The aircraft stood at hardstandings or oozed along the taxiways.

Yet she sensed something more. Out there, all around them, were crashed aircraft. The bones of the 5% lost on every raid to Berlin. Ken's Lancaster was among them. He'd gone down into the fiery inferno he had helped ignite, and his body along with those of his crewmates had been completely consumed.

Yet his spirit still haunted the mists. She sensed his presence at odd moments, particularly in weather like this. Sometimes she had the feeling that he wanted to tell her something. Today was different. Today they had simply gathered to welcome new colleagues to their macabre club. She shuddered.

False Friends
Berlin-Friedenau
Monday, 26 July
(Day 31)

Jakob Liebherr joined the delegation from the city government that went to the crash site in the Handjerystrasse. The play was to lay a wreath and speak to the inhabitants of the neighbourhood. As he stepped out of his car, he was reminded of the war. There was shattered masonry and debris everywhere. The tail section of the plane stuck out of a building, tilting to one side like a dead beast and smoke had blackened all the surrounding façades. He'd been told the aircraft and its cargo of flour had burned for hours.

Colonel Howley had called Mayor Reuter to express his condolences. He speculated that the pilot's instruments had been defective, causing him to descend too soon. Liebherr remembered reading somewhere that aircraft altimeters required the correct barometric pressure to work properly. To his old ears, that sounded like something that could easily go wrong.

Eyewitnesses reported that the aircraft's wheels had clipped the roof of the building opposite, causing it to nose-dive into the street. The forward momentum had flung it through the apartment house at ground level with enough force to bash its way almost out the other side before coming to rest and bursting into flames. Fortunately, although two balconies on the facade fell off, the floors above had not collapsed. As a result, there had been no fatalities among the residents. Three of the tenants were seriously but not mortally injured, and another six had been treated for broken bones, abrasions, and smoke inhalation. The two pilots had been killed instantly, of course, and the police had removed their bodies, or what was left of them.

The street was cordoned off by the police and the city officials picked their way across the rubble. The adults stood about gawking, while schoolboys searched for souvenirs. Louisa Schroeder, the deputy mayor, laid the wreath beside the wreckage of the tail. The ribbon read: "They died that we might live in freedom."

Afterwards, the SPD politicians spread out to talk to the people standing about mutely nearby. After about half an hour, the city council members climbed back into their car and returned to the nearby Rathaus Schoeneberg. Mayor Reuter had had his office here since the Soviets denied him access to the official rooms of the governing mayor, which were in the "*Rote Rathaus*" located in the Soviet Sector. The delegation went to report to Reuter.

The mayor was on the phone when they arrived, but he gestured for them to sit down. He said "yes, yes," into the phone several times and then hung up. Turning to his visitors, he asked simply, "And?"

Louisa answered for all of them. "Everyone's very calm. They knew this would happen eventually. They accept it is the price of an Airlift."

"No anger? No demands for an immediate end to the flights?"

They all shook their heads.

"You wouldn't know that from reading the newspapers," Reuter told them. Looking at his desk, he picked up one Soviet-controlled newspaper after another, reading off the headlines: "'Terror bomber slaughters sleeping civilians,' 'Berliners must again fear death from the sky,' 'Americans allege only three 'injured' in devastated apartment block. How dumb do they think we are?' And here's the best: 'Outraged Berliners demand end to Western air terror.'"

"My son used the same language," Jakob conceded with a deep sigh.

"How did you answer him?" Louisa Schroeder asked softly. As a close friend of the Liebherrs, she had known Karl since he was a little boy.

"I told him that with almost 30,000 kidnappings on the Soviet account, the Anglo-Americans could afford another 29,997 Airlift deaths before they drew even."

"Which reminds me," Reuter replied, "last night, Markgraf's men were again met with armed resistance while attempting to drag a man from his apartment. It was the final straw. I decided we could not risk any further escalation and sent Markgraf a letter suspending him from duty." Reuter was looking rather pleased with himself, like the cat with the canary. However, his announcement left the others speechless.

Schroeder found her voice first, "But only the Allied Kommandatura, jointly and unanimously, can dismiss Markgraf."

"True, but it occurred to me in the middle of the night that while we can't *dismiss* him, nothing says we can't *suspend* him from his duties. Which is all I've done, pending an investigation into allegations of disloyal and undemocratic conduct. Because Stumm is already his deputy, he automatically takes over the police force without the need for referring the matter to the Kommandatura."

That sounded like hair-splitting to Liebherr. Furthermore, while he sympathised with Reuter's desire to confront the situation, he reminded the mayor, "Markgraf has been systematically purging genuine police from the ranks of the police force ever since he took over. He's replaced hundreds of trained policemen with men of dubious origins — including men accused of war crimes. They're completely loyal to Markgraf because he's the only thing keeping them out of prison. They aren't suddenly going to start taking orders from Stumm."

"No, but now that Stumm is acting Chief of Police, he has the authority to dismiss anyone who refuses his orders, and anyone he dismisses needs to be replaced. We've been collecting the names of reliable, democratic volunteers for weeks," Reuter reminded him.

"Yes, but if Markgraf refuses to go and continues to give orders to his men, while Stumm hires new men, we'll end up with two competing police forces," Schroeder warned.

"Better that than one police force that is *not* loyal to the rule of law — not to mention us," Reuter countered, before changing the subject, "There is something else you need to know."

The others looked at him expectantly. "Without giving us any advance notice, the SMAD has announced that effective 1 August people — regardless of place of residence — can draw Soviet rations by registering for them. That means, without having to pack up and move to the East, residents from the Western Sectors of Berlin can obtain Soviet food allocations."

"What on earth do they hope to gain by that?" Schroeder asked. "If people rush to register, the Western Allies will have fewer mouths to feed, and the Soviets will have more. And didn't I hear that they had no meat in their Sector as it is?"

"Correct. There is also a shortage of grain across the entire Soviet Union, throughout Soviet-occupied Eastern Europe and the Soviet Zone of Germany," Reuter reminded them. "Soviet rations were notoriously bad and unpredictable before the blockade, and — thanks to the astonishing and dedicated efficiency of our colleagues in charge of — the distribution of Airlift goods has been remarkably efficient. Citizens still get their rations at the familiar distribution points, but now they can also file requests for other goods as well. We've had very positive feedback on the way things are working so far."

The others nodded their agreement. Across the city, the distribution of goods flown in by the Airlift appeared to be working like a well-oiled machine.

Reuter continued, "Soviet motives for this move are not humanitarian. They couldn't care less about people getting food or they wouldn't have started this blockade in the first place. The sole motive for this announcement is to humiliate the Western Allies by creating the *appearance* of people rushing to the East for 'a better life.'"

"I doubt the Berliners are going to embrace the Ivans for promises of more food," Schroeder scoffed.

"Maybe not, but the Soviets do have fresh milk, which the Allies cannot provide, and they also have some fresh fruit and vegetables to distribute," Reuter pointed out. "Some people will undoubtedly be tempted."

"I think we need to look beyond the sheer optics of this move," Liebherr warned. "Anyone who wants Soviet rations must go to the SMAD distribution points to receive those rations. That means they will have to show their ID, and their names and addresses will be recorded. The next thing they know, their new friends will be demanding gestures of 'thankfulness' and 'appreciation' in return. Which, if not forthcoming, will provoke admonishments and threats. Meanwhile, the SED has identified possible collaborators all across the city, people who will feel forced to do their bidding when the time comes. These actions, just like Markgraf's purge of the police force, suggest the SED is preparing a coup d'etat."

Schroeder quipped cynically, "So what else is new?"

Reuter, on the other hand, suggested, "I'd call it Plan B. Stalin expects the Airlift to collapse and the Berliners to appeal voluntarily and spontaneously to their 'Socialist brothers' for aid. But if for some reason that fails to happen, his second option is to stage a 'popular uprising' of his own. One way or another, they intend to destroy democratic government in this city — whether the Western Allies leave or not."

Chapter Nine
Adjusting to Reality

Worse than War
Michigan to Frankfurt
Tuesday, 27 July 1948
(Day 32)

One week after he'd been called up, USAF Captain J.B. Baronowsky was on his way to Frankfurt am Main, Germany. The voyage originated at Selfridge AFB in Michigan and proceeded via refuelling and refreshment stops in Presque Isle, Maine; Goosebay, Laborador; Bluie West 1 on Greenland; and Meeksfield, Iceland. Throughout that four-day trip, J.B. had been copilot, and for the former B-17 captain and 27-year-old university graduate, taking orders from a "kid" five years younger had been galling. J.B. understood the logic of it. He'd never flown a C-54 cargo plane until he'd been recalled to active duty. Jimmy Hudson, on the other hand, was a regular Air Force pilot, and he'd trained and qualified on the C-54. So, although Hudson was a first lieutenant and J.B. a captain in the reserves, Hudson was in command of the aircraft. It wasn't until they were flying from Ireland to their last transit stop in Burtonwood, England that Hudson entrusted J.B. with a take-off.

With J.B. at the controls at last, they had lifted off from Meeksfield shortly after 1:40 am. As the undercarriage clunked into position under his feet, Hudson announced, "That wasn't bad for a rookie. Think you can fly her straight and level for the next couple of hours while I get some shuteye?"

"Sure. I might be able to manage that," J.B. answered, working hard to keep the resentment out of his voice.

Hudson laid his head back, pulled his peaked cap down so it shielded his face and was snoring almost at once.

Without Hudson's nagging and commentary, J.B. discovered he rather liked the C-54. It handled easier than the B-17, seemed smoother on the controls and quieter. It also had a terrific view from the cockpit. He could see icebergs scattered on the black sea below him, and overhead the dome of stars was as perfect as a planetarium. J.B. looked for the various constellations and marvelled at how sharply they stood out in the night sky. He dropped his eyes to scan the instruments, but all were in the green. The engines hummed more than growled and Hudson's soft snoring blended into the mechanical song. It was utterly surreal.

J.B. shook his head to try to wake from the dream. Surely he wasn't flying at 15,000 feet towards the continent of Europe? It couldn't be. He was supposed to be getting married in a couple of weeks to a classy girl and starting work in a prize, well-paying job that would take him to the top of Detroit society.

Instead of all that, he was back in uniform, back in a cockpit, and back in Europe and heading back for Berlin!

God how he'd hated Berlin! Whenever he'd seen the red line of yarn stretching across almost the whole of the Continent, bending around (ha, ha!) the flak concentrations on the coast and the Ruhr or trying to weave down the Kattegat, his stomach tied itself in knots. Nowhere else had the same concentration of flak as Berlin, and fighters swarmed like gnats.

And yet, in spite of everything, J.B. had to admit to himself that he was enjoying this. He liked flying — when no one was shooting at him. Flying cargo sounded boring, yet it also meant he wouldn't have the stress of flying in close formation. This was such a great opportunity to fly a first-class aircraft and even maybe see a little of Europe from the ground while he was at it.

He checked the instrument dials, adjusted the fuel mixture a little and throttled forward slightly to increase airspeed. He reached for the clipboard with the fight plan that leaned against the base of his seat and checked the time of the next course change against his watch. Still, quite a way to go. Very gently he pressed first one foot and then the other on the rudder bar, just to feel how responsive the "Skymaster" was to his commands. Then more playfully he lifted one wing and then the other as he started to weave lazily across the sky to the sound of a waltz playing in his head.

"Everything OK up there, sir?" the question broke over his earphones from Technical Sergeant Wells, the flight engineer and third man on the crew. Since Wells was a sergeant, they didn't mingle off-duty, and with his station farther back in the fuselage, J.B. didn't have much opportunity to get to know him. He was practically a stranger.

"Just testing the controls to stay awake," J.B. assured the sergeant and settled down to flying straight and level again. Yet the joy of flying didn't go away.

Gradually, he noticed the Eastern horizon was lightening, draining the sharpness from the stars. With a start, he realised the Scottish coast was visible. Feathery breakers left streaks of dissolving white on the black surface of the sea, while the solid black of the landmass was outlined by tiny but brilliant lights that appeared and disappeared at regular but unsyncopated intervals: lighthouses. J.B. briefly wondered if he should wake Hudson, but decided against it. He was sleeping so peacefully, and J.B. was so much happier with him out cold.

Continuing inland, he noticed tiny, mellow lights scattered across the countryside and J.B. felt a different thrill. All his previous flights over the UK had been when a blackout was in effect. The sight of headlights from a car or a farmhouse exuding warm light as a farmer rose to milk his cows was elating. It encapsulated victory. The lights had gone on again — all over the world. It sent a chill of pride down his spine.

When they landed at Burtonwood to refuel, they learned that bad weather had closed Rhein-Main. They ended up spending two days there before resuming their flight on Thursday 29 July. As they lifted off in drizzling rain with visibility of less than a mile, memories again flooded J.B.'s senses. How often had he taken off in murk like this and spent nearly an hour droning around blind while hundreds of bombers took off from their grim wartime bases to collect in a huge, unwieldy gaggle? He'd hated flying circles in the fog, never seeing more than another shadow or a wingtip or tail too close for comfort.

At least today they were on their own. They climbed steadily to 14,000 feet and broke into bright summer sunshine. It was breathtaking. Soon the cockpit was as hot as a greenhouse. They stripped off their flight jackets and flew in their shirtsleeves. Jimmy Hudson was in a good mood for once. Sleep, showers and a party that included some good-looking girls the night before had cheered him up.

"So, you've been over here before, huh, Jay?" Jimmy asked conversationally.

"It's J.B. and yeah, I flew over the North Sea quite a lot."

"Doesn't look any different from the Great Lakes to me," Jimmy commented, peering down as the cloud cover started to tear apart and disintegrate.

"Not at the moment," J.B. conceded.

Later, when they made landfall, Jimmy asked, "Is that Germany?"

"No, Holland. You filed the flight plan, for God's sake," J.B. reminded him, but Jimmy just shrugged and popped another stick of Wriggley's gum into his mouth. J.B. concentrated on looking for recognizable landmarks and soon he found the distinctive line of offshore islands and the large inland lakes. The memories hovered around him like puffs of spent flak.

They turned south, picking up the radio beacons of Muenster, Hamm, Marburg, Glessen... A regular nostalgia trip, J.B. thought, shaking his head. Then he tuned their radio onto the frequency for Rhein-Main and all his memories shattered. Instead of strict radio silence punctuated by terse orders or reports, his ears were flooded with a jumble of voices coming over his earphones. It sounded like Grand Central Station at rush hour. Calls were coming in from what seemed like a dozen aircraft.

It took them five minutes just to get a response from Air Traffic Control, which then ordered them into a "holding pattern." Now they *were* circling around like those gaggles he'd hated so much in the war, but at least visibility was good. They could see a score of other planes lazily drawing large circles in the sky like a giant mobile suspended from heaven. Forty minutes passed before it was their turn to land.

As their wheels touched down with a loud squeal, the air traffic controller barked through the earphones. "534, clear the runway as rapidly as possible. Report to operations ASAP."

Well, that was a nice welcome, J.B. thought sarcastically as his eyes scanned the scene around them. There were planes everywhere, which at first reminded him of an operational base preparing for a "maximum effort" mission. Then, too, one would have seen four-engine aircraft in front of hangars with the cowlings open for maintenance. Others would have been taxiing to and from flight tests, while most would have been at their various dispersal points awaiting their fuel and cargo — the bombs dragged out to them on trailers. This felt different.

J.B. was struck by the large number of men in ragged civilian clothing unloading stuff from freight cars lined up directly beside the field. The stevedores worked energetically, transferring dirty sacks of coal from the train cars to wheeled flatbeds. The latter were hauled away as soon as they were full and replaced by empties. Like mechanical caterpillars, the tractors dragging two or three flatbeds crawled towards the waiting Skymasters. Here more ragged men set to work manhandling the coal sacks into the bellies of the planes.

Jimmy broke in on J.B.'s thoughts, exclaiming irritably, "Where the hell are we supposed to go?" There didn't seem to be any follow-me jeep to receive them and they felt lost in the chaos. Another big difference to flying in the war, J.B. reflected. There had never been a feeling of chaos. There had been plenty of emergencies when the birds came home dragging broken wings, or smashed themselves on landing because the gear wouldn't come down, or the pilot was shot up, but these only triggered efficient procedures for clearing the wounded and the wrecks out of the way.

"Call into control and ask for instructions," Jimmy ordered.

J.B. took the mic. "Rhein-Main. This is 534. We don't have a follow-me jeep. Where do you want us to go?"

After a moment, a harried voice replied, "The jeep should be there. Look harder."

J.B. would have liked to say something rude back, but just then Jimmy spotted a jeep darting out from between two planes and bouncing so hard as it hit the taxiway that they could see daylight between the driver and the seat. It pirouetted in front of them on the taxiway and, sure enough, it had a follow-me sign on its tailgate.

They docilely followed it to a recently vacated spot beside the taxiway. As they left the tarmac, the nose wheel sank into thick mud, and they wallowed as their wing wheels dug in unevenly while turning around. J.B. was happy that Jimmy was at the controls as he would have had trouble handling the unfamiliar bird in these conditions. As Jimmy cut the engines, he and J.B. exchanged a look of "What-the-hell-have-we-gotten-ourselves-into."

Sergeant Wells let down the ramp in the tail, and J.B. was the first out of the aircraft. Before he had a chance to look around, a harassed-looking lieutenant without wings on his breast came up with a clipboard. "534? Hudson, Baronowsky and Wells?"

"That's right."

"OK, follow me."

"Can we get our duffle bags first?" J.B. asked back, put off by the lieutenant's tone. Yes, this was the Army — or rather Air Force — but surely saying "Hello" or "Welcome to Rhein-Main" wouldn't have been a breach of military protocol?

"Hurry up," came the answer. "We'll be loading this bird and sending her to Berlin in the next hour."

"What about a maintenance check?" J.B. reminded him.

"Is there something wrong with her?"

"No, she's pretty new, but we did notice —"

The Lieutenant waved his objection aside. "Unless it's something that's gonna make her crash, it doesn't matter."

The three newcomers exchanged a look of disbelief. They might not know each other very well, but this casual attitude united them in a feeling of disapproval.

"What are you waiting for?" the lieutenant asked. Shaking their heads in silent disbelief, they collected their duffle bags, shouldered them, and followed their unfriendly guide. As they started towards the brick operations building, J.B. noticed one of the German loaders sweeping spilt flour into a dustpan in the wake of a C-47 that was waddling its way onto the taxiway. Another German held open an old, discarded sack and the first man emptied the flour dust into the sack. They then tied it with a piece of twine before running to jump aboard a trailer headed back in the direction of the railhead.

Was it possible the Germans were sweeping up dirty flour dust because they didn't have enough to eat? That seemed incredible. Then again, they'd damn-near starved half of Europe, so maybe being hungry themselves was the best way to teach them not to try world conquest again. And yet he found the idea unsettling in some way.

In the main admin building, the newly arrived crew was taken to an office where they had to sign some paperwork before being handed over to a sergeant who announced that since all the accommodations on the base were already occupied, they had a choice between some tents or some tar-paper shacks on the other side of the Autobahn. "I hate tents," Jimmy announced without giving J.B. or Wells a chance to comment. They were led to an exit where a weapons carrier waited. "That's the shuttle to the Zeppelinheim," their guide said.

"Looks great," Jimmy muttered sarcastically.

They dragged their duffle bags over to the weapons carrier, and the snoozing driver sat up. "Zeppelinheim?"

"Do we have a choice?" J.B. asked back.

The private grinned at him. "Not really, Captain."

They climbed in and bounced their way out of the airbase and onto a flimsy-looking improvised bridge over one of Germany's famous Autobahns. To J.B.'s disappointment, the autobahn was empty and unimpressive. The roads in Michigan looked just as good.

On the far side, the weapons carrier turned to enter a gap in a double, chain-link fence topped with barbed wire. Here they found themselves in a huge compound that consisted of rows and rows of tar-paper shacks. Christ, he thought, this place looked like the photos he'd seen of Nazi camps — not the death camps, but POW camps and slave labourer camps.

"What is this place?" he asked the driver.

"Aw, I don't know. We had to evict a bunch of foreigners. Looked like a bunch of hobos to me. All grimy and unshaven with mismatched clothes and clogs rather than shoes. All thin as sticks, too."

"We evicted people?" J.B. remembered reading somewhere that there were millions of displaced persons in Germany. They had been dragged from their homes across Eastern Europe to work as slaves for the "master race." When the war ended, they got stuck in Germany because the Soviets now occupied their homelands. Evicting them when they had no place to go seemed disgraceful. What the hell was going on here?

The driver turned to drive between two rows of huts and counted off as he drove past each hut. "One, two, three, four, five!" He came to a halt and pulled the hand brake. "This one should still be empty. We're filling them up one after another. Someone will be over with sheets and blankets in a while."

"Where are the showers and canteen?" Jimmy asked.

"The showers are over in that building there." The driver pointed to a low, grey concrete structure that looked at least half a mile away. "Meals are all served over at the base." With his thumb, the sergeant indicated the opposite side of the Autobahn.

As they climbed out, their feet sank and slipped in the mud. They dragged their duffle bags off the back of the weapons carrier and started for the open door taking big, clumsy steps to avoid puddles. Although J.B. knew it was going to be terrible even before he reached the door, he still wasn't prepared. The huts were damp, filthy, and stinking. They were empty except for a pot-bellied iron stove and eight iron cots with stained and lumpy mattresses tossed carelessly over them. The floors were concrete and dotted with clumps of partially dried mud. No washbasin, no wardrobes, or closets. Not even a chair. Nothing — except probably fleas and bedbugs.

So, this was what being a POW or a DP was like, J.B. thought — and it was to be his home for the "indefinite" future. No marriage bed and honeymoon in Niagara Falls. No modern house in the suburbs with matching furniture and Patty's colour-schemed rugs, drapes, and bathroom towels. No drive to work by car or modern office with a secretary out front. A tar-paper shack, a weapons carrier, and an outside toilet. He'd always thought that army life was pretty bad, but this was worse than any place he'd stayed during the war.

Soviet Games
RAF Gatow
Wednesday, 28 July 1948
(Day 33)

Moby Dick took off with six patients bound for Hanover at just after 8 am. In the cockpit, with Kiwi at the controls, Emily was preparing to switch over to the frequency for Area Control, when the Australian accent of S/L Garth came over her earphones. "Moby Dick," (somehow everyone had started calling them that) "Gatow Control. The Station Commander advises to be on the alert for artillery and Soviet aircraft in the corridors. Ivans are conducting manoeuvres."

"What the bloody —" Kiwi cut himself off and stared at Emily.

Into the microphone, she acknowledged, "Roger. Thanks for the warning." Then she replaced the mic and leaned back in her seat.

She was conscious of Kiwi watching her intently but tried to ignore him. He broke the silence, "Emily? You do know what that means, don't you?"

"Yes. We might be bounced or encounter ground fire."

"And we can't evade it without the risk of being shot down and tried as spies!" Kiwi reminded her of the risks of leaving the narrow corridors.

"Don't worry, Kiwi. I'm not going to panic. I've been bounced by Soviet fighters already when I was doing some formation flying soon after we arrived." Kiwi's look was so expressive that she felt compelled to add, "Yes, I remember what happened to the BEA flight, but we have a contractual and moral obligation to evacuate people for medical treatment. Charlotte says there's a large backlog of patients who need to get out of Berlin."

Kiwi drew a deep breath, nodded his agreement, and returned his attention to flying while Emily tried to think through the possible political motives for this move. The worst-case scenario was that the Soviets were fed up with 'fun and games' and intended to send the tanks into Berlin. The fact that Lt. Col. Russel was still in custody tended to support that theory. General Herbert was handling all the negotiations for his release, so Robin had no details beyond the fact that the Soviets had finally acknowledged that they were holding him for 'questioning'. They implied he was suspected of spying, which was absurd, but so was the Soviet threat to treat downed airlift pilots as "spies".

Her thoughts were interrupted by Kiwi exclaiming, "There must be hundreds of tanks down there!" Emily strained to look below the aircraft and was shaken to see tanks strung out nose-to-tail along the Berlin-Magdeburg Road as far as the eye could see. Kiwi, meanwhile, banked hard to get a better look.

"Be careful!" Emily protested. "We've got patients on board."

"I know! But we need to report what we see," Kiwi countered. "You take over the flying, while I go forward —

Before he could finish speaking, a frantic German voice asked "*Was ist los? Was ist los?*" It was their accompanying nurse.

In her calmest voice, Emily assured her in German that everything was fine.

The nurse protested indignantly that the aircraft had tipped over on its side and the patients were alarmed.

"Then please go back and explain to them that there is nothing to worry about."

As the nurse returned to the sick bay, Kiwi and Emily exchanged a look. In the short time they'd been flying since the start of the siege, they had had several nurses who were either airsick or frightened. Since losing a patient, however, they did not want to fly without. "I'd feel a lot better with a proper, British flight nurse on board," Kiwi commented.

"So would I," Emily agreed. "I'll try to talk to David about it. Now go forward and collect as much intelligence as you can."

Kiwi didn't return to the cockpit until they crossed out of Soviet airspace. As he dropped back in his seat, he announced, "They must be moving everything they have towards Berlin! I made out at least two armoured and twice as many infantry divisions."

Emily nodded. In addition to the troop movements they could see on the ground, the Soviets seemed particularly aggressive about jamming the airwaves today. Emily had had to change frequencies several times just to maintain radio contact. That too suggested the Russians might be serious, and she wondered what response HM Government would make. The British garrison in Berlin might be asked to resist — or might be told to make a hasty withdrawal. The latter would strain Gatow's capacity to the limit. Either way, it wasn't going to be pleasant. Unless, of course, these manoeuvres were just part of the war of nerves that never quite turned into a shooting war. One could hope...

A ground ambulance met them at the civil airport in Hanover and took charge of their six patients while Kiwi, Emily and the German nurse went into the terminal for a cup of coffee. The nurse became excited at the sight of so much fresh food and the smell of the coffee. "It's real!" she exclaimed several times. "And look at the shop! It is full." Opposite the restaurant was a small shop with books, magazines, chocolates, and cheap souvenirs; the nurse could hardly take her eyes off it.

They arrived back at Gatow before noon, where six more patients were awaiting evacuation to Hamburg. While Emily filed the flight plan,

Kiwi took his notes on Soviet troop movements up to Robin for forwarding to General Herbert. As Kiwi reported back to her, he wasn't alone. Based on all the reports, Robin believed the Soviets had pulled the bulk of their 300,000 occupation troops into a ring around Berlin. Nevertheless, he confided that Robertson and London did not believe the Soviets intended to take any action. "They're calling it a 'show of force' to intimidate us. I've been told to act as if they aren't there."

Moby Dick took off expeditiously at 12:12 and in Hamburg, they took time for a late lunch. Here too, just one month after the currency reform, the impact of the D-Mark was readily evident. Shop windows were full, restaurants offered choices, and the people on the streets seemed both better dressed and more energised than Berliners. Kiwi joked about envying Ron and Chips, who were stationed here rather than in beleaguered Berlin. Emily knew that he was only half-joking.

When they collected the weather report for their return trip, they were warned that a thunderstorm was brewing. It wasn't anything particularly dangerous, just a "heat storm," the Met officer said. Under normal circumstances they could have flown around it, but because they had to stay in the corridor they were going to have to fly through it. Furthermore, without patients, they were not given precedence over the Airlift freighters and spent fifty minutes in the take-off queue. By then the sky was dark and the first, thick drops of rain fell on the cockpit windscreen. With Kiwi at the controls, Emily reached forward to activate the windscreen wipers.

The skies remained dark the entire flight, although the thunderstorm never materialised. Apparently, it had passed to the north of them. Then suddenly, just twenty minutes short of Berlin, the aircraft was abruptly and violently shaken by turbulence.

Emily yelped involuntarily, and, embarrassed, confessed to Kiwi. "Sorry! I've never encountered air turbulence as abrupt and bad as that before."

"I hate to tell you this, Emily, but that wasn't turbulence. It was flak." He pointed to the distinctive puff of brown-black smoke just ahead but to the right of their track.

Emily's mouth went dry and then the Wellington was shaken a second time. Another puff of smoke erupted on their left as the nurse put her head through the curtain to ask in a panicked tone what was happening.

Emily replied it was just Soviet "war games" and they were not in danger. She persuaded her to go back into the fuselage and strap herself in.

When they were alone again, Kiwi informed her, "On the assumption that they are aiming to *miss* us, I am *not* going to take evasive action but will hold altitude, course, and speed. That way they'll know where *not* to shoot."

As a third burst of flak rattled the aircraft, however, they could hear the nurse calling on God's help.

"I'd better go back and see if I can calm her down," Emily suggested and started to unstrap herself.

Kiwi held her in place with a firm hand on her arm. "Nothing is going to calm her down and there are no patients back there for her to upset. It's better for you to stay where you are."

She looked at him blankly.

"You need to be ready to take over the controls if I get injured."

"But if they're not aiming at us—" Emily started.

Kiwi cut her off. "Shrapnel from a near miss can pierce the fuselage. The exterior is just linen and glue, remember? The aircraft is in no danger. It's designed for this. But a big piece of shrapnel could easily take off my foot, hand, or head."

Or mine, Emily added mentally, and she drew a deep breath to steady herself. The flak was still going off about three hundred feet ahead of them at 15-second intervals. It mockingly marked a corridor for them.

Emily became so transfixed by the corridor between the black puffs of smoke marking the flak bursts that she only gradually became aware of voices in her earphones. Evidently, they were within range of radio transmissions from Berlin air traffic control. A voice crackled, "... Roger, Gatow Control."

A second voice followed. "Rafair 038, Wilco. There's a white Wellington with red crosses all over it two thousand feet below and a mile ahead getting bracketed by it."

A third voice came in, "They're picking on the smaller, lower and slower aircraft."

"Moby Dick, can you read me?" Emily recognised Assistant Section Leader Hart's worried voice. Before Emily had a chance to answer, Hart urged anxiously, "Come in, Moby Dick!"

Emily had the horrible feeling that Robin was in the tower. They would have told him incoming aircraft were reporting flak and he would have gone up to hear the radio transmissions for himself. Taking the mic, she answered in a voice pitched to sound completely relaxed, "Gatow Control, this is Moby Dick." Stretching to look down and confirm their position, she added only marginally prematurely, "We're passing into Berlin airspace now. No damage or injuries." Silently she added, "This time." She hoped fervently that Robin would not ground her. Far from putting her off flying, the flak highlighted the character of the enemy they were facing and reinforced Emily's commitment to keep flying patients out of their clutches.

Russian Hospitality
Potsdam
Thursday, 29 July 1948
(Day 34)

Intelligence can be a curse, Graham realised. Because he was clever enough to think through his situation, he knew he was in deep trouble. In his windowless four-by-five cell with a neon light that never went out, he also had plenty of time to let his imagination run wild. He slept fitfully, and what sleep he snatched was filled with nightmares.

He repeatedly dreamed of Jasha — and she always rejected him. In one, she brushed aside the box of chocolates he tried to offer her. In another, she looked at him in disgust. More frequently, he chased after her, only for her to turn a corner or slam a door in his face. On the one hand, she had become the mirror in which he saw himself, and he was acutely conscious of being ugly, deformed, and contemptible. On the other, the dreams underlined the fact that he had no wife, no family, no one who cared for him enough to demand action from a notoriously timid and conflict-adverse British Military Governor.

When he didn't dream of Jasha, his semiconscious state repeated and amplified the experiences he was suffering while awake. The interrogations came at irregular intervals and lasted indeterminate lengths of time. They were conducted in other windowless rooms, and his interrogators were pale and bloodless — as if they, too, never saw the light of day or breathed fresh air. He lost all sense of day or night and passing time. He was only aware that his body was slowly breaking down as pain spread from his shoulders to his hips and back. It became more intense depending on how he moved, sat or tried to lie. There was never a moment without pain, hunger, or fear, and there was blood in his urine.

At the sound of someone outside the door, Graham felt panic bordering on hysteria. That panic had been building over time because he knew he could not take much more abuse. Yet "taking" it represented his last shred of dignity. If he broke down, he would hate himself completely and lose the last remnant of identity as an officer and a gentleman. As long as he upheld his determination not to cooperate, he told himself, he was still Lt. Col. Graham Russel of the Corps of Royal Engineers.

The NKVD thugs flung the door open so hard it bounced partially back, hitting one of them. They grabbed Graham, bound his hands behind his back and then with a Russian on either side of him, they marched/dragged him down the corridor. Unexpectedly, they turned and forced him up a long flight of stairs. He found it very hard to lift his feet high enough to clear the steps and kept tripping. Each time he fell, they cursed and yelled and sometimes cuffed or kicked him before yanking him upright. At the top of the stairs, a heavy metal door guarded by soldiers of the NKVD blocked his way. At a command, the door opened, and Graham was shoved into the fresh air and sunshine beyond.

The sunshine was blinding. Graham wanted to shade his eyes from the painful brightness, but his hands were tied behind his back. Unable to stand the light, he screwed his eyes tightly shut as they flung him into the back of a car. The NKVD men got in behind him and pushed him down onto the floor with their boots. He lay on his stomach, a boot on the back of his head crushing his face against the gravel and dirt on the floor. He heard the doors crunch shut and a key turn in the ignition. The car started vibrating and then wallowed through ruts to the sound of tires on fine stones until, with a thump, a wheel hit the edge of the paving. A moment later, all the wheels were on concrete, and the car gathered speed. Graham acknowledged to himself that this was something new, but he did not think it was good.

Sure enough, after driving fifteen or twenty minutes, they stopped. He was flung out of the car and tumbled painfully onto the road. Someone reached out and cut the ropes binding his wrists. Then they gave him a kick in the seat of his pants accompanied by a burst of Russian.

Graham knew he was supposed to run so they could gun him down for "trying to escape." He wasn't going to give them that pleasure. He dragged himself to his feet and turned to face them; his eyes had adjusted enough to the light to see that the NKVD men were gesturing for him to go away. He shook his head. They pointed behind him and again made gestures for him to leave. Someone said: "American Sector!" They must have brought him to a spot near the Sector border to make it plausible that he was "trying to escape."

His executioners were getting agitated. One of them grabbed him by the arm, turned him around and started dragging him. He could make out a river and a bridge with a heavy if elegant metal superstructure. It wasn't a suspension bridge, the engineer noted; it rested on thick, round piers standing in gently flowing water. It must be the Havel, Graham registered. Turning cautiously to look over his shoulder, he saw a street lined with villas. Turning back to face the bridge he saw a lake beyond it.

The lure of the bridge became irresistible. He started stumbling towards it. The pain from his back and hips made him wince and gasp. He struggled to right himself and then tried to master the pain enough to move more rapidly. He expected to hear the crack of a gunshot any second. His exposed back burned in expectation of a bullet slamming into it. What were they waiting for? Biting his teeth together to counter the stabbing pain from his hips, he forced himself to keep going. He took only one step at a time, so he could brace for the pain. At last, he started up the gentle incline of the bridge. If they didn't shoot him soon, they wouldn't kill him outright, he reasoned, imagining being mortally injured and left to bleed to death in agony for hours. On the far side of the bridge, US jeeps with machine guns flanked a Mercedes flying British flags.

As he passed the highest point on the bridge, the mid-way point, the driver of the Mercedes got out. He opened the back door and saluted. "My God," Graham thought in shock as he stumbled down the gentle incline. "That's General Herbert. If the Reds shoot now, it will cause an international incident."

It wasn't until that moment that he realised he was being released.

General Herbert took Graham back to the HQ of the British Brigade near Hitler's Olympic Stadium, where his batman was waiting with a complete change of clothes. He was given the opportunity to bathe and change into uniform before being subjected to a medical exam and then an intelligence debrief. The doctor gave him some painkillers and some sleeping pills but said he saw no evidence of permanent injury. The debrief, while not hostile, was rigorous, and Graham was warned that they would "talk again." By then it was 4:15 in the afternoon, and he gratefully went out to his waiting car and dozed all the way back to Gatow. At his quarters, he let himself in, removed his shoes, and then stretched down on his bed, still clothed. He fell instantly asleep.

He was awakened by the sound of the doorbell. Rearing up, still confused from his deep, escapist dream, it took him a moment to call out groggily that he was on his way. Dazed and stiff, he stumbled across the room to yank open the door. He found himself face-to-face with the Station Commander.

"Graham?" Robin asked. "I just wanted to see for myself that you were safely back. Are you all right? Is there anything I can get for you?"

The gesture of concern and the warmth of Robin's tone overwhelmed Graham. He hadn't been expecting it. General Herbert's intervention had been official; he didn't want *any* British officer in Soviet hands. Herbert had expressed regrets about the 'incident' and relief that it had ended well, but his tone had been impersonal. Robin, on the other hand, didn't care about "a British officer"; he cared about Graham Russel.

After Graham had collected himself, he stammered out. "Thank you. It's very kind of you to stop by. I'm very glad to be back. As to how I feel, if you want the truth, I'm battered and still off balance. Do you want to come in?"

Robin hesitated, "I don't mean to intrude if you'd rather just rest."

"I did rest, and after ten days in solitary confinement, a friendly face is more welcome than more sleep. Can I offer you a drink or are you in a hurry to go home? What time is it?"

"It's just gone eight, and I am on my way home — which was why

I stopped by. I thought you might prefer spending the evening with us. You're welcome to stay overnight in one of our guest rooms if you like; our friend David moved into an apartment on Kurfuerstendamm to be closer to his clients. No one will be there but Emily, Jasha, me, and the dog, of course."

Graham flinched at the mention of Jasha; the image from his dream in which she brusquely rejected his chocolates flared up in his consciousness. Yet the thought of the garden, the lake gently lapping at the foot of the property, and the birds calling in the trees was tempting. The idea of being with friends rather than alone with his thoughts, doubts, and recriminations was overwhelmingly attractive. "I'd like that very much," Graham admitted. "Come in and have a seat while I put my shoes on and throw some things together."

Graham returned to the bedroom and looked around for the small suitcase he used for short trips. He was still woozy, yet conscious of a duty to debrief the Station Commander before they were among civilians. Returning to the sitting room, he waved Robin back into a chair and explained, "Before we join the others, I'd better share some information."

"As you wish," Robin agreed, sitting down again.

"It's just that I think you should know I wasn't randomly picked up. The Reds knew exactly who I was and that I was responsible for building the concrete runway here. They were interested in everything I knew about Gatow — including you. In fact, they seemed inordinately interested in you. They wanted to know about your wife, your children, pets, your passions, and ambitions. I kept saying we didn't know each other well, stressing you are RAF and I'm Army. I said we didn't see one another socially. I'm not sure they believed me."

Robin's response was characteristically professional. "Do they know about the fuel storage tanks?"

Graham shook his head. "They didn't seem to. They didn't ask, and I certainly didn't bring them up voluntarily."

"That's all right then. I'm not important. I can be replaced, and as for the runway, it's not exactly a secret. What on earth could they hope to learn from you that they don't already know?"

"They were obsessed with finding out where I'd obtained the building materials and equipment. They were convinced 'traitors' were aiding us and wanted me to uncover them."

"The steam roller did come from the East," Robin remembered, "and some of the barrels of bitumen."

Graham found a handkerchief and wiped his forehead as he stammered, "I — I had to tell them about the steamroller. They had aerial photos of it." Graham's guilt about admitting that the steamroller had been driven across the Sector border caused some of his worst distress. Although didn't know the man's name or even the town he'd come from, Graham feared the construction worker would be identified and punished in some terrible way. He felt like a worm.

Robin focused on the consequences. "Which means we must set up camouflage nets to hide our work on the fuel storage tanks."

"I hadn't even thought of that," Graham admitted, shocked by his failure. Abruptly he was drenched by a wave of shame. "I made one stupid mistake after another, Robin. I don't know what Herbert is going to do with me, but I wouldn't blame him if he doesn't trust me anymore."

"Nonsense! We can't get along without you! I need you to build the underground fuel storage tanks, and everyone else wants you to start work on the third airfield."

Graham shook his head and admitted, "I'm not feeling very confident in my abilities at the moment."

"That's just the aftereffects of abuse. I know. I've been through it too. Maybe not quite the same, but I had a bad time as a POW. Made a couple of failed escape attempts, you see, to which the Gestapo didn't take kindly. I assure you, you'll get over it after you've had enough time to rest, heal and put things into perspective."

Graham answered by reporting, "They called me a deformed dwarf that the Red Army would have kicked into the gutter and stamped on to put me out of my misery."

"Which only underlines how stupid they are since they would have denied themselves a brilliant engineer," Robin shot back, meeting his friend's eyes.

"But the image haunted me the whole time I was in custody — something so disgusting, you just kick it aside and stamp it out like a cockroach. I started to wonder if Herbert thought of me that way and to fear he'd dismiss me as unworthy of any effort after walking so stupidly into this situation."

"Surely you knew better?" Robin countered earnestly.

"Yes, at first. But with time... They told me all ideals — patriotism, loyalty, friendship, and even courage — are jokes."

"What about Communism?" Robin shot back. "Is that a joke?"

Graham nodded. "I asked that very question, and they *laughed* at me! The interrogating officer leant closer until our eyes were inches apart and he said in this calm voice, '*Especially* Communism. Comrade Stalin lives better than the tsars ever did, and he'd rather let a million peasants starve than admit to a single mistake.' It was chilling to have one of their officers admit that," Graham conceded.

"It's chilling to think they *know* it's a sham and still support it so fanatically."

"Oh, they explained that too! They said it is simple: everything is for sale, and everyone has a price. When I protested, they laughed at me. In a sneering voice, the chief interrogator told me some men sell themselves for love, others for power, and still others for prestige and fame. All loyalty, he told me, is transactional. I tried to suggest that his worldview reflected poorly on the Soviet Union, but not necessarily on the rest of the world. He dismissed my protests as childish naivety and told me that even the most idealistic men will sell themselves to save someone or something they love. That was when I became afraid. I'm not much tempted by money or fame, but there are things I deeply love."

"You're right," Robin agreed solemnly. "Saving those we love is the strongest motivation a man has — and it can be used against us." They fell silent, each reflecting on what this meant to them personally.

Then Graham continued, "The worst was their ability to make me feel there was no point in being loyal, no point in being brave. What I mean is that they made me feel like a fool for clinging to obsolete notions like courage and loyalty. They said it was naive to believe there was any virtue in the values I cherish most: patriotism, friendship, or honour. Everyone lies, they told me, everyone pursues their own self-interest. Everyone is corrupt. Did I think Atlee or Bevin or Robertson gave a tinker's damn about me? Did I think any member of the government, parliament, or the General Staff would lift a finger to help me? Didn't I know that the British Military Governor and the City Commandant had already written me off?

I wasn't worth a demarch, let alone an incident. The sense of everything being pointless made it hard to stand up to them. I'm just not sure how much more abuse and isolation I could have withstood. I fear if it had gone on much longer, I would have broken down."

Robin answered solemnly, "Every man has his limits and none of us know where they are until we reach them. The Gestapo got very close to mine," he admitted almost inaudibly.

Their eyes met, and they recognised one another as brothers. Robin, too, had looked his weaknesses in the face. Graham nodded to him, grateful for that confession.

They sat in silence, reflecting, and then Robin switched to a lighter tone. "Enough of this brooding! Let me take you home for a strong drink, good food, and pleasant company."

"Of course!" Graham agreed, adding, "Thank you for letting me ramble a bit. I needed to share it with someone. But you're right. It's time to try and forget. Your invitation home to spend the night is exceptionally kind."

They went out to Robin's car and on the way to the residence talked about what had happened since Graham's disappearance: the USAF crash, the increasing resistance by Berliners to kidnappings, the SMAD offer to feed anyone who registered with them, and the "manoeuvres" which the Soviets used to justify flying aircraft and shooting flak in the corridors. "They're just testing our nerves," Robin commented on the latter. Graham was astonished at how much could happen in ten days.

On reaching the Priestman residence, Graham swung open the door, but his sore limbs forced him to move slowly. He'd hardly stood up before Jasha, falling more than running down the stairs, collided with him. He caught her in his arms as she tripped on the last step. When he drew back to release her, she wouldn't let him go. She clung to him, burying her face in his chest. "I was so afraid for you! So afraid! Promise me you will never go into the East again. Please!"

Overwhelmed, Graham held her to him, his heart pounding in his chest as Robin and Emily discreetly waited in the background. It took a few seconds before he was able to speak. "I promise, Jasha. Will you let me help you in your garden instead?"

Jasha nodded vigorously, then withdrew from his arms to fumble for a handkerchief in her apron pocket and blow her nose, looking flustered. Emily stepped into the breach, offering Graham her cheek as she exclaimed warmly, "I was so relieved to hear you'd been released. We've all been worried, though none of us quite as intensely as Jasha. She's been so distraught she could hardly function."

Graham turned to look at her again. She was crying uninhibitedly now and dabbing at her eyes with her crumpled handkerchief. Those dreams, he registered, had been wrong.

Emily was saying, "Come inside and Robin will find you a drink. Jasha has been cooking all day long to make something special."

Graham turned again towards Jasha. Her hands trembled as she tried to wipe her tears away. Graham reached out and took her hand in his. She looked up at him, and he nodded reassurance. Then they walked hand in hand up the stairs to enter the house behind their host and hostess.

Crewmates
Lincoln
Friday, 30 July 1948
(Day 35)

Moran had suggested that his crew meet at the King's Head in Lincoln, one of their wartime haunts, on the Friday before they were due to present themselves to the management of EAS in London. The idea was to spend the weekend together as a crew and get to know each other better. He'd run into problems finding a qualified second pilot, however, so it wasn't until Tuesday 27 July that he'd sent out a cable to the other others announcing: "Crew complete. Meet at King's Head, Lincoln as planned."

Terry promptly gave notice at the Post Office and his lodgings. Nigel and he packed their meagre belongings and travelled to Lincoln together. At the King's Head, they chose to share a twin room to save on costs. By the time they went down to the lounge bar to meet up with the others, Terry was feeling excited and elated. He kept telling Nigel he felt like a free man for the first time in ages. Nigel, on the other hand, was nervous. He kept asking Terry, "Do I look all right?" and "Have the bruises faded?" Terry assured him all was well.

Entering the bar, the first person they saw was Gordon MacDonald in his wheelchair with a pint in his hand. The smile he gave them lit up the whole room. They hastened over to him, clapping him on the back and teasing him about how good he looked. "What have you been doing? Playing golf all day?" Nigel teased.

"I've been sunbathing for three weeks!" Daddy answered. "Didn't want to look like an invalid."

"In Scotland?" Nigel quipped back. "I didn't know you had any sunshine up there."

"We get more sun than you do in Liverpool, Laddie. The air's clean, you see!"

"Is it certain you have a job, then?" Terry asked more earnestly.

"Nothing's certain, the skipper says, until we've passed muster with the company management, but they have invited me to an interview on Monday an hour before yours. Now, before the two of you rabbit on, you need to meet Richard Scott-Ross here." He indicated a tall, good-looking black man who had risen to his feet at the arrival of Terry and Nigel. He held out his hand, and Terry automatically shook it, smiling. Nigel followed suit more hesitantly.

Gordon made the introductions, "Mr Scott-Ross was a flight engineer on 640 and 9 Squadrons, the latter at the same time we were with 617. He knows both the Halifax and the Lancaster. We've been chatting engines for almost an hour, and I couldn't catch him out on anything, so he's got my approval. Which means, lads, you treat him with the same respect you showed me."

"Did we respect you?" Nigel quipped. "I don't remember that."

"For that, you buy the next round!" Gordon ordered. Nigel made a face but went to the bar. Meanwhile, Terry turned to Scott-Ross to ask, "Were you on any of the Tirpitz Raids?"

"Two of them, along with the V1 and V2 launch sites, the U-boat factory, and Berchtesgaden at the end."

"We missed that one," Terry admitted. "Let's sit," he indicated the vacant chairs. Scott-Ross settled back into the armchair he'd occupied before, and Terry took the chair opposite, so they were flanking Gordon. "I'm Terry Tibble the signaller, and Nigel's our navigator."

Scott-Ross nodded, noting, "So, we're just missing the pilots," as Nigel returned and put the pints on the table.

As if on cue, the door opened, and Moran walked in. "There's the skipper now!" Gordon exclaimed, lifting his voice and arm to call out, "We're over here, Skipper!"

Moran spotted them, smiled, and waved back. He looked very smart, Terry thought proudly, like a real gentleman in a tailored suit. Then Terry noticed that another man was shadowing him. Scott-Ross, meanwhile, had jumped up to haul an empty chair over to their table, and Nigel did the same, so there were two vacant places when Kit and his companion arrived. Moran opened, "Good to see you all! Gordon," he leaned forward to shake hands with the man in the wheelchair first, then the others in turn before introducing the man beside him. "Mr Sidney Liddel. The last member of our crew."

The four men already at the table looked up at the man who stood taller than Moran (and he was almost six feet tall). The stranger had a receding hairline over an aquiline nose and cold blue eyes. Terry tried not to make instant judgements about people, but something about this man sent a chill down his spine. "I see you've all got something to drink," Moran noted, adding, "What can I get you, Mr Liddel?"

Mister Liddel? Terry looked at Nigel. Since when did the skipper call his second pilot *mister*? Unless he was Navy, of course. When Liddel asked for rum, Nigel mouthed "Fishhead!" to Terry.

Moran left for the bar, and Liddel sat down and looked around the table critically. "Would you mind identifying your trades for me?"

Pompous ass, Terry thought, but complied with "Signaller." Scott-Ross, Gordon and finally Nigel followed suit. Nigel going last was unfortunate because it allowed Liddel to query, "You were an air gunner in the war, Moran said?"

"That's right, but I'm a qualified navigator now," Nigel answered defensively.

"Qualified yes, but you've never actually done any navigating in an aircraft, have you?"

"Look, I passed the exams and I navigated at sea—"

The snort Liddel gave in response to this statement made Terry question his earlier assumption about Liddel's RN background.

"Maybe you could say a word or two about *your* background," Gordon deftly shifted the focus of the conversation.

"Fair enough," Liddel answered. "I flew Whitleys with 102 Squadron and after time as an instructor and in staff college, I transferred to Coastal Command where I flew Liberators."

"Liberators? That's about the only aircraft we're *not* likely to fly," Nigel complained.

"Well, for those of you *ignorant* of the fact," Liddel retorted, "the skills demanded of a Liberator pilot are such that anyone who can handle a Liberator can fly anything else."

Gordon looked at Scott-Ross and muttered just loud enough to be heard over the general pub noise, "bollocks."

Moran returned with his own and Liddel's drink. "Everyone getting along?" he asked innocently. The silence that answered him made him look around the table in alarm.

"You didn't tell me the crew was composed of a bunch of insolent buggers," Liddel sneered.

"That's because they're not," Moran responded levelly.

"I think we'd better get things straight right from the start," Liddel countered. "I run a tight ship. I won't tolerate any kind of unprofessionalism or undue familiarity, much less impudence from my crew. I will be addressed as "captain," not skipper—"

"Wait a minute!" Nigel broke in, looking furiously between Moran and Liddel. "You aren't the skipper, let alone the captain, of this crew. You're the second pilot—"

Kit gestured for Nigel to stop, but it was too late. Liddel turned on Moran in outrage. "Didn't you tell them?"

"I haven't had a chance. Besides, I thought it would be more appropriate to do so when we were all together—."

Liddel didn't let him finish. He turned back to the others. "Since Moran was remiss in informing you, I shall do so now. I have more than twice as many flying hours in my logbook as Moran. I've flown a greater variety of aircraft, and I held the wartime rank of Wing Commander. I'm not flying Second Dickie to a former Flight Lieutenant with such limited experience — not to mention a blemished record—"

Nigel sprang to his feet and his voice was loud enough to make the customers at adjacent tables turn to look. "I don't give a toss how many hours you flew on what sodding aircraft much less what effing rank you had in the war! I didn't sign on to your crew, Liddel! I signed on with Kit Moran."

"Well, he doesn't have a crew. I do. So adjust your thinking and pay attention to what I'm saying."

"No. I'm not flying on your crew. You'll have to find another navigator." Nigel turned and walked out of the lounge.

In the stunned silence that followed, Terry registered that this was the end of the whole dream of flying again. What was more, he'd already resigned from his job at the Post Office, which made him unemployed. For a second he thought of chasing after Nigel and trying to get him to change his mind. Then he realised that he agreed with Nigel. He stood and said in a soft voice to Moran, "Sorry, Skipper, but I'm with Nigel." Then he too walked out of the lounge.

Terry caught up with Nigel in their room, where he was punching things — fortunately, soft things like the armchair and the bed. "How could he do this to us?" Nigel fumed.

"He didn't have a lot of choice. He didn't have a second pilot until Tuesday."

"But that turd—" Nigel picked up a pillow and threw it across the room. "*Now* what are we going to do?"

"We could go out for fish and chips over at Yates'." It had been one of their favourite places during the war.

Nigel glared at him. "I didn't mean tonight. I meant for jobs, income, our future!"

"I don't know. Let's talk about it over fish and chips."

Nigel threw the second pillow at him and then they left the room together, but they didn't make it out of the hotel. Scott-Ross intercepted them in the lobby, "Mr Moran asked me to find you and bring you back to the lounge."

"Not if that bastard Liddel's still there!" Nigel bristled.

"He's not."

Warily, they followed Scott-Ross into the lounge. Liddel was nowhere in sight, but Moran was sitting beside Gordon. Terry and Nigel gingerly sank back into their chairs. "I'm sorry about that," Moran opened. "He was the only qualified pilot I could find who was willing to take a temporary position, but his condition was that he be the first pilot."

"And you agreed to that?" Nigel challenged him.

"I didn't have a choice," Moran answered steadily, meeting his angry gaze. "He seemed like the best chance for all of us finally to get back into a job we liked."

"It's not your fault, Skipper," Terry assured him, feeling bad for them all.

"Was there absolutely no one else?" Gordon pressed him.

"There was one pilot who was very keen to fly regardless of the circumstances, but he had a grand total of 15 hours on heavies and just three of those were solo. He was in an HCU when the war ended. They aborted the course and demobbed everyone."

"Yes, but if he's just the second pilot he can get the hours and experience in the righthand seat while we're on the Airlift," Terry pointed out, perking up.

"Terry's right, Skip," Gordon seconded. "Unless the company *said* you had to bring a second pilot with a specific number of hours on heavies...."

Moran frowned. "You might be right," he admitted. "But I was told they are only buying two aircraft and will only hire two crews. I believe four captains and crews are competing for those two slots. I wanted to put forward the strongest crew possible. If the other captains have better-qualified crews, we'll lose out."

"But we can at least try!" Terry urged him anxiously, supported by a growl from Gordon.

Kit looked over at Nigel and Scott-Ross. "Do you agree? Do you want me to try to track him down and see if he's still interested?"

"Yes!" they replied in chorus.

Moran still hesitated, "There's something else you ought to know about him. I think it speaks in his favour, but I don't want any more surprises."

"Now what?" Nigel burst out in exasperation.

"He called me because he'd heard through the squadron association that I was looking." That sounded like a good thing to Terry, but Moran's tone suggested there was a drawback. Terry waited for the axe to fall. "He's Red Forrester's younger brother."

That didn't bother Terry, but Nigel kicked the table and started swearing again. Terry stared coldly at him, and Nigel went still. "All right!

All right!" He lifted his hands in surrender. "I accept. As long as he's the second pilot!"

"First we have to track him down and see if he's still available," Moran reminded them. "And we only have another 62 hours before we're due to present ourselves as a complete crew at the Savoy."

Chapter Ten
Dubious Opportunities

Berlin Economics 101
Frankfurt / Main
Saturday, 31 July 1948
(Day 36)

They were scheduled to make their first flight to Berlin at 05:50, and the wake-up call was at 4:00. The weapons carrier took their unwashed and flea-bitten bodies over to the airfield at 4:15 for a rotten, Air Force breakfast of weak coffee, burnt toast, and powdered eggs. At 4:45 they reported for an operational briefing, and at 05:25 they were dropped off beside an unfamiliar C-54 that looked as though it had flown around the world at least twice. It was also covered in coal dust. Everything they touched was coated with it, leaving their fingers, elbows, and knees grimy.

"If we sit down on those seats, our trousers are going to be ruined!" Jimmy complained with a look of disgust at the worn and sagging seats in the cockpit. A layer of black dust had been ground into the leather.

J.B. shared Jimmy's disgust. He only had three pairs of uniform trousers. But he was also a practical man, and noted, "Well, it's going to be hard to fly her standing up."

"Hey! Wells!" Jimmy called over his shoulder.

"Sir?"

"See if you can find something we can sit on. Something clean, I mean. Some old blankets or towels or *anything*."

"OK." The sergeant disappeared.

Jimmy was left looking at his dirty hands in utter disgust. J.B. reached down beside the copilot's seat and found the clipboard with the pre-flight check list, looking for something they could do standing up. Wells was back with some empty flour sacks. "How about these?"

J.B. and Jimmy looked at them with consternation but wordlessly decided that white dust was better than black dust and flour smelled better than coal. "Aw, what the hell." Jimmy put their feelings into words and started spreading the sacks over his seat. J.B. followed his example.

They reported to the tower when ready and got clearance to taxi. Jimmy released the brakes and with extra throttle convinced the C-54 to leave the mud for the concrete of the taxiway. When their turn came for take-off, they needed almost the whole runway to get airborne, and they had to pump the flaps to gain altitude. This old bird was on her last legs, J.B. thought. He hoped some newer aircraft were winging their way to Germany.

They were given a course to the Darmstadt beacon. This took them over the town at just over 3,000 feet and J.B. had a pretty good view. Although there was a lot of bomb damage, it looked like it was coming back to life with trams and buses and people moving around on the streets. Their next course took them to the Aschaffenburg beacon, which they reached as they attained their cruising altitude of 6,500 feet, by which time they were also flying at the ordained speed of 170 mph. Henceforth, they were supposed to maintain exactly five minutes of separation from the aircraft ahead of them.

Shortly after passing the Fulda beacon they crossed into Soviet airspace, which meant that from there to Berlin they had no navigational aids to help establish their position. It was a clear, summer's day, however, and J.B. could make out both the aircraft immediately ahead of them and the one beyond it. He could also see some C-47s flying at a lower altitude on the same course. It was like driving on a three-dimensional highway.

Gradually, the attractive, hilly countryside with rivers and forests grew flat. Forty minutes after passing out of the West, they could see Berlin spread out in front of them, and Jimmy told J.B. to call into the Berlin Air Safety Centre. As the outskirts of Berlin started slipping under the leading edge of their wings, Jimmy gasped, "Holy Crap! There's nothing down there but ruins! Where does anybody live?"

J.B. didn't have an answer. As far as he could see, there was nothing but broken masonry and heaps of rubble. Almost all the roofs were gone, leaving the jagged edges of the remaining walls stabbing upwards. Eventually he realised that not all the structures were complete ruins. Mostly, the roofs and upper stories had been destroyed, leaving the ground and lower floors still standing. Scattered between these half-destroyed buildings, incongruous squares of intact buildings alternated with heaps of rubble where something had been pulverised.

Wells came forward to the flight deck to get a better look and stood between the two pilots shaking his head. "Jesus," he kept saying, "Jesus. Did we do all that?"

"With a little help from the Brits," J.B. conceded.

J.B. began to discern a pattern. Infrastructure landmarks and factories were surrounded by flattened buildings and rubble. The targets seemed to be in better shape than the surrounding area. So much for "precision" bombing, he thought cynically.

Tempelhof came into view. They recognised it by the distinctive curving terminal building that had been pointed out on photos during their orientation briefing. It had been built as a landmark project for the capital of the "Thousand Year Reich," and it reared up impressively amidst the ruins. Involuntarily, J.B. thought, 'Missed again!' But at least the terminal lay to the side of the runway. In contrast, directly in their glidepath was what appeared to be the only swathe of fully intact five-storey buildings in all Berlin. Their survival might be a miracle, but they constituted a menace to aviation.

As they came closer, J.B. had the feeling they were coming in much too fast. He checked their ground speed, and he reminded Jimmy, "It's a grass field with just PSP strips."

"I know, I know," Jimmy answered, annoyed.

"And it was built for passengers, not cargo planes loaded to the gills," J.B. reminded him anyway.

"I know, J.B.! Wells, strap in! J.B., call for final clearance."

J.B. grabbed the mic. "Big Easy 381 on final approach."

"Cleared to land."

They were losing 750 feet/minute, which was a ridiculously steep glide path.

"Wheels down!" Jimmy ordered.

J.B. reached for the undercarriage lever and pulled it. With a clunk the gear went down and a green light on the panel indicated they were locked into place. When J.B. lifted his eyes from the control panel his heart missed a beat: he was looking *into* an apartment where a family was sitting around a table for breakfast. Seconds later they thumped down on the PSP surface and rumbled noisily and bumpily over the ground with Jimmy standing on the brakes to stop a few feet short of the end of the runway. J.B. let out his breath. Maybe no one was shooting at them, but this kind of flying could kill them just the same.

They turned off the runway and followed the waiting jeep to the terminal where C-47s were lined up nose-to-tail with the odd C-54 in between. Even before they had a chance to shut down all their engines, someone was banging energetically on the cargo door.

"What the —" Sergeant Wells disappeared down the fuselage to open the door, and as the last of the engines went silent, J.B. could hear voices speaking German. The next thing he, knew a man in filthy blue overalls was behind him on the flight deck, holding out his hand. "*Danke schoen!*" he exclaimed.

Dazed by the unexpected gesture, J.B. and then Jimmy shook his hand automatically but without responding verbally before he disappeared again. J.B. and Jimmy stared at one another in bafflement, then extracted themselves from their seats and walked back to the exit. A flatbed truck had already backed up to the open door and a gangplank connected it to the aircraft. A team of five men was unloading the cargo at a pace that exhausted J.B. just watching them.

J.B. and Jimmy had to squeeze past them to jump down onto the tarmac. Here the other men from the unloading crew also offered their hands, so Jimmy and J.B. dutifully shook them. The gesture embarrassed him because it seemed so heartfelt — and J.B. had dismissed Germans as heartless long ago.

After a moment of confusion, they spotted the entrance to the terminal and walked over. A large arrow pointed the way to the "Snack Bar." It was a long walk, but it was worth it. The shop was as well stocked as any Post Exchange (PX). They bought a hamburger and a hotdog respectively, Snickers bars and coffee, and then joined a bunch of other pilots sitting around tables at the back of the room.

At first, they devoted themselves to their food and just listened in on the flying talk. After he'd finished his hotdog, however, Jimmy spoke up, "We're new here. How do we know when to go back to our plane?"

The others laughed. Then someone explained, "Let's put it this way.

The staff really gets pissed off if a plane is ready and the crew is nowhere to be found, so it's better to just be there as soon as you can."

"Yeah," another took up the theme. "If they have to page you," he put his fist in front of his mouth and imitated a PA system, "'will the pilots of Big Willi 123 report *immediately* to their aircraft. It is blocking traffic!' You are in big trouble."

A third pilot took over the narrative. "The tower will cable your home base with the aircraft number, and there will be a reception committee waiting for you. When that happens, you'll wish you'd never come."

"I wish that already!" Jimmy responded, harvesting a chorus of approving laughs.

"That can only be because you haven't encountered any of the *frauleins* yet," one of the younger lieutenants declared, wriggling his hips unambiguously.

Guffaws of laughter greeted him.

"Can't go anywhere in this country without them practically assaulting you!" another agreed, shaking his head in mock disgust.

"They'll do it for a pack of cigarettes," a sergeant who looked younger than J.B.'s little brother Stan explained knowingly.

"A whole pack? You got cheated, bud. I had a *fraulein* give me a dozy of a lay for just a couple of ciggies. She was so desperate that she hardly gave me time to get my pants off."

"Yeah, they're all pretty desperate, if you ask me. Just slam, bang and hand over the cigs! It doesn't mean anything to any of them."

"Yeah, well I heard the girls here in Berlin were all screwed by the Reds for months before we got here. Even the old grandmothers and the kids. So, you know, to them an American is a real treat. At least we're clean and we pay. The problem is that the brass doesn't let us hang around here longer than it takes to offload the damn plane!"

"I'm gonna go out and get some fresh air," J.B. announced.

"How will I find you?" Jimmy protested.

"I'll wait at the aircraft," J.B. answered. As he left, the volleys of laughter continued.

He retraced his steps down the long hall, wondering if something was wrong with him. He supposed so, but he couldn't reconcile this talk with that man who had shaken his hand and thanked him for flying in a load of coal.

J.B. stepped back out onto the apron and paused to light up a cigarette, cupping his hand around the match so it wouldn't blow out in the wind. As he inhaled, he noted that whenever an aircraft landed, a bunch of men standing beside the runway dashed out to straighten the PSP plates. Some carried shovels and scraped dirt this way and that, and others stamped on everything as quickly as possible — before diving for safety as the next aircraft settled down towards the earth. He shook his head. This was crazy.

His thoughts returned to the conversation in the snack bar. It reminded him of the way some of the guys had talked about the British girls during the war. He'd told his copilot that if he spent his entire leave cruising downtown London waiting for a Piccadilly Commando to hit him up, then he was only going to meet whores. To meet nice British girls, he had to go elsewhere, but his copilot didn't really want that. He'd returned to the States swearing that the only "nice" girls in the world were those at home in Kansas.

It was easier that way, J.B. supposed. If all the girls here were whores, then you could treat them like shit and feel justified about it. No need to be a gentleman. No need to be careful. No need to even be nice. Just screw 'em and ditch 'em. So easy, so convenient, and Kansas — or Detroit — was so far away that no one at home would ever learn what an asshole you were.

He didn't think he could be like that. He didn't think he could make love to Patty if he screwed around here before going home.

Looking out towards their C-54, he saw the truck start to pull away. They had finished unloading already. Jimmy and Wells were nowhere in sight. He considered going to fetch them but opted to climb aboard and start the checks instead.

Because he hadn't finished his cigarette, he dropped it and stepped on it to put the embers out. From opposite directions, two German loaders darted towards the discarded butt. One leapt over the side of a truck, snatched it up and pocketed it as if it were gold. J.B. heard the voice in his head saying girls would put out for two cigarettes and it hit him: they *were* gold here. It was a sobering realisation.

His Brother's Shoes
London Northolt
Sunday, 1 August 1948
(Day 37)

"Put your backs into it!" the baggage supervisor shouted. "We haven't got all day!"

Bruce Forrester and another porter shoved more firmly against the trolley loaded with passenger luggage from the recently landed BOAC Skymaster. The wheels on the cart were much too small for the size and weight of the bin, making it unwieldy and awkward to push.

"Come on! Hurry up!" the supervisor called again.

"He's a right slave driver, that bloke," the other man muttered at Bruce as they pushed together, their worn-down shoes slipping on the concrete. "All that's missing is the whip!"

"Drill sergeant," Bruce answered, keeping his head down.

"Were you in the mob then?" the other man asked.

"Come on! Come on! The passengers are waiting!" their supervisor shouted.

"Yeah," Bruce admitted. "It seems like a different lifetime, though." He risked a glance over his shoulder towards the parked passenger liner. He'd taken this job at the airport just to be near aircraft again, for the smell of aviation fuel, the sound of engines, and the sight of aluminium wings glinting in the sunlight as they took to the air. What he had was an aching back, grimy hands, and barely enough pay to buy cigarettes, let alone decent lodgings or a good meal.

They entered the back of the terminal building, stopped the trolley and started to fling the luggage onto the conveyor belt. "Be careful!" their nemesis shouted. "No need to break things!"

"Well, do you want it fast or gentle?" the other luggage-handler challenged.

"Both!"

"What did you do in the war?" Bruce asked his colleague as he finished hefting a particularly heavy suitcase onto the conveyor belt.

"Armourer. Bomb depot." Saying this, the man tossed a light leather bag into the air to arc towards the moving carousel with a grin, adding, "Couldn't do that with the ordinance!"

"Sounds dangerous," Bruce muttered, and then flashed him a smile.

"Oh, there was the odd accident, but when you come down to it, our casualties were as good as nil. I'm not one of those who whined about aircrew getting perks and pay. If you ask me, they earnt it — for as long as they lived. You?"

Bruce didn't get a chance to answer. The supervisor was calling his name: "Forrester! Gentleman here wants to speak to you! Finish that load and then come here at once!"

Five minutes later, Bruce was standing beside the luggage carousel on the inside of the terminal and facing a man who looked eerily familiar although he was certain he'd never met him before. The familiar stranger offered his hand. "Moran."

Recognition clicked into place. He was the man in the photo his brother had sent him from the Heavy Conversion Unit in December 1944. Red had called him the 'bastard' that kept him from being the best pilot on the course. Bruce addressed the man opposite him in a hesitant voice, still not sure about his identification, "Zulu Moran?"

"Well, that's what your brother called me. I prefer Kit."

"Skipper to you!" A short, slender man standing behind Moran snapped.

Moran frowned at his companion before addressing Bruce again with, "Ignore Nigel. He's too cheeky for his own good, but he's my navigator. This gentleman is Richard Scott-Ross, my flight engineer." He indicated a smartly dressed and natty West Indian. Finally, he drew Bruce's attention to a thin man with a mismatched face whom he introduced as "Terry Tibble, my signaller. All we're missing is a second pilot."

Bruce gazed at him in a daze for a moment and then stammered out. "You wrote to me that I didn't have enough hours on heavies to be on your crew."

"The second pilot I hoped to engage proved unacceptable —"

"He was an effing idiot," Nigel improved.

"The fact is," Moran explained, "we're in a bit of a pickle. Tomorrow is

258

the deadline for presenting a complete crew, and without a second pilot we don't stand a chance of getting the job on the airlift. In short, if you're still interested, I'm willing to introduce you as my second pilot."

Bruce understood he was Moran's last choice, but it didn't matter. He knew just how little experience he had on heavies. Deep down, he was a little afraid he might not be up to the Airlift job. But he wanted — he *desperately* wanted — to try. Instinctively he started wiping his hands on his trousers. He felt so dirty and rundown in his work clothes. "I'd like that very much. What do I have to do?"

"We all have to be at the Savoy tomorrow morning at 8 am for an interview with the company management. My plan is to make such a good first impression that no one will drill down and ask to see logbooks and that sort of thing."

The other men looked at their skipper slightly aghast.

Moran continued. "We want to look like we're a well-oiled machine. My thought was that it would help if we all wore similar clothes. You know, dark suit, white shirt, same-coloured tie. Do you own a dark suit?"

"I can borrow one," Bruce answered.

"Good," Moran hesitated and then added, "it would also be a good idea if we got to know each other a bit better before we face the company management. We're all staying over at the Red Lion. Would you be able to join us there this evening for drinks and dinner? I'll foot the bill."

"I'd like that a lot," Bruce admitted. He still wasn't entirely sure this was happening.

"Good, then we'll let you get back to work," Moran held out his hand again.

Still dazed, Bruce took it. "What time? At the Red Lion, I mean?"

"Eight pm?"

"I'll be there."

A Voice from the Past
RAF Gatow
Sunday, 1 August 1948
(Day 37)

"Galyna? Is that you?" the woman on the other end of the telephone spoke Ukrainian, but it wasn't Galyna's friend Mila. The former partisan had a low, slightly raw and almost manly voice. Mila also spoke very fast. This voice, in contrast, was high pitched, almost unnaturally so, and each word was enunciated.

"Yes," Galyna answered warily. "This is Corporal Galyna Borisenko."

A high-pitched cry answered her — as if the woman on the other end of the line had been stabbed. Then the woman gasped out, "My puppet! My lamb!"

Galyna's blood ran cold. Those were the endearments her mother had used with her when she was little. It was eleven years since she'd last seen or heard from her mother. Then she had been an enraged and resentful fifteen-year-old, and her mother had been a semi-hysterical woman. They'd clashed almost continuously, and her mother had often declared that Galyna would "be the death of her". Their escalating fights had climaxed in the one in which her mother slapped her, and Galyna had retaliated by trying to scratch out her mother's eyes. Three weeks later, she'd been on a train bound for Helsinki and a grandmother she'd never met.

"Anastasia Sergeiovna?" Galyna asked into the phone, using her mother's first name and patronymic.

"Yes, my lamb! Yes! Don't you recognise your mother's voice?"

The longer she talked, the more familiar it sounded. How could she forget those high-pitched screams loaded with insults, recriminations and insults? Coldly, as if she were speaking to a repairman, Galyna replied, "Yes, I recognise it now. Where are you?"

"Potsdam!" Her mother answered in evident delight, but Galyna's hands started to sweat. Potsdam was where the NKVD had their headquarters and interrogation centre.

Her mother exclaimed in a tone of inane happiness, "Less than twenty miles away! Can you imagine that? We're just twenty miles apart!"

"What are you doing there and how did you get this number?"

"It's so wonderful! I'm working as an artist again!" Anastasia ignored the latter question, and Galyna recognised her mother's rapture at belonging to the exalted category "artist". Her mother viewed artists as a different species of being inherently superior to mere mortals. But no legitimate artist had any reason to live in Potsdam, and Galyna made no attempt to disguise her opinion when she asked back sarcastically, "What work is there for an artist in Potsdam?"

"I'm a freelance artist now," Anastasia assured her airily, as if her greatest pride hadn't been working for the State and the Party, as if she hadn't painted the great murals at the University at Kyiv and the railway station in Kharkiv — the murals they had covered with plaster and new paintings as soon as Galyna's father had been found guilty of treason.

"Maxim Dimitrivich is stationed here," her mother tittered. At least she had the decency to sound nervous at the mention of Galyna's stepfather. Galyna refused to answer, so her mother was forced to continue, "And you, my puppet? How are you? I've thought of you every day since we were separated."

Galyna didn't believe that. She'd seen her mother turn on her father, condemn him along with the others, and finally marry one of the men who had destroyed him. She did not believe her mother loved anyone but herself.

"Galyna?" her mother pleaded. "Talk to me, lamb! Are you well? You aren't married yet, are you?"

"No, but you haven't answered my question. How did you get this number? How did you know I was here?" As the shock of hearing her mother's voice wore off, the implications were becoming clearer. Her cover was blown! The Soviets knew who and where she was!

"Maxim Dimitrivich heard it somewhere," her mother answered vaguely and hastened to change the subject., "Are you happy?" She didn't let Galyna answer. "How can you be? The English are so cold! So arrogant and lifeless! You must miss being among your own people — people who are passionate and idealistic and artistic."

"I miss nothing. I have many English friends," Galyna insisted stubbornly, although it wasn't strictly true. She worked well with the British. She felt safe and respected among her colleagues, but she had found it difficult to connect on an emotional level. Her best friend was Mila Mikhailivna — or was she? The fact that her mother had tracked her down and knew she went under the false name of Borisenko meant that *someone* had betrayed her. The thought that it might be Mila sent chills down Galyna's spine.

"Lamb, now that we've found each other again, we must meet. I want to see how pretty you are! I want to hold you! I want to show you my latest paintings." Of course, Galyna thought bitterly. Her mother had always craved praise for her art.

"I'm sorry, mother, but I don't want to meet you and hear how happy you are while my father rots in Siberia — if he isn't already dead."

"Galyna!" It was a cry of pain — or a good imitation. Galyna cut it short by hanging up. She just sat staring at the telephone until she became aware of the routine noises in the mess around her. Her mother's call had been taken by the central switchboard. She had been paged and had taken it at one of the four public phones. Another corporal was patiently lighting up a cigarette as he waited his turn to use the public phone.

Galyna pushed open the door, cast him a brief smile of apology for taking so long, and made her way to the bar. There were several other WAAFs here, but they were recent arrivals whom Galyna did not know well. Before the blockade, when they had been barely a half dozen WAAFs, they had been a close-knit and congenial group under Kathleen's leadership. Parsons' regime had fragmented the group into little cliques, leaving Galyna feeling left out.

Galyna needed time to sort out her thoughts and emotions, and decided she needed a solitary walk around the perimeter of the field. As she walked alone beside the dark forest beyond the runways, she knew one thing was certain: she did not forgive her mother anything! The call had reawakened her grief for her father; like a deep, pervasive ache, it dimmed the sun in the sky and drained her of energy. Yet, more ominously, the call threatened her future. If *they* knew who she was and where she worked, they might strike at any time, and why should MI6 trust her under the circumstances?

Air Freight International
Savoy, London
Monday, 2 August 1948
(Day 38)

It was an indication of how bad things were in Berlin, that battered, bankrupt London looked prosperous, colourful and luxurious in contrast. When David, Emily and Kiwi flew into London Northolt on "Moby Dick" late on Sunday 1 August, they immediately felt "liberated". To celebrate their past and future successes, David invited his partners to dinner and champagne.

David felt like celebrating after seeing the first payment for their flights go into the company's bank account from the US government. It had taken roughly a month, but they were at last receiving adequate compensation in hard currency (USD) for their ambulance work. In addition, the office on the Kurfuerstendamm, located over the optometrist's office, was working out very well, and he was surprisingly comfortable in the apartment he occupied on the fourth floor. Due to war damage, the two back rooms were roofless, but the kitchen, bathroom and the large sitting room facing the street were habitable, making it a functional bedsitter. It wasn't as pleasant as the Priestmans' elegant villa on the Havel, but David was tired of being a guest and liked living in his own property. He liked being in the heart of Berlin, right over his office, and nearer to Charlotte. The only downside was that he hadn't had the heart to tear Sammy away from the ducks.

With Charlotte's help, David had hired a bookkeeper and a secretary to handle the telephone and office management. This freed Charlotte to focus on liaison with the hospitals and scheduling the flights, while David updated the financial planning. For the first time since starting the air ambulance business, the business plan projected profits within the next two months — provided, of course, that they could add two four-engine transports to their fleet.

For the freight side of the business, now officially incorporated as Air Freight International, David had options on two Halifax VIs with less than 500 flying hours each. Furthermore, both had already been converted into freighters by Transport Command in the last months of the war before being mothballed. Meanwhile, Chips had recruited two new members for their ground crew, both of whom had served on Halifax squadrons and were prepared to work in Hamburg. That just left the matter of hiring a ground crew chief for the Berlin (German) ground crew that Charlotte's cousin had recruited and, most important of all, recruiting aircrew for the Halifaxes.

Monday morning got off to a good start with the interview with Gordon MacDonald. David liked the Scotsman at once. Despite the wheelchair, he retained a military smartness that underlined his forthright and determined character. He had prepared for the interview and took the offensive by openly suggesting they could hire any number of good crew chiefs who weren't in wheelchairs. Without a pause for breath, however, he countered his own statement with the fact that he had more than twenty years' experience with aircraft engines and would repay the opportunity to work with unlimited dedication. When he finished his prepared remarks, David looked amusedly to his left and right and asked if there were any questions. Emily and Kiwi shook their heads. He turned to MacDonald. "Did you have any questions for us, Mr MacDonald?"

"Just, how soon can I start, sir?"

David laughed openly, stood up and reached out his hand. "Welcome aboard, Mr MacDonald. Mrs Priestman will complete the paperwork with you this afternoon. As far as we're concerned, you can start work as soon as you arrive in Berlin, which means either flying back with us in the Wellington tomorrow or waiting until the Halifaxes are officially transferred to the company and ready to fly to the Continent, presumably later this week."

MacDonald still had hold of David's hand and was pumping it up and down. "Thank you, sir. You won't regret this."

"I'm sure I won't," David assured him, smiling, before reminding him gently, "but first we have some other interviews."

MacDonald took the hint and released his hand. He nodded to Kiwi and Emily, then wheeled himself out of the hotel meeting room. David thought he saw tears in his eyes as he left.

"Could you call in the Dudley Crew, Emily?" David asked, and she slipped out, only to return without the crew. David looked at her in surprise.

"They're not yet complete. Do you want to see the Moran crew instead?"

"Certainly, if they're all here."

As with MacDonald, Moran and his crew made a good first impression. They all wore dark suits and blue ties, which gave them a uniform appearance. They also seemed to move as a team. There was no jostling for position as they approached the table. Moran was in the centre of course, but the others spread out to either side of him and stood attentively without nervous glances or fidgeting. David invited them to sit, and Moran opened, with a nod to Emily, by thanking David for the opportunity to present his crew. He then introduced them by name and trade.

David liked the fact that the crew was diverse. The RAF leadership had discovered that crews that mixed Englishmen with Canadians, Australians and continentals performed better than homogeneous crews. David knew from Moran's resume that he'd had been raised in Africa, his second pilot was Australian, his flight engineer was West Indian, and the remaining two crewmen were English; that sounded like a good mix to David. Since David was familiar with Moran's resume, he focused on the others, asking if any of them had experience on the Halifax. The flight engineer answered positively.

David invited questions, and Moran turned to his crew. David liked that, too. This wasn't the kind of pilot who thought he was the only one who mattered. Moran's crew shook their heads.

"Just one last question," David wrapped up the interview. "I noticed on your resume, Moran, that you have a wife and a young daughter. You do understand you'll be based in Germany?"

"Yes, sir."

"And you're both comfortable about being separated for an indefinite period?"

"My wife actively encouraged me to apply for this position, sir, believing that it would enhance my ability to obtain meaningful permanent employment in aviation in the longer term. Since she is living with her parents in a beautiful Yorkshire village and is very happy there, I'm confident that the separation will not put undue strain on our relationship."

That sounded as if Moran had anticipated the question and prepared an answer, but that too spoke in his favour. "Good. In that case, welcome aboard." David stood and shook hands first with Moran and then with the other four crew members. They departed, smiling and visibly more relaxed. Unfortunately, Dudley's crew was still incomplete.

"Who's missing?" David asked Emily, with an annoyed glance at his watch. Their interview had been scheduled for nine-thirty am and it was now nearing eleven.

"Dudley himself," Emily informed him in a neutral tone.

David winced inwardly. Dudley had been his contact and he'd been counting on him. Emily, on the other hand, had suspected a drinking problem. David hadn't wanted to believe it, while Kiwi had been quick to point out that a man down on his luck might turn to drink but would probably be fine if given a new chance. "Let's give him another few minutes," David decided.

When he still hadn't turned up forty minutes later, they invited the rest of the crew in, only to learn that the second pilot, muttering something about this all being a "cock-up," had left. "In that case, there is no crew, and we don't need to waste any more of anyone's time," David concluded sharply as his disappointment started to overwhelm him.

All David's planning had been based on two four-engine freighters and he would have to recalculate everything to see if they could break even — never mind make a profit — with just one freighter and the ambulance. He couldn't believe Dudley had left him in the lurch like this. The sense of betrayal left a bitter taste in his mouth.

"Don't you need backup signallers and navigators, sir?" a small voice broke through his anger.

David looked up and realised that although the flight engineer had left, two men were still in the room. Before he could say 'no', Emily intervened, speaking directly to the two job applicants. "Would you gentlemen please wait outside for a few more minutes? I know you've been waiting a long time, but the situation has changed, and we need to discuss this amongst ourselves."

"We can wait, ma'am," one of them answered and they withdrew.

"David," Emily started before he could protest, "I know four-engine freighters are more economical, but at the moment most aircraft on the Airlift are Dakotas. They only require one pilot, a navigator, and a signaller. If you resumed flying the ambulance, Kiwi could take command of the Dakota with Dudley's navigator and signaller, who appear keen to work regardless of captain."

David turned to Kiwi. "Would you be willing to do that?"

Kiwi shrugged eloquently. "No reason why not, mate. Emily and I have been talking about the need for some form of management presence at the freight hub in Hamburg. Ron and Chips are great with engines, but we can't expect them to make policy decisions about hangar space, a spare parts depot, liaison with BEA, or a-hundred-and-one other things."

David frowned slightly. Although what Kiwi said made sense, it bothered him that they had discussed this behind his back. Then again, they were flying together with lots of time to talk, while he'd been spending most of his time in the downtown office. After thinking the situation through again, he tried to explain, "I don't object to Kiwi taking command of a Dakota and running our office and operations in Hamburg. The problem is, if I'm flying, I can't keep our finances in order."

"Then we should recruit another pilot — or two. We need additional staff." Emily suggested, "And not just pilots. We need people who can spring in if any member of the regular crew falls ill, and — unless the blockade ends in the next couple of weeks — we are going to have to give people time off, too."

"We aren't breaking even yet!" David reminded them. "We're *still* losing money! Don't any of you understand that we can only succeed if the company is profitable!" It frustrated him that no one else thought about the financial side of their business. Or, maybe, they just thought his resources were limitless? Either way, it left him alone with all the worries about staying solvent. He was about to complain but stopped himself. He hadn't hired Kiwi or Emily to watch their revenues and expenses; that was his job. They were doing theirs. It was Dudley who had let him down. As the full weight of what it meant hit him, he felt completely deflated. He looked down at his legal pad with his jotted notes and a sense of pointlessness overwhelmed him. His father had always said he didn't have a head for business — even while he pushed him into it. As if he'd wanted to see him fail.

"There has to be a way to make this fly, David," Emily spoke softly into the tension. "Like the Airlift itself, we have to start flying first and work things out on the wing."

He turned to meet her eyes, still hesitating. He could have pointed to a dozen factors illustrating how precarious their situation was. But if they didn't *try*, then his father *would* win. He shook off his father's ghost and nodded solemnly. "You're right. We can only succeed by keeping our eyes on the stars, not the ground."

Chapter Eleven
Coping with the Unexpected

Can you Spare me a Dime?
Frankfurt / Main
Saturday, 7 August 1948
(Day 43)

"Hey, J.B.!" Jimmy Hudson shouted from the far side of the cafeteria, "There's a couple of civilians out at the front gate asking for you."

"I don't know any Germans," J.B. protested, walking towards his pilot to close the distance between them. He saw no reason why their conversation had to be shared with everyone in the room.

"Ain't Germans," Jimmy answered. "They're Americans and one's an ugly bitch. Must be an old girlfriend of yours." Jimmy laughed at his own joke.

J.B. froze. Rick and Jan? Surely, they wouldn't have come over to Germany hoping to join the Airlift? Bussing his tray without bothering to finish his doughnut, he hurried out to the gate. Even before he passed the sentry, he recognised Rick by his lanky frame. He was standing about ten yards beyond the control point with Jan in trousers beside him. J.B. called over to them and they turned and waved.

J.B. jogged over, exclaiming, "Where did you two come from?" He was grinning — and then he noticed that they weren't even smiling. Rick looked like he hadn't slept or eaten in a week; Jan looked crushed and broken.

"We're finished, J.B. We had a crash with NRJ48 — nothing serious. On the ground. But we couldn't afford the repairs. We had to sell her and thought, what the hell—"

"Wait. Slow down. Let's not talk in the street." Military jeeps and trucks were coming and going. They honked at pedestrians, stopped at the gate with squealing brakes, and belched diesel smoke into the air. Their engines growled when they moved and groaned when they changed gear. "I can get you into the club as my guests," J.B. told his friends. Returning to the sentry, he signed them in. Leading the way, he asked, "How long have you been here?"

"Almost a week."

"And you didn't stop by earlier?" J.B. asked, flabbergasted.

"We've been here five times in the last two days, but you were either flying or over at your quarters, which we were told were strictly off limits to visitors."

"Yeah, sorry about that. We've got no schedules or anything, so it's a bit crazy. Thanks for not giving up."

"Well, we didn't have any choice," Rick answered. "We're pretty desperate. In fact—"

"Wait. Wait." They had arrived at the officer's club. "Can I get you anything? A beer?"

"Do they have snacks, maybe?" Jan spoke for the first time. She sounded hesitant and timid, unlike the last time they'd met.

"Yeah, they've got potato chips and pretzels, I think. What do you want?"

"Anything salty and a coke, please. If that's ok?"

"No problem. Rick?"

"I'll have the same."

As J.B. placed the order, the bartender leaned forward and hissed at him. "Captain, sir. Your lady friend isn't dressed appropriately."

"What?"

"She's in slacks, sir. Women in slacks aren't allowed in the officers' club."

"Aw, give me a break. Rick's a wartime buddy of mine. Jan's his wife. Look the other way, will you?" J.B. slapped an extra quarter on the bar, and the enlisted man pocketed it.

J.B. returned to the table with two bags of chips and the cokes, but he also suggested they move to a less conspicuous spot. He sat between Jan and the rest of the room. "OK. Tell me the whole story from the top."

"There's not that much to tell, really," Rick started. "We had a parking accident with a luggage carrier down in Mobile, and it wrecked the alignment on the undercarriage. I don't know how such a little bump can cause so much damage, but I couldn't do the repairs myself and what the airfield maintenance workshop wanted was beyond our budget. Business wasn't all that good anyway, so we sold off NRJ48 and spent the cash to buy tickets out here. We started looking for work on the Airlift; not with the Air Force, of course, but with one of the civilian outfits, but—" he shrugged eloquently, "no dice."

"What do you mean 'no dice'?" J.B. asked back with a glance at Jan, who was nervously turning her coke around and around. "I heard the civilian carriers were desperate for everything from pilots to sparkplugs."

"Just not 'girls' — as they insist on calling me," Jan looked up and met his gaze. "The only jobs I've been offered are working in a canteen or doing laundry."

"I'm not gonna let her do that! You understand, don't you, J.B.?"

"Yeah, I understand, but I don't know how I can help," J.B. admitted. He was just a lowly pilot, a copilot to be precise, and had so little contact with the brass that he hardly recognised his squadron leader, let alone anyone more important.

Jan and Rick looked at one another, and Rick leaned towards J.B. to say in a low, earnest voice, "We came to ask for a loan — enough money for us to get back home. Or, if you don't have that much, enough for Jan to go home alone. I'll work until I can buy my own ticket and pay you back. It's just we're broke, buddy, and I don't like the looks some of the guys are giving Jan."

J.B. knew he had to help, even though he short on cash. "How much is it?"

"Third-class steamer fare from Hamburg to New York is three hundred-ninety-six bucks," Rick told him bluntly.

J.B. didn't earn that much in a month, and he didn't have it saved either. On the assumption he'd be earning good money come August, he'd spent his college savings on things for his wedding and honeymoon. Now he was back to earning peanuts. "You know I want to help," he pleaded with Rick, "but that's a lot of money. I'd have to request an advance on my pay."

"I told you he wouldn't be able to help," Jan said bitterly, getting to her feet.

"Jan! Stop! Sit down!" J.B. urged. Besides feeling bad, she'd just drawn attention to herself, and they were getting dirty looks.

"It's all right, J.B." Jan was used to talking over wide distances on a ranch or over the sound of engines. Her voice carried far, and more heads turned. Turning to address Rick, she concluded, "We should have known women pilots were no more welcome in Europe than in the States. We were dumb to come and shouldn't expect anyone else to bail us out."

"Wait," J.B. tried to soothe her. "I want to help, I just honestly don't have the money. Please sit down, Jan."

For a moment she stubbornly remained standing, but Rick coaxed her back into her seat with a gentle, "Come on, honey. J.B. didn't say he wouldn't help."

Before they could continue their conversation, a man was standing over the table. J.B. looked up and sprang to attention at the sight of a major. "Sir!"

"I need a word with you, Captain," the major said with a stiff nod to the civilians. He drew J.B. just far enough away so they couldn't be overheard. "You have no business bringing that floozy in here—"

"Sir! She's not what you think. She is the wife of my friend Rick Orloff, who flew —"

"She's in pants and that makes her a whore in my book. Get her out of here fast! And that's an order."

Resentfully, J.B. went back to his table, but Rick and Jan were already preparing to leave. "I'm really sorry about this," he stammered, embarrassed.

"Don't worry. We're used to it," Rick answered, his eyes averted, expression grim.

"I've got to see you out," J.B. reminded them, and he reached for his cap, which he'd left on the table. As they started to squeeze between a couple of other tables, a lieutenant colonel stopped them. J.B. had never seen him before, but he was in a very smart uniform with sharp creases and shiny rank insignia; he had the word "staff" stamped all over him. With an inner sigh, J.B. braced for the worst. The lieutenant colonel, however, addressed himself to Jan rather than J.B., "Weren't you one of the WAFS?"

Jan caught her breath and stood up straighter. You could see she wanted to salute but not being in uniform, she couldn't. Still, she answered with a smart, "Yes, sir! I had that privilege." She also recognised a chance when she saw one, and threw in, "I was the first woman pilot to qualify on the B-24."

He smiled and nodded, "I thought I remembered you. Bettinger," he introduced himself, holding out his hand. "I was on General Tunner's staff in the Ferry Division — and I'm on his staff for the Airlift too."

"Is General Tunner in Germany?" she asked, startled.

"We only just got here and we're still trying to organise desks and phones, but we'll be making a bunch of changes very soon. One of them might even have to do with women in pants." He flung the remark at the major. "Meanwhile, I'll mention to the General that I ran into you. We're desperate for qualified personnel and he may know of some way to reactivate you. What about you?" he turned to Rick. "Were you in the Air Force?"

"Yeah, 303rd Bombardment Group, April '43 to Jan '44, bombardier. Since the war, I've trained as an aircraft mechanic, and I worked as a flight engineer for a private company this past year."

"We could sure use you! What did you say your name was? Here!" Bettinger pulled out a notepad and handed it to Rick. "Both of you write your names down and a telephone number where we can get hold of you."

Rick and Jan willingly complied and then followed J.B. out of the club and off the base. Before the gate, J.B. pulled out his wallet. "Look, I can lend you ten bucks right away if that would help—"

"No, that's all right—" Rick started to refuse, but Jan was more practical. She reached out, took the ten-dollar bill, and smiled at J.B. "Thanks, J.B. It'll hold us over until we hear back from Bettinger. If he could talk Tunner into re-activating us, it would be the biggest break ever, and we'll pay you back in spades. Promise."

"Don't even think about it! I'll keep my fingers crossed for you. Meanwhile, give me that number so I can call if I ever get any time off."

"Sure." They wrote down the same number they'd given Bettinger and they waved good-bye to J.B. went their separate ways.

Crew Chief
RAF Gatow
Monday, 9 August 1948
(Day 45)

It was his first day on the job. The first time he'd reported to work in more than three years. The first time he was going to work since he'd crashed in a Lancaster and been dragged out with a broken back. To say that Gordon was nervous was an understatement.

The trip to Berlin had been easy. The first leg had been almost like old times with Moran at the controls and the wheelchair (against all regulations) jammed against the flight engineer's station. They'd all been a bit slap-happy finding themselves in a flying job together again, and Gordon had to admit that Red Forrester's younger brother Bruce was a marvellous addition to the team. Unlike his loud-mouthed, competitive elder brother, Bruce was soft-spoken and modest, with a sense of humour so dry they often didn't get his jokes the first time around. Not at all what one expected of an Australian. They ended up singing songs together as they had done after picking up Gee over the North Sea on the way home from an op.

In Hamburg, Gordon transferred to Moby Dick. He was less happy flying with "strange" pilots (i.e. Kiwi and Mrs Priestman) but the Wellington's conversion to an ambulance included winches for wheelchairs and a special slot facing fore-and-aft for it to sit while in flight. Once on the ground, they had been met, much to Gordon's embarrassment, by Mrs Priestman's husband, a Wing Commander and Station Commander, who welcomed him to Berlin. "I've heard a great deal about you," he said as Gordon fidgeted uncomfortably, wanting to salute or at least stand but unable to do either.

He was happy when Mrs Bell, who ran the Malcolm Club at Gatow, took over, rolling him to his "quarters" on the ground floor of the club. These were rooms intended for aircrew forced to overnight at Gatow unexpectedly due to weather or technical issues. However, AAI had arranged for one single room to be assigned to Gordon permanently. The

Malcolm Club staff made him feel welcome, and his call home to Maisy had been full of positive news and good feelings.

After dropping Gordon in Berlin, Kiwi flew the ambulance back to Hamburg for servicing at the maintenance centre one last time before the transfer to Berlin. Gordon had been given the weekend to "settle in," but he spent most of it out in the AAI hangar, which was one of the older and more dilapidated structures dating back from before the war. Based on the pictures and technical manuals still lying about, it had last been used for Ju52s. Gordon used the weekend to clean out drawers, take an inventory of tools, and get the place as "ship-shape" as he was able. One thing he couldn't do, however, was clean the windows, and they were filthy. He realised they would need more artificial lighting installed and resolved to mention this to Mr Goldman at the first opportunity.

Today the ground crew would report for work for the first time. They were all ex-Luftwaffe, he'd been told, but that didn't bother him so much as the fact that he was in a wheelchair. He presumed they'd been warned about it, but he felt strange — like when he couldn't stand up for the WingCo or had to have help with his bath at the Malcolm Club. Somehow, being an invalid hadn't been so bad when he was just a pensioner...

"Moby Dick" was scheduled to fly in around 8 am to collect six patients bound for Munich, so the ground crew had been told to report no later than seven am. Gordon was to show the crew the "quick check" procedures, confirming that all was well or responding to any concerns reported by the pilots. When Moby Dick took off, Gordon planned to introduce the ground crew to the engine manuals he'd brought with him and to show them where the tools were, etc.. If they had time, he'd put them to work washing the windows, but not until Moby Dick had made her second run of the day would the work truly begin. That was when they were to conduct the Daily Inspection (DI) to ensure she was fully serviceable to fly the next morning.

Unable to sleep, Gordon got up at 6 am, had coffee and a bun at the Malcolm Club, then rolled himself over to the hangar to wait for the Germans. He was glad he'd gone over ahead of schedule because the Germans arrived almost twenty minutes early. They came through the wide door nattering away in German. Although they'd removed all insignia, by the colour and cut of their overalls it was obvious they were wearing

Luftwaffe uniforms. For a second, Gordon felt a flash of resentment. Then they spotted him, fell silent and stood to attention.

Gordon rolled forward and in his nervousness forgot to say even "hello," greeting them instead with, "Can any of you lot speak English?"

"Yes, sir!" one of the young men answered eagerly, clicking his heels together smartly. "I am Helmut Greis, sir. I speak a little English." His English was surprisingly fluent. Not at all the way Germans spoke English in the films.

"Well, that's a good start," Gordon agreed. "And who are your friends?"

"Axel Voigt." Gries indicated an intense-looking man with thinning hair. "Voigt is the most experienced man among us. He was a *Stabsfeldwebel*, a sergeant major, Ludwig Winterfeld and I were *Oberfeldwebel*, master sergeants."

This longer speech revealed Gries' American accent, a fact that grated on Gordon's Scottish nerves. Gordon growled back, "The RAF doesn't have master sergeants — that's an American rank, or sergeant majors either. That's an army rank. Where did you learn your English? In America?"

Gries eagerness burst like a balloon, and he looked deflated, while Gordon's tone had produced a look of resentment on Voigt's face and wary uncertainty on Winterfeld's. They were not getting off to the best start, Gordon registered. He ploughed ahead just the same. "Right. Well, I'm MacDonald. You can call me 'Chiefy.'"

"Chichi?" Gries asked, not quite hearing him.

"No, ChieFy — with an F," Gordon corrected.

"Fifi?" Gries tried again.

"You make it sound like I'm some sort of bloody Chihuahua!" Gordon snarled. "It can't be all that difficult: Chi-Fi. Chi-Fi —"

Humiliated, Gries looked down at his shoes and fell silent. The other two men exchanged a look and then glared sullenly at Gordon. The set of Voigt's jaw was almost insolent. No, this was not going well at all. Gordon tried again. "So, what aircraft have you serviced?"

Gries respectfully deferred to Voigt, who answered with a list of aircraft which made it clear Voigt had no multi-engine experience at all. Gordon was beginning to wonder what the hell he was doing here. Fortunately, the other two had serviced just about every conventional aircraft the Luftwaffe had had. Next, he asked about engines, and at once wished he hadn't.

They listed what seemed like dozens of Junkers, Daimler-Benz, and BMW engines of various marks, none of which meant anything to him. Gordon was starting to feel lost and hot. He reached up and undid the top button of his overalls.

Abruptly, the Tannoy in the hangar clicked on. "AAI ground crew! AAI ground crew! Your aircraft has landed."

The three Germans broke into excited chatter, temporarily forgetting the animosity and frustration that had been building up. Meanwhile, Gordon rolled his wheelchair to the front of the hangar to look across the busy airfield. When he caught sight of the distinctive white aircraft moving sedately in their direction, he pointed and called out, "There she is!"

Taken by surprise, Gries answered, "I'm sorry, FiFi — I mean ChiChi—"

Abruptly, the humour of it hit Gordon. He broke into a loud guffaw and when his laughter died away, he advised, "Forget it, Gries. Just call me 'Mac' or 'Boss.' Whatever you prefer. Now come over here."

Warily, Gries moved up beside him with the other two men in his wake. Gordon pointed: "That white elephant out there is our aircraft. It's a Wellington, a medium bomber, with two Hercules Mark VI engines. You're not going to have any trouble with them, her — or me," he added significantly looking over at Gries and offering his hand.

Gries smiled, and taking his hand answered in his best American, "OK, MacBoss! We'll be a good team. Promise!"

Creatures of the Earth
Berlin-Kreuzberg
Tuesday, 10 August 1948
(Day 46)

"Christian? Do you have a minute?" the female voice on the other end of the telephone line was his sister-in-law, the widow of his brother Philip.

"For you, more than a minute, Alix. What is it?" Christian asked her back.

"I uncovered some significant information about Aggstein."

Christian tensed. "Yes?"

"Well, you remember we were told that your sister Theresa and her three children had been killed in a partisan attack while fleeing from Warsaw before the advancing Red Army. At the time, she and the children were travelling in a car belonging to and driven by SS Brigadefueher Max von Aggstein. Theresa's husband Walther Halle, we were told, was not in the car but remained behind in Warsaw only to later make good his escape to Switzerland, where he disappeared."

"Yes, I remember," Christian confirmed. "He had a Polish mistress. I'm sure he ran off with her."

"Well, after you asked me to see if I could find out more about Aggstein, I asked a colleague of mine, a forensics expert who had to go to Poland on official business, if he could verify the identities of the bodies in the grave where Theresa and the children are buried."

"He could do that?" Christian asked astonished.

"Such requests are more common than you may think, and it was not difficult for a man in his position to arrange. Furthermore, through your mother, I could provide him with the family dental records up to 1941. It seems the man in the car was *not* Aggstein, after all. It was Walther. So, mistress or not, he did not abandon his wife and children. He died trying to get them to safety."

"But then who's the man we traced to Switzerland?"

"I suspect it was Max von Aggstein — who had lent Walther his readily recognizable Mercedes 770. He may have expected the partisan attack, or he may just have exploited it. In either case, I believe that once Walther was dead, he assumed Walther's identity."

"What would be the advantage of that? If Aggstein wanted a disguise, surely something more innocuous would have been better?"

"I'm only speculating, of course, but SS-Brigadefuehrer Max von Aggstein was notorious for his brutality. Walther, on the other hand, was just a German factory owner. Indeed, he had a reputation for feeding and housing his slave labourers better than other German factory owners. He allegedly protected 'his workers' from the death camps. For Aggstein, the shift from brutal SS general to enlightened German industrialist may have been easier and more credible than trying to turn himself into a German deserter or a Communist activist overnight."

Christian was reminded that his sister-in-law not only had a law degree, she also had an acute understanding of human nature. Out loud, he said, "To use an American expression: I'll buy that."

"What I also discovered is that our friend SS Brigadefuehrer Max von Aggstein is the younger brother of Franz von Aggstein, who obtained his PhD in Chemistry at the University of Bern in Switzerland in 1934. Early in the war, he conducted experiments with Zyklon B to determine its suitability for use on humans, and by the end of the war, he was engaged in research on battlefield chemical weapons. He disappeared without a trace in April of 1945. Before his disappearance, he was working at a highly secret, experimental facility in Bitterfeld."

"Friedebach!" Christian exclaimed triumphantly.

"We don't have any proof," Alix reminded him.

"No, but everything fits. What about ties to Thierack, the SD man who kept his slut in our apartment and stole all our moveable goods?"

"Nothing much, I'm afraid. It appears that he and Max — not Franz — were in the same SS unit at the time of the Night of the Long Knives. That's not much."

"Unless Max is the 'butler' that smelled of SS to both Goldman and myself. Now that I think of it, there was a vague resemblance between the two."

"I know you have a good nose, Christian, but that's not exactly evidence. I'll keep looking. Your mother, by the way, was relieved to learn that Walther wasn't the rat we so readily believed him to be."

"I'm glad for her sake that it was a comfort," Christian replied. "How is she doing otherwise?"

"Hm," Alix prevaricated for a moment, then replied, "The estate is doing very well, and Yvette is more and more of a help to her every day, she says." There was just a hint of reproach in that reference to his wife.

"That's good news," Christian answered, and then expanded his response to address her unspoken suspicions: "You can assure them both that I'm not cheating on Yvette. There's simply no way for a healthy German civilian to get out of Berlin during this siege. Please try to make them understand that."

"I'll do my best," Alix promised. They said their goodbyes and hung up.

Christian was left feeling fractious. He didn't like being reminded of his duties to his wife and mother — although they hardly needed him. Yet he'd also lost all interest in selling wine in an environment where people didn't know whether they'd have enough to eat come winter. He hated feeling unproductive and superfluous.

For a moment, he considered trying to track down evidence against Friedebach/Aggstein himself, but he didn't know the first thing about detective work. However, it made sense to share the latest information with David Goldman.

It was a warm, sunny day, so he decided to walk to the AAI office on the Kurfurstendam. That was roughly 12 kilometres away, or a good two-hour walk, but he had nothing better to do with his time. Besides, it would give him a chance to take the pulse of the city.

He followed the Landwehr canal, passed the hospital where Frau Liebherr worked, and skirted around the Anhalter train station that was now an abandoned wreck. Although the damage to the façade was the work of Allied bombers, the lack of activity was the result of the blockade. Someone had painted in large white letters on the grimy façade: "Berliners awake! Those that bombed you want to enslave you! Fight back! Choose Freedom and Unity in the Democratic East!" Someone had tampered with the text in charcoal to make it read: "Berliners awake! Those that bombed you want to enslave you! Fight back! Choose Freedom and Unity in the Democratic East." Someone else had taken red paint and crossed out the "bombed" and replaced it with raped, and East with West to read: "Berliner's awake! Those that raped you want to enslave you. Fight back! Choose Freedom and Unity in the Democratic West." The two texts set out the opposing views succinctly, but there was no telling which standpoint had the wider support.

As he approached Wittenberg Platz, the old "West End" of Berlin that had once been "fashionable", Christian found more crowds and more evidence of political agitation. Young men were handing out brochures urging people to register for their rations in the eastern burroughs. "You have nothing to lose but your chains!" they reminded Berliners. Another noted, "Talk of a 'blockade' is nonsensical when you can get all you can eat just by registering with the Soviet authorities." That was a perplexing aspect of the situation, Christian conceded, and looked around wondering how many of those accepting and reading the documents were convinced of Soviet benevolence.

Some of the Soviet agitators stood on up-ended packing crates and shouted out their messages. "The Soviet Union is Peace! Any attacks on the Soviet Union will bring war! We have had enough war! Vote for peace with your feet! Vote for peace by refusing to work for the warmongers! Stop assisting the angels of death who rained fire on you!"

Except for Christian himself, no one bothered to stop and listen. Christian stopped a young man hurrying past. "What do you think? Should we help the Allies by off-loading their aircraft?"

"If only I could!" the young man lamented. "I tried to get a job first at Tempelhof and then at Gatow and finally at the new construction site in Tegel! You have to prove you can carry a 10-kilo sack 500 meters in order to get a job. I didn't make it." He hit his chest with his fist. "I took a bullet in the lung in Crimea."

Christian nodded his understanding and continued. He'd reached the start of the Kurfurstendamm, and as he continued westwards the number of political agitators declined. He reached number 168 and found the ophthalmologist's office on the ground floor that Charlotte had told him about. One flight up, he knocked on a door bearing a hand-made wooden sign reading: "Emergency Air Services."

An unfamiliar voice answered his knock with "Come in!" Three women shared the room. Two he didn't know, but Charlotte jumped to her feet in surprise. "Christian! What are you doing here?" Because the other women were staring, she hastened to explain. "Freiherr von Feldburg is my cousin! Christian, these are Fraulein Klempner, our bookkeeper, and Fraulein Dorsch, the receptionist and secretary." The women and Christian exchanged nods.

"I've come to see Mr Goldman," Christian announced.

"Oh! He's flying. Didn't I tell you?"

"You mean he's flying *all* the time?" Christian asked back, astounded. Charlotte had told him that David had gone back to flying, but he'd assumed it was only now and again.

"He has to until they find another pilot," Charlotte clarified, adding, "but he's so busy flying he doesn't have time to find any more personnel and things are happening so fast —"

"Let's go into the office to talk," Christian suggested, with an eye towards the two new employees. They went together into David's office, Christian closing the door behind him as Charlotte sank into the visitor's chair before David's empty desk. Christian noticed that she almost fell into the chair as if she was faint. "Are you all right?" he asked.

"Just a little dizzy. The real problem is that I feel overwhelmed. It's not just that there's so much to do, but I can't seem to concentrate or set priorities or — anything. I'm beginning to think I shouldn't have taken this job. I shouldn't have pretended I could manage an office like this — all the scheduling, not to mention the customer complaints—"

"Slow down, Charlotte," Christian urged. "Slow down and take a deep breath." She did, and after several seconds, seemed to relax a little as she gazed at him expectantly.

"Charlotte, what did you have for breakfast this morning?"

"A slice of toast, as usual."

"Without butter or marmalade, of course, because we have neither. Your rations are for 1,600 calories a day, and because of the blockade we are no longer getting the packages from Grandma Walmsdorf with English honey, stock cubes, hard toffee, and tea. Isn't David giving you any extras?"

"He offered to, but I could not accept," she explained, shaking her head sharply.

"Whyever not?" Christian countered, astonished. She was working for a British company that flew outside of blockaded Berlin on average twice a day. They could bring back almost five tons of cargo, and for some time now Christian had wondered why they weren't.

"It would make me feel like the women who sleep with soldiers just for the food and the nylons," Charlotte whispered, looking at the threadbare carpet at their feet.

"Are you sleeping with David?"

Charlotte turned on him so sharply that he almost got whiplash. "How dare you ask that?"

"Because I knew the answer and wanted to make the point that since you *aren't* sleeping with him, you can't be like those women who *do* sleep around for material gain. If David has offered—"

She was shaking her head furiously and told him in an angry tone. "You don't understand!" Her hands had started trembling.

Christian backed off, acknowledging that his masculine brain could not grasp the complex feelings that entangled Charlotte. He tried to soothe her by saying, "All right, I don't understand, but one thing I know is that you can't concentrate and work properly if you aren't getting enough to eat. If you don't start eating better, you will start making mistakes. You might make important mistakes — with the schedules, maybe, or the destinations or the equipment needed. You could put the company in serious difficulty."

"But you are managing on the rations," she countered. "I should be able to as well."

"I'm not living on the rations! Whenever I go to a customer, they offer me something — a hot dog, a sandwich, some cheese on toast. It's always something light and simple, but it's nourishing all the same. I should have thought to keep half for you. I'm sorry." He went down on his heels, so he was at her level and looked her straight in the eye. "Starting tonight, I will see that you have more to eat. Now, tell me what is overwhelming you. Maybe I can help."

"The hospitals — they can't cope any more. They're getting as little as five hours of electricity a day and can't fit all the necessary surgery into that period. Another problem is that they have no fresh bandages and so they have to sterilise old bandages for re-use, but that requires electricity. They're out of antiseptics and antibiotics, and are short on painkillers —"

"No morphine?"

"No," she shook her head.

"Well, we might be able to get them heroin, if they're willing to pay—"

"Don't make stupid jokes!" Charlotte admonished him. "This is very serious! The hospitals compete for the few spaces on the ambulance that we have, and the directors have pleaded with me to increase our flights, to take more patients out faster. They would send ten times as many people out if they could, but David says we can't increase our capacity because we can't afford the aircraft and can't find the crews."

"But if you were flying stuff in, wouldn't you get paid by the Allies for that as well as for the patients going out? Surely, you'd then soon earn enough to buy more aircraft?"

"It is not that simple, Christian!" Charlotte told him annoyed. "We can't carry coal and flour and fish in our ambulance! They would make it too unsanitary for patients! Also, we fly to the civil airfields closest to the hospitals, not the airlift bases where the cargoes are collected for Berlin. Not to mention that loading any return cargoes would take time and reduce rather than increase the number of evacuations we could complete each day."

"There is obviously nothing wrong with your ability to think, Charlotte. It's also obvious that David ought to be on the ground solving these issues, not flying. If he's that hard up for pilots, remind him I have about five thousand hours — all on single-engine aircraft, of course, but he was an instructor and he ought to be able to get me qualified on twins in twenty to thirty hours. For now, however, I'm going to concentrate on seeing you get a proper meal tonight, and tomorrow too."

Chapter Twelve
No Way to Run an Airlift

Keep 'em Flying
Frankfurt / Main
Wednesday, 11 August 1948
(Day 47)

"Keep 'em flying," was clearly the motto of the moment, and after just two weeks on the Airlift, J.B. was exhausted. At least during the war, you knew you'd be sent home after completing a set number of missions, but here there was no end in sight. Furthermore, with the Airlift going on "round the clock", no one worked regular shifts, either. Crews were sent to get some rest after completing two round trips no matter what time it was, and reported for duty twelve hours later. But "two round trips" didn't mean a set length of time because weather conditions sometimes kept them waiting around for thunderstorms to clear or fog to lift, stretching out their workday to unknown lengths. Whatever time one finally hit the sack for some rest, other men would be on a different schedule, crashing in or dragging themselves out to do their flying, disturbing the sleep of all the others.

J.B. had long since lost a sense of what day of the week it was, much less the date. All he knew was that his crew had just completed their second trip of the day and it was four o'clock in the afternoon. That sounded great, except they'd been up since midnight and were due to report for duty at 4 am tomorrow. He knew sleep was what he needed most, but he was too wound up. Maybe it had been seeing bandages, blankets and a box of school notebooks and pencils in their last load of "mixed cargo"? The latter reminded J.B. that innocent little kids were caught up in the political brinksmanship between the Soviets and the West. That upset him, and made him both more determined to keep flying and more frustrated with feeling like the fifth wheel on a wagon because Hudson hogged all the flying. He decided he needed a beer to wind down.

Then again, the grime on his hands and his filthy trousers made him feel too dirty to sit around drinking. The last cargo might have been "mixed", but the one before had been coal. Much as he hated returning to the Zeppelinheim and the trudge over to the communal showers, he didn't have much choice.

After collecting a change of clothes, J.B. went to the shower block to face the water that was never hot and towels that were never dry. He left all his clothes in a locker and walked naked with his bar of soap across the cold, wet concrete into the shower room. What he'd give for a hot shower in privacy! He thought wistfully of his postponed honeymoon to Niagara Falls and the classy hotel he'd booked. Hell, even the wartime base in England had offered better accommodations than they had here!

The walls of the shower room were covered with yellowing, cracked tiles, and black mould marked the mortar between them. Rows of rusting shower heads lined each wall with a drainage channel under them. Four other guys were already soaping themselves up under the lukewarm drizzle; the lather from their soap was grey with coal dust, just as his would be. With a sigh, he turned on the water and winced at the cold as he danced around under the sputtering stream of wetness until he got more used to it.

After towelling himself off, J.B. dressed in a clean uniform and headed over to the Officer's Club. On a whim, he stopped by the mail room. As he waited his turn, he noticed the calendar on the wall. It was August 11. Three days from now he *ought* to have been getting married. That seemed totally unreal.

"Name?" the mail clerk called out.

"Baronowsky, Joseph B," he answered.

To his amazement, the clerk returned with three letters. J.B. hesitated to take them with him to the Officers' Club because he didn't want a bunch of guys looking over his shoulder, but he didn't want to read in the sticky, tar-paper shack either. He decided to try his luck at the Club and was relieved to find it was practically empty. Pure luck. He ordered a beer, took it over to a corner table, and broke open the letter from Patty.

Dearest, darling Jay!

This has been the worst week of my whole life! I still can't believe what's happened. There has to be someone who can help! My Dad is calling everyone he knows, but meanwhile, we had to cancel all the wedding plans. My Mom called the Yacht Club and our honeymoon hotel, so we won't lose more than our deposit. She also called the florist, the caterer and the band. I had to write to all our guests to tell them the wedding is off indefinitely. Everyone <u>assumes</u> that you've ditched me, and I keep getting <u>condolences</u>! You don't know how embarrassing that is!

Do you have any idea how long this thing in Berlin is going to last? My Dad says the Russians are being bullies and that we have to teach them a lesson, but he doesn't think Truman will have the backbone to stick it out for long. He thinks he'll cave in pretty soon and it will all be over by September. If Truman is going to back down, why can't he do it sooner?

The newspapers are full of stories about Berlin and how brave the people are, but a couple of guys in my English lit class were there with the Army after the war. They told me nothing works and there's nothing worth seeing because there are ruins everywhere. They also said the German girls are all sluts and throw themselves at our troops so they can get nylons and cigarettes and stuff. Most of them want to get pregnant by some GI so they can get a US passport and get away from Germany since it's such a mess. I wanted to warn you about those German girls — because if you mess around with those German girls, the wedding really will be off for good!

But I know you won't be unfaithful. I shouldn't even have mentioned it. It's just my imagination running away with me because I miss you so much. Please write soon — or better yet, find a way to come back to me sooner.

Your loving baby Patty, xxxxxxxxx

J.B. sat staring at the letter for a moment and then folded it up and put it back in his pocket. He didn't know what he'd expected exactly, but he was disappointed. She hadn't asked one question about how he was doing. Not a thought about whether he was tired or in danger. She showed no curiosity about *what* he was doing whatsoever. Here he was taking part in the biggest humanitarian airlift in history, and it was as if he was just sitting around wasting time. She apparently didn't care what it was like living here — because she thought she knew already based on what some other guys said.

With a sigh, he turned to the other letters, opening his mother's letter next. It was all about whether he had enough socks, underwear and food. She ended the letter as she always had during the war with "PS: Don't forget to go to Mass." He rolled his eyes, but who knew? Maybe going to Mass was what got him through 25 missions over Germany? At least she worried about him.

He picked up the third letter, the one from his sister Barb, but before he could open it a trio of officers asked if they could sit at his table. Looking around in surprise, he realised that the club was filling up. That was the way it was here: one minute empty and crowded the next. He gestured for the others to sit down, stuffing his letters inside his pocket. Barb's letter could wait.

"Looks like you're out of beer. Can I get you another?" one of the newcomers asked, adding as he held out his hand, "Name's Timberlake. Bob Timberlake."

J.B. answered by shaking hands, supplying his name, and accepting the offer.

"What about you, Halvorsen? Crawley?" Timberlake asked his companions.

"Get me a martini, will yah?"

"One martini coming up. Halvorsen?"

"Orange juice."

"What?" the other two men said in unison, followed by "Are you sick or something?"

"No, it's just my way of life, that's all," the slender and pale Halvorsen answered.

"Aw, come on! I was raised Southern Baptist, but no one drinks more than the preacher man. Just does it in secret. After a day like this, you need a bit more than orange juice."

"I don't know," J.B. intervened with a glance at the orange juice-drinker, whose fair hair had already receded halfway back from his high forehead. "Orange juice sounds refreshing to me, too, 'though I'll stick to beer for the moment. Still, I say, let a man drink what he likes."

Timberlake shrugged and headed for the bar, while the other two officers sat down.

Halvorsen turned to J.B., holding out his hand. "Halvorsen, Gail Halvorsen. And no, Gail isn't necessarily a girl's name."

"I guessed that!" J.B. quipped back.

Halvorsen grinned and added. "Most fellas call me 'Hal.' I can't say I remember seeing you around before. Did you just get in?"

"Not really. Been here about two weeks, but we seem to either be flying or sleeping. We're housed over in Zeppelinheim, and most days it's too much trouble to come over here."

"I know what you mean," the third man chimed in, adding with a jerk of his head in the direction of J.B.'s chest, "All those bars and ribbons look like a war record."

"Eighth Air Force. And you?" J.B. asked; Crawley, too, had campaign ribbons.

"Pacific Theatre, like Timberlake."

They looked at Halvorsen with an unspoken question. "I was with Ferrying Command in the war, mostly in South America," he admitted.

"Sounds good to me," Crawley said.

"At least it means you're not new to this transport gig," J.B. noted. "It's a whole different ball game from bombing in formation with a lead navigator plotting the course there and back."

"That's true, but in the war I was flying alone over long distances without navigational aids. Flying in a narrow, crowded corridor is totally different."

"And it stinks!" Timberlake concluded as he returned and set their drinks in front of them. He sank into the vacant chair, lifted his beer mug and said, "Here's to an end to this mess!"

"I'll drink to that!" Crawley agreed, tossing back a third of his beer in one long chug. J.B. and Halvorsen exchanged a little smile before drinking more moderately.

"Any of you hear the rumour that some new, hot-shot CO has flown in from the States to take over the Airlift?" Timberlake wanted to know.

"Yeah, people have been talking about it for days now. He's already arrived in Wiesbaden and has a bunch of staff officers with him," Crawley answered.

"That's right," J.B. made the connection. "I ran into a lieutenant colonel the other day who said he was on the staff of some guy named Tunner."

"That's him, all right. People call him 'Willie the Whip' because he made the poor bastards flying the Hump clean their quarters for white glove inspections and held parades on Sundays like they were at West Point. A real hard-hosed organisational guy with no combat experience and no humour."

"Why is he here?" Timberlake asked.

"To knock us into shape," Crawley answered.

"Christ! That's just what we need!" Timberlake groaned sarcastically. He downed his beer and clunked the empty glass on the table. "I'm fed up with the whole thing and so is just about everybody else. This place is a madhouse. No one can tell us if — much less when — we get leave. No one can tell us when we're going home again. Half of us don't have our gear yet, and my wife isn't getting my pay either. The aircraft don't have regular ground crews, so there's no one to complain to when something's wrong. As far as I can see, no one even reads the snag sheets we fill out! Just 'keep 'em flying, boys!' Which means, things are going to break down in the air and we're going crash out of the sky. I don't know what the hell's so important about holding on to Berlin anyway! It's just a mound of rubble. Now, I'm going to get some shut eye. You coming, Mike?"

Crawley finished his beer and the two men pushed off, leaving J.B. and Halvorsen alone at the table. J.B. still wasn't feeling sleepy. He looked at his empty beer glass and then glanced at Halvorsen. "I could use another. What about you?"

"Yes, I'll get this one," Halvorsen offered, jumping up, which was generous given that beer cost more than orange juice.

When he returned, Halvorsen settled down and asked J.B. earnestly, "I'd be interested in how you feel about our mission here — as a man who flew in the Eighth Air Force and all."

"Oh," J.B. shrugged. "I don't think that makes much difference."

"You must have lost a lot of buddies to flak and German fighters,"

Halvorsen pressed him.

"Yeah, but when you come down to it, the Germans were just defending their country. I mean, we were bombing *them*. That doesn't excuse what the Nazis did, but not all Germans could have been war criminals. The kids certainly weren't. It seems to me the Berliners are being brave to stand up to the Reds the way they are, and we owe it to them to try to fly stuff in rather than let the Russians just take over. It's not the mission that I don't like, it's the way it's being run. All I do is sleep and sit next to Hudson while he complains about flying. It makes me feel pretty useless. Maybe that wouldn't seem so bad if I wasn't supposed to be getting married this weekend," J.B. admitted.

"You had to cancel your wedding to come out here?" Halvorsen sounded genuinely upset for him.

"Yeah. We were supposed to get hitched this coming Saturday, August 14."

"Geez! That's terrible! I'm sorry. How did your girl take it?"

"Not too good," J.B. admitted, gazing into his beer and picturing Patty as she raged.

Halvorsen left him to his memories for a moment and then raised his glass of orange juice. "Here's to pretty girls!" They clicked glasses and drank together.

After a moment, Halvorsen asked, "Who did you say you were flying with?"

"Hudson, Lt. Jimmy Hudson, and he's captain because I flew Fortresses, not C-54s. He's the 'expert' on the transport birds, even if he's a kid five years younger than me with fewer overall flying hours."

"And he doesn't let you fly much?"

"Nope. He says it's too dangerous. He doesn't trust me."

"That's short-sighted of him. In an emergency, the more experience you have the better."

"Yeah, well tell *him* that," J.B. retorted.

Halvorsen smiled but shook his head. "I don't like telling other captains how to fly their aircraft, but my copilot just got medevacked with jaundice. If you're interested, we could ask Personnel to re-assign you to my crew."

J.B. sat up straighter. "Seriously?" The USAF assigned crews more-

or-less randomly and generally didn't object to crew members swapping places.

Halvorsen smiled. "I think we'd get along, Baronowsky. You see, I agree with you on the mission. The Berliners care so much about freedom that they're willing to practically starve for it. I think we owe it to them to try to help them out. But frankly, unless this new CO whatever-his-name-is starts fixing all the problems, we're more likely to crash and burn than save Berlin."

"You said it," J.B. agreed. "LeMay ran a tight ship during the war. I can't figure out why he hasn't enforced the same kind of discipline and order on the Airlift."

Halvorsen shook his head. "I don't know, but I heard someone say all General LeMay cares about is strategic bombing. He thinks flying coal and flour is beneath his dignity."

J.B. nodded grimly. The thought made him mad because helping save lives ought to be more important than bombing people to hell. He turned his attention back to his new companion. "I'll bet you can teach me a thing or two about this cargo business and the C-54, Hal. So, let's see if we can get the crew assignment fixed up the first chance we get."

Chance Encounters
RAF Gatow
Thursday, 12 August 1948
(Day 48)

"There's been an accident on the Station, sir!" Sergeant Andrews announced, bursting into the WingCo's office.

Priestman reared up from his paperwork. "Where? What are the casualties?"

"I don't know yet," she admitted as the sound of sirens streamed through the open windows. Turning to look, Priestman saw first the fire engine then the ambulance burst from their respective bays and start speeding towards the runways. Meanwhile, his phone was ringing. Torn between the desire to follow the sirens and his duty to answer the phone,

Priestman hesitated, and Sergeant Andrews grabbed the phone for him. She listened and then handed the receiver over to her CO. "Garth, sir, with information on the accident."

"Priestman," he said into the phone.

"A Dakota from 18 Squadron had to abort take-off. Unfortunately, a 99 Squadron York, which had just landed, was taxiing across the PSP runway—"

"Damn!" That had always been the danger of parallel runways, he reminded himself, but they hadn't had a lot of alternative options. "Any word on casualties?"

"Not yet, sir. Both pilots tried to take evasive action at the last minute and swerved with the result that they are now mired in the mud. We had no choice but to suspend operations. Incoming flights have been halted until further notice."

"Understood," Priestman confirmed grimly. "Have you informed your counterparts at Tempelhof?"

"Of course."

Priestman thanked him and hung up. Accidents were inevitable in any operation carried out with the intensity of this one; he'd known Gatow could not be spared forever. He reached for his cap while ordering Sergeant Andrews to make sure the removal equipment was on the way to the crash site. "We want the runways cleared as quickly as possible — even if they have to wreck both aircraft. The Airlift takes precedence over the equipment."

Outside, he hitched a lift with a tow tug that was already lumbering towards the accident. While not the fastest means of transport, at least it kept him dry. It had been raining sporadically since noon, and there were shallow puddles everywhere.

By the time Priestman arrived, the two aircraft were surrounded by two fire trucks, the ambulance, and the follow-me Land Rover. The starboard leg of the York had sunk deep into the boggy grass beside the pavement while the port leg was still on the concrete giving the aircraft a bad list. The good news was that the undercarriage had neither crumpled nor broken. The Dakota had ploughed into the fuselage between the wings and tailplane. Priestman judged the York repairable, but he was less sure about the Dakota. It had tried to swerve too late, and the nose had crumpled up, leaving the shattered windscreen almost touching the York.

The York's five-man crew stood in a cluster under the wing looking dazed and worried — as well they should. Blame would not be assigned until after an inquiry, but a pilot aborting take-off in an emergency generally had precedence over an aircraft in the act of taxiing. Priestman had been in enough prangs himself, however, to know that a lecture at this time wouldn't help anything. Instead, he just nodded to them and moved around to the far side of the Dakota where the orderlies had boarded. Two sergeants stood beside the meat wagon wearing the brevets of a navigator and signaller respectively. That meant the pilot was the one injured.

At the sight of a senior officer with wings, the navigator volunteered, "The port engine cut out on us at take-off, sir. It had been acting up on the way down, but it suddenly made a loud bang and started to shake itself apart."

Priestman glanced over his shoulder at the engine. The cowling was misshapen, and a piece was hanging loose. Black oil streaks stained the wing. Just then, an orderly jumped out of the Dakota's belly, took the handles of the stretcher, and walked carefully backwards as his partner eased the stretcher out. Then the second man jumped down and together they carried the stretcher to the waiting ambulance to slide it inside. Priestman got a glimpse of the pilot's face, which had been bandaged. He was moving uncomfortably, but that was better than being out cold. Priestman stopped one of the orderlies to ask, "Is he badly injured?"

"He's smashed his face up a bit, but nothing that can't be put back together again. I suspect his collar and/or breastbones are fractured, as well, but I couldn't find any sign of neck or back injuries. Then again, I'm not a doctor, so I'm not supposed to give a diagnosis, sir," he ended with an apologetic smile.

Priestman nodded for him to carry on and turned back to find Captain Bateman, the army officer in charge of all off-loading. He was already consulting with Warrant Officer Abels, the officer in charge of the towing and lifting equipment. Lt Col Russel and some of his sappers had also showed up. Abels addressed Priestman, "We can't pull her out of the mud fully loaded. They're going to have to unload some of the cargo first."

Priestman turned to Bateman. "Can you do anything with it heeling over like that?"

"We can manage. With all traffic stopped, I can assign several unloading crews to shift the cargo out of the aircraft, but unless we can lay down some metal plates to bring a lorry and trailer alongside, we'll have to carry everything to the runway, which will slow us down."

"We should be able to manage that," Russel offered.

Priestman nodded his thanks to Russel and addressed Bateman again. "What do you estimate?"

"I don't expect we'll need more than half an hour, sir."

That wasn't as bad as Priestman had expected. He turned to the station maintenance chief, Flight Sergeant Lowell, who had also arrived and was inspecting the Dakota. "What's your estimate, Chiefy?"

"I won't know till we get her over to the hangar and do a full inspection, sir, but I should imagine we can have her operational again in a couple of days. If we were back in Blighty, it would be faster. I'd just switch out that duff engine, but we haven't got any spare engines here and flying one in would mean less food for the Berliners. I'm going to have to try and patch this wreck up enough for it to fly itself back to Hamburg."

"That may be what caused the accident in the first place," Priestman observed. "Take a close look at the aircraft's service record. It may be time to write it off and turn it into a spare parts depot. It sounds like we could use one here, and if the starboard engine is still in comparably good shape, keeping it here as a possible replacement makes more sense than risking another accident."

Lowell nodded. "I'll keep that in mind, sir."

With the unloading crew already at work removing cargo by hand while the sappers laid down metal plates to enable a lorry to get closer, Priestman concluded there was nothing more he could do. He looked around for any vehicle heading back towards the tower, but seeing none, he started walking.

With Gatow temporarily closed, the world seemed eerily silent. Not a breath of wind disturbed the hot, humid air, but the sharp cry of a bird of prey pierced the silence and thunder grumbled in the distance. Priestman didn't like the colour of the clouds. They were ominously dark and low. A fat raindrop fell, then a few more. Priestman started jogging and barely reached the terminal before a downpour burst from the heavens. Thousands of raindrops seemed to explode on impact and the sheet of rain blotted out the view. Bugger, he thought; that would hamper the recovery efforts.

Yet less than forty minutes later, Bateman called up to report the York had been unloaded successfully and they were ready to attempt dragging it out of the mud. "What about the Dak?" Priestman asked.

"Oh, that was hauled away five minutes ago."

"Well done."

Priestman went to the window to see if he could see what was happening, relieved to note the rain had let up temporarily. Yet the sky remained dark, and the wind was getting up. He called the Met office. "What's the forecast?"

"A storm system with several severe thunderstorms is moving in from the West. The rain we're seeing now is an early outlier. Winds are forecast to increase to 60 or 70 miles an hour. Heavy downpours and electrical storms can be expected throughout the night and all day tomorrow."

"Lovely," Priestman commented sarcastically, and hung up. Before he could get back to work, however, the phone rang again.

Abels reported, "Both runways clear, sir."

"Well done. Thank you. What about the aircraft?"

"Ah, we've written off the Dakota as you suggested, but should have the York serviceable in a few days."

"Good." Priestman hung up and called the tower with the news. Immediately, the aircraft that had been lined up awaiting clearance for take-off started moving forward. One after another, they took to the air using both runways to clear the backlog, and within another twenty minutes, the first of the inbound aircraft, which had been kept circling elsewhere, set down on the tarmac. Altogether, landings at Berlin Gatow had been interrupted for just under ninety minutes. The rain, however, had returned with a vengeance, and it was so dark that Priestman needed to switch on his desk lamp.

Roughly an hour later, the telephone rang again. It was Garth. "Sir, Tempelhof just closed due to zero visibility during rain squalls. Unfortunately, because of our earlier interruption in operations, I had to inform them that we have too much inbound traffic to allow Tempelhof to divert their aircraft here. However, I agreed to take one inbound C-47 because General Clay is aboard."

"When is it due?"

"In twelve minutes."

"Thank you." Priestman found his raincoat and an umbrella, called his driver, and they drove through the pouring rain to the hardstanding assigned to the American aircraft. Priestman did not have long to wait before a Dakota with white stars on the fuselage whisked by on the runway. Minutes later, it came to a stop at the hardstanding with the rain still pelting down as though it were an Indian monsoon. Priestman stepped out into the deluge to meet Clay at the foot of the stairs, holding an umbrella for the military governor as he guided him back to the car. Priestman then dashed around to climb in the other side with his feet drenched and his trousers soaked and clinging to his legs.

"Thank you," the General greeted him as he unfolded in the seat beside him, adding with a wry smile, "It's a bit embarrassing that you're still operational when we're closed."

"We opted for Ground Controlled Approach at all times and have the radar and controllers in place to handle it."

Clay nodded, "I won't be a burden to you for long, Wing Commander. The pilot radioed ahead, and my staff will send a car to pick me up here."

"You're no burden at all, General. Would you rather wait in the privacy of my office, or go to the Officers' Mess for a drink?"

"I could do with some bourbon if you have any."

"I'm not sure about the bourbon, sir, but we can offer Scotch whisky."

"That would be fine."

Priestman directed his driver to take them to the mess. As they left their wet outer garments in the cloakroom, Clay remarked, with a shake of his head. "I'll never get used to this terrible Berlin weather! Where I come from, it's not this cold and rainy until November."

As an Englishman, Priestman didn't feel he could complain about wet weather, but he had been surprised by the amount of heavy rain Berlin had in high summer. He'd also been warned that the weather would get worse in the autumn and winter. To Clay, he offered only a lame joke about "typical English weather," and got the expected laugh.

As he led the way to the lounge, Priestman noticed staff and officers looking twice as they passed. Clay had a distinctive face familiar to everyone from the newspapers. Priestman ordered Scotch for them both.

"Any idea how we're doing today?" Clay asked conversationally.

"Due to disruptions beyond our control, not so well, but yesterday we set a record with 707 combined USAF/RAF sorties for the delivery of 4,742 tons."

Clay nodded without commentary. They both knew that despite setting new 'records' they were still not meeting targets. They had more than doubled the number of flights and the volume of tonnage delivered since the end of the previous month, but Berlin's reserves were still being drawn down. Priestman had heard that the city was just two weeks away from a power shutdown.

Clay took out his cigarette case and politely asked, "Do you smoke?" Priestman shook his head. Clay lit up, took a long drag, and then leaned back in his chair. As if he had just remembered something, his tense, sharp face broke into a rare grin. "I've been meaning to tell you for a long time, Wing Commander: your wife is one persuasive woman! I wish I could take her along with me when I go to Washington. She's just what I need to shake up the National Security Council."

Priestman laughed shortly, but took advantage of the opening to ask, "Didn't things go well on this last trip?"

A WAAF orderly brought their drinks, giving Clay an excuse to delay his answer. He rested his cigarette on the ashtray, took a sip of Scotch, then, tapping the ash off the cigarette, took it up again before turning to his host to confide, "I'm the son of a senator, Wing Commander, and I joined the army to get away from politics. Instead, I find myself smack in the middle of the biggest political conundrum since the end of the war." Holding the burning butt of his cigarette between his fore and middle finger, he pushed the ashtray this way and that before continuing. "The consensus in the National Security Council is that the Airlift *cannot* succeed and that we must therefore prepare to withdraw in an orderly and timely fashion. However, the State Department is insistent upon a final attempt to negotiate a settlement with Stalin. As far as I can see, the only person in Washington committed to staying in Berlin is President Truman."

Priestman didn't like the sound of that, but he clung to the fact that Truman was committed. "Isn't he the one who counts?"

He was disturbed when Clay did not agree with him. Instead, the American General picked up his whisky and studied it as he swished it around in the glass before replying, "For now he is, but President Truman is facing an election in November which no one thinks he can win. He's not popular — not even in his own party. The Democrats, furthermore, are in complete disarray. The left wing has broken away to launch a third party, the Progressives, with Roosevelt's former Vice President Wallace as their candidate. Meanwhile, the reactionary southern Democrats have broken off to support a segregationist by the name of Thurmond. As a result, the democratic vote is splintered three ways, which means the Republicans are almost certain to win. They don't share Truman's commitment to Europe. Most of them want a return to isolationism. Their motto is 'America First' — and they're too short-sighted to see we can't defend American interests if Europe is economically prostrate — much less part of the Russian empire. So that's the problem, Wing Commander. We have to beat the Reds here in Berlin *before* the election in the United States brings to power a party that will just walk away from the Airlift and leave the Berliners to be eaten alive by a vengeful Russian bear."

High Winds out of the Northwest
RAF Gatow
Thursday, 12 August 1948
(Day 48)

Air Freight International's participation in the Airlift got off to a slow start. On arrival at RAF Fuhlsbuettel near Hamburg, they were told policies and procedures were still being developed regarding the integration of civilian aircraft into military operations and they would be told when things were resolved. Two days later, they were given the go-ahead, only to discover they could not communicate with the RAF aircraft because their radio crystals were outdated and no longer compatible with those used by the RAF. Fortunately, Terry managed to get that sorted out within twenty-four hours via his informal signallers' network, and they made their inaugural flight to Berlin with a load of dehydrated potatoes on the afternoon of Tuesday 10 August. Wednesday went smoothly with two round trips, and on the same day, Kiwi arrived from the UK with a Dakota and the other crew.

On Thursday, however, after a round trip in the morning and taking on a second cargo, the second flight of the day was delayed when Gatow closed temporarily. After the airfield re-opened, the RAF York squadrons were given precedence, and AFI-H (as the Halifax was officially designated) did not receive clearance for take-off until nearly 6 pm. Kit and crew arrived in Gatow in pouring rain roughly an hour later. They dashed over to the Malcolm Club for a quick meal while the Halifax was unloaded.

Kit left the others at the club while he went across to AAI's maintenance hangar to check on Gordon. He found his former flight engineer in oil-stained overalls working at a workbench that perfectly suited the height of his wheelchair.

"Where did you get that workbench?" Kit greeted him.

Gordon grinned up at him. With his thumb, he pointed to one of the three Luftwaffe mechanics who were busy working around the Wellington. "Winterfeld over there is a wizard carpenter as well as a mechanic. He set it up for me the first day."

"How are you doing?"

"Like a pig in mud. Yourself?"

"At the risk of sounding like a traitor, the Halifax VI is a dream to fly."

Gordon snorted disapprovingly.

They didn't have time for more, but Kit promised to try to find a way to stay longer on another stop-over.

It was approaching 8 pm when Kit collected his crew from the Malcolm Club, and they ran through the rain to their now-empty freighter. The crew configuration of the Halifax placed the navigator and signaller on the lower deck and the two pilots and flight engineer on the upper deck. This meant that Nigel and Terry sat close together, while Kit and the two new members of the crew crowded the cockpit. As they prepared to start engines, Kit could hear Terry and Nigel joking with one another. He flipped on the intercom to ask, "What have you two been drinking while I was looking in on Gordon?"

"Nothing to worry about, Skip," Nigel answered readily. "It was only one bottle of gin between the two of us."

Kit opened his mouth but then saw Bruce shake his head and glanced over at Richard for verification. The engineer, smiling, also shook his head.

Into the mic, he said, "Oh, that's all right then. Carry on!" Laughter from the lower deck answered him.

Bruce grinned at him. "I don't know why you look so surprised. What could be more fun than working twelve-hour days in wet shoes and eating on the run?"

Their shoes were wet, and they would have been working closer to fourteen hours by the time they got back to Hamburg, but Bruce didn't sound the least bit sarcastic. Their eyes met, and they exchanged a smile. They were exactly where they wanted to be: in the cockpit of a powerful aircraft doing useful work. "Checklist?" Bruce asked, and they got on with it.

Their Halifax was practically brand new, and all four engines sprang eagerly to life. Richard reported readings in the green across the board. Flaps, rudder, and ailerons responded smoothly. However, the airframe was vibrating as rain squalls lashed diagonally across the windscreen. The wipers were all but useless. It was going to be a rough flight.

Kit used a torch to signal to the groundcrew to remove the chocks. Instantly, he felt an unnatural wobbliness through the control column. The combination of wind and wet pavement reduced the empty aircraft's hold on the ground. With a glance over at Bruce, he asked, "Are you OK flying in this?" While waiting for the bureaucracy to get sorted out, Kit had taken Bruce up for several long and vigorous training flights. He had also allowed Bruce to fly all the return flights, but his total hours on heavy aircraft were still fewer than 30.

"Sure," Bruce answered without looking at him. He kept his eyes on the Land Rover whose flashing yellow lights were leading them to the head of the runway.

Over the radio, Kit heard the tower reporting "The wind has veered northwest. Gusting up to 60 miles per hour." That meant it would be pushing them to port during take-off. "You're going to need extra starboard rudder," Kit warned Bruce.

Bruce nodded. Kit felt Richard turn to look over his shoulder at the two pilots, but Kit did not take his eyes off the windscreen. Ahead of them, a York turned onto the runway and stood shaking in the gale for several seconds before it started to roll forward. It swerved and weaved its way down the runway and took off dragging one wing a little before banking hard to starboard.

AFI received permission from the tower to turn onto the runway. Once lined up, Bruce ran up the engines against the brakes. "You're going to need both hands on the control column," Kit told him. "I'll handle the throttles."

Bruce nodded and released the brakes. As they rolled forward, Bruce's hands clasped the wheel so hard his knuckles turned white. Because of the windspeed, lift developed sooner than normal as they accelerated, reducing their hold on the ground. The Halifax wanted to slide off the tarmac, and Bruce was fighting hard to hold them on the runway, sweat pouring down his face. "Airspeed?" Kit called to Richard.

"100, 105, 110—"

"Keep the nose down!" Kit ordered Bruce as he gave the old bomber more power. "Hold her down and straight. We need more speed."

"130, 140—"

The Halifax was veering to the left despite Bruce's efforts to keep the nose pointed at the end of the runway. If they went off the runway at this speed they'd total the aircraft and would be lucky to walk away from it. "Now!" Kit ordered as he slammed the throttles through the safety wire and called to Richard for "full flaps." Bruce hauled the nose up, but for a moment they seemed to hang uncertainly in the air. The engines screamed in protest, the rain lashed them, the gale pushed them sideways, and the trees dead ahead grinned at them. Then the Halifax seemed to recover her courage and started to lift them up and over the trees. "Ease back on the flaps," Kit ordered.

"Flaps 15," Richard answered, cool as a cucumber.

Kit checked the rpms and reduced them to 2600 from the more than 3000 he had just used to get them airborne. He glanced sidelong at Bruce, who was banking them to the north gently, sweat streaming down the side of his face. "All right?"

"I'm fine," he insisted stubbornly without looking at Kit.

They were in the murk now. Visibility nil. "What's the heading for Spandau beacon, navigator?"

"350, Skipper," Nigel answered promptly, and Bruce turned onto the designated course.

"Flaps 10," Kit ordered, watching the altimeter.

As they steadied on their course, they passed through the eye of the wind. Beyond, the squalls smashed into them from port rather than starboard. They passed over the Spandau beacon at 3,000 feet and continued climbing towards Frohnau. The storm was blowing hard almost directly on their beam. Sporadically, short showers of hail rattled the fuselage.

Kit checked the altitude; they had just passed 4,800 feet. When he looked up again, he was startled to see a star straight ahead of them. A split second later, he realised it wasn't a star but the tail light of another aircraft — and they were closing on it rapidly. There was no time to give an order. Kit grabbed the controls and pushed the nose down as hard as in any corkscrew of his operational career. Bruce yelped in shock and even Richard exclaimed something. A split-second later, the sky was blotted out by the oil-stained belly of another aircraft. Instinctively, both Kit and Bruce cringed in their seats and Richard ducked his head. Kit held his breath, waiting for the sound of their antenna being torn off. It didn't come. They were in the clear again.

Richard straightened and turned to look back along the fuselage. "A Dakota! Flying tangential to the flight path."

"Can you see any squadron letters?" Kit asked.

"No. No roundels. Stars. I can't read the ID numbers."

American aircraft did not carry large squadron IDs, only the aircraft numbers painted on their tails.

Terry called from the lower deck, "Is everything all right up there?"

"We just avoided a collision," Kit answered. "Navigator, give me a fix as soon as you can to verify our position and course."

"Yes, sir!" Nigel answered smartly.

"Where did it come from?" Bruce asked, his voice still shaky.

"He was probably blown off course by the gale," Kit answered, adding, "The poor bastards have no navigators on board." Turning the controls over to Bruce again, he reached for the radio. "AFI-H calling Berlin Air Safety Centre. We just had a near miss with a Dakota flying at 5,000 feet on a tangential course." The Berlin Air Safety Centre acknowledged the message without providing any further information. They continued the flight back to Hamburg without further incident.

On arrival in Fuhlsbuettel, Kit turned the Halifax over to the groundcrew, and told the others to go ahead to the *Goldener Loewe* or *Golden Lion*. Their accommodations in a boarding house paid for by AFI were convenient, clean and comfortable, but served neither meals nor drinks, so they spent most of their free time in the *Golden Lion*, which was located nearby.

Meanwhile, Kit reported the incident to operations. Here, his account of a near miss elicited only instructions to fill out the accident report form and an exasperated remark from a Group Captain about "these civilian outfits we now have to accommodate." He was glad to leave and even happier to discover the rain had slowed to a drizzle, although the western sky flickered irregularly. Another thunderstorm was brewing, even if it was too far off to hear the thunder.

To Kit's surprise, Bruce stepped out from the shelter of the doorway as he set off for the main gate. "Mind if I walk with you, Skipper?"

"Of course not," Kit answered. When Bruce said nothing more, he prompted gently, "Something bothering you, Bruce?"

Bruce had both his hands in his pockets and the wind blew open his flight jacket. It made him look hunched. He kept his head down and he didn't look Kit in the eye as he admitted, "I know I was your last choice and that you only gave me a chance because my brother was an exceptional pilot —"

"Bruce, your brother was an aggressive and competitive pilot who had a very high opinion of his own skills. That's not the same thing as being exceptional. Frankly, he rubbed a lot of people up the wrong way — including me. We like you just the way you are."

Bruce glanced over with a timid smile and said, "Thanks." But then his face clouded again, and he added, "But — well — liking me isn't enough, is it?"

"What do you mean?"

"Well, I nearly went off the runway on take-off and I didn't see that Dakota until we were already flying under it — thanks to you. If I'd been on my own we'd all be dead."

"Bruce, twenty-six and a half hours on heavies isn't a lot of experience for dealing with situations like we had tonight. It was my decision to let you handle the take-off, and maybe it was a bad one. On the other hand, flying is rather like riding a horse. No amount of theory can teach you how to feel an aircraft through your hands and feet. The only way to learn to fly is to do it."

They had come to a halt short of the main gate so they could talk in private. Kit continued earnestly, "There's a reason why airlines mandate two pilots in a cockpit and why we count our flying hours. Each flight shapes us and helps us to get better." Kit paused and then asked softly, "OK?"

Bruce nodded and flashed him a shy smile, "Yes, thank you."

Kit was unsettled less by Bruce's performance than the stray Dakota and the stack of near miss reports he'd seen in the ops room. Not everyone was going to be lucky all of the time, and a mid-air collision was bound to happen sooner or later. If the dangers became public he'd be putting Georgina through hell again, and for the first time since accepting the job with AFI, he wondered if he had a right to do that.

Chapter Thirteen
Course Correction

Black Friday
Frankfurt / Main
Friday, 13 August 1948
(Day 49)

Because the USAF only cared about bodies with the right skill codes rather than personalities, Halvorsen had no trouble getting J.B. assigned as his copilot. Not only were they now flying together, Halvorsen had also shown J.B. the loft of the barn at the back of the Zeppelinheim camp, where he bedded down. It was still pretty primitive, but less institutional, smelled a lot better, and was more private since only a half-dozen guys had discovered it.

This morning, with Sergeant Elkins, Halvorsen's engineer, they hopped on a crew bus to take them through the rain to their waiting aircraft. On arrival, they were told that it was grounded due to a problem with the hydraulics. Since planes flew with all kinds of minor problems, something very serious must have gone wrong during the night when someone else was flying it. Directed to a different aircraft, they found this had a "snag sheet" two pages long, which included reassuring information like "landing gear instrument panel: u/s." In other words, they couldn't know if the gear was down properly or not.

As they scrambled aboard the weary, rundown freighter, J.B. reflected that in the war they'd at least had dedicated ground crews. His crew chief had been a rock-solid, 100%-reliable Texan, who would have cut off his right hand before he let "his" aircraft fly with a defect. On the Airlift, in contrast, J.B. and Halvorsen didn't even know the names of their ground crew, much less their level of experience and competence.

As if reading his thoughts, Halvorsen said, "They do the best they can, J.B., but some bright staff officer in the States sent the squadrons out here in their aircraft and told the ground crews to come with their tools by slow boat across the Atlantic—and they haven't gotten here yet. The guys looking after our planes used to service fighters and they're so short of tools and spare parts that they're patching things together with whatever they can find on the local market — which isn't much, as you can imagine."

"That certainly makes me feel better, Hal," J.B. answered, and his pilot grinned.

They settled into their seats and started going through the checklist, while around them various leaks allowed the rain to run down the side of the cockpit, drip onto the navigation table, and collect on the floor. When they turned on the windshield wipers, they discovered these were too loose to do more than smear the water from one side of the window to the other, while the windshield itself was badly scratched.

"I'm sure glad we fly for the Air Force of the most powerful nation on earth," J.B. commented. "Just think what it would be like flying for some banana republic?"

Halvorsen chuckled.

When they received permission to taxi, they discovered they were so mired in mud they couldn't budge. Halvorsen had to use half-power to spring them loose, which meant that when the wheels hit the concrete, they almost shot off the far side of the taxiway. Halvorsen slammed on the brakes and J.B. yanked the throttles back just in time. They looked at one another and shook their heads. That had been too close for joking.

Halvorsen turned the C-54 onto the taxiway, and they started wallowing towards the runway. The persistent rain of the last few days had turned the base of the PSP taxiway into bog that sagged under the weight of the Skymaster.

They took their place in line and eventually took off into a downpour. Weather in Germany could be quite localised. Sometimes they took off in the rain and landed in sunshine — or the reverse. On this trip, however, the gloom and thunderstorms stayed with them the whole way and static interfered with the radio navigation aids, making signals weak and unreliable. Cursing under his breath, J.B. started to wonder if their compass was working properly because they seemed to be veering all over the place. Then again, they were being buffeted about by gusting winds, which made holding a steady course virtually impossible.

J.B. was relieved to get into range of Tempelhof control, until he heard what was coming over his earphones. The controller was urgently directing another incoming aircraft to adjust course. "Big Easy 761, sideslip right!" With increased volume and forcefulness, he ordered, "Big Easy 761, veer right! You are not lined up on the runway!"

"I can see the goddamned runway straight ahead of me!" the pilot replied in irritation — before he was drowned out by the sound of a loud thump, things crashing and tearing, men cursing, and then silence from the aircraft as the faint sound of sirens wafted over the microphones in the tower.

J.B. and Halvorsen just looked at one another. To their amazement, the next instruction over their headphones was an unperturbed, "Big Easy 695, you are cleared to land."

"What the devil are they doing?" Halvorsen asked.

"If he wasn't over the runway, he must have crashed beside it leaving the runway operational." J.B. surmised. They scanned the sky ahead of them for smoke or any other indication of what had happened. All they could see were clouds.

"Big Easy 328." That was them. "Turn onto 080, reduce speed to 140 mph, and descend to 2000 feet at Wedding beacon. Report on passing."

Halvorsen banked the heavy C-54 while J.B. acknowledged to the tower. As they descended they entered denser cloud. Visibility fell to a few hundred feet. They had no choice but to fly on instruments, but at least the Wedding signal came in loud and clear. As instructed, J.B. called in as they crossed over it, and the tower started to give them a new course. Before the controller finished, an excited voice yelled out, "He's overshooting! He's overshooting!" The sound of an explosion followed.

"Jeeze! That's two in ten minutes," Halvorsen exclaimed.

"Big Easy 998, abort! Abort landing!"

"Too late! I'm already on the — What the f***?" This time the squeal of brakes was audible before the signal cut off.

J.B. was sweating now.

"Tempelhof Control to all Big Easy Aircraft: the airfield is closed! Repeat the Tempelhof Airfield is closed! Stand by!" The controller snapped off and then clicked back on. "Big Easy 492, circle Tempelhof at 3000 feet. Big Easy 762, circle Tempelhof at 3,500 feet. Big Easy 689, circle

Tempelhof at 4,000—"

"Was that Big Easy 685 or 689?" a pilot asked for clarification.

"Big Easy six-eight-niner. Repeat: Six-eight-niner."

They were next and assigned to 4,500 feet.

"What direction do you want us circling up here?" a voice asked out of the blue, making J.B.'s heart miss a beat. In the Eighth, they had standing orders to "orbit" counterclockwise, but if someone could ask about it, then maybe there were no standard orders here — or J.B. and a lot of other pilots didn't know what they were! Ergo, pilots might be flying around in the murk in opposite directions, and that thought made his hair stand on end.

"Counterclockwise," the tower answered to J.B.'s relief, and he relaxed a little. He glanced over at Halvorsen and realised the experienced transport pilot's nearly bald head was glistening with sweat. He gripped the control yoke so firmly that his knuckles were white. Feeling his copilot's gaze, Hal asked, "How many aircraft do you think are now stacked up?"

"We took off at three-minute intervals, so we should be arriving at the same rate. They closed the field about 15 minutes ago, so that's just five aircraft. Nothing like mustering for a mission," J.B. assured Halvorsen. "Any one mission might involve several hundred bombers and it could take up to an hour for all the Bomb Groups to assemble. Meanwhile, we flew around in big circles in the English rain clouds."

"And there were never any problems?" Halvorsen pressed him.

J.B. drew a deep breath. "I wouldn't say that. We lost birds now and again. Once, I had a wing tip pass not more than a hundred feet in front of me. It felt more like five inches, believe me! I saw one collision, too. Or rather heard it. When two bombers fully loaded with aviation fuel and filled to the gills with high explosives run into each other at three hundred miles per hour, there's not much left to see. Just bits and pieces of propellors, fuselage and body parts floating on the fog..."

"Do you want to take her?" Halvorsen asked with a shy grin.

J.B. nodded. "I don't mind."

Halvorsen leaned back, stretching and clenching his hands to ease the tension in them. Over the earphones someone was asking for clarification. "This is Big Easy 842. Did you say I was stacked at 8,000 or 8,500 feet?"

The delay in answering was not reassuring, it was 8,500 feet.

"So, who's at 8,000 feet?" another voice asked.

"We're keeping 8,000 open for now."

Yet another voice sliced through the clouds. "How long are you planning on keeping us here? My fuel won't get me home if we're up here more than another thirty minutes."

"We will advise as soon as the runway is clear," the controller replied, not answering the question. His next transmission was, "Big Easy 481, circuit at 9,000 feet."

"You do realise we have winds gusting up to forty mph up here?" someone complained over the airwaves. He was ignored.

"Big Easy 377, circle counterclockwise at 9,500 feet."

"Just how long have we been up here?" J.B. asked Halvorsen, who checked his watch. "Twenty-eight minutes."

It felt a lot longer. J.B. forced himself to focus on his instruments, but the hiss of a sudden shower of sleet distracted him and he glanced out at the seething clouds surrounding them. If their luck ran out, the end would come very suddenly.

By the time they had been circling an hour, aircraft were stacked up to 13,000 feet and there were more than twenty aircraft turning circles in the clouds. A pilot reported, "I'm in hail. Icing conditions could develop any minute." There was an edge of panic in that voice, J.B. thought. But not in the next.

Loud, clipped and angry, a man barked: "This is Big Easy 559. Tunner talking, and you listen. Send every plane in the stack back to its base."

There was stunned silence from the tower and then an intimidated voice asked, "Please repeat."

"I said: send everybody in the stack below and above me home. Then tell me when it's OK to come down."

"Roger! Yessir, General!" the tower responded, and at once the bottom aircraft in the stack got a course for Wiesbaden. In about ten minutes, Halvorsen and J.B.'s turn came, and they turned for Frankfurt still carrying a belly full of dried eggs that Berliners desperately needed.

The Whip
RAF Gatow
Saturday, 14 August 1948
(Day 50)

Priestman called his adjutant into his office as soon as he arrived and asked what he'd been able to find out about the problems at Tempelhof the day before.

"It seems a pilot new to the Airlift mistook the building site for the operational runway and tried to land on it."

Priestman dropped his head in his hands for a second and then finished the picture, "His undercarriage sank into gravel and stopped, while ten tons of cargo continued forward."

"Not quite. He landed on the rubber underlining and I'm told the Skymaster slid, slithered, skidded and spun around like a fat figure-skater on ice. All the crew escaped without injury."

"God loves America," Priestman commented. "But that doesn't explain why they closed the airfield."

"No, it was another pilot new to Tempelhof who caught a glimpse of the apartment buildings in his glide path and lost his nerve. He pulled up a bit and couldn't land until he was halfway down the runway. By that point he couldn't stop in time, overshot, and crashed into the perimeter fence. The aircraft caught fire and burnt. A total write-off including cargo, but at least the crew was pulled to safely, albeit a bit singed. The aircraft behind, however, was unable to abort in time and to avoid colliding with the fire trucks and ambulances, the pilot stomped on his brakes so hard that both tyres burst. No one was injured, of course, but the wreck was blocking the runway and *that* was what closed the airfield."

"I should think so."

"Now, here's the interesting bit," Stan added, raising his CO's eyebrows. "Aboard one of the incoming flights was General William Tunner, the American's new Airlift commander. He ordered all aircraft back to base — fully loaded. Rumours are rife that he's going to make some big changes."

"Sounds as though we need them. What's his background?"

"He turned the supply organisation across the Himalayas from a comedy into a success — while lowering casualty rates by half. He's arguably the world's greatest expert on military transport — and knows it. You'll have the pleasure of judging for yourself. He has requested permission to land here this afternoon at 14:30 for 'consultations.'" Stan handed a notepad to Priestman on which he'd scribbled the request from US Airlift HQ.

Priestman nodded. "Then we'll roll out the red carpet and hope nobody rams anyone else in the meantime."

The USAF C-54 settled down at Gatow four minutes late and was led by the follow-me Land Rover to a hardstanding where Priestman awaited. The engines had not stopped spinning before the door opened and a US general in a khaki uniform and polished shoes jumped down onto the tarmac. He was trim, modestly good-looking with regular features, and a businesslike rather than a friendly demeanour. He returned Priestman's salute, and he offered his hand with the words, "Thank you for seeing me at such short notice, Wing Commander."

"Everything is short notice on this Airlift," Priestman replied. "How can I help you?"

"Oh, I just thought I'd take a look at your operations and see how you were handling things. If you'll wait one moment, my pilot and copilot are two of my staff officers. I want them to join us." He looked towards the aircraft, and on cue two lieutenant colonels dropped out of it to be introduced as Bettinger and Foreman.

Priestman reciprocated by introducing, "Captain Bateman, RASC, responsible for our Forward Area Supply Organisation or FASO. That is, everything to do with unloading the aircraft and moving the cargoes up to Berlin." Priestman drew attention to the fact that Tunner's aircraft was already being unloaded.

Tunner turned to watch as the trailer was backed up against the cargo door of his Skymaster. "I see you're using German stevedores, just as we do. Any problems with them?" he asked.

Priestman nodded to Bateman to answer.

"None at this end. In the early days German loaders didn't understand that the cargo capacity of aircraft varies. They knew even less about maintaining the aerodynamics of the aircraft by careful distribution of loads. Those teething problems have since been resolved. More recently we've still had had problems with overloaded aircraft, but not because of mistakes during transhipment. These were at the point of origin; in their keenness to help Berlin, flour mills and mine workers were overloading the ten-pound sacks. They stuffed in as much material as possible, sometimes cramming as much as 12% more into each sack — which, of course, translated into Dakotas carrying not six thousand pounds, but maybe 6,600 or 7000 pounds."

Tunner snorted but nodded his understanding, then looked at Priestman. Taking this to mean Tunner was finished with the topic of unloading, Priestman invited the Americans into his car and drove them over to the maintenance hangar. Here Tunner and his staff officers met Gatow's Chief Engineering Officer, Squadron Leader Holt. Tunner's sharp eye rapidly noted, "You don't have many aircraft in maintenance and almost no spare parts inventory. Why is that?"

"All Airlift aircraft are based in the West and that is where routine maintenance is carried out. We only maintain a limited supply of those essential components most likely to require immediate replacement such as tyres, brakes, etc."

"What if an aircraft lands with a different problem?" Tunner asked, adding, "You seem to have ample hangar space to manage much more maintenance."

"Our problem isn't space but personnel. We only have enough ground crew here to handle an emergency. As for spare parts, the RAF doesn't have infinite stockpiles and what we have is centralised at our main depot in the UK. If we lack something, it can be flown in within a couple of hours — a day at the most. As a rule, however, we prefer an aircraft's regular crew to handle all repairs during routine maintenance."

"You have crews assigned to individual aircraft?" Tunner sounded surprised.

"That's right."

"Isn't that a waste of manpower?" Although his expression was impassive, his disapproval was evident.

"How so, sir?" Holt asked defensively.

"Well, 50-hour checks only come due every five or six days. What is the crew doing in the meantime?"

Priestman took over from the rattled Holt, "Squadron ground crews handle two aircraft each and the RAF requires daily inspections. In addition, squadron ground crews do the 150-hour inspections which come up roughly every fortnight. Our ground crews are working twelve-hour days. There's no question of them lazing about."

"You still do daily inspections? That seems over-cautious. We've found fifty-hour checks are adequate to correct minor issues and identify major ones," Tunner countered.

Priestman was unimpressed. "Our philosophy is to carry out preventive not merely corrective maintenance. We prefer repairing an item in time rather than waiting for it to break down and need replacing."

"That sounds like an admirable approach in peacetime, Wing Commander, but in war — or warlike conditions such as we have here — the primary concern must be maximum utilisation of assets. That means aircraft should be flying, loading/unloading or undergoing maintenance. They shouldn't be sitting around on the ground being inspected for problems they don't yet have. My preference is to give them a thorough check at 200 hours. I've arranged for the C-47s to go down in Oberpfaffenhofen and the C-54s to fly to Burtonwood."

That sounded as though it would take aircraft off the Airlift longer than the RAF's daily inspections, but Priestman chose not to challenge the "expert." Instead, he suggested they move on.

Tunner's attention, however, had been caught by one of the maintenance teams and he went over for a closer look. A moment later, the American general turned to the RAF officer and asked, "I am seeing right? You have women aircraft mechanics?"

Priestman was proud of all his ground crew. They were without exception highly trained. The safety record they delivered justified his confidence in them, and the women were no exception. He was tempted to explain this, but confined himself to, "Some of our best."

The tour continued to the Malcolm Club. Priestman explained that station personnel used the messes while the Malcolm Club served the crews waiting for their aircraft to be unloaded. "The Salvation Army, NAAFI and YMCA also offer quick snacks from mobile canteens on the airfield or beside the maintenance hangars, but here men can sit down and get a bit of peace and quiet. They also have a barber shop if someone wants a haircut while waiting, and the lounge is well-stocked with newspapers and periodicals." Priestman proudly pointed to a table where these were displayed. "If an aircraft is stranded here overnight, the club offers limited but comfortable accommodation."

Tunner looked around the room critically. "The problem with nice places like this is that the crews get to chatting and smoking and reading when they ought to be flying. As of yesterday, my crews have orders not to move more than 10 feet away from their aircraft."

"I'm sure that's popular," Priestman noted.

"I'm not here to win a popularity contest," Tunner shot back. "As I said a moment ago, I want maximum utilisation of assets, and that includes pilots."

"And how do they get the weather report and file a return flight plan?"

"I send a jeep around with the operations officer, another with the weather report, and finally, a mobile snack bar manned by the prettiest girls the Red Cross could recruit in Berlin drives from plane to plane. The men don't seem to be bitching too much."

Priestman nodded acknowledgement rather than approval, and asked if his guests wanted a tour of the full station including accommodations, messes, and recreational facilities, or if they preferred to go straight over to the meteorology section, operations room and the tower. Unsurprisingly, Tunner opted for the latter.

As they mounted the steps of the main building, Tunner remarked, "I've asked my staff to work out new traffic patterns in the corridors, and I hope the RAF will cooperate."

"You'll have to talk to Group Captain Bagshot about that."

"I have." His tone suggested it had not been an entirely satisfactory conversation.

Priestman cautiously noted, "You may find it useful to get in touch with Air Commodore Merer. He's the CO of No. 46 Group in Air Transport Command and a transport expert like yourself. Bagshot's background is Bomber Command."

Tunner looked at Priestman hard and then nodded. "Thank you for that, Wing Commander."

Priestman wasn't sure if Tunner had expressed sincere thanks for a helpful tip or a rebuke for suggesting a way around his direct superior. He decided to change the subject, "What changes did you have in mind?"

"For a start, one-way traffic. Everything flies in via the northern and southern corridors and out via the central corridor."

"That would be a great improvement and something I suggested long ago," Priestman noted dryly. Tunner gave him a second look, but Priestman kept his eyes averted.

Tunner continued, "You've probably already heard that I've ordered all pilots who miss a landing to return fully loaded to avoid stacking up aircraft in the limited airspace over Berlin — and woe betide any pilot who misses his landing without good reason!"

Priestman nodded without commentary. He was not as averse to stacking aircraft as Tunner, and felt sending loaded aircraft back was a waste of aviation fuel that also delayed the delivery of desperately needed supplies to Berlin. He conceded that in a situation such as had developed at Tempelhof yesterday it was preferable to an accident, but he thought the decision should be made on a case-by-case basis.

Tunner next remarked, "I've asked the Pentagon to call up one hundred civilian air traffic controllers and send them over to improve the quality of the ATC. Some of our guys just aren't experienced enough for this environment."

Priestman nodded agreement wordlessly.

Tunner wasn't finished, "I've also put in a formal request via General LeMay to Air Marshal Sanders to base a bunch of our aircraft in your Zone."

That brought Priestman to a halt, and he looked over at the American, surprised.

"Look, the distance to Berlin from either Wiesbaden or Rhein-Main is roughly 300 miles while it's just over 120 miles from Celle or Fassberg and less than 100 from Hamburg. The same aircraft can make three trips to Berlin from Fassberg in the time it takes to make two sorties from Rhein-Main. That's 50% more."

Priestman nodded and conceded, "That makes sense."

"What it means is that most of those planes will be funnelled down the northern corridor and directed into Gatow, starting one week from today."

"Ah, I see. That's why you were so keen to visit," Priestman concluded with a faint smile.

"That was one reason. The other is that a C-74 is arriving today at Rhein-Main with vitally needed engines and other bulky replacement parts. Some genius in the Pentagon came up with the idea of stuffing it full of flour — after we've unloaded those special cargoes — and sending it on to Berlin. The problem with that is it's far too heavy to land on the PSP runways at Tempelhof. If we're going to make a show — and that's all this is since the brass refuses to dedicate any C-74s to the Airlift — it is going to have to take place here at Gatow."

"I see," Priestman commented dryly. He didn't like having something like this sprung on him at such short notice.

Tunner could read his mood and tried to make the event more palatable. "It wasn't my idea, but to be fair, something like this will highlight that this is a joint effort — even if it is still, irrationally, two separate operations."

Intentionally or not, Tunner had just shown his hand. The American general wanted a *combined* operation. More specifically, he wanted to control not just the US aircraft and airfields but the British ones as well. That way they would all have to dance to his tune.

Priestman had mixed feelings about that. He could see the sense in many of Tunner's suggestions and disliked Bagshot's small-minded approach to problems. Yet the American general also struck him as rigid and adverse to alternative approaches. Tunner appeared to believe he had all the answers already. Most damning, his obsession with "maximum utilisation of assets" struck Priestman as almost inhuman.

They had reached the top of the stairs and entered the tower. Squadron Leader Garth met them and offered to show Tunner around, starting with the radar room. Tunner showed keen interest in everything and asked good, technical questions. Priestman sensed that his radar controllers made a good impression on the American.

Finally, they went to stand behind the controllers at the windows. Garth fell silent and let Tunner just watch. As time ticked by with Tunner observing intently, Garth glanced questioningly at Priestman, but the Station Commander shook his head. The general appeared to be either looking for something or working something out in his head.

At length, the American general turned to the two RAF officers and announced more than asked, "Your planes are landing on the minute exactly, aren't they? They're spaced precisely three minutes apart in the air and they're landing three minutes apart. It's like clockwork — just the way it should be. What's the secret?"

With a nod from the WingCo, Garth answered, "Part is the GCA, of course."

"I understand the GCA part," Tunner answered frowning slightly. "But controllers can only land aircraft that are in position to land. We sometimes have gaps of up to six minutes between aircraft. Other times, we have two aircraft practically on top of each other! The orders are the same. How are your pilots getting this kind of precision flying when my guys are all over the place?" He sounded exasperated.

"Ah," Garth started, but then looked at Priestman.

Tunner looked from one to the other, and Priestman answered. "Our aircraft carry navigators and navigational equipment that allows them to know their position at all times. That enables them to adjust their speed continuously, compensating for tail or headwinds."

Tunner considered that for a moment and then clarified, "Meaning, even over the Soviet Zone, where there are no ground beacons, they know exactly where they are."

"Exactly. Over the Soviet Zone your aircraft rely entirely on dead reckoning for their position, whereas ours are equipped with the Rebecca Eureka or Gee navigation systems, which enables them to obtain reliable position fixes in the air without ground beacons."

Tunner didn't speak for several minutes as he absorbed this information. At length, he turned to one of the American officers shadowing him. "Bett, take a look into that equipment and see if we can acquire and install it. It sounds great, but I suspect it would be an expensive proposition to refit all our aircraft with additional equipment and probably would take an act of Congress or a Presidential Order to get it approved by the Pentagon."

"You'd also have to train your aircrews to use it," Priestman quietly pointed out.

"Indeed," Tunner conceded.

They had already turned away when a disembodied woman's voice came over the radio saying, "Gatow Control, this is Moby Dick. We are passing Grunewald beacon on one engine."

Priestman spun about sharply.

"Moby Dick, Gatow Control. Are you in distress?" the controller asked calmly.

"No, the fire's out, but we would appreciate priority landing."

Garth stepped in, saying to the arrival controller, "We'll land them on the PSP runway to avoid disruption of the landing stream." The controller nodded and passed the information on.

Tunner remarked, "I didn't realize you had women pilots in the RAF."

"In the Voluntary Reserve, yes, but AAI is one of the civilian contractors."

"Interesting. The women pilots did an outstanding job in Air Transport Command during the war. It's a pity that that bitch Cochrane insisted on butting her nose in and messing everything up."

"Do you mind if we see this emergency down?" Priestman asked his American guest.

"Not in the least," Tunner replied apparently interested in watching how it was handled.

Meanwhile, Garth crossed over to the departure controller and told him to hold departing traffic on the ground to clear the runway for the incoming emergency. The ground movements assistant allowed two aircraft to take off, but all other outbound aircraft waited like ducks in a row.

"There it is, sir," Garth spotted it first, and Priestman took a pair of binoculars from the table to focus on the approaching Wellington.

"Is that an air ambulance?" Tunner asked.

"Yes," Priestman answered without lowering the binoculars. He was trying to estimate the amount of damage to the engine from the exterior alone. Smoke stains had blackened the wing and part of the fuselage, but Priestman reasoned that things might look worse than they were because of the white livery of the ambulance. Emily's voice had sounded calm enough to suggest this had not been a life-threatening emergency. Still, losing an engine was never fun, and the Wellington had a nasty reputation for flying poorly on one engine. However, David was in the cockpit with her and he had extensive experience.

Garth elaborated on Priestman's answer. "The company is engaged in taking the most serious medical cases out of Berlin."

"They wouldn't be looking for more pilots, would they?" Bettinger asked. "I ran into one of our former women ferry pilots the other day. She's a first-rate pilot with a lot of ferrying experience. Unfortunately regulations prevent us from hiring her, but if this ambulance service already has a woman pilot, maybe they'd be willing to give her a chance?"

Without lowering the binoculars, Priestman agreed, "They might. They have an office in Hamburg where your acquaintance could apply. The company name is Air Freight International."

"I thought you said it was an ambulance company?"

"They have the ambulance and two freighters."

"And they're a good company?"

"My wife flies for them."

Tunner looked over sharply, but Priestman's attention remained on Moby Dick until it landed safely. Only after it had stopped at the end of the runway and turned onto the taxiway did he turn to Tunner with a faint smile.

"You run a smooth operation, Wing Commander," Tunner remarked, and Priestman suspected that was probably the highest compliment that this ice-cold American general could give.

Chapter Fourteen
Details, Details

"Don't worry."
RAF Gatow
Sunday, 15 August 1948
(Day 51)

"Halvorsen!" The voice of the base commander, Colonel Haun, boomed across the operations room.

Halvorsen winced at the tone and muttered under his breath to J.B. "What have we done now?"

With a grim expression on his face, the colonel was bearing down on them like a steamroller. "You're qualified on the C-74, right?" He addressed himself to Halvorsen and continued without letting the lieutenant answer, "You were on a C-74 squadron in Alabama before volunteering for the Airlift."

"Yes, sir," Hal admitted.

"Good, because there's a C-74 out there filled to the gills with flour for Berlin and the flight crew isn't, ahem, airworthy. Get out there — you too, Baronowsky. Fly it to Gatow and come back before anyone notices."

J.B. was on the brink of saying he'd never been near a C-74, but Halvorsen stomped on his foot.

Half an hour later, they were at the controls of the largest transport aircraft ever built. It had a wingspan 55 feet more than the C-54 Skymaster and a cargo capacity of two-and-a-half times as much. It could carry light tanks, armoured personnel carriers and howitzers, and boasted palatial crew space designed to accommodate a complete second crew. It cruised at 212 mph, which was twenty miles-an-hour faster than the C-54s and fifty mph faster than the C-47s. As a result, it could easily overtake all aircraft in the corridor as it gobbled up the distance to Berlin. To reduce the risk of them ramming something, they were ordered to 10,000 feet, the maximum height allowed in the corridor.

"Aren't we going to have trouble putting this baby down when we get to Berlin?" J.B. asked, trying to picture swooping down from ten thousand feet to squeeze between the apartment buildings and then screech to a halt before hitting the perimeter fence.

"Nope. We're going to Gatow. We'll be over forest most of the way. No apartment blocks for miles. And they have a brand-new concrete runway. It'll be a dream to land on after the PSP at Tempelhof."

Twenty minutes out of Berlin, J.B. called into the Berlin Air Safety Centre, and they received orders to throttle back almost to stalling speed. Seven minutes later they were given a new course and handed over to Gatow Control.

J.B. took the mic in his hand and called in, "Gatow Control, this is Big Easy 5414." They had a longer aircraft number to alert controllers that they were a different 'animal' from the other aircraft flying. "Do you read me?"

A woman's voice replied: "Big Easy 5414, this is Gatow Control. Reading you loud and clear. Turn left on three-one-zero and descend to five thousand feet." The disembodied voice with its clipped British accent was low, melodic and sent a shockwave of recognition to the core of J.B.'s soul. He'd heard that voice over and over in his dreams ever since that one time he'd heard it in real life.

Over Augsburg during the war, flak had blown out their # 4 engine, and as they turned for home they sank farther and farther behind the others. Soon they were alone in the hostile sky. As they crept across the face of the European continent, J.B. shamelessly prayed that the fighters and flak would concentrate on the retreating strike force rather than his lame duck.

Flak reached for them now and again, but free of the formation and their bombload, J.B. was free to take evasive action. He strained the remaining engines to gain altitude that kept them clear of most of the flak until their teeth were chattering as the wind whipped through the shrapnel holes in the fuselage. Icicles formed and hung from their oxygen masks, and when the navigator spilt some coffee from his thermos, it froze on his table in a dirty puddle of brown ice.

J.B. didn't have time to worry about the cold; the flight engineer had reported a fuel leak. The attempt to shift fuel from the damaged tank into one of the others failed because of a short circuit somewhere. The engineer resorted to pumping by hand, while J.B. wondered what other parts of the electronics and hydraulics had been damaged.

After crossing over the Dutch coast, with the flak behind them, J.B. put the Fortress into a gentle descent, and they started to relax. That was when the fighter hit them. An Me109 pounced from behind, shattering the tail turret and killing (as it turned out) the tail gunner on his first pass. He then circled out of range of the Fortress' guns to make a beam approach from starboard. His cannon fire, aimed at # 3 engine, ripped through the waist, killing the right waist gunner and mortally wounding the ball turret gunner. Then the 109 made a third pass from the other side. This time, he set # 2 engine on fire and severely injured the radio operator before turning away.

While the bombardier and navigator dealt with the injured crewmen, J.B., his engineer, and copilot struggled to douse the fire. The flames were blowing back ferociously, eating away at the fuselage abaft the wing. J.B. put the bomber in as steep a dive as he dared, and his crewmen deployed every extinguisher they had. When the last flames fizzled out, they were down to two engines and the fuel situation had become critical. They also had two badly wounded crewmen on board.

J.B. needed to land as quickly as possible, but all he could see spread out below him was cloud. He hadn't a clue where they were, although the navigator thought they might be over Suffolk. He couldn't pinpoint their position more precisely because while he had been looking after the wounded radio operator, most of his charts had been sucked out of a hole in the floor of the fuselage. J.B. had no option but to put out a "darky call," giving his call sign "Dark Maple Red Two" and reporting damage, low fuel and wounded onboard.

That voice had answered — low, melodic, well-modulated, and British. It had felt as if she was with him in the cockpit as she quipped. "I say! Am I talking to Clark Gable?" At first he'd been annoyed by the intentional misunderstanding, but as she continued in a cheerful and reassuring tone, he realised she'd broken the tension deliberately. After that, professional yet confident, she held J.B.'s nerves together as they sank lower and lower into the murk. As J.B. became aware of additional defects and reported his catalogue of calamities, she consistently replied, "Don't worry. I'll get you down safely." When he reported, with poorly disguised panic, the evaporating fuel levels, she'd jested, "Don't worry, Clark. We can't afford to lose a heartthrob like you! Flying Control has you in sight. You are only four minutes away now. You will see a flare shortly and are cleared to land as soon as it goes up."

"J.B.?" Halvorsen asked in alarm. "Are you OK?"

He shook his head to clear it of memories. "Yes, of course."

Over the radio, the voice was saying, "Big Easy 5414, repeat: turn left on two-seven-zero and descend to two thousand feet."

J.B. forced himself into the present, responding with, "Roger. Two-seven-zero, two thousand feet," yet his pulse was racing. That voice had saved not only his life, but the lives of the survivors aboard his Fortress. It had snatched them from the yawning gates of hell and set them down on an English airfield that was neat, efficient, soggy to be sure, but warm and safe nonetheless. The memory was so vivid and so powerful that J.B. was semi-bewildered throughout their arrival at Gatow.

The reception was a full-fledged circus! They were greeted by the press, civilian dignitaries, and military brass. A cute little girl gave them flowers as they came out of the cockpit. Flashbulbs went off with puffs of smoke and bursts of light. Reporters surrounded them, including one attractive-but-aggressive woman journalist. "Did you have any difficulty on the flight in?" "How is the runway?" "Will you be making many more sorties on the Airlift?" "How much cargo did you carry?" "Would it be possible to transport bulldozers, crushers and steamrollers in this aircraft?"

Halvorsen fielded the questions with a shy smile, while J.B. paid no heed to the reporters. Instead, he visually located the control tower. At the end of that flight from Augsburg, he'd tried to go to the control room to thank the WAAF who had talked him down. By the time he'd seen to his wounded and dead crewmen and put a call through to his home base, however, she'd gone off duty. He had never met her. Never seen her. Never learned her name. Yet her voice haunted him: "Don't worry. I'll get you down safely." She had calmed him down enough for him to do everything necessary to put that wounded bird down in one piece.

J.B. was desperate to break away from the reception and get to the tower. He was determined not to miss her a second time, but he was being asked to pose for pictures with the mayor of Berlin. Then he and Halvorsen had to shake hands with the German stevedores. Three teams were working to remove a load two-and-a-half times that of a C-54. After the handshakes, they were escorted to the Malcolm Club which, J.B. noted, was manned by attractive British girls, and invited to have some "English tea and scones."

Beside him, Halvorsen muttered, "Instead of English tea, don't you wish we could see something of Berlin one of these days? I'm tired of seeing nothing but airfields. I remember reading about Berlin in school, and it had a lot of interesting sights."

"Most of which we probably flattened," J.B. reminded him.

"There's still the Reichstag and what's left of Hitler's bunker. And the royal palace and armoury," Halvorsen informed him.

"Tunner won't let us go more than ten feet from our aircraft," J.B. pointed out. "How do you plan to go see the sights? It would take hours, and meanwhile our aircraft would be sitting idle and empty on the tarmac. We'd get court-martialled!"

"We'd have to do it in our free time," Halvorsen admitted.

"What free time?"

Halvorsen laughed at that but insisted, "Well, if we hopped on someone else's plane when we came off duty, we'd only miss a meal and a couple of hours sleep."

"You're welcome to do that, Hal. I'd rather relax and get some sleep. Now, I'm going to disappear if you don't mind. I have to see if there's someone I know in the tower."

J.B. excused himself with smiles and embarrassed nods, pretending he needed to go to the men's room in a hurry. He then found a back door and slipped out of the building. Outside, he burst into a jog, steering for the large building with the tower on top. In the admin building, he started up the stairs two at a time until he ran out of breath. Climbing at a slower rate, he'd almost made it to the top when an RAF officer caught sight of him. "Captain? Where are you going?"

"Ah, I just wanted — I just flew in on the C-74, and I've never been to Gatow before. I was curious what it all looked like from the tower."

"I'm sorry, sir. The tower is closed to visitors. However, you can get a good view from the operations room. I can take you there if you like."

Of course the tower was closed to visitors! J.B. didn't doubt that. He looked at the man opposite him. He looked about J.B.'s age and was wearing two rings on his sleeves. That made him a Flight Lieutenant, the same rank as J.B.. "Look," J.B. opened, taking a confidential tone, "The controller who talked me down just now. I think I met her in England when I was stationed there during the war. I wanted to say 'hello.'"

"Assistant Section Leader Hart?" the RAF officer asked back.

J.B. didn't have a clue what her name was, but if he said no he'd be lost, so he said. "Yes, that's right."

"I'll see if she's able to get away for a moment. Please go and wait in the operations room. It's just through that door and on the right." J.B. thanked him dutifully and went to the operations room. This was understandably busy and there were a half-dozen WAAF working here. Why didn't the USAF grasp what a morale booster it was to have women working beside you in an environment like this? It was all very well to have pretty German girls manning the mobile snack bars, but most men wanted women from home around them. The Brits seemed to understand that.

The operations room offered a vista of the runways, and with a jolt J.B. realised that the C-74 was almost empty. Damn! He looked at his watch. They'd been on the ground for almost ninety minutes. First the reception, then the press and the tea... Sure enough, Halvorsen and the other three crew members were approaching the C-74, Halvorsen looking around rather nervously. J.B. didn't have a choice. He had to go. But at least he had a name: Assistant Section Leader Hart. If he ever got back here again, he'd ask for her by name.

Small Miracles
RAF Gatow
Monday, 16 August 1948
(Day 52)

Moby Dick was still unserviceable, and David was slowly going insane. When he'd decided to base the ambulance in Berlin, he had not expected major maintenance problems. The aircraft had comparatively few flying hours and Wellingtons had a reputation for reliability. He had not stockpiled spare parts in Berlin. If they had to replace the whole engine, their only option would be to fly Moby Dick out on one engine because there was no way to bring a replacement engine in. He'd do that himself, of course, but since major repairs of that sort would have to be carried out in the UK, it meant the ambulance would be out of service for four to five days.

Meanwhile, the waiting list for their services just kept growing. They could have fully utilised two ambulances, but to acquire a second aircraft suitable for ambulance operations either he or Kiwi would have to return to the UK, identify an aircraft, contract and oversee the modifications, and recruit yet more air and ground crew. Furthermore, the entire process of purchasing and modifying a second ambulance would take several weeks and possibly a month — during which time the Airlift might come to an end due to a diplomatic deal.

Better focus on the aircraft he already had and the unexpected problem. He'd been flying the aircraft when it happened, so he knew there had been no exceptional strain on the engine. They had been cruising calmly at 4,000 feet and suddenly there had been a bang, then the engine had started vibrating so violently that the entire aircraft shook. Within thirty seconds it had burst into flames. That was not normal behaviour for a Hercules engine — or any other engine for that matter. Since there was no question of "pilot error," suspicion fell on the ground crew. MacDonald's watchful gaze was height-limited, so a mistake by someone unfamiliar with these engines could have evaded him. David even found himself wondering if one of the new German mechanics might have committed sabotage.

Certainly not Axel Voigt. Voigt was desperate to get his mother out of Berlin. Although Trude Liebherr had managed to put Frau Voigt on the list of evacuees from the hospital where she worked, there was already a long waiting list, and it could be weeks before Frau Voigt was aboard an outbound flight. Voigt wasn't likely to sabotage Moby Dick before his mother got out. But David wasn't so sure about the others and wanted to consult with MacDonald. He was on his way to Gatow anyway.

David took public transport as far as Spandau, where he caught one of the RAF buses that ran hourly. Robin had instituted the bus service to reduce the commuting times of their off-loading crews, most of whom lived in Spandau or just across the Havel in Charlottenburg.

There was no shortage of men willing to work, David knew. Workers on the Airlift were entitled to rations of 2,900 calories a day —1,000 to 1,500 more than many had been entitled to before. They also got a hot meal that included vegetables, meat and chocolate. In addition, wages were DM 1,20/hour, so a twelve-hour shift left them in possession of the princely sum of DM 14,40 each day. Unfortunately, there was practically nothing left to buy in Berlin legally, though, and the black market was increasingly criminalised. David had heard it was easier to get cigarettes, alcohol and guns on the black market than food.

The thought of food reminded him that Charlotte still refused to accept any "hand-outs" from him. He was afraid to insist, sensing she would be insulted. He was already frustrated that their relationship seemed to be going nowhere. He'd thought living in the city centre and having daily contact with her would foster it, but before they'd had a chance, he'd returned to flying and was hardly ever in the office. Even when he was there, the presence of two additional employees was inhibiting. Both of them were concerned about maintaining the appearance of "correct" behaviour between employee and employer, which made it awkward to treat her differently from the other two women. He longed for a day off together. Instead, all they did was work with no end in sight.

They couldn't keep this up. None of them could. Even if the current problem was not due to pilot or maintenance error, you couldn't ask men — let alone women — to fly fourteen to sixteen hours, day after day, without risking a deterioration in concentration and responses. Both of AFI's freighters were more than paying their costs, and they could have flown more if he had replacement crews. If he could hire one complete replacement crew for all three aircraft, everyone could have days off and there would always be someone available to jump in if anyone got sick. But if he, Kiwi or Emily stopped flying to recruit more personnel, they'd lose income, and the backlog of patients would increase even more. It was the sheerest good luck that a qualified pilot and flight engineer had walked into the Hamburg maintenance hub yesterday, and were even now flying in on the Dak for an interview with Emily and himself.

The woman pilot had experience with ferrying just like Emily, which meant she was used to precise and careful flying rather than trying to flog the most out of her aircraft like a fighter pilot. Charlotte had suggested her cousin could fly for them, but he *had* been a fighter pilot and had no twin-engine experience. David supposed it wouldn't take long to train Feldburg on the Wellington, yet he found himself shying away from hiring the former Luftwaffe major. Some instinct warned him they might clash. The Americans appealed to him more. If he hired them both he could take himself off flying Moby Dick altogether. He'd give Emily command with the American woman as her second pilot — no, wait: the American woman might have a four-engine rating, but she was unlikely to have flown a Wellington. Regulations required both pilots to have thirty hours on aircraft type before flying with passengers. Damn.

At the main terminal David disembarked and he continued to ponder the problem as he walked to the EAS hangar. He was tempted to ignore the regulation. After all, he wasn't flying in England with English passengers. He was evacuating Germans in an emergency. Since no one in Germany knew about the regulation, they couldn't complain, and if no one complained, then no one at the Ministry of Civil Aviation would find out. Possibly.

Looking across the field, he noticed the AFI Dakota sitting on one of the hardstandings, and the lorry beside it appeared almost full. That meant Kiwi would have to take off again soon. David picked up his pace.

As he entered the hangar, he saw MacDonald had positioned his wheelchair directly under Moby Dick's damaged engine. The cowling was off, and one of the Germans was on a ladder beside the engine while the other two were lying on their bellies on the wing. They looked grimy, sweaty and suitably focused on the repairs. David shifted his attention to a workbench against the wall where Kiwi and Emily, both in AFI's smart black uniform, were chatting with two civilians. Kiwi saw him first and called out. "I was getting worried I'd miss you. They've called my number already."

David nodded, "Go ahead, and thanks for bringing the hitchhikers." Kiwi departed, and David noted that for a man who was flying practically around the clock, Kiwi looked better than he had in six months. He'd lost weight. He had a spring in his step, and he whistled much of the time. Furthermore, he was doing a first-rate job running the maintenance hub in Hamburg. Neither freighter had had any problems that could not be put right during the daily or 150-hour inspections.

Turning his attention to the Americans, the first thing that struck him was that they looked shabby. Their clothes were worn and wrinkled and didn't seem to fit them properly. The man's shoes were scuffed while the woman wore beat-up cowboy boots. David found that ridiculous but told himself it was immaterial. He noted that the woman was as tall as her husband, lanky, and not at all good-looking. She also had a loud, harsh voice with a twang that carried a long distance in the echoing hangar. She was not the kind of woman David would have been attracted to, but he wasn't looking for a woman; he was looking for a pilot.

As he joined them, Emily made the introductions. "This is the founder and managing director of our company, Mr David Goldman. David, this is Janet Orloff. Like me, she was a ferry pilot, only in the US." They shook hands and Emily continued, "And this is her husband Rick Orloff, who was a bombardier in the war, but he has since retrained as an aircraft mechanic."

As David shook hands with Rick, he asked him about his experience as a mechanic, adding jokingly, "No chance you've worked on Hercules engines, is there?"

Rick didn't get a chance to answer because from behind them MacDonald exploded, "No! Not there! More to the right! Haven't you learnt anything from reading the bloody manuals? It's the *other* wire!" In his furious agitation, MacDonald sprang to his feet.

A stunned silence fell over the hangar.

A second later, MacDonald collapsed, but he didn't fall squarely. Hitting the edge of the wheelchair's seat, his weight sent it shooting backwards, dumping him onto the concrete floor. There was a collective gasp, and the Germans started clambering down from the wing and ladder as fast as they could.

Horrified, Emily ran towards MacDonald with David close on her heels. The crew chief looked up at them with a face full of wonder rather than pain. "I stood up," he said in a tone of disbelief. "You saw me, didn't you, lassie? Sir? I stood up."

"Are you all right?" Emily asked, reaching down to get a grip under his arms.

Before she could help, the Germans were there and together got him back into his wheelchair. MacDonald looked up at them and declared again, "I stood up." They nodded vigorously.

He turned back to Emily and repeated proudly, "I stood up."

Emily assured him with a smile, "Yes, you did."

"Do you think I should try it again?"

"I'm not sure," Emily admitted, looking worried. "What happened?"

"I was so frustrated that Gries had hold of the wrong connection, that I just jumped up to show him myself. I forgot I was crippled!"

"Well, maybe you should forget it more often!" Emily suggested, and they all burst out laughing.

Trying to be helpful, Rick offered, "Do you want me to try to figure out the connection?"

"No!" MacDonald snapped rudely. "I don't need you to 'figure' anything out! I *know* what the problem is and how to fix it! I just can't *reach* up there!" Then he seemed to realise his tone was inappropriate, and with an abrupt "Sorry!" he swung the wheelchair around and rolled away from all of them and out the hangar door.

David and Emily gazed at each other, stunned, for a moment, and then David gestured for Emily to follow the crew chief, certain that she could handle this better than he could. He trailed at a discreet distance.

Emily caught up with MacDonald in the open space between their hangar and the Salvation Army Canteen opposite. "Gordon?"

"You're going to hire that American to replace me, aren't you?" he snarled up at her.

Emily shook her head, but glanced back at David for reassurance. David shook his head in confirmation. She put a hand on MacDonald's shoulder and asked, "Is that what that was all about?"

He glared at her with an expression that mixed pride, fear and pain.

David decided it was time for him to intervene. "Mr MacDonald, you have been doing an outstanding job. No one wants to replace you."

The crippled crew chief looked from one to the other and asked in a gruff voice, "Then what is that American aircraft mechanic doing here?"

"I asked Mr Goldman to hire him as flight engineer," Emily explained. "Mrs Orloff and I were ferry pilots. We never received comprehensive training on engines, hydraulics or aerodynamics the way service pilots do. Which means that neither Mrs Orloff nor I can diagnose or respond to mechanical problems while in flight."

David picked up the thread. "I need to spend more time managing the business end of things to be sure we don't run out of money or into other kinds of problems. So Mrs Priestman and Mrs Orloff will be flying on their own and will need a flight engineer on the flight deck with them."

Again, Gordon looked from Emily to David and back, and then insisted on confirming, "And I stay on as crew chief here in Berlin?"

"Of course!"

"In that case, I'd better get back to work," he declared. He swung the wheelchair around and was about to re-enter the hangar when he stopped and looked back at them. "I think I know what caused the problems, by the way: a tiny piece of shrapnel from the flak you flew through weeks ago. It didn't hit anything vital at the time, but something must have dislodged it, and it started worming its way into the works."

David gasped as he realised he'd been wrong to doubt either MacDonald and his German mechanics. The only sabotage that had occurred here was Russian, and while David and Emily gaped at one another, Gordon went back to work inside the hangar.

That night, when Gordon rang his wife Maisy, he was too excited to let her say more than "hello" before exclaiming "I stood up, lassie! Only once and by accident. But if I did it once, I can do it again!"

Maisy couldn't believe what he was saying and made him tell her the whole story. When he finished, all he heard were sobs on the other end of the line. "I wish I were with you!" she managed to gasp out. "I want to hold you."

"I want to hold you too, Maisy," he croaked out, overwhelmed. That was saying a lot for both of them. It was several moments before he lamely suggested, "Maybe you could come over here for a visit some time."

"Yes," she agreed with a gasp.

After that, all he could think to say was, "I'll ring again tomorrow."

"Yes," she repeated, and they hung up.

Gordon sat in the phone booth at the Malcolm Club feeling lonely and miserable. He wanted to hold Maisy in his arms and dream again of dancing with her the way they used to do. He wanted to be in his own cosy home with Maisy's cooking and their memories around them. He wanted to tell his girls that their dad wasn't a cripple — or not forever. He was going to get better. He wanted to *celebrate* that hope.

But you can't celebrate anything alone among strangers in a foreign land. Gordon felt that he didn't want to be here – not in Berlin or Germany. Certainly not in an improvised Malcolm Club serving the transients of a crazy airlift. If he couldn't be with his wife and daughters, he would have liked to talk to a fellow engineer about the engine, the damage that a thumb-nail-sized chunk of metal could do, and how best to mend it. He wanted to chat and drink and laugh with friends, not sit by himself in what amounted to a transit lounge.

But wishing wouldn't change things. So, he rolled himself to the sparsely visited dining room for a dull meal. Afterwards he found a place in the institutional-looking lounge to sip a beer and try to cheer himself up. Instead, he became more and more morose as he futilely searched for a way to bring Maisy to Berlin. Every plan foundered on the political reality of the Soviet threat.

It was almost ten o'clock and he was falling asleep in his chair over a magazine he wasn't reading when the door opened and a crowd burst in calling, "Gordon! Where are you?"

Disoriented, he looked around, confused, and realised that Nigel and Terry were suddenly flanking him. Moran, Bruce Forrester and Richard Scott-Ross clustered behind them. They gathered around, clapping him on the back, congratulating and teasing. "Been dodging work, have you? Nothing wrong with you at all!" Nigel declared with a playful nudge.

Gordon started to splutter denials, but Terry and the skipper were shaking his hand and saying how happy they were, while Bruce offered to buy the first round, and Richard pulled up a chair beside Gordon declaring he wanted to know all about the engine problems.

"Where did you come from? How did you find out?" Gordon asked them as the others dragged chairs over to surround him.

"Mrs Priestman called RAF Fuhlsbuettel asking us to track down the spare parts you wanted. We couldn't draw the spares, but we loaded another cargo and flew it in tonight to celebrate with you." Moran explained.

Gordon glanced at the clock on the wall. It was almost 11 pm. It took more than two hours to unload the Halifax so they wouldn't be flying out again until nearly 2 am and wouldn't see their beds until almost dawn the next day — just to come and congratulate him. He felt himself getting choked up again and pushed back against his emotions by asking, "But what about the spare parts?"

"The RAF agreed to sell them to us, but most of them are at the central storage depot in the UK, so they'll fly them in on their daily maintenance supply flight tomorrow. Either Kiwi or we'll bring them to you the first chance we get. You should have them late tomorrow or Wednesday at the latest," Richard explained.

Gordon nodded, thinking out loud, "Moby Dick should be flying again by Friday, then." The thought filled him with immeasurable satisfaction. Suddenly, he wasn't in a foreign country or a dreary, institutional lounge; he was where he was supposed to be, doing an important job, surrounded by the best mates a man could have. And maybe, just maybe, there was a chance that one day he would walk again.

Warnings from the Underworld
Berlin-Kreuzberg
Sunday, 22 August 1948
(Day 58)

Jakob Liebherr stood at the foot of the stairwell and looked up. His apartment was on the fourth floor and there was no elevator. Even if there had been a lift, he reminded himself, there was no electricity, so he would still have had to walk up. He had no choice. He had to walk up those four flights of stairs and his lungs were hurting and his breath short from walking home after a meeting with Mayor Reuter. He had hoped that all the extra walking he'd been doing since the siege started would make him fitter, but it seemed to be having the opposite effect.

He took as deep a breath as he could and started up the stairs, one step at a time. Part of him wished that he were younger and healthier, but if he were younger he'd probably live longer. If that meant more years in a state controlled by Joseph Stalin, then he was better off being old and in poor health.

He made it to the first landing and paused to catch his breath. It was almost two months since the blockade had started and amazingly the Western Allies were still here. Even more astonishingly, Berlin still had reserves of food and coal. The deadline for surrender had been pushed back again and again by those planes that never stopped — or almost never stopped. Last Friday had been a nightmare. First, the aircraft went around in circles, and then they flew away altogether, leaving a deathly silence. It had felt as if the Americans had just given up and gone home. But they had returned the next day and shown off their wonder-plane, the C-74. The Allies, so far, were holding fast — at least for now.

Jakob turned his attention to the stairs and grimly made his way up to the second landing, where he stopped again. Two more storeys to climb, another thirty-six steps. There were so many steps because this building dated from the last century and the stairs were shallow, designed for ladies in long dresses. Breathing heavily and clinging to the banister, he continued doggedly towards the third floor.

Before he reached it, *Kapitaenleutnant* — or should he say Inspector? — Sperl overtook him on the stairs. "Herr Liebherr? What a fortunate coincidence. Could you spare me a few moments?"

"Time is one of the few things which have not been rationed, shortened, or dehydrated," Liebherr answered dryly, and Sperl laughed.

Then, assessing Liebherr's heavy breathing and grey face, Sperl suggested they stop in his apartment for their talk. Jakob gladly agreed; eighteen steps postponed until later.

Sperl led the way inside and Jakob was struck by how empty it looked without all the "inventory". Sperl had retained only a few things for his personal comfort. He invited Liebherr to sit on a stuffed sofa and offered, "What can I bring you? Water or schnapps?"

"Not your own schnapps, I hope?" Liebherr countered, remembering the moonshine Sperl and his friends and had brewed.

Sperl laughed. "That's all I have — now that I've gone over to the law."

"It is very strange, you know," Jakob reflected, relieved to be sitting down and starting to feel better because of it. "Most Berliners believe that the police keep all the things they confiscate when people are stopped for smuggling."

It was no secret that many West Berliners risked trying to smuggle things in from the Soviet Zone. Since there were still no restrictions on the movement of people, it was quite easy to get out of the blockaded Sectors and into the surrounding countryside where many fresh things were still available on the local market. The trick was getting back *into* the Western Sectors of Berlin without having the precious goods confiscated. The City Council estimated that thousands of Berliners took a chance every day. Since the Red Army and SED-controlled police couldn't be everywhere at once, not all purchases were confiscated. Enough people were lucky often enough to make it worthwhile trying. The City Council had calculated that on average Berliners were managing to add 300 calories a day by devious means. The question was for how long? Farmers had plenty of fresh crops to sell right now, but they wouldn't have much to sell come November and thereafter. Meanwhile, smuggling bands brought cigarettes and alcohol up from the Balkans, and bands of unemployed and enterprising young Berliners made a living evading the police and Red Army to bring high-margin items like alcohol, petrol, drugs and guns to black markets scattered throughout the city.

Sperl smiled faintly, "Markgraf's men think they are 'entitled' to retain anything they seize because their job is to enforce the blockade. We, on the other hand, only stop someone we suspect of dealing in drugs or contraband — according to the Western Allied lists." The British and Americans had established a "counter blockade" to protect against these harmful imports, and also to prevent certain items coveted by the Soviets from leaving West Berlin.

"Now, what did you want to talk to me about?" Jakob prompted.

"Two things. First, Freiherr von Feldburg has evidence that a certain Franz von Aggstein was involved in developing chemical weapons, and there is good reason to believe he is now going under the name of Friedebach and lives on Schwanenwerder in the American Sector. Apparently he manages pharmaceutical factories in the Soviet Zone, and we had a tip that he is the source of the high-grade heroin we're seeing in Berlin. If we could arrest Friedebach, we might land both a drug dealer and a major Nazi war criminal at the same time."

"Interesting," Jakob remarked.

Sperl considered him and noted, "Interesting, but not interested."

Jakob sighed. "I would like to see every Nazi war criminal brought to justice, but at the moment I'm more worried about avoiding a Soviet dictatorship."

"Fair enough, which brings me to my second point. My sources suggest that the SED is planning a coup d'etat against the City Council."

"Of course they're planning a coup d'etat," Liebherr answered wearily. "The SED has been planning a coup d'etat ever since they lost the last election. Since they stand no chance of winning the next election either, their only path to power is through some kind of illegal coup."

"What I'm hearing from underground sources is that they plan to incite massive riots and mobilise armed militias to topple the city council outright."

Jakob shot back tensely, "When?"

"At the next scheduled meeting of the City Council."

"Which would be six days from now," Liebherr calculated.

"Exactly," Sperl confirmed.

"What sort of numbers do you think they can mobilise?"

"Three to five thousand."

Liebherr drew a deep breath and let it out again. Five thousand paid agitators alone didn't make a successful revolution. Agitators threw stones and broke windows. They put up barricades, waved flags and shouted slogans. But such actions came to nothing unless they tapped into deeper grievances among a wider segment of the population.

And that was exactly what Jakob feared.

Another 148 factories had closed this past week — all because they did not have the raw materials or electricity necessary to operate. The closures put roughly five thousand more men out of work. The total number of unemployed in the Western Sectors was fast approaching 100,000, and unemployed workers were the "useful idiots" of every revolution. It was not empty bellies so much as the lack of meaningful work that drove men to violence. It was the promise of jobs more than hand-outs that seduced men into jumping on the nearest political bandwagon. That was what made the situation now so much more dangerous than it had been in June. Out loud, Jakob said simply, "Thank you for this intelligence, Inspector. I will share it with my colleagues urgently."

Chapter Fifteen
Out of the Blue

Red Mama Mia
Berlin-Kladow
Saturday, 21 August 1948
(Day 57)

"It's your birthday on Thursday," Galyna's mother reminded her in a voice on the brink of tears. "I can still remember it so vividly. I almost died, you know? It took heroic efforts by the doctors to save us both. But here we are, alive and separated by less than 20 miles. Why won't you meet me? I want to see what my little lamb has become! I want to give you something special on your birthday — not just food, which I'll bring too, of course, but something to show my love for you. I want to celebrate life with you, Puppet. Please, Lamb! Please!"

Twice Galyna had turned her down, but during this third call her mother offered to come to Kladow, very near to Gatow in the British Sector. "There is a little restaurant with tables out on the lawn overlooking the Havel," she coaxed. "We could meet there. It's small and discreet and very pleasant."

After asking around, Galyna learned from a corporal in the RAF regiment that the restaurant was a notorious smugglers' den. "We keep a close eye on it," he explained. "Not that we mind them bringing food in from the Zone. That saves us flying it in, but sometimes they sell things we have black-listed. You can get a good meal there, though, if that's what you're after," he'd advised. "They've got a source of fresh meat and vegetables somewhere in the Soviet Zone and a trafficker who delivers over the lake at night. The waterways are the most porous components of the blockade and rife with smuggling," he confided.

Galyna asked if it was dangerous to go there, and the corporal assured

338

that it was only dangerous after dark. So, Galyna agreed to meet her mother immediately after she came off duty.

On arrival, she gave her name to the waiter and was taken out to the lawn. Before she had a chance to get her bearings, her mother leapt to her feet and, with a cry, rushed at her. Fleshy arms pressed Galyna to an ample bust as if she were an infant, smothering Galyna's protest. Galyna had inherited her stocky figure from her mother, but her mother had gained a great deal of weight since they'd last seen each other. Almost crushing her, Anastasia babbled, "My lamb! My puppet!"

Galyna was sure everyone for miles around could hear her. Certainly, everyone at the restaurant was staring at them. Frowning, she wriggled free of her mother's embrace and scolded, "Don't make a scene! I'm not a child!"

"You'll always be a child to me!" Her mother countered, holding her by the shoulders to look into her face. "You look tired and overworked. Why did you wear that hideous uniform? It makes you look fat!"

"I am proud of it," Galyna replied, lifting her chin defiantly.

Her mother ignored her remark and led her to a table. "Sit down! Order whatever you like! It is my treat! Look they have chicken Kyiv and Stroganov." Switching to German, she called angrily "Boy! Boy!" The old man who served the tables limped over. Waving her hand irritably, Anastasia snapped. "I told you to bring the champagne as soon as my guest arrived. Bring it! Bring it!"

Galyna eased herself into one of the metal chairs and ran her eye over the menu her mother had shoved at her. She had decided before she came that regardless of what transpired, she would eat well. She deliberately chose some of the most expensive items on the menu. When the waiter returned with the bucket of ice and the bottle of Crimean champagne, she told him what she wanted and he withdrew.

Her mother filled the glasses and raised one. "To my loveliest, sweetest, most talented and never-forgotten little puppet Galyna!"

"I'm turning twenty-five today, Anastasia Sergeyevna. I am not your puppet any more, and I am not a lamb either," Galyna countered, not touching the alcohol.

"When you have children of your own, you'll learn that a child is always a child, no matter how old they are," Anastasia declared. Then she reached across the table and seized Galyna's hand to hold it. Her eyes were fixed on Galyna as if she were a rare object.

Galyna pulled her hand away, uncomfortable with all this melodrama.

Her mother answered by calling out "*Za zdarovye!*" and downing the glass of champagne in a single swig. Galyna made a point of taking a tiny sip and putting the glass back almost full.

Her mother refilled her glass and then reached under the table to remove a large shopping bag. She pulled it onto her lap and began removing items one after another, saying, "Let me show you what I've brought you. Caviar, Crimean champagne, sausage, cheese, a fresh loaf of black bread — not that horrible white stuff the English eat — and pickled beets. I'll put them all back in the bag and you can take it with you when you leave."

Galyna nodded, but told her mother, "You should not have bothered. We have plenty to eat."

"Ha! Just as Maxim said! All the planes are full of champagne, lobsters and bananas for the Americans, French and British. The Berliners are starving, he said, but not the capitalist terrorists."

"We are no more 'terrorists' than you are. We were Allies, remember? And the Berliners aren't starving." Galyna insisted.

"Puppet —" Anastasia started, but Galyna's look made her correct herself to "Galyna, I came to make peace with you, to become friends again, to—"

"And what about my father? How do you propose to 'make peace' with him, to 'become friends' with him, again?" Galyna hissed back.

Anastasia recoiled, and there was a pause. Then in a low, almost emotionless voice, so unlike her loud, melodramatic cries, she said, "That is unfair."

Galyna caught her breath. For the first time, Galyna felt her mother was serious. Now, they could talk.

"What is unfair about it?" Galyna asked back, looking her mother straight in the eye.

"There was nothing I could do for him. No one could help him. No one." Anastasia spoke in a whisper.

Galyna believed her and a chill went down her spine. It was true. No one could have saved her father once the State turned against him. But that did not absolve her mother of guilt. "Maybe you could not help him,"

Galyna conceded, "but you could have *remembered* him. You could have *honoured* him by keeping a place for him in your home, your bed, and your heart!"

"How do you know what is in my heart?" Anastasia asked back solemnly.

"You denounced him, and then you married one of the men who brought him down. Isn't that proof of what you feel?"

"No. No, it is not. Everything I did, I did for you. I could not save your father, but I could save you. Don't you see that? I did everything for you — just as I am doing now. I am trying to save you before it is too late. When this silly 'air bridge' collapses, there will be a terrible reckoning. All I want is for you to be on the right side of history."

"I already am, mother," Galyna told her steadily. "You're the one who has put your head in the sand and refuses to see what is going on around you."

Her mother frowned, seemed to consider various options, and then waved the notion aside with a gesture, announcing with forced gaiety, "Come! Let's not talk politics. It is your birthday — the first one we have spent together in thirteen years. Aren't you curious about your birthday present?"

Galyna shook her head in sadness and remarked with a faint, condescending smile, "No, Anastasia Sergeyevna, because I already know what it is."

"What?"

"It's one of your paintings, surely?"

"Ah! You do still know me! Here! Have a look! It's an entirely new style. I'm sure you'll like it."

With a deep breath, Galyna took the package, untied the string, and removed the brown wrapping paper. It was a vivid rural scene with sunburnt peasants harvesting wheat. Galyna stared at it for a long time. It merged with her memories of skeletons in rags stumbling across barren fields, of shallow graves and whispers of cannibalism. She remembered Mila's voice when she'd confided that her family had no grain to harvest and were forced to eat roots, rats and wild birds — again.

"Well?" her mother asked. "What do you think?"

"Where is it supposed to be?" Galyna asked.

"Home, of course. Ukraine."

"Then it is ridiculously unrealistic — the people in your painting are fat and happy." Galyna looked up and straight at her mother. "I am not an idiot. I know that the Soviet Union is confiscating the entire harvest of their Zone in Germany because the harvest in Ukraine has failed — again."

"You have been brainwashed! You are reading propaganda!"

"Brainwashed? Do you think I have forgotten what I saw with my own eyes? When I saw the films of the liberation of the concentration camps, I was not shocked like my English colleagues because I had seen such walking skeletons before — from the window of the train when we travelled to Kharkiv. Or do you think I have forgotten stepping over the corpses of people who had starved to death overnight on my way to school each day? Do you think I have forgotten the mothers begging for bread with babies in their arms whose heads and bellies were huge but whose arms and legs were as tiny as dolls'?"

"They were just Kulaks!" Her mother made a dismissive gesture and a disgusted face.

"Kulaks?" Galyna asked back. Mila had called herself a "Kulak." "Kulaks aren't cockroaches, Anastasia Sergeyevna! They are human beings. The question is: what are you?"

"How dare you talk to your mother like that?" Anastasia snapped back furiously, her face turning bright red.

Galyna jumped to her feet, threw her napkin on her unfinished meal and stormed out of the restaurant, leaving both the bag of food and the painting behind.

Bon-Bons Away
Frankfurt / Main
Sunday / Monday, 22 / 23 August 1948
(Day 58/59)

"The oldest of these kids couldn't have been more than twelve," Halvorsen stressed to his copilot in a breathless, excited voice. "The littlest was about eight. Yet every one of them understood that this Airlift isn't about food but freedom! It was amazing!" The American pilots were sitting together in the mess having a quick meal before bed. Halvorsen had just returned from his off-duty trip to Berlin.

"Yeah," J.B. agreed. "That is pretty amazing. Where did you say you ran into these kids?"

"They were hanging onto the perimeter fence right at the end of the runway. I'd gone over there to try to get a picture of a C-54 landing over the apartment houses, and they were clinging to the outside of the fence. They said they live nearby and come to watch the planes every day."

"And what did they say about freedom, exactly?" J.B.'s scepticism was reflected in his voice. The kids he knew didn't care about politics.

"Well, there was this little girl with blonde pigtails wearing hand-me-down trousers from probably more than one older brother and she said, 'When you bombed us and killed some of our parents and sisters and brothers —"

"She said that to your face?" J.B. asked, horrified.

"Yeah, and then she went on—"

"Wait a minute! Didn't you correct her? Didn't you tell her *you* hadn't flown bombers in the war? That you hadn't even been in the European theatre?"

"No, that wasn't important. What's important is what she said. Listen to me, J.B.! She said that during the bombing, they'd thought nothing could be worse than that — until the Russians came. She said something like, 'After the final battle for Berlin, we saw what the Russians did in the city before you arrived. And we've learned more about Communism since.' An older boy with good English added, 'We don't need lectures about freedom. We can walk on both sides of the city, and we have relatives who visit from the East. They are hungry for American newspapers and listen to RIAS.' Several then chimed in to say that everyone listened to RIAS if they could get it — East or West."

"Yeah, RIAS has a good mix of entertainment and information — and they have children's programs, too," J.B. conceded before asking, "Did you enjoy the rest of your sightseeing tour?" He had finished his meal and was wiping his hands on a paper napkin. Their next flight was scheduled to depart at 2 am and he wanted to get some sleep first.

Halvorsen nodded absently and answered between his last mouthfuls of dinner. "Sure. It was interesting, although everything's pretty wrecked. The tour got cut short when we had to hightail it back in a hurry because some Reds started chasing us. Apparently any American with a camera is treated like a spy. But I keep coming back to those kids." He put his cutlery down and wiped his hands on his napkin. "Here they are living on less than 1,000 calories a day, with no candy or chocolate or gum. Geeze, they don't even get much sugar on the rations we give them, but not one of them tried to bum something off me."

They both stood to return their trays with the dirty dishes, and Halvorsen continued, "Everywhere else in the world the kids cluster around — not begging exactly, but, you know, hinting that they could sure use some candy or gum. Brazil, Colombia, Panama, wherever — the kids would grin and wave and call out: 'Hey, chum, got any gum?' But not these kids. I'd already turned away from them before I realised that they hadn't asked me for a thing. I felt in my pockets to see what I had to share and came up with just two sticks of Wriggley's gum — for a dozen kids! I tore the sticks in half and gave a piece to each of the kids who'd done most of the talking. You know what they did? They passed the wrappers to the others so they could *sniff* them — and you should have seen their faces! You would have thought they'd just been given a whole bowl of ice cream with hot chocolate sauce and whipped cream on top."

The pilots put their trays on the counter for the mess stewards and started for the shuttle to the Zeppelinheim. "When I saw that," Halvorsen continued casually, "I promised to bring them some candy today."

"Hal! We're not allowed more than ten feet away from the aircraft, remember? You can't go wandering off across the airfield to give kids candy."

"I know, that's why I said I'd drop it from the plane, just as we come over the fence."

J.B. screeched to a halt, "You said *what*?" Then before Halvorsen repeated himself, he added, "We can't do that! It would just get blown away and scatter all over the place. Hell, it would probably shatter on impact! We're still 200 feet up and going 90 to 100 mph when we come over the fence."

"I've been thinking about it all the way back, and I figured we could make little parachutes out of handkerchiefs."

"Hal, you're crazy. Sleep deprived, that's what. Let's get some shuteye, and you'll feel better and see things straight when you wake up."

They returned to their quarters in the old barn. J.B. stripped down to his undershorts, rolled himself into his blanket and was out like a light. When he woke up, he was dismayed to find that instead of sleeping Halvorsen had been fashioning tiny parachutes from his handkerchiefs. "They work too!" he assured J.B. "I tested one from the window of the loft." Then with one of his irresistible, shy smiles, he asked, "You wouldn't happen to have any left-over candy or chocolate bars, would you? I've still got six parachutes."

Shaking his head, J.B. handed over all his candy rations, but he warned Hal, "If anyone finds out about this, we are going to get into a heap of trouble. Hell, Tunner's such a stickler for regulations, he'll probably court-martial us for something like this."

"He'll never find out," Halvorsen insisted.

Soon they had Sergeant Elkins' candy ration tied to parachutes too, and they hid the lot in Elkins' tool kit. Promptly at two am, they took off for Berlin, arriving before dawn. The C-54 was unloaded with the usual efficiency while they waited beside it, receiving one jeep after another with the weather and paperwork that went with each flight. They bought coffee at the mobile snack bar when it came by, and then flew back to Frankfurt. Here the routine was repeated with them waiting near the aircraft as it was loaded with a cargo of powdered vegetable soup, and then they were in the corridor again. It was approaching noon when they entered the traffic pattern for Tempelhof.

Halvorsen hadn't slept a wink that J.B. had seen, and he was very keyed up. J.B. had never seen him like this before. He was licking his lips every few seconds and leaning forward in his seat as he squinted against the sun. Then, sounding as excited as a kid, he exclaimed: "There they are! There they are!" He pointed ahead towards the airfield coming into view as they dropped down on their steep glide path over the apartment buildings. Sure enough, about thirty kids of all shapes and sizes were clustered at the perimeter fence and staring upwards at the approaching cargo planes.

"Sergeant Elkins, go back and prepare to drop the parachutes when I tell you to," Halvorsen ordered.

"Are you really going to go through with this?" J.B. asked.

"Yes," Halvorsen's tone brooked no contradiction, and Elkins, shaking his head but grinning, retreated to the cabin where the parachutes waited near the flare-chute.

Halvorsen started wiggling the wings of the heavily loaded freighter; that is, rolling ten to degrees first in one direction and then the other several times in succession.

"The tower is going to think we're drunk as skunks!" J.B. groaned, but his words were lost on Halvorsen. He was grinning from ear to ear as the kids started jumping up and down and waving like crazy.

"What if one of the aircraft waiting for take-off gets our number?" J.B. asked anxiously.

Halvorsen answered with: "Give me full flaps and 1800 RPM!"

Rolling his eyes, J.B. followed orders and as they almost stalled out over the end of the runway, Halvorsen called to Elkins over the intercom, "Now!"

Elkins answered with: "Bon-bons away!"

An instant later their tyres screeched on the runway and the nose wheel flopped down, but they had no way of seeing if the parachutes had landed near the children, never mind if they'd been retrieved.

The Bombers of Yesteryear
Berlin-Tempelhof
Thursday, 26 August 1948
(Day 62)

"Mrs Hart, please try to understand." Virginia Cox argued patiently with the WAAF officer. "*Everyone* is talking about these parachutes with sweets attached. There were scores and scores of witnesses, but no one has a photo of it. A picture is worth a thousand words. All I'm asking is that you lend me your adorable little daughter for a few hours. With her bright blonde hair, she looks German. We can braid it the way the Germans do and dress her in the oldest, most faded clothes she has. I've already made a parachute with one of my old scarves and have attached some Hersey's chocolate that an American friend gave me to it." Virginia held up her contraption. "We can throw the parachute out of an apartment building window and position Hope below, waiting with uplifted arms. It will be a sensational shot!"

"It would be fake," Kathleen answered tartly and indignantly. She did not like this idea at all.

"No more 'fake' than most of the films and photos we made during the war," Virginia countered. "You know as well as I do that all those laughing 'Fighter Boys' lounging around waiting for a scramble were posed for the photographers. And so were the images of Bomber Boys intently waiting to hear the 'target for tonight'. But they weren't lies. They were staged, yes, but they *replicated* reality as accurately as possible. That is what I propose to do now. What is so wrong with that?"

Kathleen didn't have an answer. She looked over at Hope, who at once started begging. "Please, Mummy! Please!" Kathleen hated being manipulated and all her instincts said this was wrong, but she lacked the arguments to plead her case.

Yes, she could slam the door in the reporter's face, but that would probably land her in more trouble. The reporter worked for the *Times*, and her father sat in Parliament. Perhaps more relevant, the WAAF OC was on very good terms with her and had brought her over, saying she was "sure" Assistant Section Leader Hart would have no objections. Kathleen and Parsons had managed to avoid clashes largely by keeping out of each other's way, but Parsons still had the power to make life very unpleasant for Kathleen if she wanted to. Kathleen preferred to find a compromise now.

She took a deep breath. "I'm sorry, but I'm not going to let you just borrow Hope. If you want to take Hope anywhere, then I am coming with you. It is my day off."

"Oh, splendid!" Virginia agreed with exaggerated enthusiasm.

An hour later, Kathleen and Virginia were sitting in the back of a confiscated "*Kuebelwagen*" with British occupation licence plates while Virginia's photographer drove them along the edge of the Havel on their way to Tempelhof. Hope was sitting in the front seat beside the photographer. She was happy as a lark in the open vehicle with the wind blowing her hair. Where Virginia had got the petrol rations for this outing, Kathleen could not fathom, but apparently the press had privileges and it was not her place to question them.

Virginia had Kathleen trapped as she turned to ask, "Why is it, Mrs Hart, that I get the feeling you disapprove of me? We're both career women, after all. We ought to be allies! We should join forces against a world that would like to shoo us both back behind the stove." Although she tried to make the question sound light-hearted, Kathleen knew she was deadly serious.

"What I don't like," Kathleen answered, meeting the reporter's eyes, "is that you are turning Hope's head, making her feel special and glamorous. It's quite misleading. She's just an ordinary seven-year-old."

"Is she?" Virginia asked with a raised eyebrow. "I think Hope is an adorable and photogenic child. She's sure to grow into an attractive girl. Every beautiful woman should learn to use her charms to get what she wants as early as possible."

That was not the way Kathleen had been raised. Then again, she hadn't been happy in the world her parents had made for her. Would she have been happier following Miss Cox's advice? She didn't think so. It was too mercenary, too exploitative, and didn't leave room for giving as well as taking. Out loud, she reminded Virginia, "Beauty is ephemeral. It can be shattered in a single accident or fade over time. Either way, it is better for a woman not to depend on it too heavily."

"Beauty is the most powerful weapon women have and ought to be used mercilessly as long as one has it," Virginia countered. "Which doesn't mean one can't develop other skills. I think it's marvellous that you're an air traffic controller. I was serious about wanting to interview you. I'm sorry you didn't get in touch with me after our last meeting."

"I am very busy."

"I'm sure you are, but we have lots of time until we get to Tempelhof. Why don't you start by telling me how you landed here? Weren't you worried about bringing a child into what is practically a warzone?"

"When I volunteered for Gatow, it was a sleepy, forgotten backwater, and I wanted to be near my husband."

"Your husband?" Virginia gasped, glancing at Kathleen's hand. Only now did she notice her wedding ring. "Silly of me! I assumed you were single. What's his role?"

"Navigator on a Lancaster. He's in the Commonwealth War Cemetery."

"Oh! You mean he's *dead*! Well, that doesn't count then, does it?"

"To me it does," Kathleen retorted, thinking how the longer she was here, the more often he seemed to visit. Mostly he came in her dreams, but sometimes she sensed his presence when she walked beside the perimeter fence to get fresh air, or when she sat alone in her flat after Hope had gone to bed.

Virginia had been talking, and when Kathleen didn't respond, she repeated her question, "Do you feel you are treated the same as your male colleagues?"

"Most of the time," Kathleen answered, appending her answer with, "it depends on the CO." Soon, without her realising what was happening, Virginia had drawn Kathleen into a conversation so successfully that Kathleen was surprised when they reached Tempelhof. American Skymasters were swooping down at them, and the roar of their engines was deafening. Their wheels and flaps were down as they passed directly overhead, and one could see the oil stains on the wings and the bolts holding the fuselage together.

"Oh, look!" Virginia exclaimed. "There's a group of German children over there. They must be hoping for a sweet drop! Let's go and talk to them. Come on!" she ordered her photographer as she flung the car door open and made a beeline for the German boys and girls, Hope and Kathleen forgotten. Kathleen took a disgruntled Hope by the hand and followed.

At the sight of three adults approaching from a car with Allied plates, the children grew still and solemn. They probably feared being chased away.

"*Sprechen Sie Englisch*?" Virginia asked.

"A little," one girl answered.

"Are you waiting for sweets to be dropped from an aeroplane?"

They all nodded energetically.

"From one of those?" Hope asked, pointing upwards as her mother hushed her.

Virginia asked the German girl, "Have you caught any sweets before?"

All the children nodded vigorously, and one of the younger children said something with a giggle that the older girl translated. "It is the first chewing gum any of us have ever had."

"Gum's bad for your teeth!" Hope informed them. Kathleen put her finger to her lips, harvesting a frown and a stamped foot as she demanded, "Why can't I say anything?"

"Because Miss Cox wants to hear what the German children have to say."

"Were you here yesterday and the day before?" Virginia asked the Germans.

They nodded solemnly.

"But no sweets were dropped?"

They shook their heads.

"But you still come every day?"

"It isn't just the sweets. Every plane brings food or coal or other things we need," the eldest girl explained. "We watched the planes before the sweets were dropped, too. As long as the planes come, my mother says, we won't have to submit to the Ivans."

Good answer, Kathleen thought, and she glanced up just in time to see a USAF Skymaster that was almost on top of them start to rock back and forth. Pilots often did that to "wave" to girlfriends or parents, but the wild reaction of the children took her by surprise. They started jumping up and down and waving with both hands, their high-pitched voices delivering ear-splitting, cacophonic yells of glee. Hope instinctively joined in without even knowing what it was all about.

The next thing Kathleen knew, tiny parachutes were opening over their heads with chocolate bars and packages of gum hanging from them. The children's shouts of joy reached a fever pitch, almost blotting out Virginia's furious screams; her photographer had left his camera in the car.

It was too late for a photo. The last of the parachutes with two Babe Ruths swaying from some strings was floating down towards outstretched little hands. Kathleen held Hope back just in time. Hope stamped her foot again and whined, "Why can't *I* have some?"

"Because we have sweets rations. These children don't," Kathleen told her firmly. "I'll give you some chocolate when we get back to Gatow."

Returning her attention to the German children, Kathleen was astonished to see that rather than tearing open the wrappers and eating whatever they could capture, the children first pooled their treasures and then shared them out with scrupulous fairness. In the end, there were three chocolate bars too many. Earnest discussion followed in German before these were handed to three children, who stowed them away in a pocket, evidently for absent siblings. This gesture more than anything struck a chord in Kathleen. She turned to look at the tail of the receding Skymaster.

Did the young men in that aircraft have any idea how happy they had just made these children? Could Americans who had never known shortages, rationing or hunger grasp what a chocolate bar meant to children like these?

They must. Otherwise, they wouldn't go to so much trouble to make little parachutes from their cotton handkerchiefs and attach candy to them. Again, she looked towards the Skymaster that had concluded its rollout and was turning off the runway. She squinted, trying to read the tail fin.

The USAF used tail fin numbers to identify themselves to the tower. If she could make out the number, then if it ever came to Gatow she would recognise it and could try to talk to the pilots. She knew the crews changed, but she'd at least have a chance of meeting the young men who'd gone to so much trouble to bring happiness to children they didn't know.

But the Skymaster was too far away. She would never have any way of knowing who had come up with this idea of dropping candy to the children of Berlin. Yet, most likely he had once dropped bombs on them. The thought moved her to unexpected tears. Ken had loved making Hope laugh and smile. She was sure he would have loved to take part in something like this — if only he'd lived to be here. She felt him beside her, smiling.

Echoes
Hamburg
Friday, 27 August 1948
(Day 63)

Kit stayed behind to talk to the ground crew about a strange noise coming from the hydraulics while the rest of the crew went ahead to pick up the mail before heading to the *Golden Lion*. By the time he arrived at the pub, he had to squeeze his way past the clusters of men in flying gear besieging the bar and blocking the stairs down to the lounge. The *Golden Lion* had become very popular with Airlift crews.

As he sank into the vacant chair at "their" table, Nigel handed him a bundle of letters with the commentary, "Four from Georgina, and one from a certain G.L. Cheshire. He wouldn't be any relation to Group Captain Leonard Cheshire VC, DSO, and bar etc., would he?"

"The same. Did you order a drink and meal for me?"

"A hot toddy is on the way," Bruce assured him, "along with the usual bratwurst."

"So, since when have you been on such friendly terms with the most highly decorated officer in the RAF?" Nigel persisted.

"Oh, we met in May after Gordon tried to join his community."

"Gordon?" Nigel and Terry asked simultaneously, turning in unison to gawk at him.

"It's rather a long story," Kit equivocated.

"The night's still young," Richard replied, leaning back with a grin that left Kit little option but to tell the tale. In due course, his meal and drink arrived, and the others ordered a second round. The conversation drifted to other topics. After about an hour, Kiwi and his crew, still wearing their wet oilskins, found them.

"What bloody awful weather!" Kiwi declared, shaking rain off his cap as he sank into the chair beside Kit. "I thought English weather —"

"Chuck, darling! What are you doing here?" A woman's voice cut through the masculine chatter and a slender blonde woman swept in and draped herself over Kiwi's chair. "I thought AAI had moved to Berlin?"

"Ah, Virginia!" Kiwi struggled to his feet, the others following. "Yes. The ambulance moved to Berlin, but I'm now captain of a freighter and head of the maintenance hub here. Let me introduce you." When he'd finished, he explained to his colleagues, "Virginia Cox is a reporter with *The Times*. Would you like to join us for a drink, Virginia?"

"I thought you'd *never* ask!" She pulled a chair from the adjacent table and placed it next to Kiwi's, then smiling up at him, she added, "I'm drinking Cuba Libres tonight, darling." Kiwi dutifully went off in the direction of the bar, while Virginia turned to smile at the others and remarked, "The weather's terrible, isn't it? I've heard it is going to get worse, too. Do you think you'll be flying tomorrow?"

She was trying too hard to be friendly, Kit thought, and her smile seemed brittle. She also reminded him he would far rather be with Georgina than here at all. He would have given half his pay to be based somewhere she and Donna could live too. It was time to leave so he could read her letters. To the reporter, he said simply, "Yes, I expect to fly tomorrow, which is why I think I'll turn in now." He stood and nodded to his crew, receiving easy waves in return. With a handshake and perfunctory, "Pleasure to have made your acquaintance," for Virginia, he departed.

Back in his room at the boarding house, he turned up the gas heater as far as possible, kicked off his shoes, and lay down on the narrow bed, still in his overcoat. Ordering the letters from Georgina by postmark, he read them one after the other. Each letter left him more disturbed than the one before. Letters had played a large role in their relationship. While he was in flight training in South Africa she had written to him several times a week — not bright, cheery letters full of gossip, but letters full of feelings, thoughts, doubts, and longings. She had laid bare her soul and allowed him to see her depths. These letters, in contrast, were stiff and wooden and false.

After thinking about this for half an hour or so, Kit concluded that she was hiding something from him. He swung his feet off the bed, put his shoes back on and went down to the reception. It was nearly 11 o'clock and the desk was manned by an old woman. In his best German, Kit explained that he had to make a phone call, but this elicited only a flood of German accompanied by much head shaking. Kit gave up and resolved to return to RAF Fuhlsbuettel.

With the Airlift operating twenty-four hours every day, he had no difficulty at the gate, and no one stopped him from going into the officer's mess either. He found a vacant phone booth and requested the international telephone operator. Just before midnight, the operator told him to insert five shillings into the slot for a three-minute call, and he was then connected to the vicarage at Foster Clough. His father-in-law was on the line, "This is Reverend Reddings. How may I help?"

"Edwin, it's me. Kit—"

"Kit! Are you all right? Nothing's happened, has it?"

"I'm all right thanks, I was just worried about Georgina. Her letters sounded so odd. How is she?"

The pause was pregnant before the reverend answered honestly, "She's very depressed. Her mother and I don't seem able to help her at all."

It was what he'd feared. "And Donna and the horses?"

"They're fine."

"But they can't cheer her up?"

"No, not really. She loves them, of course, but she needs more purpose in life. She always felt teaching was a calling — not just a job. You know that. She needs to feel she's doing something worthwhile. Her mother has tried to get her interested in — wait! She's coming down the stairs now." He put his hand over the receiver and Kit heard muffled voices. Then Georgina's anxious voice came over the line. "Kit? Are you all right?"

"Except for worrying about you, yes."

"Please don't worry. I'll be fine." There was neither conviction nor light in her voice.

"You don't sound very happy."

"I'm sorry. It's just — it's not important. I'll be fine," she repeated dully.

"Talk to me, Georgina," he pleaded.

"I — I don't — well — feel very useful, you know. Mother's much better with Donna than I am. They play together and laugh and have so much fun, but I'm — I'm just useless."

"That's not true!" Kit protested, anguished by knowing that he had no solution to her pain. "You have so many talents, G. You just need — we need — to find a way for you to get back into a position where you can do what you do best — helping others."

"I wish I could help you, Kit. It's so wonderful what you and the others are doing — keeping Berlin alive and free. I'm feel proud of you whenever I read the papers and see the pictures of the Airlift. I wish I could be part of it in some small way."

The beepers went off. The connection was about to be cut off. There was no time to say any more. Kit barely managed to call "I love you!" before the line went dead.

He hung up but did not leave the booth as he collected his thoughts. Although the call had not cheered him, it made it quite clear that quitting the Airlift would not help his wife in any way. Georgina could have coped with being separated if she'd had work she was committed to. Having them both sitting around doing nothing worthwhile would not help her. She had so much energy, enthusiasm and talent. It was absurd that it was all going to waste! He had to find some way to give her back her purpose in life.

Chapter Sixteen
Red Sun in the Morning

A Diplomatic Solution?
Allied Control Council, Berlin
Tuesday, 1 September 1948
(Day 67)

"I know how busy you are, Robin," Air Commodore Waite opened. The two RAF officers were meeting at his office in the seat of the Allied Control Council. It was one of those days that were hot, humid and vaguely threatening. Although the skies were still clear in Berlin and across the British Zone, Wiesbaden and Rhein-Main were reporting heavy thundershowers and interrupted operations. Tunner would be congratulating himself on moving two squadrons of his Skymasters to Fassberg in the British Zone. For almost a week now, the Americans had been flying into Gatow regularly, enlivening the tower with their chatter and colourful expressions. "Nevertheless," Waite continued, "even if I'm exceeding my brief somewhat, I felt I should keep you informed of what's going on here."

"*Is* something going on here?" Priestman asked back, looking around the large, elegant room in the large and imposing building that had officially been idle for five months.

"For the past month, the US Embassy in Moscow has been trying to make a deal with Stalin. They think they are on the brink of a breakthrough. The Four Powers will soon issue a joint communiqué stating that starting September 1st, the four military governors will again meet in this building to 'work out the details' of the agreement."

"The Blockade is going to be lifted?" Priestman asked in astonishment.

Waite lifted his eyebrows and opened his hands. "Let's wait and see. To say that His Majesty's Government is sceptical would be putting it mildly. Indeed, I believe the State Department and the American President are far from confident of success. They simply felt that another attempt at negotiation had to be made."

Priestman frowned. He didn't trust the Soviets. "Aren't we risking a pseudo-agreement that entails us dismantling the Airlift — only for the Soviets to impose a new blockade the moment our aircraft go home? It seems to me that the best way to win this confrontation is by keeping it up until the Soviets surrender — unconditionally." Then, reflecting on what he had just said, he added, "Not that anyone is asking my opinion."

"Nor mine, for that matter. Unfortunately, the United States is in the grip of a war scare. The upcoming presidential election has turned the crisis in Berlin into a political hot potato. The more the politicians talk about the 'confrontation' with the Soviets and exchange accusations about what *should have* been done and what *ought to be* done next, the more confused and frightened ordinary people become. It doesn't help that President Truman is universally seen as a lame duck."

"Clay said the same thing, but I don't understand why he's so unpopular. He seems such a decent, sensible man to me."

"What's doomed him is the split in the Democratic Party. There is a pacifist wing, under former Vice President Wallace, which wants the tax revenues currently spent on weapons to be used for schools and hospitals instead."

"I've heard that before," Priestman noted cynically.

"Yes, but it is appealing to many millions of war-weary Americans. Furthermore, and far more ominously, Wallace claims that the crisis in Berlin was caused by bellicose military men."

"Meaning Clay and Robertson?" Priestman asked back incredulously. Robertson had been downright deferential to the Soviets, while Clay's restraint had been admirable. It was hard to imagine two less bellicose military men.

"In a recent speech," Waite explained, "Wallace said that the United States would 'lose nothing' by withdrawing from Berlin, while the risk of releasing nuclear destruction upon innocent people should not hang upon the nerves of some second lieutenant on a train."

Priestman winced. He'd seen the images of Hiroshima and Nagasaki and he'd heard Cheshire speak about it once. It was wise to remember that

Truman had been the man to authorise both bombs, and there was no saying how he would react if the Russians started shooting down American aircraft or sent their tanks into the American Sector and took American women and children hostage. Yet appeasement wasn't the answer either. They had to resist aggression, and so far they had succeeded by non-violent means.

Turning to Waite, he asked, "Has this fellow Wallace ever been here? Has he met General Clay? Sat through a session of the Allied Control Council?"

"Of course not, but he knows that 'Uncle Joe' is a man of his word and sincerely interested in peace for all mankind — if only we'd give him a chance," Waite assured him.

Priestman responded with stunned silence before he asked, "And does this fool — or is he an NKVD mole? — stand a chance of becoming the next President of the United States?"

"No, he is simply expected to draw so many votes away from Truman that the election will go to the Republican candidate, who is beholden to the isolationists in his party who want America out of Europe and all U.S. troops to 'come home.'"

"Berlin is lost — and with it, Germany," Priestman exploded. "If Germany goes Communist, so will France, which pretty much means the Continent is lost, and we're back to where we were in June 1940, with the entire Continent under the boot of an oppressive dictator and Britain hanging on by her toenails while America retreats into a shell and plays 'neutral'." He was steaming inside — and frightened.

"That's the worst-case scenario, but do you know what has been going on here? Outside the Town Hall?"

"RIAS reported some sort of demonstration. Was it serious?"

"Yes and no. Our sources say 3,000 agitators were shipped in from the surrounding Zone — which on face value is a lot of agitators. However, it suggests the Russkies could not muster enough thugs from their Sector of Berlin and were forced to scrape together willing tools from further afield. These orchestrated hooligans chanted slogans against Reuter and the City Council in front of the town hall. Things like: 'One currency, one food supply, one police force!' or 'No Marshall Plan,' and 'No more airfields'. That's all pretty normal, but here's where it gets interesting: the Red Army stood back while the mob stormed the town hall. Fortunately, it was empty because the Chairman of the Assembly, Dr Otto Suhr, had called off the scheduled session in time to avoid a confrontation. So, the three thousand paid protesters hung their banners from the windows expressing such lofty sentiments as: 'To Socialism through Unity' and 'Peace and Brotherhood through Socialism,' and then they all went home."

"In other words, they did not strike a chord among the populace and people did not spontaneously join in," Priestman concluded.

"On the contrary. Reuter called for a counterdemonstration and some *thirty*-thousand Berliners — ten times the number who had stormed the City Hall — gathered. They cheered Reuter and other speakers who condemned Communism, denounced the use of force and intimidation to win elections, and insisted that they would not surrender their freedom for more food or more coal."

"Which puts the Allied negotiators in an awkward position. If we strike a deal with Stalin that ignores the wishes of the City Council, it'll look as though we — no, we *will* have — betrayed them."

"Precisely. At least Washington and London agreed on a deadline. Either there is a deal within a week, by September the 7th, or the US will take the issue to the United Nations."

Priestman snorted eloquently. He considered the UN a paper tiger.

Waite was still talking, "Meanwhile, the City Council voted to convene on September the 6th. I interpret that as a defiant declaration of their intention not to be intimidated by the use of force — and also a subtle reminder to us that we should not ignore them either."

Assault on Democracy
Berlin-Mitte
Monday, 6 September 1948
(Day 73)

They had miscalculated, Liebherr registered with almost paralysing shame. They had miscalculated terribly, stupidly, and criminally. Those thirty thousand Berliners who had cheered them last week had vanished.

Perhaps they had been visited in the dark of night by men whose fists reminded them which "side of history" they wanted to be on. Or maybe their rations had been cut or their jobs taken away or their children thrown out of university. Maybe little reminders had been slipped under doors about mothers and fathers in villages far away who needed housing or medicine. Whatever had happened, they had stayed at home, kept their heads down, and looked the other way when the hired thugs of the Soviet dictator again assaulted the city's historic symbol of democracy, the "*Rote Rathaus*", Berlin's town hall.

The "clever" tactic of bringing police from Stumm's new police force with them into the Soviet Zone hadn't worked either. It had not provided the deterrent and protection they had expected. They had taken a hundred trustworthy men with them, only to be confronted by thousands. They'd had to fight their way through angry crowds shouting: "Stop the Enemies of Democracy," "German Greatness through Germany Unity," "Socialism 1948!" and "Down with the Dividers!" With their police escort, the elected city councilmen managed to enter the City Hall and the president was on the brink of calling the City Assembly into session when the mob — with the obvious assistance of the Markgraf police and the Red Army — smashed its way into the building again.

The thugs were armed with sledgehammers, clubs, industrial wrenches, and crowbars. They surged into the Assembly chamber and took over the galleries. Their slogans turned violent. They screamed for blood: "Death to the Traitors!" "Death to Enemies of Peace!" "Hang Reuter! Hang Reuter!"

None of the elected assembly members could make themselves heard above the shrieks of the hate-filled horde. The shouts for violence threatened to turn into action at any second. The contorted faces and confidence of the attackers overwhelmed the psychological defences of the representatives of the people. Someone must have been the first to flee, but it felt more like a spontaneous, simultaneous, and shared act of self-preservation.

Their escort went into action. A cordon of Stumm's police protected the politicians as they fled in undignified panic. Behind them, thumps and crashes became curses and insults and then changed into howls of pain and desperate screaming. There was no doubt who was winning the battle. The hundred unarmed and orderly policemen were helpless against brutalised men wielding blunt but lethal weapons. All their escort could do was delay the mob long enough for the members of the City Assembly to escape.

They fled without hesitation, without looking back. They burst from the City Hall and scattered like leaves in the wind. They ducked behind buildings and vehicles, dashed for the nearest alleyways, and sprinted towards the closest U-Bahn stations. They bolted down the stairs to mingle and merge with the waiting passengers or leapt aboard moving trains.

Perhaps, if someone had stood up to the mob, they would all have found their courage again. But no one was brave. No one faced the violence. No one shouted defiance or declared: "Here I stand!" No, the Berlin City Assembly collapsed like a house-of-cards and the representatives of the people ran like rabbits.

Jakob Liebherr was no braver than the rest, just a little slower. He stumbled on the stairs to the U-bahn and twisted his ankle. After that, limping and hardly able to breathe, he pushed his way aboard an eastbound carriage and rode to the end of the line. There he staggered up the steps, his trousers still dusty from the fall and his shirt wet with sweat.

Once he was out into the daylight again, he took his handkerchief out of his pocket and wiped the sweat off his face; the handkerchief came away black with grime. No matter, he told himself, the coal dust was like ashes of shame. He deserved them.

Jakob sat on a public bench still struggling for breath and trying to come to terms with what had happened. They had abandoned more than the City Hall, he told himself; they had abandoned the people of Berlin. Why would anyone ever trust them again? Why *should* anyone ever trust them again? Today blotted out the heroism of voting against Hitler's enabling law. It erased the courage they had shown in voting for the currency reform. It had exposed them as the weak, helpless cowards that they were.

As he sat there still in a state of shock, the chilly, September wind cooled his sweat, and his shirt became cold and sticky. The cold started to get to him. Jakob had calmed down enough to start thinking about what came next. Three days ago, the Assembly had proudly (and in retrospect arrogantly) agreed that they would not allow the SED or the SMAD to intimidate them. They had voted by an overwhelming majority to assert their right to meet in the historic City Hall, even though this stood inside the Soviet Sector of Berlin. Only as an afterthought had Dr Suhr suggested they agree on an alternative venue to convene "just in case" something prevented them from conducting business in the "Rote Rathaus". The selected alternative was the Tabernica Academica at the Technical University. Jakob resolved he would go there and see if anyone else showed up.

Geographically, the Technical University and the more famous Humbolt University were separated by just three miles and sat on the same street. Yet the two institutions were worlds apart; the Humbolt University lay in the Soviet and the Technical University in the British Sector.

By the time Liebherr limped into the large lecture hall, it was almost six o'clock. Jakob was astonished to find it almost full — and even more moved by his reception. His colleagues jumped up to welcome him, clapping him on the back, pumping his hand, and expressing relief that he had made it. "How many of us are here?" he asked looking around.

"Almost everyone — except the traitors. None of the SED members are here."

"What about our police escort? What became of them?"

"It's not clear. We've heard that some were arrested but others took refuge in the Allied Liaison Offices. Last we heard they were still there, but there is a cordon of Markgraf police surrounding the entire building and no one can get in or out without their permission." That didn't sound good, and Jakob felt a new wave of shame. Sperl and his young colleague had been two of the police who had agreed to accompany them.

Dr Suhr called the City Assembly to order at 7 pm. The SED made up less than 20%, so they had a quorum even without a single SED representative. Dr Suhr's first motion was that future meetings would be held "in a venue where the protection and security of all members can be guaranteed." The motion passed unanimously.

The debate that followed was sober, lacking both acrimony and histrionics. The day's experience had humbled them. They shared the shame of their defeat, and no one pretended to have behaved better than the rest. The experience had shattered their confidence. After today's debacle, they doubted their instincts. No solution seemed right. If they huddled in the Western Sectors of the city, they were abandoning the one million Berliners who lived and worked in the East. If they tried to go back to the East, they risked being arrested — which would help no one.

"Let's not fool ourselves," Suhr admonished. "We have been ousted from power. The SMAD and their puppets in the SED have prevented us from exercising our duties."

Another member took up the debate. "And if *we* can't govern, then *they* will."

"More than that!" Jeannette Wolfe reminded them, "They will replace anyone and everyone who is loyal to us with their ideological puppets. It is not just the district mayors who are at risk. They will replace clerks and firemen, dustbin men and dogcatchers too. From this day forward, anyone who works for the city government will have to take their orders from the SMAD or lose their jobs."

Jakob bemoaned his stupidity. He had been too focused on the mood of the Berliners, forgetting that with the Red Army backing them, the SED did not need the masses. The thirty thousand Berliners who had stood by them a week ago had not changed their minds, they had simply been intimidated. They did not agree with the SED, but in the face of Soviet tanks, they were afraid to fight.

He thought, too, of Anton Sperl, wondering where was he now? Had he been injured or arrested while trying to defend his stupid neighbour? Was he destined for the torture chambers, the concentration camps or Siberia? Or was he crouching in one of the Allied Liaison Offices, hoping for rescue that no one would dare mount?

The debate moved on. One of the CDU members made an impassioned speech not to accept defeat but to accept reality. "Berlin is divided," he told them. "We have two police forces and two currencies already. Soon we will have two tax collection offices and two court systems. It is pointless to pretend that we can enforce our decisions in the East, but it would be stupid to stop governing in the West. Half a loaf — or this case two-thirds of a loaf — is better than none."

"Two-thirds of a loaf under siege," someone reminded them in a discouraged voice.

"But still alive and kicking," Louisa Schroeder insisted, entering the hall, and adding, "I've brought the Lord Mayor."

All discussion stopped as Reuter passed through the crowd to take the podium. "Comrades," he opened soberly. "The fate of this city hangs by a thread. No amount of food or coal flown in over the heads of the Red Army will save us if we do not stand up to the SED and resist its attempt to push us aside. We must not forget that we hold our mandate from our constituents. Until *they* have dismissed us, we have not been relieved of our responsibilities!"

They clapped, but rapidly fell silent and waited for him to continue.

Reuter argued, "We must schedule new municipal elections as soon as possible and take our case to the people. Let *them* decide whether they want unity under the heavy boot of Stalin's police or freedom even at the price of division."

Throughout the auditorium, men and women started nodding solemnly, but Reuter wasn't finished. "In the meantime, we must make clear to the Berliners what is at stake. We cannot let the SED be the sole voice screeching in their ears. We must counter that poison with truth. We cannot hide. We cannot cower. We cannot wait. We must go on the offensive."

Applause broke out again, this time vigorous and invigorating. Jakob shook his head in wonder. With only a few words, Reuter had succeeded in giving the elected representatives their courage and energy back — at least for a day or two.

"We Cannot be Bartered!"
Berlin-Tiergarten
Thursday, 9 September 1948
(Day 76)

In the three days following the aborted attempt by the City Assembly to meet in the *"Rote Rathaus"*, the newspapers and radios across Berlin spoke of nothing but the "division" of the city. Journalists, politicians, and soldiers from East and West agreed that Berlin had been "torn in two." In the East, the text was prepared and synchronised well in advance: "The terror bombers and their puppets have raped Berlin." They had "ignored the Berliners' heartfelt pleas for unity and peace." "Afraid of the people, the Western stooges cowered like curs, seeking protection behind the guns of the warmongers and capitalist aggressors." Reuter thundered back via RIAS and the free press that the SED were pathetic puppets dancing to Stalin's tune. In the name of the "elected and legitimate government of Berlin," he summoned Berliners to a demonstration before the Reichstag at 6 pm on Thursday, 9 September.

The trade unions called for all work to stop early. The public transport authority announced the trains, trams, buses, and metro would run an hour longer than usual to facilitate participation. By 4 o'clock, civilian Berlin was at a standstill. Allied aircraft still landed and took off with monotonous regularity, but work on the new airport had stopped because the construction crews laid down their tools and walked away. The factories (those that had not already been forced to close) shut their doors, as did schools and nurseries, workshops, and stores. The citizens of the Western Sectors of Berlin stopped whatever they were doing and made for the Platz der Republic, Republic Square, which stood directly on the border with the Soviet Zone.

David, too, closed and locked AAI's office on Kurfuerstendamm. With Charlotte and their other two employees, he joined the solemn and subdued crowds making their way to the Platz der Republic. They arrived around 5:20 pm and found the square in front of the derelict Reichstag already overflowing with spectators. Some of the more nimble and less sensible young men had scaled the ruins of the gutted parliament building and sat with their legs swinging from the windowsills or perched on the remains of the roof. Meanwhile, technicians from RIAS were working to set up microphones and carpenters hammered the finishing touches to the speaking platform and podium on the steps of the Reichstag.

To David's relief, the mood matched the grey, gloomy weather. He had been a little leery of joining a German demonstration, remembering too vividly the staged and choreographed spectacles that Goebbels had organised with waving flags, marching masses, uniforms and bands. This was nothing like those. There was nothing festive or happy about the crowd dressed in faded, worn and threadbare clothing. Most people wore things too big for the thin bodies wrapped inside. Shoes were scuffed and down at the heel; hats were deformed and discoloured from overuse. People didn't talk much either, and when they did, they murmured in low voices. David and Charlotte were no exception. Everyone just wanted to hear what the mayor would say.

Reuter arrived in an old Opel, escorted by a handful of city officials. The contrast to the entrance Hitler had liked to make at an organised event couldn't have been more striking. The Nazis would whip up a crowd to a state of near-orgasmic ecstasy at the sight of "der Fuehrer." There was none of that now.

The first to mount the podium was Franz Neuman, a nondescript man with no charisma. Without ado, he spoke into the microphone to ask for a moment of silence to remember the victims of National Socialism. David hadn't expected that. It took him by surprise and broke through his lingering scepticism. These Germans really were different, he concluded, as those around him solemnly bowed their heads. Some in the crowd crossed themselves while others closed their eyes, and David felt an unexpected flood of solidarity with the Berliners. He risked a glance at Charlotte, and she met his eyes with tears welling in her own. He reached out and she took his hand. That felt right and good.

Finally, Reuter mounted the podium, and a short restless rustle swept through the crowd before it fell silent with anticipation. Reuter tested the microphones and there was a pinging and humming that rapidly faded away. "Berliners!" he called out. "Today is not a day for diplomats and generals to haggle. It is the day on which the people of Berlin lift their voices. We call upon the entire world to be our witness." He paused, the audience remained tensely silent, unsure where he was going and feeling more perplexed than ever.

"We know that recently negotiations have been held in the palaces of the Kremlin. We have been told the bargaining continues in the halls of the Allied Control Council. We know our future is at stake."

An uneasy shuffling spread through the crowd, born of fear and worry. They understood the stakes very well.

Reuter resumed in a reasonable tone, "No doubt the Russians will try to confuse matters by complaining about Italian colonies or the Suez Canal, about the French in Indochina or the Americans in Panama. Yet for all such talk, the fact remains that we are the immediate object of Russian greed. The Russian bear holds us in his clenched paw and is trying to strangle us."

The crowd stirred uncomfortably. They still couldn't see where Reuter was going with this speech, but it wasn't making them feel better.

"Make no mistake! Slogans about "German unity" only highlight that the Russian bear craves not just all of Berlin but all of Germany." He paused and then raised his voice, and the microphones twanged in protest as he shouted, "I appeal to the world!" Pulling back just enough so the microphones did not interfere with his words, he demanded, "Look at this city! We do not want to be bargained! We will not be traded! And we will not be sold!"

At last, the crowd erupted in approval, cheering, clapping, and whistling enthusiastically. David tensed briefly, but the enthusiasm did not dissolve into the kind of collective and manipulated chants typical of the Nazis. He relaxed again.

Reuter allowed people to express themselves for a few moments before gesturing for silence. When their attention returned to him, he raised his voice and spoke to an audience far beyond the crowd: "People of the world, look to Berlin! This city and its people *must not* and *cannot* be sacrificed! People of the world, we must stand together!"

The crowd cheered more wildly than before. This call for solidarity was far more to David's liking than any talk of German rights, and he hoped the Allies were listening. Reuter was asking them not to make a deal behind the backs of the Berliners. He was asking them to stand firm in the face of Soviet aggression. He was asking for the Airlift to continue. David wanted that not merely because it was the basis of his business, but because he wanted to see *this* Berlin survive. His self-interest and his ideals were fortuitously married together. Moved to applaud, he let go of Charlotte's hand long enough to clap vigorously.

Reuter was speaking again, "People of the world, help us not only with the thunder of your aircraft but with your steadfast and invincible dedication to our shared values and ideals." He paused and then addressing crowd directly he added in a different yet no-less-forceful voice, "And people of Berlin, know that we are not alone in our struggle. With our friends in the West, we must, and we *will* win!"

A new roar of approval rose from the crowd, and when Reuter waved, indicating that was the end, the shouts grew louder. With new respect, David watched Reuter as he stepped down and turned reporters away. The crowd started to disperse. David's other two office employees hurriedly took their leave, saying they needed to catch their bus.

But some young men took up the words, "We will win! We will win!" and turned this into a chant. Even as Reuter climbed into his car and the crowd disintegrated around the periphery, a large, compact core of spectators started surging in the direction of the Brandenburg Gate.

David frowned, instinctively alarmed. He tried to stand still, but he and Charlotte were caught up in the human flood and were being pushed from behind. The mood of the crowd had changed radically, too. Solemn and sober concern had been replaced by excitement and anger. Again, David looked around for an escape, but they were surrounded and in danger of being trampled on if they tried to halt, much less turn.

All David could do was to hold Charlotte's hand. They exchanged a look, and he could see the fear in her eyes. He pulled her closer, hooking his arm through hers to keep them from getting separated. Ahead of them, voices were raised. It was impossible to decipher what was being said, but the tone was challenging, or was it encouraging? Some people seemed to be saying "Ja! Ja!", others shouted *"Herunter, 'runter!"* (Down! Down!). A moment later, there was an eruption of shouts and cheers and even people around them started jumping up and down and shouting "Ja! Ja! Ja!"

Following the gestures and looks of the others, David realised that the huge Soviet flag which had flapped over the badly damaged bronze statue of a four-horse chariot that crowned the Brandenburg Gate had just been thrown down. Someone hanging precariously upon the partially-collapsed bronze chariot had torn it free from its lacings. The stiff breeze carried the fluttering banner, but gravity pulled it inexorably towards the crowd. Eager hands leapt up to snatch it from the air. In a frenzy of hatred, dozens of hands tore it apart. A roar of triumphant cheering erupted from the crowd — cut short by the staccato bark of gunfire.

Charlotte recognised the sound and screamed as if she had been hit. David pulled her into his arms and held her fiercely. He pressed her to his chest while the crowd around them exploded in all directions. Someone shrieked from pain, evoking more furious shouting. People yelled, "Red scum! Murderers! Murderers!" and "Down with Communism!" while one man demanded at the top of his voice, "Death to Stalin!"

Part of the crowd surged forward with shouts of "Kill the Red scum!

Kill them!"

David stood rooted to his spot, clutching Charlotte in his arms. People jostled and bumped into them as some pressed forward while others tried to flee. He caught a glimpse of a Soviet vehicle being assaulted by the crowd. The Russians must have been disarmed somehow. While some men pummelled the cowering soldiers with their fists, others tried to overturn the Russian jeep.

Another burst of gunfire crackled through the air as Russian infantry ran onto the square, shouting and pointing their rifles at the crowd. The mob reacted with defiant shouts and taunts, which triggered a volley ending in a blood-curdling howl of pain.

David felt the crowd ball together as if preparing for a new lunge forward, even as orders were shouted in Russian. He caught a glimpse of Red soldiers lifting their rifles to their eyes. Fear almost overpowered him. He yanked at Charlotte, screaming "Get down!" And he tried to wrap himself around her as she dropped down to crouch on the cobble stones.

Instead of gunfire, a voice bellowed in English, "HALT! Or we shoot!"

Bewildered, David looked up and realised a British Army captain was standing in a Land Rover holding a megaphone to his mouth as the vehicle pushed through the crowd. He was supported by three additional lorries loaded with Royal Military Police. Behind them came what looked like several hundred German policemen.

This was their chance. David pulled Charlotte to her feet and, holding her in the crook of his arm, he pushed his way out of the crowd. As soon as they broke free they started running. They did not stop until they reached the Tiergarten. Out of breath, they stumbled to a halt and Charlotte sank onto the grass, gasping for breath. David dropped down beside her. She was sobbing, her face drenched in tears.

"Are you all right, Charlotte?" David asked, afraid that she had been injured without him noticing.

She just cried harder. David hesitated only a second, but then he pulled her into his arms and held her close. She pushed her face into the nook between his shoulder and chin, and he felt her tears and then her lips on his neck. David turned his face to her and kissed her hair, her forehead, her eyelids, and finally her lips. Suddenly, they were kissing desperately and uninhibitedly, oblivious to the world around them. "Oh, David!"

Charlotte gasped. "David! Hold me!"

He tightened his grasp around her skeletal body and kissed her again. He had never felt such a passion for anyone before. He loved her, and he wanted her, and he swore to himself that he would protect her for the rest of his life. He would never let anyone hurt her ever again.

Lucky Escape
Berlin-Kreuzberg
Friday, 10 September 1948
(Day 77)

"Jakob! Jakob!" Trude exclaimed as she shook her husband. With a grunt, Jakob awoke startled and disoriented. "Jakob!" Trude hissed in evident fear. "Someone's knocking at the door!"

Jakob went still and listened intently. She was right. There was an insistent although soft knocking coming from the front of the apartment. That was strange. The Markgraf police, not to mention the Red Army, didn't care about being quiet. They liked to make a disturbance to underline their power and impunity. This had to be someone else.

With an inarticulate groan, Jakob swung his legs over the edge of the bed, grabbed his ancient dressing gown and shuffled down the hall, knotting the ties in front as he went. Passing the kitchen, he squinted at the battery-driven wall clock. It read 3:23.

The knocking came again, and Jakob looked out of the peephole in the front door. A slender man, hunching in an overcoat with the collar turned up, leaned against the wall. In the darkness, Jakob did not recognise him, but he appeared to be alone. With the chain still on, Jakob cracked the door and hissed into the darkness. "Who's there?"

"Anton Sperl," came the slurred answer. It sounded as if the former U-boat captain was very drunk.

"Thank God!" Jakob exclaimed. "I thought the Ivans had you!" He shut the door so he could remove the chain and opened it again as rapidly as he could.

Sperl staggered into the entryway, doubled over. His face was a complete wreck.

"Oh my God!" Jakob exclaimed in horror. Sperl's right eye was swollen shut and his lips and jaw had distended so much that his entire head was misshapen. Patches of dried blood still clung to his hair and darkened every crevice. There was no need to ask how it had happened.

"Come in! Come in! You need to lie down!" Liebherr told Sperl, and then lifted his voice to call to his wife, "Trude! Hurry! Herr Sperl needs medical assistance." He tried to take Sperl's arm to help him inside, but only provoked a howl of pain.

"I think it's broken," Sperl explained after Jakob drew back in distress.

"Follow me," Jakob urged, leading Sperl to the soft sofa in the front parlour.

Sperl sank onto the upholstered couch with an audible sigh of relief, and Jakob reached down to help him out of his shoes. As he swung Sperl's legs up, the policeman gasped and with his face twisted in pain urged, "Slowly! My ribs."

Trude appeared, her long grey hair hanging down in a single braid. "Jakob! Get some candles and matches so I can see Herr Sperl better."

"And water, please," Sperl added.

Jakob hurried away and returned with a glass of water and three candles. He handed the water to Sperl and placed the candles on the coffee table in front of the sofa and the little side table beside Sperl's head on the armrest. Trude was giving his face a professional inspection. "Teeth?" she asked.

"Two broken," Sperl slurred.

Trude nodded and turned to her husband. "Bring a bowl of water and a face cloth. I need to wash off some of the dried blood."

Again, he withdrew and returned to find his wife asking, "Can you move your fingers?"

Sperl hesitantly opened and closed his swollen fingers.

"Can you turn your wrist over and show me the back?"

Sperl tried but caught his breath and shook his head.

"Your ribs?" she asked.

"Two or three broken."

"This happened on the sixth," Trude noted as she took the bowl of water from Jakob. She soaked the washcloth, and started gently cleaning Sperl's blood-encrusted face. "You've had no medical attention since?" Five days had passed since the violent assault on Berlin's elected representatives.

Sperl shook his head, and Jakob asked in amazement, "How did you escape?"

"Never got me," Sperl replied, shifting his head to try to find Jakob.

The latter moved so Sperl could see him without twisting, "How? Where have you been hiding? What happened?"

"Our line broke. Someone shouted, 'Allied Liaison Offices.' Thought they'd be safe. Rushed up stairs." Sperl had a hard time speaking because of his swollen lips and broken jaw, but Jakob nodded in understanding. Sperl continued, "Not me. Submariner. Went down. Basement. Dark. Rabbit warren. Door with a lightning bolt. Sign said: 'Danger! Keep out!' Went in." He had to pause after all that and take a sip of water. Jakob and Trude waited patiently.

"Boiler room. Lived close to boilers. Don't frighten me. Lay down. Hidden by equipment. Vents. Face bleeding. Ripped sleeve off. Made bandage. Lost consciousness." He paused for another sip of water, and Jakob urged him to take it easy.

After a little pause, he resumed in a calmer, slower voice. "Woke up in dark. No idea of time. Thought it was safe. Left boiler room. Started upstairs. Old man stopped me. Shooed me back. Janitor. Said men trapped in the Liaison Offices. Markgraf's police around building. Showed me toilet. Brought me blankets, bread and water. Said he'd tell me when safe to leave. Came tonight."

Trude and Jakob looked at one another. Jakob declared solemnly, "You did the right thing."

"The others? In Liaison Offices?"

"The French Berlin Kommandant negotiated with his counterpart General Kotikov for their release. A French military lorry collected them, and units of the Red Army escorted them almost to the Brandenburg Gate. Then, in sight of freedom, the Soviets surrounded the vehicle, dragged the Germans out, handcuffed them and dragged them off."

Sperl closed his eyes and turned his head away.

Trude and Jakob looked at one another again. This time Trude put her hand on his shoulder.

"Lothar. Second Engineer."

Jakob understood, but he had no words of comfort.

After a moment, Sperl asked, "Know Markgraf police?" Jakob didn't understand what he was trying to say, but before he could ask for clarification, Sperl added, "Concentration camp guards..." His voice faded away and they didn't speak for several moments.

Trude pulled herself together. "Herr Sperl, you must go to a hospital for a proper examination and to get your bones set. I'm going to go and call an ambulance now."

"Lothar. Second member of crew lost to Ivans. First Thomas, now Lothar. When will it end?" Sperl gazed up at Liebherr.

Jakob shook his head. "I don't know. All I can tell you is I'm not giving up. Or not yet, anyway, and neither is Reuter. The City Council has called for new elections in early December to ensure we are speaking for the majority. Meanwhile, the Allies have announced the end of their talks with the Soviets. Reuter shamed them into abandoning any bargaining that did not take our wishes into account."

Sperl tried to smile but failed. He nodded instead, and declared, "Right. Can't give up. One unconditional surrender enough. Help me. I'll fight again. Better fight than for corrupt Austrian madman."

Liebherr nodded his approval. Then he had a thought: "Maybe, while you're recovering, you could track down that war criminal you told me about a couple of weeks ago? I know I seemed uninterested at the time, but I've had a chance to give it more thought since. Shutting down the heroin source and exposing a Nazi criminal who has been protected by the Soviets would be a coup that might bolster morale."

"Friedebach? Poison," he spat out. Then he lay his head back and a faint smile crept over his misshapen face as he added, "See him in jail. Good for *my* morale!"

Liebherr nodded seriously. In Sperl's slow transformation from Nazi officer to cynical black marketeer and now democratic policeman, he saw hope for the future of Germany. Maybe Sperl was a microcosm of what was happening throughout Berlin and across the country?

Chapter Seventeen
Man Does Not Live by Bread (or Coal) Alone

Too Much of a Good Thing
RAF Wunstorf
Sunday, 19. September 1948
(Day 86)

Kit switched on the internal microphone and announced. "Skipper to crew: Fuhlsbuettel is closed due to fog. We are diverting to Wunstorf. Give me a new course, Navigator."

"Give me two secs, Skip," Nigel answered from the lower deck, "but I think we continue on 270 rather than turning north as we normally do."

From the copilot's seat, Bruce muttered that the cloud was pretty thick beneath them, while Richard let his eyes scan the engine dials. The fuel tanks were more than half empty, but Wunstorf was closer than their home base near Hamburg.

The microphone clicked and Nigel confirmed the course. Within minutes, Terry had Wunstorf control, and shortly afterwards they landed on a glistening, wet runway. Fine rain coated the windscreen, and Bruce reached forward to switch on the wipers. It was just short of 8 pm and any plans they'd had for the evening were wrecked. Not that Kit had any plans beyond writing to Georgina, but the diversion meant he had no chance of receiving a letter from her.

A follow-me jeep led them off to a parking position far from the ops room, mess and other facilities. Bruce and Kit shut down the engines one after the other, while Richard switched on an overhead light so he could make his log entries.

"Are we going to be stuck here for the night?" Nigel asked, coming up from the lower deck with Terry behind him.

"I'm afraid so," Kit answered as he unbent himself from his seat. They had been up since 5:30 am and flown their first run to Berlin at 7:00. The round-trip had put them back in Hamburg just after noon. The Halifax was re-loaded by 14:40, when they took off for a second trip, reaching Berlin at 15:50. While the cargo was unloaded, they'd had a quick meal at the Malcolm Club in Gatow, but they were all tired and would have welcomed a chance to relax.

"Someone told me the messes here are completely overcrowded and everyone's doubled up because they're now hosting two or three USAF squadrons as well as our own," Bruce remarked.

"I suppose we could see if there's anything free at the Malcolm Club," Richard responded.

"Or see what we can find off the base," Bruce suggested.

"Where off base? There's not even a town around here!" Nigel protested. Unlike their home base at Fuhlsbuettel, which was in Hamburg, Wunstorf lay in the middle of nowhere.

"Let's see what the situation is." Kit put an end to the whining. They pulled on whatever raingear they had and traipsed through the empty cargo hold to open the rear door. Using the metal stairs stored on a rack inside the fuselage, they made their way out into the rain. A moment later, headlights shone into their faces and a jeep pulled up. "Are you here to collect another cargo?" a voice called from darkness behind the headlights.

"We hadn't planned to, no," Kit answered. "We're based in Fuhlsbuettel, but it's closed due to fog."

"You're going to have to move then. This is a hardstanding for loading."

Kit looked around at the darkness behind them; being unfamiliar with this station, he hadn't a clue where else they might park. "You'll have to lead us where you want us to go," he informed the station employee, trying not to sound as annoyed as he felt. Just then a lorry bounced its way into the headlights and stopped right beside the cargo door. Stevedores jumped down and threw back the canvas covers to start transferring the boxes from the lorry to the Halifax. Kit caught a glimpse of the labels on the boxes. It was a cargo of kid's shoes. He made a snap decision. "All right, you can load up. We'll make another run to Berlin."

"Thank you, sir! Can I give you and your crew a lift back to the Ops Centre?"

"Yes. We'd appreciate that," Kit told him.

Although not a word was spoken, Kit felt the resentment of his crew as they climbed aboard the jeep and crowded together in the back. He sat in what should have been the driver's seat, but this American vehicle had left-hand drive. The driver asked what company they flew for and such like, and while Kit answered, his crew remained sullenly silent. At the far side of the field, the driver stopped before the jumble of buildings and gave Kit directions to the operations room before driving off into the dark again.

"You know," Nigel spoke up, "some of us like to get a good night's sleep. Just because you haven't got your wife here and so —"

"Let's not get personal," Richard interceded in his precise, West Indian accent.

"Well, time off *is* very personal and I'm not getting any!"

"I understand, Nigel," Kit cut in before Terry or Richard spoke up. "My thinking was we're far more likely to get a good rest at Gatow than here. If nothing else, Gordon's there and can fix something up for us. Furthermore, if we get another cargo into Berlin today, we'll only have to fly one tomorrow and can take the whole morning off."

"That makes sense to me," Bruce spoke up, and Richard echoed him.

Nigel glanced at Terry for support, but the signaller quashed his hopes by declaring, "I'd like to spend an evening with Gordon."

While waiting for their Halifax to be loaded, they headed for the Malcolm Club. As they'd been warned, it was overcrowded with both RAF and USAF crews. Conversation punctuated by laughter rose from the tables like the smoke that collected and swirled slowly under the ceiling. Not a table was free, but Bruce noticed some Americans leaving and pointed to where they had been sitting. The table was still partially occupied by two flight lieutenants with pilots' wings, a pilot-officer navigator, and two sergeants with signaller and flight engineer brevets respectively. Kit asked, "Do you mind if we join you?"

They looked up, registered the non-military uniforms, and one of the flight lieutenants remarked, "What? I didn't think you civvy boys flew at night! All strictly daytime flying and nighttime boozing, isn't it?"

"Yeah, well we're different, mate," Bruce retorted sharply before Kit got out a word. It was the first time Bruce had sounded like his more aggressive and abrasive elder brother.

Kit glanced over at him, then sought to defuse the tension by extending his hand to the flight lieutenant who had made the insulting remark and introducing himself, "Flight Lieutenant Moran, 617 Squadron. My signaller and navigator were with me in the war. Scott-Ross here flew with No 9 squadron. We fly at night."

The others looked suitably chastened and made a little more room for them at the table, introducing themselves as Fl/Lt "Tommy" Thompson, Fl/Lt Kell, P/O Gilbert and Sergeants Towersey and Watson. Kit offered to buy a round, which further mollified the others. He knew that the RAF was not entirely unjustified in their resentment of civilian fliers. Kit had heard that one company needed to employ ten pilots to ensure there would be two sober at any one time. In a more serious incident, drunken civilian airmen had welded the rails of Hamburg's tram switches overnight, creating traffic havoc the following morning. But what bothered the RAF most was that the civilians flew only if and when they liked.

When Kit returned with the non-alcoholic beverages all were drinking because they would be flying shortly, he found his crew genially swapping stories about training and assignments in the war. Kit settled into the only vacant seat as Ft/Lt Kell remarked, "I hope the tankers everyone is talking about make their appearance soon. Tonight's cargo is kerosine in barrels."

"It's a bitch of a cargo," Sergeant Towersey explained. "We flew it once before and the fumes nearly kill you, not to mention that just one electrical short in the fuselage and its curtains!"

Kit remembered that Mr Goldman had initially hoped to invest in a tanker or two but had rapidly dropped the idea because of the costs and risks involved. He was glad he had.

Just before 10 pm, the other crew excused themselves, and donning their sheepskin flight jackets, they set off into the night. Checking his watch, Kit calculated that they might be called at any moment, too, so they finished their drinks, paid their bill, and sought out the lavatories.

The rain had let up a little by the time they caught a lift back to their Halifax. Standing ten feet downwind of the aircraft, they smoked a last cigarette before boarding. Their parking position was close to the runway, and Kit automatically turned to watch as a York barrelled towards them on take-off. The wind of the aircraft buffeted him as it passed, and he observed as the nose lifted and the mechanical bird took to the air. Despite all his years of experience, Kit still found that a magical moment. The York rose above the blackness of the trees at the end of the perimeter fence, becoming a barely visible silhouette against the rough grey of the cloudy sky. Quite suddenly it coughed, shuddered, and seemed to flinch.

"He's lost Number Four engine!" Richard exclaimed in horror.

They were all staring, holding their breaths, as the York's starboard wing started to fall. The remaining engines screamed.

"Full flaps!" Kit urged pointlessly.

The York continued to heel over, losing lift and altitude at an accelerating rate until it smashed into the earth. With a dull thump, the earth beneath his feet jolted, while beyond the fence, branches, dirt and debris were hurled in all directions.

Kit started running as fast as his wooden leg allowed, but his crew overtook him. He caught up with them at the fence, but they clambered over the obstacle more agilely, leaving him behind again. He struggled forward as the others crashed through the underbrush. The surrounding forest was increasingly visible as flames from the crash lit the night. The fire also illuminated the tail fin of the York that poked skywards above the rest of the wreck. The aircraft number was clearly legible: MW 288.

Why did that trigger a memory? Kit wondered. Then he remembered. When he'd stopped in the ops room to file their flight plan, he'd noticed two aircraft were listed on the blackboard ahead of his own. MW 288 had been at the top, with Fl/Lt Thompson down as pilot.

"Get down!" Kit screamed at the top of his voice as he flung himself face down on the earth. "Get down! It's carrying kero—!"

His words were cut off by an explosion that shook the ground under him. A moment later a ball of fire rolled over them, setting the treetops aflame. From the station behind came the sound of sirens.

Forty minutes later as they swung onto the runway, Kit flipped on the intercom. "Captain to crew: ready for take-off?" The responses from his crew were dull and minimal. Aside from cuts and scrapes all were uninjured, unlike the men with whom they'd shared the evening at the Malcolm Club, none of whom had survived. As they flew over the still-smouldering wreck of MW288, Kit glanced at Bruce. He seemed to have aged overnight. Or was it just that he wore an expression Kit had seen too often during the war: an unwanted recognition of his own mortality? They might be delivering children's shoes instead of bombs, but the mission could be deadly just the same.

Flying Like Mad
USAF Bases Tempelhof / Rhein-Main
Saturday, 20. September 1948
(Day 87)

Halvorsen dodged puddles on the tarmac in his dash to reach his waiting C-54. J.B. and Elkins were already on board and together had cranked up the four engines. Hal's cap and the shoulders of his tunic were dark with rain when he clambered into the cockpit and sank into the lefthand seat. He took his cap off and wiped rain from his forehead in a single gesture.

"What took you so long?" J.B. asked. "We aren't supposed to be more than ten feet from the aircraft. If anyone had spotted—"

"We're in a heap more trouble than you think!" Hal answered, shaking his head and looking ashen, adding, "You fly her out."

That was standard practice between them now, so J.B. just nodded as he put one hand on the throttles, his feet on the brakes, and waved to the ground crew to pull the chocks away. Then he turned to Halvorsen to ask, "What's happened?"

"I found a table in the ops room covered — and I mean *covered* — with letters addressed to variations on 'Uncle Wiggly Wings' and 'Mr Candy Bomber'."

"Jesus f*** Christ—" Elkins commented from between his pilots.

"Don't insult the Lord, Elkins!" Hal admonished, frowning fiercely.

"Yeah, well, frankly, Hal, I agree with the tech sergeant on this one. I told you we were going to get in trouble," J.B. chimed in.

"Well, they don't seem to know *who* Uncle Wiggly Wings is yet—"

"Hal! Half the residents of the Zeppelinheim have been giving us candy and handkerchiefs!" J.B. protested. "All the brass has to do is ask around and every finger is going to point at us."

"Okay! Okay!" Hal agreed nervously. "We'll stop doing it."

"Yeah, and what am I supposed to do with all the candy other guys have given me? I've got a shitload of candy bars in my locker in Rhein-Main!" Elkins complained.

Neither pilot bothered to answer because the ground crew was making angry gestures for them to move off their hardstanding. J.B. nudged the throttles forward and they waddled onto the taxiway while Hal called the tower to get clearance. They started for the head of the runway, splashing through the puddles while the windshield wipers slapped from side to side, and rain dripped through the airframe in half a dozen places.

As they bounced along the taxiway, fifty or so kids hung onto the fence, waving at all the passing planes. The rain kept some kids away, but crowd was still large enough to attract attention. "Don't wave back at them!" J.B. warned his captain.

"Everybody waves at them," Hal protested, but he was unnerved enough to obey J.B. even as he remarked miserably, "I just hate to think how disappointed they're going to be when no more candy rains down on them."

"Well, they aren't going to get any more candy if we've been court-martialled and sent home, either," J.B. pointed out.

"I thought you wanted to go home?" Hal reminded him.

J.B. wasn't going to get into that thorny subject, and retorted, "Not that way! I heard a court-martial follows you around for the rest of your life just like a criminal record."

There was no time for further discussion. They were number one for take-off. Hal contacted the tower while J.B. swung the nose of their battered old freighter into the wind. Cleared, they raced down the runway and lifted off, climbing steeply. Empty, the C-54 had a powerful rate-of-climb, and they easily roared over the apartment buildings before vanishing into the cloud.

Roughly 15 minutes later, they broke clear of the low cloud layer and into sunshine. Still climbing to their designated cruising altitude for the return trip, they turned onto the central corridor and took their place in a stately convoy of aircraft.

The engines were too loud to encourage conversation, so the three men retreated into their separate thoughts. J.B. found himself reflecting on the fact that he was no longer eager to go home. Ever since they had started collecting and dropping candy to the children of Berlin, he'd felt energised and excited — and not just about the candy but, curiously, about the entire operation. Reuter's speech had struck a chord, too. The *Stars and Stripes* had printed a translation, and when he saw some footage of the mayor speaking in a news clip at the base movie theatre, he'd felt a chill run down his spine. They were doing something here that really mattered. He didn't want to stop doing it. He enjoyed the flying, now that he flew with Halvorsen who let him take the controls at least fifty per cent of the time. He glanced over at the frail, balding pilot from Utah and noticed he looked miserable and beaten.

"Hey, Hal! Cheer up!" J.B. nudged him with an elbow.

Hal looked over at him crestfallen, and remonstrated, "You'd feel different if you'd met those kids one-to-one like I did."

"I doubt it because I agree with you!" J.B. shouted over the engines. "We're not going to stop until someone tells us to. So, cheer up!"

Hal's face was transformed into sunshine. "Thanks, J.B.! You're a real pal!"

They landed back at Rhein-Main more than two hours later. It was now almost 5 pm, and the sun was streaming over the Western horizon as the clouds moved east. The pavement was already starting to dry out. They were scheduled for one more run to Berlin, and dutifully taxied behind the follow-me jeep to a loading position. Elkins went back to open the cargo door. A truck and trailer manned by a crew of five stevedores in their coal-stained, canvas overalls were already standing by to load sacks of coal into the C-54.

"Who's that guy?" Hal asked, looking out the cockpit window at a man in a clean uniform.

"I don't know, but he's got 'staff' written all over him," J.B. replied suspiciously. Then trying to be optimistic, he suggested, "Maybe he just wants to hitch a ride to Berlin for some reason." He was certainly waving at them.

Hal shoved back the cockpit window, and J.B. heard a faint voice straining to be heard over the roar of engines from the taxiing aircraft in the background. "Are you Lt. Gail Halvorsen?"

"Yup," Hal answered.

"You and your copilot are to report to HQ immediately."

"But we've got to fly another run to Berlin," Hal tried valiantly to postpone Armageddon.

"Not today you don't!" the staff officer wearing captain's bars answered. "Another crew is on their way to fly this bird back to Berlin. You and Baronowsky need to join me in my jeep. And that's an order."

There was no arguing with that.

A quarter of an hour later they were ushered into an office with a sign saying "Colonel Haun" on the door. Haun stood rigidly to one side, but the man sitting behind the desk wasn't a colonel. He was a two-star general, whose face was all-too-familiar from the newspapers and newsreels. It was Willie the Whip himself, General Tunner.

"Holy Shit," J.B. muttered involuntarily, and Hal looked at him with the eyes of a sacrificial lamb.

They came to attention and delivered the smartest salutes of their lives.

"So, do you want to tell me just what the hell the two of you have been doing?" Tunner demanded in an ice-cold voice, his steel-blue eyes pinning them to the back wall.

"Flying like mad, sir!" Hal croaked out gamely, while J.B. held his tongue, implicitly backing his captain.

It was the wrong strategy. Tunner burst out angrily, "Do you think I'm stupid?" He reached over, grabbed a newspaper and snapped it open on the desk in front of them. It was a German newspaper with text entirely in German, but front and centre was a big picture of a crowd of kids standing on ruins and looking up at the sky where tiny parachutes came drifting down. The tail-number of a C-54 from which the little packages streamed was painfully legible. They had been caught red-handed. The game was up. J.B. felt not so much fear as bottomless disappointment.

Tunner snarled, "You almost hit a reporter on the head with a candy bar yesterday, and the phones have been ringing off their handles ever since! My headquarters staff have had about a million questions about a 'candy bomber,' and I didn't know a God-damned thing about him! Didn't anyone anywhere teach you to keep your superiors informed?"

Hal wisely opted to reply with "Yes, sir."

"In that case, smart-ass, why didn't you tell Colonel Haun what you wanted to do and ask for his permission?" With a hand gesture, Tunner drew attention to Colonel Haun beside him.

Unfortunately, that question could not be answered with "yes, sir." Hal squeaked out a timid but honest, "Because I didn't think he'd approve."

Haun rolled his eyes, and Tunner answered for him. "You mean after we've dumped something like one hundred thousand sticks of bombs on Berlin, you thought we might object to you dropping a few sticks of gum?"

J.B. held his breath in disbelief, afraid to believe his ears. It sounded like Tunner was about to approve the whole business.

Hal ventured, "I guess I wasn't too smart, sir."

"Well I hope you have a steep learning curve because I've called an international press conference for tomorrow afternoon. Then I want you on the next courier flight back to Washington. The public relations guys in the Pentagon think we might be able to get you on the television program "We the People" and maybe you can do some other press conferences and publicity stuff — but don't let it go to your head. You're still just a lieutenant and an airlift pilot. Got it?"

"Yes, sir!" Halvorsen stood very stiff and kept his eyes aimed at the wall.

"Good. Then have a good time and hurry back."

J.B. risked a glance in Tunner's direction and realised the fierce general was smiling at them.

His gesture attracted the general's attention to him. Tunner turned to J.B., "Meanwhile, Captain, you take over coordinating the drops. I want a central collection point for candy donations and parachutes, and I'll put out the word that any crew that wants to participate can. Of course, you'll have to give the RAF a heads-up since we'll need to spread the drops across the city rather dumping all the goods in one place. That's all for now, gentlemen." Tunner stood up and this time he offered each his hand. J.B. and Hal were grinning like Cheshire cats as they left the office.

Paying Attention to Little Things
RAF Gatow
Monday, 22 September 1948
(Day 89)

"USAF Airlift Taskforce Headquarters is reporting that they flew nearly 7,000 tons into Berlin yesterday. They'll be making a public announcement about it later this morning," the Station adjutant handed a notepad with the figures to Wing Commander Priestman.

Priestman scanned his notes and remarked "It says 6,978 tons of coal. Is that *all* they flew in?"

"Yes, sir. For this one day. They wanted to show what could be done."

Priestman was not impressed. Berlin could not live by coal alone, yet a homogeneous cargo was easier to load and unload than a diverse one in which objects of different weights and dimensions had to be married together for an optimal aircraft load. "Well, let them boast," he told the adjutant. "We have work to do. I'd like you—" He was interrupted by the ringing of the phone on his desk, and he picked it up, "Priestman."

"Sir," his secretary was on the other end, "an American Air Force captain is here and would like to speak to you for a few moments."

"Did he say what it was about?"

"These sweets drops, sir."

"Ah. Right. Send him in."

Stan opened the door to let the American in and slipped out himself. The newcomer was a handsome young man in a brown, US Army uniform adorned with wings. He came smartly to attention to salute the more senior RAF officer. Priestman returned the salute and then asked the captain to sit down, gesturing to the chair before his desk. "What can I do for you, captain?"

"Sir. My name's Baronowsky, copilot to Lt. Gail Halvorsen. I suspect you've seen in the newspapers that we started dropping candy and chocolate to the kids who were standing around the perimeter fence at Tempelhof."

"It's been rather hard to overlook that piece of news, captain. I believe it's been on every radio programme and in every newspaper not controlled by the Soviets for a couple of days," Priestman remarked dryly.

Baronowsky looked embarrassed rather than puffed up about it, which made Priestman warm to him. "We didn't do it for the publicity, sir," Baronowsky underlined his expression. "In fact, we'd hoped to keep it secret because we were rather afraid General Tunner might not approve of it." That candidness made Priestman laugh, and the ice was broken.

Grinning himself, Baronowsky explained, "Halvorsen had met some of the kids when he visited Berlin on his time off, and he just wanted to do something to make their lives a little better. We hadn't planned to do it more than once, but somehow...." His words faded off.

"You've done a wonderful thing, captain," Priestman told him sincerely. "We envy you having the resources to share like that." It wasn't the fact that Britain didn't have enough chocolate to meet even domestic demand that saddened him. It was that the British chocolate shortage seemed like a poignant symbol of the British Empire, which could no longer shower largesse upon the poor of the world as America could.

"Yes, sir. I understand. I mean, I was in the UK during the war. I know how bad it was, and I know you still have rationing and shortages now." His earnestness was touching, and Priestman sensed not a trace of smug superiority. Baronowsky continued, "I just came to explain that General Tunner wants to ramp up the operation a bit. When Halvorsen and I started, all we had were our own rations and handkerchiefs, but Tunner is going to turn over PX resources and allow any pilot who wants to to do the drops. The problem is, if a lot of pilots take part — and I think they will — we don't want all the goodies landing in the same place."

"I can see the sense in that," Priestman conceded.

Baronowsky took an audible breath before concluding, "Tunner thinks we need to add a little flexibility into the approach pattern for those aircraft involved in what they're now calling 'Operation Little Vittles'. But of course we don't want to interfere with RAF operations and certainly don't want to do anything that would increase the risk of collisions, so we, uh, want to coordinate this with you."

Priestman nodded. "Thank you. I assure you we would like to facilitate delivery of sweets to the children of Berlin. The person you need to talk to is the Senior Flying Control Officer at the Berlin Air Safety Centre, but since you're here, why not go upstairs to the control tower and talk to Gatow's Senior Flying Control Officer, Squadron Leader Garth? If you work things out with him, I'm sure he'll be able to liaise with the Berlin Air Safety Centre for you. Would that work?"

"Yes, sir! Thank you!" Baronowsky sprang to his feet, looking happier than Priestman thought the situation warranted. He could only surmise that the American had expected 'the Brits' to be spoilsports in some way.

"Good, then I'll ask my adjutant to escort you up." The wing commander stood and came around the desk to lead him out. In the doorway, he called over to Stan to take the American up to the tower. Offering his hand to Baronowsky, he ended with, "It was a pleasure to make your acquaintance, Captain. Keep up the good work."

"Thank you, sir!"

Before Priestman could disappear into his office again, Sergeant Andrews gestured to the phone she was holding and mouthed at him "Group Captain Bagshot." With the foreboding he felt every time the Group Captain called, Priestman returned to his desk and took the call.

"Have you seen the American tonnage claims?" Bagshot barked into the phone without pleasantries or introduction.

"Yes, I have."

"And do you know what we flew in yesterday?"

"2,246 tonnes." Priestman had the figures in front of him on his desk.

Bagshot snorted. "That's less than a third of what the Americans flew! It makes us look like bumbling idiots — the tail on the dog! What are we doing wrong?"

"I don't think you can say we're doing anything wrong, sir. The RAF is roughly one-fifth the size of the USAF, yet we flew one-third of the sorties. The difference in tonnage is because they have a larger fleet of four-engine aircraft. Furthermore, yesterday's figures are distorted because they flew their C-74 in and out of Gatow six times; something they do not intend to do regularly."

"Aircraft alone can't explain the difference," Bagshot snapped irritably. "The Americans must be loading and off-loading more efficiently."

"Yesterday they hauled only coal, which is faster to load and unload than the heterogeneous cargoes we handled."

"Why don't we take more coal?" Bagshot growled.

"As you know, sir, the Berlin City government determines what they need, and they have a long list of items *other* than coal."

"You don't seem to understand!" Bagshot barked. "If the Colonials out-perform us by margins like these, they will have a very strong case for taking over the whole operation!"

So *that* was what had upset him, Priestman registered. Bagshot had learned that Tunner wanted to take over the entire Airlift and elbow the RAF Group Captain out of the way. Priestman's feelings about such a development were ambivalent. On the whole, he deplored America's rise at Britain's expense, and specifically, he resented Tunner's almost-inhuman focus on 'efficiency'. Yet there was no question that Tunner was more competent than Bagshot, and if he had to choose between the two, he would take Tunner. Given that Bagshot did not want to hear that, Priestman opted to remain silent.

"This is insufferable!" Bagshot concluded and slammed the phone down.

Wonderful, Priestman thought. The conversation left a sour taste in his mouth, and he needed to get away from his desk for a moment. He decided to go and see how Graham was getting on with the subterranean fuel storage tanks. Passing through the anteroom he noticed that the inbox on Sergeant Andrew's desk was overflowing. "Good heavens! What is all that mail?" Priestman asked in alarm. Mail usually meant work, but this mail looked surprisingly unofficial in old, tattered, even dirty envelopes and addressed by hand rather than typewriter.

"Sorry, sir. I normally pass this on to Translation before you notice."

"But what is it?"

"Just your fan mail, sir," she admitted with a smile.

"I'm still not following you."

"They are thank-you letters from the population."

"Thank you letters?"

"For the Airlift. There are also some gifts." She pointed to a cardboard box in the corner of the room. Priestman went to look inside. He was astonished to discover a cuckoo clock, a lace tablecloth, a somewhat tatty stuffed fox, and a fine set of deer antlers among other things. They appeared to be family heirlooms. They were certainly things that might have brought a pretty penny on the black market. To give them away to the occupiers instead was a touching gesture.

"Since when have these gifts been arriving?" Priestman asked Andrews.

"I think the first item came a couple of weeks ago. I mentioned it to you, but you said you didn't have time to deal with it and asked the Translation Department to draft and send thank you notes in your name."

"Yes, now I remember. But I had no idea the gifts had grown to these proportions." He stared at them a moment more and then decided. "Find a time on my calendar when I can talk to whoever in the Translation Department has been handling the gifts and letters. Tell them I'd like a summary of what is being said in the notes and that I'd also like to see their standard reply. I may want to personalise our response more. I've been neglecting public relations for too long and that is going to change."

"Yes, sir!" Her wide smile indicated her approval.

Priestman was less pleased with himself. Since the Blockade started, he'd been focusing too much on his immediate job and had lost sight of the bigger picture. Taking time to show some appreciation for gifts and thank you notes might not be much, but then nor were a handful of chocolate bars dropped on handkerchief parachutes. Sometimes, however, little things mattered out of all proportion to their objective value. It was time to pay more attention to the Berliners.

Well Met
RAF Gatow
Monday, 22 September 1948
(Day 89)

Kathleen was busy talking down a block of Dakotas when Stan brought a visitor up to the tower. She caught only a glimpse of an American officer, who turned to look over his shoulder at her as Squadron Leader Garth led him towards the window. She had not been one of those English girls who found the Americans particularly attractive during the war. The American uniform did not strike her as in any way smarter than RAF blues. Yet something about the way this officer's eyes seemed to seek her out made her pulse rate increase a little. He was certainly good-looking. When, shortly afterwards, laughter floated into the radar room from the observation deck, she surmised that the American and Garth were getting along. She risked looking away from her screen long enough to see what was happening. Garth was using his pipe to point things out on the field spread out before them. The American nodded, looking acutely interested. Maybe he was an American controller?

The disembodied voice of a pilot on approach drew her attention back to her job, and for several minutes she forgot the visitor. When the shift change came a quarter of an hour later, however, she was pleased to discover the USAF captain and Garth were still in earnest conversation. Kathleen made her way casually towards the tea urn, casting surreptitious glances at the stranger as she went. She was surprised to see he was wearing wings and a "fruit salad" of campaign ribbons. That suggested he was not a controller after all.

Her glances had not been subtle enough. The captain turned at the waist to look over at her. Their eyes met and he seemed to start and then freeze — as if he'd seen a ghost. Then he turned back to Garth and started speaking animatedly. The Squadron Leader smiled and gestured for Kathleen to join them.

Kathleen willingly complied and went over to salute smartly. Garth did the introductions: "Assistant Section Leader Hart is one of our radar operators who handles GCA approaches. Hart, Captain Baronowsky is one of the Americans who have been dropping sweets from his aircraft to the children of Berlin."

Kathleen's heart missed a beat. It was like meeting a celebrity, and a smile spread across her face. "Oh, that's wonderful! I witnessed one of your drops, and ever since I've wondered about who was behind them!"

"It's a pleasure to meet you, Assistant Flight Officer!" The intensity of his gaze was slightly unnerving; it was as if he recognized her from somewhere before although she was sure they had never met. "You talked me down when I made my first flight here in a Globemaster," he seemed to answer her thoughts, and yet that hardly seemed grounds for the look he was still giving her. "I've wanted to meet you for some time and was hoping we might find time for a short chat." He glanced at Garth.

"Oh, I think we can arrange that," Garth agreed. "It would do me good to refresh my skills a bit. Hart, why don't you take Captain Baronowsky over for a cuppa at the Malcolm Club?"

"I'd be delighted!" Kathleen agreed while the American thanked the Senior Flying Control Officer profusely.

Kathleen led the way with Baronowsky holding doors open for her, and she found herself gushing about what a splendid idea it was to give sweets to the children of Berlin. "They have so very little else in their dreary lives. We were told by some of the little tots that they haven't seen chocolate in their whole lives! But it's not just the sweets that I find wonderful! I love the idea of delivering it by parachute. That makes the whole scheme an adventure! So much better than just having some grown-up hand it out!"

The American replied modestly, giving credit for the idea to his captain, and he told her in detail about Halvorsen's first encounter at the perimeter fence. He stressed how mature these children were. She responded by telling him of her experience watching a drop and seeing how the children pooled their catch and shared everything.

By then they had reached the crowded Malcolm Club, where they bagged a table as a crew stood to leave. Baronowsky placed their order for tea, but then he removed his cap, leaned his elbows on the table, and looked at her so intently that she got flustered. "Is something the matter, Captain?"

He shook his head slowly and then modified his answer to, "No. It's just that I love the sound of your voice. Would you, by any chance, have been a controller in the war?"

"Yes, I was," Kathleen answered surprised. "Why?"

"I flew with the 303rd Bomb Group. On one mission, after we'd been badly shot up over the target, we limped back to the UK only to find it blanketed in fog. I hadn't a clue where I was. I put out a "darky call" and a voice guided me to safety. The voice sounded like yours."

"Oh, it was probably just the British accent," Kathleen dismissed the story, embarrassed by his intensity.

Baronowsky shook his head. "I've heard a lot of British accents, Assistant Section Leader. I learned to hear the difference between POSH and not-so-POSH, between Scots and Welsh and Irish and London accents. I'm not saying I have as fine an ear as you all have — right down to a 15-mile radius—" That made her laugh as he'd wanted, and he smiled gently, before continuing, "but I've never heard another British woman whose voice matches the tones and cadence of the voice in my memory as much as yours. Still, I know I might just be — I don't know — confused. So, tell me: did you ever talk down a wounded B-17?"

Kathleen's pulse was racing as she remembered. She drew a deep breath to steady her nerves. "I did, yes. Three in fact. Or, rather, two B-17s and one B-24."

"My squadron call sign was Dark Maple, and the controller pretended to hear 'Clark Gable' — just to ease the tension. It worked. Can you remember that?"

It was coming back to her, and the Malcolm Club faded behind her memories. The palpable fear in the pilot's voice, the low-hanging cloud, the knowledge that they might not be able to get him down safely. She nodded wordlessly.

"I knew it!" Baronowsky declared triumphantly. "I sensed you were my guardian angel from the moment our eyes met in the tower a few moments ago. I'm indebted to you, and I'm so grateful to have had the opportunity to say it. I tried to come to the tower that night, but by the time I'd seen to my killed and wounded crewmen, reported back to base, and done all the paperwork, you'd gone off duty."

Kathleen didn't know how to react. Finally, she said, "I suppose that makes us even because I'm grateful to you for dropping sweets to the children of Berlin."

Kathleen felt the captain's eyes shift to her left hand, apparently looking for a wedding ring. Her heart thrilled at the thought that he wanted to get to know her better, but before she could explain she was a widow, he'd already pulled back. In a more distant tone, he asked, "Do you have kids of your own, Mrs Hart?"

"Yes, a seven-year-old daughter," Kathleen admitted, adding with a bemused smile, "And she's taken it rather poorly that no one is dropping *her* sweets!"

That brought a laugh from Baronowsky, before he asked diffidently, "Your husband is RAF?"

That at last gave her the opportunity to explain. "He was, yes, but he was not as lucky as you were, Captain. His Lancaster went down over Berlin in January 1944."

Instantly, the distance he had put between them melted again. "I'm sorry," he said in a way that told her he understood both what Ken had faced and what it felt like to lose friends to the war.

Kathleen didn't want to dwell on it. "And you, captain? Do you have children?" She tried to sound casual, but she couldn't help hoping he would say 'no.' If he had looked for her ring then surely...

"Not yet," he answered.

It was her turn to recoil. The way he'd said 'yet' set off an alarm signal. It indicated he not only wanted them but was expecting them. She must have misunderstood his glance. Picturing a pregnant wife back in the States, Kathleen asked with a forced smile, "Married?"

"No, also not yet. I was due to get married on August 14, but the Russkies sort of got in the way."

"I'm so sorry. Your fiancée must have been devastated!" Kathleen tried to conjure up sympathy for J.B.'s fiancée while chiding herself for feeling disappointed. Anyway, it would have been entirely unfair to Hope to start seeing someone again so soon after the fiasco with Lionel.

"Yeah, she was pretty hysterical about it," Baronowsky responded to her words. "But I think what we're doing over here is important. A wedding can wait. This mission can't."

"Yes, I agree with you entirely," Kathleen told him, feeling more attracted to him because of his commitment and all the more disappointed that he was already engaged. Pushing her empty teacup aside, she announced, "Well, I really should get back to work, Captain. Squadron Leader Garth was kind to let me take a few minutes off, but I mustn't take advantage of him. Shall we ask for the bill?"

"Don't worry; I'll take care of it." He got to his feet. "It was a pleasure meeting you, Mrs Hart. I'm so glad I had a chance to thank you after all this time. But wait!" he put his hand in his pocket and pulled out a Hersey's chocolate bar attached to a checkered handkerchief. "I brought this along in case anyone wanted to see what we were dropping out of our flare chute. Please. Give it to your daughter. Tell her it's a personal gift from one of the candy bombers."

"Oh, that's lovely! Thank you, Captain! Hope will be delighted."

"The name's J.B.."

"Kathleen," she reciprocated.

They shook hands again, and she turned and walked away. She was angry at herself for swooning like a silly schoolgirl. The American had just wanted to thank her for what she'd done in the war. He wasn't the least bit interested in her as a woman. Yet she couldn't resist turning to look one last time at him, expecting to see him paying off the waitress. Instead, he was gazing after her. She lifted her hand to wave goodbye, and he replied with an informal salute. Something in his eyes was unfathomably sad.

Chapter Eighteen
Autumn Omens

Late Harvests
RAF Gatow
Sunday, 26 September 1948
(Day 92)

The Avro Tudor tanker left the taxiway and sedately turned to park before the new liquid fuel storage depot. In text-book fashion, the engines shut down one after another, and the pilots went through the post-flight check. Finally, the first pilot shoved the near window back and gave a thumbs up to the Royal Engineer lieutenant colonel standing to one side. Graham Russel answered with the same gesture and directed the team of aircraftmen to connect and secure the rubber fuel pipe to the metal nozzle at the tail of the tanker. When the team signalled all was fitted properly, Graham again lifted his thumb to the pilot, who opened the aircraft's tanks from the cockpit. With the gentle chug-chug-chug of a pump in operation, diesel fuel flowed down the rubber pipe into the underground storage depot. The gauge bounced upwards from the zero mark. They'd done it. The underground fuel storage tanks at Gatow were operational.

Graham gave another thumbs-up to the pilot of the Tudor, who answered with a curt nod. The pilot's coolness disappointed Graham, who had expected a little more charisma from the celebrity at the controls. Donald Bennett, the owner/manager of Airflight, had set records while flying with Imperial Airways in the '30s and was most famous for commanding the Pathfinder Force from 1942 to the end of the war. Graham would have liked to meet him, but he appeared uninterested in leaving his cockpit — presumably until his cargo of 4,000 gallons of diesel had been discharged.

Graham did not want to wait around that long. It was a warm, sunny day that felt more like late summer than autumn, and it was also almost 4 pm. He wanted to take the rest of the day off. He drove back to the main admin building, left his car out front and went directly to the Station Commander's office.

Putting his head around the door he asked, "Do you have a minute, Robin?"

"Have a seat and give me a moment to sign these papers," Robin answered, gesturing towards the coffee table. Graham sat down with a glance out the windows. This might be his last chance for gardening — and that other matter.

Robin called his secretary to collect the folder of documents and joined Graham. "How did it go?"

"Like clockwork. Your liquid fuel depot is operational."

"That's good news."

"Yes and no."

Robin looked surprised. "What's not good about it?"

"Only that with this task complete, I've been re-assigned to the airfield construction at Tegel. The Americans have the overall project management, of course, with a whole team of engineers working on the runway, taxiways, and terminal. However, they asked me to take responsibility for building the underground fuel depot."

"Ah, the punishment for success."

"You could say that. They want three times the capacity that I've put in here."

"That's fine with me," Robin assured him.

"It just seems like such an enormous investment," Graham reflected.

"After Reuter's speech, the Americans are ashamed of even *contemplating* a deal with the Russians. They're throwing everything they have into the effort."

"But surely they know that Tegel isn't going to open before the start of next year?"

"In the current political environment, that is part of the message: we're in this for the long haul and prepared to invest on this scale."

"Is that realistic? It's the 26th of September now. The equinox is five days behind us. The nights just keep getting longer and the weather worse from now until next spring. Can we keep flying at the rate necessary in the winter?"

"The Russians certainly don't think so. When General Herbert protested over the mob violence against the Berlin City Council three weeks ago, General Kotikov addressed his reply to the 'Commander of the British Garrison' and signed it as the 'Military Commandant of Berlin'. Herbert was livid, as you can imagine, and that kind of arrogant assumption of victory tends to make most Englishmen — including the PM and Foreign Secretary — dig in. Getting the third airfield up and running is more critical than ever."

Graham drew a breath. "I suppose you're right, but it isn't going to be easy. We first have to clear a lot of scrub growth and we'll also need to do considerable levelling just for the fuel depot. Not to mention that an eight thousand foot runway is a gigantic challenge with the patched together and obsolete equipment we have on hand." Robin nodded sympathetically but didn't interrupt. Graham gently steered the conversation towards his goal. "What that means, of course," Graham weighed his words carefully; he wanted Robin to understand how difficult this was for him, "...is that I'll have to live closer to Tegel. I'm going to have to move into the army officers' quarters in Charlottenburg."

"Ah," Robin nodded his understanding. "No more gardening?"

"I'd like to fit it in, but quite honestly, I don't know how I'll manage. The season's almost over anyway, which was why I was hoping to take advantage of your hospitality one last time and go over to your residence now."

"Of course," Robin replied without thinking. and then paused to suggest, "Why not stay for dinner and the night? Emily's on a flight to Hanover, which means she'll be back around seven. I'm sure she'll want to see you again before you move to Charlottenburg."

"I'd like that very much," Graham admitted gratefully.

"Excellent," Robin said as they got to their feet. "I'll ring through to Jasha and ask her to prepare one of the guestrooms for you."

"You and Emily have been exceptionally kind," Graham stressed.

"Not at all. It's been our pleasure," Robin answered sincerely. Graham started for the door and had just put his hand on the doorknob when Robin stopped him, "And Graham?"

He looked back.

"Good luck!" Something about his smile made Graham suspect he'd guessed the truth.

Back at his quarters, Graham changed into his gardening clothes and quickly packed an overnight bag. Then he started looking for the ring box he'd stowed somewhere. After looking through what seemed like every drawer, he finally found it and peeked inside. A diminutive but elegant diamond ring glittered back at him.

He'd bought it in 1926 when working on a project at the Walker Naval Yard and living in Newcastle. Every day to work and back he passed a small jeweller's shop. The objects in the window weren't exotic, but were unusual and striking nonetheless. One day when he stopped to look more closely at the things displayed, the jeweller stepped out and they had chatted. Thereafter, Graham waved a greeting whenever he went by. He noticed, too, how often the jeweller stood sadly in front of his shop looking for customers — and how seldom anyone went inside. The demand for luxuries was not great in Newcastle in 1926. At the time, Graham had fancied himself falling in love, but he'd bought the ring as much to give the jeweller a little business as to please the girl. In the end, he hadn't found the courage to offer it to her at all.

Graham closed the ring box, shoved it in his trouser pocket, and set off for the Priestman residence. As soon as he stopped the car in the drive, Jasha came out of the front door waving happily. She seemed to beam with joy, building his confidence, and she chattered cheerfully as she showed him up to his room. For a moment, he was tempted to propose right then and there, but the idea of proposing while standing beside a bed seemed unspeakably vulgar. He let the moment slip away.

They went together to the garden, where Jasha proudly showed him her pumpkins. After careful examination, however, they jointly decided it would be better to let them ripen a little more before harvesting. She decided instead to pluck a head of lettuce and cut some of her spinach. "Make salad," she told Graham. "No heat for cooking." Meanwhile, Graham noticed some snails and set to work eradicating them. One thing led to the next and the work absorbed them both. Besides, Graham found it easy to put off doing something he was afraid of — until Jasha announced it was time for her to go up to the house to make dinner. Startled, Graham looked at his watch. It was twenty past six. He could not procrastinate any longer.

"Before you go, could we have a little chat?" he asked.

Something in his voice alarmed Jasha, who asked back, "Bad news?"

"Yes, in a way — please. Let's sit down." He pointed to the edge of the lawn. A turf step about eight inches high marked where the lawn had been cut away to make the garden. Graham sat down and patted the grass beside him. Uneasily, Jasha lowered herself and waited.

Graham had fantasised about this moment many times. He had practiced speeches in his head. Now that the moment had come, however, he could find not a single word. He reached into his pocket, removed the little box, and turning it towards Jasha, opened it so the diamonds glinted in the sinking sun.

Jasha answered with a gasp. Graham smiled, thinking that was a gesture of surprised delight. Then he realised she had put her hands over her mouth and was shaking her head.

The light went out of the sun and the garden turned to ashes. His mouth went dry and his ears deaf. He slowly drew the box back, shut the lid and put it away in his pocket. Why did he do this to himself? Why did he mistake pity for love? Why couldn't he accept that women didn't want a deformed and ugly man? Would he never learn?

He was so lost in his own misery that it was several seconds before he realised that Jasha was silently sobbing beside him. He gazed at her, uncomprehending. "I don't understand," he murmured.

"I make mistake! I wrong!"

"It's not your mistake," Graham told her in a leaden voice. "I shouldn't have presumed. I'll get over it. I always have before." He didn't mean to sound bitter; he just couldn't help himself.

"No! Not understand!" Jasha cried out, tears now gushing from her eyes. "I love you! I love you! I want to — spend life — with you! Garden and cook and laugh and talk. Together. But I did bad thing." She looked as miserable as he felt. His instinct was to put his arm around her shoulders, but he was too confused to dare.

"I don't understand," he admitted. "If you want to be together, why reject my proposal?"

"Because you don't know about Russians," she gasped out.

"What don't I know about the Russians?" he asked back, baffled.

She started stammering, "At end of war — hungry — we needed food.

They surrounded us. So many of them. We couldn't get away. Screamed but no one help, and—"

Understanding hit him like lightning. He put a finger to Jasha's lips to silence her. She gazed at him with wet, red eyes filled with fear, pain and hope. He bent and kissed her forehead, then pulled her into his arms and held her tightly. She turned her face into his chest and pressed it against his sweaty shirt and started to relax in his arms. After a moment, she lifted her head and looked him in the face, demanding confirmation of what she sensed. "You don't mind?"

"I mind very much! It horrifies me and makes me angry and makes me hate the Russians more than I did before. I wish I could have prevented it. I wish I could erase every memory and every scar they left behind. But it doesn't make me love *you* less." He paused as another thought hit him. He absorbed it and sought to sound reassuring as he added, "If you are trying to say you can't face consummation, I can understand and accept that. I would be happy if you would agree just to garden and talk and grow old together."

"Not understand," Jasha admitted, drawing away and looking at him with a puzzled frown. "What is con – conmunition?"

He was bewildered until he realised his mistake. "Consummation. Don't worry about it. I'm saying we can live together like brother and sister if you prefer."

She shook her head and declared firmly, "I want to be wife, but afraid. Maybe not so good in bed."

"Probably neither am I," Graham admitted with a self-deprecating smile. Then he pulled her back into his arms. She lifted her face to him, and they kissed, tenderly at first but then with growing passion. When they pulled apart, they were both smiling through their tears.

Jasha pulled a handkerchief out of her apron pocket and blew her nose, while Graham reached for the ring box and presented it again. Jasha still shook her head, but this time she was laughing too. "Hand dirty!" she exclaimed, holding up her hands. "Must wash, change. Then you give me ring!"

Graham laughed. "My practical Jasha! Yes, we'll go up to the house and wash and change and then I'll make a proper proposal." He stuffed the ring back in his pocket a second time. They helped each other to their feet and walked hand-in-hand back to the house.

Here, Jasha darted away to take the servants' stairs up to her chamber, while Graham went into the main house and up to the guestroom. He washed and changed into uniform. When he returned downstairs, he found Jasha in the dining room wearing her blue silk dress, silk stockings and heeled shoes. She looked remarkably elegant. For a third time, he opened the ring box and formally asked her to accept his hand in marriage. She said, "Yes, please," and then held out her hand to him. He slipped the ring on her finger only to have it fall over to one side; it was too big for her.

Before Graham could apologise, Jasha declared, "No matter! I fix! You find drink for toast. I make dinner." Then she disappeared into the kitchen.

Graham looked around the elegant dining room, conscious that this was not his house. He decided he'd better ring Robin to ask permission to pilfer something.

"Sorry to bother you, Robin, but would you mind if I raided your wine cellar for something to celebrate an engagement?"

"Congratulations! Wonderful news — wait!" He covered the phone, there were muffled voices and then Emily's voice asked eagerly, "Graham? Is it true? You've proposed to Jasha? I knew Jasha had fallen for you badly, but I was a little worried her hopes might be disappointed. I'm so glad I was wrong! I can't wait to celebrate. We'll be there in a few minutes."

The Priestmans' obvious approval buoyed Graham up more than the champagne he'd dug out of the cellar. Emily went straight into the kitchen and exclaimed "Jasha, I'm so happy for you both!" Graham caught a glimpse of the women hugging, and when Emily returned to the breakfast room where the Priestmans always had their meals, she started setting the table for four, just as she had on the night he was released from Soviet detention. That little gesture of including Jasha meant the world to Graham.

Jasha soon brought a large salad, homemade vinaigrette, home-baked bread, boiled eggs, cheese and sausages, while Robin uncorked a second bottle of champagne. When they were all seated, first Robin and then Emily toasted Graham and Jasha and their future together. As they started the meal Emily ventured to ask, "Does this mean I'm losing my cook?"

"No, no!" Jasha answered, and Graham explained. "Jasha doesn't want to sit around all day doing nothing. We've agreed she'll be much happier here until the situation in Berlin is resolved one way or another. She'll come with me to my next posting as my wife, but after this rather rash engagement, we thought maybe it would be good to wait a little for the wedding."

"Rash?" Robin echoed, turning to Emily. "How long was it between when we met, and when I proposed?"

"Two months."

"How long did you wait between engagement and marriage?" Graham asked.

"Too long!" Robin shot back.

"Six weeks," Emily answered, adding, "But there was a war on. Robin was at risk every day and I feared I'd be a widow before I was a bride. Your situation is different. You're quite right not to rush things."

"What is important is that we have clarified how we feel about one another and what our long-term plans are. I'll naturally do General Herbert the courtesy of asking his permission to marry. He may even want to attend."

Robin nodded.

"There is only one thing I'm worried about," Graham started, and then paused.

"Yes?" Robin prompted.

"Well, if there is an emergency. You know, if the Russians send in the tanks, or the weather closes down the Airlift altogether, or HM Government suddenly changes its mind and decides to pull out. In short, if there is an evacuation of British personnel, would there be any difficulty getting Jasha recognised as my dependent if we *aren't* yet married?"

Before Robin could answer, Emily spoke up, "Graham, I promise: no matter what bureaucratic bumpf the RAF may come up with, if Berlin becomes unsafe, I shall personally see that Jasha flies out on the same AAI flight that I am on."

Voiceless Victims
Berlin-Kreuzberg
Monday, 27 September 1948
(Day 94)

After a chaotic week in which requests for ambulance service far exceeded AAI's capacity, Charlotte rang David in tears. The more acute demand became, the more the hospital managers tried to bully her. They used their superior understanding of medicine to justify placing their patients at the front of the established queue, and Charlotte didn't know how to counter their medical arguments. Yet giving precedence to one patient meant others were delayed. This inevitably provoked outrage and protest from the doctors of the delayed patients. Some callers had been loud, rude, and even insulting over the phone. Charlotte confided to David that she felt overwhelmed and out of her depth.

David responded by announcing that the ambulance was grounded until new procedures had been worked out. He summoned all those involved in booking AAI's services to an emergency meeting in the lecture hall at the Hospital am Urban. He scheduled the meeting for 8 am so it took place before the hospitals received their four hours of electricity a day. With any luck, they could resolve the problems by noon and still fly one or two evacuations later in the day.

The auditorium was cramped and dim because the windows had been boarded up rather than reglazed. When Emily arrived there were already more than two score men wearing white lab coats sitting on fold-down wooden seats. The room hummed with conversation. Some men leaned across others to talk to colleagues farther away. Others stood to talk to the men behind them. Voices were raised and gestures were emphatic.

Emily joined David and Charlotte at the table on the dais at the front of the room. She had come mostly to give moral support to Charlotte and find out the results of the decision made at the end of the meeting rather than to participate. Charlotte had brought a stack of papers, showing all the extra requests and changes that these had triggered. David flipped through her documents frowning with concentration. Then he nodded firmly and called the meeting to order.

Emily found his opening remarks clear and reasonable. He reminded everyone that they were facing a crisis and that AAI had limited resources. It was not going to be possible, he told them, for everyone to get what they wanted. They all had to cooperate and work together.

"But you must also be flexible!" a doctor called out in an exasperated tone, and this comment opened the floodgates. Most of the men in the room were upset and angry. They expressed themselves forcefully, often interrupting each other or talking over one another. Charlotte occasionally whispered something to David, and he nodded or jotted down notes. Eventually, Emily sensed that some of the steam had been blown off, and at that point, David stood and retook control of the meeting. Standing with his arms extended in front of him on the table, he began to summarise the points made.

"The key problem," he told them, "Is that medical conditions are not static. A patient's condition can deteriorate suddenly. Also, unexpected crises can occur with individuals who previously appeared stable. Any evacuation plan worked out a week in advance cannot take such changes into account and is consequently inadequate.

"Another issue, however, is that all of you — rightly — advocate for your particular charges, and are not willing to consider the fact that other cases might take precedence."

Someone protested, but David made a calming gesture and replied, "You recognise that *in principle*, but the reality is that you do not first inform yourselves about the condition of other patients before harassing my staff." David's words had an edge to them now and he stared down the indignant doctor with what Emily thought was great fortitude. She loved seeing him like this, breaking a lance for his lady.

She spared a glance for Charlotte, sitting on David's other side. She was looking down, slightly embarrassed by David's public advocacy, but she was glowing too, warmed by David's unstinting support.

David continued, "The office staff of AAI are doing a very difficult job, and they are doing it extremely well under the circumstances. But they are not trained medical professionals and do not have sufficient medical knowledge to moderate between you. Nor should they have to," he concluded definitively.

"Finally, there is the issue of nursing staff. The severe local shortage means that sending a nurse with an evacuee creates a severe burden for the hospital providing the nurse. This is a burden that you, understandably, want to see distributed more evenly. Is that correct?" David looked out across the room, his eyes sweeping from side to side as the audience grumbled but nodded.

When there was silence, he declared, "Good. Then the floor is open for proposed solutions," and he sat down again. Instantly, a new discussion erupted. This was less heated, but Emily recognised that her concentration was fading. She was understanding less and less of the German. In a low voice, she informed David that she was going to take up Trude's invitation to a tour. He nodded his agreement, and she slipped out.

She found Trude Liebherr at the nursing station. The older woman made her feel very welcome and started the tour at once. It was six months since Emily had visited hospitals as part of the market research she'd done for David. She noticed that the wards looked more crowded than before and the staff sparser. "Weren't you supposed to get more student nurses?" she asked Trude.

Trude shook her head. "Most of them were from the West and they did not want to come to Berlin after the siege started — even assuming the Western Allies would have allowed it. That is why it is so hard to send a nurse with the ambulance. They are gone all day, and the rest of the nursing staff must pick up the burden. Here they look after twenty or thirty patients. On the aircraft, it is just six."

Emily nodded understanding. She had wanted AAI to hire a full-time flight nurse of their own for some time. After today's meeting, she hoped David would finally agree.

She had barely completed this thought when Trude led her into a large ward filled with children. Their ages ranged from about two to roughly twelve. Regardless of age, they lay listlessly in their beds. Some had open sores, particularly around their mouths. Some whimpered or whined softly as if in pain. Some were being fed fluids intravenously. Some had distended bellies. All were thin as skeletons.

"These are the lucky ones," Trude announced. "They have been brought to us and we can start feeding them a balanced diet. But they are the tip of the iceberg. For every child in this ward, there are scores hiding in cellars or scavenging in the streets — abandoned, neglected, sometimes abused by mothers unable to cope with their situation. Many of the smaller children are the product of rape and not wanted in the first place. Even the older ones are often the children of refugees or bombed-out families, sent to live with distant relatives who didn't ask for them and don't want them."

Emily shook her head in wordless shock. For all that she thought she knew what was going on, she had not grasped that the situation was as bad as this.

"They are not acutely ill," Trude continued, "so they do not qualify for the air ambulance service. Yet they would all be better off in the Western Zones. Berlin has become a battleground. It may not be a shooting war yet, but this is a war zone nevertheless. This is a war in which the weapons are food and heat, and the targets — or at least those most likely to die — are not soldiers but these children. Regardless of who their parents were or what their parents did, these children should not be forced to live through another war — or die in an ideological conflict between East and West."

"Of course not," Emily agreed at once, but her distress did not blind her. The magnitude of this problem as depicted by Trude was beyond anything AAI could cope with. She tried to put this into words, "Frau Liebherr, we have only one aircraft with places for six stretchers. We *can't* fly all these children out no matter how much we want to!"

"I understand," Trude assured her, "but these children don't need oxygen or intravenous feeding. They don't need to be transported in an ambulance. All those planes," she pointed to the ceiling through which the incessant sound of aircraft engines droned, "fly back empty. Why can't they take the children back instead?"

"Because they would need homes and caretakers to receive them," Emily countered. "They can't just be dumped at a military airfield."

"I know that too," Trude replied with a wan smile. "I've thought of that, and I talked to my husband about it. Jakob believes the SPD could organise something. The party has cells across the Western Zones, and the Red Cross, the Salvation Army and other charities also operate there. Together they can organise homes and help. We Germans can manage all of that, but only the Allies can fly the children out."

Emily took a deep breath. This was on a scale beyond anything she had dreamed of, but Trude was right. If there was any way to get the children out, it ought to be tried. "All right. I'll raise this with my husband. I'll do my best, but please understand that I can't make any promises."

"Don't You Want to Be a Movie Star?"
Frankfurt / Main
Wednesday, 29 September 1948
(Day 96)

J.B. took the letter from Patty out of his pocket and sniffed the textured, pink envelope. Did they sell them scented, he wondered, or did Patty use perfume to seal it? It did remind him of her — and always inspired the mail clerks to make raunchy comments as they handed them over. Well, you couldn't blame them. Patty's pink and scented letters were distinctive and suggestive of, well, the bedroom — or "boudoir", as she'd word it.

J.B. chose to take his letter to the base library rather than the officers' club, to avoid attempts to snatch it out of his hand or read over his shoulder. In the library, he sat down at one of the little tables for reading periodicals that could not be checked out. He switched on the desk lamp and slid his finger under the flap to open the envelope. As he took out the letter, the scent of the perfume became stronger. Then he unfolded the textured stationary and began to read:

Dearest, darling Jay,

You can't imagine what happened! I went to see "Red Shoes" at the Odeon with Betty and Val, and there on the <u>big screen </u>was this balding, blond USAF lieutenant who was introduced as "Gail Halvorsen."

"What a funny name!" Betty giggled. "Makes him sound like a girl."

Of course, I recognised the name as <u>your</u> pilot, but I couldn't imagine <u>why</u> he was in the news. Then he started talking about dropping candy attached to these cute little parachutes from his aircraft and I realised that was <u>your</u> aircraft too!

The clip wasn't very long, but when I got home, Mom said that Halvorsen had been on "Meet the People" too.

What I don't understand is why he is getting all the attention and credit when you did just as much as he did? Besides, you're a lot better looking! You'd look great in a newsreel and do a much better job talking about the candy drops! Why didn't they send you back to the States?

On the radio, they were asking people to donate handkerchiefs and scarves to be made into parachutes, and I heard one high school domestic science class wants to start making the parachutes as a class project. Other people have asked how they can donate candy and gum and stuff. But I'm sure that if you were the face of the candy man instead of pale, balding, little Halvorsen, you'd get twice as many donations! Not to mention we could get married while you were here in the States!

You really ought to talk to someone about letting you do the publicity stuff and having Halvorsen do the flying instead of the other way around!

I've got to run now. Tomorrow I'll put together a package with some old scarves you can use for parachutes and one very special scarf for you. (You'll know which one as soon as you see it!) It's to remind you of me.

Love and kisses,

Patty

PS. Dad finally got through to our congressman, and he thinks he might be able to help get you home early, so keep your fingers crossed!

J.B. sat looking at the letter for another minute and then folded it and replaced it in its perfumed envelope. Why didn't it make him happy? Because, he answered himself, all Patty cared about was his association with the latest "celebrity". She still didn't understand what the Airlift was about, and she couldn't have cared less about the kids they were helping. Unlike Kathleen.

He knew he shouldn't be thinking about Kathleen — certainly not with the tenderness and affection he did. If he thought of her at all, it ought to be strictly as Assistant Section Leader Hart. But that wasn't who she was to him. She was Kathleen. *His* Kathleen. If he closed his eyes he could hear her low, modulated voice. It no longer just said: "Don't worry. I'll get you down safely." It also said, "I'm thankful to you for dropping sweets to the children of Berlin. They have so very little else in their dreary lives."

Patty was like a bright, glittering butterfly, he thought with a twinge of melancholy. She was blonde and beautiful with a figure and wardrobe like a movie star. At college, the guys swarmed around her, falling over themselves to catch her attention. J.B. had been proud that she'd chosen him out of the large pack. Yet this letter made him wonder if his looks had been all that attracted her. Certainly, her primary interest now was how great he'd look in a newsreel rather than the work he was doing.

Patty had everything: good looks, education, money and class — but it was Kathleen who cared about the children and the Airlift and shot-up B-17s limping home from a mission...

J.B. put the letter back in his pocket, switched off the light and left the library.

Her Master's Voice
Berlin-Kladow
Saturday, 2 October 1948
(Day 99)

Why had she let her mother talk her into another meeting? Galyna stood in the doorway of the restaurant in Kladow and searched the interior of the room. It was too cold and damp to sit outside any more, but the interior of the restaurant was dingy, and the other customers looked shady. They were either men wearing hats set to shade their eyes or nervous youths with long hair. Her instincts told her to flee.

But her mother had said she had news of her father. Was that possible? After all these years? Still, he had never been publicly executed. He had just disappeared. Maybe he could return? But why now? When it was so convenient? Or had her mother simply never bothered to find out more about his whereabouts before this?

Galyna scanned the room a third time but still couldn't find her mother. She looked at her watch. She was twenty minutes late — intentionally. She had wanted her mother to wait for her and agonise over whether she was coming. That was childish, and her gesture of petty retribution had misfired because her mother wasn't waiting.

Well, maybe that was for the best. She turned and walked back out of the restaurant, heading towards the bus stop. A car oozed along on the road beside her. It took her several seconds to register that it kept pace with her rather than continuing at a normal speed. Irritated, she looked over at it, and her heart missed a beat. Although it was an American car, it had Soviet plates on it. She spun about and started back in the opposite direction. Behind her, a car door slammed shut. She started running but wasn't fast enough. A man's arm closed around her waist and pulled her backwards. A hand smothered her mouth and nose. She struggled; she couldn't breathe. The man was tall enough to lift her off her feet. She kicked and flailed with her arms, causing him to chuckle.

"You always were an impudent girl!" a voice said in her ear, just before another man took her feet.

She kicked more violently, disregarding modesty in her desperation to escape. She knew she was being kidnapped, but her resistance was waning with her consciousness as anoxia set in. In her last conscious moment, she was aware of being stuffed into a car. Then she blacked out.

When she came to, she was still in the back seat of a car. In the driver's seat sat a Russian soldier, who stared straight ahead. Beside her was a man in civilian clothes. He slouched in the far corner blowing smoke towards the ceiling of the car. When Galyna stirred, he looked over at her from half-closed, disdainful eyes. A chill ran down her spine. It was her stepfather.

She grabbed the handle of the door and yanked it as hard as she could, but the door was locked. Frantically, she tried to release the lock, but his voice stopped her. "Stop struggling. It's locked centrally. Besides we're in Potsdam. If you run away, you'll only run into the Red Army."

She looked out of the window. They were parked next to a small, red brick house beside a lake. The scene was idyllic, peaceful, and utterly surreal. "Our humble little home," her stepfather commented. "It once belonged to the royal gardener who tended the Alter Fritz's New Garden. Some Nazi must have lived in it. It is very tastefully decorated with antique furniture and lovely paintings. Your mother has made tea for you."

Galyna turned and stared at him. "What do you want from me?"

He shrugged, and with a flick of his fingers knocked the ash from his cigarette, letting it fall on the seat of the car. "A little gratitude wouldn't be out of place. I could have sent you to a school for delinquent children instead of packing you off to your grandmother in Finland."

Galyna knew that was true, but it didn't make her feel grateful, just frightened. Even though she didn't know exactly what her stepfather's connections were, she knew that he was very dangerous. She said nothing.

"Or do you regret going to the capitalist West? Do you long to return to the Socialist Motherland?"

"No. I'm a British citizen and a member of the British armed forces. I demand to be returned to my unit."

He laughed. "All in good time, Corporal. Smoke?" he offered her a cigarette from his box. She shook her head sharply. He laughed again, took another for himself and lit it from a lighter. He inhaled, blew the smoke towards the roof of the car, and then without looking at her, drawled, "No gratitude then. What about love for your father? Your mother tells me you appeared attached to him — God knows why."

"My father was a good man! A man *genuinely* devoted to the ideals of Marxism-Leninism. He wanted to help the common man! To eliminate poverty and injustice! He was the truest and best Communist I have ever met."

"He's still alive, you know," he turned to look at her as he spoke, his eyebrows lifted over half-closed eyes.

Galyna caught her breath and held it. Was he? Or was her stepfather merely trying to manipulate her?

"I admit, he's not doing very well," her stepfather continued in a pseudo-sympathetic tone. "The hard labour in bitter cold and penetrating damp — not to mention the inadequate and almost inedible food — have worn away at his health. I'm told he may have consumption. He coughs up a lot of blood. He won't last much longer. Maybe another year. Maybe less."

Galyna couldn't breathe. He was lying to her. He was making this up to torture her.

"You could help him, Galyna Nicolaevna."

"How can I possibly help him?" she gasped out, overwhelmed by her helplessness.

Her stepfather shrugged. "You work at Gatow for the capitalist pigs. You have access to their records. You hear what they say to one another.

You see what is working and not working, and who likes whom and who sleeps with whom, and other things."

Ice water flooded her veins. She felt as though her whole body was being frozen from the inside out.

"Start with little things. Innocuous things. Tell us what you see and hear and let us decide how important it is. You don't have to steal from locked file cases, break codes or seduce the Station Commander — although I gather that would be quite a pleasure." He snickered at his little joke.

God how she hated this man! Galyna gritted her teeth together.

"Come now, that's not so difficult, is it? You meet up with your mother every now and again and have a nice little chat over tea. You gossip with her about your colleagues and superiors. Anything important — like information about facilities, personnel changes, crashes, or problems — you jot down on a piece of paper you that slip inside a napkin and leave on the table. Simple."

"What if I say no?"

"I wouldn't do that if I were you."

"I know. That doesn't answer my question. What happens if I say no?"

He inhaled deeply on the cigarette and exhaled slowly and audibly. Then he turned and faced her squarely, although his eyelids remained lowered, turning his eyes into glistening slits of grey. "*Then*, when this ridiculous charade ends — as it must when winter comes — and we take control of West Berlin, you will have the pleasure of watching your father die because you will be *with* him in Siberia."

Galyna nodded. Inwardly ice cold, she answered. "Thank you for being honest. And If I cooperate?"

"Then we will see about improving the conditions under which your father serves his sentence. And, of course, once Berlin is ours you will be given new duties in the service of the USSR."

"It seems I have no choice," Galyna concluded.

"No, not really. Not if you have any sense — or a fragment of affection for your father."

Galyna nodded. "Very well then. Let's settle the details and I'll get to work."

Chapter Nineteen
Unpleasant Facts

In for a Penny
Berlin-Kladow
Sunday, 3 October 1948
(Day 100)

Sammy was mad with joy. He dashed around, his tongue and ears flapping and his long hair flying as he raced around in circles. It was his way of saying he was happy to see David again after weeks away. Over their eight years together, there had been periodic separations like this, when Sammy stayed with "Uncle" Robin and "Aunt" Emily. Yet Sammy always made David feel he was Sammy's "real" human. His demonstrative delight when they were reunited after separation had been balm for his heart from the start, and David believed Sammy was the first being who had ever loved him completely. Yet his hopes were growing that Charlotte might also come to love him with the same kind of devotion — even if she expressed it less exuberantly!

He glanced towards the terrace where Charlotte was greeting Kit, Kiwi and Emily, who had just arrived. David had asked his partners and Moran to join Charlotte and himself for an urgent "management meeting". Emily had routed Moby Dick's last return flight via Hamburg so she could pick up Kit and Kiwi after they had completed their last cargo delivery of the day. At the end of today's meeting, they would spend the night at the Priestman villa and return to Hamburg courtesy of Rafair in the morning. This way, they could all sit down together and discuss the situation with minimal disruption to operations.

David went down on one knee and opened his arms to give Sammy a last, vigorous hug. Then he stood and approached the others. Charlotte was animatedly telling Emily that their new scheduling procedure, whereby AAI kept one bunk vacant on every flight for last-minute emergencies, seemed to be working. Kit and Kiwi were laughing about something together. As he joined them, David kissed Emily on the cheek, shook hands with Kit, and clapped Kiwi on the back, "Time to go inside and get to work," he told them.

Together they funnelled through the French windows into the winter garden, and from there into the den, a windowless but cosy room with an open fireplace and comfortable seating for six people. Emily had asked Jasha to lay out a cold buffet, but Kiwi spotted a bucket with a bottle of champagne in it. "Are we celebrating something?" he asked at once.

"Yes, we are. Emergency Air Services was cashflow positive for the first time last month," David announced proudly. "All three aircraft are more than earning their keep, particularly the Halifax. That was only possible because we have a first-rate team, both in the air and on the ground. I hope to be able to pay bonuses to everyone at the end of the year. I think that's the best way to let people know how much they are appreciated, don't you?"

"Brilliant, mate!" Kiwi agreed, while Emily chimed in with "Good idea!"

"After the events of last month," David continued, "the political commitment of both the US and UK appears certain, although we'll have to watch carefully what the new American president does. Also, as we all know, winter is coming, and if we are unlucky, that might disrupt operations significantly. Still, I do not think we should assume the worst. On the contrary, I think we are on the cusp of something bigger, and I'd personally like to make a greater contribution to this historic operation."

Emily seconded him with "Absolutely!" and the others echoed her.

"But first," David grew serious, "we need to analyse our current operations and consider how we can improve."

"Do we get to drink the champagne before or after the serious stuff?" Kiwi wanted to know.

"Go ahead and open it," David agreed with a gesture to the New Zealander.

"And please, everyone, help yourself to the food as well," Emily urged.

"I want this to be a genuine exchange of ideas and opinions," David stressed. "I don't want to do all the talking. Sometimes I get sucked too deeply into the books and lose sight of the bigger picture. Why don't you kick off, Kiwi? What do you think we could or should be doing differently?"

"That's simple," Kiwi replied pointing the bottle at the door as he eased the cork out. With a gentle pop, the cork came free in his hand. He set it down on the table and started pouring the bubbly as he answered David's question. "What we need most is backup aircrew. We were all keen to fly again when we started, but after two months we're getting run down and weary. That's when accidents happen."

David nodded, "We've talked about that right from the start. I agree. The problem is none of us has had time to stop working long enough to do serious recruiting. It was sheer luck that Jan and Rick walked through the door. Do you think placing advertisements in newspapers or aviation journals would be a good idea?"

"Yes, we should do that," Emily agreed, "but after our meeting with the hospital staff on Monday, I can't help wondering whether a flight nurse, a company flight nurse, may not be more important. I've never been able to shake off the thought that maybe we wouldn't have lost the patient with a gunshot wound to his head if we'd had a nurse on board. And you know we've had countless delays because nurses haven't shown up and we've had to find substitutes."

"Not to mention nurses that panic or chunder all over everything and everybody!" Kiwi joined in, remembering some of their worst flights when he was still flying the ambulance.

David nodded, "Point taken. Didn't you say Mrs Howley had recommended someone, Emily?"

"Yes, a former US Army nurse who speaks some German."

"See if you can find out how to get in touch with her," he urged. He next turned to Moran, who had been silent so far. "Kit? What do you think our next priorities should be?"

"Back-up air- and ground-crew and a nurse are all important, but I'd like to put forward a different, more radical idea." Because Kit was based in Hamburg, David did not know him well, but so far the former Lancaster skipper had exceeded expectations. While other civilian contractors were gaining an unsavoury reputation for unreliability, Robin reported that the RAF viewed AFI as one of the positive exceptions. Both AFI crews were invariably punctual, sober, and flying more than regulations technically allowed. But Robin had remarked that Kit's flexibility and spirit of cooperation had drawn particular praise. David nodded for Kit to continue.

"I was chatting with some USAF crews in Fassberg a couple of days ago when we were taking on cargo there. They claim the warehouses in Tempelhof are overflowing with products manufactured in Berlin."

"That's true!" Charlotte spoke up, sitting straighter in her chair. The others turned to look at her, surprised. "I overheard Herr Liebherr complaining about it to Christian. He and Mayor Reuter are upset because the factories must earn revenue if they are to stay in business, and they can only do that if they can sell their products in the West. If they can't, then they'll have to close, which would put thousands of men out of work."

"All of whom are likely to be deeply dissatisfied and resentful as a result," Emily concluded grimly.

"But why aren't the Americans shipping the stuff out?" Kiwi asked the question David had been about to raise.

"Because, unlike us, Tunner has enough crews to keep his aircraft flying around the clock. He wants to maximise equipment utilisation and that means keeping ground time to an absolute minimum," Kit explained. "We, on the other hand, can't fly around the clock unless we hire twice as many crews as we have now. A separate issue is we don't get paid for flying empty — something the USAF doesn't have to worry about. My thought is it could solve both problems if we were to back-load our aircraft with return cargoes. We could earn revenue on both legs of the sortie, and the increased ground time at both ends would reduce some of the stress and exhaustion of our aircrew."

David liked Kit's thinking and started analysing the suggestion. "What do you think the turn-around times would be with back-loading?"

"I think we're looking at three hours minimum, but the crew has to sleep sometime, and after observing the congestion at the zonal airfields first thing in the morning when the other civilian contractors wake up and start work, I thought we might benefit from basing our fleet — or at least Albie — here in Berlin." "Albie" was the crew's name for the Halifax because they'd painted an albatross on her nose. Kit continued to explain his reasoning, "It could be loaded with a return cargo overnight while the crew is sleeping. We'd then fly outbound first thing in the morning when the other contractors are just getting out of bed — figuratively at least."

David nodded seriously. Moran was making sense.

"David," Emily spoke up earnestly. "If we're going to take return cargoes, then we ought to prioritise the children I told you about. Robin raised the issue with Bagshot and — as expected — he dismissed the entire notion of the RAF flying Germans out of Berlin."

"Why?"

"Oh," she waved at the air in irritation, "he had all sorts of objections. It would look as though the Germans were fleeing. It would foment jealousy and accusations of favouritism and cause unrest. He raised security concerns, too. The point is, the RAF isn't going to handle the children."

"But we've been through this before, Emily," David reminded her. "We don't have the capacity to carry passengers." They'd discussed this on the way back from the hospital.

"The Dak still has seats from its former life as a paratrooper transport," Kiwi pointed out.

"How many? Twelve? Fourteen?" David replied exasperatedly. After Emily had put the case to him, he'd given the proposal serious thought, but they simply didn't have the means to carry the number of children who needed to be flown out.

"Twenty-four," Kiwi informed him, but David still shook his head. It was drop in the bucket and the competition for those few seats might be cut-throat — and Charlotte would be caught in the middle

Emily took up her case again, "I understand that the children we can fly out represent only a fraction of what needs to be evacuated, but even taking only a handful would draw attention to the problem, provide a precedent and maybe change the minds of some people in the RAF command."

With surprising passion Charlotte also chimed in with, "Please, David. Just because we can't help *all* the children in need is no excuse not to help *some* of them."

David's heart agreed with the women, but his brain warned him that transporting these children would open a dangerous can of worms. If nothing else, it was entirely unclear who would pay for the children? The company was not yet breaking even. He mustn't lose track of the business side of things, or there would be no business — and it would benefit no one it they went bankrupt.

Kit spoke into his thoughts, "Why not do both? The Halifax could take back cargoes and the Dakota could take the children. If Albie is earning on four flights a day — two round-trips — that should more than compensate for the Dak doing two instead of three daily sorties."

"Are you sure your crew won't mind being based in Berlin?" David asked uncertainly, remembering the way Ron and Chips had refused to work in Berlin.

"Nigel and Terry have hinted a couple of times that they'd rather be at the Malcolm Club in Berlin with Gordon. Richard and Bruce don't seem to mind one way or another."

"And you?"

Kit took a deep breath. "I don't mind one way or another where I'm based. The strain of being separated from my wife and daughter is the same either in Hamburg or Berlin."

"If you come to Berlin, your wife and daughter are welcome to stay with us here!" Emily offered at once. "We have enough room upstairs for all three of you, but there's daycare on the station for your daughter or plenty of German girls offering services as nannies, if you wife would prefer to work."

Kit seemed to start, and he turned to give Emily a penetrating look before asking, "How did you guess? About my wife wanting to work, I mean?"

"We met at your first interview, don't you recall? I was impressed then by how enthusiastically she talked about teaching, particularly vocational teaching. Now, since the start of the Blockade, many teachers have left the British school and they are very short-staffed. If you wife is interested, I'm sure she could find work there."

Kit was overwhelmed. "That would be marvellous! And whatever happens, it is extremely generous of you to allow us to stay here! You're sure your husband won't mind?"

"I'm very sure. We've always had a policy about our house being open to colleagues we *liked*." She underlined her point with a smile.

David announced. "Well then, that's settled." Addressing himself to Emily he advised, "You'd better fetch Robin. We're going to need his approval to base Albie here in Berlin *and* his permission to take on return cargoes, especially children."

"Oh, thank you, David!" Charlotte burst out, a smile transforming her face.

David reached out and took her hand in his as he continued in a businesslike tone, "Children are going to be difficult passengers. They'll need all sorts of shepherding…" The problems still seemed daunting to him, but he knew this was the right move — both for the company and for his relationship with Charlotte.

What is to be Done?
Berlin-Tiergarten
Wednesday, 6 October 1948
(Day 103)

Galyna had hardly slept, and her concentration at work had been so bad that her colleagues had commented on it. She kept saying she wasn't feeling well, which elicited suggestions for her to report to the infirmary. Instead, she tried to reach Mila. She could see no danger in meeting her. The worst-case scenario was that Mila had betrayed her to Maxim Dimitrivitch, in which case she already knew what had transpired and would be pleased Galyna had agreed to cooperate. If she had not betrayed her, then maybe she could offer advice as to what to do.

Galyna put a call through to Mila cryptically suggesting a meeting at the bar opposite the Reichstag that evening. Mila replied with, "You must have the wrong number." Galyna had to wait until Wednesday before she got a call with the message: "The film at the Red Star Cinema starts at seven. See you there!"

She felt better just knowing she would see Mila soon. She told Boyd that Mila had requested a meeting with her, and he made the usual arrangements for the MPs to be alerted to a possible "event" and for a car to wait near the Lehrter Station. After coming off duty, she took the RAF bus to Spandau and changed out of uniform in the ladies' room before going aboard the first eastbound train. On the journey, she steeled herself to face the unsavoury clientele at the horrible bar, and on arrival barged in forcefully. This time when a party of men called for her to join them at their table, she answered with the German phrase she'd taught herself: *"Fahrt zur Hoelle Ihr Schweine!"* (Go to hell, you pigs!) The response was rude, but they turned their backs. She surveyed the room a second time. No, Mila. She checked her watch. She'd been so certain the U-Bahn would be running sporadically that she'd planned extra time and now she was almost an hour early. There was nothing to do but wait.

With her nerves on edge, she found a table for two near the entrance, sat down and ordered tea. A man sauntered over and started to pull out the other chair. "Don't!" Galyna barked at him. "I'm meeting someone!" He raised his eyebrows but withdrew.

The tea arrived but when she asked for sugar, the waiter laughed at her. "Where do you think you are? New York?" There was no point asking for milk.

All she could do was sit and wait and think — think about the same things she had been thinking about ever since her encounter with her stepfather. She had been too ashamed of what had happened to tell Fl/ Lt Boyd. He had warned her about this possibility, but she had thought she was so clever! She had been so sure she would not be recognised. She needed to find out who had betrayed her.

Mila was the obvious suspect — except she had never told Mila her real family name. On the other hand, Mila might have described her to the NKVD, who had put two-and-two together based on what she had said about her birthplace, her schooling, and her father's fate.

Yet Galyna didn't *want* to believe Mila had betrayed her. Mila was the best friend she'd ever had. Not to mention that Mila had said so many things that *she* could have been shot for!

Or had she said those things explicitly to win Galyna's trust? Had she been able to say those things precisely *because* she was in the NKVD and had from the very first day been ordered to draw Galyna into a relationship? It was Mila, after all, who had approached her, not the other way around. Maybe it hadn't been innocent curiosity after all. Maybe Mila had been set on her like a hunting dog.

The more Galyna thought about it, the more plausible this explanation appeared, and she started to picture what would happen when she confronted Mila. Maybe the Hero of the Soviet Union would joyously grab her hands (as she liked to do) and say something like: "At last, I can drop this pretence of opposing Comrade Stalin and the infallible Communist Party! Now we can work together for the greater glory of the Socialist Motherland! We will defeat the capitalists just as we defeated the fascists! We will crush them under our boots! Shall I teach you how to shoot? Imagine how much damage you could do with a machine gun in the control tower of Gatow! You could end the Airlift single-handed, and you'd become a Hero of the Soviet Union just like me!"

The door opened, snapping Galyna out of her daytime nightmare. Two Royal Military Policemen walked in and scanned the room with that suspicious and cynical look unique to military police the world over. They went from table to table demanding IDs. What the hell was going on? They came to her table and one barked at her: "ID!" She reached for her handbag and fumbled around inside. Meanwhile, the other policeman was speaking in threatening tones to one of the other customers. The latter offered excuses in a broken, heavily accented English. She handed her ID to the MP. Frowning, he looked from her to the photo and back as if comparing faces. Then he winked before returning it to her with apparent disinterest and the MPs tromped back out onto the street. With a rush of relief, she registered that Boyd must have told them to look after her.

Ten minutes later, Mila arrived. Her hair was windblown and the cold had turned her face as red as the cheeks on a Matrushka doll. She waved cheerfully at Galyna the moment she saw her and squeezed her way between the tables to give her a hug. She called for tea before she sat down and took Galyna's hands to ask earnestly, "What is it? Has something happened?"

Galyna nodded but waited for the tea to be brought before lowering her voice. Then she described in chronological order and as clinically as possible everything that had happened the previous Saturday.

Mila listened intently. She kept her eyes fixed on Galyna's face and her attention never wavered. When Galyna finished, she fell silent and waited for the outburst of joy and congratulations she had anticipated. There was dead silence instead. Eventually, Mila asked warily, "Colonel Maxim Dimitrivitch Ratanov is your stepfather?"

"Yes."

Mila hesitated again before asking, "You know he is very high up in the NKVD?"

That didn't surprise Galyna. She'd guessed that long ago — when he was able to get her a passport out of Russia to Finland. She'd hoped Mila could be more specific, but if she knew any more she chose not to share it. Galyna tried to explain, "I have hated him all my life, Mila — ever since he took my father's place in our house and my mother's bed. No matter who he is officially, to me he is the man who destroyed my father and took him away from me."

Mila nodded slowly without breaking eye contact. They were probing and judging one another, and with each passing second Galyna felt hope returning. She didn't know how her stepfather had found her, but she was increasingly confident it had not been through Mila.

At last, Mila spoke again. "I speak to you as a friend, Galyna. I am trusting you not to betray me."

Galyna shook her head slowly and solemnly. "Would I be here if I did not trust you?"

Mila shrugged ambiguously and again considered her intently. Then she seemed to make a decision and announced, "Listen, Galyna. He is probably lying to you about your father, and even if he is not, he will not keep his word about improving his conditions. Nothing you do will help your father. Nothing. You must understand that. They lie whenever it is convenient. They think nothing of it. If you help them, so much the better, but they will not reward you for it. They will always want more. Today it is just information. Tomorrow they may want you to sabotage things — first little things, then bigger things. In the long run, they want to shut Gatow down because that would humiliate Britain — and it would end the Airlift. You must see that?"

"I understand that they would like to disrupt the Airlift, but I'm just a lowly translator. They can't seriously think I could close the airfield!"

"Maybe not on your own and not straight away, but for now it is enough that you agreed to cooperate. The promise to ease the conditions of your father's imprisonment was pure bait. You took it. Their next step will be to reel you in. That is, to make it more and more painful for you *not* to do what they demand."

"But what else could I do?" Galyna asked back, feeling the snare closing around her already.

"You had no choice," Mila agreed fatalistically. "You had to agree because you were in his hands. But you don't have to *comply*. Walk out of that door, Galyna Nicolaevna, go back to Gatow," Mila advised. Squaring her shoulders and speaking more forcefully still, she commanded: "Take the first aircraft out of Gatow and fly back to freedom." Then she paused, and her voice faded away until it was almost inaudible as she added, in a low, wistful and infinitely sad undertone, "You are lucky to have such a choice."

Reinforcements
RAF Gatow
Thursday, 7 October 1948
(Day 104)

The sound of the four Hercules engines was deafening and the Halifax looked huge from Emily's standpoint on the apron before the EAS hangar. It oozed its way along the taxiway and then turned to lumber ominously towards her like a malevolently growling monster crawling towards its prey. The eerie hostility of the great machine was magnified by the darkness of the night beyond the floodlights and the bright white paint of the aircraft itself. Air Freight International used the same white and red livery adopted for AAI, but the two freighters bore a broad band of red that circled the fuselage just abaft the cockpit. On this red ribbon, "AFI" stood out in large white lettering. In addition, directly underneath the cockpit window an albatross with bright, beady eyes and outstretched wings had been painted on the Halifax, which was why her crew called her "Albie". This was the first time "Albie" would overnight in Berlin, and tomorrow it would carry AFI's first return cargo composed of goods produced in Berlin.

Beside her on the tarmac, Gordon MacDonald sat in his wheelchair with the three German ground crew standing behind him. David and Charlotte had also wanted to witness the opening of this new phase of operations, but they lived in the city centre and there was no public transport at this time of night. Rick and Jan, on the other hand, could have been here but had opted to retire to the Malcolm Club. Emily understood they were tired.

"Moby Dick" had made three flights today, twice to Hannover and once to Munich. Yet she was disappointed too.

Jan was a first-rate pilot, but she had turned down Emily's invitation to stay at the house, and neither she nor Rick showed any interest in socialising with their colleagues. Emily supposed they were a self-sufficient team with many shared memories, inside jokes and a strong bond, but their insular attitude made them outsiders in what was otherwise a close-knit organisation. At the same time, their bond made Emly feel like the outsider on their flights together.

With what sounded like a sigh of relief, Albie's four engines started to wind down. The howling that had blotted out all other sounds dropped to a low whimper and then died away. The ground crew ran forward to put chocks around the wheels and a lorry hauling two empty flatbeds bounced onto the apron and pulled to a halt beside the tail. A moment later the door in the fuselage was flung open, and Richard Scott-Ross jumped down onto the flatbed and then reached back inside to pull out the internal ladder. Bruce joined him in setting up and testing the ladder, before Kit's wife emerged in the doorway.

Georgina was wearing practical, low-heeled shoes and a full skirt that fell to mid-calf, topped by a simple white blouse under a blue cardigan sweater. She navigated the metal steps carefully but not timidly and then looked around herself. When she spotted Gordon her face broke into a radiant smile, and she hastened over to throw her arms around him. He gripped her firmly in his arms for a moment and then let her go. Georgina drew back and exclaimed, "Gordon! You look marvellous!"

"Work is good for me, lassie, and I haven't forgotten whom I have to thank for that." He glanced significantly towards Kit, who had disembarked last. Gordon didn't linger on the topic, however, but hurried to introduce the German ground crew. Each man stepped forward when he called their names and, one after another, bobbed their heads and drew their heels together respectfully. The introductions to the ground crew completed, Georgina turned towards Emily and held out her hand as she crossed the distance between them. "It's marvellous to see you again, Mrs Priestman, and I can't thank you enough for your generosity and hospitality!"

Emily laughed, and with a glance at Kit, who had come to stand behind his wife, replied. "The look on your husband's face is more than enough thanks. But where's your little girl? I thought you were bringing your daughter with you?"

"My mother wouldn't hear of it. She insisted it was bad enough that Kit and I were putting ourselves at the 'tender mercies of Stalin'. She said she wouldn't allow *her* granddaughter into the bear's lair. She also told me I would be much more useful and productive if I didn't have a seven-month-old infant in tow. The truth is she couldn't stand to be separated. She fears that when Kit gets a permanent job we'll take Donna to the far ends of the earth and she won't see her again until she is grown up. So, I'm here on my own. Kit thought I might be able to find a teaching job, which I'd love. However, I hope you know that I'll do whatever kind of work you — or should I say your husband?" she glanced over at Kit a little uncertainly before finishing, "— find appropriate."

Emily had liked Georgina the first time they met at the Savoy, but she was even more impressed by her now. It was just four days since the decision to relocate Albie had been made, and here she was already. Furthermore, although Emily had hinted at a possible teaching job, Georgina made it clear she wasn't here for career advancement but to be helpful. An energetic young woman prepared to do whatever was useful was just what they needed.

Chapter Twenty
Shifting Sands

Unexpected Rewards
Gatow / Fuhlsbuettel
Friday, 8 October 1948
(Day 105)

Kids! Kiwi shook his head in amused despair.

The first twenty-two children to be flown out of Berlin had been scrupulously selected by Trude Liebherr. Trude knew this was a test and that a disaster would end all hope of further evacuations. Determined to make this first flight a spectacular success, she not chosen the children in greatest need, but rather those whose stamina and resilience seemed greatest. After all, they had to cope not only with the excitement of the trip but also separation from their familiar environment.

But kids, or crowds of kids, just weren't like other passengers, and these were no exception. They were understandably excited, which meant their voices were pitched at least an octave above normal. They couldn't sit still for more than a couple of seconds — and half the seatbelts on the fold-down seats designed for paratroopers had long since been lost. Even at take-off, Kiwi felt weight shifting in the tail and his navigator had to shout back into the cabin for the kids to sit down. They managed to stay still for maybe two minutes, but soon they were moving around again. At the controls of the Dakota, Kiwi could feel the aircraft roll to one side and then the other as they rushed in a pack from one side to the other to look out opposite windows. The groaning of the Wasp engines obliterated any recognizable words, yet the sound of their excited voices was ceaseless, reminding Kiwi of a flock of alarmed geese.

Then the airsickness started. Soon the smell of vomit was wafting into the cockpit along with wails and sobs. Kiwi shook his head and closed his eyes for a second, relieved that the flight to Hamburg lasted only fifty-five minutes. Stoically, he ordered his navigator to shut the cabin door, and his wireless operator opened the side window of the cockpit to clear out the stink.

On approach, Kiwi called the tower to report. "AFI 2 northbound with twenty-two children aboard. Repeat, twenty-two children and two adult caretakers. We are being met by a delegation of the Hamburg city council."

"Roger AFI 2. Your party is awaiting you. Turn onto..." and so on.

They were met by more than "their party". The camera flashes overwhelmed the floodlights as the AFI Dakota decorously turned onto the designated hardstanding. A delegation of civilians, including an unusual number of women in hats and gloves, was positioned near the edge of the concrete, accompanied by men in homburgs, overcoats, and scarves. The distinctly 'distinguished' appearance of the crowd suggested Hamburg society was recovering.

Fortunately, the international press was not well-represented. Kiwi had been careful to consult with David and Emily in advance about what he was to say to questions from the media. He'd jotted down some notes. Things like: 'AFI is responding to a request from the Berlin City Government.' 'This first flight is a test to see if such evacuations are viable.' 'So far (they agreed in advance) things have gone smoothly.' (Any issues, David stressed, would be discussed internally and not before the press!) Any questions about the children, their condition and their placement in homes were to be fielded by Frau Liebherr, who had accompanied them.

Taking a deep breath, Kiwi made his way down the sloping deck of the Dakota, careful to avoid the wet and slippery remnants of some child's dinner. He released the door from the inside and swung it outward. Because they had landed at the civilian side of the airport they were met by a rolling stair, and Kiwi could step out, wave briefly, and then gesture for Frau Liebherr to start disembarking the children. As she emerged leading one child by each hand, a light storm of cameras captured the moment. Kiwi stood modestly in the background. Ernst Reuter's press secretary was the other adult woman on the flight, and she disembarked last after herding the last of children in front of her.

The children were efficiently taken in hand by the welcoming committee, while the press crowded around the two women escorts, asking questions in German. Kiwi slipped past the crowd of reporters and went to talk to the ground crew. He told Ron to find some local cleaners to get the interior mopped up and then hung around under the nose of the Dakota until the excitement died down. Kiwi's German was useless, so he hadn't a clue what questions were being asked, but David had claimed the SPD was using this evacuation to boost their political popularity in both Berlin and Hamburg. Emergency Air Services, however, was billing the Americans as if these children were ambulance patients, which Kiwi thought was a little dodgy. For that reason alone, David had stressed he was not keen on additional publicity at this time.

When the children were driven away and the press dispersed, Kiwi sighed with relief and announced to his crew, "Time for a pint or two, mates!" He, his navigator, and signaller headed for the *Golden Lion* as usual, but so many of the Airlift fliers had discovered "their" pub that it was packed. It looked as if not a single table were free.

"Over there!" his signaller pointed. "Some chaps are leaving."

They pushed their way through the crowd and had hardly sat down before two hands slid down Kiwi's shoulders and onto his chest. A soft cheek touched his own. "Chuck, darling! I've been waiting for you for hours. Where have you been?"

"Flying as usual, Virginia. What else?" He tried to sound relaxed, but her touch was far too exciting. Damn her! She must know how she aroused him, and as the Airlift dragged on and with David far away, he was finding it increasingly difficult to resist temptation.

"You know something, Chuck? I think you've been avoiding me." She had a look in her eye that made him hot.

"No, nothing of the sort. Just busy."

"Well, you're not flying any more tonight, are you?"

"No. I'm here for the night."

"I'm so glad. Do you have an early start tomorrow?"

"No, not really. Start-engines tomorrow is a little later than usual, 7:40."

"Wonderful!" she exclaimed and sank into the chair beside him. His crewmates laughed. One sent him a wink, and then they moved on to join a table with RAF aircrew they'd known during the war.

"Chuck, darling, do you realise we've known each other for more than six months and you haven't yet taken me up on my suggestion for a romantic dinner for two? The restaurant I told you about in the vaulted wine cellar is just around the corner. Why don't we go there?"

Why not, indeed? Because he'd been burned once already! "Only if everything I say to you from now until tomorrow noon is strictly off the record."

Virginia sat up and held her hand up as if taking an oath. "I swear that I am off duty, and I shall neither ask journalistic questions nor report on any matter we discuss, no matter how interesting, in my newspaper. Whatever we do and say tonight will be our secret!" Then, relaxing her pose, she asked with a delightful and intimate giggle, "Is that a deal, Chuck darling?"

Kiwi thought about it again, but he couldn't find any downside. "A deal." He grabbed his cap, and they weaved their way back out of the crowd, collecting Virginia's coat as they went.

Her restaurant "just around the corner" proved to be considerably farther away, but by the time they arrived, it didn't matter. Kiwi was already in Virginia's thrall. She chatted vivaciously, interspersing her anecdotes and witty stories with meaningful smiles. She made him feel handsome, virile and desirable for the first time since his marriage had gone on the rocks.

At the restaurant they ordered cocktails and then a shrimp salad followed by roast beef. "I still can't get over how much food there is here in Hamburg and how full the shops are since they introduced the D-Mark," Kiwi remarked. The contrast with Berlin seemed to be growing exponentially.

"There are more things on offer here than in some parts of England," Virginia confirmed. "It would be worth investigating — if I had time. Is it true you flew children out of Berlin today?"

"You said no journalistic questions!" Kiwi bristled.

"But this isn't journalistic, darling, and I won't print your answer," she countered, catching his hand and rubbing her thumb in his palm soothingly. "I'm genuinely interested. You may see me as a callous career woman, but underneath my façade is a woman who longs to love and be loved and have children. I heard these children were orphans and it made me think...." Her voice faded away.

Kiwi hesitated. He was still scalded by the way she'd brushed him off in April. Yet there was no denying the attraction he felt for her. He took the chance and slipped his arm around her shoulders. She turned into him and snuggled against his chest. "Thank you," she whispered, "I needed that."

He bent his head and risked a kiss. She met his lips with an impassioned response. They broke off when the waiter arrived with their drinks. Virginia pulled back a little, but then she put her hand on his knee under the table and giggled as they toasted one another.

By the time they left the restaurant, Kiwi was in a near panic at the thought of taking her to his spartan quarters in the guest house with its narrow single bed. He wasn't even sure he'd be able to get her past the landlord, who lived on the ground floor and kept track of who came in and went out with the meticulousness of a Nazi block warden. Should he suggest a hotel?

"You'll see me to my hotel, won't you, darling?" Virginia purred in his ear.

"Of course. Where are you staying?"

"The Atlantic. Where else?"

"We'd better get a taxi." That was an option in Hamburg. Petrol didn't have to be flown in.

As they entered the elegant lobby, Virginia whispered to Kiwi. "Wait a couple of minutes, then take the lift up to the fourth floor as if you have your key with you already. Go to room 412. I'll meet you there."

Was this really happening? Kiwi nodded to Virginia and followed instructions.

A short while later, up on the fourth floor, she pulled him inside and into her arms. They fell against the door, pushing it shut, and started to undress in a frantic rush.

"Why did it take us so long to get here?" Virginia asked as they left the last of their underwear behind them and fell into the broad, soft, hotel bed.

Russian Roulette
RAF Gatow
Monday, 11 October 1948
(Day 108)

Galyna fussed with her hair net, rearranging it three times before she was satisfied. She wetted her hands before pulling on her stockings so she could get the seam centred and straight. She brushed her teeth and put on extra deodorant. Her shoes, belt buckle and buttons had been polished rigorously the night before. Yet when she caught a glimpse of herself in the mirror she still looked like a short, dumpy, boring WAAF corporal rather than an alluring Mata Hari.

Seventeen minutes later she knocked on Fl/Lt Boyd's office door and received his invitation to enter. She saluted smartly and burst out, "Sir! I have something we must talk about." Too late, she realised she might be barging in on some important intelligence work and was relieved when he closed the folder he had been reading, set it aside and invited her to take a seat.

"How can I help you, Borisenko?"

"I've been discovered, sir."

"What?" He gasped, half rising from his chair in alarm.

"My stepfather — whom I long suspected of being well-connected to powerful people in the Party — is apparently a colonel in the NKVD. Somehow he found out that I was here and used my mother as a lure. She phoned and begged to see me—"

"Wait! Stop! Your mother rang you? From where?"

"Potsdam, and she asked me to meet her in Kladow."

"Why didn't you tell me?"

"Because I thought you wouldn't let me go," Galyna admitted in a shamed voice.

"Yes! You're quite right! But you did go, it seems. And what happened next?"

'Well, the first time, we just talked. She tried to give me presents, but I refused and left. But then she talked me into a second meeting. Only this time she wasn't waiting for me; my stepfather was, and he kidnapped me in his car."

"*Kidnapped* you?" Boyd nearly jumped out of his chair a second time. Then he asked in disbelief, "And he let you go again? I don't understand."

"He said my father was still alive but was very ill, and if I cooperated with him, they would ease his conditions."

"I see," it was a sober statement that could have meant almost anything. Boyd followed it by concluding, "And you agreed to cooperate."

"I didn't have any choice, sir, but I never had any intention of complying. Not even for a second."

"When did this happen?"

"Nine days ago, sir."

"*Nine days*? Why didn't you come to me earlier?"

Galyna looked down. "I was ashamed. You'd warned me this might happen, and I wanted to talk to Mila first—"

"Yes, you reported to me about that."

"But I didn't tell you the truth. You see, I told her about my stepfather."

Boyd raised his eyebrows eloquently.

"I had to know if she had been the one to betray me!" Galyna explained passionately. "Now that I've seen her, I'm sure she had nothing to do with it. She told me to leave Berlin as fast as possible. She warned me that nothing I did would help my father."

"And that's why you're here? To request a transfer out?"

Galyna had difficulty swallowing, but she took a breath and faced the intelligence officer with great determination. "No, sir. That's why it has taken me so long to come to you. I kept procrastinating and finding excuses not to talk to you until I accepted that I couldn't ask for a transfer because I didn't want one."

"Corporal Borisenko!" Boyd exclaimed in apparent exasperation. "After agreeing to aid the NKVD, you can't just change your mind! From their point of view, it is betrayal, which puts you in acute danger. If they've kidnapped you once, they can do it again, only next time you won't be released. You'll be shot! Possibly tortured first! I simply cannot risk that. I don't want it on my conscience — not to mention the fact that you might involuntarily betray information to the Soviets in the process! It is unthinkable. You must prepare to fly out immediately."

"Please hear me out, sir! I don't want to escape — to run away. I want to be an agent, a real agent. I think the term is double agent, isn't it? I can

431

pretend to work for the Soviets but instead learn things that might be of interest MI6?"

"That's absurdly dangerous!" Boyd gasped. "The Russians have threatened to shoot our pilots, who they *know* aren't spies. You, on the other hand, would not only be a spy but a traitor as well! There's absolutely no justification for putting yourself at such risk! What could you possibly learn that would be worth your life?"

Galyna had asked herself that question at least a hundred times in the last week and she invariably came up with the same answer. "I don't know. I didn't expect to hear Russian officers talking about blockading Berlin, either. I only know that I won't have a chance to learn *anything* unless I remain in Berlin and maintain my Russian contacts."

Boyd gazed at her with an expression of disbelief and shook his head.

"All I have been asked to do is to meet my mother periodically and report the things I've seen." Galyna pleaded her case. "I was told explicitly not to worry whether it was important or not. Maxim Dimitrivitch assured—"

"Maxim Dimitrivitch? NKVD Colonel Maxim Dimitrivitch *Ratanov*?" Boyd asked for confirmation, unable to believe his ears.

"He's my stepfather," Galyna explained, unsettled by the look Boyd was giving her.

Boyd shook his head but did not explain further. Instead, he urged, "Go on."

"He told me the NKVD would assess my reports. All I had to do, he said, was gossip with my mother once a fortnight."

"Surely you understand that that is what they say *now*. The next thing you know, you'll be drawing sketches of the operations room, or jotting down aircraft numbers, or stealing documents, or — heaven knows! — putting poison in the CO's tea!" Boyd was visibly upset.

"But if I tell you everything they want of me, then you'll know what they want to know — or at least what interests them most. We can send false documents and information and flush any poison down the toilet," she pleaded. She was sure that if she hadn't been short and plump but svelte and attractive he would have been more ready to see her as a secret agent — like one of the SOE heroines she admired so intently.

"Borisenko, you haven't had any training in this business."

"Well, I can't exactly tell my stepfather that I'd be happy to help but not until I've finished my training with MI6," she pointed out.

"I don't like this," Boyd admitted, shaking his head and rapping his pen nervously on his desktop.

"I'm supposed to meet my mother again this coming Sunday. What is the harm in letting me go and see how things turn out?"

Boyd shook his head again to indicate he was still very unhappy, but after a few more tense minutes he announced, "I'll pass your request on to my superiors in London and discuss it with the WingCo. You'll have an answer by Saturday, but in the meantime, if you reconsider, just let me know."

Pride flooded through Galyna's veins as she jumped to her feet and delivered the best salute of her life.

Together we are Invincible
USAF Base Tempelhof, Berlin
Friday, 15 October 1948
(Day 112)

The brass and the brass bands were out in force. The day before, Major General William Tunner had succeeded in getting himself named commander of the newly created Combined Airlift Task Force — or CALTF. To mark the event, a small ceremony had been organised at Tempelhof. The Military Governors of the United States, Britain and France were there, as were the Berlin city commandants of the same nations. The Mayor of Berlin, with a delegation from the City Government, was likewise present on the stage, while the audience consisted of troops from the three occupiers and press from around the world. The RAF was represented by Group Captain Bagshot, now Tunner's "deputy", Air Commodore Waite and Wing Commander Priestman.

After the bands played the national anthems of the occupiers and the guards of honour did some fancy marching, Clay and Robertson spoke briefly, followed by Mayor Reuter. It was all routine stuff, and Priestman presumed it was primarily for the press. Following the official part of the program, a modest lunch was offered at the Officers' Mess at Tempelhof. The dignitaries were expertly herded in the right direction by the aides of the Base Commander and then freed to mingle at will.

Bagshot was still smouldering under the humiliation of being subordinated to the American, so Robin kept his distance and gravitated towards Graham Russel, whom he had not seen since his re-assignment to the construction of the new airfield. "How are things going at Tegel?" he asked for starters.

Curiously, Graham looked over both shoulders to see who was within hearing before lowering his voice to confide, "You aren't going to believe this, Robin, but General Herbert denied my request to marry."

"What? The bastard!" Robin exclaimed and then, like Graham, checked that Herbert was out of hearing before asking, "What could he possibly object to?"

"He thinks it's a classic case of an ugly old fool being seduced by a scheming Continental beauty only interested in acquiring a British passport."

"Jasha?" Robin answered eloquently, before adding, "At your age and rank, Graham, you don't need his permission. Marry her anyway!"

"I'm glad you feel that way, Robin, because that's exactly what I intend to do. Jasha's arranging a priest and when we have a date we'll let you know so you and Emily can be our witnesses."

"Excellent!"

"Good news?" Frank Howley asked coming up from behind. The American city commandant and Robin were friends, but their opportunities to talk had been greatly curtailed by the demands of the Airlift.

Graham, however, did not know the American, and with an informal salute excused himself. Frank addressed himself to Robin, "I gather congratulations are in order."

"Whatever for?" Robin replied, surprised, trying to remember some special landmark of the last few days. Everything was starting to blur together — or rather had been for weeks.

"For managing the busiest military airport in the world," Frank answered with a chuckle.

"Gatow?" Robin hadn't been keeping track.

"That's what I was told — and that you're fast on your way to overtaking the civilian hubs of New York, London, and Los Angeles as well."

"What about Tempelhof?" Robin looked out the tall windows towards the aircraft landing, taxiing, unloading, and taking off.

"Since Tunner threw all the US C-47s off the Airlift, the air movements are down here. The daily sorties to Gatow exceed Tempelhof's by a wide margin."

"Oh, well, the airport at Tegel is on track to open in no more than a month or two. After that the traffic will be distributed more evenly."

"Yeah, but the number of aircraft assigned is still increasing. General Clay is just back from Washington where he told President Truman that he wanted 224 C-54s. That's 172 *more* than the 52 he already has. And I heard you Brits would be adding tanker aircraft to your fleet soon?"

"We have 31 tankers on order, but so far only a handful of them have started operations. The conversion of Lancasters into tankers has proved more complicated and time-consuming than anticipated."

"Nevertheless, I'd say all three airports are going to be at capacity."

"Yes, and I suppose Tunner has lots of ideas about how to improve efficiency even more, now that he's in command."

"Ah, but he isn't," Frank remarked grimly.

That took Robin by surprise. "What do you mean? The British lion has bowed its head and deferred to your chap."

"But not the USAF. Tunner's still subordinate to the European theatre commander, and as of today that is a certain Lt. General Cannon, who — according to my usually reliable sources — thinks Tunner is a pain-in-the-butt nobody. He has no intention of working more than a forty-hour week, certainly not on weekends! And he has no intention of allowing Tunner to communicate with General Clay directly, much less talk to anyone in the Pentagon without first clearing it with him. Cannon believes the whole Airlift is a 'humanitarian effort' beneath the dignity of the USAF, and he would rather not be bothered with it at all. Which would be fine, if he'd let Tunner get on with the job, but from what I've heard, he won't."

"That's mad."

Frank held up his hands in a sign of surrender. "You didn't hear it from me."

The conversation could go no farther because Tunner himself materialised out of the crowd as if they had conjured him up. "Wing

Commander Priestman," Tunner opened the conversation, "Would you mind telling me if there is any truth to the rumours that your wife's company uses ex-Luftwaffe ground crew?"

"Yes, that's true, albeit under the supervision of an ex-RAF, eagle-eyed Scot."

"How has that worked out? Any problems? Sabotage? Tensions?"

"None whatsoever. Their work has been exemplary. Why?"

"Because General Clay is coming this way and I have a request to make of him." Even as he finished speaking, Clay joined the little circle. He nodded and murmured, "Gentlemen," before focusing on Tunner. "It's good to have a chance to chat with you, Tunner. Our schedules seem to keep us going in different directions." He made it sound as if he didn't know that the USAFE commander wanted to keep them apart, something belied by him next asking Tunner bluntly, "Any problems?"

"Yes, sir," Tunner jumped in without preliminaries or hesitation. "As I was just explaining to these gentlemen, until those extra C-54s — that you generously requested from Washington— arrive, the only way we can come close to our targets is to keep the aircraft we have flying around the clock. Maximum utilisation of equipment, however, requires regular maintenance and for that, I need a lot more trained mechanics than I have here in theatre. However, I think I might have a solution — if you'll just give me the go-ahead."

Clay considered him with an expression wavering between disapproval and amusement. Then he glanced across the room in the direction of Cannon, who was standing with champagne in hand and his back to them as he spoke with the French military governor. With a slightly cynical smile, Clay prompted, "All right, Tunner. Shoot. How do you think I can help?"

"Well, sir," Tunner tossed Priestman the slightest of nods, before forging ahead with, "While I've got only a handful of completely overworked ground crews here in Germany, there's a whole army of unemployed aircraft mechanics right under our noses — if I had your permission to disregard the regulations against hiring Germans for technical jobs."

"Um hum," Clay responded ambiguously. There was a tense pause before he expanded that to, "Go ahead and do it. And you can tell General Cannon I said so."

Tunner grinned and saluted. "Thank you, sir!"

As he exchanged a glance with Priestman, Howley raised his eyebrows. The US policy against employing Germans in anything other than menial jobs had been on the books since the start of the occupation. Howley himself had frequently complained about it. To hear Clay set it aside in such a crucial context was startling. Priestman supposed that it was an indication of how strongly Clay wanted to see the Airlift succeed.

Meanwhile, rather than continuing his rounds, Clay turned to Priestman to remark, "I ran into your wife in Frankfurt the other day. I was pleased to see she had hired a former WASP."

"Yes, and her husband, a former bomb aimer turned flight engineer."

"I hope they are pulling their weight?"

"Very much so."

"Glad to hear it." Clay nodded again and started to turn away to continue mingling with the other guests.

However, Jakob Liebherr had silently come up beside Priestman while he and Clay were talking. He did not want Clay to slip away and raised his voice, "General, I'm Jakob Liebherr from the Berlin City Council. We met at the VE celebrations. If I might have just a moment of your time?"

Clay turned back with the patient irritation of a man used to having people vying for his attention.

"The City Council is extremely grateful that you approved the operation of the Air Ambulance company and have agreed to pay for the medical evacuations."

Clay nodded graciously and would have turned away, if Liebherr hadn't continued speaking. "However, the demand far exceeds the capacity of one small, civilian company to meet. There are literally thousands of children in Berlin who are undernourished and suffering from a variety of illnesses. While their condition might not be acute now, their health will only deteriorate as the blockade drags on — not to mention if the temperatures drop. This past week, Air Freight International, the sister company of Air Ambulance International, experimented with flying twenty-two children out of Berlin in the back of their Dakota. The SPD organised foster homes for them in Hamburg and my colleagues in the West are confident that many more families all across Bizonia would be willing to take children in if we could only fly them out. Surely this shouldn't be left in the hands of a small civilian company. Surely it is something the United States Air Force should handle?"

"That's not for me to say," Clay answered with a glance at Tunner. The latter shook his head and explained, "We can't do it, sir. Three-quarters of our aircraft are hauling coal. You can't put passengers, particularly not sick people, in a filthy freighter. Patients require clean aircraft — not ones full of coal dust that could explode at any moment. Not to mention that it would slow our turn-around times to a crawl."

"Under those conditions, I'm surprised *you* authorised it, Wing Commander," Clay responded with a faint smile in Priestman's direction. The latter had the impression that Clay's unstated question was a gentlemanly rebuke to Tunner for being too single-minded.

Not wanting to rile his new indirect superior, however, Robin opted for a joke. "I really didn't have much choice, General. My wife made it quite clear that I either approve the flight for those children, or my marriage would be in the cart."

The other men burst out laughing and the latent tension was instantly dissipated. Clay, his eyes still twinkling, nodded to Robin and remarked. "I'd be afraid to cross Mrs Priestman too. Send her my compliments, Wing Commander. Good day, gentlemen."

General Tunner and Colonel Howley also drifted away, leaving Jakob Liebherr alone with Priestman. "I don't mean to sound like an alarmist, Wing Commander, but winter is inexorably approaching. When the bad weather comes, people in Berlin are going to start freezing. We must try to evacuate as many children as possible. One civilian Dakota is not enough. If the USAF won't help, perhaps the the RAF could step in?"

"What won't the USAF do?" Air Commodore Waite asked, overhearing Liebherr's remark and stopping.

"They refuse to evacuate sick children. Their policy is not entirely unreasonable," Priestman was quick to point out. "Tunner's right that you can't put sick children in what is effectively an empty coal bin. And don't forget that flour dust is also combustible. In fact, you can't load passengers safely on *any* of the larger freighters because they lack seats and seatbelts. When the children move about, they disrupt the aerodynamics of the plane. The large freighters also lack toilets, heating, and cabin pressurisation. Our Dakotas, which fly lower and most of which still have seats, are better suited for the task. The trouble is, I can't see Group Captain Bagshot approving the evacuation of children in RAF aircraft because — as Tunner keeps pointing out 'til he's blue in the face — it would slow down our turnaround times dramatically."

"Hm," Waite appeared to be thinking, and Priestman watched him alertly, waiting to see whether he would find a creative solution as he so often did. "Coastal Command's Sunderlands don't fly from airfields, so they aren't under Bagshot's command, are they?"

"No!" Priestman exclaimed, grasping the opportunity at once. "And the Sunderlands have miserable turnaround times already. How many passengers do you think they might take."

"Oh, thirty or so. I'll ring Coastal Command first thing in the morning," Waite promised with a smile, "and get back to you straight away with their answer."

"That would be much appreciated!" Priestman agreed enthusiastically, and Liebherr added his thanks.

"My pleasure," Waite assured them and continued to circulate.

Liebherr turned earnestly to Priestman, "I can't thank you enough, Wing Commander, and not just for the evacuation of the children. Flying manufactured goods produced in Berlin's factories to the West is almost as important. I'm a little concerned, however, that the scale of the problem hasn't been fully appreciated. One civilian company with a couple flights a day cannot keep up with production let alone clear the backlog. Wouldn't it be possible for the RAF could help with the back cargoes?"

Priestman drew a breath to explain all the problems he faced in that regard, but changed his mind and said simply, "I'll do my best, Herr Liebherr."

Just as unexpectedly as the others had gathered around him minutes earlier, Priestman now found himself alone in the crowd. Noticing his glass was empty, he was about to get a refill when a voice spoke from behind him. It was like being bounced by a 109 out of the sun. "I didn't approve back cargoes or passengers, Priestman," Group Captain Bagshot snapped.

"Sir?" Priestman turned to face him.

"You heard me perfectly well. I didn't approve return cargoes of *either* freight or passengers, which makes you insubordinate."

"No RAF aircraft are carrying either, sir. Only one of the civilian outfits."

"I know. And let me tell you something else," he growled like an angry bulldog. "I don't think much of an officer who can't stand up to his wife, either!" He then turned on his heel and walked away.

Return from the Dead
Berlin-Kreuzberg
Sunday, 31 October 1948
(Day 126)

As had become his habit these past weeks, David saw Charlotte back to her apartment before public transport shut down at 6 pm. Then, if he was lucky, he would catch one of the last buses back to his flat over their office on the Kurfuerstendamm. If he was unlucky, he had to walk. As the weather became colder and wetter, he became increasingly reluctant to miss the bus, yet Charlotte could also sense his reluctance to shorten their kisses on the doorstep. "Maybe I should see about finding an apartment for you nearer the office," he suggested as they broke apart.

"Finding housing in Berlin is hopeless, David."

"Well, I could try to mend the roof over the back room of my flat—"

She silenced him with a kiss. "We'll talk about it tomorrow. Hurry, or you'll miss your bus." He dropped her a final kiss and then darted in the direction of the bus stop. Charlotte stood on the doorstep watching him go. It was silly. They were together all day at work, but in front of the other employees they dared not display their affection. So, every evening he brought her home and every evening when they parted she watched him until he was out of sight. As always, he turned back once more to wave before going around the corner.

As soon as David was gone, she unlocked the front door and went inside. The apartment was already cold, and it was going to get worse. Some people whispered that there would be no coal allocations for private dwellings at all this year, but Charlotte supposed they might be spreading Russian propaganda. In any case, because of David's connections, he would be able to keep the office heated, which meant she was warm all day long. In addition, she had her mother's long underwear and the shoes David had brought her from London, which had much thicker soles. She did not believe she was going to freeze this winter, no matter how bad it was. Besides, Charlotte could face the worst with the light-heartedness of a woman in love.

She no longer doubted or denied that she was in love with David. Yes, it was a different kind of love from her juvenile infatuation with Fritz. She wasn't a sheltered, provincial girl anymore. She hadn't met David at a ball, dancing waltzes by candlelight. He wasn't a cavalry officer in polished boots and a dashing uniform. They didn't spend dreamy days together escaping reality in a rural idyll of manor houses, horses and hunting dogs. Instead, they worked side-by-side and day after day to keep an air ambulance flying. Yet it was that shared mission that had enabled Charlotte to fall in love in the first place. David had given her work to do that made her feel useful and valuable again. David had given her back her self-respect and a reason to keep on living. The work they did was saving others, and that was something noble and good. It lifted her out of the gutter into which the Russians had kicked her; it enabled her to overcome the self-loathing they had left her with. Best of all, David made her feel safe. She was certain that no matter what happened, David would look after her. He would get her out of Berlin before the Ivans took over entirely. Because she trusted him to do that, she found she could leave her fears behind. She felt stronger and more confident.

Of course, new uncertainties niggled at her. David wanted her to live "closer," and twice he had taken her to stand outside the house on Schwanenwerder that had belonged to his uncle. His determination to evict the man who lived there had not faded just because he was so busy. Inspector Sperl had taken on the case, and Christian seemed confident that they were getting very close to making an arrest. As soon as that happened, David planned to move into the house himself. Whenever he spoke about moving in, he talked of "we." "We'll clean up the garden." "We'll repair the dock." "We'll have wonderful dinner parties." Or he would say things like: "You'll love the salon with its views to the Wannsee!"

Charlotte was certain she would love everything about the house because it was beautiful and gracious and reminded her of life before the war. She also knew she would love living with David anywhere, even in his cramped rooms over the office. All that mattered was being together. Except for the bedroom part...

She still had not managed to tell him about what had happened. She just couldn't bring herself to look at him and remember the humiliation at the same time. It always made her feel filthy, disgusting and cowardly. Yet if she *didn't* tell him, then he wouldn't understand that she had terrible psychological scars that disfigured a part of her — that part of her so vital to being his wife.

Jasha had repeatedly advised her to be honest with David sooner rather than later. She claimed that because she'd procrastinated over telling Graham, he had proposed before knowing and her bad conscience had made her seem to reject him — hurting him unnecessarily. Things had turned out all right in the end. They were engaged, and Jasha's happiness surrounded her like a halo. Charlotte wished she had the courage to follow Jasha's example.

As she continued up the stairs, it was getting darker and darker. The natural light filtering up the stairway from the front hall was all that lit the stairwell. While not totally blinded, she had to watch her step carefully and did not look up until she reached the last landing. Finally, she turned to open the door, and screamed as a man rose to his feet.

He towered over her, and he stank of sweat, shit, urine and other foul things. His feet were wrapped in rags bound together by twine. His trousers were many sizes too large and bagged down between his legs, held up by more twine around his waist. He clutched a buttonless coat in front of his chest with hands so white against the dark coat that she could see three fingers were missing. The man's neck was lost in filthy scarves wrapped around his throat and his head. The face that stared out was haggard with sharp prominent bones and deep eye sockets. One eyeball drifted down and to the side, unable to stay focused. There were ugly sores on his lips.

Yet as she stood on the landing trembling in shock, those lips formed a word. It was hardly audible over the pounding of her terrified heart, but she didn't need to hear. She could read his lips; he said: "Charlotte."

Screaming 'no' inwardly, she wanted to turn away and run to safety — to David. Yet she was rooted to the spot as certainly as if she had been turned to stone. Instead of saying no, she gasped out recognition: "Fritz."

Chapter Twenty-One
General Winter

Phantoms in the Fog
RAF Gatow
Wednesday, 3 November 1948
(Day 131)

"Altitude?" J.B. asked his copilot, Barry, unwilling to take his eyes off the directional gyro and rate-of-descent instruments to read the altimeter.

"One thousand three hundred feet. When are we supposed to come out of this muck?"

"Not for another thousand feet."

Aside from struggling to keep on the precise glide path, J.B. was also trying to filter out the chatter over his earphones. There were too many voices and too many of them sounded alarmed. "Big Easy 392 you are too high. Increase rate of descent." "This is Big Easy 471, number two engine is running rough, likely to pack up any minute. Request—" "Negative. Return to base." "All inbound aircraft: barometric pressure at Tempelhof has dropped to..." "Big Easy 392. You are still too high. Come on down."

"Altitude?" J.B. asked again.

"Seven-hundred-seventy feet."

"Can you see anything yet?"

"No." They continued their descent. Over the earphones, someone was complaining. "Where's the goddamn follow-me truck? I can't see a f***ing thing out here?" and then they were on the GCA. The voice of the controller coaxed them down and in. "You're looking good, Big Easy 882. Maintain course, speed and rate of —" the controller broke off.

J.B. and his copilot looked at one another in horror. That wasn't supposed to happen on GCA. Cut off from the controller, J.B. strained to see something — anything — in the soup swirling around his windshield.

With a sharp click, the controller was back, "Big Easy 882 abort and return to base."

"That's us!" Barry exclaimed in surprise.

"He must be confused! Tell him we don't have a problem!" J.B. ordered.

Barry spoke into the microphone, "This is Big Easy 882. We have no problem. Currently at four hundred—"

"The aircraft ahead of you has yet not cleared the runway. Pull up and turn left immediately!"

J.B. pulled the nose up and pushed the throttles forward for more power. "Damn!" he exclaimed out loud. "We've got ten tons of milk powder back there. That's seventy-thousand litres of milk! Just yesterday it was all over the papers that milk supplies in Berlin are down to just three days! If we don't get this load in, kids are going to go hungry. What's the point of dropping candy if the babies don't have milk?"

Barry was a nice kid from Missouri, who'd arrived a couple of days earlier. He shook his head and muttered. "I don't know, J.B., but we've got our orders."

"Request permission to divert to Gatow," J.B. countered.

Barry shook his head but dutifully pressed the mic button and passed on J.B.'s request.

"Sure, go ahead and try," the tower answered.

"Get me Gatow," J.B. ordered Barry.

With an audible sigh of disapproval, Barry complied. When he had the channel, J.B. took over the mic. "Gatow, this is Big Easy 882. Do you read me?"

"This is Gatow 882. Reading you loud and clear. How can we help?" J.B. was disappointed that the voice was male. He longed to hear Kathleen's voice again, but told himself to concentrate on the immediate problem. "Tempelhof is temporarily closed, and I've got a load of milk here. Any chance you can squeeze me in?"

"Can you give us a waggle so we can locate you?"

J.B. yawed the C-54 first left and counted to five, then turned to the right for another five seconds. As he repeated the procedure, Gatow announced, "OK. We've got you. What is your altitude?"

"Eight-hundred-ninety."

"Right turn onto 235 and descend to five hundred feet."

"Thank you!" J.B. turned the mic over to Barry and swung his aircraft onto the course.

The voices on the Gatow frequency sounded less nervous than those approaching Tempelhof, but then there were no five-storey, brick apartment buildings in the flight path.

"Big Easy 882, turn right onto 290 and descend to two hundred feet. Lower your undercarriage." J.B. complied, noting that the clouds might be thinning a bit, but visibility was still dreadful.

Another crisp, British, male voice spoke into his ears. Still no Kathleen, J.B. registered with an inner sigh. "Big Easy 882, this is your GCA controller. Remember, do not reply to instructions unless you cannot comply. Now, start your descent to 100 feet. Give me a touch more right rudder. That looks good. Hold it. Now, just a tiny bit more. Yes. That's it. Increase rate of descent. Very good. Ease her down. You're almost there. You should see the centre line any moment now."

J.B. was tempted to say something rude because he couldn't see a damn thing, but he bit his tongue.

"There!" Barry saw it the same instant he did: a tiny white line leading deeper into the fog. A second later the rubber hit the tarmac with a distinctive screech, and then their nose flopped down with a thud. They thundered blindly through the white mist, weaving a little as J.B. applied the brakes. Ahead of them the fog seemed to be growing darker, and then J.B. registered pine forest peeping through the gloom. In a split second of panic, he jammed on the brakes, causing the Skymaster to fishtail as they slithered to a halt. It looked like they didn't have more than a dozen feet of runway left. No sign of a follow-me vehicle either. Conscious of the need to clear the runway as rapidly as possible, J.B. cautiously turned the C-54 to the right, where the taxiway ought to be. Sure enough, he found pavement peeling off and a moment later deciphered the blinking yellow lights of the follow-me vehicle as it emerged from the swirling white vapour enveloping them. The dense moisture smudged the lights as if they were dissolving into the fog. At a snail's pace, the heavy freighter followed the flashing yellow blurs, thumping over cracks in the concrete until a glowing baton signalled J.B. to turn, halt and switch off his engines. People materialised out of the clouds clinging to the ground to put chocks around his wheels.

"Can you see the offloading truck, Sgt Elkins?"

"I can't see my f***ing hand in front of my f***ing face!" came the technical sergeant's answer, but he started down the fuselage to open the loading door. J.B. and Barry ran through the post-flight cockpit drill and hung their radio headphones on the throttle handles. Finally, they pushed themselves up and out of their seats. Both men were stiff from the tension of extended instrument flying. The weather had been lousy all day, and it was getting worse.

As J.B. dropped out of the tail onto the tarmac, the unloading was in full swing. "We're going to have to report in and get the latest Met. They don't have vehicles going around to the planes here, or a mobile snack van either," he explained to Barry.

"Great," his copilot replied sarcastically, looking around at the fog eloquently. J.B. turned to the British Army corporal overseeing the German stevedores. "Could you point us in the direction of the ops room and Met office?"

"You'd better follow the tarmac right round to the end, or you might end up as strawberry jam on the runway. I know Berlin's short of jam, but for some reason, the WingCo doesn't like us scraping it off his tarmac. Interrupts incoming flights or something. Just keep walking that way," he pointed. "When the tarmac runs out, turn right. You should have the undercarriage of the incoming aircraft almost within reach overhead. Carry on from there until the tarmac opens up. At that point, I suggest you ask for a lift from the next vehicle you see."

That sounded straightforward, J.B. agreed, and they set off. As they walked blindly through the fog, J.B. counted the landings per minute. Gatow appeared to have scaled back to one-third their usual rate — which explained why they'd been able to fit him in, he supposed.

The wind of a landing Dakota nearly blew their caps off as they crossed the far end of the runway and reached the busy concrete apron beyond. Here a variety of vehicles groaned about in low gear traveling in different directions. Fortunately, none were moving very fast, and J.B. was able to flag one down. The driver agreed to take them over to the admin building. While J.B. reported to the ops centre, Barry and Sergeant Elkins headed over to the Malcolm Club for a snack and coffee.

The formalities over, J.B. thought briefly of trying to find Kathleen, but he told himself it was pointless. Nothing could come of them meeting again. He'd made a commitment to Patty, why complicate things? Hell, anyone in their right mind would envy him for being engaged with a rich, sexy girl and for having a great-paying job at one of America's leading companies all lined up. His crazy longing for Kathleen was irrational and counterproductive. He started walking towards the Malcolm Club.

A heavy tractor groaned out of the darkness behind him, and J.B. had to leap out of its way. Shortly afterwards, he registered the sound of a taxiing aircraft coming nearer. In visibility like this, a pilot high up in his cockpit could easily fail to notice a lone man wandering around on the tarmac where he didn't belong. J.B. drew up sharply and looked around, trying to orient himself. Engines were screaming as they wound up for take-off no more than a hundred yards away! Somehow he'd become disoriented and had wandered *towards* the runways. He had to get back to the buildings, but all he could see was milky murk that grew darker as daylight faded. He felt as if he were in some no-man's-land between heaven and earth and hell.

"Hello? Is someone there?" A woman's voice reached through the swirling mist like a lifeline. It was Kathleen's voice. She'd come looking for him! He turned to face her with his pulse racing in anticipation. So the feelings were mutual, he was thinking. She senses it too!

She approached out of the fog, steadily acquiring more solid shape, although he still wasn't sure whether she was real or a figment of his imagination. She stopped in front of him and looked up, astonished. "J.B.?" she asked, bewildered. "What are you doing here?"

Disappointed he registered that she had not been looking for him. It was just chance. "I managed to get lost again," he admitted. "And you?"

Kathleen looked away from him, and he sensed a strange uncertainty about her. She had always been in charge before — the confident, teasing voice over the RT, the sophisticated widow. Suddenly, in the fog she was almost a ghost, and her face was wet.

"Kathleen?" He whispered, reaching out his hand but not daring to touch her.

Kathleen shook her head as if to clear it, and a hand brushed hastily at her face. "Nothing really. Or — just silly."

His silence told her he did not believe her."

"I thought I saw Ken out here," she admitted. Then with a self-deprecating and cynical smile, she added, "I thought he had risen from the dead, restored and healthy, had walked ten miles from the patch of forest where his Lancaster crashed to climb over the perimeter fence, and come to me.... Only he didn't, did he?" she ended sadly.

J.B. registered that twilight had drained all colour from the day, so that in his battered old flight jacket and his wartime flying boots, his shape could readily be confused with that of an RAF pilot in battle dress. To Kathleen, he said simply, "No. I'm sorry. I'm not a phantom. I'm flesh and blood, and I can prove it if you'd let me hold you."

She hesitated, but then she stepped closer and let him enfold her in his arms. He did so gently, and she leaned her head on his chest. A moment later he realised she was sobbing, so he held her more firmly. Abruptly, she pulled away and started wiping at her tears with her hands and apologising nervously. "Good heavens! I don't know what's got into me. I'm being so silly! I shouldn't have — I should—" She cut herself off, pressing a hand to her mouth and closing her eyes.

"I wish I could be the answer to your prayers," he murmured, handing her his handkerchief.

"Please forget you saw me like this," she begged.

He didn't answer because he knew he wouldn't — and didn't want to.

Kathleen used his handkerchief to wipe away her tears, and firmly took hold of herself again. Avoiding his eyes, she said, "You said you were lost. Where did you want to go?"

With sudden and remarkable clarity, he saw what he wanted and it wasn't Patty or that job at GM. "I want to go wherever we can be together forever."

She caught her breath and looked over at him again questioningly. She seemed almost to want what he did, but then she shook her head. "I don't think that's possible. We are from different worlds."

"Are we?" he asked back. It wasn't Kathleen that was from a different world, it was Patty. Kathleen and he had more in common than he and Patty ever would. Awed by the realization, he confessed softly, "I love you, Kathleen."

She looked up at him intently, but then she shook her head sadly and told him gently, "No, you love a phantom who saved you from death a long

448

time ago."

"But you came to me now, too. Don't you believe in destiny? Maybe your husband led you here so we could meet again?"

"Why would Ken want me to meet an American who won't be here much longer and is already engaged to someone else?" she countered in a tone of infinite sadness.

"Because *he* knows that I love you and that we could have a life together."

"Do you really believe that?" She sounded as if she wished it might be true but had been disappointed too many times to believe in fairy tales any more.

"Yes," he assured her.

She hesitated, but then shook her head firmly. Her voice was back to being that steady, certain, commanding voice of an air traffic controller. "You're only here on temporary duty and you're still engaged to that girl at home. I think I'd better get us both out of here before something kills us." She turned and led him from the runway.

Broken Promises
Berlin-Charlottenburg
Friday, 5 November 1948
(Day 133)

Charlotte had been acting strangely all week long. David did not understand it. They had not quarrelled. They had parted warmly Sunday evening when her kisses had been more promising than ever before. Yet on Monday morning she had seemed mentally absent, and her interactions with everyone had been brusque. She kept dropping things, forgetting things, making silly mistakes. She had dismissed his concern with "I have a headache," and "I didn't sleep well." Yet she took the next three days off entirely.

He had not pressed the matter. The fog was causing havoc with their schedules. Moby Dick had been grounded all day Tuesday, and on Wednesday it had made one flight out to Hanover, only to get stuck there, meaning all subsequent evacuations had to be cancelled. It didn't return to Berlin until Thursday noon and had then managed one flight to Munich, but was now stranded there. With the weather report forecasting unbroken fog for the next two days, David had told all his employees to get some well-earned rest and suggested to Charlotte that they spend the day together.

Charlotte had nodded without meeting his eyes.

"Shall we go to Moorlake?"

She nodded again, her eyes averted, and her lips pressed shut.

David put on his hat and coat while Charlotte bundled herself up in her brother's greatcoat. She turned the collar up and wound a woollen scarf under it to hold it in place. The effect was to shield her face from view. Walking beside her on the pavement towards the S-Bahn station, David could see only the tip of her nose. She stared straight ahead. Not once did she turn to smile at him. Something was wrong.

"Charlotte?" He reached for her hand.

She yanked it back. "Please don't touch me, David."

"But why not? What has happened?"

"I — We — Our relationship has to end."

"What?" David stopped so suddenly that the people behind him ran into him. Charlotte was forced to turn and look back at him. He saw tears in her eyes. "Charlotte!" he gasped, and reached out for her again. She took a step backwards. They were attracting disapproving attention. He lowered his hands but asked more insistently. "What is it? What has happened?"

"Over the last months. We have — I have — You made me think you cared for me—"

"Charlotte! I love you! You must know that?"

She shook her head vigorously. "Don't, David! Don't make this harder than it already is! I don't want to hurt you! It's bad enough that I am in so much pain, but please, please understand."

"Understand what? You aren't making any sense. Last weekend we talked about a life together — in my house on the Wannsee. We talked of—"

"Stop it! Stop it! I know what we talked about, dreamed about. But I can't—"

"Why not? Why can you *suddenly* not think about a life with me?" Emotions raised David's voice. Because he had grown up in the Weimar

Republic, David unconsciously believed that antisemitism lay at the root of all rejection. He had believed that Charlotte was free of that poison, but if she had turned on him now then it could only be because someone had planted in her the seed that led to Auschwitz. And if she rejected him, then the hatred and anger against the people of this city that he had repressed these past months would erupt again. He could feel it boiling in his blood.

Charlotte broke through his thoughts, exclaiming, "Because I am betrothed to another man."

"Betrothed?" David recoiled. "How — you can't mean the man who was killed at Stalingrad?"

"He wasn't *killed*!" she almost shouted at him, and then her voice fell to almost a whisper as she added, "Fritz was missing. He's come back." As she spoke, her eyes were full of reflected horror.

David took several minutes to process what she had just said. The man to whom she'd been engaged in 1940 and who had been missing since late 1942 had miraculously returned? Was that credible? "Where has he been all this time?" David snapped as if in disbelief, although the rational part of his brain already knew the answer. Tens of thousands of German prisoners of war had disappeared in Russia. Ever since surrender, and still, the human wrecks of the once proud Wehrmacht had been trickling back from the horror-filled expanses of the Siberian steppe day after day.

"He was in a Soviet prisoner camp," Charlotte confirmed the obvious. "He has no toes left and has lost three fingers as well. Frostbite claimed his toes; an explosion took his fingers. His right eyeball falls off to the side and he has bad double vision — the result of a blow to the head from one of his Russian guards. He has lost most of his teeth. He's in a pitiable state."

"But you want to marry him?"

"I don't *want* to marry him," Charlotte answered, tears streaming down her face. "But I *promised* to marry him. I pledged him my troth before God. He has never needed me more. I am all he has left. We — we are fated for one another."

"Fated? What makes you more *fated* to be with him than with me?" David demanded.

"It's — I — we are more suited to one another. Being married to him would be more — more —" He could see she was struggling with the words and the tears had not stopped, but he sensed what was coming and his pity was drying up. "Fitting," she gasped out. "More appropriate."

"What's his full name?" David insisted, already guessing Fritz was someone from her class with her background, her religion. Mentally, the swastika flags were being unfurling again along the length of the avenue and rhythmic thumping of boots goose-stepping in unison set off a throbbing headache in his mind.

"Fritz von Bredow," Charlotte answered woodenly.

David nodded, and sneered, "Ah yes. You couldn't stand being a simple Frau Goldman, could you, Graefin Walmsdorf? You prefer a Nazi — even a wreck of a Nazi with no toes and one hand — to being married to a Jew. I should have known!" He turned his back on her and walked blindly in the opposite direction. He had no idea where he was going or what he was going to do. Nothing mattered any more. Certainly not his uncle's home on Schwanenwerder, nor the Airlift nor even his air ambulance business. He simply wanted to die.

Humanitarian Crisis
Berlin-Schoeneberg
Thursday, 18 November 1948
(Day 146)

The fog was so thick that Wing Commander Priestman's driver could hardly find his way through the white gloom to the Kommandatura. It had been like this for eleven out of the last fifteen days. Two days ago, they had taken the extreme measure of ordering pilots to fly even when visibility fell below RAF safety minimums. The strains on both aircrew and controllers were enormous, and accidents were inevitable. The only question was where and when. Meanwhile, the Americans were feverishly trying to install the modern radar equipment they had flown in, hoping to institute the same kind of GCA at Tempelhof that Gatow had had all along.

But sometimes it was too dangerous to fly even GCA and all flying was suspended. Yesterday, the USAF and RAF combined had managed to deliver exactly ten tons of the 5,000 tons necessary to keep Berlin's population alive. Not a single pound of coal had reached Berlin. The reserves of both food and fuel were dwindling at an alarming rate, and there was no sign of the weather breaking. The Airlift was on the brink of collapse.

While the Soviet press crowed and gloated and declared the Airlift was already a "fatal casualty" of "Capitalist hubris", the Berliners remained remarkably calm. There had been no riots, no strikes and no demonstrations since the incidents leading to the City Council's relocation to the West. There had been no formal petitions from the Berliners to the Allies demanding their withdrawal, either. And this admirable steadfastness of the city's population put the West in an awkward position. How could His Majesty's Government give up if the Berliners didn't want them to?

Not that there was any indication that political will in London or Washington was wavering. HM Government appeared immovable on the topic, while the expectations of change in the United States had proved totally wrong. Two weeks ago, President Truman had pulled off a spectacular, surprise victory in the US elections. To the astonishment and amazement of all, he had beaten off three challengers to win re-election — and Truman reiterated at every opportunity that the US wasn't leaving Berlin. Period.

Yet while the American president could insist that his troops stay put, his saying so did not magically improve visibility. Which left those responsible for implementing the Airlift in an impossible situation. Priestman found himself torn between his heart's desire to make the Airlift work *somehow*, and a nagging professional brain that said it couldn't be done. Meanwhile, Bagshot's continued snipping and oblique threats wore down his nerves and undermined his confidence. This morning's summons to an urgent meeting with the British Berlin Commandant General Herbert only added to his unease.

His car pulled up and stopped beside the four flag poles still flying the flags of all four occupying powers. The clouds hung so low to the ground that it was impossible to distinguish which flag was which as they flapped listlessly in the murk overhead. The sentries saluted as the Wing Commander passed inside, but the hallways echoed with inactivity and the corridors were damp and cold. Robin was reminded of the irony that Gatow's electricity came from the East and its heat came from boilers heated with gas siphoned off from Soviet pipes. Most of Berlin did not enjoy such luxuries.

Priestman was startled to find Colonel Howley already waiting in Herbert's office. There had been a time when Herbert detested Howley, and although they had been getting along better recently, it was still surprising to find them together in apparent harmony. Nor did Priestman like the eagerness with which they greeted him. Instinctively, he sensed a trap.

Herbert was a blunt man in the best of circumstances and got straight to the point. "Wing Commander, we asked you to meet us today because, in view of the deteriorating situation, the Berlin City Government has made a direct appeal to the Allied Kommandatura to assist in the evacuation of particularly vulnerable Berliners. What the city officials are thinking of is malnourished children, fragile, elderly people, and people suffering from chronic illnesses such as asthma, arthritis, multiple sclerosis, and so on."

"We've known for some time that Berlin's hospitals are in a deplorable state and understaffed," Priestman reminded them. "You may remember that one of the civilian charter companies and our Sunderland flying boats have been evacuating children on a small scale since early October."

"Yes, yes," Herbert brushed his remark aside and Priestman doubted if he had even been aware of the evacuations. Instead, he forged ahead exclaiming, "I'm sure you understand that we had no choice but to agree."

He'd said "we" so Priestman glanced at Howley, who nodded vigorously and added, "This really must be done, Robin, and both General Herbert and I assured the mayor it *would* be done. What else could we say, for heaven's sake? The Berliners are suffering enough as it is. How can we ask people with serious chronic illnesses, fragile old people and kids to face a winter without heat, light or adequate rations? These aren't soldiers. They're civilians." Howley, as always, spoke forcefully.

Alarms started ringing in Priestman's head. He distinctly remembered Tunner saying he would not get involved in flying civilians out of Berlin. Surely, the American and British Commandants had not made promises to the Mayor of Berlin without first checking with the Combined Airlift Task Force Commander? Out loud he asked cautiously, "Did the Mayor give you any indication of how many people are in these particularly vulnerable categories that they now want to see evacuated?"

"Reuter suggested around 17,000."

Priestman stiffened and asked at once, "Has Tunner agreed?"

"No, blast him!" Herbert answered, jumping to his feet in exasperation and starting to pace with his hands behind his back.

Howley took over, explaining, "Tunner says taking passengers on board his transport aircraft will slow down his entire supply operation — 'completely disrupt it' is the way he worded it. He says 17,000 people are a mere drop in the bucket and their departure will reduce requirements only marginally."

Priestman had heard all that from Tunner himself only a month before, so it didn't surprise him, even if he personally deplored Tunner's short-sightedness. "Mathematically speaking, he's right, of course, but saving children's lives is the right thing to do — from a humanitarian standpoint. Furthermore, if children, old people and people with chronic illnesses start dying in droves, the Soviets will be quick to accuse us of 'mass murder'. I doubt our political leaders would want either people to die or the Soviets to win a propaganda victory, so you'll have to go over Tunner's head. Have you spoken to Generals Clay and Robertson?"

"Yes," Howley replied, looking grim. "Roberston passed the buck, saying the Americans control the Airlift since the creation of the Combined Air Lift Task Force, and Clay refused to 'interfere'. He said he wasn't enough of an expert on military transport to feel he could overrule General Tunner on an operational matter."

That shook Priestman. He did not see this as a strictly 'operational' matter, and he had expected more understanding and compassion from Clay.

Herbert returned to the table, sat down and faced Priestman. "I'm pleased to hear you share my point of view on this because I hope you can help us out."

Priestman felt his pulse rate increase as he reminded the other two officers, "Tunner is my superior."

"We know," Howley assured him, "but hear us out. What Tunner said was that *his* freighters weren't going to carry one single evacuee, but he added that he had no objection to the RAF taking the passengers out." Howley and Herbert were sitting on the edge of their respective seats as they awaited Priestman's reaction.

"You're asking me if the RAF can manage this on its own?"

"Can it?" Herbert pressed him.

"Have you asked Group Captain Bagshot?"

"No, I'm asking you, Wing Commander!" Herbert admonished angrily. "I want *your* opinion as the professional who will have the main responsibility for implementation since all the passengers will have to depart from Gatow. Could you evacuate 17,000 passengers on RAF aircraft and if so, how long do you think it would take?"

Priestman did the maths out loud for them. "The RAF aircraft most suitable for flying passengers out are the Dakotas and the Sunderlands, but the latter are about to be taken off the Airlift because the fog clings to the water, reducing visibility even when Gatow is open, and we have no radar control on the Havel. Furthermore, there is an increasing risk of ice. In short, only the Dakotas are available for an evacuation of this kind. They can carry between 24 and 28 passengers, but let's be conservative and say 25 passengers per flight. Weather permitting, we average a hundred Dakota departures each 24-hour period, but not all Dakotas can carry passengers and night flights are extremely hazardous. So, let's assume passengers are evacuated on just seventy Dakota sorties per day. That would mean evacuating 1,750 people per day or all 17,000 of them in ten days — assuming good weather."

"That's jolly good!" Herbert exclaimed, evidently surprised, and Howley clapped Priestman on the back saying, "I knew we could count on you, Robin!"

"Slow down, please. Getting that many people out in one day, as I said, depends very much on the weather. Also, the evacuees will have to be ready to board at a moment's notice. They will have to be organised in groups of 25 and can't bring much luggage. I should say no more than one suitcase per person weighing one and a half stone at the most. There can be no confusion, pushing or shoving and fighting." The other two officers nodded vigorously in understanding.

Priestman continued. "Nor do the problems end there. Where are all the evacuees to go at the other end? We can't just dump them on the Airlift airfields and tell them to look after themselves—"

"No, no! Of course, not!" Herbert agreed. "The Berlin City government assured us they would organise onward transport to hospitals and homes.

They said they were already doing this on a much smaller scale — isn't that what you mentioned earlier?"

"What we've done to date is evacuate roughly 120 passengers per day using just one civilian company and the Sunderlands flying into Hamburg. However, to remove 17,000 people we'll need almost the entire RAF Dakota fleet, and it operates from a variety of different airfields. I would recommend that the evacuation flights end at the civil airport in Hannover so that from there the aircraft and crews can return to their home base to take on another load of inbound cargo for Berlin."

"That sounds first-rate, Wing Commander!" Herbert's relief added to his rare display of enthusiasm.

Howley nodded forcefully as well, adding, "Hannover has the added advantage of being centrally located, so the evacuees could readily be distributed across the West. I'm sure the City Council will agree. You'll just need to coordinate this with them."

Priestman wanted to be sure they understood the full consequences of the decision. "Bear in mind, that even if everything goes like clockwork, embarking and disembarking passengers and their luggage will delay return flights. That's why Tunner wants nothing to do with it. Realistically, it means the Dakotas won't be able to make three round trips on a good day as they have been doing, but two. Which means I must revise my earlier calculations and say we'd need closer to fifteen days of good weather to clear 17,000 passengers through Gatow using the RAF's fleet alone. If we include civilian Dakotas, we might get as many as 2,000 passengers out in a day, but don't forget we will also reduce by one-third the tonnage of goods that our Dakotas have been delivering to Berlin so far."

Herbert looked alarmed. "What would that mean in terms of supplies delivered?"

"Well, last month the RAF hauled 21% of the tonnage. The Dakotas were responsible for one-third of that — or 7% of overall tonnage. If they reduce their sorties by one-third, 2.3% less tonnage will be delivered."

"That sounds quite acceptable to me," Herbert declared with a glance at Howley, who nodded in agreement. Noting Priestman's silence, Herbert asked him directly. "Don't you agree, Wing Commander?"

"I agree, but I hope you will forgive me for noting that that's 2.3% of overall capacity — whether the RAF or the USAF takes the passengers.

There is no logical reason why the burden of removing malnourished children, feeble old people, and chronically ill patients should fall exclusively to the RAF. Even if the USAF carries more of the coal, some of their C-54, particularly from the civilian contractors, were designed as passenger liners and can easily be converted back to passenger aircraft. If both the RAF and the USAF carried their share, the entire operation could be concluded in half the time."

"We already have Tunner's answer!" Herbert snapped in annoyance, while Howley held up his hands in a gesture of surrender. "You're right! I'm not going to argue with you, Robin. But the fact is that I can't tell General Tunner what to do and General Clay isn't willing to do so. In other words, it's the RAF or no one."

Priestman had already grasped that fact and was resigned to it. He nodded. "I need to talk to whoever on the City Council is responsible for organising things at their end. I will prioritise this and try to be ready to put it into effect in three or four days' time — weather permitting."

"Well done!" General Herbert exclaimed, "I should have known the RAF would come through!"

"If there's nothing else, General, I'd better get to work," Priestman concluded.

Herbert got to his feet, thanking him. As he saw Priestman to the door, he shook his hand more energetically and warmly than ever before. Howley took his leave of Herbert at the same time and the two men walked down the corridor and stairs together. At the exit, as they prepared to go to their respective waiting cars, Priestman set his cap on his head with the peak partially covering his eyes and remarked in a low voice, "I presume you know this will be my last act as Station Commander at Gatow."

"What do you mean?" Howley asked back in astonishment.

"You and Herbert avoided asking Group Captain Bagshot about this because you knew he would say 'no.' Tunner's indirect approval is a shabby and transparent excuse that won't hold up. Bagshot will rightly view me as insubordinate, and he'll have my skin. This may cost me more than my position. It might cost me my career."

Howley took a second to absorb that and then asked, "But you'll still do it?"

"I don't see how we can maintain this Airlift for more than a few weeks, which means Berlin will most probably be in Soviet hands by Christmas. If I can help save 17,000 civilians — the bulk of them children — from Stalin, then I will. It's the moral equivalent of going down fighting."

Chapter Twenty-Two
Goetterdaemmerung

Dakota Sunset
RAF Gatow / Fuhlsbuettel
Friday, 26 November 1948
(Day 154)

The brittle sunshine was intoxicating after the seemingly endless fog. The whole world seemed to sparkle with new life. Kiwi and his crew made an early start, snapping up one of the first Dakota slots of the morning. They watched "the dawn come up like thunder" over the Communist Zone as they sped over the dreary landscape still wrapped in ground mist. Most of the trees were bare of leaves and the forests around Berlin were grey, but the sky was blue and there wasn't a cloud in the sky. Kiwi wished he were back in a Spitfire and could lark about a bit, but he maintained "convoy course and speed" (as he thought of it) and they made their landing at Gatow dead on time at the tail end of a "block" of RAF Dakotas.

Nothing had prepared him for what happened next. The Dakotas were directed, one after the other, onto the perimeter track and then told to back off onto some hastily laid PSP. Meanwhile, lorries and trailers bounced over from the direction of the terminal at a frantic pace. It was all extremely efficient, Kiwi acknowledged, but the PSP was oozing mud and he wondered how long it would stand up to this new procedure.

Before he could give it any more thought, his navigator drew his attention to some dilapidated city buses packed to the gills with civilians. No sooner had the first couple of aircraft been unloaded, than the buses pulled up alongside and started disgorging people. "Are they preparing to load passengers on those RAF crates?" Kiwi asked in disbelief.

"That's what it looks like to me."

They both stared. Sure enough, people were disembarking from the bus. Some of the passengers were so old and crippled they were doubled over and could walk only with the help of a cane. As they left the bus, however, they were efficiently organised into two lines by younger Germans wearing white armbands and holding clipboards. These officious individuals appeared to be calling out names and ticking them off on their lists as people raised their hands. One batch was sent to the Dakota to the right and another to the Dakota on the left. The passengers deposited pathetic bundles of belongings onto a trolley beside the cargo door, which German stevedores tossed into the tail of the plane. While the passengers dragged themselves up the mobile stairs, the next bus parked between the next two Dakotas in line.

Kiwi looked at his crew. "Looks like someone wants to move a lot of people out of Berlin in a hurry."

"You have to admit everything is very orderly."

"Yeah, German efficiency at work."

"Makes you wonder how we won the war, doesn't it?" they laughed together.

Before long, an RAF Land Rover brought them the latest Met and explained that the Dakota fleet would be flying some 17,000 Berliners out of the city as expeditiously as possible. They were to land at the civilian airport in Hanover to disembark their passengers and then proceed to their home base to take on more cargo for Berlin. Kiwi registered that, unlike the passengers they had been carrying out as a private initiative, these orders came from the RAF Station Commander. AFI's contract required it to comply with RAF orders, and other civilian contractors were also taking on passengers, so Kiwi assumed the details of compensation had been worked out at the appropriate levels.

The bus which parked beside Kiwi's Dakota twenty minutes later had about fifty children on board, but more adults than usual. He soon realised why; these weren't orphans, and many of the adults were taking tear-filled leave of their children. Kiwi could hardly watch as an ancient couple clung to their granddaughter, all three sobbing miserably. The little girl was shaking her head and clearly saying she didn't want to go; her grandparents were insistent. He needed no interpreter to understand that the grandmother, stroking the little girl's blonde head, was saying it was for her own good. Equally distressing was a single mother, streaming tears as she tied a scarf more firmly around her daughter's neck. Kiwi was reminded of similar scenes that had played out all across England when children were sent out of the cities to avoid German bombing at the start of the war.

He registered a difference, too. Most of the parents and children here were dressed practically in rags, and the children were tiny and frail. Although this would be Kiwi's 26th flight carrying children, the other children had been labelled "sick" and "abandoned." These children, in contrast, had loving families around them and that underlined just how widespread the malnourishment in Berlin had become.

Just then, one of the boys stopped to stare up at him. "*Bist Du der Pilot?*" he asked.

Kiwi understood the word pilot. He went down on his heels. "*Ja. Ich bin der Pilot,*" he answered. It was one of the handful of phrases he had learned in German.

The boy's eyes grew wider. "*Hast du viele Flugstunden?*"

Kiwi looked helplessly at the boy's mother. "He asked if you have many flying hours," she translated.

"More than four thousand," Kiwi answered, and the mother passed the information on to her son.

The little boy's eyes widened in wonder, and he gazed up at Kiwi with open hero worship. "*Du warst im Krieg Pilot?*"

"Did you fly in the war?" his mother mumbled.

"Yes," Kiwi admitted, feeling guilty about it for the first time in his entire life.

"*Welche Flugzeugtypen? Hast du den Lancaster oder den Halifax geflogen?*"

Lancaster and Halifax required no translation, and Kiwi was impressed that the boy knew which aircraft were RAF and didn't ask about Flying Fortresses or Liberators. Without awaiting a translation from the boy's mother. Kiwi answered with a proud smile, "Spitfires."

The boy's eyes widened further, and he started jumping up and down in excitement, jabbering, "*Wirklich? Spitfires? Du warst Jagdflieger?*"

"Yes," Kiwi confirmed. The word "Jagdflieger" was familiar from the war.

The boy's excitement made him speak louder and he was beaming as he exclaimed. "*Mein Vater auch.*" These words were followed by a flood of German far beyond Kiwi's limited capabilities. The boy's mother seemed embarrassed and summarised rather than translated the boy's words, "His father flew Me109s in France and the Mediterranean until 1941, when he was transferred to the Eastern Front and shot down. He is still being held prisoner by the Russians," she concluded. The hardness of her face revealed her bitterness over this fact.

"It must be hard for you to part with your son."

"In the West, the children will get extra milk and meat rations, they said. I want him to grow strong and big."

"How old is he?" Kiwi asked, estimating that he was about six.

"Ten," his mother answered.

Shocked, Kiwi turned to address himself to the little boy again. "What's your name?" he asked, and the boy's mother translated, "*Er fragt, wie Du heist.*"

"Uwe," the boy said solemnly. "Uwe Bildhauer."

"Well, Uwe come with me, and you can ride in the cockpit all the way to Hanover."

When his mother delivered this message, Uwe gave Kiwi a look of pure adulation. "*Danke! Danke! Das ist das Schoenste was ich mir je haette wuenschen koennen.*"

His mother said more simply, "Thank you, Captain," and held out her hand. Kiwi shook it. The other passengers had already boarded and the Dakota beside them was starting up its engines. Kiwi shook Uwe by the hand and led him to the cockpit.

The evacuation continued all day long, and word spread that Wing Commander Priestman had outflanked Group Captain Bagshot by getting permission for the operation direct from General Tunner. Bagshot wasn't popular and most of the laughs were at Bagshot's expense, but returning from the last flight of the day, Kiwi was shaken to be met by the Station Adjutant and guessed there was trouble. "Captain Murray? Air Freight International?"

"Yeah, that's me."

"Congratulations. You have just made your last flight on the Berlin Airlift. Effective immediately, all civilian Dakotas are being removed from the Airlift to make way for the tankers and larger aircraft."

"What?" Kiwi gasped.

"Those are the orders. It applies to all civilian carriers. You have twenty-four hours to remove your aircraft from the field. Thank you for your contribution and dedication. Bills can be submitted as usual." The adjutant turned and disappeared in the dark.

"Did he just say what I think he said?" Kiwi's navigator asked.

"Yeah. I'd better put a call through to Mr Goldman straight away," Kiwi answered in a daze.

No more Dakota flights by private contractors? The various charter companies operated a total of nineteen Dakotas altogether. Taking them off the Airlift would cut the Dakota fleet by more than 10% and hamper the evacuation efforts — which, Kiwi registered, was probably just what Bagshot intended. He was getting his revenge on Robin for going past him to get permission to fly the civilians out.

At the hangar, the groundcrew had already heard the news as it spread like wildfire. Some of the other companies operated only Dakotas. This decision effectively wrecked their business from one day to the next. At least EAS still had the Halifax and the ambulance.

After making three attempts to reach David without success, Kiwi gave up and decided there was nothing more he could do tonight. Leaving the others at the *Golden Lion* speculating about their future, he returned to his lodgings to freshen up and change for an evening with Virginia. Meeting her for dinner on Fridays had become a treasured ritual these last six weeks. It was the highlight of his week.

This evening, however, Kiwi found Virginia's enthusiasm for the evacuation annoying. She was so busy telling him what she'd seen and written that she hardly listened to him. It wasn't until they were in the taxi heading for Virginia's hotel that she seemed to notice he was subdued. "What is it, Chuck darling? You seem rather listless tonight. I thought you'd be as pleased as I am about this wonderful operation."

"I would be if they hadn't thrown the civilian Dakotas off the Airlift," Kiwi told her bluntly.

"What? Why would they do that?"

"Allegedly to make way for larger aircraft, but I suspect Bagshot is trying to cripple Robin's evacuation."

"Why do you call it Robin's evacuation?" She asked puzzled.

"Because he decided to go ahead with it without Bagshot's approval and organised the whole thing. Now Bagshot is gunning for him."

"What did you just say?"

"Forget it!" Kiwi growled. "It was off the record, remember? Everything I say on our night together is off the record."

Virginia backed off, giving him a delicious kiss to mollify him, but as they finished and leaned back in the taxi seat, Virginia remarked, "Robin can be so stubborn at times, and it always backfires. I mean, for example, why did he marry that stupid Communist bitch, who couldn't help his career at all?"

"Emily isn't a bitch, she isn't a Communist, and she most certainly isn't stupid," Kiwi countered firmly, deeply offended by Virginia's remark. Emily was not only a close friend, she was also what held EAS together. Without her, Kiwi knew, David and he would have clashed too often and too sharply to continue. Without her, they wouldn't have Kit and his crew or MacDonald either, not to mention the hangar at Gatow. It wasn't just that Emily understood what was needed, she had the remarkable ability to get them working together.

Virginia, of course, had not followed his thoughts and she was still ranting on about Emily. "Well, she grew up in the slums — and I mean the slums — of Portsmouth, and her parents taught in a council school. What on earth did Robin see in her?"

"Her intelligence, her compassion, her level-headedness and her love of flying — just for a start," Kiwi countered sharply. Virginia seemed to see Robin as nothing more than a glamorous Battle of Britain ace, Kiwi reflected. He, on the other hand, knew how haggard Robin had been and how close to cracking. Emily had been what saved him.

"He never gave me a chance," Virginia complained in a self-pitying voice. "I told him I wasn't just a socialite. I tried to show that I was intelligent and that I cared about the war, but he never took me seriously. He thought all I cared about was money and titles and being in the papers, but that wasn't true. I've never loved anyone as much as I loved him. If he'd given me a chance, my father could have arranged things at the Ministry, and he'd be an Air Commodore or more by now." Although she used the past tense when speaking about Robin, it did not escape Kiwi's notice that her feelings for him appeared uncomfortably strong. Fortunately, their arrival at the hotel interrupted their conversation.

As usual, Kiwi went straight to the lift, while Virginia collected her key at the front desk, flirting with the desk clerk to distract him as Kiwi slipped by. The bellboy gave Kiwi a knowing grin, however, so Kiwi tipped him a full Deutschemark to encourage him to keep his mouth shut.

Virginia was not far behind him, and they slipped inside her room. As soon as the door clicked shut, they started undressing. The only language needed between them now was that of their bodies. Yet, after six weeks, some of the excitement had gone out of the routine. Virginia took the time to hang up her dress and pile her underwear neatly; Kiwi laid his uniform trousers across the arms of a chair and hung the jacket over the back. He tucked his socks into his shoes and pushed them under the seat. When they were both naked, they climbed eagerly into the bed.

Kiwi had long since learned that Virginia didn't have a shy bone in her body. She often took the lead in bed, teaching him new ways of pleasing her. She was also vocal in her ecstasy, often gasping or crying out "aaah!" and "oooh!" and "don't stop, don't stop!"

He was surprised, therefore, when Virginia ended her climax with something more like a wail and then collapsed and started sobbing into the sheets.

Bewildered, he asked, "What is it? What is it?"

She just turned away and cried harder. When he pulled her close to comfort her, he realised she was sobbing "Robin, Robin."

Eventually, she cried herself to sleep, leaving Kiwi lying on his back staring at the ceiling. He supposed this was another defeat, but he felt more disappointed than hurt. Virginia was false gold. Just like Betty. She glittered, she sparkled, she tantalised and — to be fair — she delivered exquisite excitement in bed. But he'd never trusted her, not since that first day in Berlin when she'd teased proprietary information out of him. He certainly didn't love her. Their relationship had always been about physical attraction. With a sigh he acknowledged that he was too old for that kind of shallow relationship. Nice as these nights had been, he'd rather do without than get pulled deeper into her web of dangerous illusions.

Far more depressing was the thought that he might be out of a job. If the Dakota had become superfluous then the entire Hamburg hub was at risk. Yes, they serviced the Halifax there, but he questioned whether David would be willing to pay for five groundcrew and the facilities if a second aircraft wasn't using them. David would probably want to consolidate operations in Berlin, which meant that Ron and Chips would be out of jobs again, too. Kiwi would become the "spare" pilot, and while he recognised the economic rationality of such an arrangement, he dreaded being an "odd bod." He didn't fancy being copilot to some American woman either!

Obviously, he could make the case to David that as partner, he "out-ranked" Jan and she ought to become the "odd bod." That made more sense anyway, because she'd flown heavies and so was theoretically qualified to fly as second pilot on the Halifax, something Kiwi could not do. However, Kiwi was reluctant even to talk to David in his present mood. He had not been himself ever since Charlotte had ditched him three weeks ago. He'd withdrawn into himself and hid behind a brittle, 'businesslike' exterior. Charlotte no longer came to work, although it was unclear whether she had resigned or David had fired her. Instead, David had taken over her responsibilities, dealing directly with customers himself. That was not a viable long-term situation, but the real problems lay deeper. Kiwi feared that in losing Charlotte, David had also lost his passion for helping Berlin.

Kiwi was surprised to discover that he felt more committed than ever. Those kids today, especially little Uwe, had got under his skin. He wanted to be part of helping get the kids out of Berlin before the worst of winter — or the Russians took over. He wanted to be part of keeping Berlin free for people like Uwe's mother, Axel and his team in Berlin, and for Christian and Charlotte too. He'd come to recognise that there were many good, honest, hard-working Germans.

Thinking of today's remarkably efficient effort to get as many as two thousand Berliners out in a single day also reminded him that his friend Robin had acted without the approval of his direct superior. That was a very risky thing to do. Kiwi knew he would never have dared something like this, and he feared that Robin might have over-reached himself this time. If so, he was going to pay the price. What a lousy day it had turned out to be, after getting off to such a good start!

Kiwi turned to look at Virginia's beautiful, naked body one last time. Then he slipped as gently as he could out of the bed and dressed slowly, so as not to wake her. He tip-toed out into the hall and shut the door behind him. The party was over.

Homeward Bound
Frankfurt / Main
Saturday, 27 November 1948
(Day 155)

J.B. had barely put his head down for some well-earned sleep after an exhausting three round trips to Berlin when the public address system blared out his name and ordered him to report to the squadron adjutant. Still dead tired, he dragged himself out of bed and pulled on some clothes. He hadn't shaved in almost 24 hours, and his last shower had been before that. His uniform was wrinkled because there was no place to hang it properly in the old barn, while his shoes hadn't seen polish in a week or more.

Still yawning as he entered the adjutant's office, he'd barely saluted before the squadron adjutant hit him with: "Is your fiancée the daughter of a senator or something?"

"No, sir. Why?"

"Because I've got a goddamned 'special request cable' here that says you are to be released from Airlift duties 'forthwith' and are to return to CONUS on the first available aircraft. Your reserve status remains 'active' and you may be recalled for duty stateside, but you are hereby off the Airlift and on leave until further notice. Congratulations, buddy. Don't know how you did it, but I wish it had been me rather than you!" Despite his words, the adjutant grinned and offered his hand.

J.B. gaped at him, dazed. "I'm supposed to return to CONUS?"

"Just as soon as you can get your butt over to the flight line for the birds headed Stateside. You can fly back in the bucket seat and spell the pilots a bit. You did a fine job, Baronowsky. Those candy-drops you and Halvorsen came up with made a lot of people happy — and I don't just mean the kids here in Berlin. Been great publicity for the USAF!"

"Yeah," J.B. agreed. He didn't care so much about that, but he had a gnawing suspicion that the publicity for the candy drops had been what enabled Patty's dad to pull strings with some congressman for his transfer home.

The problem was, he didn't want to return to the States yet. On the one hand, things were getting critical in Berlin, and on the other the fog had finally lifted, so they could — and should be — flying more than ever before. It didn't feel right to just turn his back on it all.

He hesitated in the hall before the adjutant's office, wondering if he could ask to stay on for a bit, but he already knew the answer. A 'special request cable' prompted by a congressman's letter wasn't something a captain — or even an adjutant with the rank of major — could challenge. He was homeward bound whether he liked it or not. How weird.

Still in a daze, he made his way back to the Zeppelinheim, collected his meagre belongings, left his dry-cleaning chit for one of his uniforms with Barry, and asked him to send his stuff to him when he got it. He looked around the loft of the barn once more, feeling a peculiar fondness for it. Then again, it hadn't been the same since he and Hal had split up. Hal had returned from his publicity tour in the States almost two months ago, but in the meantime J.B. had been made captain of his own crew. They had not flow together since, and their schedules rarely seemed to overlap. At most they managed a fleeting coffee or orange juice now and again. They rotated J.B.'s copilots a lot too. He'd flown with so many guys in the last couple of months that they all sort of blurred together — just like the days and nights.

J.B. shouldered his duffle bag and went backwards down the ladder to the ground floor and out into the afternoon sunshine. He caught one of the "shuttles" back to the base and made his way to the flight line for the C-74s that were flying in tons of spare parts and maintenance tools for the Airlift fleet. Asking around, he found out which one was leaving next and introduced himself to the crew over at the ops room. They welcomed him and told him to just stick with them. The aircraft was fuelled up and the copilot had gone for the latest Met.

"Not some kind of emergency at home, I hope?" the pilot asked solicitously.

"Not that anybody told me about. Just orders to report to CONUS 'on the next flight.'"

The pilot shook his head. "No way to figure out the Air Force, is there?"

When the copilot arrived, they all went out together and climbed aboard the transport. J.B. stowed away his duffle bag and kept out of the way as the crew went through their checks. Eventually, they trundled out to the runway for take-off, and less than three hours after receiving his orders, J.B. was airborne, bound for the United States.

They broke out of the cloud at four thousand feet and were abruptly heading straight towards the golden orb of the setting sun. The clouds below them were painted in brilliant hues of copper and bronze. All four men in the cockpit caught their breath at the splendour of the expansive skyscape. One of the pilots remarked, awestruck, "Makes you think of Rhine Gold, doesn't it?"

"Yeah, or the twilight of the Gods," his colleague answered.

It got dark soon after that, and J.B. went to lie down and get some sleep so he could spell the pilots later. He made himself comfortable on the rest bed, and as he closed his eyes thought of Kathleen. He would never see her or hear her voice again. He knew that was for the best. When he had Patty real and alive beside him, he told himself, he would forget all the phantoms of the past and mist. He would focus on the present and the future and forget the old world with all its problems. Yet as the engines lulled him to sleep, his heart longed to be flying closer to Kathleen rather than farther away.

Abandoned Lair
Berlin-Kreuzberg
Saturday, 27 November 1948
(Day 155)

Someone was knocking on the apartment door, and Christian dragged himself off the sofa where he now slept. He'd turned his bedroom with its narrow bed over to Fritz and gratefully accepted the loan of a large, well-upholstered sofa from Jakob Liebherr. Yet while giving the ravaged Fritz the bed and privacy of a room to himself had seemed like the right thing to do a month ago, Christian was beginning to wonder when Fritz would start to pick up the pieces of his life and move out. Guests, like fish, started to stink at some point...

As he passed the kitchen door, he noted it was just after 8 am and dawn was barely making itself felt through the gloom of a November morning. It was bitterly cold in the apartment since they had too little coal to light the tile ovens except at dinner time. He went to answer the door in the clothes he'd slept in — his old, Luftwaffe great coat over his pyjamas. He put his eye to the peephole and saw Anton Sperl standing on the landing. He was properly dressed in an overcoat and hat, looking very much the police inspector these days.

Christian opened the door a crack with the words, "I'm not dressed yet. Is it something urgent?"

"No. I just wanted to bring you the bad news."

Christian opened the door all the way and stared at Sperl.

"He got away."

"What?"

"Friedebach. We surrounded the house last night and tried to deliver the arrest warrant, but the bird had flown. We searched the house from top to bottom, but both he and his 'butler' — or brother if your suspicions are correct — were nowhere to be found. They left no personal effects behind, just the furnishings, books, etc. that were in the house. We questioned the neighbours, but all claimed to have seen and heard nothing. Just as deaf and blind as when the SS dragged the Jews away," his tone of disgust did not sound artificial.

"You're saying Friedebach has disappeared?" Christian asked, and when Sperl nodded he concluded, "Someone tipped him off!"

"Very probably. But who? The Ivans or the Amis?"

"You think the *Amis* might be protecting him? But they're the ones who have pursued Nazi war criminals most actively."

"Except when it suits their purposes," Sperl retorted cynically. "Our warrant was for drug dealing, but what Herr Friedebach, or rather Aggstein, *really* sold were chemical weapons — or the formulas for producing them. The Amis don't want him working for the Ivans."

"Then it should suit their purposes to arrest him!"

"Ah, yes, but a public trial would make it difficult to put him to work in the Pentagon, wouldn't it? In the end it doesn't matter. He slipped through our fingers at the last moment." Although Sperl was trying to sound indifferent, he failed, sounding depressed instead.

"What about the house and its furnishings?" Christian asked.

Sperl glanced over his shoulder and then asked in a low voice. "May I come in for just a moment?"

Without hesitation, Christian backed up and let Sperl in, closing the door behind him. In the apartment hallway, Sperl murmured almost inaudibly. "The villa is vacant, in excellent condition by Berlin standards, and large enough to house about twenty people. The city government might want to move people who need housing into it. On the other hand, it's a beautiful villa in the American Sector, and the Americans may expropriate it for officer housing. Nevertheless, if your Jewish friend's claims are good, it will eventually be restored to him. Meanwhile," Sperl reached into his coat pocket and pulled out a set of keys, "I found these in a desk drawer. I'm not sure my colleagues even noticed them, and I don't intend to report them missing." He let them drop into Christian's hand, adding, "Who is going to want to expel the Jewish heir to the murdered owner just because the paperwork isn't complete?"

"Particularly when that man is responsible for flying sick Berliners to safety in the West," Christian finished his thought. He bowed his head formally to Sperl. "I am in your debt, Herr *Kapitaenleutnant.*"

"I'll remember that, Herr *Staffelkapitaen.* Now, I must be on my way."

Although Christian had not spoken to David Goldman since Bredow's return, their joint interest in seeing "Friedebach" brought to justice took precedence over tension arising from Charlotte's decision to break off with him. As soon as Christian explained the situation, David agreed to meet, and four hours later they stood together outside the villa on Schwanenwerder.

It looked no more dilapidated than when Christian had first seen it, but there was a notice on the door saying the former resident was wanted by the police. It asked anyone with information about him to contact the telephone number provided. The police had been forced to break into the house and had nailed the front door shut when they left.

David was unperturbed. He led Christian around to a door half-hidden by a trellis covered with dormant vines on the side of the house. He tried several keys until he found the one that worked. As the door creaked open,

David remarked in a melancholy voice, "After swimming, we'd come here, strip out of our bathing things, shower and change and then have a snack there in the servants' kitchen." As he spoke, he pointed out the shower room and kitchen before leading Christian deeper into the house.

Christian grasped that they were in the servants' quarters. He noticed blistered paint, broken tiles, rust marks and other signs of decay, yet he could sense an almost tangible benevolence that still dwelt in this house. It was not hard to imagine children's laughter and the smell of fresh-baked sweets.

Meanwhile, David led him up a few stairs and along a hallway to the large salon offering a spectacular view of the lake where Christian had first encountered Friedebach. The sun had finally penetrated the fog and was slowing burning it away. Despite the remnants of mist clinging to the trees, the water sparkled tentatively as it flirted with turning blue.

Christian had no interest in the view. He swung sharply towards the back wall where on his last visit a painting by Max Lieberman had hung. Indeed, elaborately framed oil still filled the space over the heavy buffet, but something white was stuck in the middle.

With a sharp intake of breath, Christian realised a knife stabbed into the canvas held a note in place. He rushed to the painting and together with David they lifted the heavy, gilt frame off the wall and laid it face up on the buffet. Christian then carefully extracted the knife and read the note.

"I will have my revenge, Feldburg. Traitors always get what they deserve — in your case hanging from a meat hook on piano wire."

Christian snorted and tossed the note aside to examine the damage to the painting.

David picked up the note and gasped, "How could he know you were the one who put the police onto him?"

"That was easy," Christian replied without looking up from his inspection. "In addition to the title and artist, the names of the subjects are neatly recorded on the back. If our suspicions are correct and his butler was actually his brother, Max, then he probably remembered clashing with my brother Philip in Warsaw. From there it was only a small step to realising that his vanity had given him away."

"His vanity?" David asked puzzled.

"When we first met, he couldn't resist offering me a cigarette from a silver case with the Aggstein arms on it. At the time, he only wanted to signal to me that he was my social equal. Once he realised who Philip was, however, he will have worked out that I might also know about his brother's war crimes."

"Can the painting be repaired?" David asked anxiously.

Christian's attention was still focused on the canvas as he replied cautiously. "I doubt it can ever be completely repaired, but he made a mistake. He aimed the knife at me, thinking that was what would hurt most. The image of my brother, however, appears undamaged — and that's all I care about. And you? Do you now have what you wanted?"

David surveyed the beautiful room around him and shrugged. "I am glad to have that Nazi out, but what use do I have for a house like this?"

Christian considered him solemnly. In all their encounters, David had never looked so fragile or vulnerable as now. Christian turned from David to look at the furnishings more systematically, verifying what he had long suspected. "Almost everything in this room belonged to my father. It was stolen from our apartment on the Maybachufer in the last days of the war by a senior SD officer, who housed his mistress in our apartment."

"You can have it back," David offered instantly.

"I don't want it back. I don't ever want to live in the apartment where my brother killed himself, and nor does his widow."

"Then you can move in here if you want. Send for your wife to join you. I won't charge excessive rent." David tried to make a joke, but if fell flat.

"My mother and wife are much safer and happier where they are earning D-Marks hand-over-fist in the American Zone," Christian answered. "I would much rather leave everything here so Charlotte can enjoy them when she marries you."

David turned hard, angry eyes on Christian. "Charlotte isn't going to marry me! She plans to marry Fritz von Bredow instead."

The bitterness in David's voice made Christian wince, but he replied steadily, "I know she told you that, but I believe she will come to her senses and send Fritz away. She has been badly wounded, but underneath Charlotte is a strong and sensible woman."

"You don't want her to marry Bredow?" David's tone was wary.

"Good lord, no! He may once have been a wonderful, charming and caring young man, but he is no more. What is left is cold, calculating and, I believe, brutalised beyond salvation. I've seen men like him before. I try to keep my distance."

"Charlotte doesn't see that," David told him stiffly. His face was so immobile, that Christian couldn't begin to guess what he felt.

Christian tried to explain, "Bredow is shamelessly exploiting her pity at present, but pity is no basis for marriage. The man she *loves* is you." Christian looked David in the eye and his firm voice reflected his confidence.

David broke eye contact and walked over to the windows. He stood staring out at the dissolving fog for a long time. Then he turned back to face Christian. "I'm honoured that you think I'm the better man — it proves what I have always sensed about *you*: that you are utterly untouched by antisemitism. But what about Charlotte? Aren't centuries of antisemitism, magnified to inescapable dimensions under the Nazis, at the bottom of her rejection of me? Hasn't she, possibly without even knowing it, breathed in that poison for too long to free herself of it?"

It was a fair question, but Christian shook his head. "No. She could not have looked at you and talked about you the way she did if she had ever looked down on you for any reason. While I can understand your suspicions, they are unfounded. I firmly believe that Charlotte loves you with all her heart."

"I wish I could believe that, but Charlotte was very explicit when explaining her preference for Bredow. She didn't talk about feeling sorry for him. She said he was *better* for her. If you are correct and she was not referring to me being a Jew, then she was motivated perhaps by class-consciousness. She prefers the wreck of Nazi over me because he's a nobleman."

"Charlotte doesn't have a snobbish bone in her body," Christian protested. "I'm certain there was a misunderstanding. Tell me exactly what she said."

"She talked old-fashioned nonsense about 'pledging her troth' and then said they were 'fated' for one another. When I challenged such a childish notion, she rephrased things, saying they 'fitted' one another better and marriage to him would be 'more appropriate'—"

"Jesus, Mary and Joseph," Christian whispered with so much feeling that he silenced David.

When Christian said no more, David prompted, "You see? She thinks I am beneath her."

Shaking his head, Christian took a deep breath. "No. That's not it at all." God, give me strength, he prayed. "Just the opposite. She doesn't think *she* is *worthy* of you."

"What are you talking about?" David snapped back frowning.

Christian replied by declaring, "There must be alcohol somewhere in this house!" Turning his back on David, he stormed over to the buffet on which the painting lay and started opening doors until he found a cut crystal decanter. He lifted the top, sniffed, and declared, "Brandy. That will do." He found matching crystal glasses, poured brandy into two and returned to hand one to David with the order, "Sit down and drink that."

"Why?"

"Because I am about to tell you something that you don't want to hear and which I don't want to tell you and which Charlotte doesn't want me to tell you, but which you have to know nevertheless."

David sat down on the edge of one of the satin-covered chairs and took the glass from Christian, but barely touched the liquid. Christian, on the other hand, took a large gulp and then another. He returned to the buffet, refilled his glass, and then faced David. Taking a deep breath, he started, "Charlotte arrived in Berlin in January 1945 after seeing her parents killed by a strafing Soviet fighter."

"I know," David told him coldly.

"She was here when the Russians laid siege to the city and lived for weeks in the cellar."

"Yes, she told me that."

"When the fighting was over, no one had been able to get out to get food for days. Men who ventured out were being shot. So, Jasha and Charlotte decided they had to go."

David caught his breath. "They didn't... You don't mean... The Russians!" He stared at Christian. "Charlotte?"

"A gang of them — nine that she can remember — cornered them. Three attacked Jasha. The others took turns raping, kicking, and urinating on Charlotte. They broke both her arms, and Frau Liebherr said her face was so swollen, bruised and blood-covered that she hardly recognised her.

She was hospitalised and could not walk for days."

David was staring at him, shaking his head in disbelief. Christian felt compelled to continue. "The Liebherrs nursed her back to health, but she still has nightmares and is sometimes overcome by self-loathing. She carries around a sense of worthlessness." He paused to let that sink in before underlining his point by adding, "When the blockade started and she feared you would return to Britain without her, she asked me to shoot her."

"No!" David protested. "How could she?"

"She was broken, David. She was utterly broken. I think what she hates most is that she begged and pleaded and grovelled to them. She believes she should have killed herself rather than go on living — it was the Liebherrs and two broken arms that stopped her. Thousands of other women did kill themselves, you know? Thousands of young women killed themselves from shame. Yet that shame lives on in Charlotte. That is why she does not think she is worthy of you."

"But — how — why — if she feels like that, why would she think she is worthy of Fritz von Bredow? It doesn't make sense!"

Christian came to stand directly before David. "Fritz has been tortured, insulted, starved, beaten, humiliated, and enslaved by the Russians for six years. She sees the scars he wears and equates them with her invisible scars. She thinks he will understand her and accept her because he knows what it is to be helpless in the face of Russian brutality. She thinks he won't blame her for what happened. And, because they have gone through the same hell, she believes they are better suited to one another, better 'fitted' to face the future together." He paused to let David comment, but the other man just looked dazed. Christian concluded, "That's what she meant about being fated for one another. She believes the Russians made their fate for them."

David shook his head. "I don't know what to say. I never thought — never dreamed — Charlotte? Charlotte was raped?" He seemed to be pleading with Christian to take back his words.

Christian could only nod and insist, "Six times."

David dropped his head in his hands, and Christian waited. What he missed were assurances that it didn't matter. Christian had expected David to express horror — but also sympathy. He'd expected to hear David say that he loved Charlotte regardless. Instead, David remained silent until he seemed to remember the drink Christian had brought him. He lifted his head, took the brandy and downed it all at once.

"More?" Christian asked.

David shook his head. "No. No. I need time to think. I need time alone. Would you leave me, please? Just leave me here."

Christian hesitated a moment more, and then replied, "You have the keys."

"Yes. I'll see you get the painting."

"There's no rush. You know where to find me."

Game Over
Bremen
Sunday, 28 November 1948
(Day 156)

Emily turned to scan the sky. It wasn't raining, but the air was laden with humidity. She turned up the collar of her Irvine flight jacket and buckled it to shield her face. With the weather marginally above the minimums, they had made three flights with patients out of Berlin, the last flight ending here in Bremen. The patients had long since been whisked away in an ambulance, and Rick was seeing to the refuelling while Jan got the latest weather report. The nurse was cleaning out the sick bay where one of the passengers had been air sick.

Emily was nervous without knowing why. Yes, the weather seemed to be worsening again and the last thing she wanted was to be forced to stay here overnight. They'd been stuck out six nights so far this month. That meant hotel and bar bills and being late for flying patients out the next day. Costs were going up and revenues going down. Yet her urgency to return to Berlin eclipsed such practical considerations.

Irrationally, Emily sensed that something was wrong with Robin. As important and fulfilling as her job was, he remained the mainstay of her life. She could weather losing her job, but she would be mutilated and only partly alive without Robin. She needed him, and she had experienced this nagging apprehension once before — on the day he'd been shot down over France.

The uneasy feeling had been building up all day, but she had suppressed it and concentrated on getting her job done. Now, however, the need to get back to Robin could no longer be ignored. She lifted her voice and called over to Rick. "How much longer, Rick?"

"About two minutes!" That was good.

Shortly afterwards, however, Jan emerged out of the darkness to announce, "Looks like the weather is gonna get worse. There's a new low-pressure system moving in from the West that will sweep across northern Germany in the next three to four hours."

"Bringing what?" Emily asked, irritated. She didn't want bad weather. She wanted to get back to Berlin.

"Well, rain and wind from here to Schwerin. Further south, the ceiling might drop to a thousand feet or less. We might be better off staying here for the next twelve hours or so," Jan suggested.

Easy for her to say, Emily thought. Jan and Rick formed a self-contained team. As long as they had each other they were content; overnighting in different cities was the kind of vagrant, gypsy life they'd had in the States. She glanced towards the unfamiliar German nurse, who unhelpfully shrugged and said, "Whatever you decide, Frau Kapitaen." Only Emily had a burning desire to get back to Gatow.

Emily made her decision. "No need to stay here. We have plenty of time to hop over to Hamburg and report in at Airlift operations. If we have to stay out, then we'll do so in Hamburg, ready to fly down the corridor as soon as the weather lifts."

There was no arguing either with her logic or her authority, so the others dutifully climbed back aboard Moby Dick, and they set off. At RAF Fuhlsbuettel, the weather forecast was the same, but the Airlift had not been interrupted. Emily used this to justify continuing down to Berlin.

Meanwhile, it was pitch dark and the wind was gusting strongly off the Baltic. Although this buffeted Moby Dick at take-off and made for a rough ride, as long as they had good visibility, Emily wasn't worried. They had been given a cruising altitude of 3,000 feet and a speed of 140 mph following behind a block of Dakotas flying the same speed but five hundred feet higher. Each RAF aircraft had a navigator and the RAF's latest navigation equipment on board, ensuring Dakotas did not stray from the corridor no matter how much wind there was. Since Moby Dick was equipped with the same radio crystals as the RAF, she could listen in on their transmission and piggy-back off their navigation as she usually did.

Then, halfway to Berlin, a loud, undulating whining burst out of their earphones. "What the hell is that?" Jan shouted as she shoved the earphones off her ears angrily.

Emily likewise moved her earphones partly off her ears to escape the almost painful noise, and shouted over the engines, "The Soviets are jamming the frequency! You take the controls while I try to find the alternative RAF frequency."

As she fiddled with the radio, picking up only one jamming station after another, she comforted herself with the fact that the RAF flew with their navigation lights on. That made it relatively easy to follow along behind them even without having the added benefit of hearing their progress reports.

And then the cloud ceiling dropped. Suddenly Moby Dick became suspended in impenetrable murk. The navigation lights of the Dakotas were extinguished.

Now they were in trouble.

No matter how well they held their course and speed in the air, the course made good would be distorted by the wind. Furthermore, because it was gusting irregularly, the impact would be almost incalculable. Yes, when she'd flown for the Air Transport Auxiliary, Emily had flown without radios or instruments. All navigating had been done by comparing a map to the countryside below her. But the ATA never flew by night, and if the weather closed down (as it so often did in England), ATA pilots landed at the nearest field and waited out a change in the weather. Moby Dick didn't have that option because they were flying over the Soviet Zone. Furthermore, they were at acute risk of being blown out of the corridor.

By the look Jan gave her, Emily knew she, too, was remembering that the Soviets threatened to shoot down Allied aircraft that wandered into their airspace. Any crew who survived the ensuing crash, the Russians emphasised, would be treated as spies and shot.

Without taking her eyes off the instruments, Jan yelled over the sound of the engines, "How soon can we get a ground fix from a beacon?"

"Not for another twenty minutes at best," Emily shouted back. She felt Rick shift his gaze from the instrument panel towards her.

Emily reviewed their situation. The Met had predicted winds gusting up to 35 knots out of the northeast. That was smack into their flank which meant that without constant correction they could not avoid being pushed southwest. If they laid on port rudder without a reference point, however, they risked over-compensating and flying out of the corridor to the north. They were out of range of both Hamburg and Berlin air traffic control channels, and there were no ground-based navigation beacons in the Soviet Zone. Emily concluded that the best option was to sink below the cloud and try to get a visual fix. Switching on her microphone, she announced as calmly as she could, "I think we'd better see if we can find the autobahn and follow it to Berlin."

"We don't know how low the ceiling is!" Jan reminded her.

"No, but we can't carry on blind," Emily retorted. When Jan turned to stare at her incredulously, Emily reached for the control column and announced. "I'll take her."

Jan took her hands off the controls dramatically, as if they were hot, and then sat back with a look of disapproval on her face. She and Rick exchanged a glance, clearly on the same wavelength. Emily felt isolated and intimidated. They had not wanted to make this flight and they had been right. She had insisted for the wrong reasons: her irrational concerns about Robin. Being flanked by them now with their joint disapproval was doubly intimidating. She couldn't afford the extra strain on her nerves when flying in a tricky situation. She clicked on her microphone. "Rick, please go forward into the nose and see what you can see. We're looking for the four-lane Hamburg-Berlin Autobahn. If we can find that we can ride it all the way to Berlin."

Rick hesitated, looked to Jan, and she nodded once. He then dropped down into the nose. With him no longer standing over her, Emily started to ease the column forward, putting the Wellington into a shallow dive. "Read the altimeter for me, would you please, Jan?" Emily urged.

Jan dutifully reported, "2,500... 2,200... 2,000..."

They broke into the clear at 600 feet on the altimeter and Emily could see Jan relax beside her. She put her mic to her face and called down to

Rick. "Can you see any landmarks down there?"

"Not a goddamn thing!" Rick retorted. "It's a black as — wait that might be a vehicle moving on a road, but it doesn't look like an autobahn to me. It's hardly — wait! I've got something over to the left. Swing twenty degrees to port."

Emily obeyed and thereafter Rick directed her with growing confidence. Emily was reminded that he had been a bomb aimer in the war. After a few more minutes, he called up with a triumphant. "Got it! Turn ten degrees to starboard! Good. Good. Steady. Hold this heading. We're flying the autobahn, ladies!"

That was at least something. On the other hand, rain now sporadically lashed the windscreen, and the gusts of wind shook them. Every now and again, the Wellington bucked in turbulence.

Several minutes later, Rick called up to report, "There seems to be a road junction coming up and the autobahn bends."

"Tell me how to stay on the autobahn," Emily replied.

"OK.... Turn more to starboard. That's right. Just a little more. Steady on this course."

Easier said than done, Emily thought as the Wellington dropped ten feet and then leapt up again like a steeplechaser. At least the rain squalls lashed at their quarter and the windscreen was a bit clearer.

Emily asked Jan to try to raise the Berlin Air Safety Centre, but all they got was terrible static disrupting and distorting transmissions of men singing in Russian.

"See if you can raise Gatow. Maybe the Ivans aren't jamming those frequencies." Emily suggested.

Jan tuned the radio and put out the call. There was no response, but Jan kept trying both frequencies, flipping from one to the other. Suddenly, they got a faint contact interrupted by bursts of static. "Come in, Moby Dick!" a voice pleaded several times.

Jan made several attempts to reply without success, but at last they picked up signals from the Frohnau beacon, and with considerable relief turned onto the familiar approach. Over the intercom, Emily told Rick to look for Gatow's flare path.

"Roger," Rick replied, and then a few moments later he reported, "Target in sight."

Jan glanced at Emily uncertainly at first, but when Emily smiled, she smiled back.

The mood was shattered by blinding light flooding the cockpit. Emily cried out in surprise and instinctively yanked the column up. Over the intercom came a stream of cursing from Rick. Fortunately, Jan remained calm. With a hand shading her eyes as she squinted, she declared, "I've got her. I've got her."

Emily realised that Jan had been looking down when the searchlights switched on and her night vision had been less badly impaired. She readily turned the aircraft over to her.

Minutes later they flew out of the cone of light and back into the darkness, but Emily's night vision remained diminished. She gestured for Jan to retain the controls and reached for the mic to call Gatow. The usually calm controller responded with a nervous, "What is your altitude, Moby Dick?"

"We're at 480 feet."

"You have a Tudor tanker directly overhead. Throttle back *now!* Give him space!"

Emily winced at this reminder of how risky her diversion from the flight pattern had been. She watched carefully as Jan throttled back until Moby Dick wallowed along at 100 mph then searched the sky for the Tudor. She never saw the other aircraft, and shortly afterwards they were handed over to the GCA controller and talked down onto the PSP runway.

As they touched down in drizzling rain and visibility of less than one mile, Emily felt a wave of relief sweep over her. She was buoyed up further when Jan tossed a wide, warm smile in her direction. Then Rick put his head into the cockpit and exclaimed, "Hot dang! You gals actually got us down in one piece."

Emily was disconcerted until Jan quipped back with a wink to Emily, "No thanks to you, dude."

"Yeah, well, no one's paying me for flying. What I need is a drink," he countered as their tyres thumped over the cracks in the taxiway.

"Knowing you, you need a bottle!" Jan retorted.

"Well, better a bottle in front of me than a frontal lobotomy — as *some* people have suggested to me."

It dawned on Emily that swapping insults was part of their routine, and they had been inhibited by her presence. Tonight's shared dangers had broken down their reserve, and they at last felt comfortable enough to be themselves. When the nurse came up behind Rick and admitted timidly that she'd been "a little worried," they all laughed — perhaps too loudly — but it felt good.

The double euphoria of escaping danger and forging better ties with Rick and Jan temporarily diminished Emily's anxiety about Robin. Nevertheless, she rang him as soon as she could reach a phone, but he sounded fine, just distracted. He told her it would be an hour or two before he could get away from the office. She felt a little foolish for taking such risks on account of an unfounded foreboding but comforted herself that everything had worked out in the end. Besides, now she could join Rick and Jan for a drink or two at the Malcolm Club, which would surely solidify the improvement in their relationship.

Food and drink soon lubricated the conversation, and Emily found herself listening and laughing as Jan and Rick regaled her with tales of their misadventures in civil aviation. About an hour into the evening, Kit and his crew walked in. They had just returned with a second inbound load and Albie was safe in the hangar. They were in good spirits and another round was ordered for everyone. Emily was decidedly tipsy by the time Robin walked in and said it was time to go.

Emily took an unusually warm farewell of Rick and Jan, saying, "We should do this more often," and then she and Kit followed Robin back out into the night. As she climbed into the car beside Robin, she noticed an eerie stillness had descended. It took her a second to realise what it meant, and then all her presentiments of disaster returned. "Is Gatow closed?"

"For the last half hour and probably well into tomorrow," Robin replied in a grim voice.

Some irrational voice warned her this was different from all the other times they had closed. This was more ominous. More final. Something terrible *had* happened. She could sense it. She just couldn't ask about it with Kit in the car.

On arrival at the house, Georgina and Jasha had dinner waiting for them, so they sat down together for a cold meal by candlelight. They kept their overcoats on throughout dinner because there was no heat. The chill discouraged lingering, particularly since it was already late. Kit and

Georgina excused themselves to go upstairs as soon as they finished eating.

Alone at last, Emily turned to Robin, "What is it? What's happened?"

Uncharacteristically, rather than answering, he got to his feet and went to stand staring out of the window. The fog swirled on the terrace like ghosts trying to get inside, and at the foot of the lawn wind tore through the trees causing the branches to thrash frantically like drowning souls waving for help. A knot formed in the pit of Emily's stomach, and she cautiously got to her feet to move up behind Robin. Inwardly, she waited for the axe to fall.

His back still to her, he finally spoke, "Effective this morning, I am no longer Station Commander at Gatow."

She saw no point in expressing surprise or outrage; they had talked through the possible consequences of bypassing Bagshot ten days ago when he told her what he planned to do. Still, she could not suppress an indignant, "What a petty-minded bastard!"

Robin added tensely, "I am to remain as Acting Station Commander until my replacement arrives, so I have not made a public announcement yet."

"And your onward assignment?" Emily asked apprehensively.

He shrugged. "There is none. I am to report to the Ministry. I expect to be cashiered." He said it harshly, and Emily knew that he was bleeding inside. The RAF was his life. He had not been one of those who entered the service because of the war. He had dreamt of wearing Air Force blue from the time he was a little boy. He'd gone to Cranwell. He'd grown up in the RAF; he'd matured in it. It was a part of him and he of it. It was his identity. He could not simply shrug and set it aside like an old hat.

She thought of saying something like: "We don't know that yet." Or "Let's wait and see." Yet sensible as such suggestions might be, they offered inadequate comfort. She chose instead, "Robin, whatever happens and wherever we go, I will be with you. No complaints and no recriminations."

At last, he turned around and reached out a hand. She took it, and he pulled her into his arms and held her. She laid her cheek on the rough wool of his greatcoat and waited. They had been through bad times before. They had survived the war. They would survive this crisis too, she was sure of that. Yet saying anything of the kind at this juncture would belittle the depth of Robin's pain and the magnitude of his defeat.

After several moments he spoke again. "Evacuating as many vulnerable Berliners as is humanly possible was and is our duty — both as a nation and as Christians."

Emily herself was agnostic, but Robin had a devotion to God so deep that he had no need for churchgoing. He did not speak of his "Christian" duties often, which made it all the more significant when did. She clutched his hand more firmly and assured him. "I agree one hundred per cent, Robin."

He drew back from their embrace without letting go of her hand and spoke to the fog. "I knew that Bagshot was a heartless bastard, but I honestly expected him to be overruled by someone higher up. I thought 46 Group or the Ministry would recognise that this evacuation is something we — HM Government, the United Kingdom, the British Empire — must do. By punishing me for what I've done, the RAF is effectively saying that the chain of command is more important than the lives of children. I am profoundly disillusioned."

Emily nodded. Saying that she was *not* so surprised would only add insult to injury.

Robin drew a deep breath and announced, "And much as I appreciate your loyalty, you must continue with your work. You must keep flying the ambulance. I shall return to England on my own." He paused, appeared to have a second thought, and added, "Of course, you and the Morans won't be able to live in the Station Commander's house any more. You'll have to move over to the Malcolm Club."

Emily nodded. "Of course. But realistically, this is Gotterdammerung. All EAS aircraft have been grounded more days than they could fly this past month. Meanwhile, with Charlotte no longer handling the customers, we're encountering more and more confusion and complaints, and David is effectively MIA. The company is falling apart. Most importantly, we can only fly as long as there is an Airlift. If this weather keeps up, there won't be one much longer."

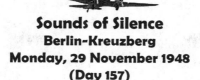

Sounds of Silence
Berlin-Kreuzberg
Monday, 29 November 1948
(Day 157)

Jakob Liebherr was torn from a deep sleep and looked around his bedroom, bewildered. It was pitch dark, although he sensed it was no longer the middle of the night. It must be close to when his alarm went off at 7 am. Sunrise wasn't until 7:50, so the gloom was natural. Yet something was wrong. So wrong that it had woken him up.

The next instant he knew what it was: the silence.

No aircraft were flying overhead. After just five days of resumed flights, the Airlift had been suspended yet again.

Jakob rolled out of bed into his old slippers and shuffled to the window to pull back the curtains and look outside. It was his worst nightmare: fog so thick he could not see the street below or the canal opposite.

My God, my God. Why hast Thou forsaken us? He asked mentally.

It was impossible to go back to sleep, so Jakob quietly collected his clothes and went to get dressed in the bathroom. With the city elections just five days away, he had a busy schedule. The SPD had rallies in two boroughs. Jakob had an interview with the *Tagesspiegel*, and for a talk Reuter would be giving on RIAS tomorrow, the mayor had asked Jakob to supply him with a variety of statistics. Reuter wanted the updated number of kidnappings; he wanted data on the number of factories the Russians had dismantled, and the number of jobs lost with them; he wanted, in short, hard facts to counter the litany of lies that came out of Karlshorst and Moscow.

Day in and day out, the Russian media hammered people with words that warped their minds and confused them with falsehoods. Through repetition alone, they appeared capable of making people believe that embracing Stalin's authoritarian dictatorship would somehow "liberate" them from the "oppression" of Western "warmongers". Bizarre as the Russian claims were, the volume, confidence and frequency with which these baseless lies were repeated seemed to lend them credence. Jakob feared that the SPD and with it the forces of democracy were about to suffer a catastrophic political defeat in the upcoming elections.

Hungry people rarely had the energy to think about anything other than their next meal — and the Berliners were getting hungry. Rations were down to 1,200 calories for the average adult, and people waited in line for as much as six hours to get their meagre rations of powdered potatoes, powdered milk, and powdered eggs. Smuggling wasn't worth the risk at this time of year, when farmers had so little to offer, and private reserves had long since been depleted. Trude had nothing left in her cupboards except a bottle of Sperl's schnapps and some Feldburg wine.

The cold also gnawed at people's nerves and spirits. It wasn't bitterly cold yet, just cold enough to remind people that winter was coming. Two years ago, the Spree had frozen over and so had Berlin's water pipes. No one had had water to wash or flush toilets. People had started going outside to the nearest heap of rubble to do their business rather than stink up their apartments. Even if it wasn't that bad yet, people knew they had less coal now than they'd had then. Everyone dreaded winter, including Jakob.

Yet the darkness, Jakob decided, was worst of all. The sun didn't rise until nearly 8 am and it set before 4 pm. If the sky was overcast even those eight hours were gloomy, and once the sun set it was as if the city had been swallowed by the underworld. There were no streetlights, no headlights, and no lighting from the shops or houses either. The darkness was more impenetrable and complete than in the wartime blackout because it didn't end when one went inside. With no electricity, people couldn't read or listen to the radio or play a gramophone. All they could do was sit together and talk about how horrible their situation was, or sit alone and despair altogether.

Jakob finished dressing. He found his way to the kitchen and took a stale "*Broetchen*" from the breadbasket and started nibbling at it. It would get him through the morning. As he pulled on his overcoat and hat, he heard his alarm go off. He returned to the bedroom to tell Trude he was on his way to work. She grunted understanding and turned over to sleep a little longer.

Holding on to the battered banister to help find his footing in the dark of the stairwell, Jakob navigated the stairs to the ground floor. At the very bottom, he tripped over a board that was missing and nearly fell on his face. Cursing, he crossed the lobby and let himself out into the chill, damp morning. As the front door clunked shut behind him, he came to an abrupt halt. He could see absolutely nothing! Not even the trees lining the canal, let alone the buildings on the other side. The fog was so thick, it would be hard to *walk* in it — never mind drive or fly.

He looked up helplessly at the silent sky. Berlin had only seven days of coal left and ten days of food. If the Airlift didn't resume soon, they would have nothing at all. And when the last reserves of coal, flour and potatoes were gone, the people of Berlin would be beaten. The Western garrisons would have no choice but to withdraw, and the vengeful Russian bear would inflict upon Berliners all the horrors of his brutish arrogance.

No one could say the Allies hadn't tried to save them. They had spared neither money nor men. They had sent their best leaders and they had sacrificed men's lives. But they could not control the weather and they could not stop the winter. As Napoleon and Hitler had already learned, winter was a Russian ally.

The End

If you enjoyed this book. Please post a review on the online retailer of your choice.

Historical Note

Although the principal characters in this novel are fictional, the main events are historical fact. The extraordinary Soviet siege of Berlin 1948-1949 and the Allied response are well documented, and many excellent, factual accounts of these events have been published. You can find selected titles under "Recommended Reading." In this short note, I wish only to highlight some of the more surprising facts and draw attention to conscious deviations from historical record.

A Word on the Characters in this Novel

- Gail Halvorsen was a real pilot, who has gone down in history as the "Candy Bomber." While dialogue and interactions with the fictional J.B. Baronowsky are invented, Halvorsen's portrayal and the opinions ascribed to him are based on his autobiography, *The Berlin Candy Bomber*, published by Horizon in 1990. His historical copilot was Captain John H. Pickering, who was not sent home mid-tour. I invented an illness for Pickering so I could put my fictional character J.B. aboard Halvorsen's aircraft for the first candy drops and thereby integrate Halvorsen's remarkable actions into the novel.

- Other historical figures include General William Tunner, General Lucius D. Clay, General Herbert, Colonel Frank Howley and Mayor Ernst Reuter. The public actions of all these men are well-recorded. Their characterisation in the novel is based largely on their respective biographies. Specifically, Tunner's *Over the Hump*, and Clay's *Decision in Germany*. For Reuter I relied on Peter Auer's biography *Ihr Voelker der Welt*.

- In contrast, the RAF airlift commander in the period covered by this book was Group Captain "Wally" Biggar. I had only scanty, anecdotal information about him that made him seem a petty-minded and bureaucratic type of officer. This offered an excellent opportunity to create a contrast and antagonist for my fictional hero Robert Priestman. Clashes between commanders and differences of opinion over policies were inevitable in an operation of this kind and portraying such clashes lends authenticity to the narrative. However, I decided to substitute a fictional figure, Bagshot, for the historical Biggar in order not to besmirch the memory of an officer I know too little about.

- Historically, the Corps of Royal Engineers lieutenant colonel responsible for the construction of the runways and other facilities at Gatow was a Lt Col R. Graham. His outstanding, professional accomplishments are depicted in this novel. However, because I also wanted to weave in personal details which are completely fictional, I opted to change the name and create a fictional character.

- Captain Bateman, the CO of the Forward Area Supply Organisation or FASO, is a historical figure and the description of him is based on secondary sources.

- Flight Officer Parsons is the name of the WAAF OC, but I found no descriptions of her and used literary license when creating her character.

- Wing Commander Robert Priestman is a fictional character invented to enable the narrative of this series to include one person with insight into the entire logistical operation. The historical Station Commander of Gatow during the Airlift was Group Captain Brian Yarde, who arrived in July 1947 and departed in November 1949. I have extended the term of his real predecessor, Group Captain Duncan Somerville, to December 1947 to accommodate the plot of the novel. The decision to make the RAF station commander the main character of this book was dictated by the fact that Gatow became the world's busiest airport and Gatow led with innovations in air traffic control, as well as being the departure point for the civilian evacuations from Berlin.

- Although the RAF employed women in air traffic control during the Airlift, Kathleen Hart is also a fictional character.

- British civil aviation companies played a critical role in the Berlin Airlift and included some of the most colourful characters of contemporary aviation such as Freddy Laker and AVM Donald Bennett. However, Air Ambulance International, Air Freight International, Emergency Air Services and all the characters associated with them were invented.

The Events and Other Facts

- The Soviet Secret police went by a variety of names during its long history. The acronyms used changed eight times between the establishment of the first organization in 1917 and the establishment of the KGB in 1954. Technically, in the period covered by this novel the predecessor of the KGB was called the MGB, but as this term is virtually unknown among readers not specialized in Soviet history, I chose a more familiar — albeit anachronistic term — the NKVD, which was the acronym used during some of the worst of Stalin's internal purges (1934-1941) and so was the organization that would have slaughtered Jasha's husband and son.

- Rationing in Germany after World War Two varied depending on the Zone/Sector of residency, the age of the recipient, the category of worker, and the date. As a rule, rations were most generous in the American Zone/Sector, but even for workers doing heavy, physical labour, rations remained below the minimum of 3,000 daily calories, which was then considered necessary for a healthy diet. Rations were worst in the French Zone.

- The French role throughout the Airlift was essentially passive. While they did not interfere with British and American efforts, allowed land in their Sector to be used for the construction of a new airfield, and attempted to free the policemen held in the *"Rote Rathaus"*, overall, their contribution was minimal.

- As depicted in the novel, the Western Allies tapped into the gas mains to keep gas-fired heating and electrical systems running courtesy of — but unbeknownst to — the Soviets.

- The power for the Soviet airfield at Staaken came from the British Sector. When, early in the Airlift, the Soviets attempted to cut power to Gatow, the issue was resolved by the British cutting the power to Staaken. Almost immediately power was restored to Gatow and neither party interfered with the other's power thereafter. While clearly an example of how integrated and complex Berlin's infrastructure connections were, I was unable to find any further details. Nor was I able to identify the exact date of this incident, although it was in the early days of the Airlift.

- The date for the construction of Gatow's concrete runway is inconsistently recorded in the available literature. Some sources claim a concrete runway already existed as early as March 1947; other sources say the concrete runway was not completed until 16 July 1948. The earlier date of 1947 is not credible because prior to the start of the mini airlift in April 1948, Gatow had almost no traffic and laying down a concrete runway would not have been a priority to a British government heavily in debt and cutting back on defence spending. After the mini blockade of April 1948, in contrast, construction of a concrete runway became imperative. Furthermore, the exceptional challenges associated with the construction of the runway are described in detail in several first-hand accounts, all of which support the thesis that completion of the concrete runway did not take place until after the start of the blockade in June 1948.

- At least one Dakota flew to Berlin carrying double its payload. There may well have been others.

- The barrels of bitumen left at the perimeter fence of Gatow, and the steamroller driven from Leipzig are historical events.

- The kidnapping of West Berliners by the Soviet controlled police continued throughout the period of this novel. The West Berliners became increasingly vociferous in resisting such "arrests" and in several documented incidents the Western Allies were forced to intervene to prevent more violence or full-scale riots.

- Likewise, at least one unidentified British officer was detained and mishandled by the Soviets for four or five days after taking photos in the East — although technically the city was still a single unit and all Allied troops allegedly had complete freedom of movement. Several American military personnel were likewise mistreated after being detained by the Soviets.

- The Soviets announced that anyone, regardless of place of residence, could register for Soviet rations on 24 July. The fatal crash in the Handjerystrasse occurred on 25 July. The Soviet threat to disrupt traffic in the corridors was issued on 26 July, and Police Chief Markgraf was suspended by the Berlin city council on 27 July. All these historical events were rolled into the single scene set on 26 July.

- The description of accommodations for USAF pilots flying the Airlift in July 1948 is based on the firsthand account of Gail Halvorsen, who was one of the first pilots to deploy. As described, he and his colleagues were housed in what had been a Displaced Persons Camp.

- General Tunner arrived in Germany at the end of July and was received coldly by the USAF commander in theatre, General Curtis LeMay. He immediately set to work trying to bring order to chaos. Among other changes, he arranged for weather reports and snacks to be brought to the aircraft and required crew to never be more than ten feet away during loading and unloading. He continued to make a variety of changes to maintenance procedures, air traffic control, and more, and is credited with professionalising the Airlift and making it successful. That said, many of the procedures attributed to Tunner (e.g. GCA approach regardless of weather) had already been instituted by the British. Likewise, the block system was already in use before his arrival.

- "Black Friday" was a real incident and (as in the novel) occurred on Friday 13 August 1948. As described, three accidents in quick succession at Tempelhof caused a stack up of aircraft. Tunner, caught in the stack, sent all the other aircraft back to their base and then ordered his staff to find ways to avoid such chaos ever again. The orders for aircraft to return loaded if landings were missed became standard, but the other aspects of the new rules are vague.

- Halvorsen does not give the date of his first candy drop in his memoirs, and different dates appear in different sources. However, there appear to have been substantial gaps between his unauthorised early drops. For the sake of the narrative pace, I have condensed events, postponing the first candy drop but speeding up the timing of subsequent drops. His conversation with the kids at the perimeter fence is a paraphrase of the description provided in his memoirs.

- Mayor Reuter's speech on 9 September 1948 is legendary. I paraphrased from the full text of that speech for the scene in the novel. His call to "Look at this city!" and a number of other phrases are direct translations, but the speech was greatly condensed.

- When the identity of the "Candy Bomber" was discovered by the USAF command, Halvorsen was first ordered to report to his squadron commander Colonel Haun, who lectured him on "keeping his superiors informed," and then sent him to Tunner. I have conflated the two scenes for brevity, but the responses are those reported by Halvorsen in his biography. The press conference was immediate; his trip to the US somewhat later, but Halvorsen gives no exact dates.

- The first fatal RAF crash was on the night of 19 September. It involved a York that experienced engine failure on take-off at c. 10:30 pm from Wunstorff. I have used the historical aircraft ID and the real names of the crew as a means of remembering them, but I do not know what cargo they were carrying.

- Tunner was named Commander of the Combined Air Lift Task Force (CALFT) on Oct. 14, the day before General Cannon replaced General LeMay as USAFE commander. Both LeMay and Cannon insisted that Tunner go through them with all requests — while refusing to work weekends. Tunner experienced extreme difficulties obtaining repair parts, maintenance tools, and many other necessities until 1949, when the Secretary of the Air Force cut the red tape for him.

- Tunner did meet General Clay "by chance" at Tempelhof, and Clay obligingly asked if he had any problems, to which Tunner explained about the lack of maintenance personnel and requested permission to hire Germans. The reported dialogue of this encounter is the basis of the exchange between them in this novel. The date, however, was earlier because at the time General LeMay was still USAFE commander.

- Although Air Commodore Merer is usually described as Tunner's deputy at CALFT, he did not assume command and control of the RAF's Airlift *airfields* until 1 December 1948, i.e. six weeks after Tunner's appointment. This suggests in the first six weeks, control of RAF assets remained split between Merer, who commanded the squadrons involved in the Airlift, and Group Captain Biggar who commanded the RAF airfields in Germany. I have used this fact to facilitate the plot.

- The British carried 78% of all passengers flown out of Berlin during the Airlift. Of those, 96,605 were Berliners flown out of Berlin by the RAF for humanitarian reasons. The backloading of German civilian passengers from Gatow commenced historically on 19 October; I moved this forward slightly to accommodate the plot. The largest single action was the evacuation of 17,000 civilians in December alone. I moved the start of this operation forward by four days to correspond with the day civilian Dakotas were taken off the Airlift enabling both events to be depicted in a single episode.

- The depiction of children moving around while in flight is based on a first-hand account by an RAF crew.

- Finally, the Americans resisted flying cargoes out because they slowed down the aircraft turnaround times, thereby reducing aircraft utilisation rates. To keep aircraft flying at Tunner's demanding but steady rate, the US authorities allowed outbound cargoes to accumulate in warehouses rather than fly them out. The British, in contrast, feared the failure to export the products would result in factory closures, unemployment and possibly discontent—even riots or rebellion. Sacrificing 'efficiency' for the greater good of fostering the Berlin economy, the British took over the burden of outbound cargoes. By the end of the airlift, the RAF and British civilian aircraft had lifted 35,843 tons of industrial goods produced in Berlin out of the besieged city and delivered them to the West. If the volume appears small, this is partly because some of these cargoes were very light, e.g., light bulbs. A better measure of their importance is their monetary value, estimated at DM 230.5 million or USD 126 million. Yet, the greatest significance of these cargoes was their immeasurable impact on morale. The products were proudly stamped 'Made in Blockaded Berlin', a cry of defiance and pride, and the packaging crates for these goods depicted the city's mascot, the Berlin Bear, breaking his chains.

Recommended Reading

- Auer, Peter. *Ihr Voelker der Welt: Ernst Reuter und die Blockade von Berlin*. Jaron, 1998.
- Cherny, Andrei. *The Candy Bombers: The Untold Story of the Berlin Airlift and America's Finest Hour*. G.P.Putnam's Sons, 2008.
- Clay, Lucius D., *Decision in Germany*. William Heinemann Ltd, 1950.
- Collier, Richard. *Bridge Across the Sky: The Berlin Blockade and Airlift 1948-1949*. MacGraw Hill, 1978.
- Gere, Edwin. *The Unheralded: Men and Women of the Berlin Blockade and Airlift*. Trafford, 2003.
- Halvorsen, Gail. *The Berlin Candy Bomber*. Horizon Publishers. 1997.
- Haydock, Michael D. *City under Siege: The Berlin Blockade and Airlift, 1948-1949*. Brassey's, 1999.
- Jackson, Robert. *The Berlin Airlift*. Patrick Stephens, 1988.
- Keiderling, Gerhard. *Rosinenbomber ueber Berlin: Waehrungsreform. Blockade, Luftbruecke, Teiling*. Dietz Verlag, 1998.
- Koenig, Peter. *Schaut auf diese Stadt! Berlin und die Luftbruecke*. Be.Brag Verlag, 1998.
- Miller, Roger G. *To Save a City: The Berlin Airlift 1948 — 1949*. Univ. Press of the Pacific, 2002
- Milton, Giles. *Checkmate in Berlin*. Henry Holt & Co, 2021.
- Parrish, Thomas. *Berlin in the Balance 1948-1949: The Blockade, The Airlift, The First Major Battle of the Cold War*. Perseus Books, 1998.
- Percy, Arthur. *Berlin Airlift*. Airlife, 1997.

- Prell, Uwe and Lothar Wilker. *Berlin-Blockade und Luftbruecke 1948-1949: Analyse und Dokumentation*. Berlin Verlag, 1987

- Reeves, Richard, *Daring Young Men*, Simon and Schuster, 2010.

- Rodrigo, Robert. *Berlin Airlift*. Cassel & Co., 1960.

- Scherff, Klaus. *Luftbruecke Berlin: Die dramatische Geschichte der Versorgung aus der Luft June 1948 — Oktober 1949*. Motorbuch Verlag, 1998.

- Schrader, Helena P. *The Blockade Breakers: The Berlin Airlift*. The History Press, 2008.

- Tunner, William H. *Over the Hump*. Office of Air Force History: USAF Warrior Studies, 1964.

- Tusa, Ann & John. *The Berlin Airlift*. Sarpedon, 1998.

RAF / USAF Rank Table

RAF	USAAF
Marshal of the Airforce	Five Star General
Air Chief Marshal	General (4 Star)
Air Marshal	Lt. General (3 Star)
Air Vice Marshal	Major General (2 Star)
Air Commodore	Brigadier General (1 Star)
Group Captain	Colonel
Wing Commander	Lt. Colonel
Squadron Leader	Major
Flight Lieutenant	Captain
Flying Officer	First Lieutenant
Pilot Officer	Second Lieutenant

Because the USAAF had ten non-commissioned ranks to the RAF's seven, it is not possible to provide exact equivalents, however, the lowest rank in the RAF was "Aircraftman." This is the term from which term "erk" derives in RAF jargon.

The RAF non-commissioned ranks from highest to lowest were:
- Warrant Officer
- Flight Sergeant
- Sergeant
- Corporal
- Leading Aircraftman (LAC)
- Aircraftman 1st and 2nd Class

Key Acronyms

AAI	Air Ambulance International, a subsidiary of Emergency Air Services
ACC	Allied Control Council
AFI	Air Freight International, a subsidiary of Emergency Air Services
AVM	Air Vice Marshal
BAFO	British Air Forces of Occupation
BAOR	British Army on the Rhine
C-47	The USAF designation for a twin-engine aircraft also known as the "Dakota" or DC3
C-54	The USAF designation for a four-engine aircraft also known as the "Skymaster" or DC4
CALTF	Combined Air Lift Task Force
CDU	Christlich Demokratische Union Deutschlands — Christian Democratic Union of Germany
CPSU	Communist Party of the Soviet Union
CRE	Corps of Royal Engineers
EAS	Emergency Air Services, the holding company for AAI and AFI
Fl/Lt	Flight Lieutenant
Fl/Sgt	Flight Sergeant
F/O	Flying Officer
G/C	Group Captain
KPD	Kommunistische Partei Deutschlands — The German Communist Party
NKVD	Soviet Secret Police
P/O	Pilot Officer
RAF	Royal Air Force
RAFVR	Royal Air Force Volunteer Reserve
R/T	Radio Telephone, the radio sets used in aircraft at this time

SED	Sozialistische Einheitspartei Deutschlands — The Socialist Unity Party, the artificial party created by the Soviet Military Government in an attempt to co-opt the SPD.
Sgt	Sergeant
S/L	Squadron Leader
SPD	Sozialdemokratische Partei Deutschlands — The German Social Democratic Party
SMAD	Soviet Military Administration in Germany
USAF	United States Air Force
USAFE	United States Air Forces Europe
Wg/Cdr	Wing Commander

About
Helena P. Schrader

Dr. Helena P. Schrader is the author of six critically acclaimed non-fiction history books and twenty historical novels, eleven of which have earned one or more awards for a total of 56 literary accolades. She holds a PhD in history from the University of Hamburg, which she earned with a ground-breaking biography of a leader of the German Resistance to Hitler and served as an American diplomat in Europe and Africa.

For readers tired of clichés and cartoons, award-winning novelist Helena P. Schrader offers nuanced insight into historical events and figures based on sound research and an understanding of human nature. Her complex and engaging characters bring history back to life as a means to better understand ourselves. Her chief areas of expertise are Aviation, the Second World War, Ancient Sparta, and the Crusader States. For more about all her books, awards, blogs and newsletter visit **helenapschrader.com**

Schrader's first published work in the English language was a comparative study of women pilots in WWII (Sisters in Arms: The Women who Flew in World War Two). This was followed by a comprehensive history of the Berlin Airlift (The Blockade Breakers: The Berlin Airlift). Her aviation novels include a novel on the Battle of Britain (Where Eagles Never Flew), a novel examining the stress of flying for Bomber Command (Moral Fibre), and a three-part series on the Berlin Airlift. Battle of Britain RAF fighter ace Wing Commander Bob Doe called Where Eagles Never Flew "the best book on the life of us fighter pilots in the Battle of Britain that I have ever seen." Moral Fibre was hailed by the Foreign Service Journal as a "tribute to those who fought for freedom." *Cold Peace*, the first book in the Bridge to Tomorrow Series, was named runner-up for BOOK OF THE YEAR 2023 by the Historical Fiction Company and took First Place (GOLD) in the Feathered Quill Book Awards 2024 in the category Historical Fiction.

Schrader's interest in ancient Sparta started when she encountered the beauty and richness of Sparta and recognized that reality conflicted with modern literary descriptions. Returning to the ancient sources, she discovered that the archaeological and historical evidence is at odds with popular myths. After stripping away the misinformation, a very different Sparta emerges. Schrader's six novels set in Ancient Sparta seek to depict this fascinating society in a manner conforming with ancient sources and common sense rather than modern politics. Her works have won the critical acclaim of classical scholars. She has participated in the "Sparta Live!" lecture series sponsored by the modern municipality of Sparti and the University of Nottingham's Centre for Spartan and Peloponnesian Studies as well as taken part on panels at international academic forums on Sparta. The third book in her Leonidas trilogy has been translated and released in Greece.

The history of the crusader states is another topic in which popular misperceptions obscure the historical record. Schrader's novels set in the Holy Land during the crusader era seek to show the Crusaders States as they really were: multi-cultural, tolerant, and sophisticated societies at crossroads of civilizations. Schrader's novels are based on the historical record and incorporate the insights gained from modern archaeological surveys. Her non-fiction history of the crusader states, *The Holy Land in the Era of the Crusades: Kingdoms at the Crossroads of Civilizations*, was the first book to pull together recent academic findings from a variety of disciplines and integrate the information into a comprehensive history and topical description of the crusader states. Schrader's focus on the crusader states rather than the crusades makes her books unique and valuable contributions to the literature on this era. Her Jerusalem Trilogy earned a total of eleven awards, including Best Biography from the Book Excellence Awards 2017 and GOLD (First Place) for Christian Historical Fiction from Readers' Favorites 2017.

Helena was born in Ann Arbor, Michigan, the daughter of a professor, and travelled abroad for the first time at the age of two, when her father went to teach at the University of Wasada in Tokyo, Japan. Later the family lived in Brazil, England and Kentucky, but home was always the coast of Maine. There, her father's family had roots, and an old, white clapboard house perched above the boatyard in East Blue Hill.

It was the frequent travel and exposure to different cultures, peoples and heritage that inspired Helena to start writing creatively and to focus on historical fiction. She wrote her first novel in second grade but later made a conscious decision not to try to earn a living from writing. She never wanted to be forced to write what was popular, rather than what was in her heart.

Helena graduated with honours in History from the University of Michigan, added a Master's degree in diplomacy and international commerce from Patterson School, University of Kentucky, and rounded off her education with a PhD in History cum Laude from the University of Hamburg. She worked in the private sector as a research analyst, and an investor relations manager in both the U.S. and Germany before joining the U.S. diplomatic corps.

She sailed the Maine coast all her life and served as a petty officer on the British three-masted schooners Sir Winston Churchill and Malcolm Miller. She owned four horses during her lifetime and was still stadium jumping at 64. She is now retired and lives with her husband Herbert and their two dogs Max and Roma.

Visit Helena's website for more about her books, awards, blogs, and newsletters visit **helenapschrader.com**

Other Aviation and WWII Books
by Helena P. Schrader

For readers interested in the backstory to Robin and Emily:

Where Eagles Never Flew:
A Battle of Britain Novel

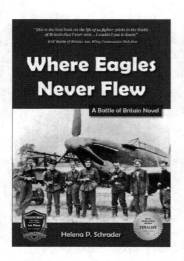

Winner of the HEMINGWAY AWARD for Twentieth Century Military Fiction, a MAINCREST MEDIA AWARD for Military Fiction, an Indie BRAG Medallion as well as a Finalist for THE BOOK EXCELLENCE AWARDS.

Summer 1940: The Battle of France is over; the Battle of Britain is about to begin. If the swastika is not to fly over Buckingham Palace, the RAF must prevent the Luftwaffe from gaining air superiority over Great Britain. Standing on the front line is No 606 (Hurricane) Squadron. As the casualties mount, new pilots find a cold reception from the clique of experienced pilots who resent them for taking the place of their dead friends. Meanwhile, despite credible service in France, former RAF aerobatics pilot Robin Priestman finds himself stuck in Training Command — and falling for a girl from the Salvation Army. On the other side of the Channel, the Luftwaffe is recruiting women as communications specialists — and naive Klaudia is about to grow up.

"... this one of the most authentic and well-told stories of the Battle of Britain we have ever read. ... The characters come to us as individuals who are authentic, relatable, and unique. ... Where Eagles Never Flew doesn't shy away from either love nor loss and, in fact, takes the opportunity to sit with the characters in their pain, their grief, and their frustration." **Chanticleer**

"This author struck gold with this story. ... The human side of war is intense and the detailed descriptions of the crafts and the fights were so vivid that they pulled me back in time... Quill says: I cannot recommend this highly enough. Do not miss this memorable, intense, amazing story." **Feathered Quill**

"Its high-octane descriptions of air maneuvers and daring escapes are breathtaking.... Because of its ambitious scope and phenomenal details, down to the last "Mae West" jacket, the novel is compelling, humanizing a historical event ....." **Foreword Clarion**

"Readers may pick up Where Eagles Never Flew for its promise of action, but will find it holds unexpected, satisfying psychological depth as its characters grow, evolve, and confront each other and the enemy during a life-changing period in Britain's history. It's a story steeped in real-life events that goes far in tracing the changing roles and influence of women in the world and is highly recommended reading for World War II history enthusiasts looking for something more than descriptions of battles." **Midwest Book Reviews**

"Helena has written a book that will become a classic. It was rated by Bob Doe, one of the top Battle of Britain fighter aces, as a book that told the story correctly and he was delighted to recommend this to a wider public. This book will be enjoyed for many years, however many times you read this." **Paul Davies, President of the Battle of Britain Historical Society**

"Scenes exploring the characters inner lives are compelling... [and] Schrader also succeeds in accurately portraying the bombing raids and defense missions.... A painstakingly researched war novel with complex characterisations." **Kirkus Reviews**

Buy now!

For readers interested in the backstory to Kit Moran:

Moral Fibre:
A Bomber Pilot's Story

Winner of a HEMINGWAY AWARD for 20th Century Wartime Fiction 2022, Silver in the 2023 HISTORICAL FICTION COMPANY BOOK AWARDS for Military Fiction, MAINCREST MEDIA AWARD for Military Fiction and An Indie BRAG Medallion. In addition, it was a finalist for a BOOK EXELLENCE AWARDS for Historical Fiction 2023 and a distinguished favorite in the INDEPENDENT PRESS AWARDS 2024.

Riding the icy, moonlit sky—
They took the war to Hitler.
Their chances of survival were less than fifty percent.
Their average age was 21.
This is the story of just one Lancaster skipper, his crew,
and the woman he loved.
It is intended as a tribute to them all.

Flying Officer Kit Moran has earned his pilot's wings, but the greatest challenges still lie ahead: crewing up and returning to operations. Things aren't made easier by the fact that while still a flight engineer, he was posted LMF (Lacking in Moral Fibre) for refusing to fly after a raid on Berlin that killed his best friend and skipper. Nor does it help that he is in love with his dead friend's fiancé, who is not yet ready to become romantically involved again.

"A richly textured, absorbing war tale that works equally well as a touching love story." **Kirkus Reviews**

"Readers will find themselves engaged in the complexities, not only of Kit, but of the men in his bomber crew." **Blue Ink Starred Review**

"For those who wish to explore different worlds, learn new things, and reflect on their life decisions, this book is a great choice." **The Moving Words Awards**

"A perfect blend of history, romance, and inspiration, Moral Fibre *[is] ... a mesmerizing look into the past."* **Maincrest Media**

"A riveting read!" **Chanticleer Reviews**

Buy now!

Grounded Eagles:
Three Tales of the RAF in WWII

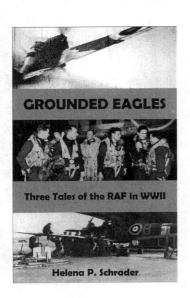

Winner of a CHANTICLEER INTERNATIONAL BOOK AWARD for Short Stories, Novellas and Collections, a MAINCREST MEDIA AWARD and an Indie BRAG Medallion

A Stranger in the Mirror: David Goldman is shot down in flames in September 1940. Not only is his face burned beyond recognition, he is told he will never fly again. While the plastic surgeon recreates his face one painful operation at a time, the 22-year-old pilot must discover who he really is.

Lack of Moral Fibre: In late November 1943, Flight Engineer Kit Moran refuses to participate in a raid on Berlin, his 37th 'op.' He is posted off his squadron for "Lacking Moral Fibre" and sent to a mysterious NYDN center. Here, psychiatrist Dr Grace must determine if he needs psychiatric treatment — or disciplinary action for cowardice.

A Rose in November: Rhys Jenkins, a widower with two teenage children, has finally obtained his dream: "Chiefy" of a Spitfire squadron. But an unexpected attraction for an upperclass woman threatens to upend his life.

"An impressive and memorable trio of works about the many costs of war." **Kirkus Reviews**

"Helena P. Schrader delivers complex plots through the eyes of characters you will wrap your arms around and cheer for to the very end." Tom Gauthier for **Readers' Favorites**

"Schrader excels at examining the nexus of physical and psychological trauma.... Grounded Eagles *will appeal to any fan of WWII fiction."* **Blue Ink Reviews**

"[These] stories are layered and told in a voice that is captivating, filled with humanity and realism...." **The Book Commentary**

Buy now!

Bridge to Tomorrow:
A Novel of the Berlin Airlift
Book I: Cold Peace

The first battle of the Cold War is about to begin.

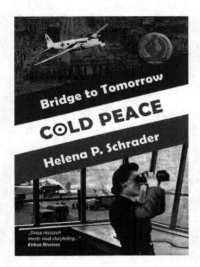

Runner-Up for BOOK OF THE YEAR 2023 and Winner of Gold from the HISTORICAL FICTION COMPANY ANNUAL BOOK AWARDS

Winner of Gold for Historical Fiction from the FEATHERED QUILL BOOK AWARDS 2024 and Silver for Political Thrillers from READERS FAVORITES AWARDS 2023.

Winner of a MAINCREST MEDIA AWARD and an Indie BRAG Medallion

Berlin 1948. The economy is broken, the currency worthless, and the Russian bear is hungry. In the ruins of Hitler's capital, war heroes and resilient women struggle in the post-war doldrums — until they discover new direction in defending Berlin's freedom. When a Soviet fighter brings down a British passenger plane, the world teeters on the brink of World War Three.

Based on historical events, award-winning novelist Helena P. Schrader brings to life the backstory of the West's bloodless victory against Russian aggression via the Berlin Airlift.

"Sharp research meets vivid storytelling in an absorbing novel of the postwar period." **Kirkus Reviews**

"In her compelling novel Cold Peace, *Helena P. Schrader delves into complexities of post-WWII Germany and the roots of the Berlin Airlift.*

... Schrader's plotting is intricate and engaging. ... [Readers] will find Cold Peace *rewarding....*" **Blue Ink**

"Cold Peace .... [is a] fast-paced, suspenseful, emotional, and riveting story that any reader will find almost impossible to put down. ... The settings are perfect, the writing is superb, and the plot is very well-crafted. ... Cold Peace is a riveting and wonderfully written example of historical fiction and definitely stands out as one of the best. ... I have become a huge fan." **Feathered Quill**

"The beauty of this narrative is that it educates wonderfully, as well as entertains completely. ... This is a wide-ranging and expansive dive into the nature of the Berlin Airlift, and I cannot wait to read the follow-up books from this superbly talented author." **Grant Leishman for Readers' Favorites**

"...a spellbinding work of historical fiction that brings a unique pocket of history to life with extraordinary detail and heart. ... Schrader puts heart and soul into the dialogue and development of everyone from cover to cover. This keen sense of reality adds to the overall attitude of the piece, giving an authentic image of people caught in a very unsettling historical time." **KC Finn for Readers' Favorites**

Buy now!

Traitors for the Sake of Humanity:
A Novel of the German Resistance to Hitler

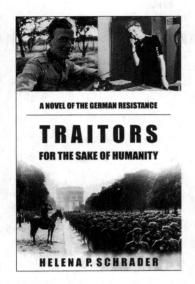

Finalist for a Forward INDIES Award 2022

They opposed Hitler's diabolical regime on moral grounds. They sought to defend human dignity and restore the rule of law — at the risk of their own lives. Traitors to Hitler, they were heroes to the oppressed. They remain an inspiration to anyone fighting against immoral and corrupt governments anywhere in the world.

Traitors opens in 1938 when Adolf Hitler seems to have captivated all of Germany. Soon one Nazi victory follows another, yet some individuals with integrity and compassion remain opposed to his regime and all it stands for — people like Philip, Alexandra, and Marianne. They feel isolated and hopeless until they discover each other — and learn that their concerns are shared by men in the very highest places in the German High Command....

"[T]he importance of this book cannot be underestimated. Traitors for the Sake of Humanity *rises as a critical, provocative, and timely book that perhaps we would all benefit from reading.... Helena P. Schrader puts a human face on some "monsters," and exposed the monster faces of others. Kudos, Dr. Schrader."* **Chanticleer Reviews**

"Truly inspiring, these awesome Traitors *keep you on the edge of your seat. Schrader has done it yet again: 5-Stars!"* **Feathered Quill**

"Anyone who would understand, on more than a factual level, the emotions and motivations of resisters and believers alike will find this powerful history captured in a story that is, yes, complex...but also thoroughly engrossing and thought-provoking." **Midwest Book Review**

Aviation Non-Fiction

Blockade Breakers
The Berlin Airlift

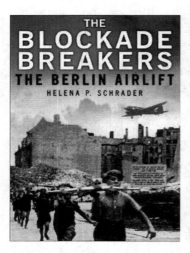

On 24 June 1948 the Soviet Union abruptly closed all land and water access to the Western Sectors of Berlin. Over 2 million civilians, dependent on the surrounding territory and the West for food, fuel, and other basic goods, were suddenly cut off from all necessities of life.

The Western Allies had the option of either withdrawing their garrisons and allowing the Soviet Union to take control of the entire city, or of trying to supply the city by air. Never before had 2 million people been supplied exclusively by air. None of the senior military commanders believed it could be done.

But the political leadership in London and Washington insisted that it must be done. A withdrawal from Berlin would discredit the West at a critical moment in history when the Soviet Union was expanding aggressively across Europe. Worse, it would endanger the political stability and economic recovery of all of Europe.

So one of the largest and most ambitious humanitarian efforts in history was set in motion. It began without the West really knowing what the Berliners needed — much less how much those supplies weighed. It was launched despite a lack of airlift expertise in theatre or a unified command structure, an almost complete absence of aircraft and aircrew resources in Germany and serious inadequacies in airfields and air traffic control. But once it began, the Berlin Airlift became an inspirational feat of organisation and collaboration and was more of a success than even its originators and advocates had ever imagined possible.

Sisters in Arms:
British & American Women Pilots
During World War II

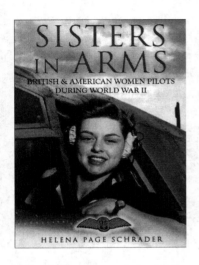

During WWII, a few carefully selected women in the United States and Great Britain were briefly given the unprecedented opportunity to fly military aircraft. In both the US and the UK, the women pilots joined auxiliary organisations, the WASP in the US and the ATA in Britain. During nearly six years of service, the women of the ATA steadily won nearly all the privileges and status enjoyed by their male colleagues. Women in the ATA could and did have command authority over men. Most exceptionally for the time, women of the ATA were awarded equal pay for equal work. The American women pilots, in contrast, were expressly denied the same status, rank, privileges, pay and benefits of their male colleagues.

What accounts for this dramatic difference in the treatment of women pilots doing essentially the same job? This book seeks to answer that question.

Buy now!

Codename Valkyrie

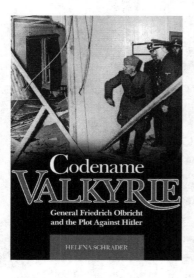

Kill the Fuehrer! A secret plot three years in the making. The main conspirator: one of Hitler's most trusted and decorated generals. His plan would have changed the course of history — if Colonel Stauffenberg had not failed.

The true story of the mastermind behind the plot to depose Hitler and re-establish the rule of law in Germany: Friedrich Olbricht.

Helena Schrader's incisive account describes the transformation of a highly decorated senior German Army officer into an active conspirator dedicated to removing Hitler from power. She convincingly shows how Olbricht's plans might just have succeeded, had Stauffenberg not failed to kill the Fuehrer on 20 July 1944.

Buy now!